SEVEN MASTERPIECES OF GOTHIC HORROR

THE CASTLE OF OTRANTO

An ancient castle is the setting for weird, supernatural events and spectral havoc.

THE OLD ENGLISH BARON

A young man spends the night with his father's corpse and uncovers the mystery of his strange birth.

MISTRUST

Witchcraft, mysterious deaths and attempted abduction culminate in a father's murder of his own son.

THE WHITE OLD MAID

The strange story of a woman's love for a dead man.

THE HEIR OF MONDOLFO

The murderous rivalry between father and son begets a strange, unnatural horror.

THE FALL
OF THE HOUSE OF USHER

Poe's famous tale of terror and madness.

CARMILLA

One of the most chillingly effective vampire tales ever written.

BANTAM LITERATURE

SEVEN
MASTERPIECES
OF GOTHIC HORROR

Edited by
ROBERT DONALD SPECTOR
LONG ISLAND UNIVERSITY

SEVEN MASTERPIECES OF GOTHIC HORROR
A Bantam Classic / published April 1963
2nd printing....November 1964   3rd printing.........July 1966
4th printing .... April 1970
Bantam edition published November 1971
6th printing
7th printing
8th printing

Library of Congress Catalog Card Number: 63-8941

Bantam Books are published by Bantam Books, Inc., a National General company. Its trade-mark, consisting of the words "Bantam Books" and the portrayal of a bantam, is registered in the United States Patent Office and in other countries. Marca Registrada. Bantam Books, Inc., 666 Fifth Avenue, New York, N.Y. 10019.

CONTENTS

Seven Masterpieces

of

Gothic Horror

INTRODUCTION

Perhaps more than any other literary genre, the Gothic novel depended for its success on what Coleridge called the reader's "willing suspension of disbelief." To be sure, its authors—like all writers of fantasy—were not always content to rely on such generous acquiescence. They sought to make credibility easier by exploiting details of scenery, appealing to contemporary social and aesthetic fashions, or explaining away the supernatural occurrences. Yet, in the end, the Gothic world of mysterious medieval castles—in whose subterranean secret passages fair maidens were pursued by unscrupulous villains and saved by noble, avenging heroes—demanded readers who would disregard its superficial absurdities and participate in a process of "co-creation" by relating the fiction to their own "emotional, imaginative, and subconscious" lives.

It is a fact that ever since Horace Walpole's *Castle of Otranto* in 1765 there have been such readers. Generally, however, they have not been critics, for that breed of rational man judges literature by standards alien to the irrational nightmare world of the Gothic. Conventional criticism, therefore, has been appalled by the fanciful plots, unreal characterizations, and morbid sentiments in the Gothic novel. Comparing Gothic medievalism with the reality of the Middle Ages, literary historians have denounced the novelists' anachronisms and scoffed at their romantic treatment of the feudal ages.

Nevertheless, the Gothic has continued to enjoy popular appeal. During the long gap between the major eighteenth-century novelists and Jane Austen and Walter Scott, it was the chief fictional form keeping alive interest in the novel. No matter how prone to ridicule, the circulating libraries and the magazines that purveyed these romances were developing not only an audience but a source for the great Victorians. Even when the genre itself no longer held the field of interest, it survived—first in the pseudo-scientific form of Mary Shelley's *Frankenstein* and the psychological probing of the Reverend Charles Maturin's *Melmoth the Wanderer,* then in the horror tales of the sub-literary monster stories and science fiction that retain a following to the present day. Moreover, no literary history of the last one hundred years, as Michael Sadleir has noted, can ignore the persistent influence of the Gothic in the popular novel.

Examining the history and characteristics of the Gothic novel, it is not difficult to account for the advent and durability of its popularity. Even before Walpole's *Castle of Otranto,* there were vague stirrings of uneasiness in the eighteenth-century rational climate of opinion. Tobias Smollett's use of terror in *Ferdinand Count Fathom,* recalling the earlier Jacobean and Elizabethan melodrama, was an example in the novel. But elsewhere, too, the restlessness was apparent. The "Graveyard School" of poets brooded upon the mysteries of existence; the antiquarians' romantic re-creations of the past developed into the ballad collections of Percy and Macpherson's legendary Ossianic poems; and the revived interest in Tasso and Ariosto's romances was given respectability by the serious scholarship of Bishop Hurd's *Letters on Chivalry and Romance.* Walpole himself was an antiquarian, builder of Strawberry Hill—a Gothic imitation complete with the ruins that had become the vogue on English estates. Whether created in jest or seriousness, his romance, like his Gothic castle, represented an attempt "to forget the unpleasant realities of life."

That was what lay behind the origin of the first Gothic novel. There had been the need to let loose the "great resources of fancy unfortunately dammed-up by common life," Walpole said; and yet he himself was so unsure of the response that he took every precaution to hide his authorship. Apart from the anonymity in the first edition, there was the pretense that it was an old work printed in Naples in 1529 and hidden away in the library of an ancient Catholic family from the north of England. Nevertheless, the reaction to the novel was successful enough for Walpole later to acknowledge his work and write a preface for the second edition, explaining his attempt to blend ancient romance, with its imagination and improbability, and modern romance, with its successful copying of nature.

Even here, however, Walpole was hedging. He was reluctant to admit that he and his readers—like his friend, the poet

Thomas Gray, who described the terrifying effect of the novel —had yielded to the irrationality of their emotions. In the Age of Reason, such unreasonability amounted to heresy, and the fact is that despite its success, *The Castle of Otranto,* which had provided the machinery for the novel of terror, generated no real successor for more than a decade.

It was not until Clara Reeve's *The Old English Baron* appeared in 1777 that the Gothic began to emerge as a literary form. But Miss Reeve, a conservative like many of the writers whose novels nevertheless were an expression of opposition to authority, was still unwilling to profess an admiration for a predominantly imaginative creation. Not only did she change her original title—*Champion of Virtue, a Gothic Story*—to emphasize its "historical" element, but she sought to explain her method by relegating the terrifying elements to a subsidiary role. Describing her technique, she declared that she had desired "a sufficient degree of the marvellous to excite attention; enough of the manners of real life to give an air of probability to the work; and enough of the pathetic to engage the heart on its behalf."

Despite their defensiveness, her remarks are not altogether disingenuous. They accurately reflect those literary changes which, together with what it borrowed from the accepted standard, enabled the Gothic novel to usurp the field. There had always been both in Walpole's and Reeve's work the insistence on a didactic purpose, no matter how vague. This in itself was a crutch of respectability, for no dictum was more characteristic of orthodox eighteenth-century values than the one based on Horace's demand that literature must entertain *and* instruct. But Clara Reeve's statement implies other literary influences as well. It suggests that the development of both the historical and sentimental novels had prepared the way for the Gothic success.

For *The Old English Baron* especially, the historical element was important. While the sense of history, no matter how distorted by those who made the past indistinguishable from the present in their treatment of ideas, contributed generally to the genre, Thomas Leland's *Longsword, Earl of Salisbury,* in 1762, directly affected Clara Reeve's novel. She sought to correct the errors in *The Castle of Otranto.* Although Walpole knew as much about the Middle Ages as any of his contemporaries, he had not bothered with historical authenticity in his novel. Whether Clara Reeve, depending on such imaginative histories as Leland's romance, was more accurate is unimportant; the fact is that she "aimed at a medieval atmosphere by the use of medieval background."

In the long run, however, the historical novel was less consequential to the success of the Gothic than the impact which had been made by the sentimental novelists, who followed a line of succession from Richardson through Sterne to Mackenzie's *The Man of Feeling.* Together with the French influence of Prevost and Marivaux, these English sentimental novelists had not only awakened a response to emotion, which was essential to acceptance of the Gothic, but they also had provided the theme of romantic love that the novelists of terror depended on to give some legitimacy and balance to their tales of terror. The truth of the relationship between the Gothic and sentimental lies somewhere between J. R. Foster's assertion that "the Gothic romance . . . is a sentimental novel in which the characters are tricked out in costumes" and Leslie Fiedler's comment that they are alike only in love treatment. While Foster ignores the darker aspects of the Gothic, Fiedler overemphasizes them, and his argument that undervalues the Gothic attempt to inculcate virtue hardly applies to the work of the many women novelists and discounts the black and white characterization in the novels which made them appropriate to an age that valued didactic literature.

At any rate, there is no question that shortly after Clara Reeve's novel appeared, the age was ready for Gothic fiction. Not only those publishing houses, like Minerva Press, that were called novel manufactures but also the magazines which served the capacious appetites of the reading public fed an English audience with Gothic romances, tales, and fragments. These were the dominant types of fiction in English periodicals from 1770-1820. They were imitative, uninspired, and plagiarized, but they are evidence enough of the readers' willingness to suspend their disbelief. However, in their insistence upon a moral, regardless of how flimsy and inappropriate, they are also an indication that at least until the German influence of "Monk" Lewis, they could still not afford to ignore the demand for didacticism.

Even Ann Radcliffe, who did not openly proclaim an instructive purpose, adhered to all the proprieties demanded for instruction. Moral retribution guided her plots; clear distinctions between good and evil marked her characterization; and as Ernest Baker has remarked, "every one of her novels provides a lesson, which is received and taken to heart through the impression upon our sensibilities." Edification climaxes all of her important novels.

But Ann Radcliffe was certainly more than a literary moralist. She was what the genre had been waiting for—a writer whose talents were of the first order. Not without reason was she called the "Shakespeare of the Romance Writers." Coleridge described her *Mysteries of Udolpho* as the "most interesting novel in the English language." If Sadleir exaggerated when he named her "the most influential woman novelist," his remark was not without basis. For Shelley she aroused an interest in natural scenery, while Byron modeled his characters on hers. To these accolades of the Romantics must be added the sober praise of Jane Austen, who held her apart from the Gothic novelists that were ridiculed in *Northanger Abbey*. Even Trollope, no friend to the flights of romanticism, admitted, "What may be done by impossible castles among impossible mountains, peopled by impossible heroes and heroines, and fraught with impossible horrors, the *Mysteries of Udolpho* have (sic) shown us."

It was a happy coincidence that Ann Radcliffe arrived at just the right time. All those forces that were to burst forth into the English Romantic Movement had been drawn together, and she somehow knew how to exploit them. From the painters of wild landscapes—Nicholas Poussin, Claude Lorraine, Salvatore Rosa, and Guido Reni—she learned the scenery that excited the imaginations of her most mature readers and provided a setting for her chilling atmosphere. Sensitivities exposed by English and French sentimental novelists had been made tender to fear by Clara Reeve, Sophia Lee, and Charlotte Smith. An age obsessed by the rational arguments of deists and French Encyclopedists required an emotional release. On the one hand, the irrational aspects that had been subdued in the Enlightenment broke forth into the excesses of the Reign of Terror; on the other hand, they were sublimated into the triumph of the Gothic Romance.

If Radcliffe was a bride of romanticism, she nevertheless was wise enough to maintain an adulterous union with the rationalists. In addition to the appeal that she made through didacticism, she offered reasonable explanations for the supernatural occurrences that might otherwise yet expose her to ridicule. Her attacks on Roman Catholicism were justified in the name of reason. Not only did the Inquisition arouse natural English antipathy on the basis of horror stories about Papist espionage, torture chambers, and secret atrocities; it also incited philosophic disapproval in the Age of the Enlightenment. Even in her aesthetic doctrine, Radcliffe relied on the effect of reason. From Edmund Burke's *Essay on the Sublime* she drew her technique that eschewed irrationality and depended instead for its effect on the dimly seen, half-seen, and the conjectured.

Yet the appeal to reason was not what made Ann Radcliffe popular. To an age that sought release from the mundane, every-day activities, she brought respectable escape. She united terror and beauty. If the reader felt uncomfortable while enjoying the liberation of sadistic and masochistic impulses, he was comforted by the passages of scenic splendor, the final morality, and the ultimate assurance of realism and reason. For pages he could yield to the excitement of horror, secure in the knowledge that in the end he would return to a world of logic. In *A Sicilian Romance* (1790), Radcliffe repeats Walpole's story of the incarcerated wife whose husband, in this instance, seeks a union with his paramour. There is the same terror in the castle—with Radcliffe's final explanation of the weird sounds and peculiar occurrences—until her heroine's final rescue and her husband's death. For all the suspense, there is the conventional assurance that all's right with the world. In the same way, *The Romance of the Forest* (1791) arouses fear and pity for the plight of a heroine threatened with death and dishonor, drawn against a background of the fascination and beauties of nature, and concluding in conventional moral satisfaction. Even in her masterpiece, *The Mysteries of Udolpho* (1794), Radcliffe alternates the excitement of melodrama with the spiritual grandeur of scenery. Hidden behind the veil of mystery, there is always the reasonable explanation: the dead body proves to be a wax image; the mysterious sounds turn out to be the lover's lute; and the supernatural happenings are the tricks of pirates. Yet the explanations are only important to cover the embarrassment of the reader, who can attribute his fancies to natural causes. Mrs. Radcliffe has not only eaten her pie but has it, too.

Only in *The Italian* (1797) does she appear to go to excess. But by then a change had taken place in the Gothic novel. Matthew Gregory Lewis, who acknowledged his indebtedness to Radcliffe, had unleashed all the horror of the German fancy, born of ghost tales, necromancy, and folklore. While the

Gothic had always been a product of international literary trade, the English tradition had been bound primarily to French and Italian products. Radcliffe had been indebted to French novelists who both absorbed and inspired English romances; she had depended upon Italian scenery for her atmosphere. But Lewis sought the raw sensationalism in the "uncanny, the grotesque, the horrific" dramas and tales of the German romances, and, in turn, what have been called his "gross voluptuousness" and "crude supernaturalism" returned to haunt the novel in Germany.

To be sure, Lewis's personality differed from that of the women novelists. He had none of the restraining conservatism of Clara Reeve or Ann Radcliffe. Son of a rich West Indian proprietor, continental traveler, homosexual, he was an outsider. Nevertheless, there was more than personal difference between Lewis and his predecessors to account for his choice of German models to convey what critics describe as the "physical agony" and "the unbridled lust" in *The Monk* (1796). Moreover, there is the need to account for the popularity of a novel whose "immorality" threatened its author with legal prosecution until he revised some of its more sensational scenes.

More than any other novel, *The Monk* characterizes the rebellion against authority which both the French Revolution and the subsequent Reign of Terror had given political and social expression to in France. It is no coincidence that the works of the Marquis de Sade, which added a new vocabulary to the personal response to repression, were being published at the same time. For the English, however, neither the bald personal reaction nor the bloody public demonstrations of a revolution were acceptable. The middle class was well in control. If on the surface, Lewis's novel—as Fiedler has said—was "intended to offend and disturb the right-minded bourgeoisie," however, it also provided the middle class with a less dangerous, vicarious means of expression. "Official guardians of morality" might be officially shocked, but privately they relished—as the large number of editions proves—the chance to savor the debaucheries, terrors, and excesses of Lewis's novel.

Lewis spared them nothing in his gory details. The story of the "Monk" Ambrosio, who gives way to lust after a youth spent in repression, combines rape, incest, and murder with all the accouterments of demonology. Between the time that Ambrosio is first seduced by the devil's disciple, who is posing as a novitiate, and the moment when he is cast from a mountaintop to his death, every sensational device of the Gothic is brought into play. Where Radcliffe was content to arouse suspense by suggesting horrors that did not exist, Lewis created a world in which genuine terror was the foremost commodity.

Actually, the "official guardians of morality" were not the only ones to complain. Critics were generally appalled by its faults of taste, and even Byron is said to have been revolted by it. Indeed, the disfavor endures in most modern criticism. Either *The Monk* is relegated to a transitional paragraph between Ann Radcliffe and the nineteenth-century novelists or it is described as an erotic nightmare. Yet such criticism does little justice to the strength of the work and rather confuses it with the cheap imitations that degenerated into the Victorian "Penny Dreadfuls." As John Berryman has pointed out, "*The Monk* is one of the authentic prodigies of English fiction, a book in spite of various crudenesses so good that even after a century and a half it is possible to consider it unhistorically." What is more, Berryman is right to concentrate his evaluation on the character of Ambrosio and to say that not only is "the point . . . to conduct a remarkable man utterly to damnation" but "it is surprising . . . how *long* it takes—how *difficult* it is—to be certain of damnation." If eighteenth-century critics missed the point, it was not Lewis's fault, for in detailing the characterization of Ambrosio, he presented a masterpiece of the deterioration of the moral fiber in the decadence of the sensualist.

At any rate, the immediate effect of *The Monk* was to create a host of bad imitations. Lewis himself wrote no other altogether original fiction, though his adaptations from the German stand as clearly his own creative work. Following him, there was the introduction of the Gothic to America by Charles Brockden Brown, who initiated a genre that was to have a profound effect on the development of the American novel. Richard Chase has argued persuasively that the great tradition in America has been the romance. Some of it has been the projection of bright, carefree dreams, but writers like Hawthorne and Poe created the black powers of Gothicism that characterized much of the American romance of the nineteenth century and mark the Faulknerian nether world of the twentieth. While historical and literary Gothicism influenced both men, they were not crucial. To be sure, both writers had antecedents in Lewis and in their own Brockden Brown and Washington Irving. Nevertheless, the very Gothic edifices that stirred the subconsciousness of Europeans were absent from the American landscape, and Poe and Hawthorne had to turn inward for their inspiration.

For Poe, as Harry Levin has pointed out, the "ruined castle was the haunted palace of the mind itself, so terrifyingly disintegrated in 'The Fall of the House of Usher.' Such terrors, Poe confessed, were 'not of Germany but of the soul.'" In much the same way, Hawthorne's "rediscovery of Gothic New England" was less indebted to historical sources than to a Puritanical temperament that thrived on the secret thrills of witches' sabbaths and black masses. Amid the pure climate of American optimism, the melancholy imaginations of Poe and Hawthorne demanded a darker picture of man's troubled soul and frightened dreams. The result is obvious. The American South ever since Poe has provided a fertile soil for transplanting Gothic castles—decadent in themselves and in their surroundings—which, together with the morose and somber New England landscape painted by Hawthorne, demonstrate that the Gothic genre can thrive wherever the imagination goes to work to explore man's subconscious disturbances.

In England, the Gothic continued on a popular level in the magazines where Lewis and the German *Schauersromane* ("shudder novels") set the fashion. With Lewis, however, the history of the English Gothic novel in the eighteenth century came to an end. For all the differences between the Radcliffe and Lewis traditions, they shared the common characteristics of *Otranto*. They were an awakening response to a coldly rational world. They were an appeal to imagination at a time when science was producing facts and demanding logical explanations. Like Dickens' rebellious child in *Hard Times*— half-a-century later—they were not content to accept the world of Gradgrinds who were demanding facts and nothing but facts.

Dickens, of course, was not alone in pointing up the excesses of materialism in the mechanistic culture of the nineteenth century. Yet his popularity, like that of Sir Walter Scott before him, demonstrates that beneath the surface acceptance of materialistic progress, exemplified by the Great Exhibition of 1851, there was a longing for imaginative and fantastic experiences. The great successes of writers like Wilkie Collins, Robert Louis Stevenson, and Sheridan Le Fanu attest to the public need for escape, and it was against such a background that the two great Gothic romances in the early nineteenth century were written. Apart from the Gothic elements in novelists like Dickens and Scott, the genre continued in the work of Mary Shelley and the Reverend Charles Maturin.

Frankenstein (1818), which has long enjoyed a reputation as a monster story, was a warning against man's domination by the machines he was creating. The evil is not inherent in the monster, but is a result of the attitude toward it. For Mary Shelley, imbued with the ideas of progress and the perfectability of man, the danger lay in a lack of proper feeling, a failing of charity and understanding. Her long passages describing the education of the monster have often been criticized as sentimental nonsense, but they were essential to her point of view. If what the monster learns about humanitarian principles comes only from books, it merely increases his wrath to discover their perversion in practice.

Mary Shelley was an artist. If Frankenstein has outlasted the juvenile attempts in Gothic fiction by her husband and the somewhat better vampire stories of his friends, it is no accident. She struck the sense of immediacy in her writing by maintaining a first person point of view under the most difficult circumstances. Retaining the Gothic atmosphere by subjecting her modern man to medieval influences, she appealed to all the romantic sympathy for the villain-hero, goaded by the melancholy and pessimism that made Byron's Childe Harold a popular success.

Yet the Gothic characteristics of Frankenstein are somewhat attenuated, and in some of her short stories Mary Shelley herself worked closer to the tradition. More immediately related to the Gothic was Maturin's masterpiece, Melmoth the Wanderer (1820). The Reverend Charles Maturin, a strange Dublin clergyman, had been nurtured by the work of Walpole, Radcliffe, and Lewis. In an earlier romance, The Fatal Revenge (1807), he had depended heavily on them. Less shocking than Lewis, he was more powerful than Radcliffe.

Melmoth the Wanderer is a Faust story that begins in contemporary Ireland but re-creates the adventures of John Melmoth, who has lived since the seventeenth century through a pact with the devil. Through six episodes of terror, Maturin creates the experiences of modern anguish. Maturin combines the myths of Faust and the Wandering Jew with all the horrible episodes of the Gothic romances, and yet he never depends on blood and gore for his effects. What Maturin does is to probe the psychological depths of fear, and in doing so, he was a little ahead of his audience. Although *Melmoth* has come to be regarded by many as the masterpiece of terror fiction, it attracted little attention until psychological Gothicists like Poe and the French Romantics resurrected it some years later.

Both *Frankenstein* and *Melmoth* give evidence of the fact that the English Gothic, as it continued, had to alter its form. To be sure, an occasional work like J. Mead Falkner's *The Lost Stradivarius* might come close to the older tradition, while *Wuthering Heights* carries the Gothic into metaphysical considerations, but for the most part it was absorbed into ghost stories, detective fiction, and science fantasy. Books like Stevenson's *Dr. Jekyll and Mr. Hyde* followed the development of *Frankenstein;* Wilkie Collins used the Gothic as trapping for mystery stories, and Sheridan Le Fanu embroidered his ghost tales with heavy Gothic trimming. The need that it served is now being met in different ways, and yet, oddly enough, there is a revived interest in the genre from a critical and historical point of view. Curious about his own "suppressed neurotic and erotic impulses," twentieth-century man has turned a Freudian and surrealistic eye upon a type of literature that once provided an outlet for those same repressions more than a century and a half ago. From the evidence, it is apparent that whenever the imagination of man is restricted unnaturally, the Gothic desire for escape into fantasy and the release of primitive emotions continues.

The texts have been altered only for greater typographical clarity and consistency of spelling.

ROBERT DONALD SPECTOR

The Castle of Otranto

A GOTHIC STORY

by

HORACE WALPOLE
Earl of Orford

HORACE WALPOLE (1717–1797)

Youngest son of England's great eighteenth-century prime minister, Horace Walpole has left his mark on literary history rather than politics. To be sure, he was an active behind-the-scenes politician, and his memoirs foreshadowed the work of Whig historians in the nineteenth century, but such transient business is nothing alongside the portrait of an age that he has given in his fantastic collection of letters. It is a record of the history and personalities of his times, written with a skill that is sufficient to guarantee an undying literary reputation.

Moreover, Walpole contributed to the development of English art and literature. If his *Catalogue of the Royal and Noble Authors of England* (1758) was no more than a gossipy account with antiquarian interest, his *Anecdotes of Painting in England* (1762–1771), drawn from the notes of George Vertue, was a pioneering effort in the history of English painting. His own estate at Strawberry Hill aided the popularity of the Gothic by giving it aristocratic sanction, and his *Castle of Otranto* (1764 —though the imprint was 1765) clearly marked the first departure from the sentimental novel to tales of terror and horror.

Walpole's novel is unlikely to affect modern readers as it did his contemporaries, but to describe the work, as a recent critic has done, as being "totally devoid of atmosphere" and thus ineffective is absurd. Vague as it is, the medieval historical background permitted Walpole to indulge his imagination in sensationalistic events cast in the gloom and decadence of a castle haunted by unknown and mysterious fears foreboding horrible discoveries. At the same time, the setting is augmented by Walpole's dramatic sense, which conveys the full feeling of terror. Yet if he had done nothing else, Walpole most certainly provided the necessary machinery for the genre in his characters and castle. The feudal tyrant, venerable ecclesiastic, forlorn and virtuous maidens; the themes of incest and usurpation; and the supernatural occurrences—all, as one literary historian has noted, were responsible for "launch[ing] 'Gothic' on its way as a critical term in prose fiction."

PREFACE TO THE FIRST EDITION

The following work was found in the library of an ancient Catholic family in the North of England. It was printed at Naples, in the black letter,[1] in the year 1529. How much sooner it was written does not appear. The principal incidents are such as were believed in the darkest ages of Christianity; but the language and conduct have nothing that savors of barbarism. The style is of the purest Italian. If the story was written near the time when it was supposed to have happened, it must have been between 1095, the era of the first crusade, and 1243, the date of the last, or not long afterward. There is no other circumstance in the work that can lead us to guess at the period in which the scene is laid; the names of the actors are evidently fictitious, and probably disguised on purpose; yet the Spanish names of the domestics seem to indicate, that this work was not composed until the establishment of the Aragonian kings[2] in Naples had made Spanish appellations familiar in that country. The beauty of the diction, and the zeal of the author (moderated, however, by singular judgment), concur to make me think that the date of the composition was little antecedent to that of the impression. Letters were then in the most flourishing state in Italy, and contributed to dispel the empire of superstition, at that time so forcibly attacked by the reformers. It is not unlikely that an artful priest might endeavor to turn their own arms on the innovators; and might avail himself of his abilities as an author to confirm the populace in their ancient errors and superstitions. If this was his view, he has certainly acted with signal address. Such a work as the following would enslave a hundred vulgar minds beyond half the books of controversy that have been written from the days of Luther to the present hour.

This solution of the author's motives is, however, offered as a mere conjecture. Whatever his views were, or whatever effects the execution of them might have, his work can only be laid before the public at present as a matter of entertainment. Even as such, some apology for it is necessary. Miracles, visions, necromancies, dreams, and other preternatural events, are exploded now even from romances. That was not the case

---

[1] Printed in Old English or Gothic type.
[2] It was not until 1442 that Alfonso V of Aragon conquered Naples, which finally was united with Aragon in 1504-1505.

when our author wrote; much less when the story itself is
supposed to have happened. Belief in every kind of prodigy
was so established in those dark ages, that an author would not
be faithful to the manners of the times who should omit all
mention of them. He is not bound to· believe them himself,
but he must represent his actors as believing them.

If this air of the miraculous is excused, the reader will find
nothing else unworthy of his perusal. Allow the possibility
of the facts, and all the actors comport themselves as persons
would do in their situation. There is no bombast, no similes,
flowers, digressions, or unnecessary descriptions. Everything
tends directly to the catastrophe. Never is the reader's attention
relaxed. The rules of the drama[3] are almost observed throughout the ·conduct of the piece. The characters are well drawn,
and still better maintained. Terror, the author's principle
engine, prevents the story from ever languishing; and it is so
often contrasted by pity, that the mind is kept up in a constant
vicissitude of·interesting passions.

Some persons may, perhaps, think the characters of the
domestics too little serious for the general cast of the story;
but, besides their opposition to the principal personages, the
art of the author is very observable in his conduct of the
subalterns. They discover many passages essential to the story,
which could not be well brought to light but by their *naïveté*
and simplicity: in particular, the womanish terror and foibles
of Bianca, in the last chapter, conduce essentially toward advancing the catastrophe.

It is natural for a translator to be prejudiced in favor of
his adopted work. More impartial readers may not be so much
struck with the beauties of this piece as I was. Yet I am not
blind to my author's defects. I could wish he had grounded
his plan on a more useful moral than this; that *the sins of the
fathers are visited on their children to the third and fourth
generation*. I doubt whether, in his time, any more than at
present, ambition curbed its appetite of dominion from the
dread of so remote a punishment. And yet this moral is weak-
ened by that less direct insinuation, that even such anathema
may be diverted by devotion to St. Nicholas.[4] Here the interest
of the monk plainly gets the better of the judgment of the au-

[3] Aristotle's rules of unity for time, place, and action. At a time when
the novel had not yet developed critical rules of its own, it was customary
to apply those that were used in the drama.

[4] The patron saint of scholars (clerics in the Middle Ages). The suggestion
is that the cleric was propagandizing against the Renaissance.

thor. However, with all its faults, I have no doubt but the English reader will be pleased with a sight of this performance. The piety that reigns throughout, the lessons of virtue that are inculcated, and the rigid purity of the sentiments, exempt this work from the censure to which romances are but too liable. Should it meet with the success I hope for, I may be encouraged to reprint the original Italian, though it will tend to depreciate my own labor. Our language falls far short of the charms of the Italian, both for variety and harmony. The latter is peculiarly excellent for simple narrative. It is difficult in English *to relate* without falling too low or rising too high; a fault obviously occasioned by the little care taken to speak pure language in common conversation. Every Italian or Frenchman, of any rank, piques himself on speaking his own tongue correctly and with choice. I cannot flatter myself with having done justice to my author in this respect: his style is as elegant as his conduct of the passions is masterly. It is a pity that he did not apply his talents to what they were evidently proper for—the theater.

I will detain the reader no longer, but to make one short remark. Though the machinery is invention, and the names of the actors imaginary, I cannot but believe that the groundwork of the story is founded on truth. The scene is undoubtedly laid in some real castle. The author seems frequently, without design, to describe particular parts. *The chamber,* says he, *on the right hand; the door on the left hand; the distance from the chapel to Conrad's apartment:* these, and other passages, are strong presumptions that the author had some certain building in his eye. Curious persons, who have leisure to employ in such researches, may possibly discover in the Italian writers the foundation on which our author has built. If a catastrophe, at all resembling that which he describes, is believed to have given rise to this work, it will contribute to interest the reader, and will make *The Castle of Otranto* a still more moving story.

CHAPTER I

MANFRED, Prince of Otranto, had one son and one daughter: the latter, a most beautiful virgin, aged eighteen, was called Matilda. Conrad, the son, was three years younger, a homely youth, sickly, and of no promising disposition; yet he was the

darling of his father, who never showed any symptoms of
affection to Matilda. Manfred had contracted a marriage for
his son with the Marquis of Vicenza's daughter, Isabella; and
she had already been delivered by her guardians into the hands
of Manfred, that he might celebrate the wedding as soon as
Conrad's infirm state of health would permit. Manfred's
impatience for this ceremonial was remarked by his family
and neighbors. The former, indeed, apprehending the severity
of their prince's disposition, did not dare to utter their surmises on this precipitation. Hippolita, his wife, an amiable
lady, did sometimes venture to represent the danger of marry-
ing their only son so early, considering his great youth, and
greater infirmities; but she never received any other answer
than reflections on her own sterility, who had given him but
one heir. His tenants and subjects were less cautious in their
discourses: they attributed this hasty wedding to the prince's
dread of seeing accomplished an ancient prophecy, which was
said to have pronounced, that *the castle and lordship of
Otranto should pass from the present family, whenever the real
owner should be grown too large to inhabit it.* It was difficult
to make any sense of this prophecy; and still less easy to conceive what it had to do with the marriage in question. Yet
these mysteries, or contradictions, did not make the populace
adhere the less to their opinion.

Young Conrad's birthday was fixed for his espousals. The
company was assembled in the chapel of the castle, and everything ready for beginning the divine office, when Conrad himself was missing. Manfred, impatient of the least delay, and
who had not observed his son retire, dispatched one of his attendants to summon the young prince. The servant, who had
not stayed long enough to have crossed the court to Conrad's
apartment, came running back breathless, in a frantic manner,
his eyes staring, and foaming at the mouth. He said nothing,
but pointed to the court. The company were struck with
terror and amazement. The Princess Hippolita, without knowing what was the matter, but anxious for her son, swooned
away. Manfred, less apprehensive than enraged at the pro-
crastination of the nuptials, and at the folly of his domestic,
asked imperiously what was the matter. The fellow made no
answer, but continued pointing toward the courtyard; and, at
last, after repeated questions put to him, cried out:

"Oh! The helmet! The helmet!"

In the meantime, some of the company had run into the

court, from whence was heard a confused noise of shrieks, horror, and surprise. Manfred, who began to be alarmed at not seeing his son, went himself to get information of what occasioned this strange confusion. Matilda remained endeavoring to assist her mother, and Isabella stayed for the same purpose, and to avoid showing any impatience for the bridegroom, for whom, in truth, she had conceived little affection.

The first thing that struck Manfred's eyes was a group of his servants endeavoring to raise something that appeared to him a mountain of sable plumes. He gazed without believing his sight. "What are you doing?" cried Manfred, wrathfully. "Where is my son?"

A volley of voices replied, "Oh, my lord! The Prince! The Prince! The helmet! The helmet!"

Shocked with these lamentable sounds, and dreading he knew not what, he advanced hastily—but, what a sight for a father's eyes—he beheld his child dashed to pieces, and almost buried under an enormous helmet, a hundred times more large than any casque[5] ever made for human being, and shaded with a proportionable quantity of black feathers.

The horror of the spectacle, the ignorance of all around how this misfortune had happened, and, above all, the tremendous phenomenon before him, took away the Prince's speech. Yet his silence lasted longer than even grief could occasion. He fixed his eyes on what he wished in vain to believe a vision; and seemed less attentive to his loss, than buried in meditation on the stupendous object that had occasioned it. He touched, he examined, the fatal casque; nor could even the bleeding, mangled remains of the young Prince divert the eyes of Manfred from the portent before him. All who had known his partial fondness for young Conrad were as much surprised at their Prince's insensibility, as thunderstruck themselves at the miracle of the helmet. They conveyed the disfigured corpse into the hall, without receiving the least direction from Manfred. As little was he attentive to the ladies who remained in the chapel; on the contrary, without mentioning the unhappy princesses, his wife and daughter, the first sounds that dropped from Manfred's lips were, "Take care of the Lady Isabella."

The domestics, without observing the singularity of this direction, were guided by their affection to their mistress to consider it as peculiarly addressed to her situation, and flew to her assistance. They conveyed her to her chamber more dead

[5] Helmet.

than alive, and indifferent to all the strange circumstances she heard, except the death of her son. Matilda, who doted on her mother, smothered her own grief and amazement, and thought of nothing but assisting and comforting her afflicted parent. Isabella, who had been treated by Hippolita like a daughter, and who returned that tenderness with equal duty and affection, was scarce less assiduous about the princess; at the same time endeavoring to partake and lessen the weight of sorrow which she saw Matilda strove to suppress, for whom she had conceived the warmest sympathy of friendship. Yet her own situation could not help finding its place in her thoughts. She felt no concern for the death of young Conrad, except commiseration; and she was not sorry to be delivered from a marriage which had promised her little felicity, either from her destined bridegroom, or from the severe temper of Manfred, who, though he had distinguished her by great indulgence, had impressed her mind with terror, from his causeless rigor to such amiable princesses as Hippolita and Matilda.

While the ladies were conveying the wretched mother to her bed, Manfred remained in the court, gazing on the ominous casque, and regardless of the crowd which the strangeness of the event had now assembled around him. The few words he articulated tended solely to inquiries, whether any man knew from whence it could have come. Nobody could give him the least information. However, as it seemed to be the sole object of his curiosity, it soon became so to the rest of the spectators, whose conjectures were as absurd and improbable, as the catastrophe itself was unprecedented. In the midst of their senseless guesses, a young peasant, whom rumor had drawn thither from a neighboring village, observed that the miraculous helmet was exactly like that on the figure in black marble of Alfonso the Good, one of their former princes, in the church of St. Nicholas.

"Villain! What sayest thou?" cried Manfred, starting from his trance in a tempest of rage, and seizing the young man by the collar; "how darest thou utter such treason? Thy life shall pay for it."

The spectators, who as little comprehended the cause of the prince's fury as all the rest they had seen, were at a loss to unravel this new circumstance. The young peasant himself was still more astonished, not conceiving how he had offended the Prince; yet, recollecting himself, with a mixture of grace and humility, he disengaged himself from Manfred's grip, and then, with an obeisance which discovered more jealousy of innocence than dismay, he asked, with respect, of what he was guilty. Manfred, more enraged at the vigor, however decently exerted, with which the young man had shaken off his hold, than appeased by his submission, ordered his attendants to seize him, and, if he had not been withheld by his friends, whom he had invited to the nuptials, would have poniarded the peasant in their arms.

During this altercation, some of the vulgar spectators had run to the great church, which stood near the castle, and came back open-mouthed, declaring that the helmet was missing from Alfonso's statue. Manfred, at this news, grew perfectly frantic; and, as if he sought a subject on which to vent the tempest within him, he rushed again on the young peasant, crying, "Villain! monster! sorcerer! 'tis thou hast done this! 'Tis thou hast slain my son!"

The mob, who wanted some object within the scope of their capacities, on whom they might discharge their bewildered reasonings, caught the words from the mouth of their lord, and re-echoed, "Ay, ay; 'tis he, 'tis he! he has stolen the helmet from good Alfonso's tomb, and dashed out the brains of our young Prince with it," never reflecting how enormous the disproportion was between the marble helmet that had been in the church, and that of steel before their eyes; nor how impossible it was for a youth, seemingly not twenty, to wield a piece of armor of so prodigious a weight.

The folly of these ejaculations brought Manfred to himself: yet, whether provoked at the peasant having observed the resemblance between the two helmets, and thereby led to the farther discovery of the absence of that in the church, or wishing to bury any fresh rumor under so impertinent a supposition, he gravely pronounced that the young man was certainly a necromancer; and that till the Church could take cognizance of the affair, he would have the magician, whom they had thus detected, kept prisoner under the helmet itself, which he ordered his attendants to raise, and place the young man under it; declaring he should be kept there without food, with which his own infernal art might furnish him.

It was in vain for the youth to represent against this preposterous sentence; in vain did Manfred's friends endeavor to divert him from this savage and ill-grounded resolution. The generality were charmed with their lord's decision, which to their apprehensions carried great appearance of justice, as the

magician was to be punished by the very instrument with
which he had offended; nor were they struck with the least
compunction at the probability of the youth being starved,
for they firmly believed that, by his diabolical skill, he could
easily supply himself with nutriment.

Manfred thus saw his commands even cheerfully obeyed; and
appointing a guard, with strict orders to prevent any food
being conveyed to the prisoner, he dismissed his friends and
attendants, and retired to his own chamber, after locking the
gates of the castle, in which he suffered none but his domestics
to remain.

In the meantime, the care and zeal of the young ladies had
brought the Princess Hippolita to herself, who, amidst the
transports of her own sorrow, frequently demanded news of
her lord, would have dismissed her attendants to watch over
him, and at last enjoined Matilda to leave her, and visit and
comfort her father. Matilda, who wanted not affectionate duty
to Manfred, though she trembled at his austerity, obeyed the
orders of Hippolita, whom she tenderly recommended to Isabella; and inquiring of the domestics of her father, was informed that he was retired to his chamber, and had commanded
that nobody should have admittance to him. Concluding that
he was immersed in sorrow for the death of her brother, and
fearing to renew his tears by the sight of his sole remaining
child, she hesitated whether she should break in upon his
affliction; yet solicitude for him, backed by the commands of
her mother, encouraged her to venture disobeying the orders
he had given, a fault she had never been guilty of before. The
gentle timidity of her nature made her pause for some minutes
at his door. She heard him traverse his chamber backward and
forward with disordered steps; a mood which increased her
apprehensions. She was however just going to beg admittance,
when Manfred suddenly opened the door; and as it was now
twilight, concurring with the disorder of his mind, he did not
distinguish the person, but asked angrily, who it was. Matilda
replied, trembling, "My dearest father, it is I, your daughter."
Manfred, stepping back hastily, cried, "Begone, I do not
want a daughter"; and, flinging back abruptly, clapped the
door against the terrified Matilda.

She was too well acquainted with her father's impetuosity to
venture a second intrusion. When she had a little recovered
the shock of so bitter a reception, she wiped away her tears,
to prevent the additional stab that the knowledge of it would

give to Hippolita, who questioned her in the most anxious terms on the health of Manfred, and how he bore his loss. Matilda assured her he was well, and supported his misfortune with manly fortitude.

"But will he not let me see him?" said Hippolita, mournfully; "will he not permit me to blend my tears with his, and shed a mother's sorrows in the bosom of her lord? Or do you deceive me, Matilda? I know how Manfred doted on his son; is not the stroke too heavy for him? Has he not sunk under it? You do not answer me:—alas! I dread the worst!—raise me, my maidens; I will, I will see my lord. Bear me to him instantly. He is dearer to me even than my children."

Matilda made signs to Isabella to prevent Hippolita's rising; and both those lovely young women were using their gentle violence to stop and calm the Princess, when a servant, on the part of Manfred, arrived, and told Isabella that his lord demanded to speak with her.

"With me!" cried Isabella.

"Go," said Hippolita, relieved by a message from her lord: "Manfred cannot support the sight of his own family. He thinks you less disordered than we are, and dreads the shock of my grief. Console him, dear Isabella, and tell him I will smother my own anguish rather than add to his."

As it was now evening, the servant who conducted Isabella bore a torch before her. When they came to Manfred, who was walking impatiently about the gallery, he started, and said hastily:

"Take away that light, and begone." Then shutting the door impetuously, he flung himself upon a bench against the wall, and bade Isabella sit by him. She obeyed trembling.

"I sent for you, lady," said he, and then stopped, under great appearance of confusion.

"My lord!"

"Yes, I sent for you on a matter of great moment," resumed he; "dry your tears, young lady;—you have lost your bridegroom. Yes, cruel fate! and I have lost the hopes of my race! but Conrad was not worthy of your beauty."

"How! my lord," said Isabella; "sure you do not suspect me of not feeling the concern I ought! My duty and affection would have always——"

"Think no more of him," interrupted Manfred, "he was a sickly, puny child; and Heaven has perhaps taken him away, that I might not trust the honors of my house on so frail a foundation. The line of Manfred calls for numerous supports. My foolish fondness for that boy blinded the eyes of my prudence—but it is better as it is. I hope, in a few years, to have reason to rejoice at the death of Conrad."

Words cannot paint the astonishment of Isabella. At first she apprehended that grief had disordered Manfred's understanding. Her next thought suggested that this strange discourse was designed to ensnare her; she feared that Manfred had perceived her indifference for his son; and in consequence of that idea she replied:

"Good my lord, do not doubt my tenderness: my heart would have accompanied my hand. Conrad would have engrossed all my care; and wherever fate shall dispose of me, I shall always cherish his memory, and regard your highness and the virtuous Hippolita as my parents."

"Curse on Hippolita!" cried Manfred. "Forget her from this moment, as I do. In short, lady, you have missed a husband undeserving of your charms; they shall now be better disposed of. Instead of a sickly boy, you shall have a husband in the prime of his age, who will know how to value your beauties, and who may expect a numerous offspring."

"Alas! my lord," said Isabella, "my mind is too sadly engrossed by the recent catastrophe in your family to think of another marriage. If ever my father returns, and it shall be his pleasure, I shall obey, as I did when I consented to give my hand to your son; but, until his return, permit me to remain under your hospitable roof, and employ the melancholy hours in assuaging yours, Hippolita's, and the fair Matilda's affliction."

"I desired you once before," said Manfred, angrily, "not to name that woman; from this hour she must be a stranger to you, as she must be to me;—in short, Isabella, since I cannot give you my son, I offer you myself."

"Heavens!" cried Isabella, waking from her delusion, "what do I hear? You, my lord! You! my father-in-law, the father of Conrad! The husband of the virtuous and tender Hippolita!"

"I tell you," said Manfred imperiously, "Hippolita is no longer my wife; I divorce her from this hour. Too long has she cursed me by her unfruitfulness. My fate depends on having sons, and this night I trust will give a new date to my hopes."

At those words he seized the cold hand of Isabella, who was half dead with fright and horror. She shrieked and started

from him. Manfred rose to pursue her, when the moon, which
was now up and gleamed in at the opposite casement, presented to his sight the plumes of the fatal helmet, which rose
to the height of the windows, waving backward and forward
in a tempestuous manner, and accompanied with a hollow and
rustling sound. Isabella, who gathered courage from her situation, and who dreaded nothing so much as Manfred's pursuit
of his declaration, cried:

"Look, my lord! See, Heaven itself declares against your
impious intentions!"

"Heaven nor hell shall impede my designs," said Manfred,
advancing again to seize the Princess. At that instant the
portrait of his grandfather, which hung over the bench where
they had been sitting, uttered a deep sigh, and heaved its
breast. Isabella, whose back was turned to the picture, saw not
the motion, nor whence the sound came but started, and said:

"Hark, my lord! what sound was that?" and at the same
time made toward the door. Manfred, distracted between the
flight of Isabella, who had now reached the stairs, and yet
unable to keep his eyes from the picture, which began to move,
had, however, advanced some steps after her, still looking
backward on the portrait, when he saw it quit its panel, and
descend on the floor with a grave and melancholy air.

"Do I dream?" cried Manfred, returning; "or are the devils
themselves in league against me? Speak, infernal specter! or,
if thou art my grandsire, why dost thou, too, conspire against
thy wretched descendant, who too dearly pays for——" Ere
he could finish the sentence, the vision sighed again, and made
a sign to Manfred to follow him.

"Lead on!" cried Manfred; "I will follow thee to the gulf
of perdition." The specter marched sedately, but dejected, to
the end of the gallery, and turned into a chamber on the right
hand. Manfred accompanied him at a little distance, full of
anxiety and horror, but resolved. As he would have entered
the chamber, the door was clapped to with violence by an
invisible hand. The Prince, collecting courage from this delay,
would have forcibly burst open the door with his foot, but
found that it resisted his utmost efforts.

"Since hell will not satisfy my curiosity," said Manfred, "I
will use the human means in my power for preserving my
race; Isabella shall not escape me."

That lady, whose resolution had given way to terror the
moment she had quitted Manfred, continued her flight to the

bottom of the principal staircase. There she stopped, not knowing whither to direct her steps, nor how to escape from the impetuosity of the Prince. The gates of the castle she knew were locked, and guards placed in the court. Should she, as her heart prompted her, go and prepare Hippolita for the cruel destiny that awaited her, she did not doubt but Manfred would seek her there, and that his violence would incite him to double the injury he meditated, without leaving room for them to avoid the impetuosity of his passions. Delay might give him time to reflect on the horrid measures he had conceived, or produce some circumstance in her favor, if she could, for that night at least, avoid his odious purpose. Yet where conceal herself? How avoid the pursuit he would infallibly make throughout the castle? As these thoughts passed rapidly through her mind, she recollected a subterraneous passage which led from the vaults of the castle to the church of St. Nicholas. Could she reach the altar before she was overtaken, she knew even Manfred's violence would not dare to profane the sacredness of the place; and she determined, if no other means of deliverance offered, to shut herself up forever among the holy virgins, whose convent was contiguous to the cathedral. In this resolution, she seized a lamp that burned at the foot of the staircase, and hurried toward the secret passage.

The lower part of the castle was hollowed into several intricate cloisters; and it was not easy for one under so much anxiety to find the door that opened into the cavern. An awful silence reigned throughout those subterraneous regions, except now and then some blasts of wind that shook the doors she had passed, and which, grating on the rusty hinges, were re-echoed through that long labyrinth of darkness. Every murmur struck her with new terror; yet more she dreaded to hear the wrathful voice of Manfred urging his domestics to pursue her. She trod as softly as impatience would give her leave—yet frequently stopped, and listened to hear if she was followed. In one of those moments she thought she heard a sigh. She shuddered, and recoiled a few paces. In a moment she thought she heard the step of some person. Her blood curdled; she concluded it was Manfred. Every suggestion that horror could inspire rushed into her mind. She condemned her rash flight, which had thus exposed her to his rage in a place where her cries were not likely to draw anybody to her assistance. Yet the sound seemed not to come from behind; if Manfred knew where she was, he must have followed her. She was still in one of the cloisters, and the steps she had heard were too distinct to proceed from the way she had come. Cheered with this reflection, and hoping to find a friend in whoever was not the Prince, she was going to advance, when a door that stood ajar, at some distance to the left, was opened gently; but ere her lamp, which she held up could discover who opened it, the person retreated precipitately on seeing the light.

Isabella, whom every incident was sufficient to dismay, hesitated whether she should proceed. Her dread of Manfred soon outweighed every other terror. The very circumstance of the person avoiding her, gave her a sort of courage. It could only be, she thought, some domestic belonging to the castle. Her gentleness had never raised her an enemy, and conscious innocence made her hope that, unless sent by the Prince's order to seek her, his servants would rather assist than prevent her flight. Fortifying herself with these reflections, and believing, by what she could observe, that she was near the mouth of the subterraneous cavern, she approached the door that had been opened; but a sudden gust of wind, that met her at the door, extinguished her lamp, and left her in total darkness.

Words cannot paint the horror of the Princess' situation. Alone, in so dismal a place, her mind impressed with all the terrible events of the day, hopeless of escaping, expecting every moment the arrival of Manfred, and far from tranquil on knowing she was within reach of somebody, she knew not whom, who for some cause seemed concealed thereabouts; all these thoughts crowded on her distracted mind, and she was ready to sink under her apprehensions. She addressed herself to every saint in heaven, and inwardly implored their assistance. For a considerable time she remained in an agony of despair. At last, as softly as was possible, she felt for the door, and having found it, entered trembling into the vault from whence she had heard the sigh and steps. It gave her a kind of momentary joy to perceive an imperfect ray of clouded moonshine gleam from the roof of the vault, which seemed to be fallen in, and from whence hung a fragment of earth or building, she could not distinguish which, that appeared to have been crushed inwards. She advanced eagerly toward this chasm, when she discerned a human form standing close against the wall.

She shrieked, believing it the ghost of her betrothed Conrad.

The figure, advancing, said in a submissive voice, "Be not alarmed, lady, I will not injure you."

Isabella, a little encouraged by the words and tone of voice of the stranger, and recollecting that this must be the person who had opened the door, recovered her spirits enough to reply, "Sir, whoever you are, take pity on a wretched princess, standing on the brink of destruction; assist me to escape from this fatal castle, or, in a few moments, I may be made miserable forever."

"Alas," said the stranger, "what can I do to assist you? I will die in your defense; but I am unacquainted with the castle, and want——"

"Oh!" said Isabella, hastily interrupting him, "help me but to find a trap-door that must be hereabout, and it is the greatest service you can do me, for I have not a minute to lose." Saying these words, she felt about on the pavement, and directed the stranger to search likewise, for a smooth piece of brass enclosed in one of the stones. "That," said she, "is the lock which opens with a spring, of which I know the secret. If we can find that, I may escape; if not, alas! courteous stranger, I fear I shall have involved you in my misfortunes. Manfred will suspect you for the accomplice of my flight, and you will fall a victim to his resentment."

"I value not my life," said the stranger; "and it will be some comfort to lose it, in trying to deliver you from his tyranny."

"Generous youth!" said Isabella, "how shall I ever requite——"

As she uttered these words, a ray of moonshine, streaming through a cranny of the ruin above, shone directly on the lock they sought. "Oh, transport!" said Isabella, "Here is the trap-door"; and, taking out the key, she touched the spring, which, starting aside, discovered an iron ring. "Lift up the door," said the Princess. The stranger obeyed; and beneath appeared some stone steps descending into a vault totally dark. "We must go down here," said Isabella; "follow me; dark and dismal as it is, we cannot miss our way; it leads directly to the church of St. Nicholas—but, perhaps," added the Princess, modestly, "you have no reason to leave the castle, nor have I farther occasion for your service; in a few minutes I shall be safe from Manfred's rage—only let me know to whom I am so much obliged."

"I will never quit you," said the stranger eagerly, "until I have placed you in safety—nor think me, Princess, more generous than I am; though you are my principal care——"

The stranger was interrupted by a sudden noise of voices that seemed approaching, and they soon distinguished these words: "Talk not to me of necromancers; I tell you she must be in the castle; I will find her in spite of enchantment."

"Oh, heavens!" cried Isabella. "It is the voice of Manfred; make haste, or we are ruined! and shut the trap-door after you." Saying this, she descended the steps precipitately; and as the stranger hastened to follow her, he let the door slip out of his hands; it fell, and the spring closed over it. He tried in vain to open it, not having observed Isabella's method of touching the spring; nor had he many moments to make an essay. The noise of the falling door had been heard by Manfred, who, directed by the sound, hastened thither, attended by his servants with torches.

"It must be Isabella," cried Manfred, before he entered the vault. "She is escaping by the subterraneous passage, but she cannot have got far." What was the astonishment of the Prince, when, instead of Isabella, the light of the torches discovered to him the young peasant, whom he thought confined under the fatal helmet. "Traitor!" said Manfred, "how camest thou here? I thought thee in durance above in the court."

"I am no traitor," replied the young man boldly, "nor am I answerable for your thoughts."

"Presumptuous villain!" cried Manfred. "Dost thou provoke my wrath? Tell me; how hast thou escaped from above? Thou hast corrupted thy guards, and their lives shall answer it."

"My poverty," said the peasant calmly, "will disculpate them; though the ministers of a tyrant's wrath, to thee they are faithful, and but too willing to execute the orders which you unjustly imposed upon them."

"Art thou so hardy as to dare my vengeance?" said the Prince. "But tortures shall force the truth from thee. Tell me; I will know thy accomplices."

"There was my accomplice!" said the youth, smiling and pointing to the roof.

Manfred ordered the torches to be held up, and perceived that one of the cheeks of the enchanted casque had forced its way through the pavement of the court, as his servants had let it fall over the peasant, and had broken through into the vault, leaving a gap through which the peasant had pressed himself some minutes before he was found by Isabella. "Was that the way by which thou didst descend?" said Manfred.

"It was," said the youth.

"But what noise was that," said Manfred, "which I heard, as I entered the cloister?"

"A door clapped," said the peasant; "I heard it as well as you."

"What door?" said Manfred hastily.

"I am not acquainted with your castle," said the peasant. "It is the first time I ever entered it; and this vault the only part of it within which I ever was."

"But I tell thee," said Manfred, wishing to find out if the youth had discovered the trap-door, "it was this way I heard the noise; my servants heard it too."

"My lord," interrupted one of them officiously, "to be sure it was the trap-door, and he was going to make his escape."

"Peace! blockhead," said the Prince angrily; "if he was going to escape, how should he come on this side? I will know from his mouth what noise it was I heard. Tell me truly, thy life depends on thy veracity."

"My veracity is dearer to me than my life," said the peasant; "nor would I purchase the one by forfeiting the other."

"Indeed, young philosopher!" said Manfred, contemptuously; "tell me, then, what was that noise I heard?"

"Ask me, what I can answer," said he, "and put me to death instantly, if I tell you a lie."

Manfred, growing impatient at the steady valor and indifference of the youth, cried, "Well, then, thou man of truth! answer; was it the fall of the trap-door that I heard?"

"It was," said the youth.

"It was!" said the Prince; "and how didst thou come to know there was a trap-door here?"

"I saw the plate of brass by a gleam of moonshine," replied he.

"But what told thee it was a lock?" said Manfred. "How didst thou discover the secret of opening it?"

"Providence, that delivered me from the helmet, was able to direct me to the spring of a lock," said he.

"Providence should have gone a little farther, and have placed thee out of the reach of my resentment," said Manfred. "When Providence had taught thee to open the lock, it abandoned thee for a fool, who did not know how to make use of its favors. Why didst thou not pursue the path pointed out for thy escape? Why didst thou shut the trap-door before thou hadst descended the steps?"

"I might ask you, my lord," said the peasant, "how I, totally unacquainted with your castle, was to know that those steps led to any outlet? But I scorn to evade your questions. Wherever those steps led to, perhaps, I should have explored the way. I could not be in a worse situation than I was. But the truth is, I let the trap-door fall; your immediate arrival followed. I had given the alarm—what imported it to me whether I was seized a minute sooner or a minute later?"

"Thou art a resolute villain for thy years," said Manfred; "yet, on reflection, I suspect thou dost but trifle with me; thou hast not yet told me how thou didst open the lock."

"That I will show you, my lord," said the peasant; and, taking up a fragment of stone that had fallen from above, he laid himself on the trap-door, and began to beat on the piece of brass that covered it; meaning to gain time for the escape of the Princess. This presence of mind, joined to the frankness of the youth, staggered Manfred. He even felt a disposition toward pardoning one who had been guilty of no crime. Manfred was not one of those savage tyrants who wanton in cruelty unprovoked. The circumstances of his fortune had given an asperity to his temper, which was naturally humane; and his virtues were always ready to operate, when his passions did not obscure his reason.

While the Prince was in this suspense, a confused noise of voices echoed through the distant vaults. As the sound approached, he distinguished the clamors of some of his domestics, whom he had dispersed through the castle in search of Isabella, calling out, "Where is my lord? Where is the Prince?"

"Here I am," said Manfred, as they came nearer; "have you found the Princess?"

The first that arrived replied, "Oh, my lord, I am glad we have found you."

"Found me!" said Manfred. "Have you found the Princess?"

"We thought we had, my lord," said the fellow, looking terrified; "but——"

"But what?" cried the Prince. "Has she escaped?"

"Jaquez and I, my lord——"

"Yes, I and Diego," interrupted the second, who came up in still greater consternation.

"Speak one of you at a time," said Manfred. "I ask you, where is the Princess?"

"We do not know," said they both together; "but we are frightened out of our wits."

"So I think, blockheads," said Manfred; "what is it has scared you thus?"

"Oh, my lord," said Jaquez, "Diego has seen such a sight! Your Highness would not believe your eyes."

"What new absurdity is this?" cried Manfred. "Give me a direct answer, or by Heaven——"

"Why, my lord, if it please your highness to hear me," said the poor fellow, "Diego and I——"

"Yes, I and Jaquez," cried his comrade.

"Did not I forbid you to speak both at a time?" said the Prince; "you, Jaquez, answer; for the other fool seems more distracted than thou art. What is the matter?"

"My gracious lord," said Jaquez, "if it please your highness to hear me, Diego and I, according to your highness' orders, went to search for the young lady; but being apprehensive that we might meet the ghost of my young lord, your highness' son, God rest his soul! as he has not received Christian burial——"

"Sot!" cried Manfred, in a rage, "is it only a ghost, then, that thou hast seen?"

"Oh, worse! worse! my lord," cried Diego; "I had rather have seen ten whole ghosts."

"Grant me patience!" said Manfred; "those blockheads distract me. Out of my sight, Diego; and thou, Jaquez, tell me, in one word, art thou sober? Art thou raving? Thou wast wont to have some sense; has the other sot frightened himself and thee too? Speak; what is it he fancies he has seen?"

"Why, my lord," replied Jaquez, trembling. "I was going to tell your highness, that since the calamitous misfortune of my young lord, God rest his precious soul, not one of us, your highness' faithful servants, indeed we are, my lord, though poor men; I say, not one of us has dared to set a foot about the castle, but two together; so Diego and I, thinking that my young lady might be in the great gallery, went up there to look for her, and tell her your highness wanted something to impart to her."

"O blundering fools!" cried Manfred; "and in the meantime she has made her escape, because you were afraid of goblins! Why, thou knave! She left me in the gallery; I came from thence myself."

"For all that, she may be there still for aught I know," said

Jaquez; "but the devil shall have me before I seek her there again. Poor Diego, I do not believe he will ever recover it!"

"Recover what?" said Manfred. "Am I never to learn what it is has terrified these rascals? But I lose my time; follow me, slave; I will see if she is in the gallery."

"For Heaven's sake, my dear good lord," cried Jaquez, "do not go to the gallery! Satan himself, I believe, is in the chamber next to the gallery."

Manfred, who hitherto had treated the terror of his servants as an idle panic, was struck at this new circumstance. He recollected the apparition of the portrait, and the sudden closing of the door at the end of the gallery—his voice faltered, and he asked with disorder, "What is in the great chamber?"

"My lord," said Jaquez, "when Diego and I came into the gallery, he went first, for he said he had more courage than I; —so, when we came into the gallery, we found nobody. We looked under every bench and stool; and still we found nobody."

"Were all the pictures in their places?" said Manfred.

"Yes, my lord," answered Jaquez, "but we did not think of looking behind them."

"Well, well," said Manfred, "proceed."

"When we came to the door of the great chamber," continued Jaquez, "we found it shut."

"And could not you open it?" said Manfred.

"Oh yes, my lord; would to Heaven we had not!" replied he; "nay, it was not I neither, it was Diego; he was grown fool-hardy, and would go on, though I advised him not; if ever I open a door that is shut again!"

"Trifle not," said Manfred, shuddering, "but tell me what you saw in the great chamber, on opening the door."

"I! my lord!" said Jaquez. "I saw nothing. I was behind Diego; but I heard the noise."

"Jaquez," said Manfred, in a solemn tone of voice, "tell me, I adjure thee by the souls of my ancestors, what was it thou sawest? What was it thou heardest?"

"It was Diego saw it, my lord, it was not I," replied Jaquez. "I only heard the noise. Diego had no sooner opened the door, then he cried out, and ran back—I ran back too, and said, 'Is it the ghost?'—'The ghost! no, no,' said Diego, and his hair stood on end—'it is a giant, I believe; he is all clad in armor, for I saw his foot and part of his leg, and they are as large as the helmet below in the court.' As he said these words, my lord, we heard a violent motion, and the rattling of armor, as if the giant was rising, for Diego has told me since that he believes the giant was lying down, for the foot and leg were stretched at length on the floor. Before we could get to the end of the gallery, we heard the door of the great chamber clap behind us, but we did not dare turn back to see if the giant was following us—yet, now I think on it, we must have heard him if he pursued us; but for Heaven's sake, good my lord, send for the chaplain, and have the castle exorcized, for, for certain, it is enchanted."

"Ay, pray do, my lord," cried all the servants at once, "or we must leave your highness' service."

"Peace, dotards," said Manfred, "and follow me. I will know what all this means."

"We! my lord? cried they, with one voice. "We would not go up to the gallery for your highness' revenue."

The young peasant, who had stood silent, now spoke. "Will your highness," said he, "permit me to try this adventure? My life is of consequence to nobody; I fear no bad angel, and have offended no good one."

"Your behavior is above your seeming," said Manfred, viewing him with surprise and admiration; "hereafter I will reward your bravery; but now," continued he with a sigh, "I am so circumstanced, that I dare trust no eyes but my own. However, I give you leave to accompany me."

Manfred, when he first followed Isabella from the gallery, had gone directly to the apartment of his wife, concluding the princess had retired thither. Hippolita, who knew his step, rose with anxious fondness to meet her lord, whom she had not seen since the death of her son. She would have flown in a transport, mixed of joy and grief, to his bosom, but he pushed her rudely off, and said, "Where is Isabella?"

"Isabella, my lord!" said the astonished Hippolita.

"Yes, Isabella," cried Manfred imperiously; "I want Isabella."

"My lord," replied Matilda, who perceived how much his behavior had shocked her mother, "she has not been with us since your highness summoned her to your apartment."

"Tell me where she is," said the prince. "I do not want to know where she has been."

"My good lord," said Hippolita, "your daughter tells you the truth: Isabella left us by your command, and has not returned since; but, my good lord, compose yourself; retire to your rest; this dismal day has disordered you. Isabella shall wait your orders in the morning."

"What, then, you know where she is?" cried Manfred. "Tell me directly, for I will not lose an instant; and you, woman," speaking to his wife, "order your chaplain to attend me forthwith."

"Isabella," said Hippolita, calmly, "is retired, I suppose to her chamber; she is not accustomed to watch at this late hour. Gracious my lord," continued she, "let me know what has disturbed you. Has Isabella offended you?"

"Trouble me not with questions," said Manfred, "but tell me where she is."

"Matilda shall call her," said the Princess. "Sit down, my lord, and resume your wonted fortitude."

"What! art thou jealous of Isabella?" replied he, "that you wish to be present at our interview?"

"Good heavens! my lord," said Hippolita; "what is it your highness means?"

"Thou wilt know ere many minutes are passed," said the cruel prince. "Send your chaplain to me, and wait my pleasure here." At these words he flung out of the room in search of Isabella, leaving the amazed ladies thunderstruck with his words and frantic deportment, and lost in vain conjectures on what he was meditating.

Manfred was now returning from the vault, attended by the peasant and a few of his servants, whom he had obliged to accompany him. He ascended the staircase without stopping, till he arrived at the gallery, at the door of which he met Hippolita and her chaplain. When Diego had been dismissed by Manfred, he had gone directly to the princess' apartment with the alarm of what he had seen. That excellent lady, who no more than Manfred doubted of the reality of the vision, yet affected to treat it as a delirium of the servants. Willing, however, to save her lord from any additional shock, and prepared by a series of grief not to tremble at any accession to it, she determined to make herself the first sacrifice, if fate had marked the present hour for their destruction. Dismissing the reluctant Matilda to her rest, who in vain sued for leave to accompany her mother, and attended only by her chaplain, Hippolita had visited the gallery and great chamber; and now, with more serenity of soul than she had felt for many hours, she met her lord, and assured him that the vision of the gigantic leg and foot was all a fable; and no doubt an impression made by fear, and the dark and dismal hour of the night, on the minds of his servants. She and the chaplain had examined the chamber, and found everything in the usual order.

Manfred, though persuaded, like his wife, that the vision had been no work of fancy, recovered a little from the tempest of mind into which so many strange events had thrown him. Ashamed, too, of his inhuman treatment of a princess, who returned every injury with new marks of tenderness and duty he felt returning love forcing itself into his eyes; but not less ashamed of feeling remorse toward one against whom he was inwardly meditating a yet more bitter outrage, he curbed the yearnings of his heart, and did not dare to lean even toward pity. The next transition of his soul was to exquisite villainy. Presuming on the unshaken submission of Hippolita, he flattered himself that she would not only acquiesce with patience to a divorce, but would obey, if it was his pleasure, in endeavoring to persuade Isabella to give him her hand—but ere he could indulge this horrid hope, he reflected that Isabella was not to be found. Coming to himself, he gave orders that every avenue to the castle should be strictly guarded, and charged his domestics, on pain of their lives, to suffer nobody to pass out. The young peasant to whom he spoke favorably, he ordered to remain in a small chamber on the stairs, in which there was a pallet-bed, and the key of which he took away himself, telling the youth he would talk with him in the morning. Then dismissing his attendants, and bestowing a sullen kind of half-nod on Hippolita, he retired to his own chamber.

CHAPTER II

Matilda, who, by Hippolita's order, had retired to her apartment, was ill-disposed to take any rest. The shocking fate of her brother had deeply affected her. She was surprised at not seeing Isabella; but the strange words which had fallen from her father, and his obscure menace to the Princess, his wife, accompanied by the most furious behavior, had filled her gentle mind with terror and alarm. She waited anxiously for the return of Bianca, a young damsel that attended her, whom she had sent to learn what was become of Isabella. Bianca soon appeared, and informed her mistress of what she had gathered from the servants, that Isabella was nowhere to be found. She related the adventure of the young peasant who had been discovered in the vault, though with many simple additions from the incoherent accounts of the domestics; and she dwelt principally on the gigantic leg and foot which had been seen in the gallery-chamber. This last circumstance had terrified Bianca so much, that she was rejoiced when Matilda told her that she would not go to rest, but would watch till the Princess should rise.

The young Princess wearied herself in conjectures on the flight of Isabella, and on the threats of Manfred to her mother. "But what business could he have so urgent with the chaplain?" said Matilda. "Does he intend to have my brother's body interred privately in the chapel?"

"Oh, madam," said Bianca, "now I guess. As you are become his heiress, he is impatient to have you married. He has always been raving for more sons; I warrant he is now impatient for grandsons. As sure as I live, madam, I shall see you a bride at last. Good madam, you won't cast off your faithful Bianca; you won't put Donna Rossara over me, now you are a great princess!"

"My poor Bianca," said Matilda, "how fast your thoughts ramble! I a great Princess! What hast thou seen in Manfred's behavior since my brother's death that bespeaks any increase of tenderness to me? No, Bianca; his heart was ever a stranger to me—but he is my father, and I must not complain. Nay, if Heaven shuts my father's heart against me, it overpays my little merit in the tenderness of my mother.—O that dear mother! Yes, Bianca, 'tis there I feel the rugged temper of Manfred. I can support his harshness to me with patience; but it wounds my soul when I am witness to his causeless severity toward her."

"Oh, madam," said Bianco, "all men use their wives so, when they are weary of them."

"And yet you congratulated me but now," said Matilda, "when you fancied my father intended to dispose of me!"

"I would have you a great lady," replied Bianca, "come what will. I do not wish to see you moped in a convent, as you would be if you had your will, and if my lady, your mother, who knows that a bad husband is better than no husband at all, did not hinder you.—Bless me! what noise is that? St. Nicholas forgive me! I was but in jest."

"It is the wind," said Matilda, "whistling through the battlements in the tower above. You have heard it a thousand times."

"Nay," said Bianca, "there was no harm neither in what I

said; it is no sin to talk of matrimony—and so, madam, as I was saying, if my Lord Manfred should offer you a handsome young prince for a bridegroom, you would drop him a curtsy, and tell him you would rather take the veil?"

"Thank Heaven! I am in no such danger," said Matilda; "you know how many proposals for me he has rejected."

"And you thank him like a dutiful daughter, do you, madam? But come, madam; suppose to-morrow morning he was to send for you to the great council-chamber, and there you should find at his elbow a lovely young prince, with large black eyes, a smooth white forehead, and manly curling locks like jet; in short, madam, a young hero resembling the picture of the good Alfonso in the gallery, which you sit and gaze at for hours together."

"Do not speak lightly of that picture," interrupted Matilda, sighing; "I know the adoration with which I look at that picture is uncommon—but I am not in love with a colored panel. The character of that virtuous prince, the veneration with which my mother has inspired me for his memory, the orisons which, I know not why, she has enjoined me to pour forth at his tomb, all have concurred to persuade me that, somehow or other, my destiny is linked with something relating to him."

"Lord, madam! how should that be?" said Bianca. "I have always heard that your family was no way related to his; and I am sure I cannot conceive why my lady, the Princess, sends you in a cold morning or a damp evening to pray at his tomb; he is no saint by the almanac.[6] If you must pray, why does she not bid you address yourself to our great St. Nicholas? I am sure he is the saint I pray to for a husband."

"Perhaps my mind would be less affected," said Matilda, "if my mother would explain her reasons to me; but it is the mystery she observes, that inspires me with this—I know not what to call it. As she never acts from caprice, I am sure there is some fatal secret at bottom—nay, I know there is. In her agony of grief for my brother's death she dropped some words that intimated as much."

"Oh, dear madam," cried Bianca, "what were they?"

"No," said Matilda, "if a parent lets fall a word, and wishes it recalled, it is not for a child to utter it."

"What! was she sorry for what she had said?" asked Bianca. "I am sure, madam, you may trust me."

[6] The calendar with ecclesiastical holidays gave the saints' days.

"With my own little secrets, when I have any, I may," said Matilda; "but never with my mother's. A child ought to have no ears or eyes, but as a parent directs."

"Well, to be sure, madam, you were born to be a saint," said Bianca, "and there is no resisting one's vocation; you will end in a convent at last. But there is my Lady Isabella would not be so reserved to me; she will let me talk to her of young men; and when a handsome cavalier has come to the castle, she has owned to me that she wished your brother Conrad resembled him."

"Bianca," said the Princess, "I do not allow you to mention my friend disrespectfully. Isabella is of a cheerful disposition, but her soul is as pure as virtue itself. She knows your idling, babbling humor, and perhaps has now and then encouraged it, to divert melancholy, and enliven the solitude in which my father keeps us."

"Blessed Mary!" said Bianca, starting. "There it is again! Dear madam, do you hear nothing? The castle is certainly haunted!"

"Peace!" said Matilda. "And listen! I did think I heard a voice—but it must be fancy; your terrors, I suppose, have infected me."

"Indeed! indeed! madam," said Bianca, half weeping with agony, "I am sure I heard a voice."

"Does anybody lie in the chamber beneath?" said the Princess.

"Nobody has dared to lie there," answered Bianca, "since the great astrologer, that was your brother's tutor, drowned himself. For certain, madam, his ghost and the young prince's are now met in the chamber below; for Heaven's sake let us fly to your mother's apartment!"

"I charge you not to stir," said Matilda. "If they are spirits in pain, we may ease their sufferings by questioning them. They can mean no hurt to us, for we have not injured them; and if they should, shall we be more safe in one chamber than in another? Reach me my beads; we will say a prayer, and then speak to them."

"Oh, dear lady, I would not speak to a ghost for the world," cried Bianca. As she said these words, they heard the casement of the little chamber below Matilda's open. They listened attentively, and in a few minutes thought they heard a person sing, but could not distinguish the words.

"This can be no evil spirit," said the Princess, in a low voice;

"it is undoubtedly one of the family—open the window, and we shall know the voice."

"I dare not, indeed, madam," said Bianca.

"Thou art a very fool," said Matilda, opening the window gently herself. The noise that the Princess made was, however, heard by the person beneath, who stopped, and they concluded had heard the casement open.

"Is anybody below?" said the Princess; "if there is, speak."

"Yes," said an unknown voice.

"Who is it?" said Matilda.

"A stranger," replied the voice.

"What stranger?" said she. "And how didst thou come here at this unusual hour, when all the gates of the castle are locked?"

"I am not here willingly," answered the voice; "but pardon me, lady, if I have disturbed your rest; I knew not that I was overheard. Sleep has forsaken me; I left a restless couch, and came to waste the irksome hours with gazing on the fair approach of morning, impatient to be dismissed from this castle."

"Thy words and accents," said Matilda, "are of a melancholy cast; if thou art unhappy, I pity thee. If poverty afflicts thee, let me know it: I will mention thee to the Princess, whose beneficent soul ever melts for the distressed; and she will relieve thee."

"I am, indeed, unhappy," said the stranger, "and I know not what wealth is; but I do not complain of the lot which Heaven has cast for me. I am young and healthy and am not ashamed of owing my support to myself; yet think me not proud, or that I disdain your generous offers. I will remember you in my orisons, and I will pray for blessings on your gracious self and your noble mistress—if I sigh, lady, it is for others, not for myself."

"Now I have it, madam," said Bianca, whispering to the Princess. "This is certainly the young peasant; and, by my conscience, he is in love;—well, this is a charming adventure! Do, madam, let us sift him. He does not know you, but takes you for one of my Lady Hippolita's women."

"Art thou not ashamed, Bianca?" said the Princess. "What right have we to pry into the secrets of this young man's heart? He seems virtuous and frank, and tells us he is unhappy. Are those circumstances that authorize us to make a property of him? How are we entitled to his confidence?"

"Lord! madam, how little you know of love!" replied

Bianca. "Why, lovers have no pleasure equal to talking of their mistress."

"And would you have me become a peasant's confidant?" said the Princess.

"Well, then, let me talk to him," said Bianca; "though I have the honor of being your highness' maid of honor, I was not always so great. Besides, if love levels ranks, it raises them too. I have a respect for a young man in love."

"Peace, simpleton," said the Princess. "Though he said he was unhappy, it does not follow that he must be in love. Think of all that has happened to-day, and tell me, if there are no misfortunes but what love causes.—Stranger," resumed the Princess, "if thy misfortunes have not been occasioned by thy own fault, and are within the compass of the Princess Hippolita's power to redress, I will take upon me to answer that she will be thy protectress. When thou art dismissed from this castle, repair to holy Father Jerome, at the convent adjoining to the church of St. Nicholas, and make thy story known to him, as far as thou thinkest meet. He will not fail to inform the Princess, who is the mother of all that want her assistance. Farewell! It is not seemly for me to hold further converse with a man at this unwonted hour."

"May the saints guard thee, gracious lady!" replied the peasant; "but, oh! if a poor and worthless stranger might presume to beg a minute's audience further—am I so happy? —the casement is not shut—might I venture to ask——"

"Speak quickly," said Matilda; "the morning dawns apace; should the laborers come into the field and perceive us—what wouldst thou ask?"

"I know not how—I know not if I dare," said the young stranger, faltering; "yet the humanity with which you have spoken to me emboldens—lady, dare I trust you?"

"Heavens," said Matilda, "what dost thou mean? With what wouldst thou trust me?—Speak boldly, if thy secret is fit to be entrusted to a virtuous breast."

"I would ask," said the peasant, recollecting himself, "whether what I have heard from the domestics is true, that the Princess is missing from the castle."

"What imports it to thee to know?" replied Matilda. "Thy first words bespoke a prudent and becoming gravity. Dost thou come hither to pry into the secrets of Manfred? Adieu. I have been mistaken in thee." Saying these words, she shut the casement hastily, without giving the young man time to reply.

"I had acted more wisely," said the Princess to Bianca, with some sharpness, "if I had let thee converse with this peasant; his inquisitiveness seems of a piece with thy own."

"It is not fit for me to argue with your highness," replied Bianca; "but perhaps the questions I should have put to him would have been more to the purpose than those you have been pleased to ask him."

"Oh, no doubt," said Matilda; "you are a very discreet personage! May I know what you would have asked him?"

"A bystander often sees more of the game than those that play," answered Bianca. "Does your highness think, madam, that his question about my Lady Isabella was the result of mere curiosity? No, no, madam; there is more in it than you great folks are aware of. Lopez told me, that all the servants believe this young fellow contrived my Lady Isabella's escape —now, pray, madam, observe—you and I both know that my Lady Isabella never much fancied the prince your brother— well, he is killed just in the critical minute—I accuse nobody. A helmet falls from the moon—so my lord, your father, says; but Lopez and all the servants say, that this young spark is a magician, and stole it from Alfonso's tomb."

"Have done with this rhapsody of impertinence," said Matilda.

"Nay, madam, as you please," cried Bianca; "yet it is very particular, though, that my Lady Isabella should be missing the very same day, and that this young sorcerer should be found at the mouth of the trap-door—I accuse nobody—but if my young lord came honestly by his death——"

"Dare not, on thy duty," said Matilda, "to breathe a suspicion on the purity of my dear Isabella's fame."

"Purity or not purity," said Bianca, "gone she is—a stranger is found that nobody knows. You question him yourself. He tells you he is in love, or unhappy, it is the same thing— nay, he owned he was unhappy about others; and is anybody unhappy about another unless they are in love with them? And, at the very next word he asks innocently, poor soul, if my Lady Isabella is missing."

"To be sure," said Matilda, "thy observations are not totally without foundation; Isabella's flight amazes me. The curiosity of the stranger is very particular; yet Isabella never concealed a thought from me."

"So she told you," said Bianca, "to fish out your secrets; but who knows, madam, but this stranger may be some prince in disguise? Do, madam, let me open the window, and ask him a few questions."

"No," replied Matilda, "I will ask him myself; if he knows aught of Isabella, he is not worthy that I should converse farther with him." She was going to open the casement, when they heard the bell ring at the postern gate of the castle, which is on the right hand of the tower where Matilda lay. This prevented the Princess from renewing the conversation with the stranger.

After continuing silent for some time, "I am persuaded," said she to Bianca, "that whatever be the cause of Isabella's flight, it had no unworthy motive. If this stranger was accessory to it, she must be satisfied of his fidelity and worth. I observed, did not you, Bianca, that his words were tinctured with an uncommon infusion of piety. It was no ruffian's speech; his phrases were becoming a man of gentle birth."

"I told you, madam," said Bianca, "that I was sure he was some prince in disguise."

"Yet," said Matilda, "if he was privy to her escape how will you account for his not accompanying her in her flight? Why expose himself unnecessarily and rashly to my father's resentment?"

"As for that, madam," replied she, "if he could get from under the helmet, he will find ways of eluding your father's anger. I do not doubt but he has some talisman or other about him."

"You resolve everything into magic," said Matilda; "but a man who has any intercourse with infernal spirits does not dare to make use of those tremendous and holy words which he uttered. Didst thou not observe with what fervor he vowed to remember me to Heaven in his prayers? Yes, Isabella was undoubtedly convinced of his piety."

"Commend me to the piety of a young fellow and a damsel that consult to elope!" said Bianca. "No, no, madam; my Lady Isabella is of another guess-mold than you take her for. She used, indeed, to sigh and lift up her eyes in your company because she knows you are a saint; but when your back was turned——"

"You wrong her," said Matilda. "Isabella is no hypocrite: she has a due sense of devotion, but never affected a call she has not. On the contrary, she always combated my inclination for the cloister; and though I own the mystery she has made to me of her flight confounds me—though it seems inconsistent with the friendship between us—I cannot forget the disinterested warmth with which she always opposed my taking the veil. She wished to see me married, though my dower would have been a loss to her and my brother's children. For her sake, I will believe well of this young peasant."

"Then you do think there is some liking between them?" said Bianca. While she was speaking, a servant came hastily into the chamber, and told the Princess that the Lady Isabella was found.

"Where?" said Matilda.

"She has taken sanctuary in St. Nicholas' church," replied the servant. "Father Jerome has brought the news himself; he is below with his highness."

"Where is my mother?" said Matilda.

"She is in her own chamber, madam, and has asked for you."

Manfred had risen at the first dawn of light, and gone to Hippolita's apartment to inquire if she knew aught of Isabella. While he was questioning her, word was brought that Jerome demanded to speak with him. Manfred, little suspecting the cause of the friar's arrival, and knowing he was employed by Hippolita in her charities, ordered him to be admitted, intending to leave them together, while he pursued his search after Isabella.

"Is your business with me or the Princess?" said Manfred.

"With both," replied the holy man. "The Lady Isabella——"

"What of her?" interrupted Manfred, eagerly.

"Is at St. Nicholas' altar," replied Jerome.

"That is no business of Hippolita's" said Manfred with confusion; "let us retire to my chamber, Father, and inform me how she came thither."

"No, my lord," replied the good man with an air of firmness and authority, that daunted even the resolute Manfred, who could not help revering the saint-like virtues of Jerome, "my commission is to both; and, with your highness' good liking, in the presence of both, I shall deliver it; but first, my lord, I must interrogate the Princess, whether she is acquainted with the cause of the Lady Isabella's retirement from your castle."

"No, on my soul," said Hippolita; "does Isabella charge me with being privy to it?"

"Father," interrupted Manfred, "I pay due reverence to your holy profession; but I am sovereign here, and will allow no meddling priest to interfere in the affairs of my domestic. If you have aught to say, attend me to my chamber. I do not use to let my wife be acquainted with the secret affairs of my state; they are not within a woman's province."

"My lord," said the holy man, "I am no intruder into the secrets of families. My office is to promote peace, to heal divisions, to preach repentance, and teach mankind to curb their headstrong passions. I forgive your highness' uncharitable apostrophe; I know my duty, and am the minister of a mightier prince than Manfred. Hearken to him who speaks through my organs."

Manfred trembled with rage and shame. Hippolita's countenance declared her astonishment and impatience to know where this would end; her silence more strongly spoke her observance of Manfred.

"The Lady Isabella," resumed Jerome, "commends herself to both your highnesses. She thanks both for the kindness with which she has been treated in your castle; she deplores the loss of your son, and her own misfortune in not becoming the daughter of such wise and noble princes, whom she shall always respect as parents. She prays for uninterrupted union and felicity between you (Manfred's color changed); but, as it is no longer possible for her to be allied to you, she entreats your consent to remain in sanctuary till she can learn news of her father, or, by the certainty of his death, be at liberty, by the approbation of her guardians, to dispose of herself in suitable marriage."

"I shall give no such consent," said the Prince; "but insist on her return to the castle without delay. I am answerable for her person to her guardians, and will not brook her being in any hands but my own."

"Your highness will recollect whether that can any longer be proper," replied the friar.

"I want no monitor," said Manfred, coloring. "Isabella's conduct leaves room for strange suspicions; and that young villain, who was at least the accomplice of her flight, if not the cause of it——"

"The cause!" interrupted Jerome. "Was a *young* man the cause?"

"This is not to be borne!" cried Manfred. "Am I to be bearded in my own palace by an insolent monk? Thou art privy, I guess, to their amours."

"I would pray to Heaven to clear up your uncharitable

surmises," said Jerome, "if your highness were not satisfied in your conscience how unjustly you accuse me. I do pray to Heaven to pardon that uncharitableness; and I implore your highness to leave the Princess at peace in that holy place, where she is not liable to be disturbed by such vain and worldly fantasies as discourses of love from any man."

"Cant not to me," said Manfred, "but return and bring the Princess to her duty."

"It is my duty to prevent her return hither," said Jerome. "She is where orphans and virgins are safest from the snares and wiles of this world; and nothing but a parent's authority shall take her thence."

"I am her parent," cried Manfred, "and demand her."

"She wished to have you for her parent," said the friar; "but Heaven, that forbade that connection, has forever dissolved all ties betwixt you; and I announce to your highness——"

"Stop! audacious man," said Manfred, "and dread my displeasure."

"Holy Father," said Hippolita, "it is your office to be no respecter of persons; you must speak as your duty prescribes; but it is my duty to hear nothing that it pleases not my lord I should hear. Attend the Prince to his chamber. I will retire to my oratory, and pray to the Blessed Virgin to inspire you with her holy counsels, and to restore the heart of my gracious lord to its wonted peace and gentleness."

"Excellent woman!" said the friar. "My lord, I attend your pleasure."

Manfred, accompanied by the friar, passed to his own apartment, where, shutting the door, "I perceive, Father," said he, "that Isabella has acquainted you with my purpose. Now hear my resolve, and obey. Reasons of state, most urgent reasons, my own and the safety of my people, demand that I should have a son. It is in vain to expect an heir from Hippolita; I have made choice of Isabella. You must bring her back, and you must do more. I know the influence you have with Hippolita; her conscience is in your hands. She is, I allow, a faultless woman; her soul is set on heaven, and scorns the little grandeur of this world. You can withdraw her from it entirely. Persuade her to consent to the dissolution of our marriage, and to retire into a monastery; she shall endow one if she will; and shall have the means of being as liberal to your order as she or you can wish. Thus you will divert the calamities that are hanging over our heads, and have the merit of saving the principality of Otranto from destruction. You are a prudent man, and, though the warmth of my temper betrayed me into some unbecoming expressions, I honor your virtue, and wish to be indebted to you for the repose of my life and the preservation of my family."

"The will of Heaven be done," said the friar. "I am but its worthless instrument. It makes use of my tongue to tell thee, Prince, of thy unwarrantable designs. The injuries of the virtuous Hippolita have mounted to the throne of pity. By me thou art reprimanded for thy adulterous intention of repudiating her; by me thou art warned not to pursue the incestuous design on thy contracted daughter. Heaven, that delivered her from thy fury, when the judgments so recently fallen on thy house ought to have inspired thee with other thoughts, will continue to watch over her. Even I, a poor and despised friar, am able to protect her from thy violence. I, sinner as I am, and uncharitably reviled by your highness as an accomplice of I know not what amours, scorn the allurements with which it has pleased thee to tempt mine honesty. I live my order; I honor devout souls; I respect the piety of thy Princess; but I will not betray the confidence she reposes in me, nor serve even the cause of religion by foul and sinful compliances; but, forsooth, the welfare of the state depends on your highness having a son! Heaven mocks the short-sighted views of man. But yester-morn, whose house was so great, so flourishing as Manfred's? Where is young Conrad now? My lord, I respect your tears, but I mean not to check them; let them flow, Prince! They will weigh more with Heaven toward the welfare of thy subjects, than a marriage which, founded on lust or policy, could never prosper. The scepter which passed from the race of Alfonso to thine cannot be preserved by a match which the Church will never allow. If it is the will of the Most High that Manfred's name must perish, resign yourself, my lord, to its decrees; and thus deserve a crown that can never pass away. Come, my lord, I like this sorrow; let us return to the Princess; she is not apprised of your cruel intentions; nor did I mean more than to alarm you. You saw with what gentle patience, with what efforts of love, she heard, she rejected hearing, the extent of your guilt. I know she longs to fold you in her arms, and assure you of her unalterable affection."

"Father," said the Prince, "you mistake my compunction. True, I honor Hippolita's virtues; I think her a saint; and wish it were for my soul's health to tie faster the knot that has united us; but, alas, Father, you know not the bitterest of my pangs; it is some time that I have had scruples on the legality of our union. Hippolita is related to me in the fourth degree—it is true, we had a dispensation; but I have been informed that she had also been contracted to another. This it is that sits heavy at my heart; to this state of unlawful wedlock I impute the visitation that has fallen on me in the death of Conrad. Ease my conscience of this burden, dissolve our marriage, and accomplish the work of godliness which your divine exhortations have commenced in my soul."

How cutting was the anguish which the good man felt, when he perceived this turn in the wily Prince! He trembled for Hippolita, whose ruin he saw was determined; and he feared if Manfred had no hope of recovering Isabella, that his impatience for a son would direct him to some other object who might not be equally proof against the temptation of Manfred's rank. For some time the holy man remained absorbed in thought. At length, conceiving some hopes from delay, he thought the wisest conduct would be to prevent the Prince from despairing of recovering Isabella. Her the friar knew he could dispose, from her affection to Hippolita, and from the aversion she had expressed to him for Manfred's addresses, to second his views till the censures of the Church could be fulminated against a divorce. With this intention, as if struck with the Prince's scruples, he at length said:

"My lord, I have been pondering on what your highness has said; and if in truth it is delicacy of conscience that is the real motive of your repugnance to your virtuous lady, far be it from me to endeavor to harden your heart. The Church is an indulgent mother; unfold your griefs to her; she alone can administer comfort to your soul, either by satisfying your conscience, or, upon examination of your scruples, by setting you at liberty, and indulging you in the lawful means of continuing your lineage. In the latter case, if the Lady Isabella can be brought to consent——"

Manfred, who concluded that he had either over-reached the good man, or that his first warmth had been but a tribute paid to appearance, was overjoyed at this sudden turn, and repeated the most magnificent promises, if he should succeed by the friar's mediation. The well-meaning priest suffered him to deceive himself, fully determined to traverse his views, instead of seconding them.

"Since we now understand one another," resumed the Prince, "I expect, Father, that you satisfy me in one point. Who is the youth that I found in the vault? He must have been privy to Isabella's flight. Tell me truly, is he her lover? Or is he an agent for another's passion? I have often suspected Isabella's indifference to my son; a thousand circumstances crowd on my mind that confirm that suspicion. She herself was so conscious of it, that while I discoursed her in the gallery she outran my suspicions, and endeavored to justify herself from coolness to Conrad."

The friar, who knew nothing of the youth but what he had learned occasionally from the princess, ignorant what was become of him, and not sufficiently reflecting on the impetuosity of Manfred's temper, conceived that it might not be amiss to sow the seeds of jealousy in his mind; they might be turned to some use hereafter, either by prejudicing the Prince against Isabella, if he persisted in that union; or, by diverting his attention to a wrong scent, and employing his thoughts on a visionary intrigue, prevent his engaging in any new pursuit. With this unhappy policy, he answered in a manner to confirm Manfred in the belief of some connection between Isabella and the youth. The Prince, whose passions wanted little fuel to throw them into a blaze, fell into a rage at the idea of what the friar had suggested.

"I will fathom to the bottom of this intrigue," cried he; and quitting Jerome abruptly, with a command to remain there till his return, he hastened to the great hall of the castle, and ordered the peasant to be brought before him.

"Thou hardened young impostor," said the Prince, as soon as he saw the youth; "what becomes of thy boasted veracity now? It was Providence, was it, and the light of the moon, that discovered the lock of the trap-door to thee? Tell me, audacious boy, who thou art, and how long thou hast been acquainted with the Princess; and take care to answer with less equivocation than thou didst last night, or tortures shall wring the truth from thee."

The young man, perceiving that his share in the flight of the Princess was discovered, and concluding that anything he should say could no longer be of service or detriment to her, replied, "I am no impostor, my lord, nor have I deserved opprobrious language. I answered to every question your highness put to me last night with the same veracity that I shall speak now; and that will not be from fear of your tortures, but because my soul abhors a falsehood. Please to repeat your questions, my lord; I am ready to give you all the satisfaction in my power."

"You know my questions," replied the Prince, "and only want time to prepare an evasion. Speak directly; who art thou, and how long hast thou been known to the Princess?"

"I am a laborer at the next village," said the peasant; "my name is Theodore. The Princess found me in the vault last night; before that hour I never was in her presence."

"I may believe as much or as little as I please of this," said Manfred; "but I will hear thy own story, before I examine into the truth of it. Tell me, what reason did the Princess give thee for making her escape? Thy life depends on thy answer."

"She told me," replied Theodore, "that she was on the brink of destruction, and that if she could not escape from the castle, she was in danger in a few moments of being made miserable forever."

"And on this slight foundation, on a silly girl's report," said Manfred, "thou didst hazard my displeasure!"

"I fear no man's displeasure," said Theodore, "when a woman in distress puts herself under my protection."

During this examination Matilda was going to the apartment of Hippolita. At the upper end of the hall, where Manfred sat, was a boarded gallery, with latticed windows, through which Matilda and Bianca were to pass. Hearing her father's voice, and seeing the servants assembled round him, she stopped to learn the occasion. The prisoner soon drew her attention; the steady and composed manner in which he answered, and the gallantry of his last reply, which were the first words she heard distinctly, interested her in his favor. His person was noble, handsome, and commanding, even in that situation, but his countenance soon engrossed her whole care.

"Heavens! Bianca," said the Princess softly, "do I dream, or is not that youth the exact resemblance of Alfonso's picture in the gallery?" She could say no more, for her father's voice grew louder at every word.

"This bravado," said he, "surpasses all thy former insolence. Thou shalt experience the wrath with which thou darest to trifle. Seize him," continued Manfred, "and bind him—the first news the Princess hears of her champion shall be that he has lost his head for her sake."

"The injustice of which thou art guilty toward me," said Theodore, "convinces me that I have done a good deed in delivering the Princess from thy tyranny. May she be happy, whatever becomes of me!"

"This is a lover," cried Manfred, in a rage; "a peasant within sight of death is not animated by such sentiments. Tell me, tell me, rash boy, who thou art, or the rack shall force thy secret from thee."

"Thou hast threatened me with death already," said the youth, "for the truth I have told thee; if that is all the encouragement I am to expect for sincerity, I am not tempted to indulge thy vain curiosity further."

"Then thou wilt not speak?" said Manfred.

"I will not," replied he.

"Bear him away into the courtyard," said Manfred; "I will see his head this instant severed from his body."

Matilda fainted at hearing those words. Bianca shrieked and cried, "Help, help! The Princess is dead!" Manfred started at this ejaculation, and demanded what was the matter. The young peasant, who heard it too, was struck with horror, and asked eagerly the same question; but Manfred ordered him to be hurried into the court, and kept there for execution, till he had informed himself of the cause of Bianca's shrieks. When he learned the meaning, he treated it as a womanish panic, and ordering Matilda to be carried to her apartment, he rushed into the court, and calling for one of his guards, bade Theodore kneel down and prepare to receive the fatal blow.

The undaunted youth received the bitter sentence with a resignation that touched every heart but Manfred's. He wished earnestly to know the meaning of the words he had heard relating to the Princess; but fearing to exasperate the tyrant more against her, he desisted. The only boon he deigned to ask was that he might be permitted to have a confessor, and make his peace with Heaven. Manfred, who hoped by the confessor's means to come at the youth's history, readily granted his request; and being convinced that Father Jerome was now in his interest, he ordered him to be called and shrive the prisoner. The holy man, who had little foreseen the catastrophe that his imprudence occasioned, fell on his knees to the Prince, and adjured him in the most solemn manner not to shed innocent blood. He accused himself in the bitterest terms for his indiscretion, endeavored to exculpate the youth, and left no method untried to soften the tyrant's rage. Manfred, more incensed than appeased by Jerome's intercession, whose retraction now made him suspect he had been imposed upon by both, commanded the friar to do his duty, telling him he would not allow the prisoner many minutes for confession.

"Nor do I ask many, my lord," said the unhappy young man. "My sins, thank Heaven, have not been numerous; nor exceed what might be expected at my years. Dry your tears, good Father, and let us dispatch; this is a bad world; nor have I had cause to leave it with regret."

"Oh, wretched youth!" said Jerome. "How canst thou bear the sight of me with patience? I am thy murderer! It is I have brought this dismal hour upon thee!"

"I forgive thee from my soul," said the youth, "as I hope Heaven will pardon me. Hear my confession, Father, and give me thy blessing."

"How can I prepare thee for thy passage as I ought?" said Jerome. "Thou canst not be saved without pardoning thy foes, and canst thou forgive that impious man there?"

"I can," said Theodore, "and do."

"And does not this touch thee, cruel Prince?" said the friar.

"I sent for thee to confess him," said Manfred, sternly; "not to plead for him. Thou didst first incense me against him; his blood be upon thy head."

"It will, it will!" said the good man, in an agony of sorrow. "Thou and I must never hope to go where this blessed youth is going."

"Dispatch," said Manfred; "I am no more to be moved by the whining of priests than by the shrieks of women."

"What!" said the youth; "is it possible that my fate could have occasioned what I heard? Is the Princess, then, again in thy power?"

"Thou dost but remember me of my wrath," said Manfred; "prepare thee, for this moment is thy last."

The youth, who felt his indignation rise, and who was touched with the sorrow which he saw he had infused into all the spectators, as well as into the friar, suppressed his emotions, and putting off his doublet, and unbuttoning his collar, knelt down to his prayers. As he stooped, his shirt slipped down below his shoulder, and discovered the mark of a bloody arrow.

"Gracious Heaven!" cried the holy man, starting. "What do I see? It is my child, my Theodore!"

The passions that ensued must be conceived; they cannot be

painted. The tears of the assistants were suspended by wonder, rather than stopped by joy. They seemed to inquire into the eyes of their lord what they ought to feel. Surprise, doubt, tenderness, respect, succeeded each other in the countenance of the youth. He received with modest submission the effusion of the old man's tears and embraces; yet, afraid of giving a loose to hope, and suspecting, from what had passed, the inflexibility of Manfred's temper, he cast a glance toward the Prince, as if to say, "Canst thou be unmoved at such a scene as this?"

Manfred's heart was capable of being touched. He forgot his anger in his astonishment; yet his pride forbade his owning himself affected. He even doubted whether this discovery was not a contrivance of the friar to save the youth. "What may this mean?" said he. "How can he be thy son? Is it consistent with thy profession or reputed sanctity to avow a peasant's offspring for the fruit of thy irregular amours?"

"Oh God!" said the holy man. "Dost thou question his being mine? Could I feel the anguish I do, if I were not his father? Spare him, good Prince! spare him! and revile me as thou pleasest."

"Spare him! spare him!" cried the attendants. "For this good man's sake."

"Peace!" said Manfred, sternly. "I must know, ere I am disposed to pardon. A saint's bastard may be no saint himself."

"Injurious lord!" said Theodore. "Add not insult to cruelty. If I am this venerable man's son, though no prince, as thou art, know, the blood that flows in my veins——"

"Yes," said the friar, interrupting him, "his blood is noble; nor is he that abject thing, my lord, you speak him. He is my lawful son; and Sicily can boast of few houses more ancient than that of Falconara—but, alas! my lord, what is blood? what is nobility? We are all reptiles, miserable, sinful creatures. It is piety alone that can distinguish us from the dust whence we sprung, and whither we must return."

"Truce to your sermon," said Manfred; "you forget you are no longer Friar Jerome, but the Count of Falconara. Let me know your history: you will have time enough to moralize hereafter, if you should not happen to obtain the grace of that sturdy criminal there."

"Mother of God!" said the friar. "Is it possible my lord can refuse a father the life of his only, his long-lost child?

Trample me, my lord, scorn, afflict me, accept my life for his, but spare my son!"

"Thou canst feel, then," said Manfred, "what it is to lose an only son! A little hour ago thou didst preach up resignation to me: *my* house, if fate so pleased, must perish—but the Count of Falconara——"

"Alas! my lord," said Jerome, "I confess I have offended; but aggravate not an old man's sufferings. I boast not of my family, nor think of such vanities; it is nature that pleads for this body; it is the memory of the dear woman that bore him—is she, Theodore, is she dead?"

"Her soul has long been with the blessed," said Theodore.

"Oh! how?" cried Jerome. "Tell me—no—she is happy! Thou art all my care now. Most dread lord! will you—will you grant me my poor boy's life?"

"Return to thy convent," answered Manfred; "conduct the Princess hither; obey me in what else thou knowest, and I promise thee the life of thy son."

"Oh, my lord!" said Jerome. "Is my honesty the price I must pay for this dear youth's safety?"

"For me!" cried Theodore. "Let me die a thousand deaths, rather than stain thy conscience. What is it the tyrant would exact of thee? Is the Princess still safe from his power? Protect her, thou venerable old man, and let all the weight of his wrath fall on me."

Jerome endeavored to check the impetuosity of the youth; and ere Manfred could reply, the trampling of horses was heard, and a brazen trumpet, which hung without the gate of the castle, was suddenly sounded. At the same instant the sable plumes on the enchanted helmet, which still remained at the other end of the court, were tempestuously agitated, and nodded thrice, as if bowed by some invisible wearer.

CHAPTER III

MANFRED's heart misgave him when he beheld the plumage on the miraculous casque shaken in concert with the sounding of the brazen trumpet. "Father," said he to Jerome, whom he now ceased to treat as Count of Falconara, "what mean these portents? If I have offended"—the plumes were shaken with greater violence than before. "Unhappy prince that I am!"

cried Manfred. "Holy Father, will you not assist me with your prayers?"

"My lord," replied Jerome, "Heaven is no doubt displeased with your mockery of its servants. Submit yourself to the Church, and cease to persecute her ministers. Dismiss this innocent youth, and learn to respect the holy character I wear. Heaven will not be trifled with. You see"—the trumpet sounded again.

"I acknowledge I have been too hasty," said Manfred. "Father, do you go to the wicket, and demand who is at the gate."

"Do you grant me the life of Theodore?" replied the friar.

"I do," said Manfred; "but inquire who is without."

Jerome, falling on the neck of his son, discharged a flood of tears that spoke the fullness of his soul.

"You promised to go to the gate," said Manfred.

"I thought," replied the friar, "your highness would excuse my thanking you first in this tribute of my heart."

"Go, dearest sir," said Theodore, "obey the Prince; I do not deserve that you should delay his satisfaction for me."

Jerome, inquiring who was without, was answered, "A herald."

"From whom?" said he.

"From the Knight of the Gigantic Saber," said the herald; "and I must speak with the usurper of Otranto."

Jerome returned to the Prince, and did not fail to repeat the message in the very words it had been uttered. The first sounds struck Manfred with terror; but when he heard himself styled usurper, his rage rekindled, and all his courage revived.

"Usurper!—Insolent villain!" cried he. "Who dares to question my title? Retire, Father; this is no business for monks: I will meet this presumptuous man myself. Go to your convent, and prepare the Princess' return; your son shall be a hostage for your fidelity; his life depends on your obedience."

"Good Heaven! my lord," cried Jerome, "your highness did but this instant freely pardon my child. Have you so soon forgot the interposition of Heaven?"

"Heaven," replied Manfred, "does not send heralds to question the title of a lawful prince. I doubt whether it even notifies its will through friars; but that is your affair, not mine. At present you know my pleasure; and it is not a saucy herald that shall save your son, if you do not return with the Princess."

It was in vain for the holy man to reply. Manfred commanded him to be conducted to the postern gate, and shut out from the castle; and he ordered some of his attendants to carry Theodore to the top of the Black Tower, and guard him strictly, scarce permitting the father and son to exchange a hasty embrace at parting. He then withdrew to the hall, and seating himself in princely state, ordered the herald to be admitted to his presence.

"Well, thou insolent!" said the Prince. "What wouldst thou with me?"

"I come," replied he, "to thee, Manfred, usurper of the principality of Otranto, from the renowned and invincible knight, the Knight of the Gigantic Saber; in the name of his lord, Frederic Marquis of Vicenza, he demands the Lady Isabella, daughter of that Prince, whom thou hast basely and traitorously got into thy power, by bribing her false guardians during his absence; and he requires thee to resign the principality of Otranto, which thou hast usurped from the said Lord Frederic, the nearest of blood to the last rightful lord, Alfonso the Good. If thou dost not instantly comply with these just demands, he defies thee to single combat to the last extremity." And so saying the herald cast down his warder.[7]

"And where is this braggart who sends thee?" said Manfred.

"At the distance of a league," said the herald; "he comes to make good his lord's claim against thee, as he is a true knight, and thou a usurper and ravisher."

Injurious as this challenge was, Manfred reflected that it was not his interest to provoke the marquis. He knew how well founded the claim of Frederic was, nor was this the first time he had heard of it. Frederic's ancestors had assumed the style of Princes of Otranto, from the death of Alfonso the Good without issue; but Manfred, his father, and grandfather, had been too powerful for the house of Vicenza to dispossess them. Frederic, a martial, amorous young prince, had married a beautiful young lady, of whom he was enamored, and who had died in childbed of Isabella. Her death affected him so much, that he had taken the cross and gone to the Holy Land, where he was wounded in an engagement against the infidels, made prisoner, and reported to be dead. When the news reached Manfred's ears, he bribed the guardians of the Lady Isabella to deliver her up to him as a bride for his son Conrad, by which alliance he had proposed to unite the claims of the

[7] A baton or truncheon used to signal the beginning of battle or hostilities.

two houses. This motive, on Conrad's death, had co-operated to make him so suddenly resolve on espousing her himself; and the same reflection determined him now to endeavor at obtaining the consent of Frederic to this marriage. A like policy inspired him with the thought of inviting Frederic's champion into his castle, lest he should be informed of Isabella's flight, which he strictly enjoined his domestics not to disclose to any of the knight's retinue.

"Herald," said Manfred, as soon as he had digested these reflections, "return to thy master, and tell him, ere we liquidate our differences by the sword, Manfred would hold some converse with him. Bid him welcome to my castle, where, by my faith, as I am a true knight, he shall have courteous reception, and full security for himself and followers. If we cannot adjust our quarrel by amicable means, I swear he shall depart in safety, and shall have full satisfaction according to the laws of arms. So help me God and his Holy Trinity!" The herald made three obeisances, and retired.

During this interview, Jerome's mind was agitated by a thousand contrary passions. He trembled for the life of his son, and his first thought was to persuade Isabella to return to the castle. Yet he was scarce less alarmed at the thought of her union with Manfred. He dreaded Hippolita's unbounded submission to the will of her lord; and though he did not doubt but he could alarm her piety not to consent to a divorce, if he could get access to her, yet, should Manfred discover that the obstruction came from him, it might be equally fatal to Theodore. He was impatient to know whence came the herald, who, with so little management, had questioned the title of Manfred; yet he did not dare absent himself from the convent, lest Isabella should leave it, and her flight be imputed to him. He returned disconsolately to the monastery, uncertain on what conduct to resolve. A monk, who met him in the porch, and observed his melancholy air, said, "Alas, brother, is it then true that we have lost our excellent Princess Hippolita?"

The holy man started, and cried, "What meanest thou, brother? I came this instant from the castle, and left her in perfect health."

"Martelli," replied the other friar, "passed by the convent but a quarter of an hour ago, on his way from the castle, and reported that her highness was dead. All our brethren are gone to the chapel to pray for her happy transit to a better life, and willed me to wait thy arrival. They know thy holy attachment to that good lady, and are anxious for the affliction it will cause thee—indeed we have all reason to weep; she was a mother to our house. But this life is but a pilgrimage; we must not murmur—we shall all follow her; may our end be like hers!"

"Good brother, thou dreamest," said Jerome; "I tell thee I come from the castle, and left the princess well;—where is the Lady Isabella?"

"Poor gentlewoman," replied the friar, "I told her the sad news, and offered her spiritual comfort; I reminded her of the transitory condition of mortality, and advised her to take the veil. I quoted the example of the holy Princess Sanchia of Arragon."

"Thy zeal was laudable," said Jerome, impatiently; "but at present it was unnecessary. Hippolita is well—at least I trust in the Lord she is; I heard nothing to the contrary—yet methinks, the Prince's earnestness—well, brother, but where is the Lady Isabella?"

"I know not," said the friar. "She wept much, and said she would retire to her chamber."

Jerome left his comrade abruptly, and hastened to the Princess, but she was not in her chamber. He inquired of the domestics of the convent, but could learn no news of her. He searched in vain throughout the monastery and the church, and dispatched messengers round the neighborhood, to get intelligence if she had been seen, but to no purpose. Nothing could equal the good man's perplexity. He judged that Isabella, suspecting Manfred of having precipitated his wife's death, had taken the alarm, and withdrawn herself to some more secret place of concealment. This new flight would probably carry the Prince's fury to the height. The report of Hippolita's death, though it seemed almost incredible, increased his consternation; and though Isabella's escape bespoke her aversion of Manfred for a husband, Jerome could feel no comfort from it while it endangered the life of his son. He determined to return to the castle, and made several of his brethren accompany him, to attest his innocence to Manfred, and, if necessary, join their intercessions with his for Theodore.

The Prince, in the meantime, had passed into the court, and ordered the gates of the castle to be flung open for the reception of the stranger knight and his train. In a few minutes the cavalcade arrived. First came two harbingers with

wands; next a herald, followed by two pages and two trum-
peters; then a hundred foot-guards. These were attended by
as many horse. After them fifty footmen, clothed in scarlet
and black, the colors of the knight; then a led horse. Two
heralds on each side of a gentleman on horseback, bearing a
banner, with the arms of Vicenza and Otranto quarterly—a
circumstance that much offended Manfred, but he stifled his
resentment. Two more pages; the knight's confessor telling
his beads;[8] fifty more footmen clad as before; two knights
habited in complete armor, their beavers[9] down, comrades to
the principal knight; the squires of the two knights, carrying
their shields and devices; the knight's own squire; a hundred
gentlemen bearing an enormous sword, and seeming to faint
under the weight of it. The knight himself, on a chestnut steed,
in complete armor, his lance in the rest, his face entirely
concealed by his visor, which was surmounted by a large plume
of scarlet and black feathers. Fifty foot-guards, with drums and
trumpets, closed the procession, which wheeled off to the right
and left, to make room for the principal knight.

As soon as he approached the gate, he stopped; and the
herald, advancing, read again the words of the challenge.
Manfred's eyes were fixed on the gigantic sword, and he scarce
seemed to attend to the cartel; but his attention was soon
diverted by a tempest of wind that rose behind him; he
turned and beheld the plumes of the enchanted helmet agitated in the same extraordinary manner as before. It required
intrepidity like Manfred's not to sink under a concurrence
of circumstances that seemed to announce his fate. Yet, scorning in the presence of strangers to betray the courage he had
always manifested, he said boldly:

"Sir Knight, whoever thou art, I bid thee welcome. If thou
art of mortal mold, thy valor shall meet its equal; and if
thou art a true knight, thou wilt scorn to employ sorcery to
carry thy point. Be these omens from heaven or hell, Manfred
trusts to the righteousness of his cause and to the aid of St.
Nicholas, who has ever protected his house. Alight, Sir Knight,
and repose thyself; to-morrow thou shalt have a fair field; and
Heaven befriend the juster side!"

The knight made no reply, but, dismounting, was conducted
by Manfred to the great hall of the castle. As they traversed

[8] Beads of the rosary were used for keeping count of the number of prayers
said.
[9] Lower part of faceguard on the helmet.

the court, the knight stopped to gaze on the miraculous casque;
and, kneeling down, seemed to pray inwardly for some minutes.
Rising, he made a sign to the Prince to lead on. As soon as
they entered the hall, Manfred proposed to the stranger to
disarm, but the knight shook his head in token of refusal.
"Sir Knight," said Manfred, "this is not courteous: but by my
good faith I will not cross thee; nor shalt thou have cause to
complain of the Prince of Otranto. No treachery is designed
on my part; I hope none is intended on thine; here, take my
gage," giving him his ring, "your friends and you shall enjoy
the laws of hospitality. Rest here until refreshments are
brought; I will but give orders for the accommodation of
your train, and return to you."

The three knights bowed, as accepting his courtesy. Manfred
directed the stranger's retinue to be conducted to an adjacent
hospital, founded by the Princess Hippolita for the reception
of pilgrims. As they made the circuit of the court to return
toward the gate, the gigantic sword burst from the supporters,
and falling to the ground opposite to the helmet, remained
immovable. Manfred, almost hardened to preternatural appearances, surmounted the shock of this new prodigy; and
returning to the hall, where by this time the feast was ready,
he invited his silent guests to take their places. Manfred,
however ill his heart was at ease, endeavored to inspire the
company with mirth. He put several questions to them, but
was answered only by signs. They raised their visors but
sufficiently to feed themselves, and that but sparingly.

"Sirs," said the Prince, "ye are the first guests I ever treated
within these walls, who scorned to hold any intercourse with
me; nor has it oft been customary, I ween, for princes to hazard
their state and dignity against strangers and mutes. You say
you come in the name of Frederic of Vicenza; I have ever
heard that he was a gallant and courteous knight; nor would
he, I am bold to say, think it beneath him to mix in social
converse with a prince who is his equal, and not unknown by
deeds in arms.—Still ye are silent—well, be it as it may, by the
laws of hospitality and chivalry, ye are masters under this roof;
ye shall do your pleasure—but come, give me a goblet of wine;
ye will not refuse to pledge me to the healths of your fair
mistresses." The principal knight sighed and crossed himself,
and was rising from the board.[10] "Sir Knight," said Manfred,
"what I said was but in sport; I shall constrain you in nothing.

[10] Table.

Use your good liking; since mirth is not your mood, let us be sad. Business may hit your fancies better; let us withdraw, and hear if what I have to unfold may be better relished than the vain efforts I have made for your pastime."

Manfred then conducting the three knights into an inner chamber, shut the door, and inviting them to be seated, began thus, addressing himself to the chief personage:

"You come, Sir Knight, as I understand, in the name of the Marquis of Vicenza, to re-demand the Lady Isabella, his daughter, who has been contracted, in the face of Holy Church, to my son, by the consent of her legal guardians; and to require me to resign my dominions to your lord, who gives himself for the nearest of blood to Prince Alfonso, whose soul God rest! I shall speak to the latter article of your demands first. You must know, your lord knows, that I enjoy the principality of Otranto from my father Don Manuel, as he received it from his father Don Ricardo. Alfonso, their predecessor, dying childless in the Holy Land, bequeathed his estates to my grandfather, Don Ricardo, in consideration of his faithful services."
—The stranger shook his head.—"Sir Knight," said Manfred, warmly, "Ricardo was a valiant and upright man; he was a pious man; witness his munificent foundation of the adjoining church and two convents. He was peculiarly patronized by St. Nicholas—my grandfather was incapable—I say, sir, Don Ricardo was incapable—excuse me, your interruption has disordered me.—I venerate the memory of my grandfather.— Well! sirs, he held this estate; he held it by his good sword and by the favor of St. Nicholas—so did my father; and so, sirs, will I, come what come will. But Frederic, your lord, is nearest in blood. I have consented to put my title to the issue of the sword—does that imply a vicious title? I might have asked, where is Frederic, your lord? Report speaks him dead in captivity. You say, your actions say, he lives. I question it not —I might, sirs, I might, but I do not. Other princes would bid Frederic take his inheritance by force, if he can; they would not stake their dignity on a single combat; they would not submit it to the decision of unknown mutes! Pardon me, gentlemen, I am too warm; but suppose yourselves in my situation; as ye are stout knights, would it not move your choler[11] to have your own and the honor of your ancestors called in question? But to the point: ye require me to deliver up the Lady Isabella. Sirs, I must ask if ye are authorized to

[11] Anger.

receive her?" The knight nodded. "Receive her!" continued Manfred. "Well, you are authorized to receive her—but, gentle knight, may I ask if you have full powers?" The knight nodded. "'Tis well," said Manfred. "Then hear what I have to offer. Ye see, gentlemen, before you the most unhappy of men." He began to weep. "Afford me your compassion; I am entitled to it; indeed I am. Know, I have lost my only hope, my joy, the support of my house—Conrad died yester-morning." The knights discovered signs of surprise. "Yes, sirs, fate has disposed of my son. Isabella is at liberty."

"Do you then restore her?" cried the chief knight, breaking silence.

"Afford me your patience," said Manfred. "I rejoice to find, by this testimony of your good will, that this matter may be adjusted without bloodshed. It is no interest of mine dictates what little I have farther to say. Ye behold in me a man disgusted with the world; the loss of my son has weaned me from earthly cares. Power and greatness have no longer any charms in my eyes. I wished to transmit the scepter I had received from my ancestors with honor to my son—but that is over! Life itself is so indifferent to me that I accepted your defiance with joy; a good knight cannot go to the grave with more satisfaction than when falling in his vocation. Whatever is the will of Heaven I submit; for, alas! sirs, I am a man of many sorrows. Manfred is no object of envy—but no doubt you are acquainted with my story." The knight made signs of ignorance, and seemed curious to have Manfred proceed. "Is it possible, sirs," continued the Prince, "that my story should be a secret to you? Have you heard nothing relating to me and the Princess Hippolita?" They shook their heads. "No! thus, then sirs, it is. You think me ambitious; ambition alas, is composed of more rugged materials! If I were ambitious, I should not for so many years have been a prey to all the hell of conscientious scruples—but I weary your patience; I will be brief. Know, then, that I have long been troubled in mind on my union with the Princess Hippolita. Oh, sirs, if ye were acquainted with that excellent woman! if ye knew that I adore her like a mistress, and cherish her as a friend—but man was not born of perfect happiness! She shares my scruples, and with her consent I have brought this matter before the Church, for we are related within the forbidden degrees. I expect every hour the definitive sentence that must separate us forever—I am sure you feel for me—I see you do—pardon these tears!"

The knights gazed on each other, wondering where this would end. Manfred continued. "The death of my son betiding while my soul was under this anxiety, I thought of nothing but resigning my dominions, and retiring forever from the sight of mankind. My only difficulty was to fix on a successor, who would be tender of my people, and to dispose of the Lady Isabella, who is dear to me as my own blood. I was willing to restore the line of Alfonso, even in his most distant kindred; and though, pardon me, I am satisfied it was his will that Ricardo's lineage should take place of his own relations, yet where was I to search for those relations? I know of none but Frederic, your lord; he was a captive to the infidels, or dead; and were he living, and at home, would he quit the flourishing state of Vicenza for the inconsiderable principality of Otranto? If he would not, could I bear the thought of seeing a hard unfeeling viceroy set over my poor faithful people? For, sirs, I love my people, and, thank Heaven, am beloved by them. But ye will ask, 'Whither tends this long discourse?' Briefly, then, thus, sirs. Heaven in your arrival seems to point out a remedy for these difficulties and my misfortunes. The Lady Isabella is at liberty; I shall soon be so—I would submit to anything for the good of my people—were it not the best, the only way to extinguish the feuds between our families if I was to take the Lady Isabella to wife. You start, but though Hippolita's virtues will ever be dear to me, a prince must not consider himself; he is born for his people." A servant, at that instant entering the chamber, apprised Manfred that Jerome and several of his brethren demanded immediate access to him.

The Prince, provoked at this interruption, and fearing that the friar would discover to the strangers that Isabella had taken sanctuary, was going to forbid Jerome's entrance. But recollecting that he was certainly arrived to notify the Princess' return, Manfred began to excuse himself to the knights for leaving them for a few moments, but was prevented by the arrival of the friars. Manfred angrily reprimanded them for their intrusion, and would have forced them back from the chamber; but Jerome was too much agitated to be repulsed. He declared aloud the flight of Isabella, with protestations of his own innocence. Manfred, distracted at the news, and not less at its coming to the knowledge of the strangers, uttered nothing but incoherent sentences, now upbraiding the friar, now apologizing to the knights; earnest to know what was become of Isabella, yet equally afraid of their knowing; impatient to pursue her, yet dreading to have them join in the pursuit. He offered to dispatch messengers in quest of her—but the chief knight, no longer keeping silence, reproached Manfred in bitter terms for his dark and ambiguous dealing, and demanded the cause of Isabella's first absence from the castle. Manfred, casting a stern look at Jerome, implying a command of silence, pretended that on Conrad's death he had placed her in sanctuary until he could determine how to dispose of her. Jerome, who trembled for his son's life, did not dare contradict this falsehood, but one of his brethren, not under the same anxiety, declared frankly that she had fled to their church in the preceding night. The Prince in vain endeavored to stop this discovery, which overwhelmed him with shame and confusion. The principal stranger, amazed at the contradictions he heard, and more than half persuaded that Manfred had secreted the Princess, notwithstanding the concern he expressed at her flight, rushing to the door, said, "Thou traitor-prince! Isabella shall be found." Manfred endeavored to hold him, but the other knights assisting their comrade, he broke from the Prince, and hastened into the court, demanding his attendants. Manfred, finding it vain to divert him from the pursuit, offered to accompany him; and summoning his attendants, and taking Jerome and some of the friars to guide them, they issued from the castle; Manfred privately giving orders to have the knight's company secured, while to the knight he affected to dispatch a messenger to require their assistance.

The company had no sooner quitted the castle, than Matilda, who felt herself deeply interested for the young peasant, since she had seen him condemned to death in the hall, and whose thoughts had been taken up with concerting measures to save him, was informed by some of the female attendants that Manfred had dispatched all his men various ways in pursuit of Isabella. He had in his hurry given this order in general terms, not meaning to extend it to the guard he had set upon Theodore, but forgetting it. The domestics, officious to obey so peremptory a Prince, and urged by their own curiosity and love of novelty to join in any precipitate chase, had to a man left the castle. Matilda disengaged herself from her women, stole up to the Black Tower, and unbolting the door, presented herself to the astonished Theodore. "Young man," said she, "though filial duty and womanly modesty condemn the step I am taking, yet holy charity, surmounting all other ties, justifies this act. Fly; the doors of thy prison are open; my father and his domestics are absent; but they may soon return; begone in safety; and may the angels of heaven direct thy course!"

"Thou art surely one of those angels!" said the enraptured Theodore. "None but a blessed saint could speak, could act, could look like thee! May I not know the name of my divine protectress? Methought thou namedst thy father; is it possible? can Manfred's blood feel holy pity? Lovely lady, thou answerest not—but how art thou here thyself? Why dost thou neglect thy own safety, and waste a thought on a wretch like Theodore? Let us fly together. The life thou bestowest shall be dedicated to thy defense."

"Alas! thou mistakest," said Matilda, sighing; "I am Manfred's daughter, but no dangers await me."

"Amazement!" said Theodore. "But last night I blessed myself for yielding thee the service thy gracious compassion so charitably returns me now."

"Still thou art in error," said the Princess; "but this is no time for explanation. Fly, virtuous youth, while it is in my power to save thee. Should my father return, thou and I both should indeed have cause to tremble."

"How?" said Theodore. "Thinkest thou, charming maid, that I will accept of life at the hazard of aught calamitous to thee? Better I endure a thousand deaths."

"I run no risk," said Matilda, "but by thy delay. Depart; it cannot be known that I assisted thy flight."

"Swear by the saints above," said Theodore, "that thou canst not be suspected; else here I vow to wait whatever can befall me."

"Oh, thou art too generous," said Matilda; "but rest assured that no suspicion can alight on me."

"Give me thy beauteous hand in token that thou dost not deceive me," said Theodore; "and let me bathe it with the warm tears of gratitude."

"Forbear," said the Princess; "this must not be."

"Alas!" said Theodore. "I have never known but calamity until this hour—perhaps shall never know other fortune again; suffer the chaste raptures of holy gratitude; 'tis my soul would print its effusions on thy hand."

"Forbear, and be gone," said Matilda; "how would Isabella approve of seeing thee at my feet?"

"Who is Isabella?" said the young man with surprise.

"Ah me! I fear," said the Princess, "I am serving a deceitful one. Hast thou forgot thy curiosity this morning?"

"Thy looks, thy actions, all thy beauteous self, seem an emanation of divinity," said Theodore; "but thy words are dark and mysterious;—speak, lady; speak to thy servant's comprehension."

"Thou understandest but too well!" said Matilda. "But once more, I command thee to be gone; thy blood, which I may preserve, will be on my head, if I waste the time in vain discourse."

"I go, lady," said Theodore, "because it is thy will, and because I would not bring the gray hairs of my father with sorrow to the grave. Say but, adored lady, that I have thy gentle pity."

"Stay," said Matilda, "I will conduct thee to the subterraneous vault by which Isabella escaped; it will lead thee to the church of St. Nicholas, where thou mayest take sanctuary."

"What!" said Theodore. "Was it another, and not thy lovely self, that I assisted to find the subterraneous passage?"

"It was," said Matilda, "but ask no more; I tremble to see thee still abide here; fly to the sanctuary."

"To sanctuary!" said Theodore. "No, Princess, sanctuaries are for helpless damsels, or for criminals. Theodore's soul is free from guilt, nor will wear the appearance of it. Give me a sword, lady, and thy father shall learn that Theodore scorns an ignominious flight."

"Rash youth," said Matilda, "thou wouldst not dare to lift thy presumptuous arm against the Prince of Otranto?"

"Not against thy father; indeed, I dare not," said Theodore. "Excuse me, lady; I had forgotten—but could I gaze on thee, and remember thou art sprung from the tyrant Manfred? But he is thy father, and from this moment my injuries are buried in oblivion." A deep and hollow groan, which seemed to come from above, startled the Princess and Theodore. "Good Heavens! we are overheard!" said the Princess. They listened, but perceived no farther noise; they both concluded it the effect of pent-up vapors.[12] And the Princess, preceding Theodore softly, carried him to her father's armory, where equipping him with a complete suit, he was conducted by Matilda to the postern-gate.

"Avoid the town," said the Princess, "and all the western side of the castle; 'tis there the search must be making by Man-

[12] Fancies or fantastic ideas.

fred and the strangers; but hie thee to the opposite quarter. Yonder, behind that forest to the east, is a chain of rocks, hollowed into a labyrinth of caverns that reach to the sea-coast. There thou mayest lie concealed till thou canst make signs to some vessel to put on shore and take thee off. Go; Heaven be thy guide! And sometimes in thy prayers remember —Matilda!" Theodore flung himself at her feet; and seizing her lily hand, which with struggles she suffered him to kiss, he vowed on the earliest opportunity to get himself knighted, and fervently entreated her permission to swear himself eternally her knight. Ere the Princess could reply, a clap of thunder was suddenly heard that shook the battlements. Theodore, regardless of the tempest, would have urged his suit, but the Princess, dismayed, retreated hastily into the castle, and commanded the youth to be gone with an air that would not be disobeyed. He sighed and retired, but with eyes fixed on the gate until Matilda, closing it, put an end to an interview in which the hearts of both had drunk so deeply of a passion, which both now tasted for the first time.

Theodore went pensively to the convent to acquaint his father with his deliverance. There he learned the absence of Jerome, and the pursuit that was making after the Lady Isabella, with some particulars of whose story he now first became acquainted. The generous gallantry of his nature prompted him to wish to assist her; but the monks could lend him no lights to guess at the route she had taken. He was not tempted to wander far in search of her, for the idea of Matilda had imprinted itself so strongly on his heart, that he could not bear to absent himself at much distance from her abode. The tenderness Jerome had expressed for him concurred to confirm this reluctance; and he even persuaded himself that filial affection was the chief cause of his hovering between the castle and monastery, until Jerome should return at night. Theodore at length determined to repair to the forest that Matilda had pointed out to him. Arriving there, he sought the gloomiest shades, as best suited to the pleasing melancholy that reigned in his mind. In this mood he roved insensibly to the caves which had formerly served as a retreat to hermits, and were now reported round the country to be haunted by evil spirits. He recollected to have heard this tradition; and being of a brave and adventurous disposition, he willingly indulged his curiosity in exploring the secret recesses of this labyrinth. He had not penetrated far before he thought he heard the steps of some person who seemed to retreat before him. Theodore, though firmly grounded in all our holy faith enjoins to be believed, had no apprehension that good men were abandoned without cause to the malice of the powers of darkness. He thought the place more likely to be infested by robbers than by those infernal agents who are reported to molest and bewilder travelers. He had long burned with impatience to approve his valor. Drawing his saber, he marched sedately onward, still directing his steps, as the imperfect rustling round before him led the way. The armor he wore was a like indication to the person who avoided him. Theodore, now convinced that he was not mistaken, redoubled his pace, and evidently gained on the person that fled, whose haste increasing, Theodore came up just as a woman fell breathless before him. He hasted to raise her; but her terror was so great that he apprehended she would faint in his arms. He used every gentle word to dispel her alarms, and assured her that, far from injuring, he would defend her at the peril of his life. The lady recovering her spirits from his courteous demeanor, and gazing on her protector, said, "Sure, I have heard that voice before!"

"Not to my knowledge," replied Theodore, "unless, as I conjecture, thou art the Lady Isabella."

"Merciful Heaven!" cried she. "Thou art not sent in quest of me, art thou?" And saying these words she threw herself at his feet, and besought him not to deliver her up to Manfred.

"To Manfred!" cried Theodore. "No, lady, I have once already delivered thee from his tyranny, and it shall fare hard with me now, but I will place thee out of the reach of his daring."

"Is it possible," said she, "that thou shouldst be the generous unknown whom I met last night in the vault of the castle? Sure thou art not a mortal, but my guardian angel. On my knees let me thank—"

"Hold, gentle Princess," said Theodore, "nor demean thyself before a poor and friendless young man. If Heaven has selected me for thy deliverer, it will accomplish its work, and strengthen my arm in thy cause; but come, lady, we are too near the mouth of the cavern; let us seek its inmost recesses; I can have no tranquillity till I have placed thee beyond the reach of danger."

"Alas, what means you, sir?" said she. "Though all your actions are noble, though your sentiments speak the purity of your soul, is it fitting that I should accompany you alone in these perplexed retreats? Should we be found together, what would a censorious world think of my conduct?"

"I respect your virtuous delicacy," said Theodore; "nor do you harbor a suspicion that wounds my honor. I meant to conduct you into the most private cavity of these rocks, and then, at the hazard of my life, to guard their entrance against every living thing. Besides, lady," continued he, drawing a deep sigh, "beauteous and all perfect as your form is, and though my wishes are not guiltless of aspiring, know, my soul is dedicated to another; and although——" A sudden noise prevented Theodore from proceeding. They soon distinguished these sounds: "Isabella! what ho! Isabella!"

The trembling Princess relapsed into her former agony of fear. Theodore endeavored to encourage her, but in vain. He assured her he would rather die than suffer her to return under Manfred's power, and begging her to remain concealed, he went forth to prevent the person in search of her from approaching.

At the mouth of the cavern he found an armed knight discoursing with a peasant, who assured him he had seen a lady enter the passes of the rock. The knight was preparing to seek her, when Theodore, placing himself in his way, with his sword drawn, sternly forbade him at his peril to advance.

"And who art thou who darest to cross my way?" said the knight haughtily.

"One who does not dare more than he will perform," said Theodore.

"I seek the Lady Isabella," said the knight, "and understand she has taken refuge among these rocks. Impede me not, or thou wilt repent having provoked my resentment."

"Thy purpose is as odious as thy resentment is contemptible," said Theodore; "return whence thou camest, or we shall soon know whose resentment is most terrible."

The stranger, who was the principal knight that had arrived from the Marquis of Vicenza, had galloped from Manfred as he was busied in getting information of the Princess, and giving various orders to prevent her falling into the power of the three knights. Their chief had suspected Manfred of being privy to the Princess' absconding; and this insult from a man who, he concluded, was stationed by that Prince to secrete her, confirming his suspicions, he made no reply, but discharging a blow with his saber at Theodore, would soon have removed all obstruction, if Theodore, who took him for one of Manfred's captains, and who had no sooner given the provocation than he prepared to support it, had not received the stroke on his shield. The valor that had so long been smothered in his breast broke forth at once; he rushed impetuously on the knight, whose pride and wrath were not less powerful incentives to hardy deeds. The combat was furious, but not long. Theodore wounded the knight in three several places, and at last disarmed him, as he fainted by the loss of blood. The peasant, who had fled on the first onset, had given the alarm to some of Manfred's domestics, who, by his orders, were dispersed through the forest in pursuit of Isabella. They came up as the knight fell, whom they soon discovered to be the noble stranger. Theodore, notwithstanding his hatred to Manfred, could not behold the victory he had gained without emotions of pity and generosity. But he was more touched when he learned the quality of his adversary, and was informed that he was no retainer, but an enemy of Manfred. He assisted the servants of the latter in disarming the knight, and in endeavoring to stanch the blood that flowed from his wounds. The knight recovering his speech, said, in a faint and faltering voice, "Generous foe, we have both been in an error. I took thee for an instrument of the tyrant; I perceive thou hast made the like mistake; it is too late for excuses—I faint—if Isabella is at hand, call her; I have important secrets to——"

"He is dying," said one of the attendants; "has nobody a crucifix about them? Andrea, do thou pray over him."

"Fetch some water," said Theodore, "and pour it down his throat, while I hasten to the Princess." Saying this, he flew to Isabella, and in few words told her modestly that he had been so unfortunate by mistake as to wound a gentleman from her father's court, who wished, ere he died, to impart something of consequence to her. The Princess, who had been transported at hearing the voice of Theodore, as he called to her to come forth, was astonished at what she heard. Suffering herself to be conducted by Theodore, the new proof of whose valor recalled her dispersed spirits, she came where the bleeding knight lay speechless on the ground—but her fears returned when she beheld the domestics of Manfred. She would again have fled, if Theodore had not made her observe that they were unarmed, and had not threatened them with instant death if they should dare to seize the Princess. The stranger, opening his eyes, and beholding a woman, said, "Art thou—pray tell me truly—art thou Isabella of Vicenza?"

"I am," said she. "Good Heaven restore thee!"

"Then thou——then thou——" said the knight, struggling for utterance, "seest—thy father. Give me one——"

"Oh, amazement! Horror! What do I hear! What do I see?" cried Isabella. "My father! You my father! How came you here, sir? For Heaven's sake speak!—Oh, run for help, or he will expire!"

"'Tis most true," said the wounded knight, exerting all his force; "I am Frederic thy father—yes, I came to deliver thee —it will not be—give me a parting kiss, and take——"

"Sir," said Theodore, "do not exhaust yourself; suffer us to convey you to the castle."

"To the castle!" said Isabella. "Is there no help nearer than the castle? Would you expose my father to the tyrant? If he goes thither, I cannot accompany him—and yet, can I leave him?"

"My child," said Frederic, "it matters not to me whither I am carried; a few minutes will place me beyond danger—but while I have eyes to dote on thee, forsake me not, dear Isabella! This brave knight, I know not who he is, will protect thy innocence. Sir, you will not abandon my child, will you?"

Theodore, shedding tears over his victim, and vowing to guard the Princess at the expense of his life, persuaded Frederic to suffer himself to be conducted to the castle. They placed him on a horse belonging to one of the domestics, after binding up his wounds as well as they were able. Theodore marched by his side, and the afflicted Isabella, who could not bear to quit him, followed mournfully behind.

CHAPTER IV

THE sorrowful troop no sooner arrived at the castle than they were met by Hippolita and Matilda, whom Isabella had sent one of the domestics before to advertise of their approach. The ladies, causing Frederic to be conveyed into the nearest chamber, retired, while the surgeons examined his wounds. Matilda blushed at seeing Theodore and Isabella together; but endeavored to conceal it by embracing the latter and condoling with her on her father's mischance. The surgeons soon came to acquaint Hippolita that none of the Marquis' wounds were dangerous, and that he was desirous of seeing his daughter and the Princesses. Theodore, under pretense of expressing his joy at being freed from his apprehensions of the combat being fatal to Frederic, could not resist the impulse of following Matilda. Her eyes were so often cast down on meeting his, that Isabella, who regarded Theodore as attentively as he gazed on Matilda, soon divined who the object was that he had told her in the cave engaged his affections. While this mute scene passed, Hippolita demanded of Frederic the cause of his having taken that mysterious course for reclaiming his daughter; and threw in various apologies to excuse her lord for the match contracted between their children. Frederic, however incensed against Manfred, was not insensible to the courtesy and benevolence of Hippolita; but he was still more struck with the lovely form of Matilda. Wishing to detain them by his bedside, he informed Hippolita of his story. He told her, that, while prisoner to the infidel, he had dreamed that his daughter, of whom he had learned no news since his captivity, was detained in a castle, where she was in danger of the most dreadful misfortunes; and that if he obtained his liberty and repaired to a wood near Joppa, he would learn more. Alarmed at this dream, and incapable of obeying the direction given by it, his chains became more grievous than ever. But while his thoughts were occupied on the means of obtaining his liberty, he received the agreeable news that the confederate princes, who were warring in Palestine, had paid his ransom. He instantly set out for the wood that had been marked in his dream. For three days he and his attendants had wandered in the forest without seeing a human form; but on the evening of the third they came to a cell, in which they found a venerable hermit in the agonies of death. Applying rich cordials, they brought the saint-like man to his speech. "My sons," said he, "I am bounden to your charity—but it is in vain—I am going to my eternal rest; yet I die with the satisfaction of performing the will of Heaven. When first I repaired to this solitude, after seeing my country become a prey to unbelievers—it is, alas! above fifty years since I was witness to that dreadful scene—St. Nicholas appeared to me, and revealed a secret, which he bade me never disclose to mortal man, but on my deathbed. This is that tremendous hour, and ye are no doubt the chosen warriors to whom I was ordered to reveal my trust. As soon as ye have done the last offices to this wretched corpse, dig under the seventh tree on the left hand of this poor cave, and your pains will—— Oh, good Heaven, receive my soul!" With those words the devout man breathed his last.

"By break of day," continued Frederic, "when we had committed the holy relics to earth, we dug according to direction; but what was our astonishment, when, about the depth of six feet, we discovered an enormous saber—the very weapon yonder in the court. On the blade, which was then partly out of the scabbard, though since closed by our efforts in removing it, were written the following lines—no; excuse me, madam," added the Marquis, turning to Hippolita, "if I forbear to repeat them. I respect your sex and rank, and would not be guilty of offending your ear with sounds injurious to aught that is dear to you."

He paused, Hippolita trembled. She did not doubt but Frederic was destined by Heaven to accomplish the fate that seemed to threaten her house. Looking with anxious fondness at Matilda, a silent tear stole down her cheek; but recollecting herself, she said, "Proceed, my lord, Heaven does nothing in vain; mortals must receive its divine behests with lowliness and submission. It is our part to deprecate its wrath, or bow to its decrees. Repeat the sentence, my lord; we listen resigned."

Frederic was grieved that he had proceeded so far. The dignity and patient firmness of Hippolita penetrated him with respect; and the tender, silent affection with which the Princess and her daughter regarded each other melted him almost to tears. Yet apprehensive that his forbearance to obey would be more alarming, he repeated, in a faltering and low voice, the following lines:

> Where'er a casque that suits this sword is found,
> With perils is thy daughter compass'd round;
> Alfonso's blood alone can save the maid,
> And quiet a long-restless prince's shade.

"What is there in these lines," said Theodore, impatiently, "that affects these Princesses? Why were they to be shocked by a mysterious delicacy, that has so little foundation?"

"Your words are rude, young man," said the Marquis; "and though fortune has favored you once——"

"My honored lord," said Isabella, who resented Theodore's warmth, which she perceived was dictated by his sentiments for Matilda, "discompose not yourself for the glozing of a peasant's son; he forgets the reverence he owes you; but he is not accustomed——"

Hippolita, concerned at the heat that had arisen, checked

Theodore for his boldness, but with an air acknowledging his zeal; and changing the conversation, demanded of Frederic where he had left her lord?

As the Marquis was going to reply, they heard a noise without, and rising to inquire the cause, Manfred, Jerome, and part of the troop, who had met an imperfect rumor of what had happened, entered the chamber. Manfred advanced hastily toward Frederic's bed to condole with him on his misfortune, and to learn the circumstances of the combat, when, starting in an agony of terror and amazement, he cried:

"Ah! What art thou? Thou dreadful specter! Is my hour come?"

"My dearest, gracious lord," cried Hippolita, clasping him in her arms, "what is it you see? Why do you fix your eyeballs thus?"

"What," cried Manfred, breathless, "dost thou see nothing, Hippolita? Is this ghastly phantom sent to me alone—to me, who did not——"

"For mercy's sweetest self, my lord," said Hippolita, "resume your soul, command your reason; there are none here, but us, your friends."

"What, is not that Alfonso?" cried Manfred. "Dost thou not see him? Can it be my brain's delirium?"

"This! my lord," said Hippolita, "this is Theodore, the youth who has been so unfortunate."

"Theodore," said Manfred mournfully, and striking his forehead—"Theodore, or a phantom, he has unhinged the soul of Manfred. But how comes he here? And how comes he in armor?"

"I believe he went in search of Isabella," said Hippolita.

"Of Isabella," said Manfred, relapsing into rage. "Yes, yes, that is not doubtful—but how did he escape from durance, in which I left him? Was it Isabella, or this hypocritical old friar, that procured his enlargement?"

"And would a parent be criminal, my lord," said Theodore, "if he mediated the deliverance of his child?"

Jerome, amazed to hear himself in a manner accused by his son, and without foundation, knew not what to think. He could not comprehend how Theodore had escaped—how he came to be armed, and to encounter Frederic. Still he would not venture to ask any questions that might tend to inflame Manfred's wrath against his son. Jerome's silence convinced Manfred that he had contrived Theodore's release.

"And is it thus, thou ungrateful old man," said the Prince, addressing himself to the friar, "that thou repayest mine and Hippolita's bounties? And not content with traversing my heart's nearest wishes, thou armest thy bastard, and bringest him into my own castle to insult me!"

"My lord," said Theodore, "you wrong my father; nor he nor I are capable of harboring a thought against your peace. Is it insolence thus to surrender myself to your highness' pleasure?" added he, laying his sword respectfully at Manfred's feet. "Behold my bosom; strike, my lord, if you suspect that a disloyal thought is lodged there. There is not a sentiment engraven on my heart that does not venerate you and yours."

The grace and fervor with which Theodore uttered these words interested every person present in his favor. Even Manfred was touched; yet still possessed with his resemblance to Alfonso, his admiration was dashed with secret horror.

"Rise," said he, "thy life is not my present purpose. But tell me thy history, and how thou camest connected with this old traitor here."

"My lord——" said Jerome, eagerly.

"Peace! impostor," said Manfred; "I will not have him prompted."

"My lord," said Theodore, "I want no assistance: my story is very brief. I was carried at five years of age to Algiers with my mother, who had been taken by corsairs from the coast of Sicily. She died of grief in less than a twelvemonth." The tears gushed from Jerome's eyes, on whose countenance a thousand anxious passions stood expressed. "Before she died," continued Theodore, "she bound a writing about my arm under my garments, which told me I was the son of the Count Falconara."

"It is most true," said Jerome; "I am that wretched father."

"Again I enjoin thee silence," said Manfred. "Proceed."

"I remained in slavery," said Theodore, "until within these two years; when, attending on my master in his cruises, I was delivered by a Christian vessel which overpowered the pirate; and discovering myself to the captain, he generously put me on shore in Sicily;—but, alas! instead of finding a father, I learned that his estate, which was situated on the coast, had, during his absence, been laid waste by the rover who had carried my mother and me into captivity; that his castle had been burned to the ground, and that my father, on his return, had sold what remained, and was retired into religion in the Kingdom of Naples,[13] but where, no man could inform me. Destitute and friendless, hopeless almost of attaining the transport of a parent's embrace, I took the first opportunity of setting sail for Naples; from whence, within these six days, I wandered into this province, still supporting myself by the labor of my hands; nor until yester-morn did I believe that Heaven had reserved any lot for me but peace of mind and contented poverty. This, my lord, is Theodore's story. I am blessed beyond my hope in finding a father; I am unfortunate beyond my desert in having incurred your highness' displeasure."

He ceased. A murmur of approbation gently arose from the audience.

"This is not all," said Frederic; "I am bound in honor to add what he suppresses. Though he is modest, I must be generous—he is one of the bravest youths on Christian ground. He is warm too; and from the short knowledge I have of him, I will pledge myself for his veracity; if what he reports of himself were not true, he would not utter it. And for me, youth, I honor a frankness which becomes thy birth. But now, and thou didst offend me; yet the noble blood which flows in thy veins may well be allowed to boil out, when it has so recently traced itself to its source. Come, my lord," turning to Manfred, "if I can pardon him, surely you may; it is not the youth's fault, if you took him for a specter."

This bitter taunt galled the soul of Manfred. "If beings from another world," replied he haughtily, "have power to impress my mind with awe, it is more than living man can do; nor could a stripling's arm——"

"My lord," interrupted Hippolita, "your guest has occasion for repose; shall we not leave him to his rest?" Saying this, and taking Manfred by the hand, she took leave of Frederic, and led the company forth. The Prince, not sorry to quit a conversation which recalled to mind the discovery he had made of his most secret sensations, suffered himself to be conducted to his own apartment, after permitting Theodore, though under engagement to return to the castle on the morrow (a condition the young man gladly accepted), to retire with his father to the convent. Matilda and Isabella were too much occupied with their own reflections and too little content with

---

[13] Naples was a separate state in Southern Italy, and consisted of Abruzzi e Molise, Apulia, Basilicata, Calabria, and Campania. Throughout its history, it underwent recurrent warfare and conquest.

each other to wish for further converse that night. They separated, each to her chamber, with more expression of ceremony
and fewer of affection than had passed between them since
their childhood.

If they parted with small cordiality, they did but meet with
greater impatience, as soon as the sun was risen. Their minds
were in a situation that excluded sleep, and each recollected a
thousand questions which she wished she had put to the other
overnight. Matilda reflected that Isabella had been twice
delivered by Theodore in very critical situations, which she
could not believe accidental. His eyes, it was true, had been
fixed on her in Frederic's chamber; but that might have been
to disguise his passion for Isabella from the fathers of both.
It were better to clear this up. She wished to know the truth,
lest she should wrong her friend by entertaining a passion
for Isabella's lover. Thus jealousy prompted, and at the same
time borrowed, an excuse from friendship to justify its curiosity.

Isabella, not less restless had better foundation for her
suspicions. Both Theodore's tongue and eyes had told her his
heart was engaged—it was true—yet perhaps Matilda might
not correspond to his passion; she had ever appeared insensible
to love; all her thoughts were set on heaven. "Why did I
dissuade her?" said Isabella to herself. "I am punished for my
generosity; but when did they meet? Where? It cannot be.
I have deceived myself; perhaps last night was the first time
they beheld each other; it must be some other object that has
prepossessed his affections. If it is, I am not so unhappy as I
thought; if it is not my friend Matilda—how! can I stoop to
wish for the affection of a man who rudely and unnecessarily
acquainted me with his indifference? And that at the very
moment in which common courtesy demanded at least expressions of civility? I will go to my dear Matilda, who will confirm
me in this becoming pride—man is false—I will advise with
her on taking the veil; she will rejoice to find me in this
disposition; and I will acquaint her that I no longer oppose
her inclination for the cloister." In this frame of mind, and
determined to open her heart entirely to Matilda, she went to
that Princess' chamber, whom she found already dressed, and
leaning pensively on her arm. This attitude, so correspondent
to what she felt herself, revived Isabella's suspicions and destroyed the confidence she had purposed to place in her friend.
They blushed at meeting, and were too much novices to disguise their sensations with address. After some unmeaning

questions and replies, Matilda demanded of Isabella the cause
of her flight. The latter, who had almost forgotten Manfred's
passion, so entirely was she occupied by her own, concluding
that Matilda referred to her last escape from the convent,
which had occasioned the events of the preceding evening,
replied, "Martelli brought word to the convent that your
mother was dead——"

"Oh!" said Matilda, interrupting her, "Bianca has explained
that mistake to me; on seeing me faint, she cried, 'The Princess
is dead'; and Martelli, who had come for the usual dole to
the castle——"

"And what made you faint?" said Isabella, indifferent to
the rest.

Matilda blushed, and stammered, "My father—he was sitting
in judgment on a criminal."

"What criminal?" said Isabella eagerly.

"A young man," said Matilda. "I believe—I think it was
that young man that——"

"What—Theodore?" said Isabella.

"Yes," answered she. "I never saw him before; I do not know
how he had offended my father—but as he has been of service
to you, I am glad my lord has pardoned him."

"Served me!" replied Isabella. "Do you term it serving me,
to wound my father and almost occasion his death? Though
it is but since yesterday that I am blessed with knowing a
parent, I hope Matilda does not think I am such a stranger to
filial tenderness as not to resent the boldness of that audacious
youth, and that it is impossible for me ever to feel any affection for one who dared to lift his arm against the author of
my being. No, Matilda, my heart abhors him; and if you still
retain the friendship for me that you have vowed from your
infancy, you will detest the man who has been on the point of
making me miserable forever."

Matilda held down her head, and replied, "I hope my
dearest Isabella does not doubt her Matilda's friendship. I
never beheld that youth until yesterday; he is almost a stranger
to me: but as the surgeons have pronounced your father out
of danger, you ought not to harbor uncharitable resentment
against one, who, I am persuaded, did not know the Marquis
was related to you."

"You plead his cause very pathetically," said Isabella, "considering he is so much a stranger to you! I am mistaken, or
he returns your charity."

THE CASTLE OF OTRANTO

"What mean you?" said Matilda.

"Nothing," said Isabella, repenting that she had given Matilda a hint of Theodore's inclination for her. Then, changing the discourse, she asked Matilda what occasioned Manfred to take Theodore for a specter?

"Bless me," said Matilda, "did you not observe his extreme resemblance to the portrait of Alfonso in the gallery? I took notice of it to Bianca even before I saw him in armor; but with the helmet on he is the very image of that picture."

"I do not much observe pictures," said Isabella; "much less have I examined this young man so attentively as you seem to have done. Ah, Matilda, your heart is in danger; but let me warn you as a friend—he has owned to me that he is in love; it cannot be with you, for yesterday was the first time you ever met—was it not?"

"Certainly," replied Matilda; "but why does my dearest Isabella conclude from anything I have said, that"—she paused, then continuing, "he saw you first, and I am far from having the vanity to think that my little portion of charms could engage a heart devoted to you. May you be happy, Isabella, whatever is the fate of Matilda!"

"My lovely friend," said Isabella, whose heart was too honest to resist a kind expression, "it is you that Theodore admires; I saw it; I am persuaded of it; nor shall a thought of my own happiness suffer me to interfere with yours." This frankness drew tears from the gentle Matilda; and jealousy, that for a moment had raised a coolness between these amiable maidens, soon gave way to the natural sincerity and candor of their souls. Each confessed to the other the impression that Theodore had made on her; and this confidence was followed by a struggle of generosity, each insisting on yielding her claim to her friend. At length the dignity of Isabella's virtue reminding her of the preference which Theodore had almost declared for her rival, made her determine to conquer her passion and cede the beloved object to her friend.

During this contest of amity, Hippolita entered her daughter's chamber.

"Madam," said she to Isabella, "you have so much tenderness for Matilda, and interest yourself so kindly in whatever affects our wretched house, that I can have no secrets with my child which are not proper for you to hear." The Princesses were all attention and anxiety.

"Know then, madam," continued Hippolita, "and you, my

dearest Matilda, that being convinced by all the events of these two last ominous days that Heaven purposes the scepter of Otranto should pass from Manfred's hands into those of the Marquis Frederic; I have been perhaps inspired with the thought of averting our total destruction by the union of our rival houses. With this view I have been proposing to Manfred, my lord, to tender this dear, dear child to Frederic your father."

"Me to Lord Frederic!" cried Matilda. "Good heavens! my gracious mother, and have you named it to my father?"

"I have," said Hippolita. "He listened benignly to my proposal, and is gone to break it to the Marquis."

"Ah, wretched Princess," cried Isabella, "what hast thou done? What ruin has thy inadvertent goodness been preparing for thyself, for me, and for Matilda!"

"Ruin from me, to you, and to my child!" said Hippolita; "what can this mean?"

"Alas!" said Isabella, "the purity of your own heart prevents your seeing the depravity of others. Manfred, your lord, that impious man——"

"Hold!" said Hippolita. "You must not, in my presence, young lady, mention Manfred with disrespect; he is my lord and husband, and——"

"Will not long be so," said Isabella, "if his wicked purposes can be carried into execution."

"This language amazes me," said Hippolita. "Your feeling, Isabella, is warm; but until this hour I never knew it betray you into intemperance. What deed of Manfred authorizes you to treat him as a murderer, an assassin?"

"Thou virtuous, and too credulous Princess!" replied Isabella; "it is not thy life he aims at—it is to separate himself from thee! to divorce thee! to——"

"To divorce me!"—"To divorce my mother!" cried Hippolita and Matilda at once.

"Yes," said Isabella, "and, to complete his crime, he meditates —I cannot speak it!"

"What can surpass what thou hast already uttered?" said Matilda.

Hippolita was silent. Grief choked her speech; and the recollection of Manfred's late ambiguous discourses confirmed what she heard.

"Excellent, dear lady—madam! mother!" cried Isabella, flinging herself at Hippolita's feet in a transport of passion, "trust me, believe me, I will die a thousand deaths sooner than consent to injure you, than yield to so odious——"

"Oh, this is too much!" cried Hippolita. "What crimes does one crime suggest! Rise, dear Isabella; I do not doubt your virtue. Oh, Matilda, this stroke is too heavy for thee! Weep not, my child; and not a murmur, I charge thee. Remember, he is *thy* father still!"

"But you are my mother, too," said Matilda, fervently; "and *you* are virtuous, *you* are guiltless! Oh, must not I, must not I complain?"

"You must not," said Hippolita; "come, all will be well, Manfred, in the agony for the loss of thy brother, knew not what he said; perhaps Isabella misunderstood him; his heart is good—and, my child, thou knowest not all. There is a destiny hangs over us; the hand of Providence is stretched out. Oh, could I but save thee from the wreck.—Yes," continued she, in a firmer tone, "perhaps the sacrifice of myself may atone for all; I will go and offer myself to this divorce—it boots not what becomes of me. I will withdraw into the neighboring monastery, and waste the remainder of life in prayers and tears for my child and—the Prince."

"Thou art as much too good for this world," said Isabella, "as Manfred is execrable—but think not, lady, that thy weakness shall determine for me. I swear, hear me all ye angels——"

"Stop, I adjure thee," cried Hippolita. "Remember thou dost not depend on thyself; thou hast a father——"

"My father is too pious, too noble," interrupted Isabella, "to command an impious deed. But should he command it; can a father enjoin a cursed act? I was contracted to the son, can I wed the father?—No, Madam, no; force should not drag me to Manfred's hated bed. I loathe him, I abhor him: divine and human laws forbid; and, my friend, my dearest Matilda, would I wound her tender soul by injuring her adored mother? My own mother—I never have known another."

"Oh, she is the mother of both," cried Matilda. "Can we, can we, Isabella, adore her too much?"

"My lovely children," said the touched Hippolita, "your tenderness overpowers me; but I must not give way to it. It is not ours to make election for ourselves; Heaven, our fathers, and our husbands must decide for us. Have patience until you hear what Manfred and Frederic have determined. If the Marquis accepts Matilda's hand, I know she will readily obey. Heaven may interpose and prevent the rest. What means my child?" continued she, seeing Matilda fall at her feet with a flood of speechless tears.—"But no; answer me not, my daughter; I must not hear a word against the pleasure of thy father."

"Oh, doubt not my obedience, my dreadful obedience to him and to you!" said Matilda. "But can I, most respected of women, can I experience all this tenderness, this world of goodness, and conceal a thought from the best of mothers?"

"What art thou going to utter?" said Isabella, trembling. "Recollect thyself, Matilda."

"No, Isabella," said the Princess, "I should not deserve this incomparable parent, if the inmost recesses of my soul harbored a thought without her permission—nay, I have offended her; I have suffered a passion to enter my heart without her avowal; but here I disclaim it; here I vow to Heaven and her——"

"My child! my child!" said Hippolita, "what words are these? What new calamities has fate in store for us? Thou, a passion! Thou, in this hour of destruction!"

"Oh, I see all my guilt," said Matilda. "I abhor myself, if I cost my mother a pang; she is the dearest thing I have on earth. Oh, I will never, never behold him more!"

"Isabella," said Hippolita, "thou art conscious to this unhappy secret, whatever it is. Speak!"

"What!" cried Matilda. "Have I so forfeited my mother's love, that she will not permit me even to speak my own guilt? Oh, wretched, wretched Matilda!"

"Thou art too cruel," said Isabella to Hippolita; "canst thou behold this anguish of a virtuous mind, and not commiserate it?"

"Not pity my child!" said Hippolita, catching Matilda in her arms. "Oh, I know she is good; she is all virtue, all tenderness and duty. I do forgive thee, my excellent, my only hope!"

The Princesses then revealed to Hippolita their mutual inclination for Theodore, and the purpose of Isabella to resign him to Matilda. Hippolita blamed their imprudence, and showed them the improbability that either father would consent to bestow his heiress on so poor a man, though nobly born. Some comfort it gave her to find their passion of so recent a date, and that Theodore had had but little cause to suspect it in either. She strictly enjoined them to avoid all correspondence with him. This Matilda fervently promised; but Isabella, who flattered herself that she meant no more than to promote his union with her friend, could not determine to avoid him, and made no reply.

"I will go to the convent," said Hippolita, "and order new masses to be said for a deliverance from these calamities."

"Oh, my mother," said Matilda, "you mean to quit us; you mean to take sanctuary, and to give my father an opportunity of pursuing his fatal intentions. Alas! on my knees I supplicate you to forbear. Will you leave me a prey to Frederic? I will follow you to the convent."

"Be at peace, my child," said Hippolita; "I will return instantly. I will never abandon thee, until I know it is the will of Heaven, and for thy benefit."

"Do not deceive me," said Matilda. "I will not marry Frederic until thou commandest it. Alas! what will become of me?"

"Why that exclamation?" said Hippolita. "I have promised thee to return."

"Ah, my mother," replied Matilda, "stay and save me from myself. A frown from thee can do more than all my fathers severity. I have given away my heart, and you alone can make me recall it."

"No more," said Hippolita; "thou must not relapse, Matilda."

"I can quit Theodore," said she, "but must I wed another? Let me attend thee to the altar and shut myself from the world forever."

"Thy fate depends on thy father," said Hippolita; "I have ill bestowed my tenderness, if it has taught thee to revere aught beyond him. Adieu! my child, I go to pray for thee."

Hippolita's real purpose was to demand of Jerome whether in conscience she might not consent to the divorce. She had oft urged Manfred to resign the principality, which the delicacy of her conscience rendered an hourly burden to her. These scruples concurred to make the separation from her husband appear less dreadful to her than it would have seemed in any other situation.

Jerome, at quitting the castle overnight, had questioned Theodore severely why he had accused him to Manfred of being privy to his escape. Theodore owned it had been with design to prevent Manfred's suspicion from alighting on Matilda; and added, the holiness of Jerome's life and character secured him from the tyrant's wrath. Jerome was heartily grieved to discover his son's inclination for that Princess; and leaving him to his rest, promised in the morning to acquaint him with important reasons for conquering his passion. Theodore, like Isabella, was too recently acquainted with parental authority to submit to its decisions against the impulse of his heart. He had little curiosity to learn the friar's reasons, and less disposition to obey them. The lovely Matilda had made stronger impressions on him than filial affection. All night he pleased himself with visions of love; and it was not till late after the morning office that he recollected the friar's commands to attend him at Alfonso's tomb.

"Young man," said Jerome, when he saw him, "this tardiness does not please me. Have a father's commands already so little weight?"

Theodore made awkward excuses and attributed his delay to having overslept himself.

"And on whom were thy dreams employed?" said the friar sternly. His son blushed. "Come, come," resumed the friar, "inconsiderate youth, this must not be; eradicate this guilty passion from thy breast."

"Guilty passion!" cried Theodore. "Can guilt dwell with innocent beauty and virtuous modesty?"

"It is sinful," replied the friar, "to cherish those whom Heaven has doomed to destruction. A tyrant's race must be swept from the earth to the third and fourth generation."

"Will Heaven visit the innocent for the crimes of the guilty?" said Theodore. "The fair Matilda has virtues enough——"

"To undo thee," interrupted Jerome. "Hast thou so soon forgotten that twice the savage Manfred has pronounced thy sentence?"

"Nor have I forgotten, sir," said Theodore, "that the charity of his daughter delivered me from his power. I can forget injuries, but never benefits."

"The injuries thou hast received from Manfred's race," said the friar, "are beyond what thou canst conceive. Reply not, but view this holy image! Beneath this marble monument rest the ashes of the good Alfonso; a prince adorned with every virtue; the father of his people; the delight of mankind! Kneel, headstrong boy, and listen, while a father unfolds a tale of horror, that will expel every sentiment from thy soul, but sensations of sacred vengeance. Alfonso! much injured prince! let thy unsatisfied shade sit awful on the troubled air, while these trembling lips—— Ha! who comes there?"

"The most wretched of women," said Hippolita, entering

the choir. "Good father, art thou at leisure? But why this
kneeling youth? What means the horror imprinted on each
countenance? Why at this venerable tomb?—Alas! hast thou
seen aught?"

"We were pouring forth our orisons to Heaven," replied the
friar, with some confusion, "to put an end to the woes of this
deplorable province. Join with us, lady; thy spotless soul may
obtain an exemption from the judgments which the portents of
these days but too speakingly denounce against thy house."

"I pray fervently to Heaven to divert them," said the pious
Princess. "Thou knowest it has been the occupation of my
life to wrest a blessing for my lord and my harmless children.
One, alas! is taken from me; would Heaven but hear me for
my poor Matilda! Father, intercede for her."

"Every heart will bless her!" cried Theodore with rapture.

"Be dumb, rash youth," said Jerome. "And thou, fond Princess, contend not with the powers above. The Lord giveth,
and the Lord taketh away; bless His holy name, and submit
to His decrees."

"I do most devoutly," said Hippolita; "but will He not
spare my only comfort? Must Matilda perish too? Ah, Father,
I came—but dismiss thy son. No ear but thine must hear
what I have to utter."

"May Heaven grant thy every wish, most excellent Princess!"
said Theodore, retiring. Jerome frowned.

Hippolita then acquainted the friar with a proposal she had
suggested to Manfred, his approbation of it, and the tender
of Matilda that he was gone to make to Frederic. Jerome could
not conceal his dislike of the motion, which he covered under
pretense of the improbability that Frederic, the nearest of
blood to Alfonso, and who was come to claim his succession,
would yield to an alliance with the usurper of his right. But
nothing could equal the perplexity of the friar when Hippolita
confessed her readiness not to oppose the separation, and
demanded his opinion on the legality of her acquiescence. The
friar seized eagerly at her request of his advice; and without
explaining his aversion to the proposed marriage of Manfred
and Isabella, he painted to Hippolita, in the most alarming
colors, the sinfulness of her consent, denounced judgments
against her if she complied, and enjoined her, in the severest
terms, to treat any such proposition with every mark of indignation and refusal.

Manfred, in the meantime, had broken his purpose to Fred-

eric, and proposed the double marriage. That weak Prince, who
had been struck with the charms of Matilda, listened but too
eagerly to the offer. He forgot his enmity to Manfred, whom he
saw but little hope of dispossessing by force; and flattering himself that no issue might succeed from the union of his daughter
with the tyrant, he looked upon his own succession to the
principality as facilitated by wedding Matilda. He made faint
opposition to the proposal; affecting, for form only, not to
acquiesce unless Hippolita should consent to the divorce.
Manfred took that upon himself. Transported with his success
and impatient to see himself in a situation to expect sons, he
hastened to his wife's apartment, determined to exhort her
compliance. He learned with indignation that she was absent
at the convent. His guilt suggested to him that she had probably been informed by Isabella of his purpose. He doubted
whether her retirement to the convent did not import an intention of remaining there until she could raise obstacles to
their divorce; and the suspicions he had already entertained of
Jerome made him apprehend that the friar would not only
traverse his views, but might have inspired Hippolita with the
resolution of taking sanctuary. Impatient to unravel this clue,
and to defeat its success, Manfred hastened to the convent, and
arrived there as the friar was earnestly exhorting the Princess
never to yield to the divorce.

"Madam," said Manfred, "what business drew you hither?
Why did you not await my return from the Marquis?"

"I came to implore a blessing on your councils," replied
Hippolita.

"My councils do not need a friar's intervention," said Manfred; "and of all men living is that hoary traitor the only one
whom you delight to confer with?"

"Profane Prince!" said Jerome; "is it at the altar thou
choosest to insult the servants of the altar? But, Manfred, thy
impious schemes are known. Heaven and this virtuous lady
know them; nay, frown not, Prince. The Church despises thy
menaces. Her thunders will be heard above thy wrath. Dare
to proceed in thy cursed purpose of a divorce until her sentence be known, and here I launch her anathema at thy head."

"Audacious rebel!" said Manfred, endeavoring to conceal
the awe with which the friar's words inspired him. "Dost thou
presume to threaten thy lawful Prince?"

"Thou art no lawful Prince," said Jerome. "Thou art no

Prince:—go, discuss thy claim with Frederic; and when that is done——"

"It is done," replied Manfred. "Frederic accepts Matilda's hand and is content to waive his claim unless I have no male issue." As he spoke those words, three drops of blood fell from the nose of Alfonso's statue. Manfred turned pale, and the Princess sunk on her knees.

"Behold!" said the friar; "mark this miraculous indication that the blood of Alfonso will never mix with that of Manfred!"

"My gracious lord," said Hippolita, "let us submit ourselves to Heaven. Think not thy ever obedient wife rebels against thy authority. I have no will but that of my lord and the Church. To that revered tribunal let us appeal. It does not depend on us to burst the bonds that unite us. If the Church shall approve the dissolution of our marriage, be it so—I have but few years, and those of sorrow, to pass. Where can they be worn away so well as at the foot of this altar, in prayers for thine and Matilda's safety?"

"But thou shalt not remain here until then," said Manfred. "Repair with me to the castle, and there I will advise on the proper measures for a divorce. But this meddling friar comes not thither; my hospitable roof shall nevermore harbor a traitor—and for thy reverence's offspring," continued he, "I banish him from my dominions. He, I ween, is no sacred personage, nor under the protection of the Church. Whoever weds Isabella, it shall not be Father Falconara's started-up son."

"They start up," said the friar, "who are suddenly beheld in the seat of lawful princes; but they wither away like the grass, and their place knows them no more."

Manfred, casting a look of scorn at the friar, led Hippolita forth; but at the door of the church whispered one of his attendants to remain concealed about the convent, and bring him instant notice if any one from the castle should repair thither.

CHAPTER V

EVERY reflection which Manfred made on the friar's behavior conspired to persuade him that Jerome was privy to an amour between Isabella and Theodore. But Jerome's new presumption, so dissonant from his former meekness, suggested still deeper apprehensions. The Prince even suspected that the friar depended on some secret support from Frederic, whose arrival coinciding with the novel appearance of Theodore seemed to bespeak a correspondence. Still more was he troubled with the resemblance of Theodore to Alfonso's portrait. The latter he knew had unquestionably died without issue. Frederic had consented to bestow Isabella on him. These contradictions agitated his mind with numberless pangs. He saw but two methods of extricating himself from his difficulties. The one was to resign his dominions to the Marquis. Pride, ambition, and his reliance on ancient prophecies, which had pointed out a possibility of his preserving them to his posterity, combated that thought. The other was to press his marriage with Isabella. After long ruminating on these anxious thoughts, as he marched silently with Hippolita to the castle, he at last discoursed with that Princess on the subject of his disquiet, and used every insinuating and plausible argument to extract her consent to, even her promise of promoting, the divorce. Hippolita needed little persuasions to bend her to his pleasure. She endeavored to win him over to the measure of resigning his dominions; but finding her exhortations fruitless she assured him that, as far as her conscience would allow, she would raise no opposition to a separation, though without better founded scruples than what he yet alleged she would not engage to be active in demanding it.

This compliance, though inadequate, was sufficient to raise Manfred's hopes. He trusted that his power and wealth would easily advance his suit at the court of Rome, whither he resolved to engage Frederic to take a journey on purpose. That Prince had discovered so much passion for Matilda that Manfred hoped to obtain all he wished by holding out or withdrawing his daughter's charms, according as the Marquis should appear more or less disposed to co-operate in his views. Even the absence of Frederic would be a material point gained until he could take further measures for his security.

Dismissing Hippolita to her apartment, he repaired to that of the Marquis; but crossing the great hall, through which he was to pass, he met Bianca. The damsel he knew was in the confidence of both the young ladies. It immediately occurred to him to sift her on the subject of Isabella and Theodore. Calling her aside into the recess of the oriel window of the hall, and soothing her with many fair words and promises, he demanded of her whether she knew aught of the state of Isabella's affections.

"I! my lord! no, my lord—yes, my lord—poor lady! She is wonderfully alarmed about her father's wounds! But I tell her he will do well; don't your highness think so?"

"I do not ask you," replied Manfred, "what she thinks about her father; but you are in her secrets. Come, be a good girl, and tell me; is there any young man—ha!—you understand me."

"Lord bless me! understand your highness, no, not I; I told her a few vulnerary herbs and repose——"

"I am not talking," replied the Prince, impatiently, "about her father; I know he will do well."

"Bless me, I rejoice to hear your highness say so; for though I thought it not right to let my young lady despond, methought his greatness had a wan look, and a something—I remember when young Ferdinand was wounded by the Venetian——"

"Thou answerest from the point," interrupted Manfred; "but here, take this jewel, perhaps that may fix thy attention; nay, no reverences; my favor shall not stop here. Come, tell me truly, how stands Isabella's heart."

"Well, your highness has such a way!" said Bianca, "to be sure; but can your highness keep a secret? If it should ever come out of your lips——"

"It shall not, it shall not," cried Manfred.

"Nay, but swear, your highness. By my halidame,[14] if it should ever be known that I said it—why, truth is truth, I do not think my Lady Isabella ever much affectioned my young lord, your son—yet he was a sweet youth, as one should see. I am sure, if I had been a princess—but bless me! I must attend my Lady Matilda; she will marvel what is become of me."

"Stay!" cried Manfred. "Thou hast not satisfied my question. Hast thou ever carried any message, any letter?"

"I! good gracious!" cried Bianca; "I carry a letter? I would not to be a queen. I hope your highness thinks, though I am poor, I am honest—did your highness never hear what Count Marsigli offered me when he came a-wooing to my Lady Matilda?"

"I have not leisure," said Manfred, "to listen to thy tales. I do not question thy honesty; but it is thy duty to conceal nothing from me. How long has Isabella been acquainted with Theodore?"

[14] Literally, Holy Dame, an oath sworn in the name of the Virgin Mary.

"Nay, there is nothing can escape your highness," said Bianca; "not that I know anything of the matter. Theodore, to be sure, is a proper young man, and, as my Lady Matilda says, the very image of good Alfonso; has not your highness remarked it?"

"Yes, yes,—no—thou torturest me," said Manfred; "where did they meet? When?"

"Who? My Lady Matilda?" said Bianca.

"No, no, not Matilda; Isabella. When did Isabella first become acquainted with this Theodore?"

"Virgin Mary!" said Bianca. "How should I know?"

"Thou dost know," said Manfred, "and I must know; I will."

"Lord! your highness is not jealous of young Theodore!" said Bianca.

"Jealous! No, no; why should I be jealous? Perhaps I mean to unite them, if I were sure Isabella would have no repugnance."

"Repugnance! No, I'll warrant her," said Bianca; "he is as comely a youth as ever trod on Christian ground. We are all in love with him; there is not a soul in the castle but would be rejoiced to have him for our prince—I mean, when it shall please Heaven to call your highness to itself."

"Indeed," said Manfred, "has it gone so far? Oh, this cursed friar! but I must not lose time. Go, Bianca, attend Isabella; but I charge thee, not a word of what has passed. Find out how she is affected toward Theodore; bring me good news, and that ring has a companion. Wait at the foot of the winding staircase; I am going to visit the Marquis, and will talk further with thee at my return."

Manfred, after some general conversation, desired Frederic to dismiss the two knights his companions, having to talk with him on urgent affairs. As soon as they were alone, he began, in artful guise, to sound the Marquis on the subject of Matilda; and finding him disposed to his wish, he let drop hints on the difficulties that would attend the celebration of their marriage, unless—, At that instant Bianca burst into the room with a wildness in her look and gestures that spoke the utmost terror.

"Oh, my lord, my lord!" cried she. "We are all undone! It is come again! It is come again!"

"What is come again?" cried Manfred, amazed.

"Oh, the hand! The giant! The hand!—Support me! I am terrified out of my senses," cried Bianca. "I will not sleep in the castle to-night. Where shall I go? My things may come after me to-morrow—would I had been content to wed Francesco!—This comes of ambition."

"What has terrified thee thus, young woman?" said the Marquis. "Thou art safe here; be not alarmed."

"Oh, your greatness is wonderfully good," said Bianca, "but I dare not—no, pray let me go. I had rather leave everything behind me than stay another hour under this roof."

"Go to, thou hast lost thy senses," said Manfred. "Interrupt us not; we were communing on important matters. My lord, this wench is subject to fits. Come with me, Bianca."

"Oh, the saints, no," said Bianca; "for certain it comes to warn your highness. Why should it appear to me else? I say my prayers morning and evening. Oh, if your highness had believed Diego! 'Tis the same hand that he saw the foot to in the gallery chamber. Father Jerome has often told us the prophecy would be out one of these days. 'Bianca,' said he, 'mark my words——' "

"Thou ravest," said Manfred in a rage. "Begone, and keep these fooleries to frighten thy companions."

"What, my lord!" cried Bianca. "Do you think I have seen nothing? Go to the foot of the great stairs yourself—as I live I saw it."

"Saw what? Tell us, fair maid, what thou hast seen," said Frederic.

"Can your highness listen," said Manfred, "to the delirium of a silly wench, who has heard stories of apparitions until she believes them?"

"This is more than fancy," said the Marquis. "Her terror is too natural and too strongly impressed to be the work of imagination. Tell us, fair maiden, what it is has moved thee thus."

"Yes, my lord, thank your greatness," said Bianca. "I believe I look very pale; I shall be better when I have recovered myself. I was going to my Lady Isabella's chamber by his highness' order——"

"We do not want the circumstances," interrupted Manfred. "Since his highness will have it so, proceed; but be brief."

"Lord! your highness thwarts one so!" replied Bianca. "I fear my hair—I am sure I never in my life—well, as I was telling your greatness, I was going, by his highness' order, to my Lady Isabella's chamber. She lies in the watchet-colored chamber, on the right hand, one pair of stairs. So when I came to the great stairs, I was looking on his highness' present here——"

"Grant me patience!" said Manfred. "Will this wench never come to the point? What imports it to the Marquis, that I gave thee a bauble for thy faithful attendance on my daughter; we want to know what thou sawest."

"I was going to tell your highness," said Bianca, "if you would permit me. So as I was rubbing the ring—I am sure I had not gone up three steps, but I heard the rattling of armor; for all the world such a clatter, as Diego says he heard when the giant turned him about in the gallery-chamber."

"What does she mean, my lord?" said the Marquis. "Is your castle haunted by giants and goblins?"

"Lord, what, has not your greatness heard the story of the giant in the gallery-chamber?" cried Bianca. "I marvel his highness has not told you—mayhap you do not know there is a prophecy——"

"This trifling is intolerable," interrupted Manfred. "Let us dismiss this silly wench, my lord; we have more important affairs to discuss."

"By your favor," said Frederic, "these are no trifles. The enormous saber I was directed to in the wood, yon casque, its fellow—are these visions of this poor maiden's brain?"

"So Jaquez thinks, may it please your greatness," said Bianca. "He says this moon will not be out without our seeing some strange revolution. For my part, I should not be surprised if it was to happen to-morrow; for, as I was saying, when I heard the clattering of armor, I was all in a cold sweat: I looked up, and, if your greatness will believe me, I saw upon the uppermost banister of the great stairs a hand in armor, as big, as big—I thought I should have swooned—I never stopped until I came hither. Would I were well out of this castle! My Lady Matilda told me but yester-morning that her highness Hippolita knows something."

"Thou art an insolent!" cried Manfred. "Lord Marquis, it much misgives me that this scene is concerted to affront me. Are my own domestics suborned to spread tales injurious to my honor? Pursue your claim by manly daring; or let us bury our feuds, as was proposed, by the intermarriage of our children. But trust me, it ill becomes a prince of your bearing to practice on mercenary wenches."

"I scorn your imputation," said Frederic; "until this hour I never set eyes on this damsel. I have given her no jewel!

My lord, my lord, your conscience, your guilt accuses you, and would throw the suspicion on me; but keep your daughter, and think no more of Isabella. The judgments already fallen on your house forbid me matching into it."

Manfred, alarmed at the resolute tone in which Frederic delivered these words, endeavored to pacify him. Dismissing Bianca, he made such submissions to the Marquis, and threw in such artful ecomiums on Matilda, that Frederic was once more staggered. However, as his passion was of so recent a date, it could not at once surmount the scruples he had conceived. He had gathered enough from Bianca's discourse to persuade him that Heaven declared itself against Manfred. The proposed marriages, too, removed his claim to a distance; and the principality of Otranto was a stronger temptation than the contingent reversion of it with Matilda. Still he would not absolutely recede from his engagements; but purposing to gain time, he demanded of Manfred if it was true in fact that Hippolita consented to the divorce. The Prince, transported to find no other obstacle, and depending on his influence over his wife, assured the Marquis it was so, and that he might satisfy himself of the truth from her own mouth.

As they were thus discoursing, word was brought that the banquet was prepared. Manfred conducted Frederic to the great hall, where they were received by Hippolita and the young Princesses. Manfred placed the Marquis next to Matilda, and seated himself between his wife and Isabella. Hippolita comported herself with an easy gravity; but the young ladies were silent and melancholy. Manfred, who was determined to pursue his point with the Marquis in the remainder of the evening, pushed on the feast until it waxed late; affecting unrestrained gaiety, and plying Frederic with repeated goblets of wine. The latter, more upon his guard than Manfred wished, declined his frequent challenges, on pretense of his late loss of blood; while the Prince, to raise his own disordered spirits, and to counterfeit unconcern, indulged himself in plentiful drafts, though not to the intoxication of his senses.

The evening being far advanced, the banquet concluded. Manfred would have withdrawn with Frederic; but the latter, pleading weakness and want of repose, retired to his chamber, gallantly telling the Prince that his daughter should amuse his highness until himself could attend him. Manfred accepted the party, and, to the no small grief of Isabella, accompanied her to her apartment. Matilda waited on her mother, to enjoy the freshness of the evening on the ramparts of the castle.

Soon as the company were dispersed their several ways, Frederic, quitting his chamber, inquired if Hippolita was alone, and was told by one of her attendants, who had not noticed her going forth, that at that hour she generally withdrew to her oratory, where he probably would find her. The Marquis, during the repast, had beheld Matilda with increase of passion. He now wished to find Hippolita in the disposition her lord had promised. The portents that had alarmed him were forgotten in his desires. Stealing softly and unobserved to the apartment of Hippolita, he entered it with a resolution to encourage her acquiescence to the divorce, having perceived that Manfred was resolved to make the possession of Isabella an unalterable condition, before he would grant Matilda to his wishes.

The Marquis was not surprised at the silence that reigned in the Princess' apartment. Concluding her, as he had been advertised, in her oratory, he passed on. The door was ajar; the evening gloomy and overcast. Pushing open the door gently, he saw a person kneeling before the altar. As he approached nearer, it seemed not a woman, but one in a long woolen weed, whose back was toward him. The person seemed absorbed in prayer. The Marquis was about to return, when the figure, rising, stood some moments fixed in meditation, without regarding him. The Marquis, expecting the holy person to come forth, and meaning to excuse his uncivil interruption, said:

"Reverend father, I sought the Lady Hippolita."

"Hippolita!" replied a hollow voice; "camest thou to this castle to seek Hippolita?" And then the figure, turning slowly round, discovered to Frederic the fleshless jaws and empty sockets of a skeleton, wrapped in a hermit's cowl.

"Angels of peace protect me!" cried Frederic, recoiling.

"Deserve their protection," said the specter.

Frederic, falling on his knees, adjured the phantom to take pity on him.

"Dost thou not remember me?" said the apparition. "Remember the wood of Joppa!"

"Art thou that holy hermit?" cried Frederic, trembling; "can I do aught for thy eternal peace?"

"Wast thou delivered from bondage," said the specter, "to

pursue carnal delights? Hast thou forgotten the buried saber, and the behest of Heaven engraven on it?"

"I have not, I have not," said Frederic; "but say, blessed spirit, what is thy errand to me? What remains to be done?"

"To forget Matilda," said the apparition, and vanished.

Frederic's blood froze in his veins. For some minutes he remained motionless. Then falling prostrate on his face before the altar, he besought the intercession of every saint for pardon. A flood of tears succeeded to this transport; and the image of the beauteous Matilda rushing, in spite of him, on his thoughts, he lay on the ground in a conflict of penitence and passion. Ere he could recover from this agony of his spirits, the Princess Hippolita, with a taper in her hand, entered the oratory alone. Seeing a man without motion on the floor, she gave a shriek, concluding him dead. Her fright brought Frederic to himself. Rising suddenly, his face bedewed with tears, he would have rushed from her presence; but Hippolita, stopping him, conjured him, in the most plaintive accents, to explain the cause of his disorder, and by what strange chance she had found him there in that posture.

"Ah, virtuous Princess!" said the Marquis, penetrated with grief, and stopped.

"For the love of Heaven, my lord," said Hippolita, "disclose the cause of this transport! What mean these doleful sounds, this alarming exclamation on my name? What woes has Heaven still in store for the wretched Hippolita?—yet silent! By every pitying angel I adjure thee, noble Prince," continued she, falling at his feet, "to disclose the purport of what lies at thy heart. I see thou feelest for me; thou feelest the sharp pangs that thou inflectest. Speak, for pity! Does aught thou knowest concern my child!"

"I cannot speak," cried Frederic, bursting from her. "Oh, Matilda!"

Quitting the princess thus abruptly, he hastened to his own apartment. At the door of it he was accosted by Manfred, who, flushed by wine and love, had come to seek him, and to propose to waste some hours of the night in music and reveling. Frederic, offended at an invitation so dissonant from the mood of his soul, pushed him rudely aside, and, entering his chamber, flung the door intemperately against Manfred, and bolted it inward. The haughty Prince, enraged at this unaccountable behavior, withdrew in a frame of mind capable of the most fatal excesses. As he crossed the court, he was met

by the domestic whom he planted at the convent as a spy on
Jerome and Theodore. This man, almost breathless with the
haste he had made, informed his lord, that Theodore and some
lady from the castle were at that instant in private conference
at the tomb of Alfonso, in St. Nicholas' church. He had
dogged Theodore thither; but the gloominess of the night had
prevented his discovering who the woman was.

Manfred, whose spirits were inflamed, and whom Isabella
had driven from her on his urging his passion with too little
reserve, did not doubt but the inquietude she had expressed
had been occasioned by her impatience to meet Theodore.
Provoked by this conjecture, and enraged at her father, he
hastened secretly to the great church. Gliding softly between
the aisles, and guided by an imperfect gleam of moonshine
that shone faintly through the illuminated windows, he stole
toward the tomb of Alfonso, to which he was directed by
indistinct whispers of the person he sought. The first sounds
he could distinguish were:

"Does it, alas, depend on me? Manfred will never permit
our union."

"No, this shall prevent it!" cried the tyrant, drawing his
dagger, and plunging it over her shoulder into the bosom of
the person that spoke.

"Ah me, I am slain!" cried Matilda, sinking. "Good Heaven,
receive my soul!"

"Savage, inhuman monster, what hast thou done?" cried
Theodore, rushing on him and wrenching his dagger from him.

"Stop, stop thy impious hand!" cried Matilda; "it is my
father!"

Manfred, waking as from a trance, beat his breast, twisted
his hands in his locks, and endeavored to recover his dagger
from Theodore to dispatch himself. Theodore, scarce less
distracted, and only mastering the transports of his grief to
assist Matilda, had now by his cries drawn some of the monks
to his aid. While part of them endeavored, in concert with the
afflicted Theodore, to stop the blood of the dying Princess, the
rest prevented Manfred from laying violent hands on himself.

Matilda, resigning herself patiently to her fate, acknowledged, with looks of grateful love, the zeal of Theodore. Yet
oft, as her faintness would permit her speech its way, she
begged the assistants to comfort her father.

Jerome, by this time, had learned the fatal news, and reached
the church. His looks seemed to reproach Theodore; but

turning to Manfred, he said, "Now, tyrant, behold the completion of woe fulfilled on thy impious and devoted head! The blood of Alfonso cried to Heaven for vengeance; and Heaven has permitted its altar to be polluted by assassination, that thou mightest shed thy own blood at the foot of that prince's sepulcher!"

"Cruel man," cried Matilda, "to aggravate the woes of a parent! May Heaven bless my father, and forgive him as I do! My lord, my gracious sire, dost thou forgive thy child? Indeed I came not hither to meet Theodore. I found him praying at this tomb, whither my mother sent me to intercede for thee, for her—dearest father, bless your child, and say you forgive her."

"Forgive thee, murderous monster," cried Manfred, "can assassins forgive? I took thee for Isabella; but Heaven directed my bloody hand to the heart of my child—oh, Matilda, I cannot utter it; canst thou forgive the blindness of my rage?"

"I can, I do, and may Heaven confirm it," said Matilda. "But while I have life to ask it—oh, my mother, what will she feel! Will you comfort her, my lord, will you not put her away? Indeed she loves you—oh, I am faint; bear me to the castle—can I live to have her close my eyes?"

Theodore and the monks besought her earnestly to suffer herself to be borne into the convent; but her instances were so pressing to be carried to the castle, that, placing her on a litter, they conveyed her thither as she requested. Theodore, supporting her head with his arm, and hanging over her in an agony of despairing love, still endeavored to inspire her with hopes of life. Jerome on the other side comforted her with discourses of Heaven; and holding a crucifix before her, which she bathed with innocent tears, prepared her for her passage to immortality. Manfred, plunged in the deepest affliction, followed her litter in despair.

Ere they reached the castle, Hippolita, informed of the dreadful catastrophe, had flown to meet her murdered child; but when she saw the afflicted procession, the mightiness of her grief deprived her of her senses, and she fell lifeless to the earth in a swoon. Isabella and Frederic, who attended her, were overwhelmed in almost equal sorrow. Matilda alone seemed insensible to her own situation; every thought was lost in tenderness for her mother. Ordering the litter to stop, as soon as Hippolita was brought to herself, she asked for her father. He approached, unable to speak. Matilda, seizing his hand and her mother's, locked them in her own, and then clasped them to her heart. Manfred could not support this act of pathetic piety. He dashed himself on the ground and cursed the day he was born. Isabella, apprehensive that these struggles of passion were more than Matilda could support, took upon herself to order Manfred to be borne to his apartment, while she caused Matilda to be conveyed to the nearest chamber. Hippolita, scarce more alive than her daughter, was regardless of everything but her; but when the tender Isabella's care would have likewise removed her, while the surgeons examined Matilda's wound, she cried:

"Remove me! never! never! never! I lived but in her, and will expire with her." Matilda raised her eyes at her mother's voice, but closed them again without speaking. Her sinking pulse and the damp coldness of her hand soon dispelled all hopes of recovery. Theodore followed the surgeons into the outer chamber, and heard them pronounce the fatal sentence with a transport equal to frenzy.

"Since she cannot live mine," cried he, "at least she shall be mine in death! Father! Jerome! Will you not join our hands?" cried he to the friar, who, with the Marquis had accompanied the surgeons.

"What means thy distracted rashness?" said Jerome. "Is this an hour for marriage?"

"It is, it is," cried Theodore; "alas! there is no other!"

"Young man, thou art too unadvised," said Frederic. "Dost thou think we are to listen to thy fond transports in this hour of fate? What pretensions hast thou to the Princess?"

"Those of a Prince," said Theodore, "of the sovereign of Otranto. This reverend man, my father, has informed me who I am."

"Thou ravest," said the Marquis. "There is no prince of Otranto but myself, now Manfred, by murder, by sacrilegious murder, has forfeited all pretensions."

"My lord," said Jerome, assuming an air of command, "he tells you true. It was not my purpose the secret should have been divulged so soon; but fate presses onward to its work. What his hot-headed passion has revealed, my tongue confirms. Know, Prince, that when Alfonso set sail for the Holy Land——"

"Is this a season for explanations?" cried Theodore. "Father, come and unite me to the Princess; she shall be mine—in every other thing I will dutifully obey you. My life; my adored

Matilda!" continued Theodore, rushing back into the inner chamber, "will you not be mine? Will you not bless your——" Isabella made signs to him to be silent, apprehending the Princess was near her end. "What, is she dead?" cried Theodore. "Is it possible?" The violence of his exclamations brought Matilda to herself. Lifting up her eyes, she looked around for her mother.

"Life of my soul! I am here," cried Hippolita, "think not I will quit thee!"

"Oh, you are too good," said Matilda; "but weep not for me, my mother! I am going where sorrow never dwells. Isabella, thou hast loved me; wo't thou not supply my fondness to this dear, dear woman? Indeed I am faint!"

"Oh, my child, my child!" said Hippolita, in a flood of tears, "can I not withhold thee a moment?"

"It will not be," said Matilda; "commend me to Heaven— where is my father? Forgive him, dearest mother—forgive him my death; it was an error. Oh, I had forgotten, dearest mother, I vowed never to see Theodore more—perhaps that has drawn down this calamity, but it was not intentional—can you pardon me?"

"Oh, wound not my agonizing soul," said Hippolita. "Thou never couldst offend me. Alas! She faints! Help! Help!"

"I would say something more," said Matilda, struggling, "but it would not be—Isabella—Theodore—for my sake— oh!" She expired. Isabella and her women tore Hippolita from the corpse; but Theodore threatened destruction to all who attempted to remove him from it. He printed a thousand kisses on her clay-cold hands, and uttered every expression that despairing love could dictate.

Isabella, in the meantime, was accompanying the afflicted Hippolita to her apartment; but in the middle of the court they were met by Manfred, who, distracted with his own thoughts, and anxious once more to behold his daughter, was advancing toward the chamber where she lay. As the moon was now at its height, he read in the countenances of this unhappy company the event he dreaded.

"What! is she dead?" cried he in wild confusion. A clap of thunder at that instant shook the castle to its foundations; the earth rocked, and the clank of more than mortal armor was heard behind. Frederic and Jerome thought the last day was at hand. The latter, forcing Theodore along with them, rushed into the court. The moment Theodore appeared, the walls of the castle behind Manfred were thrown down with a mighty force, and the form of Alfonso, dilated to an immense magnitude, appeared in the center of the ruins.

"Behold in Theodore the true heir of Alfonso!" said the vision; and having pronounced those words, accompanied by a clap of thunder, it ascended solemnly toward heaven, where the clouds parting asunder, the form of St. Nicholas was seen, and receiving Alfonso's shade, they were soon wrapped from mortal eyes in a blaze of glory.

The beholders fell prostrate on their faces, acknowledging the divine will. The first that broke silence was Hippolita.

"My lord," said she to the desponding Manfred, "behold the vanity of human greatness! Conrad is gone! Matilda is no more! In Theodore we view the true Prince of Otranto. By what miracle he is so, I know not—suffice it to us, our doom is pronounced! Shall we not—can we but—dedicate the few deplorable hours we have to live, in deprecating the further wrath of Heaven? Heaven ejects us; whither can we fly, but to yon holy cells that yet offer us a retreat?"

"Thou guiltless but unhappy woman! unhappy by my crimes!" replied Manfred, "my heart at last is open to thy devout admonitions. Oh, could—but it cannot be—ye are lost in wonder,—let me at last do justice on myself! To heap shame on my own head is all the satisfaction I have left to offer to offended Heaven. My story has drawn down these judgments; let my confession atone—but ah! what can atone for usurpation and a murdered child; a child murdered in a consecrated place? Listen, sirs, and may this bloody record be a warning to future tyrants!

"Alfonso, ye all know, died in the Holy Land—ye would interrupt me—ye would say he came not fairly to his end—it is most true—why else this bitter cup which Manfred must drink to the dregs? Ricardo, my grandfather, was his chamberlain—I would draw a veil over my ancestor's crimes, but it is in vain! Alfonso died by poison. A fictitious will declared Ricardo his heir. His crimes pursued him. Yet he lost no Conrad, no Matilda! I pay the price of usurpation for all. A storm overtook him. Haunted by his guilt, he vowed to St. Nicholas to found a church and two convents, if he lived to reach Otranto. The sacrifice was accepted; the saint appeared to him in a dream, and promised that Ricardo's posterity should reign in Otranto, until the rightful owner should be grown too large to inhabit the castle, and as long as issue-male from Ricardo's loins should remain to enjoy it. Alas! alas! nor male nor female, except myself, remains of all his wretched race! I have done—the woes of these three days speak the rest. How this young man can be Alfonso's heir, I know not—yet I do not doubt it. His are these dominions. I resign them—yet I knew not Alfonso had an heir—I question not the will of Heaven. Poverty and prayer must fill up the woeful space, until Manfred shall be summoned to Ricardo."

"What remains is my part to declare," said Jerome. "When Alfonso set sail for the Holy Land, he was driven by a storm to the coast of Sicily. The other vessel, which bore Ricardo and his train, as your *lordship* must have heard, was separated from him."

"It is most true," said Manfred; "and the title you give me is more than an outcast can claim—well! be it so—proceed."

Jerome blushed, and continued.

"For three months Lord Alfonso was wind-bound in Sicily. There he became enamored of a fair virgin, named Victoria. He was too pious to tempt her to forbidden pleasures. They were married. Yet deeming this amour incongruous with the holy vow of arms by which he was bound, he determined to conceal their nuptials, until his return from the crusade, when he purposed to seek and acknowledge her for his lawful wife. He left her pregnant. During his absence she was delivered of a daughter; but scarce had she felt a mother's pangs, ere she heard the fatal rumor of her lord's death, and the succession of Ricardo. What could a friendless, helpless woman do? would her testimony avail? Yet, my lord, I have an authentic writing——"

"It needs not," said Manfred. "The horrors of these days, the vision we have but now seen, all corroborate thy evidence beyond a thousand parchments. Matilda's death and my expulsion——"

"Be composed, my lord," said Hippolita; "this holy man did not mean to recall your griefs."

Jerome proceeded.

"I shall not dwell on what is needless. The daughter of which Victoria was delivered was, at her maturity, bestowed in marriage on me. Victoria died; and the secret remained locked in my breast. Theodore's narrative has told the rest."

The friar ceased. The disconsolate company retired to the remaining part of the castle. In the morning, Manfred signed his abdication of the principality, with the approbation of

Hippolita, and each took on them the habit of religion in the neighboring convents. Frederic offered his daughter to the new prince, which Hippolita's tenderness for Isabella concurred to promote. But Theodore's grief was too fresh to admit the thought of another love; and it was not until after frequent discourses with Isabella of his dear Matilda, that he was persuaded he could know no happiness, but in the society of one with whom he could forever indulge the melancholy that had taken possession of his soul.

The Old English Baron

A GOTHIC STORY

by
CLARA REEVE

CLARA REEVE (1729–1807)

This is the third edition of Clara Reeve's *The Old English Baron* (1780), which was originally published in 1777 as *The Champion of Virtue, a Gothic Tale,* and then again in 1778. It was the most popular of her works, which included—beside poetry, fiction, and translation—*The Progress of Romance* (1785), the first complete English book on the history of fiction. Beside going through many editions, including a reprint in the Ballantyne Novels, *The Old English Baron* was translated in 1797 and became the source for several chapbooks.

Her dedication to Samuel Richardson's daughter indicates that Clara Reeve's indebtedness was as much to the sentimental novelists as it was to Walpole's *Castle of Otranto.* While her treatment of the romance between Edmund and Lady Emma is in the best tradition of the romances, her particular obligation to Richardson's *Sir Charles Grandison* (1753-1754) is apparent in the extraordinary goodness of her heroes, whose noble speeches too often resemble the priggish expression of Sir Charles himself. Even the murderer Lovel, in his better moments, speaks with this solemnly noble pomposity.

Her restrained use of the Gothic is not surprising. Miss Reeve, daughter of an Ipswich parson, was a conservative woman who was 48 years old when her novel was first published, and she was not likely to indulge in nonsense. She looked upon her work as serious instruction. Wrapped in her historical comment is a condemnation of the manners of her own times. Her servants show the proper respect for their betters; her tone implies a longing for chivalry and nobility long dead. Moreover, her epigrammatic moral and religious statements, like her clear-cut distinctions between good and evil, were deliberately didactic. This concern for instruction partly accounts for the tempered use of mysterious occurrences, and the explanations of all except those attributable to Divine Will.

Perhaps the most interesting feature of *The Old English Baron,* however, is the early discovery of Edmund's true circumstances. In most Gothic novels the revelation comes with the climax and is the instrument for achieving suspense. Apparently Miss Reeve's didactic purpose led her to the long legalistic denouement that extends for half the novel.

PREFACE

As this story is of a species which, tho' not new, is out of the common track, it has been thought necessary to point out some circumstances to the reader, which will elucidate the design, and, it is hoped, will induce him to form a favorable, as well as a right judgment of the work before him.

This story is the literary offspring of the *Castle of Otranto,* written upon the same plan, with a design to unite the most attractive and interesting circumstances of the ancient romance and modern novel, at the same time it assumes a character and manner of its own that differs from both; it is distinguished by the appellation of a Gothic story, being a picture of Gothic times and manners. Fictitious stories have been the delight of all times and all countries, by oral tradition in barbarous, by writing in more civilized ones; and although some persons of wit and learning have condemned them indiscriminately, I would venture to affirm, that even those who so much affect to despise them under one form, will receive and embrace them under another.

Thus, for instance, a man shall admire and almost adore the epic poems of the ancients, and yet despise and execrate the ancient romances, which are only epics in prose.

History represents human nature as it is in real life;—alas, too often a melancholy retrospect! Romance displays only the amiable side of the picture; it shows the pleasing features, and throws a veil over the blemishes. Mankind are naturally pleased with what gratifies their vanity; and vanity, like other passions of the human heart, may be rendered subservient to good and useful purposes.

I confess that it may be abused, and become an instrument to corrupt the manners and morals of mankind; so may poetry, so may plays, so may every kind of composition; but that will prove nothing more than the old saying lately revived by the philosophers the most in fashion, "that every earthly thing has two handles."

The business of romance is, first, to excite the attention; and, secondly, to direct it to some useful, or at least innocent, end. Happy the writer who attains both these points—like Richardson!—and not unfortunate, or undeserving praise, he who gains only the latter, and furnishes an entertainment for the reader!

Having, in some degree, opened my design, I beg leave to conduct my reader back again, till he comes within view of the *Castle of Otranto*, a work which, as already has been observed, is an attempt to unite the various merits and graces of the ancient romance and modern novel. To attain this end, there is required a sufficient degree of the marvelous to excite the attention; enough of the manners of real life to give an air of probability to the work; and enough of the pathetic to engage the heart in its behalf.

The book we have mentioned is excellent in the two last points, but has a redundancy in the first; the opening excites the attention very strongly; the conduct of the story is artful and judicious; the characters are admirably drawn and supported; the diction polished and elegant; yet, with all these brilliant advantages, it palls upon the mind (though it does not upon the ear); and the reason is obvious, the machinery is so violent that it destroys the effect it is intended to excite. Had the story been kept within the utmost *verge* of probability, the effect had been preserved, without losing the least circumstance that excites or detains the attention.

For instance, we can conceive, and allow for, the appearance of a ghost; we can even dispense with an enchanted sword and helmet; but then they must keep within certain limits of credibility. A sword so large as to require a hundred men to lift it; a helmet that by its own weight forces a passage through a courtyard into an arched vault, big enough for a man to go through; a picture that walks out of its frame; a skeleton ghost in a hermit's cowl—when your expectation is wound up to the highest pitch, these circumstances take it down with a witness, destroy the work of imagination, and, instead of attention, excite laughter. I was both surprised and vexed to find the enchantment dissolved, which I wished might continue to the end of the book; and several of its readers have confessed the same disappointment to me. The beauties are so numerous that we cannot bear the defects, but want it to be perfect in all respects.

In the course of my observations upon this singular book, it seemed to me that it was possible to compose a work upon the same plan, wherein these defects might be avoided; and the *keeping*, as in *painting*, might be preserved.

But then I began to fear it might happen to me as to certain translators, and imitators of Shakespeare; the unities may be preserved, while the spirit is evaporated. However, I ventured to attempt it; I read the beginning to a circle of friends of approved judgment, and by their approbation was encouraged to proceed and to finish it.

By the advice of the same friends I printed the first edition in the country, where it circulated chiefly, very few copies being sent to London; and being thus encouraged, I have determined to offer a second edition to that public which has so often rewarded the efforts of those who have endeavored to contribute to its entertainment.

The work has lately undergone a revision and correction, the former edition being very incorrect; and by the earnest felicitation of several friends, for whose judgment I have the greatest deference, I have consented to a change of the title from the *Champion of Virtue* to the *Old English Baron,* as that character is thought to be the principal one in the story.

I have also been prevailed upon, though with extreme reluctance, to suffer my name to appear in the title page; and I do now, with the utmost respect and diffidence, submit the whole to the candor of the public.

IN the minority of Henry the Sixth, King of England,[1] when the renowned John Duke of Bedford was Regent of France, and Humphrey the good Duke of Gloucester was Protector of England, a worthy knight, called Sir Philip Harclay, returned from his travels to England, his native country. He had served under the glorious King Henry the Fifth with distinguished valor, had acquired an honorable fame, and was no less esteemed for Christian virtues than for deeds of chivalry. After the death of his prince, he entered into the service of the Greek emperor, and distinguished his courage against the encroachments of the Saracens.[2] In a battle there, he took prisoner a certain gentleman, by name M. Zadisky, of Greek extraction, but brought up by a Saracen officer. This man he converted to the Christian faith, after which he bound him to himself by the ties of friendship and gratitude, and he resolved to continue with his benefactor. After thirty years travel and warlike service, he determined to return to his

[1] Henry the Sixth (1421-1471) became king in 1422 when less than one year old. His minority ended in 1437. John, Duke of Bedford and Humphrey, Duke of Gloucester were brothers. Humphrey served as Protector until 1429.
[2] Commonly used to designate Moslems, then more specifically Turks.

native land, and to spend the remainder of his life in peace; and, by devoting himself to works of piety and charity, prepare for a better state hereafter.

This noble knight had, in his early youth, contracted a strict friendship with the only son of the Lord Lovel, a gentleman of eminent virtues and accomplishments. During Sir Philip's residence in foreign countries, he had frequently written to his friend, and had for a time received answers; the last informed him of the death of old Lord Lovel and the marriage of the young one; but from that time he had heard no more from him. Sir Philip imputed it not to neglect or forgetfulness, but to the difficulties of intercourse, common at that time to all travelers and adventurers. When he was returning home, he resolved, after looking into his family affairs, to visit the castle of Lovel and inquire into the situation of his friend. He landed in Kent, attended by his Greek friend and two faithful servants, one of whom was maimed by the wounds he had received in the defense of his master.

Sir Philip went to his family seat in Yorkshire; he found his mother and sister were dead, and his estates sequestered in the hands of commissioners appointed by the Protector. He was obliged to prove the reality of his claim and the identity of his person (by the testimony of some of the old servants of his family), after which everything was restored to him. He took possession of his own house, established his household, settled the old servants in their former stations, and placed those he brought home in the upper offices of his family.

He then left his friend to superintend his domestic affairs; and, attended by only one of his old servants, he set out for the castle of Lovel, in the West of England. They traveled by easy journeys; but, toward the evening of the second day, the servant was so ill and fatigued he could go no further; he stopped at an inn where he grew worse every hour, and the next day expired. Sir Philip was under great concern for the loss of his servant, and some for himself, being alone in a strange place; however, he took courage, ordered his servant's funeral, attended it himself, and, having shed a tear of humanity over his grave, proceeded alone on his journey.

As he drew near the estate of his friend, he began to inquire of every one he met whether the Lord Lovel resided at the seat of his ancestors. He was answered by one, he did not know;—by another, he could not tell;—by a third, that he never heard of such a person. Sir Philip thought it strange that a man of Lord Lovel's consequence should be unknown in his own neighborhood and where his ancestors had usually resided. He ruminated on the uncertainty of human happiness: "This world," said he, "has nothing for a wise man to depend upon. I have lost all my relations and most of my friends, and am even uncertain whether any are remaining. I will, however, be thankful for the blessings that are spared to me; and I will endeavor to replace those that I have lost. If my friend lives, he shall share my fortune with me; his children shall have the reversion of it; and I will share his comforts in return. But perhaps my friend may have met with troubles that have made him disgusted with the world. Perhaps he has buried his amiable wife or his promising children; and, tired of public life, he is retired into a monastery. At least, I will know what all this silence means."

When he came within a mile of the castle of Lovel, he stopped at a cottage and asked for a draft of water. A peasant, master of the house, brought it, and asked if his honor would alight and take a moment's refreshment. Sir Philip accepted his offer, being resolved to make further inquiry before he approached the castle. He asked the same questions of him, that he had before of others.

"Which Lord Lovel," said the man, "does your honor inquire after?"

"The man whom I knew was called Arthur," said Sir Philip.

"Ay," said the peasant, "he was the only surviving son of Richard Lord Lovel, as I think?"

"Very true, friend, he was so."

"Alas, sir," said the man, "he is dead! He survived his father but a short time."

"Dead! say you? How long since?"

"About fifteen years, to the best of my remembrance."

Sir Philip sighed deeply. "Alas," said he, "what do we, by living long, but survive all our friends! But pray tell me how he died?"

"I will, sir, to the best of my knowledge. An't please your honor, I heard say that he attended the King when he went against the Welsh rebels,[3] and he left his lady big with child; and so there was a battle fought, and the King got the better of the rebels. There came first a report that none of the

---

[3] The Welsh rebellion (1413-1417) was led by Sir John Oldcastle, English leader of the Lollards, a religious sect dedicated to the church reforms of John Wycliffe.

officers were killed; but a few days after there came a messenger with an account very different, that several were wounded, and that the Lord Lovel was slain; which sad news overset us all with sorrow, for he was a noble gentleman, a bountiful master, and the delight of all the neighborhood."

"He was indeed," said Sir Philip, "all that is amiable and good; he was my dear and noble friend, and I am inconsolable for his loss. But the unfortunate lady, what became of her?"

"Why, a'nt please your honor, they said she died of grief for the loss of her husband; but her death was kept private for a time, and we did not know it for certain till some weeks afterward."

"The will of Heaven be obeyed!" said Sir Philip; "but who succeeded to the title and estate?"

"The next heir," said the peasant, "a kinsman of the deceased, Sir Walter Lovel by name."

"I have seen him," said Sir Philip, "formerly. But where was he when these events happened?"

"At the Castle of Lovel, sir; he came there on a visit to the lady and waited there to receive my lord at his return from Wales. When the news of his death arrived, Sir Walter did everything in his power to comfort her, and some said he was to marry her; but she refused to be comforted, and took it so to heart that she died."

"And does the present Lord Lovel reside at the castle?"

"No, sir."

"Who then?"

"The Lord Baron Fitz-Owen."

"And how came Sir Walter to leave the seat of his ancestors?"

"Why, sir, he married his sister to this said lord; and so he sold the castle to him, and went away, and built himself a house in the North country, as far as Northumberland, I think they call it."

"That is very strange!" said Sir Philip.

"So it is, please your honor; but this is all I know about it."

"I thank you, friend, for your intelligence; I have taken a long journey to no purpose, and have met with nothing but cross accidents. This life is, indeed, a pilgrimage! Pray direct me the nearest way to the next monastery."

"Noble sir," said the peasant, "it is full five miles off, the night is coming on, and the ways are bad; I am but a poor man and cannot entertain your honor as you are used to; but if you will enter my poor cottage, that, and everything in it, are at your service."

"My honest friend, I thank you heartily," said Sir Philip; "your kindness and hospitality might shame many of higher birth and breeding; I will accept your kind offer. But pray let me know the name of my host?"

"John Wyatt, sir; an honest man though a poor one, and a Christian man, though a sinful one."

"Whose cottage is this?"

"It belongs to the Lord Fitz-Owen."

"What family have you?"

"A wife, two sons and a daughter, who will all be proud to wait upon your honor; let me hold your honor's stirrup while you alight."

He seconded these words by the proper action, and having assisted his guest to dismount, he conducted him into his house, called his wife to attend him, and then led his horse under a poor shed that served him as a stable. Sir Philip was fatigued in body and mind, and was glad to repose himself any where. The courtesy of his host engaged his attention and satisfied his wishes. He soon after returned, followed by a youth of about eighteen years. "Make haste, John," said the father, "and be sure you say neither more nor less than what I have told you."

"I will, father," said the lad; and immediately set off, ran like a buck across the fields, and was out of sight in an instant.

"I hope, friend," said Sir Philip, "you have not sent your son to provide for my entertainment; I am a soldier, used to lodge and fare hard; and, if it were otherwise, your courtesy and kindness would give a relish to the most ordinary food."

"I wish heartily," said Wyatt, "it was in my power to entertain your honor as you ought to be; but, as I cannot do so, I will, when my son returns, acquaint you with the errand I sent him on."

After this they conversed together on common subjects, like fellow-creatures of the same natural form and endowments, though different kinds of education had given a conscious superiority to the one, a conscious inferiority to the other; and the due respect was paid by the latter, without being exacted by the former.

In about half an hour young John returned. "Thou hast made haste," said the father.

"Not more than good speed," quoth the son.

"Tell us, then, how you speed?"

"Shall I tell all that passed?" said John.

"All," said the father; "I don't want to hide anything."

John stood with his cap in his hand, and thus told his tale. "I went straight to the castle as fast as I could run. It was my hap to light on young Master Edmund first, so I told him just as you bade me, that a noble gentleman was come a long journey from foreign parts to see the Lord Lovel, his friend; and having lived abroad many years, he did not know that he was dead, and that the castle was fallen into other hands; that upon hearing these tidings he was much grieved and disappointed, and wanting a night's lodging, to rest himself before he returned to his own home, he was fain to take up with one at our cottage; that my father thought my lord would be angry with him, if he were not told of the stranger's journey and intentions, especially to let such a man lie at our cottage, where he could neither be lodged nor entertained according to his quality."

Here John stopped, and his father exclaimed—"A good lad! You did your errand very well; and tell us the answer."

John proceeded—"Master Edmund ordered me some beer, and went to acquaint my lord of the message; he stayed a while, and then came back to me. 'John,' said he, 'tell the noble stranger that the Baron Fitz-Owen greets him well, and desires him to rest assured that, though Lord Lovel is dead and the castle fallen into other hands, his friends will always find a welcome there; and my lord desires that he will accept a lodging there, while he remains in this country'—so I came away directly, and made haste to deliver my errand."

Sir Philip expressed some dissatisfaction at this mark of old Wyatt's respect. "I wish," said he, "that you had acquainted me with your intention before you sent to inform the Baron I was here. I choose rather to lodge with you; and I propose to make amends for the trouble I shall give you."

"Pray, sir, don't mention it," said the peasant, "you are as welcome as myself; I hope no offense. The only reason of my sending was because I am both unable and unworthy to entertain your honor."

"I am sorry," said Sir Philip, "you should think me so dainty; I am a Christian soldier; and Him I acknowledge for my Prince and Master, accepted the invitations of the poor and washed the feet of his disciples. Let us say no more on this head. I am resolved to stay this night in your cottage; tomorrow

I will wait on the Baron, and thank him for his hospitable invitation."

"That shall be as your honor pleases, since you will condescend to stay here. John, do you run back and acquaint my lord of it."

"Not so," said Sir Philip, "it is now almost dark."

" 'Tis no matter," said John, "I can go it blindfolded." Sir Philip then gave him a message to the Baron in his own name, acquainting him that he would pay his respects to him in the morning. John flew back the second time, and soon returned with new commendations from the Baron, and that he would expect him on the morrow. Sir Philip gave him an angel of gold,[4] and praised his speed and abilities.

He supped with Wyatt and his family upon new laid eggs and rashers of bacon, with the highest relish. They praised the Creator for his gifts and acknowledged they were unworthy of the least of his blessings. They gave the best of their two lofts up to Sir Philip; the rest of the family slept in the other, the old woman and her daughter in the bed, the father and his two sons upon clean straw. Sir Philip's bed was of a better kind, and yet much inferior to his usual accommodations; nevertheless the good knight slept as well in Wyatt's cottage as he could have done in a palace.

During his sleep, many strange and incoherent dreams arose to his imagination. He thought he received a message from his friend Lord Lovel to come to him at the castle; that he stood at the gate and received him; that he strove to embrace him, but could not; but that he spoke to this effect. "Though I have been dead these fifteen years, I still command here, and none can enter these gates without my permission; know that it is I that invite, and bid you welcome; the hopes of my house rest upon you." Upon this he bid Sir Philip follow him; he led him through many rooms, till at last he sunk down, and Sir Philip thought he still followed him, till he came into a dark and frightful cave, where he disappeared, and in his stead he beheld a complete suit of armor stained with blood, which belonged to his friend, and he thought he heard dismal groans from beneath. Presently after, he thought he was hurried away by an invisible hand, and led into a wild heath, where the people were inclosing the ground and making preparations for two combatants; the trumpet sounded, and a voice called out

[4] Gold coin bearing the device of the archangel Michael and the dragon. Its value ranged from six to ten shillings.

still louder, "Forbear! It is not permitted to be revealed till the time is ripe for the event. Wait with patience on the decrees of Heaven." He was then transformed to his own house, where, going into an unfrequented room, he was again met by his friend, who was living, and in all the bloom of youth, as when he first knew him. He started at the sight, and awoke.

The sun shone upon his curtains, and, perceiving it was day, he sat up, and recollected where he was. The images that impressed his sleeping fancy remained strongly on his mind waking; but his reason strove to disperse them. It was natural that the story he had heard should create these ideas, that they should wait on him in his sleep, and that every dream should bear some relation to his deceased friend. The sun dazzled his eyes, the birds serenaded him and diverted his attention, and a woodbine forced its way through the window and regained his sense of smelling with its fragrance.

He arose, paid his devotions to Heaven, and then carefully descended the narrow stairs, and went out at the door of the cottage. There he saw the industrious wife and daughter of old Wyatt at their morning work, the one milking her cow, the other feeding her poultry. He asked for a draft of milk, which, with a slice of rye bread, served to break his fast. He walked about the fields alone; for old Wyatt and his two sons were gone out to their daily labor. He was soon called back by the good woman, who told him that a servant from the Baron waited to conduct him to the castle. He took leave of Wyatt's wife, telling her he would see her again before he left the country.

The daughter fetched his horse, which he mounted, and set forward with the servant, of whom he asked many questions concerning his master's family. "How long have you lived with the Baron?"

"Ten years."

"Is he a good master."

"Yes, sir, and also a good husband and father."

"What family has he?"

"Three sons and a daughter."

"What age are they?"

"The eldest son is in his seventeenth year, the second in his sixteenth, the others several years younger; but beside these my lord has several young gentlemen brought up with his own sons, two of whom are his nephews. He keeps in his house a learned clerk to teach them languages; and as for all bodily exercises, none come near them; there is a fletcher to teach them the use of the cross bow; a master to teach them to ride; another the use of the sword; another learns them to dance; and then they wrestle and run, and have such activity in all their motions, that it does one good to see them; and my lord thinks nothing too much to bestow on their education."

"Truly," says Sir Philip, "he does the part of a good parent, and I honor him greatly for it; but are the young gentlemen of a promising disposition?"

"Yes indeed, sir," answered the servant. "The young gentlemen, my lord's sons, are hopeful youths; but yet there is one who is thought to exceed them all, though he is the son of a poor laborer."

"And who is he?" said the knight.

"One Edmund Twyford, the son of a cottager in our village; he is to be sure as fine a youth as ever the sun shone upon, and of so sweet a disposition that nobody envies his good fortune."

"What good fortune does he enjoy?"

"Why, sir, about two years ago, my lord, at his sons' request, took him into his own family, and gives him the same education as his own children; the young lords doat upon him, especially Master William, who is about his own age. It is supposed that he will attend the young lords when they go to the wars, which my lord intends they shall bye and bye."

"What you tell me," said Sir Philip, "increases every minute my respect for your lord; he is an excellent father and master, he seeks out merit in obscurity, he distinguishes and rewards it. I honor him with all my heart."

In this manner they conversed together till they came within view of the castle. In a field near the house they saw a company of youths, with cross bows in their hands, shooting at a mark. "There," said the servant, "are our young gentlemen at their exercises." Sir Philip stopped his horse to observe them; he heard two or three of them cry out, "Edmund is the victor! He wins the prize!"

"I must," said Sir Philip, "take a view of this Edmund."

He jumped off his horse, gave the bridle to the servant, and walked into the field. The young gentlemen came up, and paid their respects to him; he apologized for intruding upon their sports, and asked which was the victor, upon which the youth he spoke to beckoned to another, who immediately advanced, and made his obeisance.

As he drew near, Sir Philip fixed his eyes upon him, with so much attention that he seemed not to observe his courtesy and address. At length he recollected himself, and said, "What is your name, young man?"

"Edmund Twyford," replied the youth; "and I have the honor to attend upon the Lord Fitz-Owen's sons."

"Pray, noble sir," said the youth who first addressed Sir Philip, "are not you the stranger who is expected by my father?"

"I am, sir," answered he, "and I go to pay my respects to him."

"Will you excuse our attendance, sir? We have not yet finished our exercises."

"My dear youth," said Sir Philip, "no apology is necessary; but will you favor me with your proper name, that I may know to whose courtesy I am obliged?"

"My name is William Fitz-Owen; that gentleman is my eldest brother, Master Robert; that other my kinsman, Master Richard Wenlock."

"Very well; I thank you, gentle sir; I beg you not to stir another step, your servant holds my horse."

"Farewell, sir," said Master William; "I hope we shall have the pleasure of meeting you at dinner."

The youths returned to their sports, and Sir Philip mounted his horse and proceeded to the castle; he entered it with a deep sigh, and melancholy recollections. The Baron received him with the utmost respect and courtesy. He gave a brief account of the principal events that had happened in the family of Lovel during his absence; he spoke of the late Lord Lovel with respect, of the present with the affection of a brother. Sir Philip, in return, gave a brief recital of his own adventures abroad and of the disagreeable circumstances he had met with since his return home; he pathetically lamented the loss of all his friends, not forgetting that of his faithful servant on the way, saying he could be contented to give up the world, and retire to a religious house, but that he was withheld by the consideration that some who depended entirely upon him would want his presence and assistance; and beside that, he thought he might be of service to many others. The Baron agreed with him in opinion that a man was of much more service to the world who continued in it than one who retired from it and gave his fortune to the Church, whose servants did not always make the best use of it. Sir Philip then turned the conversation, and congratulated the Baron on his hopeful family; he praised their persons and address, and warmly applauded the care he bestowed on their education. The Baron listened with pleasure to the honest approbation of a worthy heart, and enjoyed the true happiness of a parent.

Sir Philip then made further inquiry concerning Edmund, whose appearance had struck him with an impression in his favor. "That boy," said the Baron, "is the son of a cottager in this neighborhood; his uncommon merit and gentleness of manners distinguish him from those of his own class; from his childhood he attracted the notice and affection of all that knew him; he was beloved every where but at his father's house, and there it should seem that his merits were his crimes; for the peasant, his father, hated him, treated him severely, and at length threatened to turn him out of doors. He used to run here and there on errands for my people, and at length they obliged me to take notice of him. My sons earnestly desired I would take him into my family; I did so about two years ago, intending to make him their servant; but his extraordinary genius and disposition have obliged me to look upon him in a superior light; perhaps I may incur the censure of many people by giving him so many advantages and treating him as the companion of my children. His merit must justify or condemn my partiality for him; however, I trust that I have secured to my children a faithful servant of the upper kind and a useful friend to my family."

Sir Philip warmly applauded his generous host, and wished to be a sharer in his bounty to that fine youth, whose appearance indicated all the qualities that had endeared him to his companions.

At the hour of dinner the young men presented themselves before their lord, and his guest. Sir Philip addressed himself to Edmund; he asked him many questions, and received modest and intelligent answers, and he grew every minute more pleased with him. After dinner the youths withdrew with their tutor to pursue their studies. Sir Philip sat, for some time, wrapped up in meditation. After some minutes, the Baron asked him if he might not be favored with the fruits of his contemplations. "You shall, my lord," answered he, "for you have a right to them. I was thinking, that when many blessings

are lost, we should cherish those 'that remain, and even endeavor to replace the others. My lord, I have taken a strong
liking to that youth whom you call Edmund Twyford. I have
neither children nor relations to claim my fortune nor share
my affections; your lordship has many demands upon your
generosity. I can provide for this promising youth without
doing injustice to any one; will you give him to me?"

"He is a fortunate boy," said the Baron, "to gain your
favor so soon."

"My lord," said the knight, "I will confess to you, that the
first thing that touched my heart in his favor is a strong
resemblance he bears to a certain dear friend I once had,
and his manner resembles him as much as his person; his
qualities deserve that he should be placed in a higher rank.
I will adopt him for my son and introduce him into the world
as my relation, if you will resign him to me. What say you?"

"Sir," said the Baron, "you have made a noble offer, and
I am too much the young man's friend to be a hindrance to
his preferment. It is true that I intended to provide for him
in my own family; but I cannot do it so effectually as by giving
him to you, whose generous affection being unlimited by other
ties, may in time prefer him to a higher station as he shall
deserve it. I have only one condition to make; that the lad
shall have his option; for I would not oblige him to leave my
service against his inclination."

"You say well," replied Sir Philip, "nor would I take him
upon other terms."

"Agreed then," said the Baron, "let us send for Edmund
hither."

A servant was sent to fetch him; he came immediately,
and his lord thus spoke to him. "Edmund, you owe eternal
obligations to this gentleman, who, perceiving in you a certain
resemblance to a friend of his, and liking your behavior, has
taken a great affection for you, insomuch that he desires to
receive you into his family. I cannot better provide for you
than by disposing of you to him; and, if you have no objection, you shall return home with him when he goes from
hence."

The countenance of Edmund underwent many alterations
during this proposal of his lord; it expressed tenderness, gratitude, and sorrow, but the last was predominant; he bowed
respectfully to the Baron and Sir Philip, and, after some hesitation, spoke as follows: "I feel very strongly the obligations

I owe to this gentleman, for his noble and generous offer; I cannot express the sense I have of his goodness to me, a peasant boy, only known to him by my lord's kind and partial mention; this uncommon bounty claims my eternal gratitude. To you, my honored lord, I owe everything, even this gentleman's good opinion—you distinguished me when nobody else did; and, next to you, your sons are my best and dearest benefactors; they introduced me to your notice. My heart is unalterably attached to this house and family, and my utmost ambition is to spend my life in your service. But if you have perceived any great and grievous faults in me that make you wish to put me out of your family, and if you have recommended me to this gentleman in order to be rid of me, in that case I will submit to your pleasure, as I would if you should sentence me to death."

During this speech the tears made themselves channels down Edmund's cheeks; and his two noble auditors, catching the tender infection, wiped their eyes at the conclusion. "My dear child," said the Baron, "you overcome me by your tenderness and gratitude! I know of no faults you have committed that I should wish to be rid of you. I thought to do you the best service by promoting you to that of Sir Philip Harclay, who is both able and willing to provide for you; but if you prefer my service to his, I will not part with you."

Upon this Edmund kneeled to the Baron; he embraced his knees. "My dear lord! I am, and will be your servant, in preference to any man living; I only ask your permission to live and die in your service."

"You see, Sir Philip," said the Baron, "how this boy engages the heart; how can I part with him?"

"I cannot ask you any more," answered Sir Philip, "I see it is impossible; but I esteem you both still higher than ever; the youth for his gratitude, and your lordship for your noble mind and true generosity; blessings attend you both!"

"Oh, sir," said Edmund, pressing the hand of Sir Philip, "do not think me ungrateful to you, I will ever remember your goodness, and pray to Heaven to reward it; the name of Sir Philip Harclay shall be engraven upon my heart, next to my lord and his family, for ever."

Sir Philip raised the youth and embraced him, saying, "If ever you want a friend, remember me; and depend upon my protection, so long as you continue to deserve it." Edmund bowed low, and withdrew, with his eyes full of tears of sensibility and gratitude.

When he was gone, Sir Philip said, "I am thinking, that though young Edmund wants not my assistance at present, he may hereafter stand in need of my friendship. I should not wonder if such rare qualities as he possesses should one day create envy and raise him enemies, in which case he might come to lose your favor, without any fault of yours or his own."

"I am obliged to you for the warning," said the Baron, "I hope it will be unnecessary; but if ever I part with Edmund, you shall have the refusal of him."

"I thank your lordship for all your civilities to me," said the knight; "I leave my best wishes with you and your hopeful family, and I humbly take my leave."

"Will you not stay one night in the castle?" returned my lord; "you shall be as welcome a guest as ever."

"I acknowledge your goodness and hospitality, but this house fills me with melancholy recollections; I came hither with a heavy heart, and it will not be lighter while I remain here. I shall always remember your lordship with the highest respect and esteem; and I pray God to preserve you and increase your blessings!"

After some further ceremonies, Sir Philip departed, and returned to old Wyatt's, ruminating on the vicissitude of human affairs and thinking on the changes he had seen.

At his return to Wyatt's cottage, he found the family assembled together. He told them he would take another night's lodging there, which they heard with great pleasure; for he had familiarized himself to them in the last evening's conversation insomuch that they began to enjoy his company. He told Wyatt of the misfortune he had sustained by losing his servant on the way, and wished he could get one to attend him home in his place. Young John looked earnestly at his father, who returned a look of approbation. "I perceive one in this company," said he, "that would be proud to serve your honor; but I fear he is not brought up well enough."

John colored with impatience, he could not forbear speaking. "Sir, I can answer for an honest heart, a willing mind, and a light pair of heels; and though I am somewhat awkward, I shall be proud to learn to please my noble master, if he will but try me."

"You say well," said Sir Philip, "I have observed your qualifications, and if you are desirous to serve me, I am equally pleased with you; if your father has no objection I will take you."

"Objection, sir!" said the old man; "it will be my pride to prefer him to such a noble gentleman; I will make no terms for him, but leave it to your honor to do for him as he shall deserve."

"Very well," said Sir Philip, "you shall be no loser by that; I will charge myself with the care of the young man." The bargain was struck, and Sir Philip purchased a horse for John from the old man.

The next morning they set out; the knight left marks of his bounty with the good couple, and departed, laden with their blessing and prayers. He stopped at the place where his faithful servant was buried, and caused masses to be said for the repose of his soul; then, pursuing his way by easy journeys, arrived in safety at home. His family rejoiced at his return; he settled his new servant in attendance upon his person; he then looked round his neighborhood for objects of his charity; when he saw merit in distress, it was his delight to raise and support it. He spent his time in the service of his Creator and glorified Him in doing good to His creatures. He reflected frequently upon everything that had befallen him in his late journey to the West; and, at his leisure, took down all the particulars in writing.

Here follows an interval of four years, as by the manuscript; and this omission seems intended by the writer. What follows is in a different hand, and the character is more modern.

ABOUT this time the prognostics of Sir Philip Harclay began to be verified, that Edmund's good qualities might one day excite envy and create him enemies. The sons and kinsmen of his patron began to seek occasion to find fault with him and to depreciate him with others. The Baron's eldest son and heir, Master Robert, had several contests with Master William, the second son, upon his account. This youth had a warm affection for Edmund, and whenever his brother and kinsmen treated him slightly, he supported him against their malicious insinuations. Mr. Richard Wenlock and Mr. John Markham were the sisters' sons of the Lord Fitz-Owen; and there were several other more distant relations, who, with them, secretly envied Edmund's fine qualities, and strove to lessen him in the esteem of the Baron and his family. By degrees they excited a dislike in Master Robert, that in time was fixed into habit and fell little short of aversion.

Young Wenlock's hatred was confirmed by an additional circumstance: he had a growing passion for the Lady Emma, the Baron's only daughter; and, as love is eagle-eyed, he saw, or fancied he saw, her cast an eye of preference on Edmund. An accidental service that she received from him had excited her grateful regards and attentions toward him. The incessant view of his fine person and qualities had perhaps improved her esteem into a still softer sensation, though she was yet ignorant of it and thought it only the tribute due to gratitude and friendship.

One Christmas time, the Baron and all his family went to visit a family in Wales; crossing a ford, the horse that carried the Lady Emma, who rode behind her cousin Wenlock, stumbled and fell down, and threw her off into the water. Edmund dismounted in a moment and flew to her assistance; he took her out so quick that the accident was not known to some part of the company. From this time Wenlock strove to undermine Edmund in her esteem, and she conceived herself obliged in justice and gratitude to defend him against the malicious insinuations of his enemies. She one day asked Wenlock why he in particular should endeavor to recommend himself to her favor by speaking against Edmund, to whom she was under great obligations. He made but little reply; but the impression sunk deep into his rancorous heart; every word in Edmund's behalf was like a poisoned arrow that rankled in the wound and grew every day more inflamed. Sometimes he would pretend to extenuate Edmund's supposed faults in order to load him with the sin of ingratitude upon other occasions. Rancor works deepest in the heart that strives to conceal it; and, when covered by art, frequently puts on the appearance of candor. By these means did Wenlock and Markham impose upon the credulity of Master Robert and their other relations. Master William only stood proof against all their insinuations.

The same autumn that Edmund completed his eighteenth year, the Baron declared his intention of sending the young men of his house to France the following spring, to learn the art of war and signalize their courage and abilities.

Their ill-will toward Edmund was so well concealed that his patron had not discovered it; but it was whispered among the servants, who are generally close observers of the manners of their principals. Edmund was a favorite with them all, which was a strong presumption that he deserved to be so, for they seldom show much regard to dependents or to superior domestics, who are generally objects of envy and dislike. Edmund was courteous, but not familiar with them; and, by this means, gained their affections without soliciting them. Among them was an old serving man, called Joseph Howell; this man had formerly served the old Lord Lovel and his son; and when the young lord died, and Sir Walter sold the castle to his brother-in-law, the Lord Fitz-Owen, he only of all the old servants was left in the house, to take care of it and to deliver it into the possession of the new proprietor, who retained him in his service. He was a man of few words, but much reflection; and, without troubling himself about other people's affairs, went silently and properly about his own business; more solicitous to discharge his duty, than to recommend himself to notice, and not seeming to aspire to any higher office than that of a serving man. This old man would fix his eyes upon Edmund, whenever he could do it without observation; sometimes he would sigh deeply, and a tear would start from his eye, which he strove to conceal from observation.

One day Edmund surprised him in this tender emotion as he was wiping his eyes with the back of his hand. "Why," said he, "my good friend, do you look at me so earnestly and affectionately?"

"Because I love you, Master Edmund," said he, "because I wish you well."

"I thank you kindly," answered Edmund; "I am unable to repay your love otherwise than by returning it, which I do sincerely."

"I thank you, sir," said the old man; "that is all I desire, and more than I deserve."

"Do not say so," said Edmund; "if I had any better way to thank you, I would not say so much about it; but words are all my inheritance."

Upon this he shook hands with Joseph, who withdrew hastily to conceal his emotion, saying, "God bless you, master, and make your fortune equal to your deserts! I cannot help thinking you were born to a higher station than what you now hold."

"You know to the contrary," said Edmund; but Joseph was gone out of sight and hearing.

The notice and observation of strangers, and the affection of individuals, together with that inward consciousness that always attends superior qualities, would sometimes kindle the flames of ambition in Edmund's heart; but he checked them presently by reflecting upon his low birth and dependent station. He was modest, yet intrepid; gentle and courteous to all; frank and unreserved to those that loved him, discreet and complaisant to those who hated him; generous and compassionate to the distresses of his fellow-creatures in general; humble, but not servile, to his patron and superiors. Once, when he with a manly spirit justified himself against a malicious imputation, his young lord, Robert, taxed him with pride and arrogance to his kinsmen. Edmund denied the charge against him with equal spirit and modesty. Master Robert answered him sharply. "How dare you contradict my cousins? Do you mean to give them the lie?"

"Not in words, sir," said Edmund, "but I will behave so as that you shall not believe them." Master Robert haughtily bade him be silent and know himself and not presume to contend with men so much his superiors in every respect.

These heart-burnings in some degree subsided by their preparations for going to France. Master Robert was to be presented at court before his departure, and it was expected that he should be knighted. The Baron designed Edmund to be his esquire; but this was frustrated by his old enemies, who persuaded Robert to make choice of one of his own domestics, called Thomas Hewson; him did they set up as a rival to Edmund, and he took every occasion to affront him. All that Master Robert gained by this step was the contempt of those who saw Edmund's merit, and thought it want of discernment in him not to distinguish and reward it. Edmund requested to his lord that he might be Master William's attendant; "and when," said he, "my patron shall be knighted, as I have no doubt he will one day be, he has promised that I shall be his esquire." The Baron granted Edmund's request; and, being freed from servitude to the rest, he was devoted to that of his beloved Master William, who treated him in public as his principal domestic, but in private as his chosen friend and brother.

The whole cabal of his enemies consulted together in what manner they should vent their resentment against him; and it was agreed that they should treat him with indifference and neglect till they should arrive in France; and when there, they should contrive to render his courage suspected, and by putting him upon some desperate enterprise, rid themselves of him for ever. About this time died the great Duke of Bedford, to the irreparable loss of the English nation.[5] He was succeeded by Richard Plantagenet, Duke of York, as Regent of France, of which great part had revolted to Charles the Dauphin. Frequent actions ensued. Cities were lost and won; and continual occasions offered to exercise the courage and abilities of the youth of both nations.

The young men of Baron Fitz-Owen's house were recommended particularly to the Regent's notice. Master Robert was knighted with several other young men of family who distinguished themselves by their spirit and activity upon every occasion. The youth were daily employed in warlike exercises and frequent actions and made their first essay in arms in such a manner as to bring into notice all that deserved it.

Various arts were used by Edmund's enemies to expose him to danger; but all their contrivances recoiled upon themselves and brought increase of honor upon Edmund's head. He distinguished himself upon so many occasions that Sir Robert himself began to pay him more than ordinary regard, to the infinite mortification of his kinsmen and relations. They laid many schemes against him, but none took effect.

From this place the characters in the manuscript are effaced by time and damp. Here and there some sentences are legible, but not sufficient to pursue the thread of the story. Mention is made of several actions in which the young men were engaged—that Edmund distinguished himself by intrepidity in action; by gentleness, humanity, and modesty in the cessations —that he attracted the notice of every person of observation, and also that he received personal commendation from the Regent.

The following incidents are clear enough to be transcribed; but the beginning of the next succeeding pages is obliterated. However, we may guess at the beginning by what remains.

* * *

As soon as the cabal met in Sir Robert's tent, Mr. Wenlock thus began. "You see, my friends, that every attempt we make to humble this upstart turns into applause and serves only to

[5] John, Duke of Bedford died in 1435. Joan of Arc participated in the ensuing battles.

raise his pride still higher. Something must be done, or his praise will go home before us at our own expense; and we shall seem only foils to set off his glories. Any thing would I give to the man who should execute our vengeance upon him."

"Stop there, cousin Wenlock," said Sir Robert; "though I think Edmund proud and vain-glorious, and would join in any scheme to humble him, and make him know himself, I will not suffer any man to use such base methods to effect it. Edmund is brave; and it is beneath an Englishman to revenge himself by unworthy means; if any such are used, I will be the first man to bring the guilty to justice; and if I hear another word to this purpose, I will inform my brother William, who will acquaint Edmund with your mean intentions." Upon this the cabal drew back, and Mr. Wenlock protested that he meant no more than to mortify his pride, and make him know his proper station. Soon after Sir Robert withdrew, and they resumed their deliberations.

Then spoke Thomas Hewson. "There is a party to be sent out to-morrow night to intercept a convoy of provisions for the relief of Rouen; I will provoke Mr. Edmund to make one of this party, and when he is engaged in the action, I and my companions will draw off, and leave him to the enemy, who I trust will so handle him that you shall no more be troubled with him."

"This will do," said Mr. Wenlock; "but let it be kept from my two cousins, and only known to ourselves; if they offer to be of the party, I will persuade them off it. And you, Thomas, if you bring this scheme to a conclusion, may depend upon my eternal gratitude." "And mine," said Markham; and so said all.

The next day the affair was publicly mentioned; and Hewson, as he promised, provoked Edmund to the trial. Several young men of family offered themselves, among the rest, Sir Robert and his brother William. Mr. Wenlock persuaded them not to go and set the danger of the enterprise in the strongest colors. At last Sir Robert complained of the toothache, and was confined to his tent; Edmund waited on him; and judging by the ardor of his own courage of that of his patron, thus bespoke him. "I am greatly concerned, dear sir, that we cannot have your company at night; but as I know what you will suffer in being absent, I would beg the favor of you to let me use your arms and device, and I will promise not to disgrace them."

"No, Edmund, I cannot consent to that. I thank you for your noble offer, and will remember it to your advantage; but I cannot wear honors of another man's getting. You have awakened me to a sense of my duty. I will go with you and contend with you for glory; and William shall do the same."

In a few hours they were ready to set out. Wenlock and Markham, and their dependents, found themselves engaged in honor to go upon an enterprise they never intended, and set out, with heavy hearts, to join the party. They marched in silence in the horrors of a dark night and wet roads; they met the convoy where they expected, and a sharp engagement ensued. The victory was some time doubtful; but the moon rising on the backs of the English gave them the advantage. They saw the disposition of their enemies and availed themselves of it. Edmund advanced the foremost of the party; he drew out the leader on the French side; he slew him. Mr. William pressed forward to assist his friend; Sir Robert, to defend his brother; Wenlock and Markham, from shame to stay behind.

Thomas Hewson and his associates drew back on their side; the French perceived it and pursued the advantage. Edmund pushed them in front; the young nobles all followed him; they broke through the detachment and stopped the wagons. The officer who commanded the party encouraged them to go on; the defeat was soon complete, and the provisions carried in triumph to the English camp.

Edmund was presented to the Regent as the man to whom the victory was chiefly owing. Not a tongue presumed to move itself against him; even malice and envy were silenced.

"Approach, young man," said the Regent, "that I may confer upon you the honor of knighthood, which you have well deserved."

Mr. Wenlock could no longer forbear speaking: "Knighthood," said he, "is an order belonging to gentlemen; it cannot be conferred on a peasant."

"What say you, sir!" returned the Regent; "is this youth a peasant?"

"He is," said Wenlock; "let him deny it if he can."

Edmund, with a modest bow, replied, "It is true indeed I am a peasant, and this honor is too great for me: I have only done my duty."

The Duke of York, whose pride of birth equaled that of any man living or dead, sheathed his sword immediately.

"Though," said he, "I cannot reward you as I intended, I will take care that you shall have a large share in the spoils of this night; and, I declare publicly, that you stand first in the list of gallant men in this engagement."

Thomas Hewson and his associates made a poor figure in their return; they were publicly reproved for their backwardness. Hewson was wounded in body and more in mind for the bad success of his ill-laid design. He could not hold up his head before Edmund, who, unconscious of their malice, administered every kind of comfort to them. He spoke in their behalf to the commanding officer, imputing their conduct to unavoidable accidents. He visited them privately; he gave them a part of the spoils allotted to himself; by every act of valor and courtesy he strove to engage those hearts that hated, envied, and maligned him. But where hatred arises from envy of superior qualities, every display of those qualities increases the cause from whence it arises.

Another pause ensues here.

The young nobles and gentlemen who distinguished Edmund were prevented from raising him to preferment by the insinuations of Wenlock and his associates, who never failed to set before them his low descent and his pride and arrogance in presuming to rank with gentlemen.

Here the manuscript is not legible for several pages. There is mention, about this time, of the death of the Lady Fitz-Owen; but not the cause.

Wenlock rejoiced to find that his schemes took effect and that they should be recalled at the approach of winter. The Baron was glad of a pretense to send for them home; for he could no longer endure the absence of his children, after the loss of their mother.

The manuscript is again defaced for many leaves; at length the letters become more legible, and the remainder of it is quite perfect.

FROM the time the young men returned from France, the enemies of Edmund employed their utmost abilities to ruin him in the Baron's opinion and get him dismissed from the family. They insinuated a thousand things against him that happened, as they said, during his residence in France and therefore could not be known to his master; but when the Baron privately inquired of his two elder sons, he found there was no truth in their reports. Sir Robert, though he did not love him, scorned to join in untruths against him. Mr. William spoke of him with the warmth of fraternal affection. The Baron perceived that his kinsmen disliked Edmund; but his own good heart hindered him from seeing the baseness of theirs. It is said that continual dropping will wear away a stone; so did their incessant reports, by insensible degrees, produce a coolness in his patron's behavior toward him. If he behaved with manly spirit, it was misconstrued into pride and arrogance; his generosity was imprudence; his humility was hypocrisy, the better to cover his ambition. Edmund bore patiently all the indignities that were thrown upon him; and, though he felt them severely in his bosom, scorned to justify his conduct at the expense even of his enemies. Perhaps his gentle spirit might at length have sunk under this treatment, but Providence interposed in his behalf, and, by seemingly accidental circumstances, conducted him imperceptibly toward the crisis of his fate.

Father Oswald, who had been preceptor to the young men, had a strong affection for Edmund from a thorough knowledge of his heart; he saw through the mean artifices that were used to undermine him in his patron's favor; he watched their machinations and strove to frustrate their designs.

This good man used frequently to walk out with Edmund; they conversed upon various subjects; and the youth would lament to him the unhappiness of his situation and the peculiar circumstances that attended him. The Father, by his wholesome advice, comforted his drooping heart and confirmed him in his resolution of bearing unavoidable evils with patience and fortitude from the consciousness of his own innocence and the assurance of a future and eternal reward.

One day, as they were walking in a wood near the castle, Edmund asked the Father what meant those preparations for building, the cutting down trees and burning of bricks. "What," said Oswald, "have you not heard that my lord is going to build a new apartment on the West side of the castle? "And why," said Edmund, "should my lord be at that expense when there is one on the East side that is never occupied?"

"That apartment," said the friar, "you must have observed is always shut up."

"I have observed it often," said Edmund; "but I never presumed to ask any questions about it."

"You had then," said Oswald, "less curiosity, and more discretion, than is common at your age."

"You have raised my curiosity," said Edmund; "and, if it be not improper, I beg of you to gratify it."

"We are alone," said Oswald, "and I am so well assured of your prudence that I will explain this mystery in some degree to you.

"You must know, that apartment was occupied by the last Lord Lovel when he was a bachelor. He married in his father's life-time, who gave up his own apartment to him and offered to retire to this himself; but the son would not permit him; he chose to sleep here rather than in any other. He had been married about three months, when his father, the old lord, died of a fever. About twelve months after his marriage, he was called upon to attend the King, Henry the Fourth, on an expedition into Wales, whither he was attended by many of his dependents. He left his lady big with child and full of care and anxiety for his safety and return.

"After the King had chastised the rebels, and obtained the victory, the Lord Lovel was expected home every day; various reports were sent home before him; one messenger brought an account of his health and safety—soon after another came with bad news, that he was slain in battle. His kinsman, Sir Walter Lovel, came here on a visit to comfort the lady; and he waited to receive his kinsman at his return. It was he that brought the news of the sad event of the battle to the Lady Lovel.

"She fainted away at the relation; but, when she revived, exerted the utmost resolution; saying, it was her duty to bear this dreadful stroke with Christian fortitude and patience, especially in regard to the child she went with, the last remains of her beloved husband and the undoubted heir of a noble house. For several days she seemed an example of patience and resignation; but then, all at once, she renounced them and broke out into passionate and frantic exclamations; she said that her dear lord was basely murdered; that his ghost had appeared to her, and revealed his fate. She called upon Heaven and earth to revenge her wrongs, saying, she would never cease complaining to God, and the King, for vengeance and justice.

"Upon this, Sir Walter told the servants that Lady Lovel was distracted from grief for the death of her lord; that his regard for her was as strong as ever; and that, if she recovered, he would himself be her comforter and marry her. In the mean time she was confined in this very apartment, and in less than a month the poor lady died. She lies buried in the family vault in St. Austin's church in the village. Sir Walter took possession of the castle and all the other estates, and assumed the title of Lord Lovel.

"Soon after, it was reported that the castle was haunted and that the ghosts of Lord and Lady Lovel had been seen by several of the servants. Whoever went into this apartment were terrified by uncommon noises and strange appearances; at length this apartment was wholly shut up, and the servants were forbidden to enter it or to talk of any thing relating to it. However, the story did not stop here; it was whispered about that the new Lord Lovel was so disturbed every night that he could not sleep in quiet; and, being at last tired of the place, he sold the castle and estate of his ancestors to his brother-in-law the Lord Fitz-Owen, who now enjoys it, and left this country."

"All this is news to me," said Edmund; "but, Father, tell me what grounds there were for the lady's suspicion that her lord died unfairly."

"Alas!" said Oswald, "that is only known to God. There were strange thoughts in the minds of many at that time; I had mine; but I will not disclose them, not even to you. I will not injure those who may be innocent; and I leave it to Providence, who will doubtless, in its own best time and manner, punish the guilty. But let what I have told you be as if you had never heard it."

"I thank you for these marks of your esteem and confidence," said Edmund; "be assured that I will not abuse them; nor do I desire to pry into secrets not proper to be revealed. I entirely approve your discretion, and acquiesce in your conclusion that Providence will in its own time vindicate its ways to man. If it were not for that trust, my situation would be insupportable. I strive earnestly to deserve the esteem and favor of good men; I endeavor to regulate my conduct so as to avoid giving offense to any man; but I see, with infinite pain, that it is impossible for me to gain these points."

"I see it too, with great concern," said Oswald; "and every thing that I can say and do in your favor is misconstrued; and, by seeking to do you service, I lose my own influence. But I will never give my sanction to acts of injustice, nor join to oppress innocence. My dear child, put your truth in God. He who brought light out of darkness can bring good out of evil."

"I hope and trust so," said Edmund; "but, Father, if my enemies should prevail, if my lord should believe their stories against me, and I should be put out of the house with disgrace, what will become of me? I have nothing but my character to depend upon; if I lose that, I lose every thing; and I see they seek no less than my ruin."

"Trust in my lord's honor and justice," replied Oswald; "he knows your virtue, and he is not ignorant of their ill-will toward you."

"I know my lord's justice too well to doubt it," said Edmund; "but would it not be better to rid him of this trouble and his family of an incumbrance? I would gladly do something for myself, but cannot without my lord's recommendation; and, such is my situation that I fear the asking for a dismission would be accounted base ingratitude. Beside, when I think of leaving this house, my heart saddens at the thought, and tells me I cannot be happy out of it. Yet I think I could return to a peasant's life with cheerfulness rather than live in a palace under disdain and contempt."

"Have patience a little longer, my son," said Oswald; "I will think of some way to serve you and to represent your grievances to my lord without offense to either. Perhaps the causes may be removed. Continue to observe the same irreproachable conduct; and be assured that Heaven will defend your innocence and defeat the unjust designs of your enemies. Let us now return home."

About a week after this conference, Edmund walked out in the fields ruminating on the disagreeable circumstances of his situation. Insensible of the time, he had been out several hours without perceiving how the day wore away, when he heard himself called by name several times; looking backward, he saw his friend Mr. William, and hailed him. He came running toward him; and, leaping over the stile, stood still a while to recover his breath. "What is the matter, sir?" said Edmund; "your looks bespeak some tidings of importance."

With a look of tender concern and affection, the youth

pressed his hand and spoke. "My dear Edmund, you must come home with me directly; your old enemies have united to ruin you with my father; my brother Robert has declared that he thinks there will be no peace in our family till you are dismissed from it, and told my father, he hoped he would not break with his kinsmen rather than give up Edmund."

"But what do they lay to my charge?" said Edmund.

"I cannot rightly understand," answered William, "for they make a great mystery of it; something of great consequence, they say; but they will not tell me what. However, my father has told them that they must bring their accusation before your face, and he will have you answer them publicly. I have been seeking you this hour to inform you of this that you might be prepared to defend yourself against your accusers."

"God reward you, sir," said Edmund, "for all your goodness to me! I see they are determined to ruin me if possible. I shall be compelled to leave the castle; but, whatever becomes of me, be assured you shall have no cause to blush for your kindness and partiality to your Edmund."

"I know it, I am sure of it," said William; "and here I swear to you, as Jonathan did to David, I beseech Heaven to bless me, as my friendship to you shall be steady and inviolable!"

"Only so long as I shall deserve so great a blessing," interrupted Edmund.

"I know your worth and honor," continued William; "and such is my confidence in your merit, that I firmly believe Heaven designs you for something extraordinary; and I expect that some great and unforeseen event will raise you to the rank and station to which you appear to belong. Promise me, therefore, that whatever may be your fate you will preserve the same friendship for me that I bear to you."

Edmund was so much affected that he could not answer but in broken sentences. "Oh my friend, my master! I vow, I promise, my heart promises!" He kneeled down with clasped hands and uplifted eyes. William kneeled by him, and they invoked the Supreme to witness to their friendship, and implored his blessing upon it. They then rose up and embraced each other, while tears of cordial affection bedewed their cheeks.

As soon as they were able to speak, Edmund conjured his friend not to expose himself to the displeasure of his family out of kindness to him. "I submit to the will of Heaven," said he; "I wait with patience its disposal of me; if I leave the castle, I will find means to inform you of my fate and fortunes."

"I hope," said William, "that things may yet be accommodated; but do not take any resolution, let us act as occasions arise."

In this manner these amiable youths conferred, till they arrived at the castle. The Baron was sitting in the great hall, on a high chair with a footstep before, with the state and dignity of a judge; before him stood Father Oswald, as pleading the cause for himself and Edmund. Round the Baron's chair stood his eldest son and his kinsmen with their principal domestics. The old servant, Joseph, at some distance, with his head leaning forward, as listening with the utmost attention to what passed. Mr. William approached the chair. "My lord, I have found Edmund, and brought him to answer for himself."

"You have done well," said the Baron. "Edmund, come hither; you are charged with some indiscretions, for I cannot properly call them crimes. I am resolved to do justice between you and your accusers; I shall therefore hear you as well as them; for no man ought to be condemned unheard."

"My lord," said Edmund, with equal modesty and intrepidity, "I demand my trial; if I shall be found guilty of any crimes against my benefactor, let me be punished with the utmost rigor. But if, as I trust, no such charge can be proved against me, I know your goodness too well to doubt that you will do justice to me, as well as to others; and if it should so happen that by the misrepresentations of my enemies (who have long sought my ruin privately, and now avow it publicly), if by their artifices your lordship should be induced to think me guilty, I would submit to your sentence in silence, and appeal to another tribunal."

"See," said Mr. Wenlock, "the confidence of the fellow! He already supposes that my lord must be in the wrong if he condemns him; and then this meek creature will appeal to another tribunal. To whose will he appeal? I desire he may be made to explain himself."

"That I will immediately," said Edmund, without being compelled; "I only meant to appeal to Heaven that best knows my innocence."

"'Tis true," said the Baron, "and no offense to any one; man can only judge by appearances, but Heaven knows the heart. Let every one of you bear this in mind, that you may not bring a false accusation, nor justify yourselves by concealing the truth. Edmund, I am informed that Oswald and you have made very free with me and my family in some of your conversations; you were heard to censure me for the absurdity of building a new apartment on the West side of the castle, when there was one on the East side uninhabited. Oswald said that apartment was shut up because it was haunted; that some shocking murder had been committed there; adding many particulars concerning Lord Lovel's family, such as he could not know the truth of, and, if he had known, was imprudent to reveal. But, further, you complained of ill treatment here; and mentioned an intention to leave the castle and seek your fortune elsewhere. I shall examine into all these particulars in turn. At present I desire you, Edmund, to relate all that you can remember of the conversation that passed between you and Oswald in the wood last Monday."

"Good God!" said Edmund. "Is it possible that any person could put such a construction upon so innocent a conversation?"

"Tell me then," said the Baron, "the particulars of it."

"I will, my lord, as nearly as my memory will allow me." Accordingly he related most of the conversation that passed in the wood; but, in the part that concerned the family of Lovel, he abbreviated as much as possible. Oswald's countenance cleared up, for he had done the same before Edmund came.

The Baron called to his eldest son, "You hear, Sir Robert, what both parties say. I have questioned them separately; neither of them knew what the other would answer, yet their accounts agree almost to a word."

"I confess they do," answered Sir Robert; "but, sir, it is very bold and presuming for them to speak of our family affairs in such a manner; if my uncle, Lord Lovel, should come to know it, he would punish them severely; and, if his honor is reflected upon, it becomes us to resent and to punish it."

Here Mr. Wenlock broke out into passion, and offered to swear to the truth of his accusation. "Be silent, Dick," said the Baron; "I shall judge for myself. I protest," said he to Sir Robert, "I never heard so much as Oswald has now told me concerning the deaths of Lord and Lady Lovel; I think it is best to let such stories alone till they die away of themselves. I had, indeed, heard of an idle story of the East apartment's being haunted, when first I came hither, and my brother advised me to shut it up till it should be forgotten;

but what has now been said, has suggested a thought that may make that apartment useful in future. I have thought of a punishment for Edmund that will stop the mouth of his accusers for the present; and, as I hope, will establish his credit with everybody. Edmund, will you undertake this adventure for me?"

"What adventure, my lord?" said Edmund. "There is nothing I would not undertake to show my gratitude and fidelity to you. As to my courage, I would show that at the expense of my malicious accusers, if respect to my lord's blood did not tie up my hands; as I am situated, I beg it may be put to the proof in whatever way is most for my master's service."

"That is well said," cried the Baron. "As to your enemies, I am thinking how to separate you from them effectually; of that I shall speak hereafter. I am going to try Edmund's courage; he shall sleep three nights in the East apartment, that he may testify to all whether it be haunted or not; afterward I will have that apartment set in order, and my eldest son shall take it for his own; it will spare me some expense, and answer my purpose as well, or better. Will you consent, Edmund?"

"With all my heart, my lord," said Edmund, "I have not wilfully offended God or man; I have, therefore, nothing to fear."

"Brave boy!" said my lord; "I am not deceived in you, nor shall you be deceived in your reliance on me. You shall sleep in that apartment to-night, and to-morrow I will have some private talk with you. Do you, Oswald, go with me; I want to have some conversation with you. The rest of you, retire to your studies and business; I will meet you at dinner."

Edmund retired to his own chamber, and Oswald was shut up with the Baron; he defended Edmund's cause and his own, and laid open as much as he knew of the malice and designs of his enemies. The Baron expressed much concern at the untimely deaths of Lord and Lady Lovel and desired Oswald to be circumspect in regard to what he had to say of the circumstances attending them, adding that he was both innocent and ignorant of any treachery toward either of them. Oswald excused himself for his communications to Edmund, saying they fell undesignedly into the subject and that he mentioned it in confidence to him only.

The Baron sent orders to the young men to come to dinner; but they refused to meet Edmund at table; accordingly he ate in the steward's apartment. After dinner, the Baron tried to reconcile his kinsmen to Edmund, but found it impossible. They saw their designs were laid open; and, judging of him by themselves, thought it impossible to forgive or be forgiven. The Baron ordered them to keep in separate apartments; he took his eldest son for his own companion, as being the most reasonable of the malcontents, and ordered his kinsmen to keep to their own apartment with a servant to watch their motions. Mr. William had Oswald for his companion. Old Joseph was bid to attend on Edmund; to serve him at supper; and, at the hour of nine, to conduct him to the haunted apartment. Edmund desired that he might have a light and his sword, lest his enemies should endeavor to surprise him. The Baron thought his request reasonable and complied with it.

There was a great search to find the key of the apartment; at last it was discovered by Edmund himself among a parcel of old rusty keys in a lumber room. The Baron sent the young men their suppers to their respective apartments. Edmund declined eating and desired to be conducted to his apartment. He was accompanied by most of the servants to the door of it; they wished him success and prayed for him as if he had been going to execution.

The door was with great difficulty unlocked, and Joseph gave Edmund a lighted lamp and wished him a good night; he returned his good wishes to them all with the utmost cheerfulness, took the key on the inside of the door, and dismissed them.

He then took a survey of his chamber; the furniture, by long neglect, was decayed and dropping to pieces; the bed was devoured by the moths, and occupied by the rats, who had built their nests there with impunity for many generations. The bedding was very damp, for the rain had forced its way through the ceiling; he determined, therefore, to lie down in his clothes. There were two doors on the further side of the room, with keys in them. Being not at all sleepy, he resolved to examine them; he attempted one lock and opened it with ease; he went into a large dining-room, the furniture of which was in the same tattered condition; out of this was a large closet with some books in it, and hung round with coats of arms, with genealogies and alliances of the house of Lovel; he amused himself here some minutes, and then returned into the bed-chamber.

He recollected the other door and resolved to see where it led to. The key was rusted into the lock and resisted his attempts; he set the lamp on the ground, and, exerting all his strength, opened the door, and at the same instant the wind of it blew out the lamp, and left him in utter darkness. At the same moment he heard a hollow rustling noise, like that of a person coming through a narrow passage. Till this moment not one idea of fear had approached the mind of Edmund; but, just then, all the concurrent circumstances of his situation struck upon his heart, and gave him a new and disagreeable sensation. He paused a while; and, recollecting himself, cried out aloud—"What should I fear? I have not wilfully offended God or man; why then should I doubt protection? But I have not yet implored the divine assistance; how then can I expect it!" Upon this, he kneeled down and prayed earnestly, resigning himself wholly to the will of Heaven; while he was yet speaking, his courage returned, and he resumed his usual confidence; again he approached the door from whence the noise proceeded; he thought he saw a glimmering light upon a staircase before him. "If," said he, "this apartment is haunted, I will use my endeavors to discover the cause of it; and if the spirit appears visibly, I will speak to it."

He was preparing to descend the staircase, when he heard several knocks at the door by which he first entered the room; and, stepping backward, the door was clapped to with great violence. Again fear attacked him, but he resisted it and boldly cried out—"Who is there?"

A voice at the outer door answered, "It's I—Joseph, your friend!"

"What do you want?" said Edmund.

"I have brought you some wood to make a fire," said Joseph.

"I thank you kindly," said Edmund; "but my lamp is gone out; I will try to find the door, however." After some trouble he found, and opened it; and was not sorry to see his friend Joseph, with a light in one hand, a flagon of beer in the other, and a fagot upon his shoulder. "I come," said the good old man, "to bring you something to keep up your spirits; the evening is cold; I know this room wants airing; and beside that, my master, I think your present undertaking requires a little assistance."

"My good friend," said Edmund, "I never shall be able to deserve or requite your kindness to me."

"My dear sir, you always deserved more than I could do for you; and I think I shall yet live to see you defeat the designs of your enemies, and acknowledge the services of your friends."

"Alas!" said Edmund. "I see little prospect of that!"

"I see," said Joseph, "something that persuades me you are designed for great things; and I perceive that things are working about to some great end. Have courage, my master, my heart beats strangely high upon your account!"

"You make me smile," said Edmund."

"I am glad to see it, sir; may you smile all the rest of your life!"

"I thank your honest affection," returned Edmund, "though it is too partial to me. You had better go to bed, however; if it is known that you visit me here, it will be bad for us both."

"So I will presently; but, please God, I will come here again to-morrow night, when all the family are a-bed; and I will tell you some things that you never yet heard."

"But pray tell me," said Edmund, "where does that door lead to?"

"Upon a passage that ends in a staircase that leads to the lower rooms; and there is likewise a door out of that passage into the dining-room."

"And what rooms are there below stairs?" said Edmund.

"The same as above," replied he.

"Very well; then I wish you a good-night, we will talk further to-morrow."

"Aye, to-morrow night; and in this place, my dear master."

"Why do you call me your master? I never was, nor ever can be, your master."

"God only knows that," said the good old man; "good-night, and Heaven bless you!"

"Good-night, my worthy friend!"

Joseph withdrew, and Edmund returned to the other door and attempted several times to open it in vain; his hands were benumbed and tired; at length he gave up. He made a fire in the chimney, placed the lamp on a table, and opened one of the window-shutters to admit the day-light; he then recommended himself to the divine protection and threw himself upon the bed; he presently fell asleep, and continued in that state, till the sun saluted him with his orient beams through the window he had opened.

As soon as he was perfectly awake, he strove to recollect his dreams. He thought that he heard people coming up the staircase that he had a glimpse of; that the door opened, and there entered a warrior, leading a lady by the hand, who was young and beautiful, but pale and wan. The man was dressed in complete armor; and his helmet down. They approached the bed; they drew aside the curtains. He thought the man said, "Is this our child?"

The woman replied, "It is; and the hour approaches that he shall be known for such."

They then separated, and one stood on each side of the bed; their hands met over his head, and they gave him a solemn benediction. He strove to rise and pay them his respects, but they forbade him; and the lady said, "Sleep in peace, oh my Edmund! For those who are the true possessors of this apartment are employed in thy preservation. Sleep on, sweet hope of a house that is thought past hope!" Upon this, they withdrew and went out at the same door by which they entered, and he heard them descend the stairs.

After this, he followed a funeral as chief mourner; he saw the whole procession, and heard the ceremonies performed. He was snatched away from this mournful scene to one of a contrary kind, a stately feast, at which he presided; and he heard himself congratulated as a husband, and a father. His friend William sat by his side; and his happiness was complete. Every succeeding idea was happiness without allay; and his mind was not idle a moment till the morning sun awakened him. He perfectly remembered his dreams and meditated on what all these things should portend. "Am I then," said he, "not Edmund Twyford, but somebody of consequence in whose fate so many people are interested? Vain thought that must have arisen from the partial suggestion of my two friends, Mr. William and old Joseph!"

He lay thus reflecting, when a servant knocked at his door and told him it was past six o'clock and that the Baron expected him to breakfast in an hour. He rose immediately; paid his tribute of thanks to Heaven for its protection, and went from his chamber in high health and spirits.

He walked in the garden till the hour of breakfast, and then attended the Baron. "Good morrow, Edmund!" said he; "how have you rested in your new apartment?"

"Extremely well, my lord," answered he.

"I am glad to hear it," said the Baron; "but I did not know your accommodations were so bad, as Joseph tells me they are."

" 'Tis of no consequence," said Edmund; "if they were much worse, I could dispense with them for three nights."

"Very well," said the Baron; "you are a brave lad. I am satisfied with you, and will excuse the other two nights."

"But, my lord, I will not be excused; no one shall have reason to suspect my courage. I am determined to go through the remaining nights upon many accounts."

"That shall be as you please," said my lord. "I think of you as you deserve; so well, that I shall ask your advice bye and bye in some affairs of consequence."

"My life and services are yours, my lord; command them freely."

"Let Oswald be called in," said my lord; "he shall be one of our consultation." He came; the servants were dismissed; and the Baron spoke as follows. "Edmund, when first I took you into my family, it was at the request of my sons and kinsmen; I bear witness to your good behavior; you have not deserved to lose their esteem; but, nevertheless, I have observed for some years past, that all but my son William have set their faces against you. I see their meanness, and I perceive their motives. But they are, and must be, my relations; and I would rather govern them by love than fear. I love and esteem your virtues. I cannot give you up to gratify their humors.[6] My son William has lost the affections of the rest, for that he bears to you; but he has increased my regard for him. I think myself bound in honor to him and you to provide for you; I cannot do it, as I wished, under my own roof. If you stay here, I see nothing but confusion in my family; yet I cannot put you out of it disgracefully. I want to think of some way to prefer you, that you may leave this house with honor; and I desire both of you to give me your advice in this matter. If Edmund will tell me in what way I can employ him to his own honor and my advantage, I am ready to do it; let him propose it, and Oswald shall moderate between us."

Here he stopped; and Edmund, whose sighs almost choked him, threw himself at the Baron's feet, and wet his hand with his tears. "Oh, my noble, generous benefactor! Do you condescend to consult such a one as me upon the state of your family? Does your most amiable and beloved son incur the ill-will of his brothers and kinsmen for my sake? What am I, that I should disturb the peace of this noble family? Oh, my lord, send me away directly! I should be unworthy to live, if

[6] Whims.

I did not earnestly endeavor to restore your happiness. You have given me a noble education, and I trust I shall not disgrace it. If you will recommend me and give me a character, I fear not to make my own fortune."

The Baron wiped his eyes. "I wish to do this, my child, but in what way?"

"My lord," said Edmund, "I will open my heart to you. I have served with credit in the army, and I should prefer a soldier's life."

"You please me well," said the Baron. "I will send you to France, and give you a recommendation to the Regent; he knows you personally, and will prefer you, for my sake, and for your own merit."

"My lord, you overwhelm me with your goodness! I am but your creature, and my life shall be devoted to your service."

"But," said the Baron, "how to dispose of you till the spring?"

"That," said Oswald, "may be thought of at leisure; I am glad that you have resolved, and I congratulate you both."

The Baron put an end to the conversation by desiring Edmund to go with him into the manège to see his horses. He ordered Oswald to acquaint his son William with all that had passed, and to try to persuade the young men to meet Edmund and William at dinner.

The Baron took Edmund with him into his manège to see some horses he had lately purchased; while they were examining the beauties and defects of these noble and useful animals, Edmund declared that he preferred Cardoc, a horse he had broken himself, to any other in my lord's stables. "Then," said the Baron, "I will give him to you; and you shall go upon him to seek your fortune." He made new acknowledgments for this gift, and declared he would prize it highly for the giver's sake. "But I shall not part with you yet," said my lord; "I will first carry all my points with these saucy boys, and oblige them to do you justice."

"You have already done that," said Edmund; "and I will not suffer any of your lordship's blood to undergo any further humiliation upon my account. I think, with humble submission to your better judgment, the sooner I go hence the better."

While they were speaking, Oswald came to them and said that the young men had absolutely refused to dine at the table, if Edmund was present. " 'Tis well," said the Baron; "I shall find a way to punish their contumacy hereafter: I will make them know that I am the master here. Edmund and you, Oswald, shall spend the day in my apartment above stairs. William shall dine with me alone; and I will acquaint him with our determination. My son Robert and his cabal shall be prisoners in the great parlor. Edmund shall, according to his own desire, spend this and the following night in the haunted apartment; and this for his sake and my own; for if I should now contradict my former orders, it would subject us both to their impertinent reflections."

He then took Oswald aside, and charged him not to let Edmund go out of his sight; for if he should come in the way of those implacable enemies, he trembled for the consequences. He then walked back to the stables, and the two friends returned into the house.

They had a long conversation on various subjects; in the course of it, Edmund acquainted Oswald with all that had passed between him and Joseph the preceding night, the curiosity he had raised in him, and his promise to gratify it the night following. "I wish," said Oswald, "you would permit me to be one of your party."

"How can that be?" said Edmund; "we shall be watched, perhaps; and, if discovered, what excuse can you make for coming there? Beside, if it were known, I shall be branded with the imputation of cowardice; and, though I have borne much, I will not promise to bear that patiently."

"Never fear," replied Oswald, "I will speak to Joseph about it; and, after prayers are over and the family gone to bed, I will steal away from my own chamber and come to you. I am strongly interested in your affairs; and I cannot be easy unless you will receive me into your company. I will bind myself to secrecy in any manner you shall enjoin."

"Your word is sufficient," said Edmund; "I have as much reason to trust you, Father, as any man living; I should be ungrateful to refuse you any thing in my power to grant. But suppose the apartment should really be haunted, would you have resolution enough to pursue the adventure to a discovery?"

"I hope so," said Oswald; "but have you any reason to believe it is?"

"I have," said Edmund; "but I have not opened my lips upon this subject to any creature but yourself. This night I purpose, if Heaven permit, to go all over the rooms; and, though I had formed this design, I will confess that your company will strengthen my resolution. I will have no reserves to you in any respect; but I must put a seal upon your lips." Oswald swore secrecy till he should be permitted to disclose the mysteries of that apartment; and both of them waited, in solemn expectation, the event of the approaching night.

In the afternoon Mr. William was allowed to visit his friend. An affecting interview passed between them. He lamented the necessity of Edmund's departure; and they took a solemn leave of each other, as if they foreboded it would be long ere they should meet again.

About the same hour as the preceding evening, Joseph came to conduct Edmund to his apartment. "You will find better accommodations than you had last night," said he, "and all by my lord's own order."

"I every hour receive some new proof of his goodness," said Edmund.

When they arrived, he found a good fire in the chamber and a table covered with cold meats and a flagon of strong beer. "Sit down and get your supper, my dear master," said Joseph; "I must attend my lord; but as soon as the family are gone to bed, I will visit you again."

"Do so," said Edmund; "but first, see Father Oswald; he has something to say to you. You may trust him, for I have no reserves to him."

"Well, sir, I will see him if you desire it; and I will come to you as soon as possible." So saying, he went his way; and Edmund sat down to supper.

After a moderate refreshment, he kneeled down, and prayed with the greatest servency; he resigned himself to the disposal of Heaven: "I am nothing," said he, "I desire to be nothing but what Thou, O Lord, pleasest to make me. If it is Thy will that I should return to my former obscurity, be it obeyed with cheerfulness! and, if thou art pleased to exalt me, I will look up to Thee, as the only fountain of honor and dignity." While he prayed, he felt an enlargement of heart beyond what he had ever experienced before; all idle fears were dispersed, and his heart glowed with divine love and affiance. He seemed raised above the world and all its pursuits. He continued wrapped up in mental devotion, till a knocking at the door obliged him to rise and let in his two friends, who came without shoes and on tiptoe to visit him.

"Save you, my son!" said the friar; "you look cheerful and happy."

"I am so, Father," said Edmund; "I have resigned myself to the disposal of Heaven, and I find my heart strengthened above what I can express."

"Heaven be praised!" said Oswald; "I believe you are designed for great things, my son."

"What! do you too encourage my ambition?" says Edmund; strange concurrence of circumstances! Sit down, my friend; and do you, my good Joseph, tell me the particulars you promised last night." They drew their chairs round the fire, and Joseph began as follows.

"You have heard of the untimely death of the late Lord Lovel, my noble and worthy master; perhaps you may have also heard that, from that time, this apartment was haunted. What passed the other day, when my lord questioned you both on this head, brought all the circumstances fresh into my mind. You then said there were suspicions that he came not fairly to his end. I trust you both and will speak what I know of it. There was a person suspected of this murder; and whom do you think it was?"

"You must speak out," said Oswald.

"Why then," said Joseph, "it was the present Lord Lovel."

"You speak my thoughts," said Oswald; "but proceed to the proofs."

"I will," said Joseph. "From the time that my lord's death was reported, there were strange whisperings and consultations between the new lord and some of the servants; there was a deal of private business carried on in this apartment. Soon after, they gave out that my poor lady was distracted; but she threw out strong expressions that favored nothing of madness. She said, that the ghost of her departed lord had appeared to her and revealed the circumstances of this murder. None of the servants, but one, were permitted to see her. At this very time, Sir Walter, the new lord, had the cruelty to offer love to her; he urged her to marry him; and one of her women overheard her say, she would sooner die than give her hand to the man who caused the death of her lord. Soon after this, we were told my lady was dead. The Lord Lovel made a public and sumptuous funeral for her."

"That is true," said Oswald; "for I was a novice and assisted at it."

"Well," says Joseph, "now comes my part of the story. As I was coming home from the burial, I overtook Roger our plowman. Said he, 'What think you of this burying?' 'What should I think,' said I 'but that we have lost the best master and lady that we shall ever know?' 'God he knows,' quoth Roger, 'whether they be living or dead; but if ever I saw my lady in my life, I saw her alive that night they say she died.' I tried to convince him that he was mistaken; but he offered to take his oath that the very night they said she died, he saw her come out at the garden-gate into the fields; that she often stopped, like a person in pain, and then went forward again until he lost sight of her. Now it is certain that her time was out, and she expected to lie down any day: and they did not pretend that she died in childbed. I thought upon what I heard, but nothing I said. Roger told the same story to another servant; so he was called to an account, the story was hushed up, and the foolish fellow said he was verily persuaded it was her ghost that he saw. Now you must take notice that, from this time, they began to talk about, that this apartment was troubled; and not only this, but at last the new lord could not sleep in quiet in his own room; and this induced him to sell the castle to his brother-in-law and get out of this country as fast as possible. He took most of the servants away with him, and Roger among the rest. As for me, they thought I knew nothing, and so they left me behind; but I was neither blind nor deaf, though I could hear, and see, and say nothing."

"This is a dark story," said Oswald.

"It is so," said Edmund; "but why should Joseph seem to think it concerns me in particular?"

"Ah, dear sir," said Joseph, "I must tell you, though I never uttered it to mortal man before; the striking resemblance this young man bears to my dear lord, the strange dislike his reputed father took to him, his gentle manners, his generous heart, his noble qualities so uncommon in those of his birth and breeding, the sound of his voice—You may smile at the strength of my fancy, but I cannot put it out of my mind but that he is my own master's son."

At these words Edmund changed color and trembled; he clapped his hand upon his breast, and looked up to Heaven in silence; his dream recurred to his memory, and struck upon his heart. He related it to his attentive auditors. "The ways of Providence are wonderful," said Oswald. "If this be so, Heaven in its own time will make it appear."

Here a silence of several minutes ensued; when, suddenly, they were awakened from their reverie by a violent noise in the rooms underneath them. It seemed like the clashing of arms, and something seemed to fall down with violence.

They started, and Edmund rose up with a look full of resolution and intrepidity. "I am called!" said he; "I obey the call!" He took up a lamp and went to the door that he had opened the night before. Oswald followed with his rosary in his hand, and Joseph last with trembling steps. The door opened with ease, and they descended the stairs in profound silence.

The lower rooms answered exactly to those above; there were two parlors and a large closet. They saw nothing remarkable in these rooms, except two pictures that were turned with their faces to the wall. Joseph took the courage to turn them. "These," said he, "are the portraits of my late lord and lady. Father, look at this face; do you know who is like it?"

"I should think," said Oswald, "it was done for Edmund!"

"I am," said Edmund, "struck with the resemblance myself. But let us go on; I feel myself inspired with unusual courage. —Let us open the closet-door."

Oswald stopped him short. "Take heed," said he, "lest the wind of the door put out the lamp. I will open this door." He attempted it without success; Joseph did the same, but to no purpose. Edmund gave the lamp to Joseph; he approached the door, tried the key, and it gave way to his hand in a moment. "This adventure belongs," said he, "to me only; that is plain; bring the lamp forward." Oswald repeated the paternoster, in which they all joined, and then entered the closet.

The first thing that presented itself to their view was a complete suit of armor that seemed to have fallen down on an heap. "Behold!" said Edmund. "This made the noise we heard above." They took it up, and examined it piece by piece; the inside of the breast-plate was stained with blood. "See here!" said Edmund; "what think you of this?"

" 'Tis my lord's armor," said Joseph; "I know it well. Here has been bloody work in this closet!"

Going forward, he stumbled over something; it was a ring with the arms of Lovel engraved upon it. "This is my lord's ring," said Joseph; "I have seen him wear it. I give it to you, sir, as the right owner; and most religiously do I believe you his son."

"Heaven only knows that," said Edmund; "and, if it permits, I will know who was my father before I am a day older." While he was speaking, he shifted his ground, and perceived that the boards rose up on the other side of the closet; upon farther examination they found that the whole floor was loose, and a table that stood over them concealed the circumstance from a casual observer. "I perceive," said Oswald, "that some great discovery is at hand."

"God defend us!" said Edmund, "but I verily believe that the person that owned this armor lies buried under us." Upon this, a dismal hollow groan was heard, as if from underneath. A solemn silence ensued, and marks of fear were visible upon all three; the groans was thrice heard. Oswald made signs for them to kneel, and he prayed audibly that Heaven would direct them how to act; he also prayed for the soul of the departed, that it might rest in peace. After this, he arose; but Edmund continued kneeling. He vowed solemnly to devote himself to the discovery of this secret, and then avenging the death of the person there buried. He then rose up. "It would be to no purpose," said he, "for us to examine further now; when I am properly authorized, I will have this place opened. I trust that time is not far off."

"I believe it," said Oswald; "you are designed by Heaven to be its instrument in bringing this deed of darkness to light. We are your creatures; only tell us what you would have us do and we are ready to obey your commands."

"I only demand your silence," said Edmund, "till I call for your evidence; and then, you must speak all you know, and all you suspect."

"Oh," said Joseph, "that I may but live to see that day, and I shall have lived long enough!"

"Come," said Edmund, "let us return up stairs, and we will consult further how I shall proceed." So saying, he went out of the closet, and they followed him. He locked the door, and took the key out. "I will keep this," said he, "till I have power to use it to purpose, lest any one should presume to pry into the secret of this closet. I will always carry it about me to remind me of what I have undertaken."

Upon this, they returned up stairs into the bed-chamber; all was still, and they heard nothing more to disturb them. "How," said Edmund, "is it possible that I should be the son of Lord Lovel? For, however circumstances have seemed to encourage such a notion, what reason have I to believe it?"

"I am strangely puzzled about it," said Oswald. "It seems unlikely that so good a man as Lord Lovel should corrupt the wife of a peasant, his vassal; and, especially, being so lately married to a lady with whom he was passionately in love."

"Hold there!" said Joseph. "My lord was incapable of such an action. If Master Edmund is the son of my lord, he is also the son of my lady."

"How can that be?" said Edmund.

"I don't know how," said Joseph, "but there is a person who can tell if she will. I mean Margery Twyford, who calls herself your mother."

"You meet my thoughts," said Edmund; "I had resolved, before you spoke, to visit her and to interrogate her on the subject. I will ask my lord's permission to go this very day."

"That is right," said Oswald; "but be cautious and prudent in your inquiries."

"If you," said Edmund, "would bear me company, I should do better; she might think herself obliged to answer your questions; and, being less interested in the event, you would be more discreet in your interrogations."

"That I will most readily," said he; "and I will ask my lord's permission for us both."

"This point is well determined," said Joseph; "I am impatient for the result; and I believe my feet will carry me to meet you whether I consent or not."

"I am as impatient as you," said Oswald; "but let us be silent as the grave, and let not a word or look indicate any thing knowing or mysterious."

The day-light began to dawn upon their conference; and Edmund, observing it, begged his friends to withdraw in silence. They did so, and left Edmund to his own recollections. His thoughts were too much employed for sleep to approach him; he threw himself upon the bed and lay meditating how he should proceed; a thousand schemes offered themselves and were rejected. But he resolved, at all events, to leave Baron Fitz-Owen's family the first opportunity that presented itself.

He was summoned, as before, to attend my lord to breakfast, during which, he was silent, absent, and reserved. My lord observed it and rallied him, inquiring how he had spent the night. "In reflecting upon my situation, my lord; and in laying plans for my future conduct." Oswald took the hint, and asked permission to visit Edmund's mother in his company and acquaint her with his intentions of leaving the country soon. He consented freely; but seemed unresolved about Edmund's departure.

They set out directly, and Edmund went hastily to old Twyford's cottage, declaring that every field seemed a mile to him. "Restrain your warmth, my son," said Oswald; "compose your mind, and recover your breath, before you enter upon a business of such consequence." Margery met them at the door, and asked Edmund, what wind blew him thither. "Is it so very surprising," said he, "that I should visit my parents?"

"Yes, it is," said she, "considering the treatment you have met with from us; but since Andrew is not in the house, I may say I am glad to see you. Lord bless you, what a fine youth you be grown! 'Tis a long time since I saw you; but that is not my fault. Many a cross word and many a blow have I had on your account; but I may now venture to embrace my dear child."

Edmund came forward and embraced her fervently; the starting tears, on both sides, evinced their affection. "And why," said he, "should my father forbid you to embrace your child? What have I ever done to deserve his hatred?"

"Nothing, my dear boy! You were always good and tender-hearted, and deserved the love of every body."

"It is not common," said Edmund, "for a parent to hate his first-born son without his having deserved it."

"That is true," said Oswald; "it is uncommon, it is unnatural; nay, I am of opinion it is almost impossible. I am so convinced of this truth that I believe the man who thus hates and abuses Edmund, cannot be his father." In saying this, he observed her countenance attentively; she changed color apparently. "Come," said he, "let us sit down; and do you, Margery, answer to what I have said."

"Blessed Virgin!" said Margery, "what does your Reverence mean? What do you suspect?"

"I suspect," said he, "that Edmund is not the son of Andrew your husband."

"Lord bless me!" said she, "what is it you do suspect?"

"Do not evade my question, woman! I am come here by authority to examine you upon this point."

The woman trembled in every joint. "Would to Heaven!" said she, "that Andrew was at home!"

"It is much better as it is," said Oswald. "You are the person we are to examine."

"Oh, Father," said she, "do you think that I—that I—am to blame in this matter? What have I done?"

"Do you, sir," said he, "ask your own questions."

Upon this, Edmund threw himself at her feet, and embraced her knees. "Oh my mother!" said he. "For as such my heart owns you, tell me for the love of Heaven! tell me, who was my father?"

"Gracious Heaven," said she, "what will become of me?"

"Woman!" said Oswald, "confess the truth, or you shall be compelled to do it? By whom had you this youth?"

"Who, I?" said she; "I had him! No, Father, I am not guilty of the black crime of adultery; God he knows my innocence. I am not worthy to be the mother of such a sweet youth as that is."

"You are not his mother, then, nor Andrew his father?"

"Oh, what shall I do?" said Margery; "Andrew will be the death of me!"

"No, he shall not," said Edmund; "you shall be protected and rewarded for the discovery."

"Goody,"[7] said Oswald, "confess the whole truth, and I will protect you from harm and from blame; you may be the means of making Edmund's fortune, in which case he will certainly provide for you; on the other hand, by an obstinate silence you will deprive yourself of all advantages you might receive from the discovery; and, beside, you will soon be examined in a different manner, and be obliged to confess all you know, and nobody will thank you for it."

"Ah," said she, "but Andrew beat me the last time I spoke to Edmund; and told me he would break every bone in my skin, if ever I spoke to him again."

"He knows it then?" said Oswald.

"He know it! Lord help you, it was all his own doing."

"Tell us then," said Oswald; "for Andrew shall never know it, till it is out of his power to punish you."

"'Tis a long story," said she, "and cannot be told in a few words."

"It will never be told at this rate," said he; "sit down and begin it instantly."

"My fate depends upon your words," said Edmund; "my soul is impatient of the suspense! If ever you loved me and cherished me, show it now, and tell while I have breath to ask it."

[7] A title applied to married women in humble circumstances.

He sat in extreme agitation of mind; his words and actions were equally expressive of his inward emotions. "I will," said she; "but I must try to recollect all the circumstances. You must know, young man, that you are just one-and-twenty years of age."

"On what day was he born?" said Oswald.

"The day before yesterday," said she, "the 21st of September."

"A remarkable era," said he.

"'Tis so, indeed," said Edmund. "Oh, that night! that apartment!"

"Be silent," said Oswald; "and do you, Margery, begin your story."

"I will," said she. "Just one-and-twenty years ago, on that very day, I lost my first-born son. I got a hurt by over-reaching myself when I was near my time, and so the poor child died. And so, as I was sitting all alone, and very melancholy, Andrew came home from work. 'See, Margery,' said he, 'I have brought you a child instead of that you have lost.' So he gave me a bundle, as I thought; but sure enough it was a child; a poor helpless babe just born, and only rolled up in a fine handkerchief, and over that a rich velvet cloak, trimmed with gold lace. 'And where did you find this?' said I. 'Upon the foot-bridge,' says he, 'just below the clay field. This child,' said he, 'belongs to some great folk, and perhaps it may be inquired after one day, and may make our fortunes; take care of it,' said he, 'and bring it up as if it was your own.' The poor infant was cold, and it cried, and looked up at me so pitifully that I loved it; beside, my milk was troublesome to me, and I was glad to be eased of it; so I gave it the breast, and from that hour I loved the child as if it were my own, and so I do still if I dared to own it."

"And this is all you know of Edmund's birth?" said Oswald.

"No, not all," said Margery; "but pray look out and see whether Andrew is coming, for I am all over in a twitter."

"He is not," said Oswald; "go on, I beseech you!"

"This happened," said she, "as I told you, on the 21st. On the morrow, my Andrew went out early to work, along with one Robin Rouse, our neighbor; they had not been gone above an hour, when they both came back seemingly very much frightened. Says Andrew, 'Go you, Robin, and borrow a pick-axe at neighbor Styles's.' 'What is the matter now?' said I. 'Matter enough!' quoth Andrew; 'we may come to be hanged, perhaps, as many an innocent man has before us.' 'Tell me what is the matter,' said I. 'I will,' said he; 'but if ever you open your mouth about it, woe be to you!' 'I never will,' said I. But he made me swear by all the blessed saints in the calendar; and then he told me, that, as Robin and he were going over the foot-bridge, where he found the child the evening before, they saw something floating upon the water; so they followed it, till it stuck against a stake, and found it to be the dead body of a woman. 'As sure as you are alive, Madge,' said he, 'this was the mother of the child I brought home.' "

"Merciful God!" said Edmund; "am I the child of that hapless mother?"

"Be composed," said Oswald. "Proceed, good woman, the time is precious."

"And so," continued she, "Andrew told me they dragged the body out of the river, and it was richly dressed, and must be somebody of consequence. "I suppose," said he, "when the poor lady had taken care of her child, she went to find some help; and, the night being dark, her foot slipped, and she fell into the river, and was drowned.'

" 'Lord have mercy!' said Robin, 'what shall we do with the dead body? We may be taken up for the murder; what had we to do to meddle with it?' 'Aye, but,' says Andrew, 'we must have something to do with it now; and our wisest way is to bury it.' Robin was sadly frightened, but at last they agreed to carry it into the wood, and bury it there; so they came home for a pick-axe and shovel. 'Well,' said I, 'Andrew, but will you bury all the rich clothes you speak of?' 'Why,' said he, 'it would be both a sin and a shame to strip the dead.' 'So it would,' said I; 'but I will give you a sheet to wrap the body in, and you may take off her upper garments and any thing of value; but do not strip her to the skin for any thing.' 'Well said, wench!' said he; 'I will do as you say.' So I fetched a sheet, and by that time Robin was come back, and away they went together.

"They did not come back again till noon, and then they sat down and ate a morsel together. Says Andrew, 'Now we may sit down and eat in peace.' 'Aye,' says Robin, 'and sleep in peace too, for we have done no harm.' 'No, to be sure,' said I; 'but yet I much concerned that the poor lady had not Christian burial.' 'Never trouble thyself about that,' said Andrew; 'we have done the best we could for her. But let us see what we have got in our bags; we must divide them.' So they opened their bags, and took out a fine gown and a pair of rich shoes; but, besides these, there was a fine necklace with a golden locket, and a pair of ear-rings. Says Andrew, and winked at me, 'I will have these, and you may take the rest.' Robin said he was satisfied, and so he went his way. When he was gone, 'Here, you fool,' says Andrew, 'take these, and keep them as safe as the bud of your eye. If ever young master is found, these will make our fortune.' "

"And have you them now?" said Oswald.

"Yes, I have," answered she; "Andrew would have sold them long ago, but I always put him off it."

"Heaven be praised!" said Edmund.

"Hush," said Oswald, "let us not lose time; proceed, Goody!"

"Nay," said Margery, "I have not much more to say. We looked every day to hear some inquiries after the child, but nothing passed, nobody was missing."

"Did nobody of note die about that time?" said Oswald.

"Why yes," said Margery, "the widow Lady Lovel died that same week. By the same token, Andrew went to the funeral, and brought home a 'scutcheon,[8] which I keep unto this day."

"Very well; go on."

"My husband behaved well enough to the boy, till such time as he had two or three children of his own; and then he began to grumble and say it was hard to maintain other folks's children when he found it hard enough to keep his own. I loved the boy quite as well as my own; often and often have I pacified Andrew, and made him to hope that he should one day or other be paid for his trouble; but at last he grew out of patience and gave over all hopes of that kind.

"As Edmund grew up, he grew sickly and tender, and could not bear hard labor; and that was another reason why my husband could not bear with him. 'If,' quoth he, 'the boy could earn his living, I did not care; but I must bear all the expense.' There came an old pilgrim into our parts; he was a scholar, and had been a soldier, and he taught Edmund to read; then he told him histories of wars, and knights, and lords, and great men; and Edmund took such delight in hearing him that he would not take to anything else.

"To be sure, Edwin was a pleasant companion; he would tell old stories, and sing old songs, that one could have sat all night to hear him; but, as I was a saying, Edmund grew more and more fond of reading and less of work; however,

[8] Escutcheon, a shield bearing the arms of a noble family.

he would run errands and do many handy turns for the neighbors; and he was so courteous a lad that people took notice of him. Andrew once caught him alone reading, and then told him that if he did not find some way to earn his bread, he would turn him out of doors in a very short time; and so he would have done, sure enough, if my Lord Fitz-Owen had not taken him into his service just in the nick."

"Very well, Goody," said Oswald; "you have told your story very well. I am glad, for Edmund's sake, that you can do it so properly. But now, can you keep a secret?"

"Why, an't please your Reverence, I think I have showed you that I can."

"But can you keep it from your husband?"

"Aye," said she, "surely I can; for I dare not tell it him."

"That is a good security," said he; "but I must have a better. You must swear upon this book not to disclose anything that has passed between us three, till we desire you to do it. Be assured you will soon be called upon for this purpose; Edmund's birth is near the discovery. He is the son of parents of high degree; and it will be in his power to make your fortune, when he takes possession of his own."

"Holy Virgin! What is it you tell me? How you rejoice me to hear that what I have so long prayed for will come to pass!" She took the oath required, saying after Oswald. "Now," said he, "go and fetch the tokens you have mentioned."

When she was gone, Edmund's passions, long suppressed, broke out in tears and exclamations; he kneeled down, and, with his hands clasped together, returned thanks to Heaven for the discovery. Oswald begged him to be composed, lest Margery should perceive his agitation and misconstrue the cause. She soon returned with the necklace and ear-rings. They were pearls of great value; and the necklace had a locket, on which the cypher of Lovel was engraved.

"This," said Oswald, "is indeed a proof of consequence. Keep it, sir, for it belongs to you."

"Must he take it away?" said she.

"Certainly," returned Oswald; "we can do nothing without it. But if Andrew should ask for it, you must put him off for the present, and hereafter he will find his account in it." Margery consented reluctantly to part with the jewels; and, after some further conversation, they took leave of her.

Edmund embraced her affectionately. "I thank you with my whole heart," said he, "for all your goodness to me! Though I confess, I never felt much regard for your husband, yet for you I had always the tender affection of a son. You will, I trust, give your evidence in my behalf when called upon; and I hope it will one day be in my power to reward your kindness. In that case, I will own you as my foster-mother, and you shall always be treated as such."

Margery wept. "The Lord grant it!" said she; "and I pray Him to have you in His holy keeping. Farewell, my dear child." Oswald desired them to separate for fear of intrusion; and they returned to the castle. Margery stood at the door of her cottage, looking every way to see if the coast was clear.

"Now, sir," said Oswald, "I congratulate you as the son of Lord and Lady Lovel; the proofs are strong and indisputable."

"To us they are so," said Edmund; "but how shall we make them so to others? And what are we to think of the funeral of Lady Lovel?"

"As of a fiction," said Oswald; "the work of the present lord, to secure his title and fortune."

"And what means can we use to dispossess him?" said Edmund. "He is not a man for a poor youth like me to contend with."

"Doubt not," said Oswald, "but Heaven, who has evidently conducted you by the hand thus far, will complete its own work; for my part, I can only wonder and adore!"

"Give me your advice then," said Edmund; "for Heaven assists us by natural means."

"It seems to me," said Oswald, "that your first step must be to make a friend of some great man of consequence enough to espouse your cause and to get this affair examined into by authority."

Edmund started, and crossed himself; he suddenly exclaimed, "A friend! Yes; I have a friend! A powerful one too; one sent by Heaven to be my protector, but whom I have too long neglected."

"Who can that be?" said Oswald.

"Who should it be," said Edmund, "but that good Sir Philip Harclay, the chosen friend of him, whom I shall from henceforward call my father."

" 'Tis true indeed," said Oswald; "and this is a fresh proof of what I before observed, that Heaven assists you and will complete its own work."

"I think so myself," said Edmund, "and rely upon its direction. I have already determined on my future conduct, which

I will communicate to you. My first step shall be to leave the castle; my lord has this day given me a horse, upon which I purpose to set out this very night, without the knowledge of any of the family. I will go to Sir Philip Harclay; I will throw myself at his feet, relate my strange story, and implore his protection. With him I will consult on the most proper way of bringing this murderer to public justice; and I will be guided by his advice and direction in every thing."

"Nothing can be better," said Oswald, "than what you propose; but give me leave to offer an addition to your scheme. You shall set off in the dead of night, as you intend; Joseph and I will favor your departure in such a manner as to throw a mystery over the circumstances of it. Your disappearing at such a time from the haunted apartment will terrify and confound all the family; they will puzzle themselves in vain to account for it, and they will be afraid to pry into the secrets of that place."

"You say well, and I approve your addition," replied Edmund. "Suppose, likewise, there was a letter written in a mysterious manner, and dropt in my lord's way, or sent to him afterward; it would forward our design and frighten them away from that apartment."

"That shall be my care," said Oswald; "and I will warrant you that they will not find themselves disposed to inhabit it presently."

"But how shall I leave my dear friend Mr. William without a word of notice of this separation?"

"I have thought of that too," said Oswald; "and I will so manage as to acquaint him with it in such a manner as he shall think out of the common course of things, and which shall make him wonder and be silent."

"How will you do that?" said Edmund.

"I will tell you hereafter," said Oswald; "for here comes old Joseph to meet us."

He came, indeed, as fast as his age would permit him. As soon as he was within hearing, he asked them what news. They related all that had passed at Twyford's cottage; he heard them with the greatest eagerness of attention, and as soon as they came to the great event—"I knew it! I knew it!" exclaimed Joseph. "I was sure it would prove so! Thank God for it! But I will be the first to acknowledge my young lord, and I will live and die his faithful servant!"

Here Joseph attempted to kneel to him, but Edmund prevented him with a warm embrace. "My friend! My dear friend!" said he, "I cannot suffer a man of your age to kneel to me; are you not one of my best and truest friends? I will ever remember your disinterested affection for me; and if Heaven restores me to my rights, it shall be one of my first cares to render your old age easy and happy." Joseph wept over him, and it was some time before he could utter a word.

Oswald gave them both time to recover their emotion by acquainting Joseph with Edmund's scheme for his departure. Joseph wiped his eyes and spoke. "I have thought," said he, "of something that will be both agreeable and useful to my dear master. John Wyatt, Sir Philip Harclay's servant, is now upon a visit at his father's; I have heard that he goes home soon; now he would be both a guide, and companion, on the way."

"That is, indeed, a happy circumstance," said Edmund; "but how shall we know certainly the time of his departure?"

"Why, sir, I will go to him, and inquire; and bring you word directly."

"Do so," said Edmund, "and you will oblige me greatly."

"But, sir," said Oswald, "I think it will be best not to let John Wyatt know who is to be his companion; only let Joseph tell him that a gentleman is going to visit 'his master. And, if possible, prevail upon him to set out this night."

"Do so, my good friend," said Edmund; "and tell him, further, that this person has business of great consequence to communicate to his master and cannot delay his journey on any account."

"I will do this, you may depend," said Joseph, "and acquaint you with my success as soon as possible; but, sir, you must not go without a guide, at any rate."

"I trust I shall not," said Edmund, "though I go alone; he that has received such a call as I have, can want no other, nor fear any danger."

They conversed on these points till they drew near the castle, when Joseph left them to go on his errand and Edmund attended his lord at dinner. The Baron observed that he was silent and reserved; the conversation languished on both sides. As soon as dinner was ended, Edmund asked permission to go up into his own apartment, where he packed up some necessaries and made a hasty preparation for his departure.

Afterward he walked into the garden, revolving in his mind the peculiarity of his situation and the uncertainty of his future prospects; lost in thought, he walked to and fro in a covered walk, with his arms crossed and his eyes cast down, without perceiving that he was observed by two females who stood at a distance watching his motions. It was the Lady Emma and her attendant who were thus engaged. At length, he lifted up his eyes and saw them; he stood still, and was irresolute whether to advance or retire.

They approached him; and, as they drew near, fair Emma spoke. "You have been so wrapped in meditation, Edmund, that I am apprehensive of some new vexation that I am yet a stranger to. Would it were in my power to lessen those you have already! But tell me if I guess truly?"

He stood still irresolute; he answered with hesitation. "Oh, lady—I am—I am grieved, I am concerned, to be the cause of so much confusion in this noble family, to which I am so much indebted. I see no way to lessen these evils but to remove the cause of them."

"Meaning yourself?" said she.

"Certainly, madam; and I was meditating on my departure."

"But," said she, "by your departure you will not remove the cause."

"How so, madam?"

"Because you are not the cause, but those you will leave behind you."

"Lady Emma!"

"How can you affect this ignorance, Edmund? You know well enough it is that odious Wenlock, your enemy and my aversion, that has caused all this mischief among us, and will much more, if he is not removed."

"This, madam, is a subject that it becomes me to be silent upon. Mr. Wenlock is your kinsman; he is not my friend; and for that reason I ought not to speak against him, nor you to hear it from me. If he has used me ill, I am recompensed by the generous treatment of my lord your father, who is all that is great and good; he has allowed me to justify myself to him, and he has restored me to his good opinion, which I prize among the best gifts of Heaven. Your amiable brother William thinks well of me, and his esteem is infinitely dear to me; and you, excellent lady, permit me to hope that you honor me with your good opinion. Are not these ample amends for the ill-will Mr. Wenlock bears me?"

"My opinion of you, Edmund," said she, "is fixed and fettled. It is not founded upon events of yesterday, but upon long knowledge and experience; upon your whole conduct and character."

"You honor me, lady! Continue to think well of me, it will excite me to deserve it. When I am far distant from this place, the remembrance of your goodness will be a cordial[9] to my heart."

"But why will you leave us, Edmund? Stay and defeat the designs of your enemy; you shall have my wishes and assistance."

"Pardon me, madam, that is among the things I cannot do, even if it were in my power, which it is not. Mr. Wenlock loves you, lady, and if he is so unhappy as to be your aversion that is a punishment severe enough. For the rest, I may be unfortunate by the wickedness of others, but if I am unworthy, it must be my own fault."

"So then you think it is an unworthy action to oppose Mr. Wenlock! Very well, sir. Then I suppose you wish him success; you wish that I may be married to him?"

"I, madam!" said Edmund, confused; "what am I that I should give my opinion on an affair of so much consequence? You distress me by the question. May you be happy! May you enjoy your own wishes!" He sighed, he turned away. She called him back; he trembled, and kept silence.

She seemed to enjoy his confusion; she was cruel enough to repeat the question. "Tell me, Edmund, and truly, do you wish to see me give my hand to Wenlock? I insist upon your answer."

All on a sudden he recovered both his voice and courage; he stepped forward, his person erect, his countenance assured, his voice resolute and intrepid. "Since Lady Emma insists upon my answer, since she avows a dislike to Wenlock, since she condescends to ask my opinion, I will tell her my thoughts, my wishes." The fair Emma now trembled in her turn; she blushed, looked down, and was ashamed to have spoken so freely. Edmund went on: "My most ardent wishes are that the fair Emma may reserve her heart and hand till a certain person, a friend of mine, is at liberty to solicit them; whose utmost ambition is, first to deserve, and then to obtain them."

"Your friend, sir!" said Lady Emma, her brow clouded, her eye disdainful.

Edmund proceeded: "My friend is so particularly circumstanced that he cannot at present with propriety ask for Lady

[9] Medicine or liquor taken to stimulate the circulation.

Emma's favor; but as soon as he has gained a cause that is yet in suspense, he will openly declare his pretensions, and if he is unsuccessful, he will then condemn himself to eternal silence."

Lady Emma knew not what to think of this declaration; she hoped, she feared, she meditated; but her attention was too strongly excited to be satisfied without some gratification. After a pause, she pursued the subject. "And this friend of yours, sir, of what degree and fortune is he?"

Edmund smiled; but, commanding his emotion, he replied: "His birth is noble, his degree and fortune uncertain." Her countenance fell, she sighed. He proceeded: "It is utterly impossible," said he, "for any man of inferior degree to aspire to Lady Emma's favor; her noble birth, the dignity of her beauty and virtues, must awe and keep at their proper distance, all men of inferior degree and merit; they may admire, they may revere; but they must not presume to approach too near, lest their presumption should meet with its punishment."

"Well, sir," said she, suddenly; "and so this friend of yours has commissioned you to speak in his behalf?"

"He has, madam."

"Then I must tell you, that I think his assurance is very great, and yours not much less."

"I am sorry for that, madam."

"Tell him that I shall reserve my heart and hand for the man to whom my father shall bid me give them."

"Very well, lady; I am certain my lord loves you too well to dispose of them against your inclination."

"How do you know that, sir? But tell him, that the man that hopes for my favor must apply to my lord for his."

"That is my friend's intention, his resolution I should say, as soon as he can do it with propriety; and I accept your permission for him to do so."

"My permission did you say? I am astonished at your assurance! Tell me no more of your friend. But perhaps you are pleading for Wenlock all this time. It is all one to me; only, say no more."

"Are you offended with me, madam?"

"No matter, sir."

"Yes, it is."

"I am surprised at you, Edmund."

"I am surprised at my own temerity; but, forgive me."

"It does not signify; good-by ty'e, sir."

"Don't leave me in anger, madam; I cannot bear that. Perhaps I may not see you again for a long time."

He looked afflicted; she turned back. "I do forgive you, Edmund. I was concerned for you; but, it seems, you are more concerned for everybody than for yourself." She sighed. "Farewell!" said she. Edmund gazed on her with tenderness; he approached her, he just touched her hand; his heart was rising to his lips, but he recollected his situation; he checked himself immediately; he retired back, he sighed deeply, bowed low, and hastily quitted her.

The lady turning into another walk, he reached the house first, and went up again to his chamber; he threw himself upon his knees; prayed for a thousand blessings upon every one of the family of his benefactor, and involuntarily wept at mentioning the name of the charming Emma, whom he was about to leave abruptly, and perhaps for ever. He then endeavored to compose himself, and once more attended the Baron; wished him a good night; and withdrew to his chamber, till he was called upon to go again to the haunted apartment.

He came down equipped for his journey, and went hastily for fear of observation; he paid his customary devotions, and soon after Oswald tapped at the door. They conferred together upon the interesting subject that engrossed their attention, until Joseph came to them, who brought the rest of Edmund's baggage and some refreshment for him before he set out. Edmund promised to give them the earliest information of his situation and success. At the hour of twelve they heard the same groans as the night before in the lower apartment; but, being somewhat familiar with it, they were not so strongly affected. Oswald crossed himself and prayed for the departed soul; he also prayed for Edmund and recommended him to the divine protection. He then arose and embraced that young man, who, also, took a tender leave of his friend Joseph. They then went, with silence and caution, through a long gallery; they descended the stairs in the same manner; they crossed the hall in profound silence, and hardly dared to breathe, lest they should be overheard. They found some difficulty in opening one of the folding doors, which at last they accomplished; they were again in jeopardy at the outward gate; at length they conveyed him safely into the stables. There they again embraced him and prayed for his prosperity.

He then mounted his horse and set forward to Wyatt's

cottage; he hailed at the door, and was answered from within. In a few minutes John came out to him. "What, is it you, Master Edmund?"

"Hush!" said he; "not a word of who I am. I go upon private business, and would not wish to be known."

"If you will go forward, sir, I will soon overtake you."

He did so; and they pursued their journey to the North. In the meantime, Oswald and Joseph returned in silence into the house; they retired to their respective apartments without hearing or being heard by anyone.

About the dawn of day Oswald intended to lay his packets in the way of those to whom they were addressed; after much contrivance he determined to take a bold step, and, if he were discovered, to frame some excuse. Encouraged by his late success, he went on tip-toe into Master William's chamber, placed a letter upon his pillow, and withdrew unheard. Exulting in his heart, he attempted the Baron's apartment, but found it fastened within; finding this scheme frustrated, he waited till the hour the Baron was expected down to breakfast and laid the letter and the key of the haunted apartment upon the table.

Soon after, he saw the Baron enter the breakfast room; he got out of sight, but stayed within call, preparing himself for a summons. The Baron sat down to breakfast; he saw a letter directed to himself, he opened it, and to his great surprise, read as follows:

"The guardian of the haunted apartment to Baron Fitz-Owen. To thee I remit the key of my charge, until the right owner shall come, who will both discover and avenge my wrongs; then, woe be to the guilty! But let the innocent rest in peace. In the meantime, let none presume to explore the secrets of my apartment, lest they suffer for their temerity."

The Baron was struck with amazement at the letter. He took up the key, examined it, then laid it down, and took up the letter; he was in such confusion of thought, he knew not what to do or say for several minutes. At length he called his servants about him; the first question he asked was, "Where is Edmund?"

They could not tell.

"Has he been called?"

"Yes, my lord, but nobody answered, and the key was not in the door."

"Where is Joseph?"

"Gone into the stables."

"Where is Father Oswald?"

"In his study."

"Seek him, and desire him to come hither."

By the time the Baron had read the letter over again, he came.

He had been framing a steady countenance to answer to all interrogatories; as he came in he attentively observed the Baron, whose features were in strong agitation; as soon as he saw Oswald, he spoke as one out of breath. "Take that key, and read this letter!"

He did so, shrugged up his shoulders, and remained silent.

"Father," said my lord, "what think you of this letter?"

"It is a very surprising one."

"The contents are alarming; where is Edmund?"

"I do not know."

"Has nobody seen him?"

"Not that I know of."

"Call my sons, my kinsmen, my servants."

The servants came in. "Have any of you seen or heard of Edmund?" "No," was the answer. "Father, step upstairs to my sons and kinsmen, and desire them to come down immediately."

Oswald withdrew; and went, first, to Mr. William's chamber. "My dear sir, you must come to my lord now directly; he has something extraordinary to communicate to you."

"And so have I, Father; see what I have found upon my pillow."

"Pray, sir, read it to me before you show it to anybody; my lord is alarmed too much already and wants nothing to increase his consternation."

William read his letter, while Oswald looked as if he was an utter stranger to the contents, which were these:

"Whatever may be heard or seen, let the seal of friendship be upon thy lips. The peasant Edmund is no more. But there still lives a man who hopes to acknowledge and repay the Lord Fitz-Owen's generous care and protection; to return his beloved William's vowed affection, and to claim his friendship on terms of equality."

"What," said William, "can this mean?"

"It is not easy to say," replied Oswald.

"Can you tell what is the cause of this alarm?"

"I can tell you nothing, but that my lord desires to see you directly; pray may haste down; I must go up to your brothers and kinsmen. Nobody knows what to think or believe."

Master William went downstairs, and Father Oswald went to the malcontents. As soon as he entered the outward door of their apartment, Mr. Wenlock called out. "Here comes the friend; now for some new proposal!"

"Gentlemen," said Oswald, "my lord desires your company immediately in the breakfast parlor."

"What! To meet your favorite Edmund, I suppose?" said Mr. Wenlock.

"No, sir."

"What, then, is the matter?" said Mr. Robert.

"Something very extraordinary has happened, gentlemen. Edmund is not to be found; he disappeared from the haunted apartment, the key of which was conveyed to my lord in a strange manner, with a letter from an unknown hand. My lord is both surprised and concerned and wishes to have your opinion and advice on the occasion."

"Tell him," said Sir Robert, "we will wait upon him immediately."

As Oswald went away, he heard Wenlock say, "So Edmund is gone, it is no matter how, or whither." Another said, "I hope the ghost has taken him out of the way." The rest laughed at the conceit, as they followed Oswald downstairs. They found the Baron and his son William commenting upon the key and the letter. My lord gave them to Sir Robert, who looked on them with marks of surprise and confusion. The Baron addressed him: "Is not this a very strange affair? Son Robert, lay aside your ill humors, and behave to your father with the respect and affection his tenderness deserves from you, and give me your advice and opinion on this alarming subject."

"My lord," said Sir Robert, "I am as much confounded as yourself. I can give no advice. Let my cousins see the letter; let us have their opinion." They read it in turn; they were equally surprised.

But when it came into Wenlock's hand, he paused and meditated some minutes; at length—"I am indeed surprised, and still more concerned, to see my lord and uncle the dupe of an artful contrivance; and, if he will permit me, I shall endeavor to unriddle it, to the confusion of all that are concerned in it."

"Do so, Dick," said my lord, "and you shall have my thanks for it."

"This letter," said he, "I imagine to be the contrivance of Edmund, or some ingenious friend of his, to conceal some designs they have against the peace of this family, which has been too often disturbed upon that rascal's account."

"But what end could be proposed by it?" said the Baron.

"Why, one part of the scheme is to cover Edmund's departure, that is clear enough; for the rest, we can only guess at it. Perhaps he may be concealed somewhere in that apartment, from whence he may rush out in the night, and either rob or murder us; or, at least, alarm and terrify the family."

The Baron smiled: "You shoot beyond the mark, sir, and overshoot yourself, as you have done before now; you show only your inveteracy against that poor lad, whom you cannot mention with temper. To what purpose should he shut himself up there, to be starved?"

"Starved! No, no! He has friends in the house" (looking at Oswald), "who will not suffer him to want any thing. Those who have always magnified his virtues and extenuated his faults will lend a hand to help him in time of need; and, perhaps, to assist his ingenious contrivances." Oswald shrugged his shoulders, and remained silent.

"This is a strange fancy of yours, Dick," said my lord, "but I am willing to pursue it; first, to discover what you drive at; and, secondly, to satisfy all that are here present of the truth or falsehood of it, that they may know what value to set upon your sagacity hereafter. Let us all go over that apartment together; and let Joseph be called to attend us thither."

Oswald offered to call him, but Wenlock stopped him. "No, Father," said he, "you must stay with us; we want your ghostly counsel and advice. Joseph shall have no private conference with you."

"What mean you," said Oswald, "to insinuate to my lord against me or Joseph? But your ill-will spares nobody. It will one day be known who is the disturber of the peace of this family; I wait for that time, and am silent."

Joseph came; when he was told whither they were going, he looked hard at Oswald. Wenlock observed them. "Lead the way, Father," said he, "and Joseph shall follow us."

Oswald smiled. "We will go where Heaven permits us," said he. "Alas! the wisdom of man can neither hasten nor retard its decrees."

They followed the Father upstairs, and went directly to the haunted apartment. The Baron unlocked the door; he bid Joseph open the shutters and admit the daylight, which had been excluded for many years. They went over the rooms above stairs, and then descended the staircase, and through the lower rooms in the same manner. However, they overlooked the closet in which the fatal secret was concealed; the door was covered with tapestry, the same as the room, and united so well that it seemed but one piece. Wenlock tauntingly desired Father Oswald to introduce them to the ghost. The Father, in reply, asked them where they should find Edmund. "Do you think," said he, "that he lies hid in my pocket, or in Joseph's?"

" 'Tis no matter," answered he; "thoughts are free."

"My opinion of you, sir," said Oswald, "is not founded upon thoughts: I judge of men by their actions; a rule, I believe, it will not suit you to be tried by."

"None of your insolent admonitions, Father!" returned Wenlock. "This is neither the time nor the place for them."

"That is truer than you are aware of, sir; I meant not to enter into the subject just now."

"Be silent," said my lord. "I shall enter into this subject with you hereafter; then look you be prepared for it! In the meantime, do you, Dick Wenlock, answer to my questions. Do you think Edmund is concealed in this apartment?"

"No, sir."

"Do you think there is any mystery in it?"

"No, my lord."

"Is it haunted, think you?"

"No, I think not."

"Should you be afraid to try?"

"In what manner, my lord?"

"Why, you have shown your wit upon the subject, and I mean to show your courage; you and Jack Markham, your confidant, shall sleep here three nights, as Edmund has done before."

"Sir," said Sir Robert, "for what purpose? I should be glad to understand why."

"I have my reasons, sir, as well as your kinsmen there. No reply, sirs! I insist upon being obeyed in this point. Joseph, let the beds be well aired and everything made agreeable to the gentlemen. If there is any contrivance to impose upon me, they, I am sure, will have pleasure in detecting it; and, if not,

I shall obtain my end in making these rooms habitable. Oswald, come with me; and the rest may go where they list[10] till dinner-time."

The Baron went with Oswald into the parlor. "Now tell me, Father," said he, "do you disapprove what I have done?"

"Quite the contrary, my lord," said he. "I entirely approve it."

"But you do not know all my reasons for it. Yesterday Edmund's behavior was different from what I have ever seen it; he is naturally frank and open in all his ways; but he was then silent, thoughtful, absent; he sighed deeply, and once I saw tears stand in his eyes. Now, I do suspect there is something uncommon in that apartment; that Edmund has discovered the secret; and, fearing to disclose it, he is fled away from the house. As to this letter, perhaps he may have written it to hint that there is more than he dares reveal; I tremble at the hints contained in it, though I shall appear to make light of it. But I and mine are innocent; and if Heaven discloses the guilt of others, I ought to adore and submit to its decrees."

"That is prudently and piously resolved, my lord; let us do our duty, and leave events to Heaven."

"But, Father, I have a further view in obliging my kinsmen to sleep there. If anything should appear to them, it is better that it should only be known to my own family; if there is nothing in it, I shall put to the proof the courage and veracity of my two kinsmen, of whom I think very indifferently. I mean shortly to inquire into many things I have heard lately to their disadvantage; and, if I find them guilty, they shall not escape with impunity."

"My lord," said Oswald, "you judge like yourself; I wish you to make inquiry concerning them, and believe the result will be to their confusion, and your lordship will be enabled to re-establish the peace of your family."

During this conversation, Oswald was upon his guard, lest anything should escape that might create suspicion. He withdrew as soon as he could with decency, and left the Baron meditating what all these things should mean. He feared there was some misfortune impending over his house, though he knew not from what cause.

He dined with his children and kinsmen and strove to appear cheerful; but a gloom was perceivable through his

10 Like.

deportment. Sir Robert was reserved and respectful; Mr. William was silent and attentive; the rest of the family dutifully assiduous to my lord; only Wenlock and Markham were fallen and chagrined. The Baron detained the young men the whole afternoon; he strove to amuse and to be amused; he showed the greatest affection and parental regard to his children, and endeavored to conciliate their affections and engage their gratitude by kindness. Wenlock and Markham felt their courage abate as the night approached. At the hour of nine, old Joseph came to conduct them to the haunted apartment; they took leave of their kinsmen, and went upstairs with heavy hearts.

They found the chamber set in order for them, and a table spread with provision and good liquor to keep up their spirits. "It seems," said Wenlock, "that your friend Edmund was obliged to you for his accommodations here."

"Sir," said Joseph, "his accommodations were bad enough the first night; but, afterward, they were bettered by my lord's orders."

"Owing to your officious cares?" said Wenlock.

"I own it," said Joseph, "and I am not ashamed of it."

"Are you not anxious to know what is become of him?" said Markham.

"Not at all, sir; I trust he is in the best protection; so good a young man as he is, is safe everywhere."

"You see, cousin Jack," said Wenlock, "how this villain has stolen the hearts of my uncle's servants. I suppose this canting old fellow knows where he is, if the truth were known."

"Have you any further commands for me, gentlemen?" said the old man.

"No, not we."

"Then I am ordered to attend my lord, when you have done with me."

"Go, then, about your business." Joseph went away, glad to be dismissed.

"What shall we do, cousin Jack," said Wenlock, "to pass away the time? It is plaguy dull sitting here."

"Dull enough," said Markham; "I think the best thing we can do, is to go to bed and sleep it away."

"Faith," says Wenlock, "I am in no disposition to sleep! Who would have thought the old man would have obliged us to spend the night here?"

"Don't say us, I beg of you; it was all your own doing," replied Markham.

"I did not intend he should have taken me at my word."

"Then you should have spoken more cautiously. I have always been governed by you, like a fool as I am; you play the braggart, and I suffer for it. But they begin to see through your fine-spun arts and contrivances, and I believe you will meet with your deserts one day or other."

"What now? Do you mean to affront me, Jack? Know, that some are born to plan, others to execute; I am one of the former, thou of the latter. Know your friend, or——"

"Or what?" replied Markham. "Do you mean to threaten me? If you do!"

"What then?" said Wenlock.

"Why, then, I will try which of us two is the best man, sir!" Upon this Markham arose, and put himself into a posture of defense. Wenlock perceiving he was serious in his anger began to soothe him; he persuaded, he flattered, he promised great things if he would be composed. Markham was sullen, uneasy, resentful; whenever he spoke, it was to upbraid Wenlock with his treachery and falsehood. Wenlock tried all his eloquence to get him into a good humor, but in vain; he threatened to acquaint his uncle with all that he knew and to exculpate himself at the other's expense. Wenlock began to find his choler[11] rife; they were both almost choked with rage; and, at length, they both rose with a resolution to fight.

As they stood with their fists clenched, on a sudden they were alarmed with a dismal groan from the room underneath. They stood like statues petrified by fear, yet listening with trembling expectation. A second groan increased their consternation; and, soon after, a third completed it. They staggered to a seat and sunk down upon it, ready to faint; presently, all the doors flew open, a pale shimmering light appeared at the door, from the staircase, and a man in complete armor entered the room. He stood, with one hand extended, pointing to the outward door; they took the hint, and crawled away as fast as fear would let them; they staggered along the gallery, and from thence to the Baron's apartment, where Wenlock sank down in a swoon, and Markham had just strength enough to knock at the door.

The servant who slept in the outward room alarmed his lord. Markham cried out—"For Heaven's sake, let us in!"

[11] Anger.

Upon hearing his voice, the door was opened, and Markham approached his uncle in such an attitude of fear as excited a degree of it in the Baron. He pointed to Wenlock, who was with some difficulty recovered from the fit he had fallen into; the servant was terrified, he rung the alarm-bell; the servants came running from all parts to their lord's apartment. The young gentlemen came likewise, and presently all was confusion, and the terror was universal. Oswald, who guessed the business, was the only one that could question them; he asked, several times, "What is the matter?"

Markham, at last, answered him: "We have seen the ghost!" All regard to secrecy was now at an end; the echo ran through the whole family: "They have seen the ghost!"

The Baron desired Oswald to talk to the young men, and endeavor to quiet the disturbance. He came forward; he comforted some, he rebuked others; he bade the servants retire into the outward room. The Baron, with his sons and kinsmen, remained in the bed-chamber. "It is very unfortunate," said Oswald, "that this affair should be made so public; surely these young men might have related what they had seen, without alarming the whole family. I am very much concerned upon my lord's account."

"I thank you, Father," said the Baron, "but prudence was quite overthrown here. Wenlock was half dead, and Markham half distracted; the family were alarmed without my being able to prevent it. But let us hear what these poor terrified creatures say."

Oswald demanded, "What have you seen, gentlemen?"

"The ghost!" said Markham.

"In what form did it appear?"

"A man in armor."

"Did it speak to you?"

"No."

"What did it do to terrify you so much?"

"It stood at the farthest door, and pointed to the outward door, as if to have us leave the room; we did not wait for a second notice, but came away as fast as we could."

"Did it follow you?"

"No."

"Then you need not have raised such a disturbance."

Wenlock lifted up his head, and spoke: "I believe, Father, if you had been with us, you would not have stood upon ceremonies any more than we did. I wish my lord would send you to parley with the ghost; for, without doubt, you are better qualified than we."

"My lord," said Oswald, "I will go thither, with your permission; I will see that everything is safe and bring the key back to you. Perhaps this may help to dispel the fears that have been raised; at least, I will try to do it."

"I thank you, Father, for your good offices; do as you please."

Oswald went into the outward room. "I am going," said he, "to shut up the apartment. The young gentlemen have been more frightened than they had occasion for; I will try to account for it. Which of you will go with me?" They all drew back, except Joseph, who offered to bear him company. They went into the bedroom in the haunted apartment, and found everything quiet there. They put out the fire, extinguished the lights, locked the door, and brought away the key. "As they returned, I thought how it would be," said Joseph. "Hush! not a word," said Oswald; "you find we are suspected of something, though they know not what. Wait till you are called upon, and then we will both speak to purpose." They carried the key to the Baron.

"All is quiet in the apartment," said Oswald, "as we can testify."

"Did you ask Joseph to go with you," said the Baron, "or did he offer himself?"

"My lord, I asked if anybody would go with me, and they all declined it but he; I thought proper to have a witness beside myself, for whatever might be seen or heard."

"Joseph, you were servant to the late Lord Lovel; what kind of man was he?"

"A very comely man, please your lordship."

"Should you know him if you were to see him?"

"I cannot say, my lord."

"Would you have any objection to sleep a night in that apartment?"

"I beg—I hope—I beseech your lordship not to command me to do it!"

"You are then afraid; why did you offer yourself to go thither?"

"Because I was not so much frightened as the rest."

"I wish you would lie a night there; but, I do not insist upon it."

"My lord, I am a poor ignorant old man, not fit for such an undertaking. Beside, if I should see the ghost, and if it should be the person of my master, and if it should tell me anything, and bid me keep it secret, I should not dare to disclose it; and then, what service should I do your lordship?"

"That is true, indeed," said the Baron.

"This speech," said Sir Robert, "is both a simple and an artful one. You see, however, that Joseph is not a man for us to depend upon; he regards the Lord Lovel, though dead, more than Lord Fitz-Owen, living; he calls him his master, and promises to keep his secrets. What say you, Father, is the ghost your master or your friend? Are you under any obligation to keep his secrets?"

"Sir," said Oswald, "I answer as Joseph does; I would sooner die than discover a secret revealed in that manner."

"I thought as much," said Sir Robert; "there is a mystery in Father Oswald's behavior that I cannot comprehend."

"Do not reflect upon the Father," said the Baron, "I have no cause to complain of him; perhaps the mystery may be too soon explained. But let us not anticipate evils. Oswald and Joseph have spoken like good men; I am satisfied with their answers. Let us, who are innocent, rest in peace, and let us endeavor to restore peace in the family; and do you, Father, assist us."

"With my best services," said Oswald. He called the servants in. "Let nothing be mentioned out of doors," said he, "of what has lately passed within, especially in the East apartment; the young gentlemen had not so much reason to be frightened as they apprehended; a piece of furniture fell down in the rooms underneath, which made the noise that alarmed them so much. But I can certify that all things in the rooms are quiet, and there is nothing to fear. All of you attend me in the chapel in an hour; do your duties, put your trust in God, and obey your lord, and you will find everything go right as it used to do."

They dispersed; the sun rose, the day came on, and everything went on in the usual course. But the servants were not so easily satisfied; they whispered that something was wrong and expected the time that should set all right. The mind of the Baron was employed in meditating upon the circumstances that seemed to him the forerunners of some great events. He sometimes thought of Edmund; he sighed for his expulsion and lamented the uncertainty of his fate; but, to his family, he appeared easy and satisfied.

From the time of Edmund's departure, the fair Emma had

many uneasy hours; she wished to inquire after him, but feared to show any solicitude concerning him. The next day, when her brother William came into her apartment, she took courage to ask a question. "Pray, brother, can you give any guess what is become of Edmund?"

"No," said he, with a sigh. "Why do you ask me?"

"Because, my dear William, I should think if anybody knew, it must be you; and I thought he loved you too well to leave you in ignorance. But don't you think he left the castle in a very strange manner?"

"I do, my dear; there is a mystery in every circumstance of his departure. Nevertheless (I will trust you with a secret), he did not leave the castle without making a distinction in my favor."

"I thought so," said she; "but you might tell *me* what you know about him."

"Alas, my dear Emma! I know nothing. When I saw him last, he seemed a good deal affected, as if he were taking leave of me; and I had a foreboding that we parted for a longer time than usual."

"Ah! so had I," said she, "when he parted from me in the garden."

"What leave did he take of you, Emma?" She blushed, and hesitated to tell him all that passed between them; but he begged, persuaded, insisted; and, at length, under the strongest injunctions of secrecy, she told him all.

He said that Edmund's behavior on that occasion was as mysterious as the rest of his conduct; "but, now you have revealed your secret, you have a right to know mine."

He then gave her the letter he found upon his pillow; she read it with great emotion. "Saint Winifred[12] assist me!" said she. "What can I think? 'The peasant Edmund is no more, but there lives one,'—that is to my thinking, Edmund lives, but is no peasant."

"Go on, my dear," said William; "I like your explanation."

"Nay, brother, I only guess; but what think you?"

"I believe we think alike in more than one respect, that he meant to recommend no other person than himself to your favor; and, if he were indeed of noble birth, I would prefer him to a prince for a husband to my Emma!"

"Bless me!" said she, "do you think it possible that he should be of either birth or fortune?"

[12] Guardian saint of virgins.

"It is hard to say what is impossible! We have proof that the East apartment is haunted. It was there that Edmund was made acquainted with many secrets, I doubt not; and, perhaps, his own fate may be involved in that of others. I am confident that what he saw and heard there was the cause of his departure. We must wait with patience the unraveling of this intricate affair. I believe I need not enjoin your secrecy as to what I have said; your heart will be my security."

"What mean you, brother?"

"Don't affect ignorance, my dear; you love Edmund, so do I; it is nothing to be ashamed of. It would have been strange, if a girl of your good sense had not distinguished a swan among a flock of geese."

"Dear William, don't let a word of this escape you; but you have taken a weight off my heart. You may depend that I will not dispose of my hand or heart till I know the end of this affair."

William smiled: "Keep them for Edmund's *friend*. I shall rejoice to see him in a situation to ask them."

"Hush, my brother! Not a word more; I hear footsteps." They were her eldest brother's, who came to ask Mr. William to ride out with him, which finished the conference.

The fair Emma from this time assumed an air of satisfaction; and William frequently stole away from his companions to talk with his sister upon their favorite subject.

While these things passed at the Castle of Lovel, Edmund and his companion John Wyatt proceeded on their journey to Sir Philip Harclay's seat; they conversed together on the way, and Edmund found him a man of understanding, though not improved by education; he also discovered that John loved his master and respected him even to veneration; from him he learned many particulars concerning that worthy knight. Wyatt told him that Sir Philip maintained twelve old soldiers who had been maimed and disabled in the wars and had no provision made for them; also six old officers, who had been unfortunate and were grown gray without preferment; he likewise mentioned the Greek gentleman, his master's captive and friend, as a man eminent for valor and piety; "but, beside these," said Wyatt, "there are many others who eat of my master's bread and drink of his cup, and who join in blessings and prayers to Heaven for their noble benefactor; his ears are ever open to distress, his hand to relieve it, and he shares in every good man's joys and blessings."

"Oh, what a glorious character!" said Edmund; "how my heart throbs with wishes to imitate such a man! Oh that I might resemble him, though at ever so great a distance!" Edmund was never weary of hearing the actions of this truly great man, nor Wyatt with relating them; and, during three days journey, there were but few pauses in their conversation.

The fourth day, when they came within view of the house, Edmund's heart began to raise doubts of his reception. "If," said he, "Sir Philip should not receive me kindly, if he should resent my long neglect and disown my acquaintance, it would be no more than justice."

He sent Wyatt before, to notify his arrival to Sir Philip, while he waited at the gate, full of doubts and anxieties concerning his reception. Wyatt was met and congratulated on his return by most of his fellow-servants; he asked, "Where is my master?"

"In the parlor."

"Are any strangers with him?"

"No, only his own family."

"Then I will show myself to him."

He presented himself before Sir Philip. "So, John," said he, "you are welcome home! I hope you left your parents and relations well?"

"All well, thank God! and send their humble duty to your honor, and they pray for you every day of their lives; I hope your honor is in good health."

"Very well."

"Thank God for that! but, sir, I have something further to tell you. I have had a companion all the way home, a person who comes to wait on your honor, on business of great consequence, as he says."

"Who is that, John?"

"It is Master Edmund Twyford, from the Castle of Lovel."

"Young Edmund!" says Sir Philip, surprised. "Where is he?"

"At the gate, sir."

"Why did you leave him there?"

"Because he bade me come before, and acquaint your honor that he waits your pleasure."

"Bring him hither," said Sir Philip; "tell him I shall be glad to see him."

John made haste to deliver his message, and Edmund followed him in silence into Sir Philip's presence. He bowed low and kept at distance. Sir Philip held out his hand and bade him approach. As he drew near, he was seized with an universal trembling; he kneeled down, took his hand, kissed it, and pressed it to his heart in silence.

"You are welcome, young man!" said Sir Philip; "take courage, and speak for yourself."

Edmund sighed deeply; he at length broke silence with difficulty. "I am come thus far, noble sir, to throw myself at your feet and implore your protection. You are, under God, my only reliance."

"I receive you," said Sir Philip, "with all my heart! Your person is greatly improved since I saw you last, and I hope your mind is equally so. I have heard a great character of you from some that knew you in France. I remember the promise I made you long ago, and am ready now to fulfil it, upon condition that you have done nothing to disgrace the good opinion I formerly entertained of you; and am ready to serve you in any thing consistent with my own honor."

Edmund kissed the hand that was extended to raise him. "I accept your favor, sir, upon this condition only; and if ever you find me to impose upon your credulity, or incroach on your goodness, may you renounce me from that moment!"

"Enough," said Sir Philip; "rise, then, and let me embrace you. You are truly welcome!"

"Oh, noble sir!" said Edmund, "I have a strange story to tell you; but it must be by ourselves, with only Heaven to bear witness to what passes between us."

"Very well," said Sir Philip; "I am ready to hear you. But first, go and get some refreshment after your journey, and then come to me again; John Wyatt will attend you."

"I want no refreshment," said Edmund; "and I cannot eat or drink till I have told my business to your honor."

"Well then," said Sir Philip, "come along with me." He took the youth by the hand, and led him into another parlor, leaving his friends in great surprise, what this young man's errand could be. John Wyatt told them all that he knew relating to Edmund's birth, character, and situation.

When Sir Philip had seated his young friend, he listened in silence to the surprising tale he had to tell him. Edmund told him briefly the most remarkable circumstances of his life, from the time when he first saw and liked him till his return from France; but from that era, he related at large everything that had happened, recounting every interesting particular, which was imprinted on his memory in strong and lasting characters.

Sir Philip grew every moment more affected by the recital;
sometimes he clasped his hands together, he lifted them up
to heaven, he smote his breast, he sighed, he exclaimed aloud;
when Edmund related his dream, he breathed short, and
seemed to devour him with attention; when he described the
fatal closet, he trembled, sighed, sobbed, and was almost suf-
focated with his agitations. But when he related all that
passed between his supposed mother and himself, and finally
produced the jewels, the proofs of his birth, and the death
of his unfortunate mother—he flew to him, he pressed him to
his bosom, he strove to speak, but speech was for some minutes
denied.

He wept aloud, and, at length, his words found their way
in broken exclamations. "Son of my dearest friend! Dear
and precious relic of a noble house! Child of Providence!—
The beloved of Heaven!—Welcome! Thrice welcome to my
arms!—To my heart!—I will be thy parent from henceforward, and thou shalt be indeed my child, my heir! My mind
told me from the first moment I beheld thee, that thou wert
the image of my friend! My heart then opened itself to receive
thee, as his offspring. I had a strange foreboding that I was
to be thy protector. I would then have made thee my own;
but Heaven orders things for the best; it made thee the instrument of this discovery, and in its own time and manner
conducted thee to my arms. Praise be to God for his wonderful doings toward the children of men! Everything that has
befallen thee is by his direction, and he will not leave his work
unfinished; I trust that I shall be his instrument to do justice
on the guilty, and to restore the orphan of my friend to his
rights and title. I devote myself to this service, and will make
it the business of my life to effect it."

Edmund gave vent to his emotions in raptures of joy and
gratitude. They spent several hours in this way without thinking of the time that passed; the one inquiring, the other explaining, and repeating, every particular of the interesting
story.

At length they were interrupted by the careful John Wyatt,
who was anxious to know if anything was likely to give trouble
to his master. "Sir," said John, "it grows dark, do you want a
light?"

"We want no light but what Heaven gives us," said Sir
Philip; "I knew not whether it was dark or light."

"I hope," said John, "nothing has happened, I hope your

honor has heard no bad tidings,—I—I—I hope no offense."

"None at all," said the good knight; "I am obliged to your solicitude for me. I have heard some things that grieve me, and others that give me great pleasure; but the sorrows are past, and the joys remain."

"Thank God!" said John. "I was afraid something was the matter to give your honor trouble."

"I thank you, my good servant! You see this young gentleman; I would have you, John, devote yourself to his service. I give you to him for an attendant on his person, and would have you show your affection to me by your attachment to him."

"Oh, sir!" said John in a melancholy voice, "what have I done to be turned out of your service?"

"No such matter, John," said Sir Philip; "you will not leave my service."

"Sir," said John, "I would rather die than leave you."

"And, my lad, I like you too well to part with you; but in serving my friend you will serve me. Know, that this young man is my son."

"Your son, sir!" said John.

"Not my natural son, but my relation; my son by adoption, my heir!"

"And will he live with you, sir?"

"Yes, John; and I hope to die with him."

"Oh, then, I will serve him with all my heart and soul; and I will do my best to please you both."

"I thank you, John, and I will not forget your honest love and duty. I have so good an opinion of you that I will tell you of some things concerning this gentleman that will entitle him to your respect."

"'Tis enough for me," said John, "to know that your honor respects him to make me pay him as much duty as yourself."

"But, John, when you know him better, you will respect him still more; at present, I shall only tell you what he is not; for you think him only the son of Andrew Twyford."

"And is he not?" said John.

"No; but his wife nursed him, and he passed for her son."

"And does old Twyford know it, sir?"

"He does, and will bear witness to it; but he is the son of a near friend of mine, of quality superior to my own, and as such you must serve and respect him."

"I shall, to be sure, sir; but what name shall I call him?"

"You shall know that hereafter; in the meantime bring a light, and wait on us to the other parlor."

When John was withdrawn, Sir Philip said, "That is a point to be considered and determined immediately. It is proper that you should assume a name till you can take that of your father; for I choose you should drop that of your foster-father; and I would have you be called by one that is respectable."

"In that, and every other point, I will be wholly governed by you, sir," said Edmund.

"Well then, I will give you the name of Seagrave. I shall say that you are a relation of my own; and my mother was really of that family."

John soon returned, and attended them into the other parlor. Sir Philip entered, with Edmund, hand in hand. "My friends," said he, "this gentleman is Mr. Edmund Seagrave, the son of a dear friend and relation of mine. He was lost in his infancy, brought up by a good woman out of pure humanity, and is but lately restored to his own family. The circumstances shall be made known hereafter. In the meantime, I have taken him under my care and protection and will use all my power and interest to see him restored to his fortune, which is enjoyed by the usurper who was the cause of his expulsion and the death of his parents. Receive him as my relation, and friend. Zadisky, do you embrace him first. Edmund, you and this gentleman must love each other for my sake; hereafter you will do it for your own."

They all rose, each embraced and congratulated the young man. Zadisky said, "Sir, whatever griefs and misfortunes you may have endured, you may reckon them at an end, from the hour you are beloved and protected by Sir Philip Harclay."

"I firmly believe it, sir," replied Edmund; "and my heart enjoys, already, more happiness than I ever yet felt, and promise me all that I can wish in future. His friendship is the earnest Heaven gives me of its blessings hereafter."

They sat down to supper with mutual cheerfulness; and Edmund enjoyed the repast with more satisfaction than he had felt a long time. Sir Philip saw his countenance brighten up, and looked on him with heart-felt pleasure. "Every time I look on you," said he, "reminds me of your father; you are the same person I loved twenty-three years ago. I rejoice to see you under my roof. Go to your repose early, and tomorrow we will consult further." Edmund withdrew, and enjoyed a night of sweet undisturbed repose.

The next morning Edmund arose in perfect health and spirits; he waited on his benefactor. They were soon after joined by Zadisky, who showed great attention and respect to the youth, and offered him his best services without reserve. Edmund accepted them with equal respect and modesty; and finding himself at ease, began to display his amiable qualities. They breakfasted together; afterward, Sir Philip desired Edmund to walk out with him.

As soon as they were out of hearing, Sir Philip said, "I could not sleep last night for thinking of your affairs; I laid schemes for you and rejected them again. We must lay our plan before we begin to act. What shall be done with this treacherous kinsman! This inhuman monster! This assassin of his nearest relation? I will risk my life and fortune to bring him to justice. Shall I go to court, and demand justice of the King? Or shall I accuse him of the murder and make him stand a public trial? If I treat him as a Baron of the realm, he must be tried by his peers; if as a commoner, he must be tried at the county assize. But we must show reason why he should be degraded from his title. Have you anything to propose?"

"Nothing, sir; I have only to wish that it might be as private as possible, for the sake of my noble benefactor, the Lord Fitz-Owen, upon whom some part of the family disgrace would naturally fall; and that would be an ill return for all his kindness and generosity to me."

"That is a generous and grateful consideration on your part; but you owe still more to the memory of your injured parents. However, there is yet another way that suits me better than any hitherto proposed. I will challenge the traitor to meet me in the field; and, if he has spirit enough to answer my call, I will there bring him to justice; if not, I will bring him to a public trial."

"No, sir," said Edmund, "that is my province. Should I stand by and see my noble, gallant friend expose his life for me, I should be unworthy to bear the name of that friend whom you so much lament. It will become his son to vindicate his name and revenge his death. I will be the challenger, and no other."

"And do you think he will answer the challenge of an unknown youth with nothing but his pretentions to his name and title? Certainly not. Leave this matter to me. I think of a way that will oblige him to meet me at the house of a third person who is known to all the parties concerned, and where we will have authentic witnesses of all that passes between him and me. I will devise the time, place, and manner, and satisfy all your scruples." Edmund offered to reply; but Sir Philip bade him be silent, and let him proceed in his own way.

He then led him over his estate and showed him everything deserving his notice; he told him all the particulars of his domestic economy, and they returned home in time to meet their friends at dinner.

They spent several days in consulting how to bring Sir Walter to account and in improving their friendship and confidence in each other. Edmund endeared himself so much to his friend and patron that he declared him his adopted son and heir before all his friends and servants, and ordered them to respect him as such. He every day improved their love and regard for him, and became the darling of the whole family.

After much consideration, Sir Philip fixed his resolutions and began to execute his purposes. He set out for the seat of the Lord Clifford, attended by Edmund, M. Zadisky, and two servants. Lord Clifford received them with kindness and hospitality.

Sir Philip presented Edmund to Lord Clifford and his family as his near relation and presumptive heir. They spent the evening in the pleasures of convivial mirth and hospitable entertainment. The next day Sir Philip began to open his mind to Lord Clifford, informing him that both his young friend and himself had received great injuries from the present Lord Lovel, for which they were resolved to call him to account; but that, for many reasons, they were desirous to have proper witnesses of all that should pass between them, and begging the favor of his lordship to be the principal one. Lord Clifford acknowledged the confidence placed in him; and besought Sir Philip to let him be the arbitrator between them. Sir Philip assured him that their wrongs would not admit of arbitration, as he should hereafter judge; but that he was unwilling to explain them further till he knew certainly whether or not the Lord Lovel would meet him; for, if he refused, he must take another method with him.

Lord Clifford was desirous to know the grounds of the quarrel; but Sir Philip declined entering into particulars at present, assuring him of a full information hereafter. He then sent M. Zadisky, attended by John Wyatt and a servant of Lord Clifford, with a letter to Lord Lovel; the contents were as follows:

"My Lord Lovel!

"Sir Philip Harclay earnestly desires to see you at the house of Lord Clifford, where he waits to call you to account for the injuries done by you to the late Arthur Lord Lovel, your kinsman. If you accept his demand, he will make the Lord Clifford a witness and a judge of the cause; if not, he will expose you publicly as a traitor and a coward. Please to answer this letter, and he will acquaint you with the time, place and manner of the meeting.

PHILIP HARCLAY."

Zadisky presented the letter to Lord Lovel, informing him that he was the friend of Sir Philip Harclay. He seemed surprised and confounded at the contents; but, putting on a haughty air; "I know nothing," said he, "of the business this letter hints at! But wait a few hours, and I will give you an answer." He gave orders to treat Zadisky as a gentleman in every respect, except in avoiding his company; for the Greek had a shrewd and penetrating aspect, and he observed every turn of his countenance. The next day he came and apologized for his absence, and gave him the answer, sending his respects to the Lord Clifford. The messengers returned with all speed, and Sir Philip read the answer before all present.

"Lord Lovel knows not of any injuries done by him to the late Arthur Lord Lovel, whom he succeeded by just right of inheritance; nor of any right Sir Philip Harclay has to call to account a man to whom he is barely known, having seen him only once, many years ago, at the house of his uncle, the old Lord Lovel. Nevertheless, Lord Lovel will not suffer any man to call his name and honor into question with impunity; for which reason he will meet Sir Philip Harclay at any time, place, and in what manner he shall appoint, bringing the same number of friends and dependents, that justice may be done to all parties.

LOVEL."

" 'Tis well," said Sir Philip; "I am glad to find he has the spirit to meet me; he is an enemy worthy of my sword."

Lord Clifford then proposed that both parties should pass the borders and obtain leave of the warden of the Scottish marshes to decide the quarrel in his jurisdiction, with a select number of friends on both sides. Sir Philip agreed to the proposal; and Lord Clifford wrote in his own name to ask permission of the Lord Graham that his friends might come there; and obtained it, on condition that neither party should exceed a limited number of friends and followers.

Lord Clifford sent chosen messengers to Lord Lovel, acquainting him with the conditions, and appointing the time, place, and manner of their meeting, and that he had been desired to accept the office of judge of the field. Lord Lovel accepted the conditions and promised to be there without fail. Lord Clifford notified the same to Lord Graham, warden of the marshes, who caused a piece of ground to be inclosed for the lists and made preparations against the day appointed.

In the interim, Sir Philip Harclay thought proper to settle his worldly affairs. He made Zadisky acquainted with every circumstance of Edmund's history, and the obligation that lay upon him to revenge the death of his friend and see justice done to his heir. Zadisky entered into the cause with an ardor that spoke the affection he bore to his friend. "Why," said he, "would you not suffer me to engage this traitor? Your life is of too much consequence to be staked against his. But though I trust that the justice of your cause must succeed, yet, if it should happen otherwise, I vow to revenge you; he shall never go back from us both. However, my hope and trust is, to see your arm the minister of justice." Sir Philip then sent for a lawyer and made his will, by which he appointed Edmund his chief heir, by the name of Lovel, alias Seagrave, alias Twyford; he ordered that all his old friends, soldiers, and servants, should be maintained in the same manner during their lives; he left to Zadisky an annuity of a hundred a year and a legacy of two hundred pounds; one hundred pounds to a certain monastery; the same sum to be distributed among disbanded soldiers, and the same to the poor and needy in his neighborhood.

He appointed Lord Clifford joint executor with Edmund, and gave his will into that nobleman's care, recommending Edmund to his favor and protection. "If I live," said he, "I will make him appear to be worthy of it; if I die, he will want a friend. I am desirous your lordship, as a judge of the field, should be unprejudiced on either side, that you may judge impartially. If I die, Edmund's pretentions die with me; but my friend Zadisky will acquaint you with the foundation of them. I take these precautions because I ought to be prepared for everything; but my heart is warm with better hopes, and I trust I shall live to justify my own cause, as well as that of my friend, who is a person of more consequence than he appears to be." Lord Clifford accepted the truth and expressed the greatest reliance upon Sir Philip's honor and veracity.

While these preparations were in the making for the great event that was to decide the pretensions of Edmund, his enemies at the Castle of Lovel were brought to shame for their behavior to him.

The disagreement between Wenlock and Markham had by degrees brought on an explanation of some parts of their conduct. Father Oswald had often hinted to the Baron, Wenlock's envy of Edmund's superior qualities, and the artifices by which he had obtained such an influence with Sir Robert, as to make him take his part upon all occasions. Oswald now took advantage of the breach between these two incendiaries to persuade Markham to justify himself at Wenlock's expense and to tell all he knew of his wickedness; at length, he promised to declare all he knew of Wenlock's conduct, as well in France as since their return, when he should be called upon; and, by him, Oswald was enabled to unravel the whole of his contrivances against the honor, interest, and even life of Edmund.

He prevailed on Hewson and Kemp, his associate, to add their testimony to the others. Hewson confessed that he was touched in his conscience when he reflected on the cruelty and injustice of his behavior to Edmund, whose behavior toward him, after he had laid a snare for his life, was so noble and generous that he was cut to the heart by it and had suffered so much pain and remorse that he longed for nothing so much as an opportunity to unburden his mind; but the dread of Mr. Wenlock's anger, and the effects of his resentment, had hitherto kept him silent, always hoping there would come a time when he might have leave to declare the whole truth.

Oswald conveyed this information to the Baron's ear, who waited for an opportunity to make the proper use of it. Not long after, the two principal incendiaries came to an open rupture, and Markham threatened Wenlock that he would show his uncle what a serpent he had harbored in his bosom. The Baron arrested his words and insisted upon his telling all he knew, adding, "if you speak the truth, I will support you; but if you prove false, I will punish you severely. As to Mr. Wenlock, he shall have a fair trial; and, if all the accusations I have heard are made good, it is high time that I should put him out of my family." The Baron, with a stern aspect, bade them follow him into the great hall, and sent for all the rest of the family together.

He then, with great solemnity, told them he was ready to hear all sides of the question. He declared the whole substance of his informations, and called upon the accusers to support the charge. Hewson and Kemp gave the same account they had done to Oswald, offering to swear to the truth of their testimony; several of the other servants related such circumstances as had come to their knowledge. Markham then spoke of everything, and gave a particular account of all that had passed on the night they spent in the East apartment; he accused himself of being privy to Wenlock's villainy, called himself fool and blockhead for being the instrument of his malignant disposition, and asked pardon of his uncle for concealing it so long.

The Baron called upon Wenlock to reply to the charge, who, instead of answering, flew into a passion, raged, swore, threatened, and finally denied everything. The witnesses persisted in their assertions. Markham desired leave to make known the reason why they were all afraid of him; "he gives it out" (said he), "that he is to be my lord's son-in-law; and they, supposing him to stand first in his favor, are afraid of his displeasure."

"I hope," said the Baron, "I shall not be at such a loss for a son-in-law as to make choice of such a one as him; he never but once hinted at such a thing, and then I gave him no encouragement. I have long seen there was something very wrong in him; but I did not believe he was of so wicked a disposition. It is no wonder that princes should be so frequently deceived, when I, a private man, could be so much imposed upon within the circle of my own family. What think you, son Robert?"

"I, sir, have been much more imposed on; and I take shame to myself on the occasion."

"Enough, my son," said the Baron; "a generous confession is only a proof of growing wisdom. You are now sensible that the best of us are liable to imposition. The artifices of this unworthy kinsman have set us at variance with each other, and driven away an excellent youth from this house to go I know not whither. But he shall no longer triumph in his wickedness; he shall feel what it is to be banished from the house of his protector. He shall set out for his mother's this very day; I will write to her in such a manner as shall inform her that he has offended me, without particularizing the nature of his faults. I will give him an opportunity of recovering his credit with his own family, and this shall be my security against his doing further mischief. May he repent, and be forgiven!

"Markham deserves punishment, but not in the same degree."

"I confess it," said he, "and will submit to whatever your lordship shall enjoin."

"You shall only be banished for a time, but he forever. I will send you abroad on a business that shall put you in a way to do credit to yourself and service to me. Son Robert, have you any objection to my sentence?"

"My lord," said he, "I have great reason to distrust myself; I am sensible of my own weakness, and your superior wisdom, as well as goodness; and I will henceforward submit to you in all things."

The Baron ordered two of his servants to pack up Wenlock's clothes and necessaries, and to set out with him that very day; he bade some others keep an eye upon him lest he should escape. As soon as they were ready, my lord wished him a good journey, and gave him a letter for his mother. He departed without saying a word, in a sullen kind of resentment, but his countenance showed the inward agitations of his mind.

As soon as he was was gone, every mouth was opened against him; a thousand stories came out that they never heard before. The Baron and his sons were astonished that he should go on so long without detection. My lord sighed deeply at the thoughts of Edmund's expulsion, and ardently wished to know what was become of him.

Sir Robert took the opportunity of coming to an explanation with his brother William; he took shame to himself for some part of his past behavior. Mr. William owned his affection to Edmund, and justified it by his merit and attachment to him, which were such that he was certain no time or distance could alter them. He accepted his brother's acknowledgment as a full amends for all that had passed, and begged that henceforward an entire love and confidence might ever subsist between them. These new regulations restored peace, confidence, and harmony in the Castle of Lovel.

At length, the day arrived for the combatants to meet. The Lord Graham, with twelve followers gentlemen, and twelve servants, was ready at the dawn of day to receive them.

The first that entered the field was Sir Philip Harclay,

knight, armed completely, excepting his headpiece; Hugh Rugby, his esquire, bearing his lance; John Barnard, his page, carrying his helmet and spurs; and two servants in his proper livery. The next came Edmund, the heir of Lovel, followed by his servant John Wyatt; Zadisky, followed by his servant.

At a short distance came the Lord Clifford, as judge of the field, with his esquire, two pages, and two livery-servants; followed by his eldest son, his nephew, and a gentleman his friend, each attended by one servant. He also brought a surgeon of note to take care of the wounded.

The Lord Graham saluted them; and, by his order, they took their places without the lists, and the trumpet sounded for the challenger. It was answered by the defendant, who soon after appeared, attended by three gentlemen his friends, with each one servant, beside his own proper attendants.

A place was erected for the Lord Clifford, as judge of the field; he desired Lord Graham would share the office, who accepted it, on condition that the combatants should make no objection, and they agreed to it with the greatest courtesy and respect. They consulted together on many points of honor and ceremony between the two combatants.

They appointed a marshal of the field and other inferior officers usually employed on these occasions. The Lord Graham sent the marshal for the challenger, desiring him to declare the cause of his quarrel before his enemy. Sir Philip Harclay then advanced, and thus spoke:

"I Philip Harclay, knight, challenge Walter, commonly called Lord Lovel, as a base, treacherous, and bloody man, who, by his wicked arts and devices, did kill, or cause to be killed, his kinsman, Arthur Lord Lovel, my dear and noble friend. I am called upon, in an extraordinary manner, to revenge his death; and I will prove the truth of what I have affirmed at the peril of my life."

Lord Graham then bade the defendant answer to the charge. Lord Lovel stood forth before his followers, and thus replied:

"I Walter, Baron of Lovel, do deny the charge against me, and affirm it to be a base, false, and malicious accusation of this Sir Philip Harclay, which I believe to be invented by himself, or else framed by some enemy and told to him for wicked ends; but, be that as it may, I will maintain my own honor, and prove him to be a false traitor, at the hazard of my own life and to the punishment of his presumption."

Then said the Lord Graham, "Will not this quarrel admit of arbitration?"

"No," replied Sir Philip. "When I have justified this charge, I have more to bring against him. I trust in God and the justice of my cause, and defy that traitor to the death!"

Lord Clifford then spoke a few words to Lord Graham, who immediately called to the marshal, and bade him open the lists and deliver their weapons to the combatants.

While the marshal was arranging the combatants and their followers, Edmund approached his friend and patron; he put one knee to the ground, he embraced his knees with the strongest emotions of grief and anxiety. He was dressed in complete armor, with his visor down; his device was a hawthorn, with a graft of the rose upon it, the motto—*This is not my true parent;*—but Sir Philip bade him take these words— *E fructu arbor cognoscitur.*[13]

Sir Philip embraced the youth with strong marks of affection. "Be composed, my child!" said he. "I have neither guilt, fear, nor doubt in me; I am so certain of success, that I bid you be prepared for the consequence."

Zadisky embraced his friend, he comforted Edmund, he suggested everything that could confirm his hopes of success.

The marshal waited to deliver the spear to Sir Philip; he now presented it with the usual form. "Sir, receive your lance, and God defend the right!" Sir Philip answered, "Amen!" in a voice that was heard by all present.

He next presented his weapon to Lord Lovel with the same sentence, who likewise answered, "Amen!" with a good courage. Immediately the lists were cleared, and the combatants began the fight.

They contended a long time with equal skill and courage; at length Sir Philip unhorsed his antagonist. The judges ordered that either he should alight or suffer his enemy to remount; he chose the former, and a short combat on foot ensued. The sweat ran off their bodies with the violence of the exercise. Sir Philip watched every motion of his enemy, and strove to weary him out, intending to wound, but not to kill him, unless obliged for his own safety.

He thrust his sword through his left arm, and demanded

[13] "And the tree is known from its fruit." *Matthew* XII, 33.

whether he would confess the fact? Lord Lovel enraged, answered, he would die sooner. Sir Philip then passed the sword through his body twice, and Lord Lovel fell, crying out that he was slain.

"I hope not," said Sir Philip, "for I have a great deal of business for you to do before you die. Confess your sins and endeavor to atone for them, as the only ground to hope for pardon."

Lord Lovel replied, "You are the victor, use your good fortune generously!"

Sir Philip took away his sword, and then waved it over his head, and beckoned for asistance. The judges sent to beg Sir Philip to spare the life of his enemy. "I will," said he, "upon condition that he will make an honest confession."

Lord Lovel desired a surgeon and a confessor. "You shall have both," said Sir Philip; "but you must first answer me a question or two. Did you kill your kinsman or not?"

"It was not my hand that killed him," answered the wounded man.

"It was done by your own order, however? You shall have no assistance till you answer this point."

"It was," said he, "and Heaven is just!"

"Bear witness, all present," said Sir Philip; "he confesses the fact!"

He then beckoned Edmund, who approached. "Take off your helmet," said he. "Look on that youth, he is the son of your injured kinsman."

"It is himself!" said the Lord Lovel, and fainted away.

Sir Philip then called for a surgeon and a priest, both of which Lord Graham had provided; the former began to bind up his wounds, and his assistants poured a cordial into his mouth. "Preserve his life, if it be possible," said Sir Philip; "for much depends upon it."

He then took Edmund by the hand and presented him to all the company. "In this young man," said he, "you see the true heir of the house of Lovel! Heaven has in its own way made him the instrument to discover the death of his parents. His father was assassinated by order of that wicked man, who now receives his punishment; his mother was, by his cruel treatment, compelled to leave her own house; she was delivered in the fields, and perished herself in seeking a shelter for her infant. I have sufficient proofs of everything I say, which I am ready to communicate to every person who desires to know the particulars. Heaven, by my hand, has chastised him; he has confessed the fact I accuse him of, and it remains that he make restitution of the fortune and honor he hath usurped so long."

Edmund kneeled, and with uplifted hands returned thanks to Heaven that his noble friend and champion was crowned with victory! The lords and gentlemen gathered round them; they congratulated them both while Lord Lovel's friends and followers were employed in taking care of him. Lord Clifford took Sir Philip's hand. "You have acted with so much honor and prudence that it is presumptuous to offer you advice; but what mean you to do with the wounded man?"

"I have not determined," said he; "I thank you for the hint, and beg your advice how to proceed."

"Let us consult Lord Graham," replied he.

Lord Graham insisted upon their going all to his castle. "There," said he, "you will have impartial witnesses of all that passes." Sir Philip was unwilling to give so much trouble. The Lord Graham protested he should be proud to do any service to so noble a gentleman. Lord Clifford enforced his request, saying it was better upon all accounts to keep their prisoner on this side the borders till they saw what turn his health would take, and to keep him safely till he had settled his worldly affairs.

This resolution being taken, Lord Graham invited the wounded man and his friends to his castle as being the nearest place where he could be lodged and taken proper care of, it being dangerous to carry him further. They accepted the proposal with many acknowledgments; and, having made a kind of litter of boughs, they all proceeded to Lord Graham's castle, where they put Lord Lovel to bed, and the surgeon dressed his wounds and desired he might be kept quiet, not knowing at present whether they were dangerous or not.

About an hour after, the wounded man complained of thirst; he asked for the surgeon, and inquired if his life was in danger. The surgeon answered him doubtfully. He asked "Where is Sir Philip Harclay?"

"In the castle."

"Where is that young man whom he calls the heir of Lovel?"

"He is here, too."

"Then I am surrounded with my enemies. I want to speak to one of my own servants without witnesses; let one be sent to me."

The surgeon withdrew, and acquainted the gentlemen below. "He shall not speak to any man," said Sir Philip, "but in my presence." He went with him into the sick man's room.

Upon the sight of Sir Philip, he seemed in great agitation. "Am I not allowed to speak with my own servant?" said he.

"Yes, sir, you may; but not without witnesses."

"Then I am a prisoner, it seems?"

"No, not so, sir; but some caution is necessary at present. But compose yourself, I do not wish for your death."

"Then why did you seek it? I never injured you."

"Yes, you have, in the person of my friend, and I am only the instrument of justice in the hand of Heaven; endeavor to make atonement while life is spared to you.—Shall I send the priest to you? Perhaps he may convince you of the necessity of restitution in order to obtain forgiveness of your sins."

Sir Philip sent for the priest and the surgeon, and obliged the servant to retire with him. "I leave you, sir, to the care of these gentlemen; and whenever a third person is admitted, I will be his attendant. I will visit you again within an hour." He then retired, and consulted his friends below; they were of opinion that no time should be lost. "You will then," said he, "accompany me into the sick man's apartment in an hour's time."

Within the hour, Sir Philip, attended by Lord Clifford and Lord Graham, entered the chamber. Lord Lovel was in great emotion; the priest stood on one side of the bed, the surgeon on the other; the former exhorted him to confess his sins, the other desired he might be left to his repose. Lord Lovel seemed in great anguish of mind; he trembled, and was in the utmost confusion. Sir Philip intreated him, with the piety of a confessor, to consider his soul's health before that of his body. He then asked Sir Philip, by what means he knew that he was concerned in the death of his kinsman?

"Sir," replied he, "it was not merely by human means this fact was discovered. There is a certain apartment in the Castle of Lovel, that has been shut up these one and twenty years, but has lately been opened and examined into."

"Oh Heaven!" exclaimed he, "then Geoffry must have betrayed me!"

"No, sir, he has not, it was revealed in a very extraordinary manner to that youth whom it most concerns."

"How can he be the heir of Lovel?"

"By being the son of that unfortunate woman whom you

cruelly obliged to leave her own house to avoid being compelled to wed the murderer of her husband. We are not ignorant, moreover, of the fictitious funeral you made for her. All is discovered, and you will not tell us any more than we know already; but we desire to have it confirmed by your confession."

"The judgments of Heaven are fallen upon me!" said Lord Lovel. "I am childless, and one is arisen from the grave to claim my inheritance."

"Nothing, then, hinders you to do justice and make restitution; it is for the ease of your conscience; and you have no other way of making atonement for all the mischief you have done."

"You know too much," said the criminal, "and I will relate what you do not know."

"You may remember," proceeded he, "that I saw you once at my uncle's house?"

"I well remember it."

"At that time my mind was disturbed by the baleful passion of envy; it was from that root all my bad actions sprung."

"Praise be to God!" said the good priest. "He hath touched your heart with true contrition, and you show the effect of His mercies; you will do justice, and you will be rewarded by the gift of repentance unto salvation." Sir Philip desired the penitent to proceed.

"My kinsman excelled me in every kind of merit, in the graces of person and mind, in all his exercises, and in every accomplishment. I was totally eclipsed by him, and I hated to be in his company; but what finished my aversion was his addressing the lady upon whom I had fixed my affections. I strove to rival him there, but she gave him the preference that, indeed, was only his due; but I could not bear to see, or acknowledge, it.

"The most bitter hatred took possession of my breast, and I vowed to revenge the supposed injury as soon as opportunity should offer. I buried my resentment deep in my heart, and outwardly appeared to rejoice at his success; I made a merit of resigning my pretensions to him, but I could not bear to be present at his nuptials. I retired to my father's seat, and brooded over my revenge in secret. My father died this year, and soon after my uncle followed him; within another year my kinsman was summoned to attend the King on his Welsh expedition.

"As soon as I heard he was gone from home, I resolved to prevent his return, exulting in the prospect of possessing his title, fortune, and his lady. I hired messengers, who were constantly going and coming to give me intelligence of all that passed at the castle; I went there soon after, under pretense of visiting my kinsman. My spies brought me an account of all that happened; one informed me of the event of the battle, but could not tell whether my rival was living or dead; I hoped the latter, that I might avoid the crime I meditated. I reported his death to his lady, who took it very heavily.

"Soon after a messenger arrived with tidings that he was alive and well, and had obtained leave to return home immediately.

"I instantly dispatched my two emissaries to intercept him on the way. He made so much haste to return, that he was met within a mile of his own castle. He had outridden his servants, and was alone. They killed him and drew him aside out of the highway. They then came to me with all speed and desired my orders; it was then about sunset. I sent them back to fetch the dead body, which they brought privately into the castle. They tied it neck and heels, and put it into a trunk, which they buried under the floor in the closet you mentioned. The sight of the body stung me to the heart; I then felt the pangs of remorse, but it was too late. I took every precaution that prudence suggested to prevent the discovery; but nothing can be concealed from the eye of Heaven.

"From that fatal hour I have never known peace, always in fear of something impending to discover my guilt, and to bring me to shame. At length I am overtaken by justice. I am brought to a severe reckoning here, and I dread to meet one more severe hereafter."

"Enough," said the priest; "you have done a good work, my son! Trust in the Lord; and, now this burden is off your mind, the rest will be made easy to you."

Lord Lovel took a minute's repose, and then went on. "I hope by the hint you gave, Sir Philip, the poor lady is yet alive?"

"No, sir, she is not; but she died not till after she brought forth a son, whom Heaven made its instrument to discover and avenge the death of both his parents."

"They are well avenged!" said he. "I have no children to lament for me; all mine have been taken from me in the bloom of youth; only one daughter lived to be twelve years old;

I intended her for a wife for one of my nephews, but within three months I have buried her." He sighed, wept, and was silent.

The gentlemen present lifted up their hands and eyes to Heaven in silence. "The will of Heaven be obeyed!" said the priest. "My penitent hath confessed all; what more would you require?"

"That he make atonement," said Sir Philip; "that he surrender the title and estate to the right heir, and dispose of his own proper fortune to his nearest relations, and resign himself to penitence and preparation for a future state. For this time I leave him with you, Father, and will join my prayers with yours for his repentance."

So saying, he left the room, and was followed by the barons and the surgeon, the priest alone remaining with him. As soon as they were out of hearing, Sir Philip questioned the surgeon concerning his patient's situation, who answered that at present he saw no signs of immediate danger, but he could not yet pronounce that there was none; "if he were mortally wounded," said he, "he could not be so well, nor speak so long without faintness; and it is my opinion that he will soon recover, if nothing happens to retard the cure."

"Then," said Sir Philip, "keep this opinion from him; for I would suffer the fear of death to operate on him until he hath performed some necessary acts of justice. Let it only be known to these noblemen, upon whose honor I can rely, and I trust they will approve my request to you, sir."

"I join in it," said Lord Clifford, "from the same motives."

"I insist upon it," said Lord Graham; "and I can answer for my surgeon's discretion."

"My lords," said the surgeon, "you may depend on my fidelity; and, after what I have just heard, my conscience is engaged in this noble gentleman's behalf, and I will do everything in my power to second your intentions."

"I thank you, sir," said Sir Philip, "and you may depend on my gratitude in return. I presume you will sit up with him to-night; if any danger should arise, I desire to be called immediately; but, otherwise, I would suffer him to rest quietly, that he may be prepared for the business of the following day."

"I shall obey your directions, sir; my necessary attendance will give me a pretense not to leave him, and thus I shall hear all that passes between him and all that visit him."

"You will oblige me highly," said Sir Philip, "and I shall go to rest with confidence in your care."

The surgeon returned to the sick man's chamber, Sir Philip and the barons to the company below. They supped in the great hall, with all the gentlemen that were present at the combat. Sir Philip and his Edmund retired to their repose, being heartily fatigued; and the company stayed to a late hour, commenting upon the action of the day, praising the courage and generosity of the noble knight, and wishing a good event to his undertaking.

Most of Lord Lovel's friends went away as soon as they saw him safely lodged, being ashamed of him and of their appearance in his behalf; and the few that stayed were induced by their desire of a further information of the base action he had committed, and to justify their own characters and conduct.

The next morning Sir Philip entered into consultation with the two barons on the methods he should take to get Edmund received and acknowledged as heir of the house of Lovel. They were all of opinion that the criminal should be kept in fear till he had settled his worldly affairs and they had resolved how to dispose of him. With this determination they entered his room, and inquired of the surgeon how he had passed the night. He shook his head and said but little.

Lord Lovel desired that he might be removed to his own house. Lord Graham said he could not consent to that as there was evident danger in removing him, and appealed to the surgeon, who confirmed his opinion. Lord Graham desired he would make himself easy, and that he should have every kind of assistance there.

Sir Philip then proposed to send for the Lord Fitz-Owen, who would see that all possible care was taken of his brother-in-law and would assist him in settling his affairs. Lord Lovel was against it; he was peevish and uneasy, and desired to be left with only his own servants to attend him. Sir Philip quitted the room with a significant look; and the two lords endeavored to reconcile him to his situation. He interrupted them. "It is easy for men in your situation to advise, but it is difficult for one in mine to practice; wounded in body and mind, it is natural that I should strive to avoid the extremes of shame and punishment. I thank you for your kind offices, and beg I may be left with my own servants."

"With them, and the surgeon, you shall," said Lord Graham; and they both retired.

Sir Philip met them below. "My lords," said he, "I am desirous that my Lord Fitz-Owen should be sent for, and that he may hear his brother's confession; for I suspect that he may hereafter deny what only the fear of death has extorted from him. With your permission I am determined to send messengers today."

They both expressed approbation, and Lord Clifford proposed to write to him, saying, a letter from an impartial person will have the more weight: "I will send one of my principal domestics with your own." This measure being resolved upon, Lord Clifford retired to write, and Sir Philip to prepare his servants for instant departure. Edmund desired leave to write to Father Oswald, and John Wyatt was ordered to be the bearer of his letter. When the Lord Clifford had finished his letter, he read it to Sir Philip and his chosen friends, as follows:

"Right Hon. my good Lord,
"I have taken upon me to acquaint your lordship that there has been a solemn combat at arms between your brother-in-law, the Lord Lovel, and Sir Philip Harclay, knt. of Yorkshire. It was fought in the jurisdiction of the Lord Graham, who, with myself, was appointed judge of the field; it was fairly won, and Sir Philip is the conqueror. After he had gained the victory he declared at large the cause of the quarrel, and that he had revenged the death of Arthur Lord Lovel his friend, whom the present Lord Lovel had assassinated that he might enjoy his title and estate. The wounded man confessed the fact; and Sir Philip gave him his life, and only carried off his sword as a trophy of his victory. Both the victor and the vanquished were conveyed to Lord Graham's castle, where the Lord Lovel now lies in great danger. He is desirous to settle his worldly affairs and to make his peace with God and man. Sir Philip Harclay says there is a male heir of the house of Lovel, for whom he claims the title and estate; but he is very desirous that your lordship should be present at the disposal of your brother's property that of right belongs to him, of which your children are the undoubted heirs. He also wants to consult you in many other points of honor and equity. Let me intreat you, on the receipt of this letter,

to set out immediately for Lord Graham's castle, where you
will be received with the utmost respect and hospitality.
You will hear things that will surprise you as much as they
do me; you will judge of them with that justice and honor
that speaks your character; and you will unite with us in
wondering at the ways of Providence and submitting to its
decrees in punishing the guilty and doing justice to the
innocent and oppressed. My best wishes and prayers attend
you and your hopeful family. My lord, I remain your humble servant,

"CLIFFORD."

Everyone present expressed the highest approbation of this
letter. Sir Philip gave orders to John Wyatt to be very circumspect in his behavior, to give Edmund's letter privately to
Father Oswald, and to make no mention of him or his pretensions to Lovel Castle.

Lord Clifford gave his servant the requisite precautions.
Lord Graham added a note of invitation, and sent it by a
servant of his own. As soon as all things were ready, the
messengers set out with all speed for the Castle of Lovel.

They stayed no longer by the way than to take some refreshment, but rode night and day till they arrived there.

Lord Fitz-Owen was in the parlor with his children. Father
Oswald was walking in the avenue before the house, when he
saw three messengers whose horses seemed jaded and the riders
fatigued like men come a long journey. He came up just as
the first had delivered his message to the porter. John Wyatt
knew him, he dismounted, and made signs that he had something to say to him; he retired back a few steps, and John,
with great dexterity, flipped a letter into his hand. The Father
gave him his blessing, and a welcome. "Who do you come
from?" said he aloud.

"From the Lords Graham and Clifford to the Lord Fitz-
Owen; and we bring letters of consequence to the Baron."

Oswald followed the messengers into the hall; a servant
announced their arrival. Lord Fitz-Owen received them in the
parlor. Lord Clifford's servant delivered his master's letter,
Lord Graham's his, and they said they would retire and wait
his lordship's answer. The Baron ordered them some refreshment. They retired, and he opened his letters. He read them
with great agitations, he struck his hand upon his heart, he

exclaimed—"My fears are all verified! The blow is struck, and it has fallen upon the guilty!"

Oswald came in a minute after. "You are come in good time," said the Baron. "Read that letter, that my children may know the contents."

He read it with faltering voice and trembling limbs. They were all in great surprise. William looked down and kept a studied silence. Sir Robert exclaimed—"Is it possible? Can my uncle be guilty of such an action?"

"You hear," said the Baron, "he has confessed it!"

"But to whom?" said Sir Robert.

His father replied, "Lord Clifford's honor is unquestionable, and I cannot doubt what he affirms."

Sir Robert leaned his head upon his hand, as one lost in thought. At length he seemed to awake. "My lord, I have no doubt that Edmund is at the bottom of this business. Do you not remember that Sir Philip Harclay long ago promised him his friendship? Edmund disappears; and, soon after, this man challenges my uncle. You know what passed here before his departure. He has suggested this affair to Sir Philip and instigated him to this action. This is the return he has made for the favors he has received from our family, to which he owes everything."

"Softly, my son!" said the Baron; "let us be cautious of reflecting upon Edmund. There is a greater hand in this business. My conjecture was too true. It was in that fatal apartment that he was made acquainted with the circumstances of Lord Lovel's death; he was, perhaps, enjoined to reveal them to Sir Philip Harclay, the bosom friend of the deceased. The mystery of that apartment is disclosed, the woe to the guilty is accomplished! There is no reflection upon anyone; Heaven effects its purposes in its own time and manner. I and mine are innocent; let us worship, and be silent!"

"But what do you propose to do?" said Sir Robert.

"To return with the messengers," answered the Baron. "I think it highly proper that I should see your uncle, and hear what he has to say. My children are his heirs; in justice to them, I ought to be acquainted with everything that concerns the disposal of his fortune."

"Your lordship is in the right," answered Sir Robert, "it concerns us all. I have only to ask your permission to bear you company."

"With all my heart," said the Baron. "I have only to ask

of you in return, that you will command yourself and not speak your mind hastily; wait for the proofs before you give judgment, and take advice of your reason before you decide upon anything; if you reflect upon the past, you will find reason to distrust yourself. Leave all to me, and be assured I will protect your honor and my own."

"I will obey you in all things, my lord; and will make immediate preparation for our departure." So saying, he left the room.

As soon as he was gone, Mr. William broke silence. "My lord," said he, "if you have no great objection, I beg leave also to accompany you both."

"You shall, my son, if you desire it; I think I can see your motives, and your brother's also; your coolness will be a good balance to his warmth. You shall go with us. My son Walter shall be his sister's protector in our absence, and he shall be master here till we return."

"I hope, my dear father, that will not be long; I shall not be happy till you come home," said the fair Emma.

"It shall be no longer, my dearest, than till this untoward affair is settled."

The Baron desired to know when the messengers were expected to return. Oswald took this opportunity to retire; he went to his own apartment, and read the letter, as follows:

"The heir of Lovel, to his dear and reverend friend, Father Oswald.

"Let my friends at the Castle of Lovel know that I live in hopes one day to see them there. If you could by any means return with the messengers, your testimony would add weight to mine; perhaps you might obtain permission to attend the Baron. I leave it to you to manage this. John Wyatt will inform you of all that has passed here, and that hitherto my success has outrun my expectation, and, almost, my wishes. I am in the high road to my inheritance; and trust that the Power who hath conducted me thus far will not leave His work unfinished. Tell my beloved William that I live, and hope to embrace him before long. I recommend myself to your holy prayers and blessing, and remain your son and servant,

EDMUND."

Oswald then went to the messengers; he drew John Wyatt to a distance from the rest and got the information he wanted.

He stayed with him till he was sent for by the Baron, to whom he went directly, and prevented his questions by saying, "I have been talking with the messengers. I find they have traveled night and day to bring the letters with all speed; they only require one night's rest, and will be ready to set out with you tomorrow."

"'Tis well," said the Baron; "we will set out as soon as they are ready."

"My lord," said Oswald, "I have a favor to beg of you; it is, that I may attend you. I have seen the progress of this wonderful discovery, and I have a great desire to see the conclusion of it; perhaps my presence may be of service in the course of your business."

"Perhaps it may," said the Baron; "I have no objection, if you desire to go." They then separated and went to prepare for their journey.

Oswald had a private interview with Joseph, whom he informed of all that he knew and his resolution to attend the Baron in his journey to the North. "I go," said he, "to bear witness in behalf of injured innocence. If it be needful, I shall call upon you; therefore hold yourself in readiness in case you should be sent for."

"That I will," said Joseph, "and spend my last remains of life and strength to help my young lord to his right and title; but do they not begin to suspect who is the heir of Lovel?"

"Not in the least," said Oswald; "they think him concerned in the discovery, but have no idea of his being interested in the event."

"Oh, Father!" said Joseph, "I shall think every day a week till your return; but I will no longer keep you from your repose."

"Good-night," said Oswald; "but I have another visit to pay before I go to rest."

He left Joseph, and went on tip-toe to Mr. William's room, and tapped at his door; he came and opened it. "What news, Father?"

"Not much; I have only orders to tell you that Edmund is well and as much your friend as ever."

"I guessed," said William, "that we should hear something of him. I have still another guess."

"What is that, my child?"

"That we shall see or hear of him where we are going."

"It is very likely," said Oswald; "and I would have you

be prepared for it. I am confident we shall hear nothing to his discredit."

"I am certain of that," said William, "and I shall rejoice to see him. I conclude that he is under the protection of Sir Philip Harclay."

"He is so," said Oswald; "I had my information from Sir Philip's servant, who is one of the messengers and was guide to the others in their way hither." After some further conversation they separated, and each went to his repose.

The next morning the whole party set out on their journey; they traveled by easy stages on account of the Baron's health, which began to be impaired, and arrived in health and spirits at the castle of Lord Graham, where they were received with the utmost respect and kindness by the noble master.

The Lord Lovel had recovered his health and strength as much as possible in the time, and was impatient to be gone from thence to his own house. He was surprised to hear of the arrival of his brother and nephews, and expressed no pleasure at the thoughts of seeing them. When Sir Philip Harclay came to pay his respects to Baron Fitz-Owen, the latter received him with civility, but with a coldness that was apparent. Sir Robert left the room, doubting his resolution. Sir Philip advanced, and took the Baron by the hand. "My lord," said he, "I rejoice to see you here. I cannot be satisfied with the bare civilities of such a man as you. I aspire to your esteem, to your friendship, and I shall not be happy till I obtain them. I will make you the judge of every part of my conduct, and where you shall condemn me, I will condemn myself."

The Baron was softened, his noble heart felt its alliance with its counterpart, but he thought the situation of his brother demanded some reserve toward the man who sought his life; but, in spite of himself, it wore off every moment. Lord Clifford related all that had passed, with the due regard to Sir Philip's honor; he remarked how nobly he concealed the cause of his resentment against the Lord Lovel till the day of combat, that he might not prepossess the judges against him. He enlarged on his humanity to the vanquished, on the desire he expressed to have justice done to his heirs; finally, he mentioned his great respect for the Lord Fitz-Owen, and the solicitude he showed to have him come to settle the estate of the sick man in favor of his children. Lord Clifford also employed his son to soften Sir Robert and to explain to him every doubtful part of Sir Philip's behavior.

After the travelers had taken some rest, the Lord Graham proposed that they should make a visit to the sick man's chamber. The lords sent to acquaint him when they were coming to visit him, and they followed the messenger. The Lord Fitz-Owen went up to the bedside; he embraced his brother with strong emotions of concern. Sir Robert followed him; then Mr. William. Lord Lovel embraced them, but said nothing; his countenance showed his inward agitations. Lord Fitz-Owen first broke silence. "I hope," said he, "I see my brother better than I expected?"

Lord Lovel bit his fingers; he pulled the bed-clothes; he seemed almost distracted; at length he broke out—"I owe no thanks to those who sent for my relations! Sir Philip Harclay, you have used ungenerously the advantage you have gained over me! You spared my life, only to take away my reputation. You have exposed me to strangers, and, what is worse, to my dearest friends; when I lay in a state of danger, you obliged me to say anything, and now you take advantage of it, to ruin me in my friends' affection. But, if I recover, you may repent it!"

Sir Philip then came forward. "My lords, I shall take no notice of what this unhappy man has just now said; I shall appeal to you, as to the honorable witnesses of all that has passed. You see it was no more than necessary. I appeal to you for the motives of my treatment of him, before, at, and after our meeting. I did not take his life, as I might have done; I wished him to repent of his sins and to make restitution of what he unjustly possesses. I was called out to do an act of justice; I had taken the heir of Lovel under my protection; my chief view was to see justice done to him; what regarded this man was but a secondary motive. This was my end, and I will never, never lose sight of it."

Lord Lovel seemed almost choked with passion to see everyone giving some mark of approbation and respect to Sir Philip. He called out, "I demand to know who is this pretended heir, whom he brings out to claim my title and fortune?"

"My noble auditors," said Sir Philip, "I shall appeal to your judgment in regard to the proofs of my ward's birth and family; every circumstance shall be laid before you, and you shall decide upon them.

"Here is a young man, supposed the son of a peasant, who, by a train of circumstances that could not have happened by human contrivance, discovers not only who were his real parents, but that they came to untimely deaths. He even discovers the different places where their bones are buried, both out of consecrated ground, and appeals to their ashes for the truth of his pretensions. He has also living proofs to offer that will convince the most incredulous. I have deferred entering into particulars till the arrival of Baron Fitz-Owen; I know his noble heart and honorable character from one that has long been an eye-witness of his goodness; such is the opinion I have of his justice, that I will accept him as one of the judges in his brother's cause. I and my ward will bring our proofs before him and the company here present; in the course of them, it will appear that he is the best qualified of any to judge of them, because he can ascertain many of the facts we shall have occasion to mention. I will rest our cause upon their decision."

Lord Graham applauded Sir Philip's appeal, affirming his own impartiality, and calling upon Lord Clifford and his son, and also his own nephews who were present. Lord Clifford said, "Sir Philip offers fairly, and like himself; there can be no place nor persons more impartial than the present, and I presume the Lord Lovel can have no objection."

"No objection!" answered he; "what, to be tried like a criminal, to have judges appointed over me, to decide upon my right to my own estate and title? I will not submit to such a jurisdiction!"

"Then," said Sir Philip, "you had rather be tried by the laws of the land, and have them pronounce sentence upon you? Take your choice, sir; if you refuse the one, you shall be certain of the other."

Lord Clifford then said, "You will allow Lord Lovel to consider of the proposal; he will consult his friends, and be determined by their advice."

Lord Fitz-Owen said, "I am very much surprised at what I have heard. I should be glad to know all that Sir Philip Harclay has to say for his ward, that I may judge what my brother has to hope or fear; I will then give my best advice, or offer my mediation, as he may stand in need of them."

"You say well," replied Lord Graham, "and pray let us come directly to the point. Sir Philip, you will introduce your ward to this company and enter upon your proofs."

Sir Philip bowed to the company; he went out and brought in Edmund, encouraging him by the way; he presented him to Baron Fitz-Owen, who looked very serious. "Edmund Twyford," said he, "are you the heir of the house of Lovel?"

"I am, my lord," said Edmund, bowing to the ground; "the proofs will appear; but I am, at the same time, the most humble and grateful of all your servants, and the servant of your virtues."

Sir Robert rose up, and was going to leave the room. "Son Robert, stay," said the Baron. "If there is any fraud, you will be pleased to detect it, and, if all that is affirmed be true, you will not shut your eyes against the light; you are concerned in this business; hear it in silence, and let reason be arbiter in your cause." He bowed to his father, bit his lip, and retired to the window. William nodded to Edmund, and was silent. All the company had their eyes fixed on the young man, who stood in the midst, casting down his eyes with modest respect to the audience; while Sir Philip related all the material circumstances of his life, the wonderful gradation by which he came to the knowledge of his birth, the adventures of the haunted apartment, the discovery of the fatal closet, and the presumptive proofs that Lord Lovel was buried there.

At this part of his narration, Lord Fitz-Owen interrupted him—"Where is this closet you talk of? For I and my sons went over the apartment since Edmund's departure, and found no such place as you describe."

"My lord," said Edmund, "I can account for it; the door is covered with tapestry, the same as the room, and you might easily overlook it; but I have a witness here," said he, and putting his hand into his bosom, he drew out the key. "If this is not the key of that closet, let me be deemed an impostor, and all I say a falsehood; I will risk my pretensions upon this proof."

"And for what purpose did you take it away?" said the Baron.

"To prevent any person from going into it," replied Edmund; "I have vowed to keep it till I shall open that closet before witnesses appointed for that purpose."

"Proceed, sir," said the Baron Fitz-Owen. Sir Philip then related the conversation between Edmund and Margery Twyford, his supposed mother. Lord Fitz-Owen seemed in the utmost surprise. He exclaimed, "Can this be true? Strange discovery! Unfortunate child!" Edmund's tears bore witness to his veracity; he was obliged to hide his face; he lifted up his clasped hands to Heaven and was in great emotions during all this part of the relation, while Lord Lovel groaned, and seemed in great agitation.

Sir Philip then addressed himself to Lord Fitz-Owen. "My lord, there was another person present at the conversation between Edmund and his foster-mother, who can witness to all that passed; perhaps your lordship can tell who that was?"

"It was Father Oswald," replied the Baron; "I well remember that he went with him at his request; let him be called in." He was sent for, and came immediately. The Baron desired him to relate all that passed between Edmund and his mother.

Oswald then began. "Since I am now properly called upon to testify what I know concerning this young man, I will speak the truth, without fear or favor of anyone; and I will swear, by the rules of my holy order, to the truth of what I shall relate." He then gave a particular account of all that passed on that occasion, and mentioned the tokens found on both the infant and his mother.

"Where are these tokens to be seen?" said the Lord Clifford.

"I have them here, my lord," said Edmund, "and I keep them as my greatest treasures." He then produced them before all the company.

"There is no appearance of any fraud or collusion," said Lord Graham; "if any man thinks he sees any, let him speak."

"Pray, my lord, suffer me to speak a word," said Sir Robert. "Do you remember that I hinted my suspicions concerning Father Oswald, the night our kinsmen lay in the East apartment?"

"I do," said the Baron.

"Well, sir, it now appears that he did know more than he would tell us; you find he is very deep in all Edmund's secrets, and you may judge what were his motives for undertaking this journey."

"I observe what you say," answered his father, "but let us hear all that Oswald has to say. I will be as impartial as possible."

"My lord," returned Oswald, "I beg you also to recollect what I said, on the night your son speaks of, concerning secrecy in certain matters."

"I remember that also," said the Baron; "but proceed."

"My lord," continued Oswald, "I knew more than I thought myself at liberty to disclose at that time; but I will now tell you everything. I saw there was something more than common in the accidents that befell this young man, and in his being called out to sleep in the East apartment; I earnestly desired him to let me be with him on the second night, to which he consented reluctantly; we heard a great noise in the rooms underneath; we went downstairs together. I saw him open the fatal closet; I heard groans that pierced me to the heart; I kneeled down and prayed for the repose of the spirit departed. I found a seal with the arms of Lovel engraven upon it, which I gave to Edmund and he now has it in his possession. He enjoined me to keep secret what I had seen and heard, till the time should come to declare it. I conceived that I was called to be a witness of these things; besides, my curiosity was excited to know the event; I, therefore, desired to be present at the interview between him and his mother, which was affecting beyond expression. I heard what I have now declared as nearly as my memory permits me. I hope no impartial person will blame me for any part of my conduct; but if they should, I do not repent it. If I should forfeit the favor of the rich and great, I shall have acquitted myself to God and my conscience. I have no worldly ends to answer; I plead the cause of the injured orphan; and I think, also, that I second the designs of Providence."

"You have well spoken, Father," said the Lord Clifford; "your testimony is indeed of consequence."

"It is amazing and convincing," said Lord Graham; "and the whole story is so well connected, that I can see nothing to make us doubt the truth of it. But let us examine the proofs." Edmund gave into their hands the necklace and ear-rings; he showed them the locket with the cipher of Lovel, and the seal with the arms; he told them the cloak, in which he was wrapped, was in the custody of his foster-mother, who would produce it on demand. He begged that some proper persons might be commissioned to go with him to examine whether or no the bodies of his parents were buried where he affirmed, adding that he put his pretensions into their hands with pleasure, relying entirely upon their honor and justice.

During this interesting scene, the criminal covered his face, and was silent; but he sent forth bitter sighs and groans that denoted the anguish of his heart. At length, Lord Graham, in compassion to him, proposed that they should retire and consider of the proofs, adding, "Lord Lovel must needs be fatigued; we will resume the subject in his presence, when he is disposed to receive us."

Sir Philip Harclay approached the bed. "Sir," said he, "I now leave you in the hands of your own relations; they are men of strict honor, and I confide in them to take care of you and of your concerns." They then went out of the room, leaving only the Lord Fitz-Owen and his sons with the criminal. They discoursed of the wonderful story of Edmund's birth and the principal events of his life.

After dinner, Sir Philip requested another conference with the lords and their principal friends. There were present also Father Oswald and Lord Graham's confessor, who had taken the Lord Lovel's confession, Edmund, and Zadisky. "Now, gentlemen," said Sir Philip, "I desire to know your opinion of our proofs and your advice upon them."

Lord Graham replied, "I am desired to speak for the rest. We think there are strong presumptive proofs that this young man is the true heir of Lovel; but they ought to be confirmed and authenticated. Of the murder of the late lord there is no doubt; the criminal hath confessed it, and the circumstances confirm it; the proofs of his crime are so connected with those of the young man's birth, that one cannot be public without the other. We are desirous to do justice; and yet are unwilling, for the Lord Fitz-Owen's sake, to bring the criminal to public shame and punishment. We wish to find out a medium; we therefore desire Sir Philip to make proposals for his ward, and let Lord Fitz-Owen answer for himself and his brother, and we will be moderators between them." Here everyone expressed approbation, and called upon Sir Philip to make his demands.

"If," said he, "I were to demand strict justice, I should not be satisfied with anything less than the life of the criminal; but I am a Christian soldier, the disciple of Him who came into the world to save sinners; for His sake," continued he (crossing himself), "I forego my revenge; I spare the guilty. If Heaven gives him time for repentance, man should not deny it. It is my ward's particular request, that I will not bring shame upon the house of his benefactor, the Lord Fitz-Owen, for whom he hath a filial affection and profound veneration. My proposals are these: First, that the criminal make restitution of the title and estate, obtained with so much injustice and cruelty, to the lawful heir, whom he shall acknowledge such before proper witnesses. Secondly, that he shall surrender his own lawful inheritance and personal estate into the hands of the Lord Fitz-Owen, in trust for his sons, who are his heirs of blood. Thirdly, that he shall retire into a religious house or else quit the kingdom in three months time; and, in either case, those who enjoy his fortune shall allow him a decent annuity, that he may not want the comforts of life. By the last, I disable him from the means of doing further mischief and enable him to devote the remainder of his days to penitence. These are my proposals, and I give him four-and-twenty hours to consider of them; if he refuses to comply with them, I shall be obliged to proceed to severer measures and to a public prosecution. But the goodness of the Lord Fitz-Owen bids me expect, from his influence with his brother, a compliance with proposals made out of respect to his honorable character."

Lord Graham applauded the humanity, prudence, and piety of Sir Philip's proposals. He enforced them with all his influence and eloquence. Lord Clifford seconded him; and the rest gave tokens of approbation. Sir Robert Fitz-Owen then rose up. "I beg leave to observe to the company, who are going to dispose so generously of another man's property, that my father purchased the castle and estate of the house of Lovel. Who is to repay him the money for it?"

Sir Philip then said, "I have also a question to ask. Who is to pay the arrears of my ward's estate, which he has unjustly been kept out of these one-and-twenty years? Let Lord Clifford answer to both points, for he is not interested in either."

Lord Clifford smiled. "I think," returned he, "the first question is answered by the second, and that the parties concerned should set one against the other, especially as Lord Fitz-Owen's children will inherit the fortune, which includes the purchase-money."

Lord Graham said, "This determination is both equitable and generous, and I hope will answer the expectations on all sides."

"I have another proposal to make to my Lord Fitz-Owen," said Sir Philip; "but I first wait for the acceptance of those already made."

Lord Fitz-Owen replied, "I shall report them to my brother, and acquaint the company with his resolution tomorrow."

They then separated; and the Baron, with his sons, returned to the sick man's chamber; there he exhorted his brother, with the piety of a confessor, to repent of his sins and make atonement for them. He made known Sir Philip's proposals and observed on the wonderful discovery of his crime and the punishment that followed it. "Your repentance," continued he, "may be accepted, and your crime may yet be pardoned. If you continue refractory and refuse to make atonement, you will draw down upon you a severer punishment." The criminal would not confess, and yet could not deny, the truth and justice of his observations. The Baron spent several hours in his brother's chamber; he sent for a priest, who took his confession; and they both sat up with him all night, advising, persuading, and exhorting him to do justice and to comply with the proposals. He was unwilling to give up the world, and yet more so to become the object of public shame, disgrace, and punishment.

The next day, Lord Fitz-Owen summoned the company into his brother's chamber, and there declared, in his name, that he accepted Sir Philip Harclay's proposals; that, if the young man could, as he promised, direct them to the places where his parents were buried, and if his birth should be authenticated by his foster-parents, he should be acknowledged the heir of the house of Lovel. That, to be certified of these things, they must commission proper persons to go with him for this purpose; and, in case the truth should be made plain, they should immediately put him in possession of the castle and estate, in the state it was. He desired Lord Graham and Lord Clifford to choose the commissioners, and gave Sir Philip and Edmund a right to add to them, each, another person.

Lord Graham named the eldest son of Lord Clifford; and the other, in return, named his nephew; they also chose the priest, Lord Graham's confessor, and the eldest son of Baron Fitz-Owen, to his great mortification. Sir Philip appointed Mr. William Fitz-Owen, and Edmund named Father Oswald; they chose out the servants to attend them, who were also to be witnesses of all that should pass. Lord Clifford proposed to Baron Fitz-Owen that, as soon as the commissioners were set out, the remainder of the company should adjourn to his seat in Cumberland, whither Lord Graham should be invited to accompany them and to stay till this affair was decided. After some debate, this was agreed to; and, at the same time, that the criminal should be kept with them till everything was properly settled.

Lord Fitz-Owen gave his son William the charge to receive and entertain the commissioners at the castle. But, before they set out, Sir Philip had a conference with Lord Fitz-Owen, concerning the surrender of the castle, in which he insisted on the furniture and stock of the farm, in consideration of the arrears. Lord Fitz-Owen slightly mentioned the young man's education and expenses. Sir Philip answered, "You are right, my lord; I had not thought of this point; we owe you, in this respect, more than we can ever repay. But you know not half the respect and affection Edmund bears for you. When restitution of his title and fortune are fully made, his happiness will still depend on you."

"How on me?" said the Baron.

"Why, he will not be happy unless you honor him with your notice and esteem; but this is not all, I must hope that you will do still more for him."

"Indeed," said the Baron, "he has put my regard for him to a severe proof; what further can he expect from me?"

"My dear lord, be not offended, I have only one more proposal to make to you; if you refuse it, I can allow for you; and I confess it requires a greatness of mind, but not more than you possess, to grant it."

"Well, sir, speak your demand."

"Say rather my request; it is this: Cease to look upon Edmund as the enemy of your house; look upon him as a son, and make him so indeed."

"How say you, Sir Philip? My son!"

"Yes, my lord, give him your daughter. He is already your son in filial affection; your son William and he are sworn brothers; what remains but to make him yours? He deserves such a parent, you such a son; and you will, by this means, ingraft into your family, the name, title, and estate of Lovel, which will be entailed on your posterity forever."

"This offer requires much consideration," returned the Baron.

"Suffer me to suggest some hints to you," said Sir Philip. "This match is, I think, verily pointed out by Providence, which hath conducted the dear boy through so many dangers and brought him within view of his happiness; look on him as the precious relic of a noble house, the son of my dearest friend! Or look on him as my son and heir, and let me, as his father, implore you to consent to his marriage with your daughter."

The Baron's heart was touched, he turned away his face.

"Oh, Sir Philip Harclay, what a friend are you! Why should
such a man be our enemy?"

"My lord," said Sir Philip, "we are not, cannot be enemies;
our hearts are already allied; and I am certain we shall one
day be dear friends."

The Baron suppressed his emotions, but Sir Philip saw into
his heart. "I must consult my eldest son," returned he.

"Then," replied Sir Philip, "I foresee much difficulty; he
is prejudiced against Edmund, and thinks the restitution of
his inheritance an injury to your family. Hereafter he will see
this alliance in a different light, and will rejoice that such a
brother is added to the family; but, at present, he will set his
face against it. However, we will not despair; virtue and resolution will surmount all obstacles. Let me call in young
Lovel."

He brought Edmund to the Baron, and acquainted him
with the proposal he had been making in his name, my lord's
answers, and the objections he feared on the part of Sir
Robert. Edmund kneeled to the Baron; he took his hand and
pressed it to his lips. "Best of men! of parents! of patrons!"
said he, "I will ever be your son in filial affection, whether I
have the honor to be legally so or not; not one of your own
children can feel a stronger sense of love and duty."

"Tell me," said the Baron, "do you love my daughter?"

"I do, my lord, with the most ardent affection; I never
loved any woman but her; and, if I am so unfortunate as to
be refused her, I will not marry at all. Oh, my lord, reject
not my honest suit! Your alliance will give me consequence
with myself; it will excite me to act worthy of the station to
which I am exalted; if you refuse me, I shall seem an abject
wretch, disdained by those whom my heart claims relation to.
Your family are the whole world to me. Give me your lovely
daughter! Give me also your son, my beloved William! And
let me share with them the fortune Providence bestows upon
me. But what is title or fortune, if I am deprived of the society
of those I love?"

"Edmund," said the Baron, "you have a noble friend; but
you have a stronger in my heart, which I think was implanted
there by Heaven to aid its own purposes. I feel a variety of
emotions of different kinds, and am afraid to trust my own
heart with you. But answer me a question: Are you assured of
my daughter's consent? Have you solicited her favor? Have
you gained her affections?"

"Never, my lord! I am incapable of so base an action. I ave loved her at a humble distance; but, in my situation, should have thought it a violation of all the laws of gratitude nd hospitality to have presumed to speak the sentiments of ay heart."

"Then you have acted with unquestionable honor on this, nd, I must say, on all other occasions."

"Your approbation, my lord, is the first wish of my life; it s the seal of my honor and happiness."

Sir Philip smiled. "My Lord Fitz-Owen, I am jealous of Edmund's preferable regard for you; it is just the same now s formerly."

Edmund came to Sir Philip, he threw himself into his arms, e wept, he was overpowered with the feelings of his heart; e prayed to Heaven to strengthen his mind to support his nexpressible sensations. "I am overwhelmed with obligations!" aid he. "Oh, best of friends, teach me, like you, to make my ctions speak for me!"

"Enough, Edmund; I know your heart, and that is my secu-ity. My lord, speak to him, and bring him to himself, by ehaving coldly to him, if you can."

The Baron said, "I must not trust myself with you; you make a child of me! I will only add, gain my son Robert's avor, and be assured of mine. I owe some respect to the heir of my family; he is brave, honest, and sincere; your enemies are separated from him; you have William's influence in your ehalf; make one effort, and let me know the result."

Edmund kissed his hand in transports of joy and gratitude. 'I will not lose a moment," said he; "I fly to obey your commands."

Edmund went immediately to his friend William and re-lated all that had passed between the Baron, Sir Philip, and himself. William promised him his interest in the warmest manner. He recapitulated all that had passed in the castle since his departure; but he guarded his sister's delicacy, till it should be resolved to give way to his address. They both consulted young Clifford, who had conceived an affection to Edmund for his amiable qualities and to William for his gen-erous friendship for him. He promised them his assistance, as Sir Robert seemed desirous to cultivate his friendship. Accordingly, they both attacked him with the whole artillery of friendship and persuasion. Clifford urged the merits of Edmund, and the advantages of his alliance. William enforced his arguments by a retrospect of Edmund's past life and observed that every obstacle thrown in his way had brough his enemies to shame, and increase of honor to himself. "I say nothing," continued he, "of his noble qualities and affec tionate heart; those who have been so many years his compan ions, can want no proofs of it."

"We know your attachment to him, sir," said Robert, "and, in consequence, your partiality."

"Nay," replied William, "you are sensible of the truth of my assertions; and, I am confident, would have loved him yourself, but for the insinuations of his enemies. But if he should make good his assertions, even you must be convinced of his veracity."

"And you would have my father give him your sister upon this uncertainty?"

"No, sir, but upon these conditions."

"But suppose he does not make them good?"

"Then I will be of your party, and give up his interest."

"Very well, sir; my father may do as he pleases; but I cannot agree to give my sister to one who has always stood in the way of our family and now turns us out of our own house."

"I am sorry, brother, you see his pretensions in so wrong a light; but if you think there is any imposture in the case, go with us, and be a witness to all that passes."

"No, not I; if Edmund is to be master of the castle, I will never more set my foot in it."

"This matter," said Mr. Clifford, "must be left to time, which has brought stranger things to pass. Sir Robert's honor and good sense will enable him to subdue his prejudices, and to judge impartially." They took leave, and went to make preparations for their journey.

Edmund made his report of Sir Robert's inflexibility to his father in presence of Sir Philip, who again, ventured to urge the Baron on his favorite subject.

"It becomes me to wait for the further proofs," said he; "but, if they are as clear as I expect, I will not be inexorable to your wishes. Say nothing more on this subject till the return of the commissioners." They were profuse in their acknowl edgments of his goodness.

Edmund took a tender leave of his two paternal friends. "When," said he, "I take possession of my inheritance, I must hope for the company of you both to complete my happiness."

"Of me," said Sir Philip, "you may be certain; and, as far

as my influence reaches, of the Baron." He was silent. Edmund assured them of his constant prayers for their happiness.

Soon after, the commissioners, with Edmund, set out for Lovel Castle; and the following day the Lord Clifford set out for his own house with Baron Fitz-Owen and his son. The nominal Baron was carried with them, very much against his will. Sir Philip Harclay was invited to go with them by Lord Clifford, who declared his presence necessary to bring things to a conclusion. They all joined in acknowledging their obligations to Lord Graham's generous hospitality, and besought him to accompany them; at length he consented, on condition they would allow him to go to and fro as his duty should call him.

Lord Clifford received them with the greatest hospitality and presented them to his lady and three daughters, who were in the bloom of youth and beauty. They spent their time very pleasantly, excepting the criminal, who continued gloomy and reserved, and declined company.

In the meantime, the commissioners proceeded on their journey. When they were within a day's distance from the castle, Mr. William and his servant put forward, and arrived several hours before the rest to make preparations for their reception. His sister and brother received them with open arms, and inquired eagerly after the event of the journey to the North. He gave them a brief account of everything that had happened to their uncle, adding, "but this is not all. Sir Philip Harclay has brought a young man who he pretends is the son of the late Lord Lovel, and claims his estate and title. This person is on his journey hither, with several others who are commissioned to inquire into certain particulars, to confirm his pretensions. If he make good his claim, my father will surrender the castle and estate into his hands. Sir Philip and my lord have many points to settle; and he has proposed a compromise, that you, my sister, ought to know, because it nearly concerns you."

"Me! brother William; pray explain yourself."

"Why, he proposes that, in lieu of arrears and other expectations, my father shall give his dear Emma to the heir of Lovel, in full of all demands."

She changed color. "Holy Mary!" said she; "and does my father agree to this proposal?"

"He is not very averse to it; but Sir Robert refuses his consent. However, I have given him my interest with you."

"Have you indeed? What! A stranger, perhaps an impostor, who comes to turn us out of our dwelling?"

"Have patience, my Emma! See this young man without prejudice, and perhaps you will like him as well as I do."

"I am surprised at you, William!"

"Dear Emma, I cannot bear to see you uneasy. Think of the man who of all others you would wish to see in a situation to ask you of your father, and expect to see your wishes realized."

"Impossible!" said she.

"Nothing is impossible, my dear; let us be prudent, and all will end happily. You must help me to receive and entertain these commissioners. I expect a very solemn scene; but when that is once got over, happier hours than the past will succeed. We shall first visit the haunted apartment; you, my sister, will keep in your own till I shall send for you. I go now to give orders to the servants." He went and ordered them to be in waiting; and himself, and his youngest brother, stood in readiness to receive them.

The sound of the horn announced the arrival of the commissioners; at the same instant a sudden gust of wind arose, and the outward gates flew open. They entered the courtyard, and the great folding-doors into the hall were opened without any assistance. The moment Edmund entered the hall, every door in the house flew open; the servants all rushed into the hall, and fear was written on their countenances. Joseph only was undaunted. "These doors," said he, "open of their own accord to receive their master! This is he indeed!"

Edmund was soon apprised of what had happened. "I accept the omen!" said he. "Gentlemen, let us go forward to the apartment! Let us finish the work of fate! I will lead the way." He went on to the apartment, followed by all present. "Open the shutters," said he, "the daylight shall no longer be excluded here; the deeds of darkness shall now be brought to light."

They descended the staircase; every door was open, till they came to the fatal closet. Edmund called to Mr. William: "Approach, my friend, and behold the door your family overlooked!" They came forward; he drew the key out of his bosom, and unlocked the door; he made them observe that the boards were all loose; he then called to the servants, and bid them remove everything out of the closet. While they were doing this, Edmund showed them the breast-plate all stained with blood; he then called to Joseph: "Do you know whose was this suit of armor?"

"It was my lord's," said Joseph; "the late Lord Lovel; I have seen him wear it."

Edmund bade them bring shovels and remove the earth. While they were gone, he desired Oswald to repeat all that passed the night they sat up together in that apartment, which he did till the servants returned. They threw out the earth, while the bystanders in solemn silence waited the event. After some time and labor they struck against something. They proceeded till they discovered a large trunk, which with some difficulty they drew out. It had been corded round, but the cords were rotted to dust. They opened it and found a skeleton which appeared to have been tied neck and heels together, and forced into the trunk. "Behold," said Edmund, "the bones of him to whom I owe my birth!"

The priest from Lord Graham's advanced. "This is undoubtedly the body of the Lord Lovel; I heard his kinsman confess the manner in which he was interred. Let this awful spectacle be a lesson to all present, that though wickedness may triumph for a season, a day of retribution will come!"

Oswald exclaimed, "Behold the day of retribution! of triumph to the innocent, of shame and confusion to the wicked."

The young gentlemen declared that Edmund had made good his assertions; "what then," said they, "remains?"

"I propose," said Lord Graham's priest, "that an account be written of this discovery and signed by all the witnesses present; that an attested copy be left in the hands of this gentleman, and the original be sent to the barons and Sir Philip Harclay to convince them of the truth of it."

Mr. Clifford then desired Edmund to proceed in his own way. "The first thing I propose to do," said he, "is to have a coffin made for these honored remains; I trust to find the bones of my other parent, and to inter them all together in consecrated ground. Unfortunate pair! You shall at last rest together! Your son shall pay the last duties to your ashes!" He stopped to shed tears, and none present but paid this tribute to their misfortunes. Edmund recovered his voice and proceeded.—"My next request is, that Father Oswald and this reverend father, with whoever else the gentlemen shall appoint, will send for Andrew and Margery Twyford, and examine them concerning the circumstances of my birth, and the death and burial of my unfortunate mother."

"It shall be done," said Mr. William; "but first let me intreat you to come with me and take some refreshment after your journey, for you must be fatigued. After dinner we will proceed in the inquiry."

They all followed him into the great hall, where they were entertained with great hospitality, and Mr. William did the honors in his father's name. Edmund's heart was deeply affected, and the solemnity of his deportment bore witness to his sincerity; but it was a manly sorrow that did not make him neglect his duty to his friends or himself. He inquired after the health of the Lady Emma. "She is well," said William, "and as much your friend as ever." Edmund bowed in silence.

After dinner the commissioners sent for Andrew and his wife. They examined them separately and found their accounts agreed together and were in substance the same as Oswald and Edmund had before related, separately also. The commissioners observed that there could be no collusion between them and that the proofs were indisputable. They kept the foster parents all night; and the next day Andrew directed them to the place where the Lady Lovel was buried between two trees which he had marked for a memorial. They collected the bones and carried them to the castle, where Edmund caused a stately coffin to be made for the remains of the unfortunate pair. The two priests obtained leave to look in the coffin buried in the church, and found nothing but stones and earth in it. The commissioners then declared they were fully satisfied of the reality of Edmund's pretensions.

The two priests were employed in drawing up a circumstantial account of these discoveries in order to make their report to the barons at their return. In the meantime Mr. William took an opportunity to introduce Edmund to his sister. "My Emma," said he, "the heir of Lovel is desirous to pay his respects to you."

They were both in apparent confusion; but Edmund's wore off, and Emma's increased. "I have been long desirous," said he, "to pay my respects to the lady whom I most honor, but unavoidable duties have detained me; when these are fully paid, it is my wish to devote the remainder of my life to Lady Emma!"

"Are you, then, the heir of Lovel?"

"I am, madam; and am also the man in whose behalf I once presumed to speak."

" 'Tis very strange indeed!"

"It is so, madam, to myself; but time that reconciles us to all things, will, I hope render this change in my situation familiar to you."

William said, "You are both well acquainted with the wishes of my heart; but my advice is, that you do not encourage a further intimacy till my lord's determination be fully known."

"You may dispose of me as you please," said Edmund; "but I cannot help declaring my wishes; yet I will submit to my lord's sentence, though he should doom me to despair."

From this period, the young pair behaved with solemn respect to each other, but with apparent reserve. The young lady sometimes appeared in company, but oftener chose to be in her own apartment, where she began to believe and hope for the completion of her wishes. The uncertainty of the Baron's determination threw an air of anxiety over Edmund's face. His friend William, by the most tender care and attention, strove to dispel his fears and encourage his hopes; but he waited with impatience for the return of the commissioners, and the decision of his fate.

While these things passed at the Castle of Lovel, the nominal baron recovered his health and strength at the house of Lord Clifford. In the same proportion he grew more and more shy and reserved, avoided the company of his brother and nephew, and was frequently shut up with his two servants. Sir Robert Fitz-Owen made several attempts to gain his confidence, but in vain; he was equally shy to him as the rest. M. Zadisky observed his motions with the penetration for which his countrymen have been distinguished in all ages. He communicated his suspicions to Sir Philip and the barons, giving it as his opinion that the criminal was meditating an escape. They asked what he thought was to be done. Zadisky offered to watch him in turn with another person and to lie in wait for him; he also proposed that horses should be kept in readiness, and men to mount them, without knowledge of the service they were to be employed in. The barons agreed to leave the whole management of this affair to Zadisky. He took his measures so well that he intercepted the three fugitives in the fields adjoining to the house, and brought them all back prisoners. They confined them separately, while the lords and gentlemen consulted how to dispose of them.

Sir Philip applied to Lord Fitz-Owen, who begged leave to

be silent. "I have nothing," said he, "to offer in favor of this bad man; and I cannot propose harsher measures with so near a relation."

Zadisky then begged to be heard. "You can no longer have any reliance upon the word of a man who has forfeited all pretensions to honor and sincerity. I have long wished to revisit once more my native country, and to inquire after some very dear friends I left there; I will undertake to convey this man to a very distant part of the world, where it will be out of his power to do further mischief, and free his relations from an ungrateful charge, unless you should rather choose to bring him to punishment here." Lord Clifford approved of the proposal; Lord Fitz-Owen remained silent, but showed no marks of disapprobation.

Sir Philip objected to parting with his friend; but Zadisky assured him he had particular reasons for returning to the Holy Land, of which he should be judge hereafter. Sir Philip desired the Lord Fitz-Owen to give him his company to the criminal's apartment, saying, "We will have one more conversation with him, and that shall decide his fate."

They found him silent and sullen, and he refused to answer their questions. Sir Philip then bespoke him. "After the proofs you have given of your falsehood and insincerity, we can no longer have any reliance upon you, nor faith in your fulfilling the conditions of our agreement; I will, therefore, once more make you a proposal that shall still leave you indebted to our clemency. You shall banish yourself from England forever and go in pilgrimage to the Holy Land with such companions as we shall appoint; or, secondly, you shall enter directly into a monastery, and there be shut up for life; or, thirdly, if you refuse both these offers, I will go directly to court, throw myself at the feet of my Sovereign, relate the whole story of your wicked life and actions, and demand vengeance on your head. The King is too good and pious to let such villainy go unpunished; he will bring you to public shame and punishment. And be you assured, if I begin this prosecution, I will pursue it to the utmost. I appeal to your worthy brother for the justice of my proceeding. I reason no more with you, I only declare my resolution. I wait your answer one hour, and the next I put in execution whatever you shall oblige me to determine."

So saying, they retired, and left him to reflect and to resolve. At the expiration of the hour they sent Zadisky to receive his answer; he insinuated to him the generosity and charity of Sir Philip and the lords, and the certainty of their resolutions, and begged him to take care what answer he returned, for that his fate depended on it. He kept silent several minutes, resentment and despair were painted on his visage; at length he spoke: "Tell my proud enemies that I prefer banishment to death, infamy, or a life of solitude."

"You have chosen well," said Zadisky. "To a wise man all countries are alike; it shall be my care to make mine agreeable to you."

"Are you, then, the person chosen for my companion?"

"I am, sir; and you may judge by that circumstance that those whom you call your enemies are not so in effect. Farewell, sir; I go to prepare for our departure."

Zadisky went and made his report, and then set immediately about his preparations. He chose two active young men for his attendants and gave them directions to keep a strict eye upon their charge, for that they should be accountable if he should escape them.

In the meantime the Baron Fitz-Owen had several conferences with his brother; he endeavored to make him sensible of his crimes and of the justice and clemency of his conqueror; but he was moody and reserved to him as to the rest. Sir Philip Harclay obliged him to surrender his worldly estates into the hands of Lord Fitz-Owen. A writing was drawn up for that purpose, and executed in the presence of them all. Lord Fitz-Owen engaged to allow him an annual sum and to advance money for the expenses of his voyage. He spoke to him in the most affectionate manner, but he refused his embrace. "You will have nothing to regret," said he, haughtily; "for the gain is yours."

Sir Philip conjured Zadisky to return to him again, who answered, "I will either return, or give such reasons for my stay as you shall approve. I will send a messenger to acquaint you with my arrival in Syria and with such other particulars as I shall judge interesting to you and yours. In the meantime remember me in your prayers, and preserve for me those sentiments of friendship and esteem that I have always deemed one of the chief honors and blessings of my life. Commend my love and duty to your adopted son; he will more than supply my absence, and be the comfort of your old age. Adieu, best and noblest of friends!" They took a tender leave of each other, not without tears on both sides.

The travelers set out directly for a distant seaport where they heard of a ship bound for the Levant, in which they embarked and proceeded on their voyage.

The commissioners arrived at Lord Clifford's a few days after the departure of the adventurers. They gave a minute account of their commission and expressed themselves entirely satisfied of the justice of Edmund's pretensions; they gave an account in writing of all that they had been eye-witnesses to, and ventured to urge the Baron Fitz-Owen on the subject of Edmund's wishes. The Baron was already disposed in his favor; his mind was employed in the future establishment of his family. During their residence at Lord Clifford's, his eldest son Sir Robert had cast his eye upon the eldest daughter of that nobleman, and he besought his father to ask her in marriage for him. The Baron was pleased with the alliance, and took the first opportunity to mention it to Lord Clifford, who answered him, pleasantly, "I will give my daughter to your son, upon condition that you will give yours to the heir of Lovel." The Baron looked serious. Lord Clifford went on. "I like that young man so well that I would accept him for a son-in-law, if he asked me for my daughter; and if I have any influence with you, I will use it in his behalf."

"A powerful solicitor indeed!" said the Baron; "but you know my eldest son's reluctance to it; if he consents, so will I."

"He shall consent," said Lord Clifford, "or he shall have no daughter of mine. Let him subdue his prejudices, and then I will lay aside my scruples."

"But, my lord," replied the Baron, "if I can obtain his free consent, it will be the best for all. I will try once more, and if he will not, I will leave it wholly to your management."

When the noble company were all assembled, Sir Philip Harclay revived the subject and besought the Lord Fitz-Owen to put an end to the work he had begun by confirming Edmund's happiness. The Baron rose up and thus spoke: "The proofs of Edmund's noble birth, the still stronger ones of his excellent endowments and qualities, the solicitations of so many noble friends in his behalf, have altogether determined me in his favor; and I hope to do justice to his merit, without detriment to my other children. I am resolved to make them all as happy as my power will allow me to do. Lord Clifford has been so gracious to promise his fair daughter to my son Robert, upon certain conditions, that I will take upon me to

atify, and which will render my son worthy of the happiness
that awaits him. My children are the undoubted heirs of my
unhappy brother, Lovel; you, my son, shall therefore immediately take possession of your uncle's house and estate, only
obliging you to pay to each of your younger brothers, the
sum of one thousand pounds; on this condition, I will secure
that estate to you and your heirs forever. I will by my own
act and deed surrender the castle and estate of Lovel to the
right owner, and at the same time marry him to my daughter.
I will settle a proper allowance upon my two younger sons,
and dispose of what remains by a will and testament; and then
I shall have done all my business in this world, and shall have
nothing to do but prepare for the next."

"Oh, my father!" said Sir Robert, "I cannot bear your generosity! You would give away all to others, and reserve nothing
for yourself."

"Not so, my son," said the Baron. "I will repair to my old
castle in Wales, and reside there. I will visit my children, and
be visited by them; I will enjoy their happiness, and by that
means increase my own; whether I look backward or forward,
I shall have nothing to do but rejoice, and be thankful to
Heaven that has given me so many blessings. I shall have the
comfortable reflection of having discharged my duties as a
citizen, a husband, a father, a friend; and, whenever I am
summoned away from this world, I shall die content."

Sir Robert came forward with tears on his cheeks; he
kneeled to his father. "Best of parents, and of men!" said he;
"you have subdued a heart that has been too refractory to
your will; you have this day made me sensible how much I
owe to your goodness and forbearance with me. Forgive me
all that is past, and from henceforward dispose of me; I have
no will but yours, no ambition but to be worthy of the name
of your son."

"And this day," said the Baron, "do I enjoy the true happiness of a father! Rise, my son, and take possession of the
first place in my affection without reserve." They embraced
with tears on both sides. The company rose, and congratulated
both father and son. The Baron presented his son to Lord
Clifford, who embraced him, and said, "You shall have my
daughter, for I see that you deserve her."

Sir Philip Harclay approached; the Baron gave his son's
hand to the knight. "Love and respect that good man," said

he; deserve his friendship, and you will obtain it." Nothing
but congratulations were heard on all sides.

When their joy was in some degree reduced to composure,
Sir Philip proposed that they should begin to execute the
schemes of happiness they had planned. He proposed that my
Lord Fitz-Owen should go with him to the Castle of Lovel,
and settle the family there. The Baron consented; and both
together invited such of the company as liked it to accompany
them thither. It was agreed that a nephew of Lord Graham's,
another of Lord Clifford's, two gentlemen, friends of Sir
Philip Harclay, and Father Oswald, should be of the party;
together with several of Sir Philip's dependents and domestics,
and the attendants on the rest. Lord Fitz-Owen gave orders
for their speedy departure. Lord Graham and his friends took
leave of them, in order to return to his own home; but,
before he went, he engaged his eldest nephew and heir to the
second daughter of the Lord Clifford. Sir Robert offered himself to the eldest, who modestly received his address, and
made no objection to his proposal. The fathers confirmed
their engagement.

Lord Fitz-Owen promised to return to the celebration of
the marriage; in the meantime he ordered his son to go and
take possession of his uncle's house, and to settle his household. He invited young Clifford and some other gentlemen to
go with him. The company separated with regret, and with
many promises of friendship on all sides; and the gentlemen
of the North were to cultivate the good neighborhood on both
sides of the borders.

Sir Philip Harclay and the Baron Fitz-Owen, with their
friends and attendants, set forward for the Castle of Lovel;
a servant went before, at full speed, to acquaint the family
of their approach. Edmund was in great anxiety of mind,
now the crisis of his fate was near at hand. He inquired of
the messenger who were of the party and finding that Sir
Philip Harclay was there, and that Sir Robert Fitz-Owen
stayed in the North, his hopes rose above his fears. Mr. William, attended by a servant, rode forward to meet them; he
desired Edmund to stay and receive them. Edmund was under
some difficulty with regard to his behavior to the lovely Emma;
a thousand times his heart rose to his lips, as often he suppressed his emotions; they both sighed frequently, said little,
thought much, and wished for the event. Master Walter was

too young to partake of their anxieties, but he wished for the arrival of his father to end them.

Mr. William's impatience spurred him on to meet his father; as soon as he saw him, he rode up directly to him. "My dear father, you are welcome home!" said he.

"I think not, sir," said the Baron, and looked serious.

"Why so, my lord?" said William.

"Because it is no longer mine, but another man's home," answered he, "and I must receive my welcome from him."

"Meaning Edmund?" said William.

"Whom else can it be?"

"Ah, my lord! he is your creature, your servant; he puts his fate into your hands, and will submit to your pleasure in all things!"

"Why comes he not to meet us?" said the Baron.

"His fears prevent him," said William; "but speak the word, and I will fetch him."

"No," said the Baron, "we will wait on him."

William looked confused. "Is Edmund so unfortunate," said he, "as to have incurred your displeasure?"

Sir Philip Harclay advanced, and laid his hand on William's saddle. "Generous impatience! noble youth!" said he; "look round you, and see if you can discover in this company one enemy of your friend! Leave to your excellent father the time and manner of explaining himself; he only can do justice to his own sentiments." The Baron smiled on Sir Philip. William's countenance cleared up; they went forward, and soon arrived at the Castle of Lovel.

Edmund was walking to and fro in the hall when he heard the horn that announced their arrival; his emotions were so great that he could hardly support them. The Baron and Sir Philip entered the hall hand in hand; Edmund threw himself at their feet, and embraced their knees, but could not utter a word. They raised him between them, and strove to encourage him; but he threw himself into the arms of Sir Philip Harclay, deprived of strength and almost of life. They supported him to a seat, where he recovered by degrees, but had no power to speak his feelings; he looked up to his benefactors in the most affecting manner, he laid his hand upon his bosom, but was still silent. "Compose yourself, my dear son," said Sir Philip; "you are in the arms of your best friends. Look up to the happiness that awaits you; enjoy the blessings that Heaven sends you; lift up your heart in gratitude to the

Creator, and think less of what you owe to the creature! You will have time enough to pay us your acknowledgment hereafter."

The company came round them, the servants flocked into the hall, shouts of joy were heard on all sides; the Baron came and took Edmund's hand. "Rise, sir," said he, "and do the honors of your house! It is yours from this day. We are your guests, and expect from you our welcome!"

Edmund kneeled to the Baron, he spoke with a faltering voice, "My lord, I am yours! All that I have is at your devotion! Dispose of me as it pleases you best."

The Baron embraced him with the greatest affection. "Look round you," said he, "and salute your friends; these gentlemen came hither to do you honor."

Edmund revived, he embraced and welcomed the gentlemen. Father Oswald received his embrace with peculiar affection and gave him his benediction in a most affecting manner. Edmund exclaimed—"Pray for me, Father! that I may bear all these blessings with gratitude and moderation!" He then saluted and shook hands with all the servants, not omitting the meanest; he distinguished Joseph by a cordial embrace, he called him his dear friend. "Now," said he, "I can return your friendship, and I am proud to acknowledge it!"

The old man, with a faltering voice, cried out—"Now I have lived long enough! I have seen my master's son acknowledged for the heir of Lovel!" The hall echoed with his words: "Long live the heir of Lovel!"

The Baron took Edmund's hands in his own: "Let us retire from this crowd," said he. "We have business of a more private nature to transact." He led to the parlor, followed by Sir Philip and the other gentlemen. "Where are my other children?" said he. William retired, and presently returned with his brother and sister. They kneeled to their father, who raised and embraced them. He then called out, "William!—Edmund!—Come and receive my blessing also." They approached hand in hand, they kneeled, and he gave them a solemn benediction. "Your friendship deserves our praise, my children! Love each other always! and may Heaven pour down its choicest blessings upon your heads!" They rose, and embraced in silent raptures of joy.

Edmund presented his friend to Sir Philip. "I understand you," said he; "this gentleman was my first acquaintance of this family, he has a title to the second place in my heart:

I shall tell him, at more leisure, how much I love and honor him for his own sake as well as yours." He embraced the youth, and desired his friendship.

"Come hither, my Emma!" said the Baron. She approached, with tears on her cheek, sweetly blushing, like the damask rose, wet with the dew of the morning. "I must ask you a serious question, my child; answer me with the same sincerity you would to Heaven. You see this young man, the heir of Lovel; you have known him long; consult your own heart, and tell me whether you have any objection to receive him for your husband. I have promised to all this company to give you to him; but upon condition that you approve him. I think him worthy of you; and, whether you accept him or not, he shall ever be to me a son; but Heaven forbid that I should compel my child to give her hand, where she cannot bestow her heart! Speak freely, and decide this point for me and for yourself."

The fair Emma blushed, and was under some confusion; her virgin modesty prevented her speaking for some moments. Edmund trembled; he leaned upon William's shoulder to support himself. Emma cast her eye upon him, she saw his emotion, and hastened to relieve him; she thus spoke, in a soft voice which gathered strength as she proceeded—"My lord and father's goodness has always prevented my wishes; I am the happiest of all children in being able to obey his command without offering violence to my own inclinations. As I am called upon in this public manner, it is but justice to this gentleman's merit to declare, that, were I at liberty to choose a husband from all the world, he only should be my choice, who I can say, with joy, is my father's choice also."

Edmund bowed low, he advanced toward her; the Baron took his daughter's hand and presented it to him; he kneeled upon one knee, he took her hand, kissed it, and pressed it to his bosom. The Baron embraced and blessed them; he presented them to Sir Philip Harclay. "Receive and acknowledge your children!" said he.

"I do receive them as the gift of Heaven!" said the noble knight; "they are as much mine as if I had begotten them. All that I have is theirs, and shall descend to their children forever." A fresh scene of congratulation ensued; and the hearts of all the auditors were too much engaged to be able soon to return to the ease and tranquillity of common life.

After they had refreshed themselves, and recovered from

the emotions they had sustained on this interesting occasion, Edmund thus addressed the Baron: "On the brink of happiness I must claim your attention to a melancholy subject. The bones of both my parents lie unburied in this house; permit me, my honored lord, to perform my last duties to them, and the remainder of my life shall be devoted to you and yours."

"Certainly," said the Baron; "why have you not interred them?"

"My lord, I waited for your arrival, that you might be certified of the reality, and that no doubts might remain."

"I have no doubts," said the Baron. "Alas, both the crime and punishment of the offender leave no room for them!" He sighed. "Let us now put an end to this affair; and, if possible, forget it forever."

"If it will not be too painful to you, my lord, I would intreat you, with these gentlemen our friends, to follow me into the East apartment, the scene of my parents' woes, and yet the dawning of my better hopes."

They rose to attend him; he committed the Lady Emma to the care of her youngest brother, observing that the scene was too solemn for a lady to be present at it. They proceeded to the apartment; he showed the Baron the fatal closet, and the place where the bones were found, also the trunk that contained them; he recapitulated all that passed before their arrival; he showed them the coffin where the bones of the unfortunate pair were deposited. He then desired the Baron to give orders for their interment. "No," replied he, "it belongs to you to order, and everyone here is ready to perform it." Edmund then desired Father Oswald to give notice to the Friars of the Monastery of St. Austin that, with their permission, the funeral should be solemnized there and the bones interred in the church. He also gave orders that the closet should be floored, the apartment repaired, and put in order. He then returned to the other side of the castle.

Preparations being made for the funeral, it was performed a few days after. Edmund attended in person as chief-mourner, Sir Philip Harclay as the second; Joseph desired he might assist, as servant to the deceased. They were followed by most people of the village. The story was now become public, and everyone blessed Edmund for the piety and devotion with which he performed the last duties to his parents.

Edmund appeared in deep mourning the week after; he assisted at a mass for the repose of the deceased.

Sir Philip Harclay ordered a monument to be erected to the memory of his friends, with the following inscription.

"Pray for the souls of Arthur Lord Lovel and Marie his wife, who were cut off in the flower of their youth by the treachery and cruelty of their near kinsman. Edmund their only son, one and twenty years after their death, by the direction of Heaven, made the discovery of the manner of their death, and at the same time proved his own birth. He collected their bones together and interred them in this place—a warning and proof to late posterity of the justice of Providence and the certainty of Retribution."

The Sunday after the funeral, Edmund threw off his mourning, and appeared in a dress suitable to his condition. He received the compliments of his friends with ease and cheerfulness and began to enjoy his happiness. He asked an audience of his fair mistress, and was permitted to declare the passion he had so long stifled in his own bosom. She gave him a favorable hearing, and in a short time confessed that she had suffered equally in that suspense that was so grievous to him. They engaged themselves by mutual vows to each other, and only waited the Baron's pleasure to complete their happiness; every cloud was vanished from their brows, and sweet tranquillity took possession of their bosoms. Their friends shared their happiness; William and Edmund renewed their vows of everlasting friendship, and promised to be as much together as William's other duties would permit.

The Baron once more summoned all his company together; he told Edmund all that had passed relating to his brother-in-law, his exile, and the pilgrimage of Zadisky; he then related the circumstances of Sir Robert's engagement to Lord Clifford's daughter, his establishment in his uncle's seat, and his own obligations to return time enough to be present at the marriage. "But before I go," said he, "I will give my daughter to the heir of Lovel, and then I shall have discharged my duty to him and my promise to Sir Philip Harclay."

"You have nobly performed both," said Sir Philip, "and whenever you depart I shall be your companion."

"What," said Edmund, "am I to be deprived of both my fathers at once? My honored lord, you have given away two houses, where do you intend to reside?"

"No matter," said the Baron; "I know I shall be welcome to both."

"My dear lord," said Edmund, "stay here and be still the master; I shall be proud to be under your command and to be your servant as well as your son!"

"No, Edmund," said the Baron, "that would not now be proper; this is your castle, you are its lord and master, and it is incumbent on you to show yourself worthy of the great things Providence has done for you."

"How shall I, a young man, acquit myself of so many duties as will be upon me, without the advice and assistance of my two paternal friends? Oh, Sir Philip! Will you too leave me? Once you gave me hopes"—he stopped, greatly affected.

Sir Philip said, "Tell me truly, Edmund, do you really desire that I should live with you?"

"As truly, sir, as I desire life and happiness!"

"Then, my dear child, I will live and die with you!" They embraced with tears of affection, and Edmund was all joy and gratitude.

"My good lord," said Sir Philip, "you have disposed of two houses, and have none ready to receive you; will you accept of mine? It is much at your service, and its being in the same county with your eldest son will be an inducement to you to reside there."

The Baron caught Sir Philip's hand. "Noble sir, I thank you, and I will embrace your kind offer; I will be your tenant for the present; my castle in Wales shall be put in repair in the meantime; if I do not reside there, it will be an establishment for one of my younger sons. But what will you do with your old soldiers and dependents?"

"My lord, I will never cast them off. There is another house on my estate that has been shut up many years; I will have it repaired and furnished properly for the reception of my old men. I will endow it with a certain sum to be paid annually, and will appoint a steward to manage their revenue; I will continue it during the lives of the first inhabitants, and after that I shall leave it to my son here, to do as he pleases."

"Your son," said Edmund, "will make it the business of his life to act worthy of such a father."

"Enough," said Sir Philip, "I am satisfied that you will. I purpose to reside myself in that very apartment which my dear friend your father inhabited; I will tread in his footsteps, and think he sees me acting his part in his son's family.

I will be attended by my own servants; and, whenever you desire it, I will give you my company; your joys, your griefs shall be mine, I shall hold your children in my arms, and their prattle shall amuse my old age. And, as my last earthly wish, your hands shall close my eyes."

"Long, very long," said Edmund (with eyes and hands lifted up), "may it be ere I perform so sad a duty!"

"Long and happily may you live together," said the Baron! "I will hope to see you sometimes, and to claim a share in your blessings. But let us give no more tears to sorrow, the rest shall be those of joy and transport. The first step we take shall be to marry our Edmund; I will give orders for the celebration, and they shall be the last orders I shall give in this house." They then separated, and went to prepare for the approaching solemnity.

Sir Philip and the Baron had a private conference concerning Edmund's assuming the name and title of Lovel. "I am resolved," said Sir Philip, "to go to the King; to acquaint him briefly with Edmund's history; I will request that he may be called up to parliament by a writ, for there is no need of a new parent, he being the true inheritor; in the meantime he shall assume the name, arms, and title, and I will answer anyone that shall dispute his right to them." Sir Philip then declared his resolution to set out with the Baron at his departure, and to settle all his other affairs before he returned to take up his residence at the castle.

A few days after, the marriage was celebrated, to the entire satisfaction of all parties. The Baron ordered the doors to be thrown open and the house free for all comers with every other token of joy and festivity. Edmund appeared full of joy without levity, of mirth without extravagance; he received the congratulations of his friends, with ease, freedom, and vivacity. He sent for his foster father and mother, who began to think themselves neglected, as he had been so deeply engaged in affairs of more consequence that he had not been particularly attentive to them; he made them come into the great hall, and presented them to his lady.

"These," said he, "are the good people to whom I am, under God, indebted for my present happiness; they were my first benefactors; I was obliged to them for food and sustenance in my childhood, and this good woman nourished my infancy at her own breast." The lady received them graciously and saluted Margery. Andrew kneeled down and, with great humility, begged Edmund's pardon for his treatment of him in his childhood. "I heartily forgive you," said he, "and I will excuse you to yourself; it was natural for you to look upon me as an intruder that was eating your children's bread; you saved my life, and afterward you sustained it by your food and raiment. I ought to have maintained myself and to have contributed to your maintenance. But, besides this, your treatment of me was the first of my preferment; it recommended me to the notice of this noble family. Everything that happened to me since has been a step to my present state of honor and happiness. Never man had so many benefactors as myself; but both they, and myself, have been only instruments in the hands of Providence to bring about its own purposes. Let us praise God for all! I shared your poverty, and you will share my riches; I will give you the cottage where you dwell and the ground about it; I will also pay you the annual sum of ten pounds for the lives of you both; I will put out your children to manual trades, and assist you to provide for them in their own station; and you are to look upon this as paying a debt, and not bestowing a gift. I owe you more than I can ever pay; and, if there be anything further in my power that will contribute to your happiness, you can ask nothing in reason that I will deny you."

Andrew hid his face. "I cannot bear it!" said he. "Oh what a brute was I to abuse such a child as this! I shall never forgive myself!"

"You must indeed, my friend, for I forgive and thank you."

Andrew retired back, but Margery came forward; she looked earnestly on Edmund, she then threw her arms about his neck, and wept aloud—"My precious child! My lovely babe! thank God, I have lived to see this day! I will rejoice in your good fortune, and your bounty to us, but I must ask one more favor yet; that I may sometimes come hither and behold that gracious countenance, and thank God that I was honored so far as to give the food from my own breast and to bring thee up to be a blessing to me and to all that know thee!" Edmund was affected, he returned her embrace; he bade her come to the castle as often as she pleased, and she should always be received as his mother; the bride saluted her, and told her the oftener she came, the more welcome she should be. Margery and her husband retired, full of blessings and prayers for their happiness; she gave vent to her joy, by relating to the servants and neighbors every circumstance of Edmund's birth, infancy, and childhood. Many a tear was dropped by the auditors, and many a prayer wafted to Heaven for his happiness.

Joseph took up the story where she left it; he told the rising dawn of youth and virtue, darting its ray through the clouds of obscurity, and how every stroke of envy and malignity brushed away some part of the darkness that veiled its luster. He told the story of the haunted apartment and all the consequences of it; how he and Oswald conveyed the youth away from the castle, no more to return till he came as master of it. He closed the tale with praise to Heaven for the happy discovery that gave such an heir to the house of Lovel; to his dependents such a lord and master; to mankind a friend and benefactor. There was truly a house of joy; not that false kind, in the midst of which there is heaviness, but that of rational creatures, grateful to the supreme Benefactor, raising their minds by a due enjoyment of earthly blessings to a preparation for a more perfect state hereafter.

A few days after the wedding, the Lord Fitz-Owen began to prepare for his journey to the North. He gave to Edmund the plate, linen, and furniture of the castle, the farming stock and utensils; he would have added a sum of money, but Sir Philip stopped his hand. "We do not forget," said he, "that you have other children, we will not suffer you to injure them; give us your blessing and paternal affection, and we have nothing more to ask. I told you, my lord, that you and I should one day be sincere friends.

"We must be so," answered the Baron; "it is impossible to be long your enemy. We are brothers, and shall be to our lives' end."

They regulated the young man's household; the Baron gave leave to the servants to choose their master; the elder ones followed him (except Joseph, who desired to live with Edmund, as the chief happiness of his life); most of the younger ones chose the service of the youthful pair. There was a tender and affectionate parting on all sides. Edmund besought his beloved William not to leave him. The Baron said he must insist on his being at his brother's wedding, as a due attention to him; but after that he should return to the castle for some time.

The Baron and Sir Philip Harclay, with their train, set forward. Sir Philip went to London and obtained all he desired for his Edmund; from thence he went into Yorkshire, and settled his affairs there, removing his pensioners to his other house, and putting Lord Fitz-Owen in possession of his own. They had a generous contention about the terms; but Sir Philip insisted on the Baron's accepting the use of everything there. "You hold it in trust for a future grandchild," said he, "whom I hope to live to endow with it."

During Sir Philip's absence, the young Lord Lovel caused the haunted apartment to be repaired and furnished for the reception of his father by adoption. He placed his friend Joseph over all his men servants, and ordered him to forbear his attendance; but the old man would always stand at the sideboard and feast his eyes with the countenance of his own master's son, surrounded with honor and happiness. John Wyatt waited upon the person of his lord and enjoyed his favor without abatement. Mr. William Fitz-Owen accompanied Sir Philip Harclay from the North country, when he returned to take up his residence at the Castle of Lovel.

Edmund, in the arms of love and friendship, enjoyed with true relish the blessings that surrounded him, with an heart overflowing with benevolence to his fellow creatures, and raptures of gratitude to his Creator. His lady and himself were examples of conjugal affection and happiness. Within a year from his marriage she brought him a son and heir, whose birth renewed the joy and congratulations of all his friends. The Baron Fitz-Owen came to the baptism, and partook of his children's blessings. The child was called Arthur, after the name of his grandfather.

The year following was born a second son, who was called Philip Harclay; upon him the noble knight of that name settled his estate in Yorkshire; and by the King's permission, he took the name and arms of that family.

The third son was called William; he inherited the fortune of his uncle of that name, who adopted him, and he made the Castle of Lovel his residence, and died a bachelor.

The fourth son was called Edmund; the fifth Owen; and there was also a daughter called Emma.

When time had worn out the prejudices of Sir Robert Fitz-Owen, the good old Baron of that name proposed a marriage between his eldest son and heir, and the daughter of Edmund Lord Lovel, which was happily concluded. The nuptials were honored with the presence of both families; and the old Baron was so elevated with this happy union of his descendants, that he cried out—"Now I am ready to die! I have lived long enough! This is the band of love that unites all my children to me, and to each other!" He did not long survive this happy event; he died full of years and honors, and his name was never mentioned but with the deepest marks of gratitude, love and veneration. Sweet is the remembrance of the virtuous, and happy are the descendants of such a father! They will think on him and emulate his virtues; they will remember him, and be ashamed to degenerate from their ancestor.

Many years after Sir Philip Harclay settled at the castle, he received tidings from his friend Zadisky by one of the two servants who attended him to the Holy Land. From him he learned that his friend had discovered, by private advices, that he had a son living in Palestine, which was the chief motive of his leaving England; that he had met with various adventures in pursuit of him; that at length he found him, converted him to the Christian religion, and then persuaded him to retire from the world into a monastery by the side of Mount Libanus, where he intended to end his days.

That Walter, commonly called Lord Lovel, had entered into the service of the Greek emperor, John Paleologus,[14] not bearing to undergo a life of solitude and retirement; that he made up a story of his being compelled to leave his native country by his relations, for having accidentally killed one of them, and that he was treated with great cruelty and injustice; that he had accepted a post in the Emperor's army, and was soon after married to the daughter of one of the chief officers of it.

Zadisky foresaw and lamented the downfall of that empire, and withdrew from the storm he saw approaching. Finally, he bade the messenger tell Sir Philip Harclay and his adopted son that he should not cease to pray for them and desired their prayers in return.

Sir Philip desired Lord Lovel to entertain this messenger in his service. That good knight lived to extreme old age in honor and happiness and died in the arms of his beloved Edmund, who also performed the last duties to his faithful Joseph.

Father Oswald lived many years in the family as chaplain; he retired from thence at length, and died in his own monastery.

Edmund Lord Lovel lived to old age, in peace, honor and happiness; and died in the arms of his children.

[14] Byzantine emperor, ruled from 1425 to 1448.

Sir Philip Harclay caused the papers relating to his son's history to be collected together; the first part of it was written under his own eye in Yorkshire, the subsequent parts by Father Oswald at the Castle of Lovel. All these, when together, furnish a striking lesson to posterity, of the over-ruling hand of Providence, and the certainty of retribution.

Mistrust, or
Blanche and Osbright

A FEUDAL ROMANCE

by

MATTHEW GREGORY LEWIS

MATTHEW GREGORY LEWIS (1775–1818)

By the time he came to his collection of *Romantic Tales* (1808), in which *Mistrust* appeared, Matthew Gregory Lewis had toned down the ghastly, supernatural elements which had made *The Monk* (1795) a sensational, although infamous, success. He had from his earliest reading been interested in the sentimental novel, and even in the full flight of his Gothic imagination he was concerned with the psychological probing of his characters' minds, and it is upon these elements that *Mistrust* depends for much of its effect. Yet the Gothic is no less genuine in this adaptation of a German romance from which Lewis acknowledged he had "borrowed a great part of the plot, and one of the most striking scenes," while occasionally inserting in his narrative "such speeches" as pleased him.

If the occurrences in *Mistrust* are not supernatural, they nevertheless display all the other accouterments of the Gothic tradition. The scenes in the crypt, the witchcraft in the forest, the tyrannical parent, the mysterious deaths, the attempted abduction, and the father's murder of his own son are pure Gothic. Here Lewis appeals to horror through human rather than supernatural passions, but this was always a primary interest of the novelist. In the figure of Rudiger, he depends on the eighteenth-century concept of the "ruling passion" to explain his tragedy; yet the technique is not different from the one employed with the Monk Ambrosio, who is dominated by his overpowering lust.

Those elements of blood and slaughter which had brought disrepute to Lewis, even with his masterpiece, surely have not been abjured in this later work. The graphic description of the slaughter of Baron Ottokar, Eugene's attempted ravaging of Blanche, Rudiger's fateful discovery of his misdirected murder and his subsequent suicide—all match point by point the sensational events in *The Monk*. In adapting *Mistrust*, Lewis gave it those characteristics that most interested his own taste in erotic, sadistic, and brutal subject matter.

Mistrust was only one of his German adaptations. Others appeared in his collections of ballads and stories: *Tales of Terror* (1799) and *Tales of Wonder* (1801), while his free translation of Schiller's tale in *The Bravo of Venice* (1805) appeared as well as a popular drama.

CHAPTER I

—"The bird is dead,
That we have made so much on! I had rather
Have skipped from sixteen years of age to sixty,
To have turned my leaping time into a crutch,
Than have seen this!"

CYMBELINE.

PEACE was concluded, and the waters of the Rhine again flowed through plains unpolluted with blood. The Palatine[1] saw his enemies at his feet; it rested in his own pleasure to trample or to raise them, and the use which he made of the victory proved how well he merited to be victorious. His valor had subdued his enemies; his clemency converted those enemies into friends. The Duke of Saxony,[2] the hereditary foe of his family, had been made his prisoner in the last engagement; he restored him to liberty without ransom or conditions; and he could have framed none so binding as those, which this fearless generosity imposed on the Duke's gratitude. Henry of Saxony became from that moment his firmest ally; and the Palatine found in his powerful friendship more real strength than if he had surrounded his whole dominions with a triple wall of brass.

The Saxons departed to their own country; the Palatine dismissed his feudatory troops; and their chiefs led back their vassals, loaded with the presents of their liege-lord, and proud of the wounds which they had received in his service. Among these warriors few had displayed more valor than the youthful Osbright of Frankheim; but no sooner was the war concluded than none panted with more impatience for the permission to depart. It was given, and the next hour saw him spring upon his courser; he committed the care of his vassals to a gray-headed knight, in whose prudence he could confide; and then, while his heart swelled high with joy and expectation, he gave his horse the spur, and sped toward his native towers.

But it was not the recollection of those native towers, nor

---

[1] A ruler (count) of the Palatinate, one of two districts in Southwest Germany.
[2] Henry the Lion, Duke of Saxony (in Northwest Germany) and Bavaria, died in 1195.

of any one whom his castle-walls contained, which now made his cheeks glow and his eyes blaze with such impatient fire. It was not to embrace his beloved and loving mother; nor to kneel at the feet of his respected father, who held his two sons precious as the two apples of his eyes; nor yet to behold once more his little darling, the young Joscelyn, who looked upon his elder brother as the masterpiece of creation; none of these was the motive, which now hurried Osbright onward: none of these, while the mountains, woods, and wilds were left behind him with inconceivable rapidity, made him wonder at the unaccustomed sluggishness of his courser. No! It was the hope of once more beholding the avowed enemy of himself and of his whole house, that being to whom he was an object of the wildest alarm, and by whom his very name was held in abhorrence; this was the hope, which made the young warrior's heart swell with eagerness almost to bursting.

There was not a fleeter steed in the whole Palatinate than Osbright's; his speed was stretched to the utmost, but in vain. Night was at hand, and he had not yet arrived at the wished-for goal. The knight abandoned the fruitless attempt to reach it, checked his courser, and stopped for a few moments to gaze upon the hostile towers of Orrenberg, as they rose proudly in the distance, all golden and glittering with the splendors of the setting sun.

"Oh! yes!" he sighed to himself, "the day must at length arrive when I need no longer gaze at distance on yonder walls, and envy every pilgrim who dares approach the portals with the prayer of hospitality! The day shall surely come when my name, now never mentioned but with curses, or at least with alarm within the precincts of yonder castle, shall call down blessings only inferior to those given to its lord's; when the sound of my courser's tramp on the drawbridge shall seem to the hearer sweet as the merry bells which announce a victory; and when to proclaim that Osbright of Frankheim draws near shall be to announce a holiday throughout Orrenberg. Till then, peace dwell in all your hearts, my beloved enemies! With every bead that he tells, with every orison that he breathes, Osbright of Frankheim shall call down blessings on the heads of those, who now call down curses on his!"

Again he set forward, but now suffered his horse to choose what pace he pleased. The wearied animal gladly profited by the permission. Osbright, plunged in melancholy but not unpleasing thought, observed not the moderate rate, at which he was now performing his journey; till the moon, emerging from behind a cloud, suddenly poured her radiance full upon his sight, and the unexpected light startled him from his reverie. He looked up, and saw the place before him, to reach which had been the object of his proceeding with such unwearied expedition. But it was already night, and the spell, which had drawn him thither so forcibly, had ceased to operate.

Still, though he knew well that the search must be fruitless, he could not refuse himself the satisfaction of revisiting that place, whose remembrance was so dear to his imagination, so consecrated by his heart. He bound his steed to the branch of a shattered oak, and entered a narrow path, which wound among the mountains. He soon reached an open space, nearly square in its form, surrounded on three sides with flowering shrubs and branches, and presenting on the fourth the entrance to a grotto, whose mouth was thickly overgrown with ivy, woodbines, and a variety of tangling weeds. Osbright heard the well-known murmur of the waterfall; his heart beat quicker as he listened to the sound, and his eyes sparkled in the moonbeams with tears of melancholy pleasure.

He entered the cavern; as he expected and feared, it was vacant; but the moonshine, penetrating through an opening in the rocky roof, and converting the cataract into a flood of silver light, enabled him to see a wreath of flowers still fresh, which was lying on a stone seat at no great distance from the water. With an exclamation of joy he seized the wreath, and pressed it to his lips. The cave then had been visited that very day! Ah! if he had but reached it before sunset. . . . But the sun was not set forever; tomorrow it would rise again, and he now doubted no longer that it would rise a sun of joy to him. He kissed off the dew-drops, with which the flowers were heavy, and which he could not help flattering himself were tears of sorrow for his absence. He then hung the garland round his neck, and having deposited his well-known scarf in place of the flowers, he quitted the cavern with a lightened heart, and with hopes increased by the certainty that in his absence he had not been forsaken.

And now this first and chief anxiety dispelled, he was at liberty to bestow his thoughts on those friends who were the next dearest objects of his affection, and on that home where his unexpected arrival was certain to diffuse such joy. Again he spurred his horse forward; but the animal needed no in-

ducement to make him exert all his speed, while retracing
road whose goal was so well known to him. He darted forward
with the rapidity of an arrow and would not have paused
till his arrival at the castle of Frankheim had not Osbright
checked him when within half a mile of his paternal towers.
The sound of a bell tolling heavily attracted his attention and
gave his imagination the alarm; from the quarter whence it
sounded, he guessed that it must proceed from St. John's
chapel, a building raised by the piety of one of his ancestors
long deceased, and whose vaults were appropriated to the sole
purpose of receiving the reliques of those who expired within
the walls of Frankheim. Vespers must have long been past; it
was not yet midnight; nor indeed was it usual to celebrate
religious rites within that chapel except on particular festivals
or occasions of extraordinary solemnity. His heart beat high
while he paused to listen. The bell continued to toll, so slow,
so solemn, as to permit his doubting no longer that it was
sounding for the departure of some enfranchised spirit. Was
there a death then in his family? Had he to lament the loss of
a relation, of a friend, of a parent? Anxiety to have this question answered without delay, would not permit him to pursue
his destined course. Hastily he turned the bridle of his horse
and darted into the grove of cypress, whose intervening shades
hid the chapel from his observation.

It was situated in the bosom of this grove, and a few minutes
were sufficient to bring him to the place whence the sound
proceeded. But the bell had already ceased to toll, and in its
place, after a momentary silence, a strain of solemn choral
music and the full swell of the organ burst upon the ear of
Osbright. He knew well those sad melodious sounds: it was
the "De Profundis" chanted by the nuns and monks of the
two neighboring monasteries, St. Hildegarde and St. John.
The chapel was brilliantly illuminated; the painted windows
poured a flood of light upon the surrounding trees and stained
their leaves with a thousand glowing colors; it was evident
that a burial was performing and that the deceased must be a
person of no mean consideration. Osbright sprang from his
horse, and without allowing himself time to secure the animal
from escape, he rushed into the chapel, while anxiety almost
deprived him of the powers of respiration.

The chapel was crowded; and as he had lowered the visor
of his casque,[3] no one was disposed to make way for him; but

[3] Helmet.

within a few paces of the principal entrance there was a low
door conducting to a gallery, the access to which was prohibited
to all, except the members of the noble family of Frankheim.
Too impatient to ask questions, which he dreaded to hear
answered, Osbright without a moment's delay hastened toward
the private door. It was not without difficulty that he forced
his way to it; but all present were too much engaged by the
mournful business which they had come thither to witness to
permit their attending to his motions, and he reached the
gallery unquestioned and unobserved.

Alas! It was empty! With every moment the conviction
acquired new force that the funeral bell had knelled for some
one of his family. His whole frame shook with alarm as he
cast his eyes upon the aisle beneath. It was hung with black
throughout; but the blaze of innumerable torches dispelled the
double gloom of night and of the sable hangings. The sweet
sad requiem still rose from the choir, where the nuns of St.
Hildegarde were stationed. The avenues to the aisle were
thronged with the vassals of Frankheim; but the middle of
the aisles was left free, for there stood the chief actors in this
mournful ceremony, and the crowd kept a respectful distance.
By the side of an open grave, which occupied the center of
the aisle, stood the Abbot of St. John's, the venerable Sylvester.
His arms were extended over the grave, as if bestowing on
the already consecrated earth an additional benediction. An
awe-inspiring air of sanctity pervaded his tall thin figure; his
eyes seemed to shine with a mild celestial brightness when he
raised them with all the rapture of enthusiasm toward Heaven;
but their fires were quenched by tears of pity when he cast a
glance of benevolence toward a stately tomb of white marble
which rose upon his left hand. Against that tomb (which was
raised in honor of Ladislaus the first Count of Frankheim,
and which was exactly opposite to Osbright's retreat) reclined
the two chief mourners: a warrior and a lady; and the youth's
heart felt itself relieved from a weight almost intolerable,
when he recognized the beloved authors of his being.

Now then he no longer trembled for the life of one of those
parents, whose undeviating affection through the whole course
of his existence had made them so justly dear to him. But for
whom then were they mourning? The loss must needs touch
Osbright nearly, which could occasion such extreme affliction
to his parents; and that their affliction *was* extreme, it was
not permitted him to cherish even a doubt. The noble Magda-

lena stood with her hands clasped, her eyes raised to Heaven, while unconscious tears coursed each other down her cheeks; motionless as a statue; pale as the marble tomb, against which she was leaning; the very image of unutterable despair.

Widely different was the expression produced by anguish upon the noble and strongly-marked features of Count Rudiger. His heart was the seat of agony; a thousand scorpions seemed every moment to pierce it with their poisonous stings; but not one tear forced itself into his blood-shot eyeballs; not the slightest convulsion of his gigantic limbs betrayed the silent tortures of his bosom. A gloom settled and profound reigned upon his dark and high-arched eyebrows. He bent his gaze immutably upon a bier, which stood between himself and Magdalena, and which supported a coffin richly adorned with the escutcheons of the house of Frankheim. He rested one hand on the coffin; his other hand grasped firmly the jeweled handle of his dagger. His glaring eyes were stretched widely, as if their strings were on the point of breaking, and the flames which blazed in them were red and lurid. Disdain seemed to curl his lips and expand his nostrils; an expression of restrained fury pervaded his whole deportment; and his resolute attitude, and something almost like a sullen smile which marked itself round his mouth, gave the prophetic assurance of revenge dreadfully satisfied. His long sable mantle was wrapped round his right arm; it had fallen from his left shoulder, and hung round him in loose drapery; while its folds rustled wildly in the night wind, in whose blast the tapers were flaring, and whose murmurs seemed to sigh for the deceased, when the nuns pausing in their mournful melody permitted its hollow voice to be heard. With every fresh gust the white plumes, which decorated the four corners of the bier, waved themselves backward and forward with a melancholy motion; and then did the tears stream faster from Magdalena's eyes to think that now nothing of motion remained to the being whom she had ever loved so fondly, except the waving plumes with which his hearse was decorated.

And now the moment was come for depositing the coffin in the earth. The music ceased; a profound and awful silence reigned in the chapel, only interrupted by the loud sobbing of a young page, who had thrown himself on his knees and who, by enveloping his head in his cloak, had endeavored without success to prevent his grief from becoming audible. Though his face was thus concealed, his light and graceful form, the long tresses of his dark golden hair which streamed in the night wind, and still more the enthusiastic extravagance of his sorrow, left Osbright no doubt who was the mourner. It was the young Eugene, Count Rudiger's beloved but unacknowledged offspring.

Four of the friars had now approached the bier; they raised the coffin in silence and bore it toward the open grave. The heavy sound of their departing footsteps roused Magdalena; she extended her arms toward the coffin and started forward a few paces, as if she wished to detain the bearers. But a moment's recollection was sufficient to make her feel the inutility of delay; and folding her arms across upon her bosom, she bowed her head in humble resignation. Her lord still remained without motion.

The coffin was lowered gently into the grave; it disappeared, and the attendants were on the point of covering it with the appointed marble, when Eugene uttered a loud shriek.

"Oh! Not yet! Not yet!" he cried, while he started from the ground, and rushing forward, he arrested the arm of one of the friars, who held the monumental stone. His eyes were swollen with weeping, his gestures were wild as a maniac's, and his voice was the very accent of despair.—"Oh! not yet!" he exclaimed. "He was the only being in the world that ever really loved me! The slightest drop of blood in his veins was dearer to me than those which warm my own heart! I cannot endure to part with him for ever! Oh! not yet, father! good father, not yet!"

The youth was now kneeling on the verge of the grave, and he bent down his head and bathed the friar's feet with his tears in all the humility of supplication. As yet Magdalena had borne her sorrow like a heroine; but the unexpected shriek of Eugene, the heart-piercing hopeless tone in which he pronounced the words of "for ever!" was more than her fortitude could bear. She uttered a deep sigh, and sank insensible into the arms of her attendants; while Rudiger (whom the page's cry of agony had also roused from his gloomy meditations) sprang forward with a furious look, and plunged into the grave.

With involuntary horror the friars started back, and then as if changed to stone by a Gorgon's head, they remained gazing upon the dreadful countenance, which presented itself before them. Count Rudiger's stature was colossal; the grave in which he stood, scarcely rose above his knees. His eyes blazed; his mouth foamed; his coal-black hair stood erect, in which he twisted his hands, and tearing out whole handsful by the roots, he strewed them on the coffin, which stood beside his feet.

"Right! right!" he cried, while his thundering voice shook the vaults above him, and while he stamped upon the hallowed earth with impotent fury. "Right, Eugene! Not yet shall the earth cover the innocent victim of avarice! Not yet shall the lips of holiness pronounce the last long farewell! Not till I have sworn upon his coffin never to know rest, till his death is avenged most amply; not till I have devoted to the demons of darkness the murderer and his accursed offspring! Yes, yes! Not he alone, but his whole serpent-brood shall pay the penalty of his crime, his wife, his children, his servants, all! all! His vassals shall be hunted through the woods like wolves, slaughtered wherever found; his towers shall be wrapped by my hand in flames, and its shrieking inmates hurled back into the burning ruins! You hear me, friends! You see the agony which tortures my heart, and yet do I curse alone? And yet does no voice join mine in the vow of revenge? —Nay then, look here!—Observe this pallid face! Observe this mangled bosom! Look on these, look on these, and join with me in one dreadful irrevocable curse. "Vengeance! Everlasting vengeance on the bloody house of Orrenberg."

As he said this, he violently forced open the coffin, tore from the shroud a lifeless body, and held it up to the gaze of the shuddering multitude around him. It was the corpse of a child apparently not more than nine years old; a large wound disfigured the ivory bosom; yet even in death the countenance was that of a sleeping angel. His eyes were closed; as Rudiger held it forth at his arm's length, the profusion of its light flaxen hair fell over the pale lovely features of the child; but Osbright had already seen enough to confirm his worst suspicions. His brain whirled round, his sight grew dim, and he sank lifeless upon a bench which stood behind him. Yet as his eyes closed, and before his senses quite forsook him, he could hear the exasperated multitude answer his father's demand by a general shout of—"Vengeance! Everlasting vengeance on the bloody house of Orrenberg."

CHAPTER II

—"Suspicion's lurking frown and prying eye."—
R. P. KNIGHT'S, *"Landscape."*

THE visor of Osbright's helmet was closed, and the exclusion of air necessarily prolonged his insensibility. When he recovered himself, the chapel was vacant, and the lamps and torches all extinguished. The total darkness, which surrounded him, added to the confusion of his ideas; and a considerable time elapsed, before he could recollect himself sufficiently to arrange in their proper order the dreadful circumstances which had just occurred. The image of his murdered brother haunted his imagination, and resisted all his efforts to chase it away. Though his own education had been received principally at the court of the Bishop of Bamberg, and therefore he had seen but little of the young Joscelyn, that little was sufficient to make him feel an affection most truly fraternal for the amiable child. Deeply therefore did he regret his loss; but yet he regretted the circumstances which attended it even more than the loss itself. His father's horrible curse still rang in his ears; the sentence of death pronounced upon himself would have sounded to him less dreadful, than that general shout of the incensed vassals—"Vengeance on the house of Orrenberg!"

Bewildered, irresolute, daring scarcely to admit the possibility of his father's solemn assertion being unfounded, and heaving many a sigh of anguish over the probable ruin of all his schemes of happiness, did Osbright quit the gallery and pursue his way to the great entrance of the chapel. The darkness was profound, and he reached the gates with some difficulty; but here he found his intention of departure completely frustrated. During his swoon the doors had been carefully locked and barred, and though his strength was great, it was still insufficient to enable him to force them open.

Exhausted with his fruitless efforts, he abandoned the attempt, and had made up his mind to return to the matted gallery and remain there quietly till morning should enable him to regain his liberty; when he recollected, that at the further extremity of the aisle there existed a cell, which generally was tenanted by one of the Brethren of St. John, whose office it was to keep the chapel in order, and by whose care in all probability the doors had been so carefully secured. Thither he bent his way, hoping to obtain his freedom by the friar's assistance, and at least certain of finding a less damp and unwholesome shelter for the night.

Feeling his way from pillar to pillar he proceeded slowly and cautiously. It was not long, before a ray of light at some distance guided his steps, and a low murmuring voice assured him that the cell was inhabited. He pushed the door gently open. A lamp, which was placed in the nook of a narrow Gothic window, threw its light full upon the pale face and gray locks of the friar, who was kneeling before a crucifix, with an immense rosary in his hand, and his eyes fixed devoutly upon the Redeemer's countenance. Osbright was both too unwell and too impatient to wait for the conclusion of his prayer; he stepped into the cell, and the sound of his heavy spurs, which clattered as he trod, roused the monk from his devotions. He started up and looked round, amazed at so unusual an intrusion. But no sooner did he cast his eye upon his visitor than he fell prostrate upon the earth before him, loaded him with benedictions, and poured forth a profusion of thanks to Heaven, which had thought the meanest of its servants worthy of so unusual and distinguished an honor. Osbright had raised his visor for the benefit of air; and the singular beauty of his features, the noble expression of his countenance, the symmetry of his form, and the dazzling brilliance of his armor, made the pious brother conclude that he was honored by a celestial vision, and that the form who stood before him was no other than the Archangel Michael. He was so convinced of this that he was on the very point of asking news of the Dragon when the knight hastened to dissipate his illusion.[4]

"Rise, good father!" said he; "I am a mortal like yourself, and what is more, am a mortal who greatly needs your assistance. During the late mournful ceremony, a sudden illness overpowered me. I became insensible; no one observed me, and I found myself on my recovery alone, in darkness, and inclosed within the chapel. Doubtless, you possess the means of opening the gate, and can restore me to liberty."

"Truly can I, my son," answered the monk; "and it is but just that I should be the person to let you out, as I was the

---

[4] St. Michael, prince of angels, was commonly depicted in art as a dragon-slayer.

person who locked you in so carefully. Mercy on me, poor old man! I little thought, that I was locking in anything better than the dead, and myself, and my old raven Jojo. But oh! all ye blessed spirits! You must have been ill indeed, sir knight; for the poor child that Count Rudiger tore out of its shroud did not look paler than *you* do at this moment. Nay, in truth, it was your paleness, which made me be so sure of your being a spirit when I· first looked on you; for I thought, that no living thing could have had a countenance so bloodless. But how I stand here talking when I ought to be doing somewhat to assist you!—Here, sir knight!" he continued, at the same time hastening to a small walnut-tree cupboard, and spreading his whole store of provisions before the stranger; "here is some refreshment—here is bread—and fruit—and hard eggs—and here is even some venison for you; for alas, the day! I am old and weak, and our Abbot has forbidden my fasting and keeping the spare holy diet, which I used, and which I *ought* to keep. Ah! I shall never have the good fortune to be a saint, nor even a martyr, Heaven help me! But I will not murmur at Providence, sinner that I am for saying so! Now, good sir knight, eat, and refresh yourself, for it makes my heart bleed to see you look so pale. And see! I protest, I had like to have forgotten the best of all. Here is a small bottle of a most rare cordial; it was given me by Sister Radigonda, the fat portress of St. Hildegarde's, and she assured me that its virtue was sovereign. Now taste it, good son, I beseech you! I am sure it will do you service; not that I ever tried its good qualities myself; but Sister Radigonda has, and she's a devouted person, who (I warrant you) knows what's good. Now taste it, dear sir knight! In the name of St. Ursula and the eleven thousand virgins[5] (rest their souls, though nobody was ever lucky enough to find their blessed bodies!) I beseech you, now, taste it!"

The benevolent manner of the old man was irresistible. Osbright partook of the cordial, and the warmth which immediately diffused itself through his chilled veins, and the glow which it produced upon his cheeks, sufficiently testified that Sister Radigonda had not said too much in favor of her present. Brother Peter now pressed the youth to partake of the viands placed before him; and Osbright, finding that his person was totally unknown to the monk, thought that by

[5] A legendary Cornish princess, supposedly slain by the Huns along with the 11,000 virgins that she was escorting in eleven galleys to France.

engaging him in conversation he might most easily and expe-
ditiously learn the meaning of the melancholy transactions,
which he had just witnessed in the chapel. Accordingly, he
took some of the refreshments, which his host presented to
him, and found no difficulty in leading the conversation to
the funeral and its cause; while on the other hand Father
Peter, believing his discourse to be directed to a stranger,
whom curiosity alone had led to the chapel, and who had no
personal interest in the transaction, felt no hesitation in
answering the questions put to him without disguise and in
their fullest extent.

"You shall hear all that I know, sir knight," said the old
man; "and I believe, I know more of the matter than most
people. Indeed, you'll marvel perhaps, how I came to know
so much; but did you remark a young page at the funeral
who sobbed so piteously that one heard him in spite of the
organ? His name is Eugene; he is the Countess's page, and
(between ourselves) they do say that he is more nearly related
to the Count, than law and religion allow of; but the Count
wishes this to be kept a secret, and so I shall not say a syllable
upon the subject. Well! this Eugene is an excellent pious
youth, and often comes to the chapel, and prays upon his
knees for whole hours together before the Virgin's image,
and employs all the money he can procure in purchasing
masses in hopes of removing the soul of his poor sinful mother
out of purgatory—and so he used often to bring the poor little
murdered Joscelyn to visit me in my cell, and he told me the
whole matter exactly, as I now tell it you. You must know,
sir knight, that some twenty years ago, there was an old Count
of Frankheim, by name Jeronymus, who bequeathed his large
domains. . . ."

"Nay, pry'thee, my good Father," interrupted Osbright impatiently, "proceed to the murder at once, and leave out the
bequest of Count Jeronymus!"

"Leave out the bequest?" cried Brother Peter. "Heaven help
us! you might as well bid me tell the story of the Fall of Man,
and leave out the Apple! Why, that bequest has made the
whole mischief; and into the bargain, sir knight, I must tell
my own story my own way, or I shall never be able to tell it
at all.—Well! as I was saying, this Count Jeronymus had but
one child, a daughter; and as his ruling passion was family
pride (of which, however, the present Count has a hogshead,
where the old one had but a drop), he resolved to bestow her

hand and his large domains upon the next heir. Unluckily, before his intentions were made known to him, the next heir was already affianced to another. Rudiger of West Frankheim and his cousin Gustavus of Orrenberg, equally needy and equally related to Jeronymus (only Rudiger was the eldest branch) were both suitors to Magdalena, the rich heiress of Helmstadt, who at this very moment chose to make her election in favor of the former. Now who was puzzled but the old Count? What should he do? Family pride forbade his alienating the patrimony of Frankheim from the man who at his death would be the reigning Count; and yet paternal affection would not suffer him to leave his unoffending daughter quite destitute. To reconcile these two jarring passions, he bequeathed the whole hereditary estates to Count Rudiger, and gave his daughter the Lady Ulrica his whole personal property, besides several purchased estates of considerable value, together with permission to bestow them and her hand according to her own free choice. That choice fell on Gustavus of Orrenberg, who was too greedy of wealth to refuse so advantageous a match; though he never forgave the Lady Magdalena's rejection of him; but cherished a secret spite in his heart against her and his successful rival."

"Indeed? Is that quite certain?"

"Oh! quite, quite! Why, Count Rudiger always said so himself! Though to be sure Gustavus carried himself artfully enough toward him, and would fain have been on friendly terms at Frankheim. But Rudiger was too prudent to be deceived, and guessed that all these fair speeches and mild looks were intended to lull him into a dangerous security, till an opportunity should offer of doing him an injury without danger."

"And did Gustavus ever betray any such intention by his actions?"

"Oh! Blessed Virgin! No, to be sure not! My lord was too much on his guard to give him an opportunity! It's true, the families still kept up an appearance of being on decent terms, and even visited; but my lord never went to the castle of Orrenberg but well armed and attended, and kept an eye of suspicion on everything that was passing around him; and when Gustavus returned the visit, he must easily have seen by my lord's looks and manner that he was aware of his being come for no good; and so he never ventured to put his evil designs in execution.—But how my old head rambles! I forget to tell you that there was a worse cause of enmity than their joint-suit to Magdalena! You must know that when Coun Jeronymus found his daughter's choice to have fallen upor Gustavus (who, after Rudiger, would inherit the titles of Frankheim), he bethought himself of a way to render the union of that beloved name and his large possessions more durable than ever. Accordingly in a clause to his will he enacted, that in case either Gustavus or Rudiger should die without heirs, the property, which he had bequeathed to the one, should descend to the other undiminished. Neither of them had children at the time of the old Count's decease; but within a twelvemonth after it, Rudiger fell dangerously ill. He lay for two days insensible; the physicians believed him to be dead. The report spread over the whole country; and oh! in what haste was Gustavus to take possession of the castle and its domains! He came galloping over in all joy, when lo and behold! he found our good lord still in the land of the living, and was obliged to return home quite chapfallen! If the plague had broken out among them, it could not have produced more sorrow in the castle of Orrenberg than the tidings of this recovery!"

"Indeed! Who told you that, Father?"

"Oh! I remember that it was the common report throughout Frankheim; I never heard anyone say otherwise. Well! sir knight, Gustavus had scarcely got the better of this disappointment when he met with another. The Lady Magdalena proved with child, and was safely delivered of a fine boy, who was christened Osbright. When Gustavus heard this, he turned as white as a corpse!"

"How know you that? Did you see him?"

"I? St. Chrysostom[6] forbid! I never saw the hypocritical assassin (Heaven pardon me for calling him so, who am myself so hardened a sinner!). I say, I never saw him in my whole life, not I! I would as soon look on Beelzebub in person! No, no! I might indeed have seen him once; but I cast down my eyes, crossed myself, and passed on. Well, the house of Orrenberg comforted itself with thinking that Rudiger had but *one* son, while the Lady Ulrica had borne four, besides a daughter. It's true, Count Rudiger's prudence had made him send the young Osbright out of the reach of their enmity; but still he might be taken off by a thousand natural accidents.

[6] St. John Chrysostom (345-407), Greek churchman, Bishop of Constantinople.

This hope also received its death-blow about nine years ago by the birth of a second son to Rudiger, this very little luckless Joscelyn. The two boys increased in bloom and strength, as they increased in years; while the Orrenberg children were all weak sickly creatures. One after another, the three eldest sank into the grave; but when about six months ago the fourth boy expired and left them with only a daughter and without hopes of further progeny, Gustavus's spite and avarice could no longer contain itself within bounds. He resolved to remove the objects of his aversion, cost what it might; and you saw in the mangled body of Joscelyn the effects of this diabolical resolution! Heaven pardon him and me, and all sinners, Amen!"

"Aye, that murder, Father! That murder. . . . that is what I would fain hear! Oh! Proceed, proceed, for pity's sake! Let me know every cruel circumstance. . . . even though to hear it should break my heart!"

"Ah! and that would be a thousand pities, for it must needs be a kind heart to take on so grievously at hearing a story in which you have no concern.—Well then! You must know, that one morning the Count set forth to hunt the hart, and his young son pleaded so earnestly to accompany him, that the father could not resist his entreaties. The sport was excellent; and in the eagerness of pursuit everyone forgot to look after Joscelyn. At length the animal was taken; the hunters found themselves at a considerable distance from home; by degrees they all assembled, all except Joscelyn. Now then a hue and cry commenced; the Count was half frantic with apprehensions, and his alarm was increased tenfold, when he discovered that the chase had beguiled them into the woods of Orrenberg. Away rode the hunters, some one way, some another; four of the most trusty followed Rudiger, and while he made the forests ring again with the name of Joscelyn, the hand of Providence, in order that the murderer might be punished, guided him to the place where the poor child had already breathed his last; it was near a small river; the ground was stained with blood, and a huge wound stood gaping upon his ivory bosom. Search was made for the assassin, who (it was evident) could not have gone far, for the body was not yet cold! And a man, whose garments were still crimsoned with blood, and whose countenance pronounced him capable of committing any mischief, was found concealed in a thicket at no great distance."

"And what reason had he for. . . ."

"Oh! sir knight, every one guessed at the reason as soon a
Martin (the Count's squire) exclaimed that he knew the assa
sin, and that he was one of the Count of Orrenberg's dome
tics. The villain too knew in whose presence he was, an
addressing Count Rudiger by his name, he fell on his knee
and entreated him not to hurt him; a sure proof of his bein
conscious of some crime, else why should he have been appre
hensive of receiving hurt, sir knight? Well! He could not den
his belonging to Gustavus, but for a long time he persiste
in swearing that he had found the child already insensibl
in the wood, and that the blood had stained his clothes whil
conveying him to the rivulet, in hopes that by bathing his fac
with water he might restore him to his senses. Truly, th
fellow was artful enough, and made out a good plausible story
but Rudiger was not easily to be deceived. He had the villai
conveyed to the castle of Frankheim, and there proper mean
were taken for extorting from him a confession of the truth."

"And what was that confession?"

"Exactly what everyone expected; that he had been com
manded to murder the child by his master, Gustavus o
Orrenberg."

"He confessed it?—Almighty powers! Are you *sure*, that he
confessed it?"

"Sure of it? Why, alas-the-day! I heard him say it with my
own ears. He was asked by the Count who set him on to
commit the murder, and I heard him answer as plain as I
now hear you—'Gustavus of Orrenberg.'"

"Is it possible!" exclaimed Osbright in agony. His last lin
gering hope was now destroyed, and with all his anxiety to
believe Gustavus innocent, he found himself unable to exclude
the irresistible conviction of his guilt.

"Ah! It is but too certain!" resumed the friar with a deep
sigh. "One would willingly disbelieve the existence of such
villainy, but I heard the assassin own it myself; and a hard
ened sinner he was! In spite of all my pious exhortations to
repentance, not a word would he confess, though I begged
him with tears in my eyes; for wicked as he was, it almost
broke my heart to see the tortures which he endured, and all
out of his own obstinacy! Since the very moment that he
made the desired confession, my lord ordered him to be taken
from the rack, though it was then but to little purpose."

"The rack?" exclaimed Osbright, seizing the old man's hand

with a convulsive grasp. "Was it then only on the rack, that he made this confession?"

"No truly; till Count Rudiger had recourse to torture, not a syllable would he utter, but assertions of his own and his master's innocence. Nay, even when he was actually on the rack, he persisted in his obstinate falsehood. He had already remained there so long that he was scarcely unbound, before he breathed his last, poor sinful wretch! Heaven pardon him and take him to its mercy!"

Now then the heart of Osbright again beat freely. It is true, the death of his brother made that heart the abode of deep sorrow; but to banish from it the belief that Gustavus was the boy's assassin was to relieve it from a burden of insupportable agony. That belief grew weaker with every question which he put to Brother Peter; he found that while in possession of his strength and faculties the supposed culprit had most strenuously denied all knowledge of the crime; that the excess of torture alone had forced from him the declaration that Gustavus of Orrenberg had any concern in it; that the name of Gustavus had been suggested by the prejudices of the suspicious and already exasperated father; and that the whole confession was comprised in the mere pronouncing that name when the speaker was seduced into uttering it by the certainty of immediate release from tortures the most excruciating. Osbright had been educated at a distance from his family, and his mind therefore had not imbibed the prejudices which made the Count of Orrenberg be considered as an incarnate fiend throughout the domains of Frankheim. His liberal nature inclined him to wish all hearts to be as pure and as benevolent as his own; and his judgment was both too candid and too keen to mistake assertions for proofs or to be deluded by the artful coloring in which prejudice ever paints the actions of a detested object. In defiance therefore of all his father's endeavors, he had resolved to suspend his opinion of Gustavus, even while his character was a matter of indifference to him; but now that the dearest of all interests made him wish to find him worthy, to have found him so deeply culpable would have wrung with excess of torture the most susceptible fibers of his heart.

On reflection, he found that his plans must be delayed till the innocence of Gustavus in this bloody business could be fully cleared to the satisfaction of Count Rudiger and of all Germany; and he silently vowed never to know rest till he had proved that innocence, and ascertained, beyond the power of doubting, the real name of the monster whose dagger had sent the blooming Joscelyn to an untimely grave.

But how was he to commence his inquiries? Brother Peter was so fully convinced of the guilt of Gustavus that his answers to Osbright's questions only served to mislead his search, instead of furnishing the unraveling clue to this mystery of iniquity. The youth anxiously desired to talk over the business with some unprejudiced person; and for this purpose he resolved to depart immediately for the castle of Sir Lennard of Kleeborn. This worthy knight was, in spite of their alienation, considered equally as a friend by the two families of Frankheim and Orrenberg; Osbright had seen enough of his character, during his last visit at his father's, to feel for him the highest sentiments of esteem and reverence; and he resolved to lay his difficulties, his hopes, and his fears before this excellent man without disguise, and entreat his assistance in forwarding the one and removing the others.

The moon shone bright; in defiance of the friar's entreaties he resolved not to wait for morning, since grief and anxiety would have prevented sleep from visiting his couch. However, being anxious to avoid the presence of Count Rudiger till the first emotions of grief for the loss of his child, and of passion against the house of Orrenberg, should have subsided, he requested the monk to allow him to find hospitality within his cell on the succeeding night, when (as he said) his affairs would necessitate his being again in the chapel's neighborhood. His request being readily granted, he charged the old man to conceal his visit from everyone; and then having enforced his charge, by a considerable present to be appropriated to the use of Brother Peter's patron saint, Osbright vaulted upon his courser, whom fidelity had detained near the chapel, and whose frequent neighing had already announced his impatience at the absence of his lord.

CHAPTER III

"Alas! the spring-time's pleasant hours returning
Serve but to waken me to sharper pain,
Recalling scenes of agony and mourning,
Of baffled hopes, and prayers preferred in vain!

Thus was the sun his vernal beams displaying,
Thus did the woods in early foliage wave,
While dire disease on all I loved was preying,
And flowers seemed rising, but to strew his grave."
                                          CHARLOTTE SMITH.

WHILE the castle of Frankheim resounded with cries of agony
and threats of vengeance, the spirit of tranquil sorrow reigned
on every brow and in every heart throughout the domains of
Orrenberg. Seven months had elapsed since the death of the
heir of those domains, the young and amiable Philip; the
wound was skinned over, but the pain was still felt; tears had
ceased to trickle, but the heart had not yet ceased to bleed.

Gustavus stood at an oriel-window, and contemplated the
fertile fields, which he hoped on his deathbed to have bequeathed to his darling. The Lady Ulrica was employed at
her tapestry-frame; but her work was often suspended, while
she cast a look of anxious tenderness on the lovely Blanche
(who was at work beside her), and while she breathed a
mental prayer that Heaven in mercy to an almost broken
heart would preserve to her this, her loveliest, her dearest, her
only remaining child.

The silence was interrupted by the entrance of an old
female domestic, who informed Blanche that she had at length
found the canvas bag which had been so long missing, and
which she now presented to her. Blanche hastily quitted the
tapestry-frame, while her cheek alternately colored with anger,
and grew pale with apprehension.

"Oh! Rachel!" she exclaimed in a tone of reproach, "how
thoughtless to bring it hither! ah! and see! My dear mother
has recognized it but too surely, for her eyes are already filled
with tears!"—And she threw her arms affectionately round the
waist of Ulrica, and entreated her pardon for being the occasion of suggesting such painful recollections.

"What is the matter?" demanded her father, advancing from
the window. "What distresses you, Ulrica?" Then glancing
his eye on the canvas bag, which Blanche had suffered to fall
upon the ground, "Ah!" he continued, "I need no answer!
Those are the playthings of my poor dead boy! What would
you do with them, Blanche?"

"I meant to give them to the gardener's children; they were
Philip's playfellows and friends, and they have not forgotten
yet, how dearly he loved them. It was only yesterday that as I

passed toward St. Hildegarde's grotto, I met the poor children going to adorn Philip's grave with their choicest flowers; and their father tells me, that they mention him every night in their prayers, and never pass a day without visiting his monument—and so I fancied that by giving these playthings. . . . But I wish that I had never thought at all about them, since the sight of them has distressed you so much, dear mother! Nay now, pry'thee, weep no more! You know, my father says that 'tis sinful to murmur at the dispensations of Providence, and that it gives him pain whenever he sees our tears!"

"And should not that reflection check your own, my Blanche?" inquired Gustavus. "Why are your cheeks so wet? Fie! fie, my child!"

"Ah! Dear father, I cannot prevent their flowing, do all that I can! When anyone seems happy, I cannot help smiling; and when anyone dies, surely I needs must weep. But at least I obey you better than my mother; indeed neither of us *talk* of Philip, but then she always *thinks* of him and is always melancholy. Now I am always gay, and endeavor *not* to think of him; except when something brings him suddenly before me, and then I cannot choose but weep, or else my heart would break in two;—for instance, when I look at these playthings, it seems to me as if Philip were present. I think I see him arranging his troops so busily on the ground; I think I hear him entreating me to leave my tiresome tapestry and observe how bravely he will fight the battle. 'The blue,' he used to say, 'are the vassals of Orrenberg, and the red are the vassals of Frankheim; and now. . . .'"

"Of Frankheim, Blanche?" interrupted Gustavus, "no, no; that was not what Philip called them. 'The red,' he used to say, 'are our enemies.'"

"Yes, yes; our enemies, the vassals of Frankheim."

"You misunderstood him, Blanche; why should Philip call the vassals of Frankheim our enemies?"

"Nay, dear father, are they *not* so? Everyone in the castle thinks and says it."

"They, who say so, had better not say it in my hearing. The Count of Frankheim is my nearest relation, a man of singular military prowess and distinguished by many noble qualities. It is true, the dissimilarity of our manners and habits, together with various other impediments, has prevented so cordial an intimacy between the families as should exist between such near connections; but still I entertain a high respect for the character of the owners of Frankheim, and shall not hear without displeasure those persons called my enemies, whom I would willingly boast of as my friends."

"Your friends? Oh! Father! Would you call those your friends who have poisoned your only remaining son, who have deprived me of an only remaining brother? Ah! Should I not call these cruel people our enemies, our worst of enemies?"

"Poisoned my son? Poisoned Philip?"

"Nay, it is the common talk of the whole castle! Every child on the domains knows it, as well as I do, and trembles at the name of Rudiger, the ruthless child-murderer! Nay; has not my mother openly acknowledged that. . . ."

"Blanche!" interrupted Ulrica hastily, "you go too far. You misrepresent the fact. What have I ever openly acknowledged? I merely, in confidential conversation, let fall a hint, a sort of suspicion. . . . that it was just possible. . . . that to judge from appearances. . . . that I was almost tempted to imagine. . . ."

"Aye, Ulrica," replied her husband, "I feared from the very first that *you* were the original cause of this ill-founded report. Is there no hope then that my entreaties and advice will ever eradicate from your mind the only dark speck which deforms it? Of all the defects of the human heart, there is none more encroaching, more insidious, more dangerous than mistrust; viewed through her distorted optics, there is no action so innocent, no everyday occurrence so insignificant, that does not assume the appearance of offense. Words are misconstrued; looks are interpreted! Thoughts are guessed at and acted upon, as if thoughts were facts; the supposed fault is retaliated by a real one; that one gives birth to more; injury succeeds injury, and crime treads upon the heels of crime, till the web of mischief and misery is complete; and the suspector starts in surprise and horror to find both himself and his adversary equally involved in that guilt which but for his suspicions would probably have been the lot of neither."

"Nay, Gustavus, why thus severe? What have I done? I assert nothing; I accuse no one. I merely hinted at the possibility. . . . and *that,* while I have life and conscience, I *must* maintain—to die so suddenly! today in all the bloom of health, and tomorrow in his coffin! Oh! That fatal inheritance! To that shall I ever ascribe the loss of my child!—And then the livid spots, which broke out upon my poor boy's corpse. . . . and the agonies which he suffered. . . . the burning heat, and the insatiable thirst which tormented him. . . . and above all the rapid putrefaction. . . . Yes! yes! the moment that I beheld that, I exclaimed—'such a death cannot be natural.' A dreadful light broke in upon me, and. . . ."

"—And at that light you have kindled a torch, capable of burning to the very ground the house of your unsuspecting neighbor, of your nearest relation! You have inflamed the imaginations of the giddy unthinking multitude, whose rage if once let loose and countenanced by their superiors. . . ."

"*I* inflamed them? Oh! You injure me, my husband! It is true, their rage, their hatred against the Count of Frankheim is at this moment extreme; but I have done my utmost to prevent their breaking out into violence. I dread Count Rudiger; but I hate him not, for I will not hate any one; and though your former love for Magdalena once made me fear her influence over your heart, your uniform kindness during many long years has totally erased all such apprehensions from my bosom. Do not then suspect me of stirring up our people to vengeance upon the Frankheimers. Alas! It needed no instigation of mine to make them understand a tale so clear, a fact so evident that the murder circulated from lip to lip, ere I had time to impose silence on the deathbed attendants; and every man's own consciousness suggested to him the murderer's name."

"A tale so clear, Ulrica? Before your father's fatal bequest had raised suspicions of each other between the families, you attended Magdalena's lying-in—the child lived but a few hours, and expired in your arms. Had Magdalena been as mistrustful as yourself, how well would the tale have been told that, jealous of my former attachment to the mother, you had privately, while pretending to kiss it, confined the windpipe of the child, or pressed its skull together, or else. . . ."

"Oh! spare me, my husband! Yes, such a tale might have been told. . . . Oh! horror! might perhaps have been believed. I will say nothing more; I will accuse no one in future; I will bury all my suspicions in oblivion; I will forgive all. . . . if they will but leave me this one blessing, this one darling, this my last, my only existing child!"

As she said this, Ulrica threw her arms round her kneeling daughter; and she was still weeping upon her neck, when a domestic entered, and announced a herald from the castle of Frankheim. As all intimacy between the families had ceased, and they now only met on great festivals, or at tournaments, or on some solemn occasion, it was concluded that the herald's business related to some public occurrence, some imperial edict, or some regulations for the welfare of the Palatinate. The women, therefore, thought proper to withdraw. Ulrica, greatly agitated by the conversation which had just taken place, retired to indulge the agony of maternal regret in her own solitary apartment; and Blanche. . . . ?

The war was concluded; the troops were dismissed; the knights were returning home.

"*Perhaps!*" said Blanche, and with a light step and heart full of hope, she fled through the secret passage toward the cave among the rocks.

CHAPTER IV

—"*Oh! my soul come not thou into their counsels; unto their assembly, mine honor, be not thou united; for in their anger they slew a man, and in their self-will they digged a wall. Cursed be their anger, for it was fierce, and their wrath, for it was cruel.*"—

GENESIS.

AND the hopes of Blanche were not quite disappointed. It is true, the cave was vacant: but he had been there; but he had left a token that she was not forgotten by him. Tomorrow according to their mutual agreement she might depend upon seeing once more the youth whose image gratitude had engraved upon her heart in characters never to be effaced; and then might she claim his promise of revealing to her his real name and clearing up the mystery in which he had hitherto enveloped all that related to him, except his adoration of herself. Satisfied of that most material point, she had hitherto been content to leave every other in obscurity; but now she should know everything; now her lover would disclose himself, and authorize her disclosing their attachment to her parents; and precious as they held her, she still feared not their opposing her union with a man whom she loved so tenderly and by whom she was so tenderly beloved. Besides, her father was sinking into the vale of years; the family required some younger and more active champion to defend them against the nefarious designs of their mortal foe, the cruel and insidious Count of Frankheim; and where could they find a fitter protector than this unknown knight who had already proved the strength of his arm and valor of his heart so successfully when he rescued her from the banditti? Oh! When once his bride, she should no longer tremble at the dreadful name of Rudiger! All then would be peace, security, and happiness! And while she made these reflections, she pressed the well-known scarf to her lips a thousand and a thousand times.

The sun was setting, and it was time for her to return home. She threw herself on her knees before the crucifix which she had herself placed on the rough-hewn altar; she poured forth a prayer of fervent gratitude to St. Hildegarde, traced a cross upon her forehead and bosom with the same holy water which had formerly quenched the thirst of that virgin martyr, and then bidding a tender adieu to the cavern in which she had passed so many happy moments, she sped back toward the castle, the scarf fluttering in the evening breeze as she retraced the secret passages.

She was proceeding toward her own apartment, when in crossing a gallery which was connected with the great hall, she was alarmed at seeing several of the domestics hurrying backward and forward in confusion; she stopped, and listened; she heard her father's name frequently repeated, and at length caught some words, as if some accident had happened to him. Now then everything else was forgotten in the apprehension of his being in danger. She flew toward his apartment, which was on the other side of the castle; but in crossing the great hall, she was detained by the young Baron of Hartfeld.

"Heaven be thanked, that I have found you, lady!" said he, taking her hand affectionately. "The Countess charged me to seek you, and prevent your being suddenly alarmed. Nay, look not so terrified! On my knightly word there is no danger, and a few hours will restore your father to that fortitude, of which the too great sensibility of his nature has at present deprived him."

"Oh! what has happened? What has overcome his fortitude? Something dreadful surely! Is he ill, Sir Ottokar? Oh! Assure me at least, that he is not ill!"

"His illness is merely temporary; by this time no doubt it is quite past. It is true, his senses forsook him for a time; he fainted, and. . . ."

"He fainted? Oh! Heavens! Let me hasten to him this moment. . . ."

"You must not, till you are more calm. Your present agitation would affect him and probably occasion a relapse. Suffer me to lead you into a less public apartment; there you shall hear all that has happened, and when your spirits are composed, you shall then carry peace and consolation to the wounded feelings of your father."

But the emotions of Blanche could admit of no delay; she still hurried onward; and as in fact Sir Ottokar had only wished to detain her, in order that he might enjoy her society for a few minutes without restraint, all that he had to communicate was told, before they reached the Count's chamber-door.

Interlarding his discourse with many compliments to his auditress and insinuations of the tender interest which he felt for her, the Baron now related that the business of the Count of Frankheim's herald was to accuse Gustavus of the assassination of the Count's youngest son, and to proclaim open and inveterate feuds between the families of Frankheim and Orrenberg. This the herald had not only announced to Gustavus in the most disrespectful manner, but had thought proper to repeat the purport of his mission publicly in the courtyard; at the same time accompanying his speech with such insulting remarks upon their master and his whole family, that the indignation of the vassals became outrageous, and threatened the insolent herald with consequences the most dangerous. The Count of Orrenberg was alarmed at the tumult and hastened to the courtyard to appease his incensed people, whose affection for them was unbounded. Gustavus was but lately recovered from a perilous malady, occasioned by grief for the loss of his last male heir; he was still in a state of lamentable weakness, and the shock of being so unexpectedly accused of assassination had greatly increased the irritability of his nerves, which naturally was excessive; yet still he exerted himself most strenuously in endeavoring to quell the confusion. But in vain did he command his vassals to be silent and temperate; in vain did he conjure the herald to be gone, if he valued his own safety. The insolent emissary persisted in heaping taunt upon taunt, and slander upon slander. The people grew more incensed with every word that he uttered; and at length overcome with agitation, heat, fatigue, and weakness, Gustavus sank into the arms of his attendants, and was conveyed to his apartment in a state of insensibility. However, he was already nearly recovered when

Ulrica requested Sir Ottokar to seek her daughter and relate what had happened, lest she should be unnecessarily alarmed.

But Blanche loved her father too dearly to believe that he was quite out of danger till her own eyes had convinced her of his health and safety. She found him very pale and feeble, and his recollection was yet scarcely clear enough to permit his perfectly understanding the events which had taken place. Blanche sank on her knees by the couch, on which he was reposing, and threw her white arms round his neck affectionately.

"You have heard it all, my child?" said Gustavus. "You know, of how dreadful a crime your father is accused? But surely you will not believe me capable of. . . ."

"Nor she nor anyone can believe it," interrupted Ulrica, "except those who are interested in working the destruction of you and all your house. Nay more; everyone, except yourself, knew well, that sooner or later the rancor and avarice of Count Rudiger must end in open war; but I little thought that he would have advanced so gross a falsehood as an excuse for commencing hostilities! They to accuse you of murdering a child! They, who themselves but seven months ago deprived us. . . ."

"Peace! Peace! Ulrica; no more of that!—But tell me. . . . my ideas are still so wandering. . . . Is it then true, that Rudiger's son is murdered?"

"It is but too certain. He was found dead in one of our forests, and what makes the fact more distressing is that one of our domestics was the assassin. He confessed his crime on the rack, and died in a few minutes afterward; died (horrible to tell!) with a lie still warm upon his lips. For oh! my husband, in his last moments he declared that he had been bribed by you to assassinate the poor child!"

"By me?" exclaimed Gustavus, and started from his couch. "Confessed it? No, this is not to be endured! Under such an imputation there is no living. Bring my armor; saddle my steed! I will hasten this moment to Frankheim; I will assert my innocence with all the irresistible energy of truth; I will demand to be tried by every ordeal, by fire, by water. . . . Nay, nay, detain me not, I must to Rudiger this instant, and either convince him that I am guiltless, or perish by his hand."

He was rushing toward the door, but all present hastened to impede his passage.

"Count, this is insanity!" exclaimed Sir Ottokar. "You are

rushing on inevitable destruction! Rudiger is not to be convinced. He has vowed your destruction with the most solemn and terrible adjurations; nor your destruction only; his vengeance includes all who are related to you, all who love you! Your wife, your daughter, your very domestics. . . ."

"My daughter?" repeated Gustavus, clasping his hands in an agony of horror, "my innocent Blanche?"

"All! All are involved in Count Rudiger's plan of vengeance! He has sworn to give your castle a prey to the flames, and to feed them with its wretched inmates. No man, no woman, no child, no, not the very dog that now licks your hand, shall be suffered to escape! This did I myself hear the Count of Frankheim swear last night at the burial of his murdered child; and his friends, his servants, his vassals, all made St. John's vaults echo, while with one voice they repeated the bloody, the diabolical oath. My friendship for you, my lord, and my alarm for the safety of the Lady Blanche, made me hasten homeward to summon the assistance of my followers; they are mounted to the number of forty, well-armed and accoutered, and I have conducted them hither prepared to spill the last drop of their blood in vindication of your innocence, and in defense of the Countess and your lovely daughter."

"I thank you, Sir Ottokar, and should there be no means of avoiding this unnatural war, I shall profit with gratitude by your kind and ready friendship. But still I indulge the hopes of peace. I have no real fault toward Rudiger; and could I but contrive a personal interview with him. . . . could I but explain the injustice of his suspicions. . . . at least I will make the attempt; and perhaps. . . . Ha! well remembered! Kurt," he continued, addressing himself to a gray-headed domestic, who was standing near the door, "is the herald yet gone?"

"Gone?" repeated the old man, shaking his head with a smile of satisfaction. "No, truly, nor likely to go, the villain!"

"Then call him hither instantly. He shall bear my request for an interview with Rudiger, and . . . How is this, Kurt? Why do you still linger here? I would have the herald come to me; bring him this moment!"

"Bring him? Why, aye, to be sure I could easily do that; but as to his *coming,* he'd find that a difficult matter. . . . unless he can walk without his head. Nay, my lord, it is even so, and now all's out—the people's rage was not to be bridled;

when they saw you fall, they thought that the herald had stabbed you; they fell upon him, men, women, and children, like so many mad people, and before one could say 'Ave' his head was off his shoulders, and nailed over the gateway between the two great kites."

"Ulrica! Ottokar!" stammered the Count, and seemed, as if he had been struck by a thunderbolt. "Is this true? Has my castle indeed been polluted by so horrible an outrage?—Almighty powers! the murder of a herald. . . . a character, ever held sacred even among the most barbarous nations. . . . murdered in my own castle. . . . almost in my own sight. . . . Now then indeed the mischief is irremediable. From the imputation of this guilt never shall I be able to clear myself in Rudiger's eyes!"

"Nay, my dear lord," replied Sir Ottokar, "let not this misfortune affect you so deeply. The insolent menial merited well such a fate; a fate which (*I* can witness, as I arrived in the heat of the tumult) you did your utmost to avert. But to save him was not within the power of a mortal. His calumnies. . . . his threats against your whole family. . . . Your people's hatred of Rudiger. . . . their consciousness, that he had deprived you of your son Philip by poison. . . ."

"Aye, aye!" exclaimed Gustavus, "hear you that, Ulrica? Now then you see the fatal effects of your mistrust! Now then you enjoy the bloody fruits of those ungrounded suspicions, which you so lightly infused into the minds of the rash and wanton multitude! Oh! my wife, I fear greatly, that at the day of judgment when this murder is cited, your hands will not appear quite bloodless! God forgive you!"

The Countess shuddered, but only answered by a flood of tears.

"Spare your lady, my noble friend," said Ottokar, taking the Count's hand. "Even if your reproaches are deserved, they now come too late, and the present difficulties demand our attention too much to admit of reflections on the past. The Frankheimers are powerful and inveterate. Rudiger has sworn the extirpation of your whole family; Osbright is returned from the wars to assist his father's plans of vengeance; these human wolves thirst for your blood, and. . . . earth and heavens! can it be possible? It is. . . . it *must* be the same! Pardon me, Lady Blanche; by what strange accident do I see that scarf in your possession?"

"This scarf? You know it, sir knight?—I came by it. . . .

that is. . . . I found it. . . . as I was passing through the secret passages, which lead. . . ."

"The secret passages? Osbright of Frankheim lurking in the secret passages of Orrenberg Castle?"

"Osbright?" exclaimed Ulrica in the greatest alarm. "And you traversed those passages alone?—Oh! my child, from what a danger have you escaped! No doubt, his purpose there. . . ."

"Must needs have been hostile to the inmates of this castle!" interrupted Ottokar eagerly. "Perhaps. . . . perhaps, he was aware that the lovely Blanche frequented those secret passages and hoped that his dagger might unobserved revenge. . . ."

"Oh! no, sir knight," exclaimed the affrighted Blanche, "you misunderstood me! No one was lurking in the secret paths! It was not there that I found the scarf, it was in the cavern of St. Hildegarde. . . . and perhaps you mistake about the scarf, too! Perhaps, it is not Osbright's! Oh! no, no, no! Heavenly mercy forbid that it should be!"

"Indeed?" said Ottokar, while jealousy whispered a thousand suspicions to his mind, "nay, of that there is no doubt. It is the work of the Lady Magdalena, and too remarkable to be mistaken. Besides, in saving the Palatine's life in battle, Osbright's bosom was slightly wounded; his scarf was stained with blood, and I heard him swear that the blood shed in his sovereign's defense was the noblest ornament of his scarf, and should never be effaced—look, lady, look! Osbright has kept his oath."

Blanche looked on the bloody marks; the scarf fell from her hands, and she clasped them in an agony of despair. With every moment did Sir Ottokar's jealous fears grow more strong, and his desire to impress Blanche with an idea of Osbright's animosity more keen and anxious.

"But one thing more!" said Blanche with difficulty, while she almost gasped for breath—"that horrible curse, which you spoke of. . . . which Rudiger. . . . which his vassals pronounced. . . . was it pronounced by Osbright? Was Osbright in the chapel, when it was pronounced?"

"He was, lady! He was!" replied Ottokar, eagerly and peremptorily. "I was near the chapel door, and saw him rush into the chapel with a maniac's look, his eyes burning with vengeance, his lips pale with passion, his whole frame trembling with eagerness, and with fear lest he should be too late to join in the horrible execration. I heard Count Rudiger devote to destruction your father, your mother, your innocent self!

I saw Osbright rush furiously forward to join his father; and instantly every voice except my own re-echoed the dreadful words—'vengeance! everlasting vengeance on the bloody house of Orrenberg!'"

"And did not one kind voice," said Blanche faintly, "did no suggestion of pity. . . . ah! did no one utter one word to plead for the poor Blanche?"

"No one, lady! No one, as I have a soul to save!"

"Oh! I am very faint, my mother!" murmured Blanche, and bursting into tears she sank upon the bosom of Ulrica.

Her pale looks and trembling frame greatly alarmed her parents; but believing her agitation to be solely produced by apprehension and by horror at the dreadful threats pronounced against her life by the Frankheimers, they advised her to retire to rest and compose herself. Blanche willingly accepted the permission of departing, and hastened to meditate in the solitude of her chamber on the fatal discovery, which accident had just made.

CHAPTER V

> "Let no one say, that there is need
>   Of time for love to grow;
> Oh! no; the love, which kills indeed,
>   Dispatches at a blow.
>
> "Love all at once should from the earth
>   Start up full-grown and tall;
> If not an Adam at his birth,
>   He is no love at all."
>   LORD HOLLAND from Lope de Vega.

WHILE these transactions were passing at Orrenberg, Osbright was anxiously employed in finding means to remove all existing prejudices, and establish a close and lasting amity between the rival kinsmen. He found Sir Lennard of Kleeborn willing to assist his design, and scrupled not to lay before him the dearest secret of his bosom.

So great had been his father's apprehensions of treachery on the part of Orrenberg, that Osbright was seldom suffered to visit his paternal mansion. Year after year, however, having passed away without any fatal effects arising from the supposed avaricious views of Gustavus, and the youth being now of an age to take his own part, Count Rudiger about nine months before had gratified himself and his fondly anxious consort by the recall of his first-born son. The breaking out of hostilities compelled Osbright to leave the Castle of Frankheim a second time; but previous to his departure it had been his fortune to rescue the lovely Blanche from the hands of ruffians, and at the same moment to receive and impart a passion the most ardent and irradicable.

Blanche declared her name to her deliverer and earnestly entreated him to accompany her to the castle of Orrenberg, where her parents would receive their child's deliverer with all the warmth of heartfelt gratitude; but Osbright's prudence forbade his taking so dangerous a step, especially when the discourse of his mistress convinced him how deeply engraved, and how odious in their nature, were the prejudices attached to the name of Frankheim in the minds of the inmates of Orrenberg. Educated himself at the court of Bamberg, his heart was untainted by the gloomy mistrust which (with the solitary exception of Magdalena) he found prevailing throughout his father's domains; and the knowledge of Blanche's family name instantly suggested to his fancy the pleasing hope that their union might be the means of extinguishing the animosity which prevailed between two families so nearly related; but he found that the mind of Blanche was very differently modeled. The Lady Ulrica was naturally of a temper timid and suspicious. Jealousy of her lord's early attachment to Magdalena had originally disposed her to consider the actions of the Frankheimers in no favorable point of view; her father's unfortunate bequest made her regard them as persons whose interest must necessarily lead them to wish for the extinction of her family; a variety of trifling circumstances, which her jaundiced imagination made her see in false colors, strengthened her in this persuasion; and the successive deaths of four sons thoroughly persuaded her that she had not evil wishes alone to fear on the part of those who would benefit so greatly by depriving her of her children. All these ideas had been imbibed by her only remaining offspring. Blanche from her infancy had been accustomed to pray, that the Virgin would preserve her from Satan and the Frankheimers; at the mention of Rudiger's name she never failed to cross herself; and while she was thanking Osbright for her rescue from the ruffians, he could scarcely help smiling at the positiveness, with which she assured him of their having been emissaries either of his wicked father or of his bloodthirsty self!

Till these prejudices so deeply-rooted could be effaced, Osbright thought it absolutely necessary to conceal his name and to refuse Blanche's invitation to visit the castle of Orrenberg. At the drawbridge he respectfully took his leave, and in return for his service, he only requested her word of honor, that she would not mention her adventure to any human being. Though surprised at the entreaty, Blanche could not refuse to give this promise; not to mention that she was herself apprehensive that if the danger which she had run should be made public, her mother's anxious care would never again suffer her to pass the walls of Orrenberg. This promise therefore she gave readily; but she hesitated a little when the unknown youth expressed an ardent hope that he should in future be permitted to thank the Lady Blanche for her compliance. To permit such interviews unknown to her parents, and when even herself was ignorant of his name and quality, she felt, would be highly imprudent; but he implored so earnestly, yet with such diffidence; he had treated her with such respectful delicacy, while she was in his power unprotected; his manners were so noble; her obligations to him were so recent; and above all, her own inclination to see him again was so strong, that before she was herself aware of her intention, she hinted that she generally visited the Grotto of St. Hildegarde about two hours before sunset. The youth pressed her hand to his lips with respectful gratitude, breathed a fervent prayer for her welfare, and she then hastened into the castle, her cheeks glowing with blushes and her heart beating high with hope.

To one interview another still succeeded, and still did the unknown knight acquire a greater influence over the heart of the innocent Blanche. That influence he chiefly exerted in efforts to eradicate her antipathy to everything belonging to Frankheim; but he found it a less easy task to destroy her ill opinion of his relations than to inspire her with a favorable one of himself. However, his own interest in her heart appeared to be so firmly established that he no longer dreaded lest the knowledge of his connections should make him the object of Blanche's aversion; and when the Palatine's summons compelled him to lead his retainers to Heidelberg, he gave his mistress at parting a solemn promise that when next they met, he would disclose to her his real name and situation;

a secret which she was most anxious to know, and to arrive at which, she had exhausted all the little arts of which she was mistress, though all were exhausted in vain. However, he had assured her of his rank being equal to her own; and the splendor of his dress, at once simple and magnificent, and (still more) the variety of his accomplishments and dignified frankness of his manners, convinced her that the sphere in which he moved must needs be elevated.

Such was the present situation of the lovers which Osbright now laid before the good Sir Lennard. His host heard him with evident satisfaction; and his excellent heart exulted in the prospect of a reconciliation between two families, the chiefs of which had both been his earliest friends, and with whom (in despite of their disunion) he was still upon the most amicable terms. He therefore said everything in his power to confirm Osbright in his attachment. He exclaimed loudly against the injustice of supposing Gustavus to be concerned in the death of Joscelyn; he described him as the most humane of mortals, a man whose fault was rather to push compassion and benevolence beyond the limits of reason and prudence than to be seduced into the commission of a crime so atrocious as the murder of an unoffending child; and as to the temptation which was supposed to have influenced Gustavus in this transaction, he quoted a thousand acts of disinterestedness and generosity, each strong enough to convince even the most prejudiced, that the man who performed them must possess a mind totally free from the pollution of avarice. In conclusion Sir Lennard promised the youth his best offices; and as he judged it most advisable to make the whole business known to Gustavus as soon as possible, he engaged to visit the castle of Orrenberg the next day, where he was certain that Osbright's proposals would be received with eagerness. The great point, however, was to remove from Rudiger's mind the persuasion that Gustavus had caused his younger son to be assassinated, and he advised Osbright to spare no pains to discover the real murderers; that mystery once cleared up, all other difficulties he looked upon as trifles. Osbright received Sir Lennard's advice with gratitude, promised to obey it implicitly, and having passed the night at his friend's castle, he returned with renovated hopes to the Chapel of St. John.

Father Peter gave him the most cordial welcome, though still ignorant that his humble cell was honored by affording a refuge to the heir of Frankheim. Osbright made him repeat the story of the murder circumstantially, and among other things the old man mentioned that the little finger of Joscelyn's left hand was missing when his corpse was found, and that it had been repeatedly sought on the fatal spot, but without success. This circumstance struck Osbright as very singular, and he thought it not impossible but that it might furnish a clue to unravel the whole mystery. But with much more sanguine expectations did he learn from Father Peter that the assassin had left a wife, for whom (even while enduring the agony of the rack) he expressed the most ardent affection. Was it not probable then that this beloved wife was in her husband's confidence and could explain the motive which tempted him to commit the crime? Osbright resolved to examine her himself; but he found that she had gone to visit a relation at some distance, where she was said to be inconsolable for the loss of her ill-fated husband. To depart without seeing Blanche was too much to be expected; he therefore determined to pass the day in Father Peter's cell, to visit St. Hildegarde's Grotto in the evening, and after assuring himself that the heart of Blanche was still his own, to set forward on his expedition without suffering a moment's longer delay.

Evening approached; and Osbright was crossing the aisle which led toward the principal gate of the chapel when his attention was arrested by the murmuring of a voice, proceeding from a small oratory dedicated to the Virgin. The door was open, and he cast a passing glance within. A youth was kneeling at the shrine in fervent prayer, and a second glance assured Osbright that the youth was the page, Eugene.

Enthusiasm seemed to have marked Eugene for her own, even from his earliest infancy; and succeeding events had given to that enthusiasm a universal cast of tender melancholy. Rudiger esteemed and admired the Lady Magdalena; but a visit to the Convent of St. Hildegarde several years after his marriage convinced him that he had never loved till then. He there saw a sister of the order who made upon his heart the most forcible impression; and though Rudiger possessed many noble qualities, the mastery of his passions was not numbered among them. The personal attractions which had gained for him the heart of Magdalena were equally triumphant over the principles of the Sister Agatha; she eloped with him from the convent, and became the mother of Eugene.

But all the blandishments of her seducer, whose love sur-

vived the gratification of his desires, could not stifle in her
bosom the cries of remorse. She saw herself the disgrace of
her noble family, and the violator of the sacred marriage-bed;
the dread of discovery constantly tormented her; her perjury
to Heaven made her look upon herself as a mark for divine
vengeance; she trembled every moment with apprehension of
punishment in *this* world, and she despaired of obtaining
pardon in the next. At length her mental sufferings became
too exquisite for endurance; she resolved to break the disgraceful chains which united her to Rudiger and endeavor
to atone for her past errors by the penitence of her future
life. She made by letter a full confession to the Lady Magdalena; entreated pardon for herself and protection for her
helpless infant; and then hastened to conceal her ignominy
in a retreat, to discover which baffled all the inquiries of her
forsaken seducer.

Magdalena forgave her husband's faults, pitied his sufferings, and became the benevolent protectress of his child. It was
thought highly advisable for the sake of his own respectability
that Rudiger should be supposed to have no concern in this
business, and that the disgraceful circumstances attending the
child's birth should be suppressed as much as possible. Accordingly, Eugene was educated as a foundling, whose helpless
situation had attracted Magdalena's notice and compassion;
but this fortunate delusion was not suffered to last. The
wretched mother felt that her end was approaching and could
not resist her desire to see and bless her child, though she
prudently resolved to keep her relation to him still unknown.

Remorse, and self-enforced penance the most cruel, had
worn her to the very bone. Oppressed with long travel, her
feet bleeding, fainting, dying, she arrived at the castle of
Frankheim. She sought out her boy; she saw him; and in an
agony of tenderness and grief the mother's heart betrayed her
secret. The boy's character had ever appeared singular. He
entered into no childish sports; he would listen for hours to
stories of murders, or robbers, but above all he delighted in
the narrative of religious miracles and the sufferings of mar-
tyrs. His favorite walk was in the churchyard, where he passed
whole evenings, learning by heart the rhymes engraved upon
the tombstones. He was seldom moved to laughter; even in his
smile there was something melancholy; nor had he any way
of expressing joy or gratitude, except by tears. Every word,
look, and gesture already betrayed the enthusiast; and from

his fondness for all church ceremonies and his continually chanting religious hymns, he had obtained among the domestics of Frankheim the name of the Little Abbot.

Such was the boy, who at ten years old saw himself unexpectedly clasped in the arms of an expiring mother, whom he had long numbered among the dead. The sudden recognition; her wild and emaciated appearance; her tattered garments, her bleeding feet; the passion of her kisses, the agony of her tears; the description of her faults, of her remorse, of her terrors of the future, of her dreadful and unexampled penance; all these united were too much for Eugene's sensibility to endure! When in spite of all Magdalena's efforts to prolong her existence, the wretched mother breathed her last, the son was forcibly torn from the corpse delirious.

No sooner had the report reached the Countess that a dying beggar had declared herself to be Eugene's mother than she hastened to assist the sufferer and rescue the feeling child from a scene so terrible. But she arrived too late; a few moments terminated the nun's existence, and Eugene had already received a shock, which during a twelvemonth set the physician's skill at defiance.

His senses at length returned; but his heart never seemed to recover from the wound, which had agonized it so exquisitely. Pale, drooping, absorbed in thought, nothing seemed capable of affording him pleasure. He declined all amusements; he neglected all attainments, both literary and warlike: and when chided by the chaplain for inattention to his lessons, and when mocked by the military vassals for effeminacy, he listened to their reproofs and taunts with indifference and answered both with silence. His time was passed in listless indolence; he would stand hour after hour dropping pebbles in the river and gazing upon the circles as they formed themselves and then vanished into nothing. Vain were the exertions of Magdalena and her husband to awaken him from this torpor of the mind; though compelled to endure their kindness, he evidently felt it a burden, and sedulously avoided it. Agatha's sad story occupied his whole soul; he could not but consider Magdalena as filling the place which his mother should have occupied; he could not but consider Rudiger as the author of his mother's sufferings; and though the Count almost doted upon the boy with a truly paternal tenderness, the most that he could obtain from him was implicit submission and cold respect.

Eugene only saw in himself a forlorn being, whose odious birth had branded his mother with infamy, and whose existence was given under circumstances too disgraceful to permit his being avowed by his surviving parent. Magdalena's kindness was the offspring of mere compassion; the memory of his mother's wrongs was inseparably connected with the sight of his father: he felt that he had no claim to the love of anyone, nor did he see anyone toward whom his heart felt love, till accident made him the preserver of the little Joscelyn. The child had strayed from its careless nurse, and fell into the river. No one but Eugene saw its danger, who having obstinately refused to practice all manly exercises was totally ignorant of the art of swimming. The river was deep, the stream was strong; to attempt to save Joscelyn was to expose himself to equal danger; yet without a moment's hesitation did the effeminate Eugene plunge into the river, grasp the child's garments with one hand and the bough of a neighboring willow with the other; and thus did he sustain his already insensible burden, till his frantic cries attracted the notice of the domestics. They hastened to the place, and arriving at the very moment when the bough giving way menaced the child and his preserver with inevitable destruction.

From that moment Joscelyn became the object of Eugene's whole solicitude and affection. He was his *brother*, was a being who had no faults in his eyes, and was one who but for him would have been numbered with the dead. Attachment to Joscelyn now divided his heart with grief for the earthly sufferings of his mother and with religious terrors for her eternal salvation. However, as he increased in years, it was suspected in the castle, that other passions would ere long possess no inconsiderable influence over his bosom. Though he still shunned society, it was remarked that he only shunned that of men; in the company of women, his habitual gloom seemed to melt into a voluptuous languor. The Countess's damsels perceived that when they addressed him in the language of kindness, his large eyes swam in tears and sparkled with fire, and the rush of blood spread a hectic crimson over his pale fair cheeks. Moreover it was observed that, though his devotions were performed with unabated ardor, after he reached the age of fifteen Eugene prayed to no saints but female ones.

Even now it was to the Virgin that he was kneeling when Osbright discovered him in the oratory. During his short visits at Frankheim, the knight's attention had been engaged by the singularity of the page's demeanor; and though respect for his own character had induced Rudiger to conceal the relationship between himself and Eugene from his son's knowledge, still Osbright, prompted by his own feelings, had neglected no means of showing the boy that he bore him much good-will. But his advances were all rejected with the most obstinate coldness; Eugene only looked upon him as the possessor of that place which, if his own mother had filled Magdalena's, he should himself have occupied; he could not help envying Count Rudiger's fortunate heir and avowed offspring; and when he reflected that but for this odious elder brother his darling Joscelyn would one day be lord of the extensive domains of Frankheim, a sentiment mingled itself with his envy and repugnance, which nothing but his religious principles prevented from becoming hatred. As a Christian, he would not hate anyone; but as a human being, he felt that it was impossible for him to love Count Rudiger's eldest son and Joscelyn's elder brother.

Finding his attentions so ill repaid, Osbright bestowed no further thought on the wayward lad; and the interest with which he at this moment surveyed him arose from the recollection of Eugene's ardent attachment to the murdered child. He listened in mournful silence while the page poured forth his lamentations in a strain of devotion the most ardent; with a thousand touching expressions, with enthusiasm almost delirious, he described his favorite's perfections, and bewailed his own irreparable loss; but what was the knight's astonishment to hear the page conclude his orisons by imploring the blessed spirit of Joscelyn to protect from every danger and watch with celestial care the precious life of Blanche of Orrenberg!

An exclamation of surprise burst from Osbright's lips, and warned Eugene of his being overheard. The page started from the ground, and in his confusion a rosary formed of ebony and coral escaped from his hands. Osbright sprang forward, and seized it, for he knew that rosary well; and had he doubted its identity, the name of Blanche engraved upon the golden crucifix would have removed all hesitation on the subject; in an instant a thousand jealous fears rushed before his fancy. The lad was singularly beautiful; his figure, light and exquisitely formed, might have served the statuary as a model for a zephyr;[7] confusion had spread over his cheeks an unusual glow, and his bright and flowing hair glittered in the sunbeams like dark gold. Osbright eyed him with displeasure and asked him haughtily how that rosary came into his hands.

"Noble sir," replied Eugene, trembling and embarrassed; "I. . . . I found it.—I found it near the caves of St. Hildegarde."

"And of course you know not its owner, or I should not find it still in your possession?"—(Eugene was silent.)

"Well! the workmanship pleases me; there is a diamond of price; take it, Eugene, and let the rosary be mine."

He drew a ring from his finger, and presented it to the page; but it was not accepted.

"Oh! Sir Osbright," exclaimed Eugene, and sank upon his knee; "take my life from me; it is at your disposal; but while I live, do not deprive me of that rosary. It is my only remembrance of an event so dear to me. . . . Of the day in which I first found existence valuable!—Three months are passed, since while following my lord, your father, to the chase, my horse became ungovernable and bore me to the brink of a precipice. My efforts to restrain him were in vain. I at length sprang from his back, but too late to save myself. I rolled down the declivity and was dashed to the bottom of the precipice. I lost my senses, but projecting shrubs doubtless broke my descent and preserved me from destruction. On opening my eyes, I believed that my fall had killed me and that I was in Heaven already; for near me knelt a form so angelic, with looks so benevolent, with eyes so expressive of compassion! And she questioned me about my safety in so sweet a voice! And she related with an air of such interest, how in returning from St. Hildegarde's Grotto she had observed my fall; how she had trembled for my life, and had brought water from the cave to wash off the blood, and had torn her veil to bind up my wounded head! And then, she bade me so tenderly be of good cheer, for that the danger was passed, and that she hoped I should soon be quite well! Oh! How valuable did my life then become in my own eyes when I found that it had some worth in hers!"

"And you knew not her name?"

"Oh! no, my lord, not then; but alas! her terror too soon made me guess it; for no sooner did I mention the castle of

[7] In classical mythology, the west wind, son of Aeolus and Aurora.

Frankheim as my abode, then she uttered a loud shriek, started from the ground with every mark of horror and alarm, and fled from me with the rapidity of an arrow. Then did my foreboding heart tell me too truly that she, in whom the bare mention of Frankheim could excite such aversion, must needs belong to the hostile family of Orrenberg. That suspicion was confirmed when I observed lying near me this rosary, which she had forgotten in her haste, and whose crucifix bears the dear, dear name of Blanche!—a name, which from that moment I blessed in every prayer! A name, which has ever since been held in my fancy sacred as that of my patron saint!"

"And you saw her no more? And you spoke to her no more? Nay, answer me with frankness, boy, or I swear. . . ."

"Oh! be patient, good my lord; I mean not to deceive you. Yes; once more, only once I addressed her; I would have restored her rosary; I wished to thank her for her timely succor; but the moment that she beheld me, her former terrors returned. She shrieked out 'a Frankheimer!' and hastened away, as if flying from an assassin. Thenceforward I accosted her no more. I found that the sight of me alarmed her, and I forbode to intrude upon her, whom my whole soul adores, a presence so hateful! You now know all; noble knight, restore my rosary."

The frankness of this narration dissipated entirely Osbright's jealous terrors. The impassioned yet respectful manner, in which Blanche was mentioned, and the height of admiration which the sight of her had inspired, both pleased and softened him; and he could not help feeling himself strongly influenced in favor of the young enthusiast, whose heart beat so perfectly in unison with his own. Yet he judged it prudent to conceal that favorable impression and accompany the surrender of the rosary with a lecture on the folly of his nourishing so hopeless a passion.

"There is your rosary," said he, assuming a severity of tone and manner very foreign to his feelings; "though I know not, whether in restoring it I do you any kindness. Imprudent youth, for whom do you feel this excess of adoration? For the daughter of your patron's most inveterate enemy; of a man accused of the murder of your dearest friend; of one against whom scarce forty hours ago you vowed in this very chapel. . . ."

"Oh! No, no, no!" exclaimed the page with a look of horror. "I vowed nothing; I took no oath; I heard, but joined not in the blasphemy; and when all around me cursed the devoted family of Orrenberg, I prayed for the angel Blanche!"

"For the daughter of Joscelyn's supposed assassin? Joscelyn, whom you professed to love so truly, that your life. . . ."

"Oh! and I did love Joscelyn, truly, dearly! But I feel that I love Blanche even better than Joscelyn, a thousand, oh! and a thousand times!"

"Love her indeed? Alas, poor youth! Love whom? The only child of the rich and noble Count of Orrenberg; after me, the heiress of all those domains, on which you have been educated through my father's charity. Blanche, Countess of Orrenberg, and the orphan page, Eugene, a foundling, without family, without friend; how ill do these names sound together! My good lad, I mean not to wound your feelings, but observe, how hopeless is your present pursuit; rouse yourself from your romantic dream, and erase from your heart this frantic passion!"

During this speech, the glow faded from the cheeks of Eugene; the fire of enthusiasm no longer blazed in his eyes; the deepest gloom of melancholy overspread his countenance. His head sank upon his bosom, and his eyes were filled with tears.

"True! true! sir knight," said he after a short pause. "I know it well! I *am* an orphan boy, without family, without friends! God help me!"

He pressed the crucifix to his trembling lips, bowed his head to Osbright with humility, and turned to leave the chapel.

Osbright was deeply affected, and he suffered him to pass him in silence; but soon recollecting himself. "Stay, Eugene," said he, calling after him, and the page stopped. "I would not have my parents know that I am in their neighborhood; should you reveal that I am here, my displeasure. . . ."

"I reveal?" interrupted Eugene proudly. "I am no tale-bearer, sir knight!"—and he quitted the chapel, his passion for Blanche inflamed by the opposition made to it, and his antipathy to Osbright strengthened by resentment at his being the person who opposed it.

CHAPTER VI

*—"My life! my soul! my all that Heaven can give! Death's
life with thee, without thee death to live!"*

DRYDEN.

WHILE Osbright was employed in smoothing the real obstacles
to their union, his mistress was the victim of imaginary terror.
She had discovered in her unknown lover the son of her
father's most inveterate enemy; a man too, whom from her
cradle she had been taught to consider with horror, and who
(according to Sir Ottokar's account) had taken a most solemn
and irrevocable oath to exterminate herself and her whole
family. She now believed that Osbright's protestations were
all false and only calculated to beguile her to destruction; or
else that he was ignorant of her origin, when he pretended
affection; or that, even if in spite of her bearing the detested
name of Orrenberg, he had still formerly felt a real love for
her, she doubted not that grief for his brother's murder and
thirst of vengeance had converted that love into hatred, and
that he would seize the first opportunity of fulfilling his horrible vow by plunging his dagger in her bosom.

But she prudently resolved to afford him no such opportunity. The image of her loved preserver no longer beckoned
her to the grotto; she only saw there him whom her prejudiced
fancy had delighted to load with every vice, and who thirsted
to sign in her blood his claim to the rich inheritance of her
parents. No! To St. Hildegarde's Grotto she would venture
no more; that was a point determined! And it remained
determined for a whole long day and night; but when the
second morning arrived, her resolution faltered; and when the
evening was at hand, her prudence totally failed. Yet another
hour, and the knight would be waiting for her in the cave;
and for what purpose he waited now appeared to her but of
little consequence. He might murder her, it's true; but to see
him no more, she felt, was but to perish by a more painful
though more lingering death, and she determined to ascertain
the worst immediately. Her mother was occupied by household
arrangements. Gustavus was in close conference with Sir Lennard of Kleeborn, who was just arrived; no one observed her

movements, and she employed her liberty in hastening to the Grotto of St. Hildegarde.

No one was there; and now a new terror seized her, lest Osbright should not mean to come. She seated herself on a broken stone which had rolled from the rock above, and was lost in melancholy reflections when someone took her hand gently. She looked up; Osbright stood before her; but in the moment of surprise she only saw in him the dreaded assassin, and uttering a cry of terror, her first movement was to fly from the place. The knight started back in astonishment. But she soon recollected herself, and returned.

"Is it you then?" she said, endeavoring to assume a tranquil look, and extending her hand with a smile, equally expressive of tenderness and melancholy; "I feared. . . . I thought. . . ."

"What did you think? What could your innocence have to fear?" And he gently drew her back to the seat which she had quitted and took his place by her side.

"I feared. . . . that some enemy. . . . that some assassin. . . . that some emissary of the Count of Frankheim. . . ."

"Ah! Blanche! Still this aversion? To belong to Frankheim is sufficient to become the object of your hate."

"All who belong to Frankheim hate *me*."

"Not *all*, Blanche, certainly."

"The Count at least."

"Dearest Blanche! did you but know the pain which I feel when you calumniate the Count. . . . ! He is stern and passionate I confess, but he has ever been an honorable man. Shall I own to you the truth, my Blanche? The Count is my friend, is my *best* friend! His affection is my proudest boast; his commands I have never disobeyed. . . ."

"Indeed?—and never will?"

"Never; at least, I hope not! His commands from my earliest infancy have ever been to me as a law, and. . . . my love! why thus pale? What alarms you? What distresses you?"

" 'Tis nothing! It will soon be past! I am not quite well, and. . . ."

"You speak still more faintly! Stay one moment! I will bring water for you from the grotto."

"Oh! no, no, no!" she exclaimed, and detained him by his arm. He stopped, surprised at the eagerness with which she spoke. "Yet 'tis no matter!" she continued; "bring it, if you will; I will drink it."

"I will return instantly!" said he, and hastened to the

waterfall. Blanche started wildly from her seat; she sank upon her knees, covered her face with her hands, and prayed for a few moments fervently and silently.

"Now then," she said in a firm voice, while she rose from the ground; "now then I am prepared for everything. Let him bring me what he will, be it water or be it poison, from his hands will I receive it without hesitation, and die, if he will have it so, without a murmur."

A consecrated goblet ever stood upon the rustic altar of St. Hildegarde; it was supposed to be that, which had once pressed the blessed lips of the saint, and even the starving robber respected its sanctity. Osbright hastily filled it, and returning to his mistress, urged her to taste the water which it contained.

Blanche received the cup with a trembling hand, and fixing her eyes upon his countenance. "Will it not *chill* me too suddenly?" she asked.

"You need not drink much of it; a few drops will be sufficient to produce the effect desired."

"Indeed? Is it so powerful then? Nay, it is all the better. See, sir knight, you are obeyed; from your hands even this is welcome!" And she placed the goblet to her lips, nor doubted that she drank a farewell to the world. "Look!" she resumed restoring the cup; "have I swallowed enough? Are you satisfied?"

"Blanche!" exclaimed the youth, his surprise at her demeanor increasing with every moment; "what is the matter? What means this mysterious conduct? You seem to me so much altered. . . ."

"Already? Does it then work so speedily? Nay, then I must be sudden, and here all disguise shall end. You promised, when I saw you last, that at our next meeting you would disclose your name. I know it already, Osbright of Frankheim; know the hatred which you bear to me and mine; know the dreadful oath which was taken last night in the chapel of St. John, and know also that you have now made one step toward fulfilling it. Osbright, when I raised yonder goblet to my lips, I was not ignorant that it contained poison. . . ."

"Poison?" interrupted Osbright. "What! you believe then. . . . you suspect. . . . yet believe it still! Yes, Blanche, yes! Let this convince you that the cup which *you* have tasted, Osbright will raise to his lips with joy, even though that cup be poisoned!"—and he seized the goblet, and drank its contents with eagerness.

"Osbright! My own Osbright!" exclaimed Blanche, and sank upon her lover's bosom. "Oh! that it were indeed poison, and that I might die with you in this moment, for to live with you I feel myself unworthy! Shame upon me! How could I for one instant belie your generous nature so grossly! Never, no, never more will I suspect. . . ."

"Nor me, nor any one, my Blanche, I hope, without some better reason. Oh! banish from your bosom the gloomy fiend, Mistrust; so pure a shrine should never be polluted by an inmate so odious! Away with the prejudices, which have been so carefully instilled into your youthful mind; see no more with the eyes of parents; see with your own, my Blanche, and judge by your own good heart of the feelings of others. Then will the world again become lovely in your sight, for you will see it the abode of truth, of virtue, of affection; then will this host of imagined enemies be converted into a band of real friends; then will your mind be freed from these visionary terrors, so injurious to others, so painful to yourself, which now fill your waking thoughts with anxiety and your nightly dreams with gloomy recollections. You have told me yourself, that you have frequently started from sleep exclaiming that Count Rudiger of Frankheim was at hand; and yet this Count Rudiger is Osbright's father! You have mistaken *me;* you are mistaken in *him,* and. . . . ?"

"In the Count? Oh! no, no, no, Osbright! Impossible! Indeed, indeed the Count is a very fierce, a very cruel man! ah! your partiality blinds you; but if you knew as well as I do. . . . but I was forbidden to mention it. . . . ?"

"And have you still secrets from *me,* Blanche? From this moment I have none to you."

"Nay, look not so sad; you shall know all; and you should have known it before, but that you ever spoke so warmly in favor of the Count that I was unwilling to grieve you. Well then, Osbright; it is certain (*quite* certain!) that the Count of Frankheim caused my poor brother Philip to be poisoned."

"Indeed? *Quite* certain? And do *you* know, Blanche, that it is equally certain, nay, much *more* certain, that the Count of Orrenberg caused my brother to be assassinated in Burnholm wood?"

"Oh! most atrocious calumny! Oh! Falsehood most incredible! What! My father, whose actions. . . ."

"*My* father never did an unworthy action, either, Blanche."

"Nay, but I saw with my own eyes the livid spots with which Philip's neck. . . ."

"I too saw with mine the deep wound which gaped on poor Joscelyn's bosom."

"The attendants, the physician, all have told me themselves. . . ."

"Every inmate of Frankheim Castle heard the confession. . . ."

"That your father had bribed Philip's nurse, who left us about a week before his illness. . . ."

"That assassins were bribed by your father to murder Joscelyn while hunting."

"Nay, what is more strong, my mother herself assured me. . . ."

"But what is still stronger than that is that your father's crime was actually confessed by the very assassins themselves."

"Well, Osbright, your surely cannot expect me to see everything with *your* eyes. . . ."

"Should *I* see everything with *yours*, Blanche?"

"Nor to believe my dear good father, whose heart I know so well, guilty of a crime so base and so atrocious!"

"Does not the argument hold equally good for me, Blanche? Your father may be innocent of Joscelyn's death, but so is mine of Philip's; you love your father well, but not better than I love mine. Each thinks the other's father to be guilty; why may not each be wrong? Both believe their own father to be innocent, and why should not both be right?"

"Oh! that it were so! How gladly should I banish from my bosom these gloomy terrors which now torture it so cruelly. No, Osbright; the heart may feel, but the tongue can never utter, how painful it is for me to hate one who is so much beloved by you!"

Osbright thanked her by a kiss, the purest and the warmest that ever was sealed upon the lip of woman; and he now proceeded to unfold to her his intentions of seeking the widow of the assassin, and endeavoring to learn from her the real motives of her husband for murdering the innocent Joscelyn. She approved of his design, and then urged his immediate departure, as the evening was already closing round them and Osbright's road lay through a forest rendered dangerous in several parts by pit-falls and not entirely free from wild beasts. Osbright obeyed; but he first advised her to visit St. Hildegarde's Grotto no more till his return, of which he could easily apprise her by means of Sir Lennard of Kleeborn.

"For I must confess," he added, "though I am certain, that nothing could induce my father to act ill deliberately, yet his passions are so violent, and so frequently overcome his better judgment, that I know not what extremes he might be hurried in a momentary ebullition of fury. My brother's death (I understand) has almost driven him frantic; he breathes vengeance against the whole family of Orrenberg; it is rumored also that the herald whom he dispatched to signify to your father. . . ."

"Alas! It is but too true! The wild cruel people murdered the poor man; but my father did his utmost to prevent the crime; indeed, indeed, Osbright, my father was not in fault!"

"Heaven grant that it may be found so; but at present appearances are greatly against Count Gustavus, and this unlucky event will make my father's resentment burn with tenfold fury. He is noble, generous, benevolent, friendly. . . . But in his rage he is terrible, and he cherishes in his heart with unjustifiable fondness the thirst for vengeance. Some officious vassal may observe your visits hither, and unprotected as you are, may easily purchase his lord's favor by delivering you into his power. Dearest Blanche, enraged as he is at this moment, I would not even answer that your life. . . ."

"Mine? One, who never offended him by word or deed? One, who for your sake would so willingly love him? And you really think. . . . Ah! Osbright, say what you will, I fear that your father is a very wicked man!"

"He has his faults, but they are greatly overbalanced by his virtues. Yet I confess. . . . there have been moments when. . . . But let us drop this unpleasant subject. Time presses; I must be gone. Give me your promise not to visit this spot during my absence, one sweet kiss to confirm that promise, and then farewell, my Blanche."

The promise was given; the kiss was taken; the farewell was said; and then Osbright, having conducted his mistress in safety to the spot which concealed the private entrance to Orrenberg Castle (and which was within a very short distance of the cave) returned to the place, where he had fastened his courser, and giving him the spur, was soon concealed within the shades of the neighboring forest.

But scarcely had he quitted her, when Blanche recollected that the consecrated goblet was left on the outside of the cave. To replace this, her reverence for the saint made her think absolutely necessary; yet the close of her conversation with Osbright made her feel no small degree of repugnance to revisiting the grotto by herself. However, it was so near that she could not suppose it possible for her to meet with any danger during the few minutes which it would take her to perform this duty, and therefore after some little hesitation she retraced her steps.

Trembling as she ran, she traversed the space which divided her from the cave, threaded the rocky passages, and soon reached the mouth of the cave. The goblet was replaced; an *Ave* was murmured before the altar in all haste, and she now hurried back again; when as she rushed out of the grotto—"Stay!"—exclaimed a voice, and springing from the rock above, a man stood before her. She shrieked and started back; the moon, which was now risen, showed her what seemed rather to be a specter than any mortal being. His tall thin form (viewed through the medium of her fears and seen but indistinctly among the shadows of the surrounding rocks) dilated to a height which appeared gigantic, his tresses fluttering wildly in the evening blast, his limbs trembling with agitation, his face colorless as the face of a corpse, his large eyes almost starting from their sockets and glaring with all the fires of delirium, his hands filled with locks of bright hair torn from his own head, and stained with blood which had flowed from his own self-mangled bosom, such was the stranger; such was the wretched Eugene.

The terror which the sight of him evidently caused in Blanche had prevented the page from obtruding his presence upon her any more; but he could not prevail upon himself to abstain from the delight of gazing upon that beauty which had made so forcible an impression upon his youthful heart. He watched her and observed that regularly every evening she visited the cave of St. Hildegarde; and regularly every evening did Eugene climb the rocks among which it was situated, and feed his hopeless passion by gazing for whole hours upon the lovely form of Blanche. He admired the celestial expression of her countenance, as she knelt in prayer before the shrine; he listened in silent ecstasy, when, seated before the grotto's mouth and weaving into garlands the wild-flowers which sprouted among the rocks, she chanted some sweet though simple ballad; he smiled, when he saw her smile at the dexterity with which her flowery work had been completed; and when some melancholy thought glanced across her mind, he echoed back the sigh which escaped from her bosom. He knew not that the wreaths were woven to deck the seat which had been hallowed by sustaining a rival; he knew not that the sigh proceeded from grief for that rival's absence.

And thus had whole months rolled away; and with every day did the charms of Blanche inflame his heart with more glowing passion and exalt his imagination to a higher pitch of enthusiasm. At length came the fatal blow which at once destroyed this solitary source of ideal happiness; he found not only that he had a beloved rival, but that this rival was the man who possessed that place in his father's affections which he would so gladly have possessed in them himself; was Count Rudiger's avowed offspring, while *he* was rejected and pointed out to the world as nothing better than an orphan and an outcast; was the heir of the rich domains of Frankheim, while *he* was condemned to a life of servitude and obscurity; in short, was the very man toward whom of all existing beings he cherished, and had cherished from his childhood, the most inveterate and uncontrollable antipathy.

Breathless with agitation, and fixing his nails in his bosom in order to distract the sense of mental agony by the infliction of bodily pain, he had witnessed from the rock above them the interview between the lovers. He heard not their words; but he saw, as they sat, the arm of Osbright tenderly encircling the waist of Blanche, and witnessed the kiss which he pressed upon her lips at parting. They were gone; yet the boy still lay extended upon the rock, stupefied by a blow so unexpected. A few minutes restored him to sensation, but not to himself. Horror at Joseclyn's death had shaken his nerves most cruelly; since that event grief had scarcely permitted his tasting food; that constitutional infirmity which the knowledge of his mother's sad story had inflamed into delirium now exerted itself with dreadful violence upon his enfeebled frame and exalted imagination; his brain was unable to support the shock, and he now stood a maniac before the affrighted Blanche.

"It is she indeed!" he exclaimed. "She here again? Here, and alone! Oh! Then it was no illusion! The night-wind murmured in my ear—'death!'—And the screech-owl shrieked in my ear—'death!'—And the wind and the screech-owl told me true, for you are returned on purpose! Yes, yes; I feel it well, angel; you are here, and the hour is come!"

"What hour? I know you not. You terrify me."

She attempted to pass him, but he grasped her by the wrist. "Terrified? Are you not a blessed spirit, and what can you fear? I must away to the skies, and there will I kneel and implore for you and pray that you may speedily follow me thither! You will soon be made a saint in Heaven, but I must prepare the way for you; take this sword, and plunge it. . . . Nay, nay! Why should you dread to use it? Have you not plunged a dagger in my heart already? You have, you have! And oh! That wound was a wound so painful. . . . Take it, I say; take it; here is my naked bosom!"

And as he said this, he tore open his doublet with one hand, while with frantic eagerness he endeavored to force her to take the sword with the other; when summoning up all her strength Blanche rushed swiftly past him, and with loud shrieks fled through the rocky passage. The frantic youth pursued her, in vain imploring her to stay; with fruitless efforts did Blanche exert her speed; the maniac gained upon her; and overcome by terror she fell breathless at his feet, at the moment when guided by her shrieks Baron Ottokar arrived to her assistance. He heard her scream for help; he saw her pursued by one who held an unsheathed sword; he beheld her sink upon the earth and doubted not that she had perished by the blow of an assassin.

"Inhuman ruffian!" exclaimed the knight, and instantly his sword struck the supposed murderer to the earth. Then raising the trembling Blanche in his arms, he hastened toward the castle to procure surgical assistance for his lovely burden.

During Blanche's absence, Sir Lennard of Kleeborn was employed in the performance of his promise to Osbright. He requested an audience of the Count of Orrenberg, which was readily granted; but Gustavus added that as what Sir Lennard had to state was announced to be of importance, he begged that Baron Ottokar might share the communication; the nature of his engagements to that young nobleman being such that they possessed a common interest in everything. Sir Lennard foreboded from this declaration an obstacle to his negotiation; however, he immediately commenced it, disclosed to the astonished Count the mutual attachment between Osbright and his daughter, and concluded by advising him most strenuously to seize so favorable an opportunity of putting a final close to the disputes which had so long separated the kindred houses of Orrenberg and Frankheim.

While Gustavus listened to this narrative, a variety of emo-

tions expressed themselves by turns on his countenance. Sir
Lennard had finished. The Count passed a few minutes in
silence; but at length taking his resolution decisively, he
assured Sir Lennard, that most earnestly did he desire to see
amity established between the two families; that there was no
personal sacrifice which he would not joyfully make to accomplish an event so desirable; but that unfortunately, he had
already contracted such engagements as formed an insuperable
obstacle to the union of Blanche and Osbright.

"No, my lord," hastily interrupted Ottokar; "you have contracted none, at least if you allude to those which you have
contracted with me. It is true, last night I received your
knightly word that the hand of Blanche should be mine; and
had you promised me the Imperial crown, I should have
thought the boon less valuable. But when the object is, to
prevent the effusion of kindred blood, to establish peace
between the two noblest families in the whole Palatinate, nay
more, to procure the happiness of Blanche herself, shall I
suffer my own selfish wishes to interfere? Shall I hesitate for
one moment to sacrifice them to the general welfare? No,
my lord, read the heart of Ottokar more justly. Were the
affections of your daughter the prize, I would dispute it
against Osbright, against the world, and would never resign
my claim but with the last sigh of my bosom; but the possession
of her *hand* alone could only make me wretched. The heart
of Blanche is Osbright's; Blanche can only be happy in being
his, and unless *she* is happy, *I* must be miserable myself. Count
of Orrenberg, I restore your promise; I resume my own; let
this wished-for union take place. Heaven itself surely lighted
up this flame in the bosoms of the lovers; and the hour which
gives Blanche to the envied Osbright will doubtless bury in
eternal oblivion all past offenses, all existing prejudices, all
future mistrust. It is true, my heart will bleed; but the applause
of my conscience will repay me for every selfish pang most
amply. Still consider me as your warmest friend, Gustavus; but
for the sake of Blanche, I must now refuse to be your son."

In vain did Gustavus combat this generous resignation.
Ottokar was firm, and at length the Count honestly confessed
to Sir Lennard the joy which he should feel at the accomplishment of the union in question. The difficulty now was how to
convince Rudiger of the injustice of his suspicions respecting
Joscelyn's murder, and to bring him to view Osbright's attachment in the same favorable light. In this also Ottokar prof-

fered his assistance. As nephew to the Lady Magdalena, though he was no favorite with her lord, he had ready access to the castle of Frankheim; that lady was well aware of the strength of his attachment to Blanche, and the generosity of her own nature rendered her fully capable of appreciating the sacrifice which he made in surrendering his claims in favor of Osbright's. He knew also that the feuds between the families had long been to her a source of mental uneasiness the most acute; that she had ever vindicated the conduct of Gustavus, as far as Rudiger's violence would permit her prudence to give such an opinion; and he was certain, that she would seize with joy an opportunity of terminating disputes so odious. He therefore proposed his immediate departure for the castle of Frankheim, where he would make a confidential communication of the whole business to the Countess, and discuss with her the most likely means of gaining over to their side the inclinations of her stormy husband. This plan was universally approved of; and without an hour's delay Ottokar set out for Frankheim Castle, accompanied by the warmest gratitude of Gustavus, and the highest admiration of Sir Lennard.

It was on his progress to Frankheim that the shrieks of the alarmed Blanche had summoned him to her assistance. On his arrival with her at the castle, immediately all was anxiety and confusion; but it was soon ascertained that she had received no wound, though some time elapsed before she could recollect herself sufficiently to give an account of what had happened. Even then, her narrative was greatly confused; alarm and anxiety to escape had prevented her from hearing much of what the maniac addressed to her. She could only relate, that a youth (whom she remembered to have seen twice before, and who had confessed himself to be a Frankheimer) had surprised her among the rocks; had accosted her with much violence and passion, frequently mentioning the word— "death"—and (as she believed) had told her that her hour was come. She was however quite certain that he accused her of having attempted "to plunge a dagger in his heart," had threatened "to make her a saint in Heaven," and had drawn his sword to put his threats in execution; at which she had fled, still pursued by him, till her strength failed her, and she sank on the earth before him. Having given this imperfect account, Blanche was committed to the care of her female attendants and advised by the physician to retire to rest, and endeavor to compose her ruffled spirits; advice, which she readily adopted, and immediately withdrew to her own apartment.

Gustavus had listened to her narrative with surprise, Ulrica with horror; and when Ottokar confirmed the assertion of Blanche that the supposed assassin was in the service of the Count of Frankheim (adding, that he had seen him occasionally in attendance upon Magdalena, and that he rather believed his name to be Eugene), the Countess darted a triumphant glance upon her husband. The latter ordered some domestics to go in quest of the assassin and convey him to the castle.

"Perhaps," said he, "his wound may not be mortal, and we may induce him to explain this mysterious business. I confess, that at present it wears a most hideous aspect; yet I cannot believe that the noble and brave Count Rudiger would descend to so base an action as to instigate a menial to take away the life of an innocent girl by assassination. If indeed, he should really be guilty of an action so atrocious. . . ."

"If?" interrupted his wife impatiently. "And is it possible any longer to doubt his guilt? Is not everything confirmed? Does not this agree with my suspicions respecting Philip? Suspicions, did I say? 'Twas certainty! 'Twas fact, supported by proofs too clear to be mistaken by any eyes, but by those of wilful blindness! Nay, I could tell you more. . . ."

"Indeed?" said Gustavus with a look of incredulity.

"Yes, Gustavus, yes! You remember well the fever which about two years ago brought you to the very gates of the sepulcher? You were recovering; you were pronounced out of danger; when a present of sweetmeats arrived for you from the Lady Magdalena."

"And what inference. . . ."

"Be patient; I come to the point. I warned you not to taste them, and presented you with some conserves prepared by my own hand. You were obstinate; you first ridiculed my fears, then chided me for entertaining such unjust suspicions. What was the result? You ate freely of Magdalena's present, and the very next day your fever returned with such violence as made the physician for several days despair of your recovery."

"It was very singular! You are perfectly correct, Ulrica; and certainly. . . . But stay! I think I recollect one little circumstance, which. . . . Exactly so! Our dispute took place in the honeysuckle bower on the south-side of the garden, and out of patience at (what you termed) my obstinacy, you left me in displeasure. Scarcely were you gone, when old Grim the wolf-dog came bounding to caress me, and springing upon me unexpectedly, Magdalena's present fell from my hands, and the vessel broke into a thousand pieces. This accident made me have recourse to *your* conserves, which were still standing on the table; and what is something singular, old Grim (who had appropriated the fallen sweetmeats to himself without hesitation) suffered not the least inconvenience; while I had scarcely tasted those prepared by your own hand, before my fever returned with violence, and I was declared to be in danger of my life."

"Why, certainly," said Ulrica, hesitating and embarrassed, "there are two ways of telling everything. Appearances seemed strong. . . . I argued to the best of my knowledge. . . . Everybody is liable to be mistaken. . . ."

"Are they so? Then, good Ulrica, since you find yourself mistaken in one instance, allow the possibility of your having been mistaken in another. In short, I insist upon it, and will not be disobeyed, that you are henceforth silent on the subject of Philip's malady. Were he poisoned or were he not, it is my pleasure that he should be mentioned only as dead, and nothing further. Nay, Ulrica! Not a syllable more, I entreat you!—My friends," he continued, turning to Ottokar and Sir Lennard, "advise me what to do. This new adventure, I own, wears a very embarrassing appearance; and yet appearances are no less strong against myself respecting the herald's death, and still more respecting the murder of young Joscelyn. One of my own people was found near the corpse; he declared upon the rack with his last breath that I had instigated him to commit the crime; and yet God sees the heart and knows that I am innocent. Rudiger may be equally guiltless of this attack upon my child; if fortunately, there should still be life in the assassin, and he could be brought to confess. . . ."

"Nay," exclaimed Ottokar, "he *must* confess; he *shall* confess! If he refuses, the rack shall force from him. . . ."

"And if he then declares that Rudiger set him on. . . ."

"Then the business is ended! Then Rudiger's guilt is clear, and. . . ."

"Indeed? Then it is also clear that *I* am Joscelyn's murderer. Is not that equally well proved, Sir Ottokar, and by means exactly the same?"

The youth colored, and hung his head in confusion; nor

did any one break the silence, till a domestic entering informed the Count, that the assassin had been removed from the place where Sir Ottokar left him. On inquiry he had learned from some peasants that they had found the youth bleeding profusely, but that his wound appeared not to be dangerous; that they were preparing to convey him to the castle, when a party of Frankheimers accidently passed that way, and, recognizing a favorite domestic of their liege-lord, had forced him from them and hastened to convey him out of the domains of Orrenberg.

All hopes of Eugene's clearing up this mystery being thus removed, it was thought best that Ottokar should resume his intended visit to the Lady Magdalena, should inform her of all that had happened, should entreat her to account for the highly culpable conduct of the page, and ascertain whether Rudiger was disposed to bury all mutual injuries in oblivion; a measure which for his own part Gustavus professed himself still perfectly ready to adopt in spite of the suspicious transactions of that eventful evening. Ottokar immediately set forth; but Sir Lennard remained at the castle of Orrenberg to wait the issue of the young warrior's negotiation.

CHAPTER VII

—*"The image of a wicked heinous fault lives in his eye; that close aspect of his doth show the mood of a much troubled bosom."*—

King John.

THE arrival of Ottokar at Frankheim Castle appeared to create no trifling astonishment and embarrassment in the domestics. Suspicion and ill-humor were expressed on every countenance; and Wilfred, the seneschal,[8] only answered the youth's inquiries for the Lady Magdalena by a dry and sullen —"this way, sir knight!" The Countess was alone; his appearance seemed to excite in her almost as much surprise as it had produced on her attendants, and her reception of him was studiously cold. But the frankness and impetuosity of Ottokar's nature soon banished this constraint; he opened his embassy without loss of time; and as she listened, the countenance of his auditress gradually brightened.

[8] A major-domo for a medieval lord, generally his steward.

The mutual attachment of Osbright and Blanche equally surprised and pleased her; she bestowed the highest encomia on that generosity of sentiment which had prompted Ottokar to sacrifice his own passion to the general welfare; she declared her thorough persuasion of the merits of the fair Blanche, and her anxiety to see these odious feuds terminated in an amicable manner. She was also willing to give credit to Ottokar's solemn protestations, that Gustavus was innocent of Joscelyn's death; but she greatly feared that it would be difficult to inspire her husband with the same confidence; especially at the present moment when his persuasion of Gustavus's animosity had gained additional strength from several late occurrences. The account of the herald's murder, she said, had inspired Rudiger with a degree of indignation, which (often as she had witnessed the strength of his emotions) had far surpassed anything, of which she had before believed him capable.

Ottokar hastened to clear up this transaction, at which he was present; and his account perfectly exculpated Gustavus in Magdalena's eyes, though (conscious of Rudiger's innate obstinacy) she was doubtful of its being equally successful with her husband. Ottokar, whose chief virtue was by no means that of patience, took fire at this; and it escaped him to say that it ill became a person to be so difficult in believing the innocence of another, who lay himself under such strong suspicions of having instigated an assassin to commit the very same crime. The Countess eagerly demanded an explanation and heard with surprise and resentment which increased with every word that in the course of that very evening a domestic of Count Rudiger had attempted to stab the Lady Blanche and would have succeeded in his diabolical attempt had not Ottokar arrived in time to fell the assassin to the ground.

Ottokar was still expatiating with all the warmth of a lover on the atrocity of the attempt; the Countess was still listening to this dreadful charge in such horror as deprived her of all power to interrupt her nephew; when the door was thrown open with violence, and Count Rudiger rushed into the room. "Have you heard it, Magdalena?" he exclaimed in a thundering voice, while he stamped upon the floor with passion; "have you heard. . . ."—at that moment his eyes rested upon Ottokar, and instantly they appeared to flash out fire. He started back; all the blood in his body seemed at once to rush into his face; for some moments he gazed upon the youth in terrific silence, as if he would have devoured him with his eyes.

At length—"So!" he exclaimed in a satisfied tone; "*here!* He is *here!*—What hoa! Wilfred!"—And he rushed again from the apartment, as abruptly as he had entered.

"What can this mean?" said the amazed and trembling Magdalena; "those looks. . . . that well-known terrible expression. . . . Oh! This very moment I must be satisfied."—She hastened to a window which overlooked the principal court, and summoned the old porter, who was then crossing it. He soon entered the apartment, and the Countess hastily inquired whether within the last hour any strangers had arrived at the castle and whether her lord had seen them.

"No, lady, no strangers!" replied the old man, "but truly Martin and his son Hans, the farmers of Helmstadt, are arrived, and sad news they bring to be sure. By your inquiry, lady, I suppose, that you have not yet heard what has happened at Orrenberg? Ah! the hard hearts! Ah! the barbarians! How could they be so cruel as to hurt the poor harmless innocent lad! One so gentle, that. . . . the Lord have mercy! It is you, Sir Ottokar? Why, surely you must be distracted to show your face within these walls, after committing an act so barbarous!"

Ottokar declared his ignorance of the old man's meaning.

"Indeed? Nay, then perhaps the story is not true; Martin and Hans may have mistaken the name, and Heaven grant it may prove so! But to be plain, sir knight, Martin told me himself that on his road hither he found the young page Eugene bleeding and fainting; that the peasants who stood near him had assured him that the lad was stabbed by no hand but yours, and that you had perpetrated this barbarous action by the command of the Lady Blanche, under whose very eyes it was committed. Finding that Eugene still lived, and knowing how much my lord and yourself, noble lady, value him, Martin and his companions rescued him from the hands of the Orrenbergers, and endeavored to bring him home to the castle. But his wound being dangerous, they thought it safest to stop with him at the Convent of St. John, where they left him under the care of the good fathers, and then hastened hither to inform my lord of what had happened. But, bless my heart! I quite forget, lady; the Count ordered me to summon Wilfred immediately to his chamber, and I doubt, even this little delay will bring me into anger. Your pardon, lady; I must away this instant!"—And he hurried out of the apartment.

"Eugene?" repeated Magdalena; "Eugene wounded? And wounded by *your* hand, Ottokar? A boy, a poor harmless boy? Oh! impossible! This is some egregious mistake, and...."

"No, lady: there is no mistake in this; the peasants told the truth. It *was* my hand, which struck Eugene to the ground; for Eugene was the wretch who (as I before mentioned to you) attempted this evening the precious life of Blanche."

"You rave, Sir Ottokar! Eugene, an assassin? The assassin of a *female*, too? He, who bears to the very name of woman a love, a reverence almost idolatrous? He, the gentlest, tenderest...."

"Lady, I saw him myself; I heard the shrieks of Blanche with my own ears! I saw her sink at his feet in terror; I saw Eugene with his sword drawn on the very point of plunging it in her bosom...."

"Nay, nay! Let us not waste our time in disputing about Eugene. Be he innocent, or be he guilty, your hands are stained with his blood, and here you are no longer in safety. So dear as Eugene is to my husband...."

"Surely, Countess, surely, he will be no longer dear to him, when Rudiger learns his guilt; or if he still protects him, that protection will prove, that Rudiger himself cannot be innocent. Criminal as Eugene is, if he can still inspire his master with any sentiment, but indignation, but hatred...."

"Hatred? His master? Oh! Ottokar, you know not. . . . there is a mystery about that boy. . . . there is a secret reason. . . . Rudiger hate Eugene? Eugene, who is his own. . . . I mean. . . . I would say. . . . Eugene, whom Rudiger loves as dearly, as *if* he were his own son!"

The eagerness with which she endeavored to recall her words; the hesitation with which she pronounced the correcting phrase; the color which crimsoned her cheeks at having so nearly divulged her husband's secret; all these immediately dispelled the cloud which overhung the birth of Eugene. Ottokar instantly comprehended how dear an interest Rudiger took in the page's welfare, and how odious the man must appear in his eyes who had plunged his sword in the boy's bosom. He hesitated, what course to pursue; Magdalena advised his leaving her to reconcile the mind of her husband to what had happened, and not to repeat his visit at the castle, till she should inform him, that his present offense was forgotten and forgiven; and the knight was on the point of following her counsels when the door was again thrown open, and the Count of Frankheim re-entered the room.

The Countess shuddered, as she cast an anxious glance upon his countenance. His face was of a deadly paleness; the deepest gloom sat upon his frowning brows; his burning eyes glared with terrible expression: yet a smile of forced urbanity played round his bloodless lips, and on his entrance he bowed his proud head toward Ottokar with an air of unusual condescension.

"You are welcome, sir knight!" said he. "This visit affords me a satisfaction totally unexpected. Magdalena, your nephew will need some refreshment; will you not see that it is prepared?"

The tone in which this question was asked converted it into a command; she was obliged to obey, and could only whisper to Ottokar in passing—"Be on your guard, for God's sake!"

"Be seated, Sir Ottokar," resumed the Count. "Nay, no ceremony! And now may I inquire, what lucky circumstance brings you hither? It is not often, that Frankheim Castle is honored by your presence. You come, I understand, from Orrenberg; you are a friend of Gustavus, and a suitor of his daughter; is it not so? A fair lady and an excellent choice; I am told that her influence over you is unbounded; that what *she* desires, be it right, or be it wrong, you perform with all the ardor of a true lover; and in truth, it is fitting that you should. But as I said before, you come straight from Orrenberg; perhaps, you bring some message from your friend Gustavus? Some conciliatory proposal. . . . some explanation of past circumstances. . . . or perhaps, he has sent me a defiance in return for mine, and your friendship for him induces you to appear before me in the sacred character of his herald. Am I right, Sir Ottokar?"

"As the herald of Gustavus? No, Count Rudiger: I come here as your *friend,* if you will permit me to be so; as your *guest,* unless you have forsworn the rights of hospitality."

"My guest? Oh! undoubtedly! You do me but too much honor! But. . . . am I to understand, then, that you bring no commission from Orrenberg?"

"Yes; one which I trust will convince you that I am not more the friend of Orrenberg than of Frankheim. Count, Gustavus wishes to hold with you a personal conference."

"A conference? With me?"

"You may well be surprised; I was so myself when he first

mentioned it; but he asserts with such solemn adjurations his innocence...."

"His innocence? Indeed?"

"He declares himself so certain of proving to your complete satisfaction that he had no hand in Joscelyn's murder, and he is so anxious of laying before you a plan for putting an end to all feuds in a manner equally beneficial and agreeable to both families, that if you will but listen to him...."

"Listen to him? Oh! by all means. When you see him again, pray, assure him that an interview with him will give me the highest satisfaction."

"When I see him? Dear Count, since you charge me with so welcome a commission, I will hasten back to Orrenberg without a moment's delay. Oh! From what a weight shall I relieve his mind, and how wisely do you act in showing this readiness to conciliation! Rudiger, may the right hand, which I thus stretch toward Heaven, wither and rot away if I am perjured in swearing that I believe Gustavus to be innocent. Now then, farewell! Yet hold! there are two points.) . . two unlucky accidents, which have lately happened. . . . and which while unexplained. . . . must have produced a disadvantageous impression upon your mind, and may be the source of future dissension. Permit me therefore to mention, that Eugene...."

"I know it; I have heard it already. Eugene has been mortally wounded in the neighborhood of Orrenberg Castle. You need say no more about it."

"Not *mortally,* Count. I am assured, that his wounds are not mortal; I trust that he will recover."

"*Not* mortal, you say? Nay, just as you please!"

"Count Rudiger!"

"Anything more? You mentioned *two* accidents, I think, and...."

"Before I enter upon the second, permit me to explain that if there was any fault in the first, it proceeded entirely from the conduct of Eugene himself. He attempted to assassinate the Lady Blanche this evening, and...."

"Oh! to be sure! Extremely probable, and extremely wrong; the boy deserved his fate! And I make no doubt that Gustavus supposes him to have been instigated by *me* to commit this crime? Nay, I confess, that seems highly probable too!"

"No, Rudiger, you wrong him. It is true, everyone else at Orrenberg accuses you, but Gustavus himself loudly asserts his conviction of your innocence."

"Fiend! fiend! Oh! artful devil. . . . ten thousand pardons, Baron! A sudden pain. . . . but 'tis gone; I am quite myself again. Now then; the second little accident. . . . ?"

"The herald whom you sent to Orrenberg two days ago. . . ."

"Was knocked on the head; they told me so before; but of course, Gustavus had no hand in the affair!"

"He had none, indeed. I was present myself and witnessed his exertions to calm the fury of the mob; till unluckily, exhausted with fatigue, and overcome with apprehension, he fainted, and while he was insensible. . . ."

"He fainted? That *was* unlucky indeed!"

"This misfortune has distressed Gustavus beyond measure; he has commissioned me to say that any reparation which you can demand in honor. . . ."

"Reparation for such a trifle? Oh! absurd! The thing is really not worth talking of."

"Count of Frankheim!"

"For after all, the man was but a herald; and what is a herald, you know!"

"What is he? Permit me to say. . . ."

"How is this, Sir Ottokar? You espouse the cause of heralds so warmly that one would think you were a herald yourself; and in fact you are so! You bring the Count of Orrenberg's messages; you make the Count of Orrenberg's conciliatory proposals; and therefore to all intents and purposes you are the Count of Orrenberg's herald. Is it not so, sir knight?"

"Rudiger, I repeat it, I am here only as your friend, and as the Lady Magdalena's near kinsman—and even should the laws of chivalry not induce you to respect the herald, the rights of hospitality must surely make you consider the person of your guest as sacred."

"Sacred? My guest? Oh! Undoubtedly! Nothing can be better said, or more certain—the person of my guest must always be considered as sacred by me; only. . . . there is one trifling point, of which it may be as well to make you aware.— *I* also am very subject to *fainting*."

"Indeed?" exclaimed Ottokar, starting; then fixing his eyes on those of Rudiger, he read in them an expression which almost froze the marrow in his bones—"Farewell, Count Rudiger!" said he, and hastily quitted the room.

The Count remained in his seat, reclining his head upon his hand, silent, motionless, and gloomy. Some minutes elapsed, and still he moved not.

"Save him! Save him!" shrieked Magdalena, as she rushed into the chamber, pale as death; "hasten to his rescue, Rudiger! For God's sake, hasten! Look! Look"—and she threw open the window which commanded the courtyard, and from whence the light of the full moon and the blaze of numerous torches permitted her to observe distinctly what was passing below. "He is surrounded. . . . Ottokar. . . . the people, the whole crowd of them, with swords, with clubs. . . . fly, fly, Rudiger, and rescue him!—Merciful Heaven! They drag him from his horse. . . . they throw him on the earth. . . . they will kill him! They will murder him!—Nay, look yourself! Come to the window; speak to the wild rabble, or their fury. . . . Ha! he forces himself out of their clutches! He draws his sword. . . . he fights. . . . he drives them back. . . . now, now, my lord! Now they can hear you! Seize this interval of fear, and command them. . . . Alas! alas! Now they all rush upon him at once, like madmen; he defends himself still, but their numbers. . . . Rudiger! Rudiger! For mercy's sake, for God's sake, call to them from the window. . . . speak one word, speak but one word, and. . . . Ah! his head. . . . a blow. . . . he staggers. . . . and now another. . . . and another. . . . it's done! it's done! —He falls! He is dead!—Oh! Blessed Mary, receive his soul to mercy!"

She sank upon her knees, pressed to her lips the golden cross, which hung at her bosom, and passed some minutes in fervent supplication for the sins of her unhappy nephew. As she prayed, the excess of horror gradually abated; religion already poured balm into her still bleeding wounds; the thought of eternal happiness hereafter, enabled her to sustain the weight of her present afflictions; the agony of grief was softened into melancholy tenderness; she found, that she could again breathe freely; and a torrent of grateful tears rushed into her burning eyes and relieved the burden of her overcharged bosom.

She rose from her knees; she turned toward her husband, who still sat motionless in his chair.

"Rudiger!" she said, "your guest, your kinsman has been murdered in your castle, almost before your eyes; it would have cost you but one word, but one look, nay, the very sight of their lord's countenance, his mere presence would have been sufficient to recall the rabble to their duty, and terrify them from accomplishing their barbarous purpose! I told you what would happen; I called you; I implored you; and still you were deaf to my cries; and still you moved not! Oh! what cruel insensibility! Oh! what inhuman obstinacy! Now God grant that in that bitter hour when you most want his help, *he* may not be as slow to afford it as *you* have been to the wretched Ottokar!"

The Count replied not. The door opened, and Wilfred entered.

"Noble lord!" said he, "your orders are obeyed."

"Obeyed? His orders?" repeated Magdalena with a shriek of surprise and horror. She fixed her eyes upon the countenance of her husband with a look of dreadful inquiry. Every muscle in his gigantic form seemed convulsed by some horrible sensation; the deepest gloom darkened every feature; the wind from the unclosed window agitated his raven locks, and every hair appeared to writhe itself. His eyeballs glared; his teeth chattered; his lips trembled; and yet a smile of satisfied vengeance played horribly round them. His complexion appeared suddenly to be changed to the dark tincture of an African; the expression of his countenance was dreadful, was diabolical. Magdalena, as she gazed upon his face, thought that she gazed upon the face of a demon.

"Obeyed?" After a long pause she repeated once more, "Rudiger! Obeyed!"—He raised his eyes to hers, but he could not support their gaze. He turned hastily away, and concealed his countenance with his robe.

"Now then," she resumed, "the whole is clear! Fool that I was! And I called *you* to the innocent youth's rescue! Fye, oh! fye!—This is not the action of a warrior, of a man! This is so odious, so despicable, that *I*, your wife, your fond, your humble, your much-injured, your ever-enduring wife, even I pronounce it odious and despicable, and dare to proclaim aloud my hatred and my contempt. Oh! shame! shame!—How the man sits there, and must endure to hear the just reproaches of one whom he knows so inferior in all things but virtue; of a woman, weak in mind, weak in body, but strong in conscious innocence, and therefore stronger than himself! Heaven can witness with what truth, with what fondness, with what adoration, I have ever loved you, Rudiger; but the feeling of what is right is superior to all other feelings; but the voice of justice *will* be heard; and not even the husband of my heart, not even the father of my children is to me a character so sacred as to stifle the sentence of my reason, of my conscience, which cries to me aloud 'The husband of your heart, the father of your children, is a *murderer!*' Your caprice, your pride, your wayward humors, your infidelities, I have borne them all, and loved you still; but when I see your hands stained with the blood of your kinsman, of your guest, of a man who came hither solely for your service, who had sacrificed to your welfare all his heart's dearest wishes; when I see your hands stained with his blood, with his innocent blood. . . . Oh! Rudiger! Rudiger! is it possible that I should ever love you more!"

Her heart agonized, her brain almost distracted, she fled from her husband's presence, and inclosing herself within her oratory, passed the night in prayer equally for the souls of the murdered one and of his unhappy murderer!

CHAPTER VIII

—"*Semina, floresque, et succos incoquit acres;*
   Addit et exceptas lunâ pernocte pruinas,
   Et strigis infames ipsis cum carnibus alas,
   Vivacisque jecur cervi; quibus insuper addit
   Ora caputque novem cornicis sæcula passæ."—
                                                OVID.

—"*Here boil'd she many a seed, and herb, and flower,*
   And dews in moonshine culled at midnight hour,
   Bat's wings, a stag's still-panting heart, and last
   A raven's head, o'er which nine hundred years had past."—

WHILE his father was thus plunging himself in an abyss of real guilt, Osbright was hastening in eager pursuit of means to elucidate the imaginary crime of Gustavus. The forest was thick; the way was long, and difficult to find without a guide. Osbright had obtained ample instructions respecting the course which he was to hold, and he believed it impossible to make a mistake; but his mind occupied with canvassing the obstacles, which impeded his union with Blanche and the reconciliation of the families, and in weighing the arguments for and against success in his present pursuit, he suffered himself to fall into a reverie, during which his steed directed his course entirely at his own pleasure. At length the animal thought proper to stop. The cessation of motion recalled Osbright to himself;

he looked around and found himself in the deepest part of the wood and where no beaten path was discernible.

Which way to guide his horse he had not the most distant idea. Highly incensed at his own negligence, he urged his courser on at random, being only able to decide that to remain where he was then was the worst thing that he could do; whereas by proceeding he might possibly either regain the proper road, or might find some peasant to direct him how to find it. He therefore continued to hasten onward, till his horse put his foot into a pit-fall, and entangled himself too completely to be extricated by any efforts of his rider.

Osbright was now at a complete loss, what to do. The groans of the animal announced that he had received some injury, though the thickness of the boughs excluding all assistance from the moon, the knight was unable to ascertain the nature of his hurt. A sound, like distant thunder, seemed to foretell a coming storm, and to remind him that it was probable in a short time that his situation would become still more disagreeable; while his meditations on the means of extricating himself from his present embarrassment received very unpleasant interruptions from the howling of wolves and other wild beasts by whom the forest was infested. Suddenly Osbright fancied that he saw something glimmer among the trees. He hastily hewed away with his sword some of the intervening branches, which impeded his view, and was delighted to perceive the light of a fire, which evidently shed its rays through the casement of a cottage-window at no great distance. Thither he resolved to hasten, and request its owners to assist him in recovering his horse.

He arrived at the spot, whence the light proceeded. Here stood a low and wretched-looking hut, rudely constructed, and covered with fern and withered boughs. Before he gave notice of his presence, the youth judged it prudent to ascertain the nature of the inhabitants. Accordingly he approached the small window without noise, whence he had a perfect view into the hut's interior.

A young girl, who seemed to be about fifteen, and whose patched garments declared her to be the child of poverty, sat upon a low stool by the hearth. Sometimes she fed the fire with dry sticks, and at others she cast different materials into an iron kettle, which was boiling before her. She frequently stirred its contents and seemed extremely intent upon her occupation. Osbright doubted not that she was preparing the repast of her parents, or perhaps of her master, and he was on the point of lifting the latch of the door, when he heard the girl speak, as if addressing someone in an adjoining room.

"Yes! yes!" said she; "I hear you; all is going on well!" And then turning again to the cauldron, "Now then," she continued; "once again! First for father.

> "Peace to his bones! May they sleep in the cell,
> Ne'er mingled for mischief in poison, nor spell!
> Rest in the coffin! All ghastly and pale,
> By night may his ghost never wander and wail!
> Joy to the soul! May he rise without fears,
> When the trumpet, to sinners so dreadful, he hears."

"Now for my grandmother.

> "Feuds with the Fiends! May the Hag's evil eye
> Ne'er cause...."

"Barbara! Barbara!" screamed a cracked voice, from the inner room. "Idle hussy, what are you thinking about? I'm sure, you're not repeating the three wishes!"

"Sure, are you? Nay, for certain, if the saints are half as deaf as *you* are, I repeat them to little purpose. Set your heart at rest, I tell you; I warrant you, all goes right.

> "Joy to the soul! May he rise...."

"No, no! I said that; where was I? Stay! Oh! Aye, now I remember.

> "Feuds with the Fiends! May the Hag's evil eye
> Ne'er cause our cow Brindle to droop and to die!
> Mercy to man! May her limbs cease to ache,
> Which the ague now forces to shiver and shake!
> Safety with Saints! Let not Satan succeed
> In laming her tongue, when she's saying her creed!"

"And now for myself!

> "Holy and sweet! May the knot soon be tied
> By the priest, which shall make me some honest man's bride!
> Sorrow and Joy! When in childbirth I lie,
> Light be my labor, and...."

Here her eye fell upon Osbright, who, having lifted up
the latch of the door softly, had entered, and was now standing
beside her. "Oh! preserve me, all blessed saints and angels!"
cried the girl with a loud shriek, and sprang from her seat.
"Mercy upon me, sir knight; who are you, and what brings
you here?"

"Be not alarmed, my pretty lass!" answered Osbright. "My
horse has fallen into a pit-fall, and I need assistance to draw
him out. Are there any men belonging to this cottage, who...."

"Oh! no, sir knight; there is no one here, but myself and
my old grandmother, who is confined to her bed with a terrible
ague-fit! But to the right, you will find a narrow path which
leads to the village of Orrenberg; there you may procure assistance in plenty; it is not above a mile off; and now, good sir
knight, be gone, I entreat you!"—And she turned again to
the hearth.

"To the right, I think, you said?" inquired the youth. "My
good girl, leave your cookery to itself for a few minutes, and
just point out the path of which you spoke, and an ample
reward...."

"Oh! no, no, no! I could not stir a step out of this room for
the universe, sir knight! So, pry'thee, interrupt me no longer,
or you'll certainly.... look you there now!" she exclaimed,
running to the cauldron, and beginning to stir it again with
great eagerness. "I thought what would come of talking to me!
The brewage was just going to boil over, and then all the
charm would have been to do over again!"

"The charm?"

"No, no! Not a *charm*! I did not mean to say, *charm*....
I don't know what I meant to say; but I know, I wish, that
you would not interrupt me any longer. Now do go away,
there's a good young knight; now go!"—And she began again
to mutter her rhymes.

"Barbara!" called again the cracked voice from the inner
room. "For Heaven's love, don't forget the ague!"

"No, no!" replied Barbara, "nor the cow either."

"Did I tell you," resumed the voice, "did I tell you, that
the snail-shells must be whole? If they are cracked in the least
part, the broth will be spoiled, and then the child's finger
will have no power or virtue."

"A child's finger?" Osbright started, and his heart beat
violently at the sound. He recollected that Father Peter had
mentioned the loss of Joscelyn's little finger of the right hand.

Should this prove to be the same, here was a clue furnished which might lead to the most important discoveries! While he made this reflection, Barbara answered her grandmother that she had observed her caution respecting the shells, and bade her make herself quite easy.

"Good! good!" said again the old woman. "Only be sure that you put in cobwebs enough, for that is a prime ingredient."—And now Barbara resumed her entreaties that the stranger would leave the cottage.

"By no means!" answered he resolutely, "there seems to be something improper going on here. A child's finger is boiling in that cauldron, and I must know for what purpose you procured it, and in what manner you came by it, before I stir one step from this apartment."

"Now indeed, sir knight!" cried the girl evidently alarmed, "the purpose for which it is intended is a very harmless one. A child's finger is boiling yonder, I must confess; but it is only to make a spell of great virtue, though so innocent that the Virgin herself need not have scrupled to make use of it. The kettle contains the broth of good-luck, and whatever wishes I pronounce, while it is making, sooner or later will all come to pass. And then when it is done, the child's finger being passed nine times through a wedding-ring, it affords an infallible cure for the ague and the earache; and being wrapped in the skin of a dormouse with a sprig of St. John's wort, and laid under the threshold of the door, it is better than an old horseshoe, and neither witch nor devil will venture to put their noses over it; and being dipped in bat's blood, and well rubbed in . . . but mercy on me, what am I about? I ought to be alone while the broth is brewing, for my grandmother herself must not set her foot in the room, because she's not a virgin. Now, dear, good young knight, go along, for if any impure person is present, the charm is quite spoiled."

"Very possibly," observed Osbright; "but though an impure person may do so much mischief, the presence of another pure person ought to make the work go on still better."

"Indeed? Why, as to that point, my grandmother gave no instructions, and it may very well be, as you say, sir knight! Stay a moment, and I'll ask her."

"By no means!" resumed Osbright, detaining her with a look of feigned severity. "It would be quite superfluous, as I am determined not only to remain where I am, but to know by what means the child's finger came into your possession."

"Oh! Gracious! Sir knight! My grandmother charged me not to say a word about the finger to any soul breathing. She said that it might bring us into much trouble, in spite of our innocence."

"It will bring you into much more trouble, if you do not obey me without a moment's hesitation; for I shall hasten to the next village and depose that I found you in the very act of composing an unlawful potion. Both yourself and your grandmother will be seized as witches, and. . . ."

"Oh! all ye blessed saints protect us!" cried the girl trembling in every limb. "That is exactly what we are afraid of; that is it which has obliged us to take refuge in this wild forest out of the reach of every human eye. Indeed, sir knight, we are honest creatures; but my grandmother is a wise woman and knows a power of strange secrets and all the hidden virtues of herbs and plants; and so some ignorant evil-minded person accused her of dealing in sorcery, and if she had not escaped in time, the poor innocent woman would most probably have been burnt for a witch, only because she knew a little more than her neighbors. Now, good sir knight, do not depose against us; only promise to keep our secret, and you shall know every syllable of the matter as faithfully, as if I was kneeling at confession before the Father-Abbot of St. John's himself!"

Osbright gave the required promise—and now he listened with interest, which almost deprived him of the power of breathing, while the girl related that a fortnight had scarcely elapsed, since she found in the wood a young boy, apparently not above nine years old, and at the point of death. She endeavored to save his life but in vain; he had only time to tell her that while separated from his friends during the chase, he had been seized by a wolf; that he had drawn his little dagger and had defended himself so successfully, that though in the contest he gave himself several wounds with his own weapon, he achieved the death of the ferocious animal; but before he could accomplish this, his bosom was dreadfully lacerated, and he had lost so much blood before the girl's arrival, that in spite of all her efforts to succor him, he soon breathed his last. Assured that he was quite dead, she left the fatal spot but took with her the dead wolf, whose skin, she knew, would be an acceptable winter-gift to her grandmother. The old woman, however, on hearing the story, informed her that she had left something behind much more valuable than the skins of all the wolves in the forest. This was the little finger of the child's left hand, which, being boiled with certain mystical ingredients, possessed a thousand important and beneficial properties. Barbara greatly regretted her not having been aware of its virtue; especially as she had taken notice, that in struggling with the wolf the boy had broken that identical finger, and as it seemed only to hang by the skin, nothing would have been more easy for her than to make herself mistress of it. However, it might possibly not be too late, and she hurried back to the scene of death. The corpse was still lying there; no one observed her, and she secured the finger; but in one minute more she would have been too late. She heard footsteps approaching, and had scarcely time to conceal herself behind a bush, when a man arrived at the place whom she well knew to be a domestic of the Count of Orrenberg, having frequently seen him at the castle, when she occasionally ventured thither to dispose of the eggs of her poultry and the milk of the aforesaid cow Brindle. The man, she said, seemed to be greatly distressed and shocked at finding the poor child weltering in his blood; he lifted him in his arms, and she watched him to the river's side, where she left him bathing the child's forehead, washing the blood from the wounds, and using all those efforts to recover him, which, experience had already assured her, must be ineffectual. However, she judged it unwise to tell him so, lest seeing her clothes stained with the blood which had trickled from the dead wolf, and perhaps missing the little finger from the child's hand, he might be induced to suspect her of having been accessory to his death. She thereupon left him still engaged in his charitable endeavors, and returned to her grandmother with her important prize; the use of which, however, had been deferred till the present evening, on account of the difficulty of collecting the other ingredients of the charm.

Such was Barbara's narrative, and Osbright heard with rapture the confirmation of Gustavus's innocence. He asked the girl why she had not disclosed these circumstances when inquiry was made respecting the child's supposed murder; but no such inquiry had reached this secluded hut, whose existence was unknown even at Orrenberg, though so near, and whose inhabitants had no intercourse with the rest of the world, except when necessity compelled Barbara to venture with fear and trembling, either to the castle to dispose of her ware or to the village to purchase those few articles of life which were indispensable.

Osbright rewarded the girl's information liberally, and then having received certain instructions for reaching the neighboring village, he set forward to request assistance for his embarrassed horse. His plans were now changed; and instead of prosecuting his journey, he determined to hasten to Sir Lennard of Kleeborn with the explanation of those circumstances which (as the warrior had assured him) formed the principal objection to his union with Blanche and to a reconciliation between the hostile kinsmen.

CHAPTER IX

"To you my soul's affections move,
Devoutly, warmly true;
My life has been a task of love,
One long, long thought of you."

T. Moore.

OSBRIGHT found the castle of Kleeborn in all the hurry of warlike preparation. The courtyard was strewn with swords and lances; on every side vassals were seen employed in furbishing up their shields and breastplates, and from every quarter resounded the noise of the busy armorers. The youth was too eager to impart the purport of his visit to Sir Lennard to allow himself time for inquiring the cause of all this bustle. He hastened to his friend's apartment, and started back in surprise and disappointment at the marked coldness with which he was received.

With all the frankness and impetuosity of his age, he demanded the reason of this altered treatment; and he now learned, with equal grief and horror the crime with which his father had burdened his soul, and the effect which it had produced at Orrenberg. Sir Ottokar had always been particularly acceptable to Gustavus and his wife; his deference to their opinions, and the partial interest which he had ever taken in their concerns, had not only flattered their pride, but had even been of essential benefit on many most important occasions. His wealth, his power, his high birth and military talents rendered his friendship and support a treasure

to those on whom it was conferred; his evident adoration of
Blanche had made them for some time past consider him as
their future son; and the generosity, with which in their last
interview he had sacrificed his own pretensions to the wishes
of Blanche and the welfare of her family, had exalted their
esteem to a pitch of the highest admiration; a sentiment which
was shared by Sir Lennard, whose heart Ottokar's disinterested
conduct had completely won. When, therefore, the news of
his murder reached Orrenberg, the consternation, the astonishment, the grief, the thirst for revenge, and the bursts of frantic
anger, which it excited, exceeded all powers of description.
Ulrica poured forth without restraint the effusions of all that
jealousy and mistrust which she had so long stifled within her
bosom against the house of Frankheim. The gentle Blanche
wept floods of tears, alternately pitying the kind youth, who
from her childhood had been to her as a brother, and bewail-
ing this fresh obstacle to a reconciliation with her lover's
family; while Gustavus now mourned the loss of his friend,
whom he considered as having fallen a victim to the warmth
with which he had espoused the interests of Orrenberg, now
expatiated on his numerous merits and his own extensive
obligations to him, and now vowed to enact a dreadful vengeance for his death on the barbarous bloody Rudiger. Sir Lennard, inspired with similar indignation, agreed that no
vengeance could be exacted too severe for such a crime; he
promised to assist Gustavus in obtaining it with his whole
power; and having sworn to renounce all intercourse with the
house of Frankheim, he hastened to his own castle to arm his
vassals, and lead them to the assistance of Gustavus.

Osbright listened in the utmost consternation, while the
above circumstances were narrated by his host; but the vehemence with which he reprobated Ottokar's murder and the
agony which he evidently felt at hearing the guilt of his father
were such as speedily to remove from Sir Lennard's mind every
unfavorable impression respecting the youth himself. The
good knight, therefore, gave him his hand with his accustomed
cordiality, and assured him of his undiminished anxiety for his
welfare. Heartily did he wish his future happiness; but he
added that after his solemn promise to Gustavus, he must
confine himself to merely wishing it. Osbright must now
prosecute his love-suit entirely by his own address; if he could
obtain the lady, no one would feel more joy at his success
than Sir Lennard. But never more should the name of Osbright

be pronounced by him at the castle of Orrenberg; he had
sworn it, and nothing could induce him to violate his oath.

Entreaties, that he would change this resolution, proved
unavailing, and Osbright departed with a heavy heart. Yet a
hint which had fallen from Sir Lennard had not been wasted
in the air. Could Blanche be induced to fly with him and
unite her fate to his, the Castle of Kleeborn would afford them
a secure refuge during the first storm of paternal indignation.
He was himself innocent of any offense, and doubtless Gustavus
would soon forbear to confound the son with the father. The
irrevocable knot once tied, the two families must needs reconcile themselves to a measure which could no longer be avoided.
Time, the great healer of wounds, might even obliterate the
remembrance of this atrocious act from the minds of the
different parties; and their respective interests being inseparably blended by this marriage, Mistrust (that odious and malignant monster, which for so long had blasted the happiness
of the hostile kinsmen) must needs perish for want of aliment.
That Blanche could be persuaded to abandon those parents,
whom she loved so passionately, Osbright with justice greatly
doubted; but he resolved that at least the attempt should be
made. An interview with her must be immediately procured;
then if she refused to share his fate, he determined to bid an
eternal adieu both to Blanche and to Germany, to join the
Crusaders who were on the point of departing on their holy
mission, and to lose on the ensanguined plains of Palestine
at once his sorrows, his affection, and his life.

But how was he to obtain this interview? Blanche was not
to visit the grotto till informed of his return by Sir Lennard,
and Sir Lennard had positively refused to interfere any further
in the business. He in vain looked round for some other friend
to render him this service; and after much deliberation, he
determined that under pretense of disposing of her ware at the
castle, the young Barbara might easily deliver a letter to
Blanche. He, therefore, hastened once more to the cottage in
the wood. His liberality soon induced the girl to undertake
the commission. Writing materials were procured at the next
village; and Barbara soon departed with a most pressing
letter, for the answer to which he determined to wait at the
cottage.

But Blanche was no longer mistress of her actions. In the
height of their indignation at Ottokar's murder, her parents
had insisted upon her renouncing all thoughts of a union with

Osbright of Frankheim. Her heart would not allow her to make this renunciation. She protested against the injustice of implicating the son in the father's guilt and avowed the impossibility of withdrawing her affection. Ulrica, whose passions were violent and whose understanding was not strong, was highly indignant at her daughter's disobedience, declared that she would see her no more till she was awakened to a proper sense of duty, and order her to be confined to her own apartment; as to Gustavus, though he disapproved in his heart of such compulsory measures, yet having entirely given up the management of Blanche to his wife hitherto, he forbore on this occasion also to interfere with her orders.

Willingly would the poor Blanche have complied with her lover's request for a last parting interview, to which he had confined himself in his letter, thinking the plan of elopement more likely to be adopted by her if presented without allowing her time for consideration; but how was that compliance to be effected? She was a captive, and could not even leave her own apartment, much less the castle. In this dilemma she resolved to appeal to her nurse, the only person who had access to her, and one who had ever showed toward her the affection of a mother.

The good woman at first remonstrated loudly against the impropriety of her lady's quitting her father's home clandestinely, and insisted upon the danger of her being encountered by the emissaries of the Count of Frankheim, from whose bloody designs she had so lately and so narrowly escaped. But the prayers and tears of Blanche conquered all resistance; and on her promising to be absent but a single hour and to wear such a disguise as must effectually prevent her being recognized either by friend or foe, Margaret consented to assist her temporary evasion.

Her son, a young peasant, was at that time on a visit to her and resident in the castle. His stature was nearly the same as that of Blanche; it was accordingly agreed, that Margaret should procure permission for him to take leave of his young mistress, who was also his foster sister, previous to his quitting the castle; that Blanche arrayed in a suit of his clothes might easily elude the vigilance of her guards, while he remained concealed in her apartment till her return; for which his being supposed to have remembered something of importance to say to his mother would afford a plausible reason; and that, as the late occurrences had occasioned the

private passage to be shut up, Barbara should wait near the
drawbridge to conduct Blanche to the grotto by a path through
the woods, by which means she would be less exposed to observation and discovery than if obliged to traverse the usual
and beaten road. Blanche adopted this plan with eagerness,
and rewarded her kind nurse for her invention with a thousand benedictions and caresses; but as this discussion had
lasted till the approach of night, it was agreed to defer the
interview till the succeeding evening.

This being arranged, Barbara hastened back to the cottage
with a letter whose assurances of undiminished affection filled
the heart of Osbright with hope, joy, and gratitude. To prevent by his presence even the possibility of danger, he engaged
to meet Barbara near the drawbridge at the appointed hour;
and he now sought the villager, to whose care he had intrusted
his wounded horse, and from whom he had borrowed a sorry
beast for his excursion to the Castle of Kleeborn. He found
his courser perfectly recovered, rewarded the villager for his
attention, and he now resolved to return to Frankheim; where
his plans made it necessary for him to furnish himself with
gold and jewels for the expenses of his journey in case of his
departure for the Holy Land, or for the sustenance of his wife
in case he should be so fortunate as to prevail on Blanche to
accompany him in his proposed flight. His course was again
directed to St. John's Chapel; where the intelligence communicated by Brother Peter, respecting Ottokar's murder, Eugene's
illness, and the state of Castle Frankheim, confirmed him in
the prudence of his determinations. He found that under the
present circumstances there was no hope of getting his father
to countenance his affection for the daughter of Gustavus; but
his knowledge of Magdalena's character and of the warm undeviating affection she had ever borne him convinced him
that he ran no danger of her betraying him should he venture
to confess to her his love and his designs; and that if they were
once made known to her, she would assist his wishes to the
very utmost of her power. Accordingly, he requested Brother
Peter to convey a letter to the Countess, which must be delivered with the greatest secrecy into her own hands; in this,
he disclosed to her his irrevocable vows to Blanche, entreated
her to use every means to soften his father's heart toward the
family of Orrenberg, and finally requested her to transmit to
him by the bearer a casket containing gold and some jewels

of value, which she would find in a particular part of his bed chamber.

The good friar, though still ignorant of the name of his young guest, already was too much fascinated by his manners and conversation to refuse him any honest service; accordingly, without requiring to have his curiosity gratified by an explanation of its nature, he readily accepted the commission, and departed with the letter for the Castle of Frankheim.

CHAPTER X

"Horror and doubt distract
  His troubled thoughts, and in his bosom stir
  The hell within him——Now conscience wakes despair
  Which slumbered; wakes the better memory
  Of what he was, what is, and what must be,
  Worse; of worse deeds, worse sufferings must ensue."
                                                    MILTON.

ANGER had satiated itself with blood; the tempest was past; the voice of conscience now could be heard again, and dreadful was its sound in the ears of the guilty Rudiger. Blinded by passion, he had persuaded himself that in putting Ottokar to death he had exercised a just retaliation for the murder of his herald; but now that the illusion was dissipated, he shuddered at perceiving that the two actions wore a very different complexion. Gustavus at least had given no positive orders for the one; but no such excuse could be alleged for the other: the one at least was sudden, and *might* have occurred through accident; the other was premeditated, and *could* only have happened through design; again, the herald was the partisan of a foe, and was indeed a foe himself; but Ottokar was a friend, was a kinsman, was a guest who had trusted to the laws of knightly hospitality and knightly honor—laws which had been found insufficient to preserve his life.

Conscience and his wife's reproaches had awakened Rudiger to a full sense of his guilt; but instead of being beneficial, fatally dreadful were the effect which this conviction produced upon his character. He was not a villain; on the contrary, crimes filled his soul with horror and indignation; nay, he possessed a thousand noble, generous, and heroic feelings; but he was the slave of tempestuous passions, and even in the most laudable movements of his nature, he might rather be said to detest vice than to love virtue.

Now then, when he saw himself on a sudden the object of his own abhorrence, of that abhorrence which he had formerly expressed so loudly and so warmly against others; when he heard the bitter reproaches of Magdalena, and felt in all the agony of his soul, that her reproaches were deserved; he sank at once into the deepest gloom of despondency, into all the horrors of self-loathing, and all the bitterness of mental misery. He indulged no wish of reparation; he formed no plan of repentance; he sought no excuse for his crime; he rather exaggerated its atrocity. What he now felt toward Gustavus was no longer suspicion, or jealousy, or ill-will! No—it was the deepest, deadliest hatred; it was a burning thirst for vengeance, which the blood of the whole family of Orrenberg seemed scarcely enough to quench. He was guilty, he was the most execrable of mortals, he was odious in his own eyes; and what punishment could be inflicted too severe on the man, who had made him so? That man was Gustavus; on Gustavus he swore to be revenged with the most dreadful imprecations; the magnitude of this one crime made him consider all future ones as but of little account, and he became the more a villain from his very abhorrence of vice.

When the first emotions of grief and horror had subsided, and Magdalena's heart no longer prevented her better judgment from exercising its influence, she regretted bitterly her having exposed her feelings so plainly before her lord. She was well aware that with his temper reproaches could only serve to exasperate his passions, and unqualified opposition to confirm him in a course of error. With the dawn of morning, therefore, she hastened to his chamber, determined to remove as much as possible the impression which she had left on his mind at their last parting. She wished to soothe the agonies of his bleeding conscience, to convince him gently and gradually that all these mischiefs arose from the long-subsisting and unnatural enmity of the two houses, and (if possible) by using the gentlest persuasion to win from him a consent that the occurrence of similar disasters should be prevented by the union of Blanche and Osbright, and consequently of the dearest interests of the two families. But her good intentions were frustrated; she was refused admittance to Rudiger, who passed the next four-and twenty hours in the solitude of his chamber, alternately execrating himself and others, and passing by turns from the depth of the blackest gloom to the extreme of the wildest fury.

No one but Wilfred was suffered to approach him; nor would he quit his chamber, till informed of the arrival of Eugene, whom (though his wound was not mortal) it had been at first judged imprudent to remove from the monastery of St. John. Though he had hitherto endeavored to conceal it even from himself, partly through prudence, partly through pride, it was in truth this unacknowledged boy who possessed the whole paternal love of Rudiger. The difference of his sensations toward him and Osbright partook of those which he had felt toward their respective mothers. His esteem, his admiration were bestowed in the highest degree on Magdalena; but his heart had never melted with love but for the unhappy Agatha. Osbright was his heir, was a hero; he was fond of him, but on Eugene he doted. In the one, he prized the transmitter of his name, which was so precious to his vanity; but he cherished Eugene for his own sake. It is true, if he had been asked—"which of the youths should perish"—he would have sacrificed Eugene without a moment's hesitation; for, in the bosom of Rudiger pride ever bore a sway far superior to that of tenderness; but had he been asked—"which of them he could consent never to see again"—he would have felt as little doubt in answering—"Osbright"—nor perhaps would have felt very deeply the deprivation, though the being his heir was the strongest claim to his attention. Still the reflection, that he *must* be his heir, made Rudiger entertain some little jealousy toward him; and in the presence of Osbright, the father's self-love felt painfully wounded by being sensible, that the perfection of his son made the defects of his own character appear in a more glaring light. On the other hand he saw in Eugene a poor defenseless being, whom he had brought into a world of sorrow, where his lot was hard, and against whose difficulties he was ill calculated to struggle. He pitied him for his destitute situation, and he loved him for his likeness to his wretched mother. In short, Eugene was dearer to him than Osbright; but the pride of blood was a thousand times dearer to him than either: he would have sacrificed his own life to preserve Eugene's; but he would have sacrificed Eugene's as well as his own to preserve in Osbright "the future Count of Frankheim."

No sooner was he informed of the youth's arrival, than he hastened to visit him; but he had scarcely passed the threshold

of his chamber, when Magdalena stood before him. He started
back, and a deep gloom darkened all his features. In vain did
she address him in the most soothing language, and endeavor
to extenuate the atrocity of Ottokar's murder; he listened in
silence, and only replied by a look of scornful incredulity. In
vain did she recant the too hasty declaration of her sentiments
toward him, and assure him of her undiminished affection;
the bending of his head with constrained politeness and a smile
of the bitterest irony was the only manner in which he expressed his gratitude. His coldness hurt, and his sullenness
alarmed her. Her eyes filled with tears; she motioned to take
his hand and press it to her lips; but he drew it back, haughtily
and gloomily, and passing her without uttering a word, proceeded to the chamber of Eugene.

But no comfort awaited him there. He found the wretched
youth tortured by one of his most violent paroxysms. He raved
incessantly of his mother and of the murdered Joscelyn; of the
lovely cruel Blanche, and the happy hated Osbright. Every
word which fell from his lips either tore open a scarcely healed
wound in his father's bosom or inflicted upon it a new one.
Rudiger listened with horror and remorse to the recapitula-
tion of the poor Agatha's injuries and sufferings; the mention
of Joscelyn's murder re-kindled in his heart the flames of
vengeance against Gustavus; but when he collected from
Eugene's ravings that the child of that very Gustavus was likely
to become his daughter-in-law; that she, whose fatal beauty
had robbed his darling son of his reason, and almost of his life,
had also fascinated the affections of his heir; and that the
proud name of Frankheim was destined to be perpetuated
through a descendant of the detested race of Orrenberg; no
sooner was this discovery made to him, than his surprise, his
alarm, his indignation were extreme, extravagant, ungovernable. He rushed from Eugene's apartment, hastened to that
of Magdalena, and entering abruptly, assailed her at once with
such a storm of passion, of threats, of vows of vengeance against
Blanche, against Osbright, against herself if he should find her
privy to her son's attachment, that it was long before the
Countess could discover the origin of his frantic behavior.

But when she *did* discover it, she found all efforts to appease
his fury totally unavailing. On the contrary, the attempt to
soothe him, and the bare suggestion of the advantages likely
to result from Osbright's attachment only served to increase
his passion; and after loading his wife with the bitterest re-

proaches, he was rushing from the chamber, when his eye rested on a letter, which in her agitation had fallen from her bosom unobserved. At the same moment with her lord, she also had perceived the paper; with a cry of terror she hastily caught it from the ground; but Rudiger had recognized his son's handwriting, and Magdalena's evident alarm convincing him that it contained some mystery and *that* a mystery of no slight importance, he rudely forced the letter from her. One half, however, remained in the hand of the Countess, and she hastened to conceal its contents from discovery by throwing it into a brazier which was burning on the hearth.

It was Osbright's letter, which Brother Peter had delivered not an hour before. Pale and trembling with passion, Rudiger read the avowal of his son's love for Blanche expressed in the most glowing terms, his urgent entreaties that Magdalena would prevail on his father to consent to their union, and his confession that for several days he had remained in concealment at the cell of Brother Peter. He also mentioned that he was to have an interview with Blanche that evening. . . .—and here the letter broke off. The object of that interview, the place of rendezvous, the precise time of meeting, these points were contained in the burned half of the letter; and on these points the alarmed Magdalena resolutely refused to give any information. Threats and entreaties were employed in vain; and having placed guards at her chamber door, lest she should make Osbright aware that his incensed father was apprised of the intended meeting, Rudiger left her to meditate on the most certain means of getting the defenseless Blanche into his power.

Wilfred was summoned to his counsels; but the seneschal refused his assistance, till assured that his lord's designs aimed at the liberty, but not at the life of Blanche; though perhaps had he reasoned justly, he would have known that with a man like Rudiger, whose passions were so impetuous, and who was ever swayed by the impulse of the moment, her liberty once lost, her life could not for one instant be secure. However, at present Rudiger's object was, by getting Blanche into his hands, to prevent the possibility of her marriage with Osbright, and to inflict the bitterest agony on Gustavus by making him tremble with every minute for the life of his darling daughter. He also fancied that her presence might be of great efficacy in restoring Eugene to his senses; but he swore with dreadful imprecations that if she failed to produce that beneficial effect, she should be the lunatic's only nurse and continual attendant and should pass the remainder of her existence in witnessing the frantic transports of the wretch whom her fatal charms had ruined. Such being his avowed objects, Wilfred made no longer any scruple of giving his advice. It was accordingly agreed that St. John's Chapel should be watched; that Osbright should be followed to the place of rendezvous; and that Rudiger should hasten thither with a small body of chosen men to seize and convey Blanche to the castle of Frankheim. But Wilfred (who dreaded the resentment of his young lord, should he be known to have had any hand in this business, and in whose power he should be left entirely after Rudiger's decease) stipulated that every possible means should be used to surprise the lady, either previous to her meeting with Osbright or after she had parted from him, but not when the lovers were together. By taking this precaution, he trusted that Osbright would be kept in ignorance of the persons by whom his mistress had been carried off; all resistance on his part would also be precluded, which otherwise was likely to be very desperate and dangerous to the assailants; and it might even be possible to conceal from him that the scene of his mistress' captivity was the castle of his own father.

To these stipulations Rudiger readily consented; and everything being now arranged, he waited with the utmost impatience for the information that Osbright had set forward from the Chapel of St. John.

CHAPTER XI

> "Why does she stop, and look often around,
>   As she glides down the secret stair;
> And why does she pat the shaggy bloodhound,
>   As he rouses him up from his lair;
> And though she passes the postern alone,
> Why is not the watchman's bugle blown?"
>
> W. Scott's "Lay of the Last Minstrel."

THE time was arrived at which Osbright had engaged to meet Barbara near the drawbridge; but some suspicious circumstances had alarmed Brother Peter and made him intimate to his guest that spies were certainly watching near the chapel gate. There was no other outlet. Osbright, however unwillingly, thought it advisable to protract his departure for a short time; after which Brother Peter was sent out to examine whether the persons whose appearance had excited his suspicions were still loitering near the place. The old man soon returned with the report that all seemed quiet and that in his belief his guest might now set forward without danger of a discovery. But as much time had been lost by this hesitation, the youth doubted not that Blanche and her companion must have long since quitted the castle of Orrenberg and probably had already sheltered themselves within the cave.

Thither he therefore hastened with all possible expedition, and found his conjectures verified. Blanche and Barbara were safe within St. Hildegarde's Grotto and extremely uneasy at his not arriving. In two hours the drawbridge of Orrenberg Castle would be raised, and Blanche's return prevented; while on the other hand Barbara was uneasy at being so long absent from her decrepit grandmother, and yet could not think of leaving Blanche in the cavern without a companion. The arrival of Osbright at once dispelled their uneasiness. Blanche received him with mingled joy and sorrow; and Barbara, having congratulated the lovers on their meeting, stated her own presence to be now superfluous and entreated permission to return to her grandmother, who (she was certain) must be extremely uneasy at her absence. The permission was readily granted, and she lost no time in profiting by it.

And now did Osbright employ every resource of his eloquence to persuade Blanche that the hour was come when they must either part forever or must part no more. Blanche heard the assurance with agony; but the proposal of flight, of marriage unauthorized by her parents, was rejected by her, not merely with firmness, but even with abhorrence. She owned that to see Osbright no more was the bitterest of all earthly misfortunes, except to live under the consciousness of having merited paternal displeasure. She said that in truth her parting with him would break her heart, but her flight with him would break the hearts of her parents; and she prayed that the vengeance of offended Heaven might fall heavy on her head if she ever planted a single painful feeling in those bosoms, which from the first moment of her birth had only palpitated with love and with anxiety for her.

In answer to this, Osbright said everything that despairing passion could suggest. In vain did Blanche assure him that no persuasion could induce her to act in contradiction to her

sense of duty. The youth persisted in pointing out all the
advantages likely to result from so slight and so temporary a
deviation from the path of strict propriety; and he was still
urging his hopeless suit, when a stone fell through the chasm
in the grotto's roof, which was at some little distance from the
rocky bank on which the lovers were seated. Osbright turned
round; a second stone fell, and was followed by a third,
accompanied by a low murmuring noise. He listened and
fancied that he could distinguish his own name. He rose, and
advanced to the chasm.

"Is any one above?" said he aloud; "did any one call. . . ."

"Hush! hush! sir knight!" interrupted a voice, still whispering. "Speak softly for Heaven's sake; I am Barbara! Oh! Sir
knight, I fear that we are all undone, or at least that the Lady
Blanche has got into the saddest hole that ever poor lady put
her head into. Would you think it, sir knight? I had scarcely
set my foot on the outside of the narrow passage. . . . I was
going along gaily, singing to myself, and (the Lord knows)
thinking of no harm. . . . all on a sudden—'Seize her,' cries
a voice like thunder, and in an instant I found myself surrounded by armed men. I fell on my knees, and begged for
my life, and with good reason; for one tall terrible knight
had got his dagger drawn as if ready to stab me, only his companion caught him by the arm, and bade him remember his
oath. 'Right,' said the fierce-one, 'then away with her to the
castle! Confine her in the dungeons of the south tower!'—When
I heard the word 'dungeon,' I thought, that I should have died
outright; so I fell to crying and entreating more than ever,
and as luck would have it, the moon just then happened to
come from behind a cloud. 'Ha!' cried the quiet one, as soon
as he saw my face, 'this cannot be the Lady Blanche?' 'Oh! no,
no, no!' said I, before I gave myself time to think; 'I am not
the Lady Blanche indeed. She is yonder in the cave with Sir
Osbright, disguised in boy's clothes, and. . . ."

"You told them so? Imprudent girl! You have undone us
all!"

"Alas the day! Sir knight! I was in such a flutter that I
scarcely knew what I did or what I said; but as soon as they
knew who I really was, they released me and bade me go my
ways. I would fain have returned to tell you what had happened; but they would not suffer me, and I was obliged to set
forward as if going to my own home. Yet I could not bear to
leave you in ignorance of their evil designs; so after a little

while I stole back again without noise, and by help of the shrubs and bushes I crept behind the two who appeared to be the chief of the party, so that I could overhear their whole design."

"And that design is. . . . . ."—

"To seize the Lady Blanche on her leaving the grotto and convey her to the castle of Frankheim, where she is to be shut up in a dungeon, till she consents to marry some young madman who (it seems) has lost his wits for love of her. The fierce one was for going to the grotto and dragging her away this moment; but his companion reminded him of his promise of seizing her if possible after she had parted with Sir Osbright. 'But suppose,' says the fierce one, 'he should not part with her till she is safe within the walls of Orrenberg?' At last it was agreed between them that they should still wait an hour to see whether Blanche would come out alone; but if that time should elapse without your quitting the cave, sir knight, then the fierce one swore with a thousand dreadful oaths that he would tear her from you with his own hands—'And if he resists,' continued he in a dreadful voice, and he clenched his hands, and I could hear him gnash his teeth, 'if he resists, I will either plunge my sword in the hated girl's heart, or he shall bury his in his father's.'"

"Your father, Osbright? Your dreadful father?" exclaimed Blanche, wringing her hands. "Now you see, in what danger even this trifling breach of duty has involved me! Oh! My parents, my dear, good parents! How severely am I punished for having clandestinely left for one hour the shelter of your protecting arms!"

"No! no!" said Barbara eagerly, while Osbright vainly endeavored to calm the terrors of his mistress, though his own alarm was scarcely less, "all is not lost yet, dear lady; calm yourself, and listen to me; for as soon as I knew the designs of these villains, I bethought me of a means to save you, and it was for this purpose, that I hazarded to climb the rock and steal hither unobserved to give you this intelligence. It seems that Sir Osbright is in no danger; they will let him pass forth without hindrance, and will rejoice in getting rid of him, in order that they may bear you away to their horrible dungeons without resistance. Now mark what you must do; throw off that long cloak in which Dame Margaret wrapped you up so carefully; array yourself instead in Sir Osbright's armor, and then march forth with a stout heart, his shield on your arm, and his helmet on your head. The shadows of night will doubtless prevent the strangers from observing any difference in your height; the clattering of the armor will confirm them in their mistake; and though to be sure the moon shines brightly just at present, that is a circumstance in your favor; for I heard one of the villains tell the other, that though you were in boy's clothes, there could be no mistaking you for Sir Osbright, who would be known by the device of his shield, and by the scarlet and white plumes on his helmet. Come, come, make haste, lady; for I warrant you, there is but little time to spare."

Osbright had already divested himself of his breastplate and his glittering casque, and he now hastened to adorn with them the delicate form of Blanche. Confused and terrified in the extreme, she yielded to his entreaties, but frequently compelled both him and Barbara to repeat their assurances that he ran no danger in remaining in the grotto. At length her disguise was complete, and with a beating heart and trembling limbs, she set forward on her dangerous expedition.

No sooner had the lady left the cave than Barbara resumed her discourse. "And now, sir knight," said she, "it will be necessary for *you* also to play a part. I warrant you, the lady will be no sooner out of hearing than the strangers will hurry hither to secure their prize; and should they discover her flight immediately, they may still be in time to prevent her escape. Therefore wrap yourself up in her scarlet mantle, and conceal your face under the large slouched hat which she has left behind her; they are aware that she is in male apparel, and by disguising your voice a little, you may easily persuade them that you are the person whom they seek till she is safe at Orrenberg. That's right! Now then the hat!—Hark! I hear the noise of armor. Keep up the deception as long as you can; you know, they can but carry you to your own castle; and as it seems that the chief of these strangers is your own father, at worst you have only to discover. . . . they are here! Hush!"

Barbara was correct. Count Rudiger and his attendants had suffered the trembling Blanche to pass unmolested through their ambuscade; they only marked the clank of her arms and the waving of her parti-colored plumes; while the faintness of her step, and that she tottered under the weight of the ponderous shield, passed entirely unobserved. Yet as she drew near the outlet of the rocky path, she once heard a voice whisper from among some bushes—"Now then! Now!"—and the sound appeared to her the sentence of death. Her pulse ceased to beat; she staggered, and caught at a projection of the rock; but presently another voice whispered eagerly in reply—"No! No! Be silent, fool! 'Tis Sir Osbright! I know him by that casque";—and she felt her hopes and her spirits revive. She rushed forward with renewed vigor, and in a few minutes found herself in the great road leading to Orrenberg.

"Now praised be the Virgin!" she exclaimed in a rapture of gratitude, "I am safe!"—when at that moment she found herself seized with violence; her lance was wrested from her hand, and on looking round she perceived herself surrounded by armed men. A shout of exultation immediately followed her capture.

"What is the matter?" exclaimed a warrior, at whose approach the crowd gave way, and in whose voice Blanche recognized with shame and terror the voice of her father. But the visor of her casque was closed, and he little guessed that the warrior who stood before him was the daughter whom he believed secure in the castle of Orrenberg.

"The business is half done, my lord!" was the answer. "I should know that helmet and shield among a thousand; and I here present you (without the capture costing you a single blow) with that redoubtable warrior, Osbright of Frankheim."

"Sir Osbright?" cried Gustavus. "Maurice, are you certain of what you assert?—Nay then, this is indeed a prize! But time permits not. . . . . Fear nothing, sir knight; your treatment shall be noble, but for the present you must remain my prisoner. Let six of you convey him to the castle, and confine him in the state-chamber, adjoining to the great hall. Guard him honorably, but closely, and see that no one has access to him. Now then for Rudiger! Away!" Gustavus said, and hastened toward the grotto; and now Blanche found herself compelled to visit the castle of her parents, as an enemy and a captive. However, her plan was already arranged. She determined to keep her secret till safe within the walls of Orrenberg. Once arrived there, she meant to request an interview with her mother, confess to her the whole of her imprudence, and entreat her assistance in repairing it. She doubted not that the strength of maternal tenderness would soon conquer the first emotions of resentment; that Ulrica would find some means of enabling her to regain her own chamber undiscovered; and that as the disappearance of the supposed Osbright might easily be accounted for by his having effected his

escape by bribing his guards, or any other artifice, her fault
and her danger on this adventurous night might effectually be
kept from the knowledge of her father. Such were the designs
of Blanche; and having thus arranged them to her satisfaction,
she prosecuted her journey to Orrenberg with a less heavy
heart.

CHAPTER XII

——"Even-handed Justice
Commends the ingredients of the poisoned chalice
To our own lips."——

MACBETH.

A DOMESTIC, whom Count Rudiger had chastised for some
trivial fault with unjustifiable severity, in revenge had fled to
the castle of Orrenberg and informed its lord that both Osbright and his father were in St. Hildegarde's Grotto, slightly
attended, and might easily be surprised. Gustavus failed not
to employ so fortunate and unhoped-for an opportunity of
getting his chief enemies into his power. He immediately set
forward with all the forces which he could muster—and so
great was the superiority of his numbers, that in spite of
Rudiger's resistance (who exposed his life on this occasion with
all the inconsiderate fury of a madman and performed prodigies of valor almost incredible) the small body of Frankheimers
were soon put to flight, and their chief was conveyed a prisoner
to the castle of Orrenberg.

Now then it was in the power of Gustavus to take a full
revenge on his furious kinsman and secure to himself, by the
deaths of Rudiger and his son, the entire possessions of the
haughty house of Frankheim; but to profit by this opportunity
was not in the noble and forgiving nature of Gustavus; he
meditated a more honorable vengeance. His own injuries were
already forgotten; the death of Ottokar was still remembered,
but remembered with grief, not rage. His enemies were totally
in his power; that consideration was sufficient to make him
view them no longer as enemies; and he seized with eagerness
this opportunity of evincing the disinterestedness of his wishes
and the sincerity of his professions of good will by a proof so
clear and striking as should effectually banish all future mistrust, even from the suspicious bosom of Rudiger. He com-

municated his intentions to Sir Lennard, who on that evening had arrived with his promised succors at Orrenberg. The worthy knight sanctioned the plan with his warmest approbation, and Gustavus now hastened, with a heart glowing with delight at the thought of doing a great and generous act, to explain himself to his indignant prisoner.

The great hall was the scene of this interview between the hostile kinsmen. His guards had caused Rudiger's wounds to be carefully dressed, but had thought it proper to restrain him by chains from committing acts of violence. Gustavus, however, no sooner observed this precaution, than he ordered the fetters to be removed; but the sullen captive neither thanked the servants for their care of his wounds nor the master for the restoration of his liberty. He looked on all around him with an air of haughty indifference; but while he listened to Gustavus's professions of good will and proposals for a mutual oblivion of past injuries, the expression of gratified malice glared terribly in his burning eyeballs.

"In short," said Gustavus in conclusion, "I am convinced that the numerous causes which have occasioned the mutual alienation of our hearts and families arose entirely from misinterpretation of accidental circumstances, and not from any intention of offense, or desire to inflict a premeditated injury. Your suspicions are easily excited; those of my wife are not more difficult to rouse; every trifle was exaggerated, every fact was misrepresented, and suppositions were counted as facts. It is my most earnest wish to root out all misunderstanding forever, and I know of no more certain means than a union of our children, the union of Osbright and Blanche."

"Blanche?" repeated Rudiger "Blanche? Nay, 'tis a most fortunate idea! I only doubt the facility of. . . ."

"Nothing can be effected more easily!" interrupted Gustavus, rejoiced to find his proposal so favorably received. "They love each other. . . . have loved each other long, and. . . ."

"True! I have heard so! Osbright loves your daughter fondly; and no doubt *you* love her fondly, too?"

"Fondly? Passionately! She is the joy of my existence, the being on whom alone I depend for the whole happiness of my future life!"

"Indeed? That is still better—I rejoice to hear it—there is a youth at home. . . . His name is Eugene. . . . He too loves her passionately. . . . madly, indeed, I *might* say. . . . But she, you think, loves Osbright?"

"*Think* it? I know it! It was but this morning that she assured me so ardently that her heart burned for him with such true affection. . ."

"Nay, it may be so; you must know best; and yet I cannot help suspecting, that her heart feels colder toward him now than it did this morning."

"Your suspicions are unjust, Count Rudiger. Blanche is no capricious. . . . But you shall hear her own lips declare her sentiments. She shall be called hither instantly, and. . ."

"By no means," cried Rudiger hastily, while he detained his host. "By no means! She is probably retired to rest; I do not wish her to be disturbed; I do not even wish to see her. . . . till Osbright shall present her to me as his bride."

"That may be done this instant; you are not yet aware, Count Rudiger that you are not the only captive of rank whom this night's adventure has thrown into my power. Your son inhabits yonder chamber."

Instantly the expression of Rudiger's countenance changed. He turned pale, and starting from his chair grasped the arm of his seneschal, who had been captured with him in the cave and had accompanied him to Orrenberg.

"My son *here?*" he exclaimed. "Here! in your power!"

A similar dismay seemed to have taken possession of the seneschal.

"I warned you," he replied in broken accents; "I told you. . . . I charged you. . ."

"Peace, babbler!" interrupted his lord passionately; while Gustavus thus resumed his discourse.

"Yes; Osbright, on leaving the cave, was seized by my followers, and conveyed hither; but calm this agitation, Count, which doubtless is caused by your unjust suspicions respecting the death of your younger son. Your elder, your only one, is now in my hands, and with a single word could I annihilate your whole race. But fear nothing; I would rather perish myself than pronounce that word. Osbright's liberty shall prove to you that I am innocent of the death of Joscelyn; he shall be immediately restored to you, and I only ask in return your consent to his union with my sole heiress, with my darling child."

"I consent!" cried Rudiger eagerly. "I consent to that, to everything! Only give me back my son; suffer us to depart this instant, and to-morrow name your own conditions."

"You shall be obeyed," answered Gustavus, and ordered

the doors of the captive's chamber to be thrown open, and himself conducted to their presence. "But," he continued, addressing himself to Rudiger, "surely you will not depart immediately. 'Tis late; the espousals may take place to-morrow; a messenger may be dispatched to inform the Lady Magdalena of the cause which detains you; then tarry here this night, and. . . ."

"This night?" exclaimed Rudiger wildly; "no, no! Not an hour! Not an instant! Count of Orrenberg, would you *extort* my consent to this union? Would you believe this reconciliation to be sincere, if made with your captives? No! Be generous! Give me back my son without conditions; restore us to liberty; then send your herald to the castle of Frankheim to-morrow and receive my answer, free and uncontrolled."

"Be it so!" said Gustavus; and at the same moment the captive knight entered the hall. The Count of Frankheim, in spite of his agitation (which increased with every moment), recognized the well-known shield and helmet; and before Gustavus had time to explain what had happened, he hastily commanded the youth to follow him. But the youth obeyed not the command. Again it was repeated, and still he remained motionless. Rudiger, whose impatience by this time amounted almost to frenzy, rushed forward to grasp his son's hand, and draw him by force from the apartment. The youth started back with a cry of terror, and retreating nearer to the Count of Orrenberg, seemed to implore his protection against his incensed father. Gustavus endeavored to reassure him.

"Fear nothing, noble youth!" said he. "Your father knows your attachment and approves it. We are no longer enemies; your union with my daughter is settled, and you will only leave this castle to-night that you may return to it to-morrow as the acknowledged bridegroom of your Blanche."

"Indeed?" exclaimed the young knight in joyful surprise. "Oh! Happy tidings! Now then I need nothing more to complete my happiness. . . . nothing but my father's pardon—then pardon me, my father," he continued, at the same time throwing off his ponderous casque, and falling at the feet of Gustavus. "Oh! Pardon your penitent, your imprudent child!"

"Amazement!" exclaimed the Count of Orrenberg. "'Tis Blanche!"

"Blanche?" cried Rudiger, "Blanche in Osbright's armor? Oh! Wilfred, Wilfred! Whom then. . . . ? Speak, girl, speak!

Explain. . . . oh! Lose not a moment. . . . you know not the fears. . . . . . the agonies. . . . speak, oh! Speak!"

Agitated by hope, blushing at her imprudence, confused by the rapidity and violence with which Rudiger questioned her, it was with difficulty that Blanche related the adventures of the cave to her astonished auditors; but Rudiger soon heard enough to guess the rest. He understood that the lovers had been aware of his approach; that they had changed habits; that disguised as Blanche, Osbright had remained in the cavern; he required to know no more! A shriek of horror interrupted the narrative; his countenance expressed all the agonies of despair; he seemed to be some fiend rather than a human being.

"The blow is struck!" he exclaimed; "'tis past! All is over!—Agony!—Madness!—Yet 'tis possible. . . . To the cave! To the cave! To save him, or to die!" he said, and rushed out of the hall.

"Oh! follow him!" cried Wilfred, wringing his hands; "drag him from the cavern! Nay, nay! Detain me not! His brain will turn. . . . his heart will break. . . . He promised so solemnly. . . . but his violence. . . . . . his passions. . . . a sudden burst of fury. . . . let me be gone! For the love of Heaven, oh! Let me depart this moment."

And breaking from Gustavus, who wished him to explain the cause of this excessive agitation, the seneschal followed his master, who had already crossed the drawbridge with the rapidity of an eagle.

After a few words to tranquilize his affrighted daughter, the Count of Orrenberg judged it best to pursue the fugitives and learn the cause of their alarm; but before he could leave the hall, a fresh incident obstructed his progress. A young girl, bathed in tears, pale as a specter, and her garments spotted with blood, rushed wildly into the room, and threw herself sobbing at the feet of Blanche. It was Barbara.

"He is gone!" she exclaimed, wringing her hands. "Oh! Lady, lady; he is gone! From the rock above I heard the clank of the assassin's armor as he rushed into the cavern. 'Blanche! Blanche!' he cried; 'Blanche of Orrenberg!' 'Here I am!' answered the poor victim, 'what would you with Blanche?' 'Ha! sorceress!' cried again the terrible voice; 'take this! 'Tis Eugene who sends it you!'—and then. . . . oh! then I saw the weapon gleam. . . . I heard a dreadful shriek. . . . I heard no more!—I lost my senses. When they returned, all was hushed—I ventured down from the rock. . . . I stole into the cave. . . . I dragged him into the light. . . . he was bloody. . . . he was cold. . . . he was dead!"

"Whom? Whom?" exclaimed Blanche, almost frantic with alarm.

"Oh! Osbright! Osbright!" answered the sobbing girl; and Blanche fell lifeless at the feet of her father.

At the door of St. Hildegarde's cave stood the wretched Rudiger; before him lay a corpse, on which he gazed for a few moments in silent agony. At length with desperate resolution he drew away the large hat which overshadowed the face of the dead person, and the moonbeams shone full upon his features. Rudiger knew those features well! He tore off the scarlet robe in which the body was enveloped; he saw a large wound on the breast; he saw his own dagger in the wound; he snatched it forth, plunged it in his heart, and then murmuring the name of Osbright, the slave of passion sank upon his victim's body, and sank to rise no more!

Blanche was restored to life, but her happiness was fled forever. She languished through a few mournful years, and then sought the grave, whither her broken-hearted father soon followed his darling. Then fatal inheritance passed into another family, and the proud race of Frankheim closed its illustrious line forever.

At the expiration of some years, Eugene was unhappy enough to recover his senses sufficiently to know that Blanche was already numbered among the dead. He visited her tomb, wept, and prayed there; then fixed the Cross upon his bosom, and wandered in pilgrim's weeds to the Holy Land. He was never heard of more; but with a frame so delicate, intellect so shattered, and a heart so wounded, doubtless his sufferings could not be long.

Magdalena and Ulrica, these sisters in calamity, retired to the convent of St. Hildegarde, where they soon after assumed the veil, and in whose chapel they caused a stately tomb to be erected over the ashes of their departed children. Here every day they met to indulge their common sorrows; here every night they joined in prayer for the eternal happiness of those dear ones; here during many years of unavailing anguish they bathed with tears the marble tablet on which stood engraved these words, so mournful, so fatal, and so true,

"Here rest the Victims of Mistrust."

The Heir of Mondolfo

by

MARY SHELLEY

MARY SHELLEY (1797–1851)

Mary Shelley's "The Heir of Mondolfo"—which was first published in *Appleton's Journal* in 1877, more than 25 years after her death—is an excellent example not only of one of the directions that the later Gothic took, but also of what happened to it along the way. In its thirteenth- or fourteenth-century setting, in the tyrannical cruelty of Fernando, in its concern for the problems of a legitimate heir, in the abduction and imprisonment in the tower of Viola, in her escape during a violent storm and her salvation among the ancient ruins, "The Heir of Mondolfo" makes good use of the Gothic tradition. Yet the castle itself has ceased to be the location of action; the supernatural has been reduced to the terrors of the weather, and both sentimental and didactic interests are egalitarian rather than aristocratic.

Like her father, William Godwin, who in *Caleb Williams* (1794) had found a fictional medium for his political philosophy, Mary Shelley was most concerned that her Gothic story should demonstrate that true nobility was of the heart and not of birth. Godwin was England's foremost anti-authoritarian philosopher. His wife, Mary Wollstonecraft, was widely known as the author of *Vindication of the Rights of Women* (1792). With such a background, it is not surprising that their daughter Mary, who scorned propriety in running off with Shelley while he was still married, should have looked upon her fiction as serving a radical political and social purpose. The child of rationalistic parents, she was hardly disposed to the re-creation of medieval superstitions to demonstrate the miracles of God in the world. Yet the elements of romanticism influenced her contrast of the idyllic pastoral life with society's inhumanity to man; they led her to descriptions of nature in the Italy that she knew so well at first hand; and they furnished her Byronic hero with the melancholy, passionate, and restless characteristics that had become fashionable.

Most famous for *Frankenstein* (1818), she also wrote *Valperga* (1823), an historical novel of the Italian Middle Ages; *The Last Man* (1825), a Utopian story; *Perkin Warbeck* (1830); *Lodore* (1835); and *Falkner* (1837), modeled on Godwin's *Caleb Williams*.

IN the beautiful and wild country near Sorrento, in the Kingdom of Naples, at the time it was governed by monarchs of the house of Anjou,[1] there lived a territorial noble, whose wealth and power overbalanced that of the neighboring nobles. His castle, itself a stronghold, was built on a rocky eminence, toppling over the blue and lovely Mediterranean. The hills around were covered with ilex-forests, or subdued to the culture of the olive and vine. Under the sun no spot could be found more favored by nature.

If at eventide you had passed on the placid wave beneath the castellated rock that bore the name of Mondolfo, you would have imagined that all happiness and bliss must reside within its walls, which, thus nestled in beauty, overlooked a scene of such surpassing loveliness; yet if by chance you saw its lord issue from the portal, you shrunk from his frowning brow, you wondered what could impress on his worn cheek the combat of passions. More piteous sight was it to behold his gentle lady, who, the slave of his unbridled temper, the patient sufferer of many wrongs, seemed on the point of entering upon that only repose "where the wicked cease from troubling and the weary are at rest."[2] The Prince Mondolfo had been united early in life to a princess of the regal family of Sicily. She died in giving birth to a son. Many years subsequently, after a journey to the northern Italian states, he returned to his castle, married. The speech of his bride declared her to be a Florentine. The current tale was that he married her for love, and then hated her as the hindrance of his ambitious views. She bore all for the sake of her only child—a child born to its father's hate; a boy of gallant spirit, brave even to wildness. As he grew up, he saw with anger the treatment his mother received from the haughty Prince. He dared come forward as her defender; he dared oppose his boyish courage to his father's rage: the result was natural— he became the object of his father's dislike. Indignity was heaped on him; the vassals were taught to disobey him, the menials to scorn him, his very brother to despise him

---

[1] For the description of the Kingdom of Naples see note 13 to *The Castle of Otranto* on page 76. The reign of the monarchs of Anjou began with Charles I in 1266 and continued, with many interruptions, until the fifteenth century.

[2] The quotation is from *Job* III, 17.

as of inferior blood and birth. Yet the blood of Mondolfo was his; and, though tempered by the gentle Isabel's more kindly tide, it boiled at the injustice to which he was a victim. A thousand times he poured forth the overflowings of his injured spirit in eloquent complaints to his mother. As her health decayed, he nurtured the project, in case of her death, of flying his paternal castle, and becoming a wanderer, a soldier of fortune. He was now thirteen. The Lady Isabel soon, with a mother's penetration, discovered his secret, and on her death-bed made him swear not to quit his father's protection until he should have attained the age of twenty. Her heart bled for the wretchedness that she foresaw would be his lot; but she looked forward with still greater horror to the picture her active fancy drew of her son at an early age wandering forth in despair, alone and helpless, suffering all the extremities of famine and wretchedness; or, almost worse, yielding to the temptations that in such a situation would be held out to him. She extracted this vow, and died satisfied that he would keep it. Of all the world, she alone knew the worth of her Ludovico—had penetrated beneath the rough surface, and become acquainted with the rich store of virtue and affectionate feeling that lay like unsunned ore in his sensitive heart.

Fernando hated his son. From his earliest boyhood he had felt the sentiment of aversion, which, far from endeavoring to quell, he allowed to take deep root, until Ludovico's most innocent action became a crime, and a system of denial and resistance was introduced that called forth all of sinister that there was in the youth's character, and engendered an active spirit of detestation in his father's mind. Thus Ludovico grew, hated and hating. Brought together through their common situation, the father and son, lord and vassal, oppressor and oppressed, the one was continually ready to exert his power of inflicting evil, the other perpetually on the alert to resist even the shadow of tyranny. After the death of his mother, Ludovico's character greatly changed. The smile that, as the sun, had then often irradiated his countenance, now never shone; suspicion, irritability, and dogged resolution, seemed his master-feelings. He dared his father to the worst, endured that worst, and prevented from flying by his sacred observance of his vow, nurtured all angry and even revengeful feelings till the cup of wrath seemed ready to overflow. He was loved by none, and loving none his good qualities expired, or slept as if they would never more awaken.

His father had intended him for the Church; and Ludovico, until he was sixteen, wore the priestly garb. That period past, he cast it aside, and appeared habited as a cavalier of those days, and in short words told his parent that he refused to comply with his wishes; that he should dedicate himself to arms and enterprise. All that followed this declaration—menace, imprisonment, and even ignominy—he bore, but he continued firm; and the haughty Fernando was obliged to submit his towering will to the firmer will of a stripling. And now, for the first time, while rage seemed to burst his heart, he felt to its highest degree the sentiment of hatred; he expressed this passion—words of contempt and boundless detestation were heaped upon Ludovico's head. The boy replied; and the bystanders feared that a personal encounter would ensue. Once Fernando put his hand on his sword, and the unarmed Ludovico drew in and collected himself, as if ready to spring and seize the arm that might be uplifted against him. Fernando saw and dreaded the mad ferocity his son's eye expressed. In all personal encounters of this kind the victory rests not with the strong, but the most fearless. Fernando was not ready to stake his own life, or even with his own hand to shed his son's blood; Ludovico, not as aggressor, but in self-defense, was careless of the consequences of an attack—he would resist to the death; and this dauntless feeling gave him an ascendency his father felt and could not forgive.

From this time Fernando's conduct toward his son changed. He no longer punished, imprisoned, or menaced him. This was usage for a boy, but the Prince felt that they were man to man, and acted accordingly. He was the gainer by the change; for he soon acquired all the ascendency that experience, craft, and a court education, must naturally give him over a hot-headed youth, who, nerved to resist all personal violence, neither saw nor understood a more covert mode of proceeding. Fernando hoped to drive his son to desperation. He set spies over him, paid the tempters that were to lead him to crime, and by a continued system of restraint and miserable thwarting hoped to reduce him to such despair that he would take refuge in any line of conduct that promised freedom from so irksome and degrading a slavery. His observance of his vow saved the youth; and this steadiness of purpose gave him time to read and understand the motives of the tempters. He saw his father's master-hand in all, and his heart sickened at the discovery.

He had reached his eighteenth year. The treatment he had endured and the constant exertion of fortitude and resolution had already given him the appearance of manhood. He was tall, well made, and athletic. His person and demeanor were more energetic than graceful, and his manners were haughty and reserved. He had few accomplishments, for his father had been at no pains for his education; feats of horsemanship and arms made up the whole catalogue. He hated books, as being a part of a priest's insignia; he was averse to all occupation that brought bodily repose with it. His complexion was dark— hardship had even rendered it sallow; his eyes, once soft, now glared with fierceness; his lips, formed to express tenderness, were now habitually curled in contempt; his dark hair, clustering in thick curls round his throat, completed the wild but grand and interesting appearance of his person.

It was winter, and the pleasures of the chase began. Every morning the huntsmen assembled to attack the wild-boars or stags which the dogs might arouse in the fastnesses of the Apennines. This was the only pleasure that Ludovico ever enjoyed. During these pursuits he felt himself free. Mounted on a noble horse, which he urged to its full speed, his blood danced in his veins, and his eyes shone with rapture as he cast his eagle glance to Heaven; with a smile of ineffable disdain, he passed his false friends or open tormentors, and gained a solitary precedence in the pursuit.

The plain at the foot of Vesuvius and its neighboring hills was stripped bare by winter; the full stream rushed impetuously from the hills; and there was mingled with it the baying of the dogs and the cries of the hunters; the sea, dark under a lowering sky, made a melancholy dirge as its waves broke on the shore; Vesuvius groaned heavily, and the birds answered it by wailing shrieks; a heavy sirocco hung upon the atmosphere, rendering it damp and cold. This wind seems at once to excite and depress the human mind: it excites it to thought, but colors those thoughts, as it does the sky, with black. Ludovico felt this; but he tried to surmount the natural feelings with which the ungenial air filled him.

The temperature of the air changed as the day advanced. The clouded sky spent itself in snow, which fell in abundance; it then became clear, and sharp frost succeeded. The aspect of earth was changed. Snow covered the ground and lay on

the leafless trees, sparkling, white, and untrod. Early in the
morning a stag had been roused, and, as he was coursed along
the plain skirting the hills, the hunters went at speed. All
day the chase endured. At length the stag, who from the
beginning had directed his course toward the hills, began to
ascend them, and, with various windings and evolutions, almost
put the hounds to fault. Day was near its close when Ludovico
alone followed the stag, as it made for the edge of a kind
of platform of the mountain, which, isthmus-like, was connected with the hill by a small tongue of land, and on three
sides was precipitous to the plain below. Ludovico balanced
his spear, and his dogs drew in, expecting that the despairing
animal would there turn to bay. He made one bound, which
conducted him to the very brow of the precipice—another,
and he was seen no more. He sprang downward, expecting
more pity from the rocks beneath than from his human adversary. Ludovico was fatigued by the chase and angry at the
escape of his prey. He sprang from his horse, tied him
to a tree, and sought a path by which he might safely descend
to the plain. Snow covered and hid the ground, obliterating
the usual traces that the flocks or herds might have left as
they descended from their pastures on the hills to the hamlets
beneath; but Ludovico had passed his boyhood among mountains: while his hunting-spear found sure rest on the ground,
he did not fear, or while a twig afforded him sufficient support
as he held it, he did not doubt to secure his passage; but the
descent was precipitous, and necessary caution obliged him to
be long. The sun approached the horizon, and the glow of
its departure was veiled by swift-rising clouds which the wind
blew upward from the sea—a cold wind, which whirled the
snow from its resting-place and shook it from the trees.
Ludovico at length arrived at the foot of the precipice. The
snow reflected and enhanced the twilight, and he saw four
deep marks that must have been made by the deer. The
precipice was high above, and its escape appeared a miracle.
It must have escaped; but those were the only marks it had
left. Around lay a forest of ilex, beset by thick, entangled
underwood, and it seemed impossible that any animal so large
as the stag in pursuit could have broken its way through the
apparently impenetrable barrier it opposed. The desire to find
his quarry became almost a passion in the heart of Ludovico.
He walked round to seek for an opening, and at last found
a narrow pathway through the forest, and some few marks

seemed to indicate that the stag must have sought for refuge up the glen. With a swiftness characteristic even of his prey, Ludovico rushed up the pathway, and thought not of how far he ran, until, breathless, he stopped before a cottage that opposed itself to his further progress. He stopped and looked around. There was something singularly mournful in the scene. It was not dark, but the shades of evening seemed to descend from the vast woof of cloud that climbed the sky from the West. The black and shining leaves of the ilex and those of the laurel and myrtle underwood were strongly contrasted with the white snow that lay upon them. A breeze passed among the boughs, and scattered the drift that fell in flakes, and disturbed by fits the silence around; or, again, a bird twittered, or flew with melancholy flap of wing, beneath the trees to its nest in some hollow trunk. The house seemed desolate; its windows were glassless, and small heaps of snow lay upon the sills. There was no print of footing on the equal surface of the path that led right up to the door, yet a little smoke now and then struggled upward from its chimney, and, on paying fixed attention, Prince Ludovico thought he heard a voice. He called, but received no answer. He put his hand on the latch; it yielded, and he entered. On the floor, strewed with leaves, lay a person sick and dying; for, though there was a slight motion in the eyes that showed that life had not yet deserted his throne, the paleness of the visage was that of death only. It was an aged woman, and her white hair showed that she descended to no untimely grave. But a figure knelt beside her which might have been mistaken for the angel of heaven waiting to receive and guide the departing soul to eternal rest, but for the sharp agony that was stamped on the features, and the glazed but earnest gaze of her eye. She was very young, and beautiful as the star of evening. She had apparently despoiled herself to bestow warmth on her dying friend, for her arms and neck were bare but for the quantity of dark and flowing hair that clustered on her shoulders. She was absorbed in one feeling, that of watching the change in the sick person. Her cheeks, even her lips, were pale; her eyes seemed to gaze as if her whole life reigned in their single perception. She did not hear Ludovico enter, or, at least, she made no sign that indicated that she was conscious of it. The sick person murmured; as she bent her head down to catch the sound, she replied, in an accent of despair:

"I can get no more leaves, for the snow is on the ground; nor have I any other earthly thing to place over you."

"Is she cold?" said Ludovico, creeping near, and bending down beside the afflicted girl.

"Oh, very cold!" she replied, "and there is no help."

Ludovico had gone to the chase in a silken mantle lined with the choicest furs: he had thrown it off, and left it with his horse that it might not impede his descent. He hastened from the cottage, he ran down the lane, and, following the marks of his footsteps, he arrived where his steed awaited him. He did not again descend by the same path, reflecting that it might be necessary for him to seek assistance for the dying woman. He led his horse down the hill by a circuitous path, and, although he did this with all possible speed, night closed in, and the glare of the snow alone permitted him to see the path that he desired to follow. When he arrived at the lane he saw that the cottage, before so dark, was illuminated, and, as he approached, he heard the solemn hymn of death as it was chanted by the priests who filled it. The change had taken place, the soul had left its mortal mansion, and the deserted ruin was attended with more of solemnity than had been paid to the mortal struggle. Amid the crowd of priests Ludovico entered unperceived, and he looked around for the lovely female he had left. She sat, retired from the priests, on a heap of leaves in a corner of the cottage. Her clasped hands lay on her knees, her head was bent downward, and every now and then she wiped away her fast-falling tears with her hair. Ludovico threw his cloak over her. She looked up, and drew the covering round her, more to hide her person than for the sake of warmth, and then, again turning away, was absorbed in her melancholy thoughts.

Ludovico gazed on her in pity. For the first time since his mother's death, tears filled his eyes, and his softened countenance beamed with tender sympathy. He said nothing, but he continued to look on as a wish arose in his mind that he might wipe the tears that one by one fell from the shrouded eyes of the unfortunate girl. As he was thus engaged, he heard his name called by one of the attendants of the castle, and, throwing the few pieces of gold he possessed into the lap of the sufferer, he suddenly left the cottage, and, joining the servant who had been in search of him, rode rapidly toward his home.

As Ludovico rode along, and the first emotions of pity

having, as it were, ceased to throb in his mind, these feelings merged into the strain of thought in which he habitually indulged, and turned its course to something new.

"I call myself wretched," he cried—"I, the well-clad and fed, and this lovely peasant-girl, half famished, parts with her necessary clothing to cover the dying limbs of her only friend. I also have lost my only friend, and that is my true misfortune, the cause of all my real misery—sycophants would assume that name—spies and traitors usurp that office. I have cast these aside—shaken them from me as yon bough shakes to earth its incumbrance of snow, not as cold as their iced hearts, but I am alone—solitude gnaws my heart and makes me savage—miserable—worthless."

Yet, although he thought in this manner, the heart of Ludovico was softened by what he had seen, and milder feelings pressed upon him. He had felt sympathy for one who needed it; he had conferred a benefit on the necessitous; tenderness molded his lips to a smile, and the pride of utility gave dignity to the fire of his eye. The people about him saw the change, and, not meeting with the usual disdain of his manner, they also became softened, and the alteration apparent in his character seemed ready to effect as great a metamorphosis in his external situation. But the time was not come when this change would become permanent.

On the day that succeeded to this hunt, Prince Fernando removed to Naples, and commanded his son to accompany him. The residence at Naples was peculiarly irksome to Ludovico. In the country he enjoyed comparative freedom. Satisfied that he was in the castle, his father sometimes forgot him for days together; but it was otherwise here. Fearful that he should form friends and connections, and knowing that his commanding figure and peculiar manners excited attention and often curiosity, he kept him ever in sight; or, if he left him for a moment, he first made himself sure of the people around him, and left such of his own confidants whose very presence was venom to the eye of Ludovico. Add to which, Prince Mondolfo delighted to insult and browbeat his son in public, and, aware of his deficiencies in the more elegant accomplishments, he exposed him even to the derision of his friends. They remained two months at Naples, and then returned to Mondolfo.

It was spring; the air was genial and spirit-stirring. The white blossoms of the almond-trees and the pink ones of the

peach just began to be contrasted with the green leaves that
shot forth among them. Ludovico felt little of the exhilarating
effects of spring. Wounded in his heart's core, he asked nature
why she painted a sepulcher; he asked the airs why they fanned
the sorrowful and the dead. He wandered forth to solitude.
He rambled down the path that led to the sea; he sat on the
beach, watching the monotonous flow of the waves; they
danced and sparkled; his gloomy thoughts refused to imbibe
cheerfulness from wave or sun.

A form passed near him—a peasant-girl, who balanced a
pitcher, urn-shaped, upon her head; she was meanly clad,
but she attracted Ludovico's regard, and when, having approached the fountain, she took her pitcher and turned to fill
it, he recognized the cottager of the foregoing winter. She
knew him also, and, leaving her occupation, she approached
him and kissed his hand with that irresistible grace that
southern climes seem to instill into the meanest of their
children. At first she hesitated, and began to thank him in
broken accents, but words came as she spoke, and Ludovico
listened to her eloquent thanks—the first he had heard addressed to him by any human being. A smile of pleasure stole
over his face—a smile whose beauty sank deep into the gazer's
heart. In a minute they were seated on the bank beside the
fountain, and Viola told the story of her poverty-stricken
youth—her orphan lot—the death of her best friend—and it
was now only the benign climate which, in diminishing human
wants, made her appear less wretched than then. She was alone
in the world—living in that desolate cottage—providing for
her daily fare with difficulty. Her pale cheek, the sickly languor that pervaded her manner, gave evidence of the truth
of her words; but she did not weep, she spoke words of good
heart, and it was only when she alluded to the benefaction of
Ludovico that her soft dark eyes swam with tears.

The youth visited her cottage the next day. He rode up the
lane, now grass-grown and scented by violets, which Viola was
gathering from the banks. She presented her nosegay to him.
They entered the cottage together. It was dilapidated and
miserable. A few flowers placed in a broken vase was a type
only of poor Viola herself—a lovely blossom in the midst of
utter poverty; and the rose-tree that shaded the window could
only tell that sweet Italy, even in the midst of wretchedness,
spares her natural wealth to adorn her children.

Ludovico made Viola sit down on a bench by the window,

and stood opposite to her, her flowers in his hand, listening.
She did not talk of her poverty, and it would be difficult to
recount what was said. She seemed happy and smiled and
spoke with a gleeful voice, which softened the heart of her
friend, so that he almost wept with pity and admiration.
After this, day by day, Ludovico visited the cottage and bestowed all his time on Viola. He came and talked with her,
gathered violets with her, consoled and advised her, and
became happy. The idea that he was of use to a single human
being instilled joy into his heart; and yet he was wholly
unconscious how entirely he was necessary to the happiness of
his *protégée*. He felt happy beside her, he was delighted to
bestow benefits on her, and to see her profit by them; but
he did not think of love, and his mind, unawakened to
passion, reposed from its long pain without a thought for the
future. It was not so with the peasant-girl. She could not see
his eyes bent in gentleness on her, his mouth lighted by its
tender smile, or listen to his voice as he bade her trust in
him, for that he would be father, brother, all to her, without
deeply, passionately loving him. He became the sun of her
day, the breath of her life—her hope, joy, and sole possession.
She watched for his coming, she watched him as he went, and
for a long time she was happy. She would not repine that he
replied to her earnest love with calm affection only—she was
a peasant, he a noble—and she could claim and expect no
more; he was a god—she might adore him; and it were blasphemy to hope for more than a benign acceptation of her
worship.

Prince Mondolfo was soon made aware of Ludovico's visits
to the cottage of the forest, and he did not doubt that Viola
had become the mistress of his son. He did not endeavor to
interrupt the connection, or put any bar to his visits. Ludovico,
indeed, enjoyed more liberty than ever, and his cruel father
confined himself alone to the restricting of him more than
ever in money. His policy was apparent: Ludovico had resisted every temptation of gambling and other modes of
expense thrown in his way. Fernando had long wished to
bring his son to a painful sense of his poverty and depend-
ence, and to oblige him to seek the necessary funds in such a
career as would necessitate his desertion of the paternal roof.
He had wound many snares around the boy, and all were
snapped by his firm but almost unconscious resistance; but
now, without seeking, without expectation, the occasion came

of itself which would lead him to require far more than his father had at any time allowed him, and now that allowance was restricted, yet Ludovico did not murmur—and until now he had had enough.

A long time Fernando abstained from all allusion to the connection of his son; but one evening, at a banquet, gayety overcame his caution—a gayety which ever led him to sport with his son's feelings, and to excite a pain which might repress the smile that his new state of mind ceased to make frequent visits to his countenance.

"Here," cried Fernando, as he filled a goblet—"here, Ludovico, is to the health of your violet-girl!" and he concluded his speech with some indecorous allusion that suffused Ludovico's cheek with red. Without replying he arose to depart.

"And whither are you going, sir?" cried his father. "Take yon cup to answer my pledge, for, by Bacchus! none that sit at my table shall pass it uncourteously by."

Ludovico, still standing, filled his cup and raised it as he was about to speak and retort to his father's speech, but the memory of his words and the innocence of Viola pressed upon him and filled his heart almost to bursting. He put down his cup, pushed aside the people who sought to detain him, and left the castle, and soon the laughter of the revelers was no more heard by him, though it had loudly rung and was echoed through the lofty halls. The words of Fernando had awakened a strange spirit in Ludovico. "Viola! Can she love me? Do I love her?" The last question was quickly answered. Passion, suddenly awake, made every artery tingle by its thrilling presence. His cheeks burned and his heart danced with strange exultation as he hastened toward the cottage, unheeding all but the universe of sensation that dwelt within him. He reached its door. Blank and dark the walls rose before him, and the boughs of the wood waved and sighed over him. Until now he had felt impatience alone—the sickness of fear— fear of finding a cold return to his passion's feeling now entered his heart; and, retreating a little from the cottage, he sat on a bank, and hid his face in his hands, while passionate tears gushed from his eyes and trickled from between his fingers. Viola opened the door of her cottage; Ludovico had failed in his daily visit, and she was unhappy. She looked on the sky—the sun had set, and Hesperus glowed in the West; the dark ilex-trees made a deep shade, which was broken by innumerable fire-flies, which flashed now low on the ground,

discovering the flowers as they slept hushed and closed in
night, now high among the branches, and their light was
reflected by the shining leaves of ilex and laurel. Viola's
wandering eye unconsciously selected one and followed it as
it flew, and ever and anon cast aside its veil of darkness and
shed a wide pallor around its own form. At length it nestled
itself in a bower of green leaves formed by a clump of united
laurels and myrtles; and there it stayed, flashing its beautiful
light, which, coming from among the boughs, seemed as if the
brightest star of the heavens had wandered from its course,
and, trembling at its temerity, sat panting on its earthly perch.
Ludovico sat near the laurel—Viola saw him—her breath came
quick—she spoke not—but stepped lightly to him—and looked
with such mazed ecstasy of thought that she felt, nay, almost
heard, her heart beat with her emotion. At length she spoke—
she uttered his name, and he looked up on her gentle face,
her beaming eyes and her sylph-like form bent over him. He
forgot his fears, and his hopes were soon confirmed. For the
first time he pressed the trembling lips of Viola, and then tore
himself away to think with rapture and wonder on all that
had taken place.

Ludovico ever acted with energy and promptness. He returned only to plan with Viola when they might be united.
A small chapel in the Apennines, sequestered and unknown,
was selected; a priest was easily procured from a neighboring
convent and easily bribed to silence. Ludovico led back his
bride to the cottage in the forest. There she continued to
reside; for worlds he would not have had her change her
habitation; all his wealth was expended in decorating it;
yet his all only sufficed to render it tolerable. But they were
happy. The small circlet of earth's expanse that held in his
Viola was the universe to her husband. His heart and imagination widened and filled it until it encompassed all of beautiful,
and was inhabited by all of excellent, this world contains.
She sang to him; he listened, and the notes built around him
a magic bower of delight. He trod the soil of paradise, and
its winds fed his mind to intoxication. The inhabitants of
Mondolfo could not recognize the haughty, resentful Ludovico
in the benign and gentle husband of Viola. His father's taunts
were unheeded, for he did not hear them. He no longer
trod the earth, but, angel-like, sustained by the wings of love,
skimmed over it, so that he felt not its inequalities nor was
touched by its rude obstacles. And Viola, with deep gratitude

and passionate tenderness, repaid his love. She thought of him only, lived for him, and with unwearied attention kept alive in his mind the first dream of passion.

Thus nearly two years passed, and a lovely child appeared to bind the lovers with closer ties, and to fill their humble roof with smiles and joy.

Ludovico seldom went to Mondolfo; and his father, continuing his ancient policy, and glad that in his attachment to a peasant-girl he had relieved his mind from the fear of brilliant connections and able friends, even dispensed with his attendance when he visited Naples. Fernando did not suspect that his son had married his low-born favorite; if he had, his aversion for him would not have withheld him from resisting so degrading an alliance; and, while his blood flowed in Ludovico's veins, he would never have avowed offspring who were contaminated by a peasant's less highly-sprung tide.

Ludovico had nearly completely his twentieth year when his elder brother died. Prince Mondolfo at that time spent four months at Naples, endeavoring to bring to a conclusion a treaty of marriage he had entered into between his heir and the daughter of a noble Neapolitan house, when this death overthrew his hopes, and he retired in grief and mourning to his castle. A few weeks of sorrow and reason restored him to himself. He had loved even this favored eldest son more as the heir of his name and fortune than as his child; and the web destroyed that he had woven for him, he quickly began another.

Ludovico was summoned to his father's presence. Old habit yet rendered such a summons momentous; but the youth, with a proud smile, threw off these boyish cares, and stood with a gentle dignity before his altered parent.

"Ludovico," said the Prince, "four years ago you refused to take a priest's vows, and then you excited my utmost resentment; now I thank you for that resistance."

A slight feeling of suspicion crossed Ludovico's mind that his father was about to cajole him for some evil purpose. Two years before he would have acted on such a thought, but the habit of happiness made him unsuspicious. He bent his head gently.

"Ludovico," continued his father, while pride and a wish to conciliate disturbed his mind and even his countenance, "my son, I have used you hardly; but that time is now past."

Ludovico gently replied:

"My father, I did not deserve your ill-treatment; I hope I shall merit your kindness when I know—"

"Yes, yes," interrupted Fernando, uneasily, "you do not understand—you desire to know why—in short, you, Ludovico, are now all my hope—Olympio is dead—the house of Mondolfo has no support but you—"

"Pardon me," replied the youth. "Mondolfo is in no danger; you, my lord, are fully able to support and even to augment its present dignity."

"You do not understand. Mondolfo has no support but you. I am old, I feel my age, and these gray hairs announce it to me too glaringly. There is no collateral branch, and my hope must rest in your children—"

"My children, my lord!" replied Ludovico. "I have only one; and if the poor little boy—"

"What folly is this?" cried Fernando, impatiently. "I speak of your marriage and not—"

"My lord, my wife is ever ready to pay her dutious respects to you—"

"Your wife, Ludovico! But you speak without thought. How? Who?"

"The violet-girl, my lord."

A tempest had crossed the countenance of Fernando. That his son, unknown to him, should have made an unworthy alliance, convulsed every fiber of his frame, and the lowering of his brows and his impatient gesture told the intolerable anguish of such a thought. The last words of Ludovico restored him. It was not his wife that he thus named—he felt assured that it was not. He smiled somewhat gloomily, still it was a smile of satisfaction.

"Yes," he replied, "I understand; but you task my patience— you should not trifle with such a subject or with me. I talk of your marriage. Now that Olympio is dead, and you are, in his place, heir of Mondolfo, you may, in his stead, conclude the advantageous, nay, even princely, alliance I was forming for him."

Ludovico replied with earnestness:

"You are pleased to misunderstand me. I am already married. Two years ago, while I was still the despised, insulted Ludovico, I formed this connection, and it will be my pride to show the world how, in all but birth, my peasant-wife is able to follow the duties of her distinguished situation."

Fernando was accustomed to command himself. He felt as

if stabbed by a poniard; but he paused till calm and voice returned, and then he said:

"You have a child?"

"An heir, my lord," replied Ludovico, smiling—for his father's mildness deceived him—"a lovely, healthy boy."

"They live near here?"

"I can bring them to Mondolfo in an hour's space. Their cottage is in the forest, about a quarter of a mile east of the convent of Santa Chiara."

"Enough, Ludovico; you have communicated strange tidings, and I must consider of them. I will see you again this evening."

Ludovico bowed and disappeared. He hastened to his cottage, and related all that he remembered or understood of this scene, and bade Viola prepare to come to the castle at an instant's notice. Viola trembled; it struck her that all was not so fair as Ludovico represented; but she hid her fears, and even smiled as her husband with a kiss hailed his boy as heir of Mondolfo.

Fernando had commanded both look and voice while his son was within hearing. He had gone to the window of his chamber, and stood steadily gazing on the drawbridge until Ludovico crossed it and disappeared. Then, unrestrained, he strode up and down the apartment, while the roof rang with his impetuous tread. He uttered cries and curses, and struck his head with his clenched fist. It was long ere he could think—he felt only, and feeling was torture. The tempest at length subsided, and he threw himself in his chair. His contracted brows and frequently-convulsed lips showed how entirely he was absorbed in consideration. All at first was one frightful whirl; by degrees, the motion was appeased; his thoughts flowed with greater calmness; they subsided into one channel whose course he warily traced until he thought that he saw the result.

Hours passed during this contemplation. When he arose from his chair, as one who had slept and dreamed uneasily, his brows became by degrees smooth; he stretched out his arm, and, spreading his hand, cried:

"So it is! and I have vanquished him!"

Evening came, and Ludovico was announced. Fernando feared his son. He had ever dreaded his determined and fearless mode of action. He dreaded to encounter the boy's passions with his own, and felt in the clash that his was not the master-passion. So, subduing all of hate, revenge, and wrath, he received him with a smile. Ludovico smiled also; yet there was no similarity in their look: one was a smile of frankness, joy, and affection—the other the veiled grimace of smothered malice. Fernando said:

"My son, you have entered lightly into a marriage as if it were a child's game, but, where principalities and noble blood are at stake, the loss or gain is too momentous to be trifled with. Silence, Ludovico! Listen to me, I entreat. You have made a strange marriage with a peasant, which, though I may acknowledge, I cannot approve, which must be displeasing to your sovereign, and derogatory to all who claim alliance with the house of Mondolfo."

Cold dew stood on the forehead of Fernando as he spoke; he paused, recovered his self-command, and continued:

"It will be difficult to reconcile these discordant interests, and a moment of rashness might cause us to lose our station, fortune, everything! Your interests are in my hands. I will be careful of them. I trust, before the expiration of a very few months, the future Princess Mondolfo will be received at the court of Naples with due honor and respect. But you must leave it to me. You must not move in the affair. You must promise that you will not, until I permit, mention your marriage to any one, or acknowledge it if you are taxed with it."

Ludovico, after a moment's hesitation, replied:

"I promise that, for the space of six months, I will not mention my marriage to any one. I will not be guilty of falsehood, but for that time I will not affirm it or bring it forward in any manner so as to annoy you."

Fernando again paused; but prudence conquered, and he said no more. He entered on other topics with his son; they supped together, and the mind of Ludovico, now attuned to affection, received all the marks of his father's awakening love with gratitude and joy. His father thought that he held him in his toils, and was ready to sweeten the bitterness of his intended draft by previous kindness.

A week passed thus in calm. Ludovico and Viola were perfectly happy. Ludovico only wished to withdraw his wife from obscurity from that sensation of honest pride which makes us desire to declare to the whole world the excellence of a beloved object. Viola shrank from such an exhibition; she loved her humble cottage—humble still though adorned with all that taste and love could bestow on it. The trees bent over its low roof and shaded its windows, which were filled with flowering shrubs; its floor shone with marble, and vases of antique shape and exquisite beauty stood in the niches of the room. Every part was consecrated by the memory of their first meeting and their loves—the walks in snow and violets; the forest of ilex with its underwood of myrtle and its population of fire-flies; the birds; the wild and shy animals that sometimes came in sight, and, seen, retreated; the changes of the seasons, of the hues of nature influenced by them; the alterations of the sky; the walk of the moon; and the moving of the stars—all were dear, known, and commented on by this pair, who saw the love their own hearts felt reflected in the whole scene around, and in their child, their noisy but speechless companion, whose smiles won hopes, and whose bright form seemed as if sent from Heaven to reward their constant affection.

A week passed, and Fernando and Ludovico were riding together, when the Prince said:

"Tomorrow, early, my son, you must go to Naples. It is time that you should show yourself there as my heir, and the best representative of a princely house. The sooner you do this the quicker will arrive the period for which, no doubt, you long, when the unknown Princess Mondolfo will be acknowledged by all. I cannot accompany you. In fact, circumstances which you may guess make me desire that you should appear at first without me. You will be distinguished by your sovereign, courted by all, and you will remember your promise as the best means of accomplishing your object. In a very few days I will join you."

Ludovico readily assented to this arrangement, and went the same evening to take leave of Viola. She was seated beneath the laurel tree where first they had made their mutual vows; her child was in her arms, gazing with wonder and laughter on the light of the flies. Two years had passed. It was summer again, and as the beams from their eyes met and mingled each drank in the joyous certainty that they were still as dear to one another as when he, weeping from intense emotion, sat under that tree. He told her of his visit to Naples which his father had settled for him, and a cloud passed over her countenance, but she dismissed it. She would not fear; yet again and again a thrilling sense of coming evil made her heart beat, and each time was resisted with greater difficulty. As night came on, she carried the sleeping child into the cottage, and placed him on his bed, and then walked up and down the pathway of the forest with Ludovico until the moment of his departure should arrive, for the heat of the weather rendered it necessary that he should travel by night. Again the fear of danger crossed her, and again she with a smile shook off the thought; but, when he turned to give her his parting embrace, it returned with full force on her. Weeping bitterly, she clung to him, and entreated him not to go. Startled by her earnestness, he eagerly sought an explanation, but the only explanation she could give excited a gentle smile as he caressed and bade her to be calm; and then, pointing to the crescent moon that gleamed through the trees and checkered the ground with their moving shades, he told her he would be with her ere its full, and with one more embrace left her weeping. And thus it is a strange prophecy often creeps about, and the spirit of Cassandra inhabits many a hapless human heart, and utters from many lips unheeded forebodings of evils that are to be: the hearers heed them not—the speaker hardly gives them credit—the evil comes which, if it could have been avoided, no Cassandra could have foretold, for if that spirit were not a sure harbinger so would it not exist; nor would these half revealings have place if the to come did not fulfill and make out the sketch.

Viola beheld him depart with hopeless sorrow, and then turned to console herself beside the couch of her child. Yet, gazing on him, her fears came thicker; and in a transport of terror she rushed from the cottage, ran along the pathway, calling on Ludovico's name, and sometimes listening if she might hear the tread of his horse, and then again shrieking aloud for him to return. But he was far out of hearing, and she returned again to her cot, and, lying down beside her child, clasping his little hand in hers, at length slept peacefully.

Her sleep was light and short. She arose before the sun, and hardly had he begun to cast long shadows on the ground when, attiring herself in her veil, she was about to go with the infant to the neighboring chapel of Santa Chiara, when she heard the trampling of horses come up the pathway; her heart beat quick, and still quicker when she saw a stranger enter the cottage. His form was commanding, and age, which had grizzled his hair, had not tempered the fire of his eye nor marred the majesty of his carriage; but every lineament was impressed by pride and even cruelty. Self-will and scorn

were even more apparent. He was somewhat like what
Ludovico had been, and so like what he then was that Viola
did not doubt that his father stood before her. She tried to
collect her courage, but the surprise, his haughty mien, and,
above all, the sound of many horses, and the voices of men
who had remained outside the cottage, so disturbed and distracted her that her heart for a moment failed her, and she
leaned trembling and ashy white against the wall, straining her
child to her heart with convulsive energy. Fernando spoke:

"You are Viola Amaldi, and you call yourself, I believe, the
wife of Ludovico Mandolfo?"

"I am so"—her lips formed themselves to these words, but
the sound died away.

Fernando continued:

"I am Prince Mondolfo, father of the rash boy who has
entered into this illegal and foolish contract. When I heard
of it my plan was easily formed, and I am now about to put
it into execution. I could easily have done so without coming
to you, without enduring the scene which, I suppose, I shall
endure; but benevolence has prompted me to the line of
conduct I adopt, and I hope that I shall not repent it."

Fernando paused; Viola had heard little of what he had
said. She was employed in collecting her scattered spirits, in
bidding her heart be still, and arming herself with the pride
and courage of innocence and helplessness. Every word he
spoke was thus of use to her, as it gave her time to recollect
herself. She only bowed her head as he paused, and he continued:

"While Ludovico was a younger son, and did not seek to
obtrude his misalliance into notice, I was content that he
should enjoy what he termed happiness unmolested; but circumstances have changed. He has become the heir of Mondolfo, and must support that family and title by a suitable marriage. Your dream has passed. I mean you no ill. You will be
conducted hence with your child, placed on board a vessel, and
taken to a town in Spain. You will receive a yearly stipend,
and, as long as you seek no communication with Ludovico,
or endeavor to leave the asylum provided for you, you are
safe; but the slightest movement, the merest yearning for a
station you may never fill, shall draw upon you and that boy
the vengeance of one whose menaces are but the uplifted arm
—the blow quickly follows!"

The excess of danger that threatened the unprotected Viola gave her courage. She replied:

"I am alone and feeble, you are strong, and have ruffians waiting on you to execute such crimes as your imagination suggests. I care not for Mondolfo, nor the title, nor the possession, but I will never, oh! never, never! renounce my Ludovico—never do aught to derogate from our plighted faith. Torn from him, I will seek him, though it be barefoot and a-hungered, through the wide world. He is mine by that love he has been pleased to conceive for me; I am his by the sentiment of devotion and eternal attachment that now animates my voice. Tear us asunder, yet we shall meet again, and, unless you put the grave between us, you cannot separate us."

Fernando smiled in scorn.

"And that boy," he said, pointing to the infant, "will you lead him, innocent lamb, a sacrifice to the altar of your love, and plant the knife yourself in the victim's heart?"

Again the lips of Viola became pale as she clasped her boy and exclaimed, in almost inarticulate accents:

"There is a God in Heaven!"

Fernando left the cottage, and it was soon filled by men, one of whom threw a cloak over Viola and her boy, and, dragging them from the cottage, placed them in a kind of litter, and the cavalcade proceeded silently. Viola had uttered one shriek when she beheld her enemies, but, knowing their power and her own impotence, she stifled all further cries. When in the litter she strove in vain to disengage herself from the cloak that enveloped her, and then tried to hush her child, who, frightened at his strange situation, uttered piercing cries. At length he slept; and Viola, darkling and fearful, with nothing to sustain her spirits or hopes, felt her courage vanish. She wept long with despair and misery. She thought of Ludovico and what his grief would be, and her tears were redoubled. There was no hope, for her enemy was relentless, her child torn from her, a cloister her prison. Such were the images constantly before her. They subdued her courage, and filled her with terror and dismay.

The cavalcade entered the town of Salerno, and the roar of the sea announced to poor Viola that they were on its shores.

"O bitter waves!" she cried. "My tears are as bitter as ye, and they will soon mingle!"

Her conductors now entered a building. It was a watchtower at some distance from the town, on the sea-beach. They lifted Viola from the litter and led her to one of the dreary apartments of the tower. The window, which was not far from the ground, was grated with iron; it bore the appearance of a guardroom. The chief of her conductors addressed her, courteously asked her to excuse the rough lodging; the wind was contrary, he said, but change was expected, and the next day he hoped they would be able to embark. He pointed to the destined vessel in the offing. Viola, excited to hope by his mildness, began to entreat his compassion, but he immediately left her. Soon after another man brought in food, with a flask of wine and a jug of water. He also retired; her massive door was locked, the sound of retreating footsteps died away.

Viola did not despair; she felt, however, that it would need all her courage to extricate herself from her prison. She ate a part of the food which had been provided, drank some water, and then, a little refreshed, she spread the cloak her conductors had left on the floor, placed her child on it to play, and then stationed herself at the window to see if any one might pass whom she might address, and, if he were not able to assist her in any other way, he might at least bear a message to Ludovico, that her fate might not be veiled in the fearful mystery that threatened it; but probably the way past her window was guarded, for no one drew near. As she looked, however, and once advanced her head to gaze more earnestly, it struck her that her person would pass between the iron grates of her window, which was not high from the ground. The cloak, fastened to one of the stanchions, promised a safe descent. She did not dare make the essay; nay, she was so fearful that she might be watched, and that, if she were seen near the window, her jailers might be struck with the same idea, that she retreated to the farther end of the room, and sat looking at the bars with fluctuating hope and fear, that now dyed her cheeks with crimson, and again made them pale as when Ludovico had first seen her.

Her boy passed his time in alternate play and sleep. The ocean still roared, and the dark clouds brought up by the sirocco blackened the sky and hastened the coming evening. Hour after hour passed; she heard no clock; there was no sun to mark the time, but by degrees the room grew dark, and at last the Ave Maria tolled, heard by fits between the howling of the winds and the dashing of the waves. She knelt, and put up a fervent prayer to the Madonna, protector of innocence—prayer for herself and her boy—no less innocent than the Mother and Divine Child, to whom she made her orisons. Still she paused. Drawing near to the window, she listened for the sound of any human being: that sound, faint and intermittent, died away, and with darkness came rain that poured in torrents, accompanied by thunder and lightning that drove every creature to shelter. Viola shuddered. Could she expose her child during such a night? Yet again she gathered courage. It only made her meditate on some plan by which she might get the cloak as a shelter for her boy after it had served for their descent. She tried the bars, and found that, with some difficulty, she could pass, and, gazing downward from the outside, a flash of lightning revealed the ground not far below. Again she commended herself to divine protection; again she called upon and blessed her Ludovico; and then, not fearless but determined, she began her operations. She fastened the cloak by means of her long veil, which, hanging to the ground, was tied by a slip-knot, and gave way when pulled. She took her child in her arms, and, having got without the bars, bound him with the sash to her waist, and then, without accident, she reached the ground. Having then secured the cloak, and enveloped herself and her child in its dark and ample folds, she paused breathlessly to listen. Nature was awake with its loudest voice—the sea roared—and the incessant flashes of lightning that discovered that solitude around her were followed by such deafening peals as almost made her fear. She crossed the field, and kept the sight of the white sea-foam to her right hand, knowing that she thus proceeded in an opposite direction from Mondolfo. She walked as fast as her burden permitted her, keeping the beaten road, for the darkness made her fear to deviate. The rain ceased, and she walked on, until, her limbs falling under her, she was fain to rest, and refresh herself with the bread she had brought with her from the prison. Action and success had inspired her with unusual energy. She would not fear—she believed herself free and secure. She wept, but it was the overflowing emotion that found no other expression. She doubted not that she should rejoin Ludovico. Seated thus in the dark night—having for hours been the sport of the elements, which now for an instant paused in their fury—seated on a stone by the roadside— a wide, dreary, unknown country about her—her helpless child in her arms—herself having just finished eating the only food she possessed—she felt triumph, and joy, and love, descend into her heart, prophetic of future reunion with her beloved.

It was summer, and the air consequently warm. Her cloak
had protected her from the wet, so her limbs were free and
unnumbed. At the first ray of dawn she arose, and at the
nearest pathway she struck out of the road, and took her
course nearer the bordering Apennines. From Salerno as far
south as the eye could reach, a low plain stretched itself along
the seaside, and the hills at about the distance of ten miles
bound it in. These mountains are high and singularly beautiful in their shape; their crags point to Heaven and streams
flow down their sides and water the plain below. After several
hours' walking, Viola reached a pine forest, which descended
from the heights and stretched itself in the plain. She sought
its friendly shelter with joy, and, penetrating its depths until
she saw trees only on all sides of her, she again reposed. The
sirocco had been dissipated by the thunderstorm, and the sun,
vanquishing the clouds that at first veiled its splendor, glowed
forth in the clear majesty of noon. Southern born, Viola did
not fear the heat. She collected pine nuts, she contrived to
make a fire, and ate them with appetite; and then, seeking a
covert, she lay down and slept, her boy in her arms, thanking
Heaven and the Virgin for her escape. When she awoke, the
triumph of her heart somewhat died away. She felt the solitude, she felt her helplessness, she feared pursuers, yet she
dashed away the tears, and then reflecting that she was too near
Salerno—the sun being now at the sea's verge—she arose and
pursued her way through the intricacies of the wood. She got
to the edge of it so far as to be able to direct her steps by the
neighboring sea. Torrents intercepted her path, and one rapid
river threatened to impede it altogether; but, going somewhat
lower down, she found a bridge; and then, approaching still
nearer to the sea, she passed through a wide and desolate kind
of pasture-country, which seemed to afford neither shelter nor
sustenance to any human being. Night closed in, and she was
fearful to pursue her way, but, seeing some buildings dimly
in the distance, she directed her steps thither, hoping to discover a hamlet where she might get shelter and such assistance
as would enable her to retrace her steps and reach Naples
without being discovered by her powerful enemy. She kept
these high buildings before her, which appeared like vast
cathedrals, but that they were untopped by any dome or spire;
and she wondered much what they could be, when suddenly
they disappeared. She would have thought some rising ground
had intercepted them, but all before her was plain. She

paused, and at length resolved to wait for dawn. All day she
had seen no human being; twice or thrice she had heard the
bark of a dog, and once the whistle of a shepherd, but she
saw no one. Desolation was around her; this, indeed, had
lulled her into security at first. Where no men were, there
was no danger for her. But at length the strange solitude
became painful—she longed to see a cottage, or to find some
peasant, however uncouth, who might answer her inquiries
and provide for her wants. She had viewed with surprise the
buildings which had been as beacons to her. She did not wish
to enter a large town, and she wondered how one could exist
in such a desert; but she had left the wood far behind her,
and required food. Night passed—balmy and sweet night—
the breezes fanned her, the glowing atmosphere encompassed
her, the fire-flies flitted round her, bats wheeled about in the
air, and the heavy-winged owl hooped anigh, while the beetle's
constant hum filled the air. She lay on the ground, her babe
pillowed on her arm, looking upon the starry heavens. Many
thoughts crowded upon her: the thought of Ludovico, of her
reunion with him, of joy after sorrow; and she forgot that
she was alone, half-famished, encompassed by enemies in a
desert plain of Calabria[3]—she slept.

She awoke not until the sun had risen high—it had risen
above the temples of Pæstum,[4] and the columns threw short
shadows on the ground. They were near her, unseen during
night, and were now revealed as the edifices that had attracted
her the evening before. They stood on a rugged plain, despoiled of all roof, their columns and cornices encompassing
a space of high and weed-grown grass; the deep-blue sky
canopied them and filled them with light and cheerfulness.
Viola looked on them with wonder and reverence; they were
temples to some god who still seemed to deify them with his
presence; he clothed them still with beauty, and what was
called their ruin might, in its picturesque wildness and sublime
loneliness, be more adapted to his nature than when, roofed
and gilded, they stood in pristine strength; and the silent
worship of air and happy animals might be more suited to
him than the concourse of the busy and heartless. The most
benevolent of spirit-gods seemed to inhabit that desert, weed-
grown area; the spirit of beauty flitted between those columns

---

[3] Part of the Kingdom of Naples, a peninsula forming the heel of the
Italian boot. Today it is the southern part of Apulia.
[4] In Southern Italy, modern Pesto.

embrowned by time, painted with strange color, and raised a genial atmosphere on the deserted altar. Awe and devotion filled the heart of lonely Viola; she raised her eyes and heart to Heaven in thanksgiving and prayer—not that her lips formed words, or her thoughts suggested connected sentences, but the feeling of worship and gratitude animated her; and, as the sunlight streamed through the succession of columns, so did joy, dove-shaped, fall on and illumine her soul.

With such devotion as seldom before she had visited a saint-dedicated church, she ascended the broken and rude steps of the larger temple, and entered the plot that it inclosed. An inner circuit of smaller columns formed a smaller area, which she entered, and, sitting on a huge fragment of the broken cornice that had fallen to the ground, she silently waited as if for some oracle to visit her sense and guide her.

Thus sitting, she heard the near bark of a dog, followed by the bleating of sheep, and she saw a little flock spread itself in the field adjoining the farther temple. They were shepherded by a girl clothed in rags, but the season required little covering; and these poor people, moneyless, possessing only what their soil gives them, are in the articles of clothing poor even to nakedness. In inclement weather they wrap rudely-formed clothes of undressed sheepskin around them—during the heats of summer they do little more than throw aside these useless garments. The shepherd-girl was probably about fifteen years of age; a large black straw hat shaded her head from the intense rays of the sun; her feet and legs were bare; and her petticoat, tucked up, Diana-like, above one knee, gave a picturesque appearance to her rags, which, bound at her waist by a girdle, bore some resemblance to the costume of a Greek maiden. Rags have a costume of their own, as fine in their way, in their contrast of rich colors and the uncouth boldness of their drapery, as kingly robes. Viola approached the shepherdess and quietly entered into conversation with her; without making any appeal to her charity or feelings, she asked the name of the place where she was, and her boy, awake and joyous, soon attracted attention. The shepherd-girl was pretty, and, above all, good-natured; she caressed the child, seemed delighted to have found a companion for her solitude, and, when Viola said that she was hungry, unloaded her scrip of roasted pine nuts, boiled chestnuts, and coarse bread. Viola ate with joy and gratitude. They remained together all day; the sun went down, the glowing light of its setting faded, and the shepherdess would have taken Viola home with her. But she dreaded a human dwelling, still fearing that, wherever there appeared a possibility of shelter, there her pursuers would seek her. She gave a few small silver-pieces, part of what she had about her when seized, to her new friend, and, bidding her bring sufficient food for the next day, entreated her not to mention her adventure to any one. The girl promised, and, with the assistance of her dog, drove the flock toward their fold. Viola passed the night within the area of the larger temple.

Not doubting the success of his plan, on the very evening that followed its execution, Prince Mondolfo had gone to Naples. He found his son at the Mondolfo Palace. Despising the state of a court, and careless of the gaieties around him, Ludovico longed to return to the cottage of Viola. So, after the expiration of two days, he told his father that he should ride over to Mondolfo, and return the following morning. Fernando did not oppose him, but, two hours after his departure, followed him, and arrived at the castle just after Ludovico, leaving his attendants there, quitted it to proceed alone to his cottage. The first person Prince Mondolfo saw was the chief of the company who had had the charge of Viola. His story was soon told: the unfavorable wind, the imprisonment in a room barricaded with the utmost strength, her incomprehensible escape, and the vain efforts that had subsequently been made to find her. Fernando listened as if in a dream; convinced of the truth, he saw no clue to guide him—no hope of recovering possession of his prisoner. He foamed with rage, then endeavored to suppress as useless his towering passion. He overwhelmed the bearer of the news with execrations; sent out parties of men in pursuit in all directions, promising every reward, and urging the utmost secrecy, and then, left alone, paced his chamber in fury and dismay. His solitude was of no long duration. Ludovico burst into his room, his countenance lighted up with rage.

"Murderer!" he cried. "Where is my Viola?"

Fernando remained speechless.

"Answer!" said Ludovico. "Speak with those lips that pronounced her death-sentence—or raise against me that hand from which her blood is scarcely washed.—Oh, my Viola! thou and my angel-child, descend with all thy sweetness into my heart, that this hand write not parricide on my brow!"

Fernando attempted to speak.

"No!" shrieked the miserable Ludovico; "I will not listen to her murderer. Yet—is she dead? I kneel—I call you father— I appeal to that savage heart—I take in peace that hand that often struck me, and now has dealt the death-blow—oh, tell me, does she yet live?"

Fernando seized on this interval of calm to relate his story. He told the simple truth; but could such a tale gain belief? It awakened the wildest rage in poor Ludovico's heart. He doubted not that Viola had been murdered; and, after every expression of despair and hatred, he bade his father seek his heir among the clods of the earth, for that such he should soon become, and rushed from his presence.

He wandered to the cottage, he searched the country round, he heard the tale of those who had witnessed any part of the carrying off of his Viola. He went to Salerno. He heard the tale there told with the most determined incredulity. It was the tale, he doubted not, that his father forged to free himself from accusation, and to throw an impenetrable veil over the destruction of Viola. His quick imagination made out for itself the scene of her death. The very house in which she had been confined had at the extremity of it a tower jutting out over the sea; a river flowed at its base, making its confluence with the ocean deep and dark. He was convinced that the fatal scene had been acted there. He mounted the tower; the higher room was windowless, the iron grates of the windows had for some cause been recently taken out. He was persuaded that Viola and her child had been thrown from that window into the deep and gurgling waters below.

He resolved to die! In those days of simple Catholic faith, suicide was contemplated with horror. But there were other means almost as sure. He would go a pilgrim to the Holy Land, and fight and die beneath the walls of Jerusalem. Rash and energetic, his purpose was no sooner formed than he hastened to put it in execution. He procured a pilgrim's weeds at Salerno, and at midnight, advising none of his intentions, he left that city, and proceeded southward. Alternate rage and grief swelled his heart. Rage at length died away. She whose murderer he execrated was an angel in Heaven, looking down on him, and he in the Holy Land would win his right to join her. Tender grief dimmed his eyes. The world's great theater closed before him—of all its trappings his pilgrim's cloak was alone gorgeous, his pilgrim's staff the only scepter—they were the symbols and signs of the power he possessed beyond the

earth, and the pledges of his union with Viola. He bent his
steps toward Brundusium.[5] He walked on fast, as if he grudged
all space and time that lay between him and his goal. Dawn
awakened the earth and he proceeded on his way. The sun
of noon darted its ray upon him, but his march was uninterrupted. He entered a pine wood, and, following the track of
flocks, he heard the murmurs of a fountain. Oppressed with
thirst, he hastened toward it. The water welled up from the
ground and filled a natural basin; flowers grew on its banks
and looked on the waters unreflected, for the stream paused
not, but whirled round and round, spending its superabun-
dance in a small rivulet that, dancing over stones and glancing
in the sun, went on its way to its eternity—the sea. The trees
had retreated from the mountain, and formed a circle about
it; the grass was green and fresh, starred with summer flowers.
At one extremity was a silent pool that formed a strange contrast with the fountain that, ever in motion, showed no shape,
and reflected only the color of the objects around it. The pool
reflected the scene with greater distinctness and beauty than
its real existence. The trees stood distinct, the ambient air
between, all grouped and pictured by the hand of a divine
artist. Ludovico drank from the fount, and then approached
the pool. He looked with half wonder on the scene depicted
there. A bird now flitted across in the air, and its form,
feathers, and motion, were shown in the waters. An ass
emerged from among the trees, where in vain it sought herb-
age, and came to grass near these waters; Ludovico saw it
depicted therein, and then looked on the living animal, almost
appearing less real, less living, than its semblance in the
stream. Under the trees from which the ass had come lay someone on the ground, enveloped in a mantle, sleeping. Ludovico
looked carelessly—he hardly at first knew why his curiosity
was roused; then an eager thought, which he deemed madness,
yet resolved to gratify, carried him forward. Rapidly he approached the sleeper, knelt down, and drew aside the cloak,
and saw Viola, her child within her arms, the warm breath
issued from her parted lips, her love-beaming eyes hardly
veiled by the transparent lids, which soon were lifted up.

Ludovico and Viola, each too happy to feel the earth they
trod, returned to their cottage—their cottage dearer than any
palace—yet only half believing the excess of their own joy.
By turns they wept, and gazed on each other and their child,

[5] On the east-southeast coast of Italy.

holding each other's hands as if grasping reality and fearful it would vanish.

Prince Mondolfo heard of their arrival. He had long suffered keenly from the fear of losing his son. The dread of finding himself childless, heirless, had tamed him. He feared the world's censure, his sovereign's displeasure—perhaps worse accusation and punishment. He yielded to fate. Not daring to appear before his intended victim, he sent his confessor to mediate for their forgiveness, and to entreat them to take up their abode at Mondolfo. At first, little credit was given to these offers. They loved their cottage, and had small inclination to risk happiness, liberty, and life, for worthless luxury. The Prince, by patience and perseverance, at length convinced them. Time softened painful recollections; they paid him the duty of children, and cherished and honored him in his old age; while he caressed his lovely grandchild, he did not repine that the violet-girl should be the mother of the heir of Mondolfo.

The White Old Maid

by
NATHANIEL HAWTHORNE

NATHANIEL HAWTHORNE (1804–1864)

First printed in the *New-England Magazine* in 1835, "The White Old Maid" has never been one of Hawthorne's more popular stories. Poe, reviewing the enlarged edition of *Twice-Told Tales* (1842) in which the story was republished, praised the collection as belonging "to the highest region of Art," but called "The White Old Maid" "objectionable . . . on the score of its mysticism. Even with the thoughtful and analytic [reader]," he concluded, "there will be much trouble in penetrating its entire import."

Poe's criticism, odd for a writer whose own necromantic vision everywhere traverses the bounds of reality, seems limited by its failure to distinguish between allegory and symbolism. Where Hawthorne in much of his short fiction restricts himself to allegorical simplicity, in "The White Old Maid" he seems deliberately to have practiced the more complex art of the symbolist. The decadence in his Gothic tale is, to be sure, not easily translatable into any one-for-one relationship with a surface reality, but that is precisely its virtue. Not only does it resemble the technique that Hawthorne employs in *The Scarlet Letter* (1850), his masterpiece, but it foreshadows the manner in which William Faulkner, about a century later, used the Gothic detail and atmosphere in "A Rose for Emily." The decay of a way of life and its institutions is paralleled by the macabre events of the narrative.

T. S. Eliot has objected to Hawthorne's use of the "Walter Scott-Mysteries of Udolpho upholstery" in *The Marble Faun* (1860), his only Europeanized novel, but stories like "Young Goodman Brown" (1835), "The Minister's Black Veil" (1836), "Lady Eleanore's Mantle" (1838), and "Rappacini's Daughter" (1844), as well as "The White Old Maid," suggest that Hawthorne was acclimatizing the European Gothic to an American, and particularly a New England, environment. The appearance of these stories, along with those of Poe, in early nineteenth-century American periodicals, indicates the popularity of the genre that had dominated English magazines a few years before.

Despite the common notion that Hawthorne's writing was directly related to his life as a recluse, recent scholarship has demonstrated that for most of his life he was a public figure who was capable of warm, affable conduct and social urbanity.

THE moonbeams came through two deep and narrow windows, and showed a spacious chamber richly furnished in an antique fashion. From one lattice the shadow of the diamond panes was thrown upon the floor; the ghostly light, through the other, slept upon a bed, falling between the heavy silken curtains, and illuminating the face of a young man. But, how quietly the slumberer lay! How pale his features! And how like a shroud the sheet was wound about his frame! Yes; it was a corpse, in its burial clothes.

Suddenly, the fixed features seemed to move with dark emotion. Strange fantasy! It was but the shadow of the fringed curtain waving betwixt the dead face and the moonlight, as the door of the chamber opened and a girl stole softly to the bedside. Was there delusion in the moonbeams, or did her gesture and her eye betray a gleam of triumph, as she bent over the pale corpse—pale as itself—and pressed her living lips to the cold ones of the dead? As she drew back from that long kiss, her features writhed as if a proud heart were fighting with its anguish. Again it seemed that the features of the corpse had moved responsive to her own. Still an illusion! The silk curtain had waved, a second time, betwixt the dead face and the moonlight, as another fair young girl unclosed the door, and glided, ghost-like, to the bedside. There the two maidens stood, both beautiful, with the pale beauty of the dead between them. But she who had first entered was proud and stately, and the other a soft and fragile thing.

"Away!" cried the lofty one. "Thou hadst him living! The dead is mine!"

"Thine!" returned the other, shuddering. "Well hast thou spoken! The dead is thine!"

The proud girl started, and stared into her face with a ghastly look. But a wild and mournful expression passed across the features of the gentle one; and weak and helpless, she sank down on the bed, her head pillowed beside that of the corpse, and her hair mingling with his dark locks. A creature of hope and joy, the first draft of sorrow had bewildered her.

"Edith!" cried her rival.

Edith groaned, as with a sudden compression of the heart; and removing her cheek from the dead youth's pillow, she stood upright, fearfully encountering the eyes of the lofty girl.

"Wilt thou betray me?" said the latter, calmly.

"Till the dead bid me speak, I will be silent," answered Edith. "Leave us alone together! Go, and live many years, and then return, and tell me of thy life. He, too, will be here! Then, if thou tellest of sufferings more than death, we will both forgive thee."

"And what shall be the token?" asked the proud girl, as if her heart acknowledged a meaning in these wild words.

"This lock of hair," said Edith, lifting one of the dark, clustering curls that lay heavily on the dead man's brow.

The two maidens joined their hands over the bosom of the corpse, and appointed a day and hour, far, far in time to come, for their next meeting in that chamber. The statelier girl gave one deep look at the motionless countenance, and departed—yet turned again and trembled ere she closed the door, almost believing that her dead lover frowned upon her. And Edith, too! Was not her white form fading into the moonlight? Scorning her own weakness she went forth, and perceived that a Negro slave was waiting in the passage with a wax-light, which he held between her face and his own, and regarded her, as she thought, with an ugly expression of merriment. Lifting his torch on high, the slave lighted her down the staircase, and undid the portal of the mansion. The young clergyman of the town had just ascended the steps, and bowing to the lady, passed in without a word.

Years, many years, rolled on; the world seemed new again, so much older was it grown since the night when those pale girls had clasped their hands across the bosom of the corpse. In the interval, a lonely woman had passed from youth to extreme age, and was known by all the town as the "Old Maid in the Winding Sheet."[1] A taint of insanity had affected her whole life, but so quiet, sad, and gentle, so utterly free from violence, that she was suffered to pursue her harmless fantasies, unmolested by the world, with whose business or pleasures she had nought to do. She dwelt alone, and never came into the daylight, except to follow funerals. Whenever a corpse was borne along the street in sunshine, rain, or snow; whether a pompous train of the rich and proud thronged after it, or few and humble were the mourners, behind them came the lonely woman in a long white garment which the people called her shroud. She took no place among the kindred or the friends, but stood at the door to hear the funeral prayer, and

[1] The sheet in which a corpse is wrapped.

walked in the rear of the procession, as one whose earthly charge it was to haunt the house of mourning, and be the shadow of affliction, and see that the dead were duly buried. So long had this been her custom that the inhabitants of the town deemed her a part of every funeral, as much as the coffin pall, or the very corpse itself, and augured ill of the sinner's destiny unless the "Old Maid in the Winding Sheet" came gliding, like a ghost, behind. Once, it is said, she affrighted a bridal party with her pale presence, appearing suddenly in the illuminated hall, just as the priest was uniting a false maid to a wealthy man, before her lover had been dead a year. Evil was the omen to that marriage! Sometimes she stole forth by moonlight and visited the graves of venerable Integrity, and wedded Love, and virgin Innocence, and every spot where the ashes of a kind and faithful heart were moldering. Over the hillocks of those favored dead would she stretch out her arms, with a gesture, as if she were scattering seeds; and many believed that she brought them from the garden of Paradise; for the graves which she had visited were green beneath the snow, and covered with sweet flowers from April to November. Her blessing was better than a holy verse upon the tombstone. Thus wore away her long, sad, peaceful, and fantastic life, till few were so old as she, and the people of later generations wondered how the dead had ever been buried, or mourners had endured their grief, without the "Old Maid in the Winding Sheet."

Still years went on, and still she followed funerals, and was not yet summoned to her own festival of death. One afternoon the great street of the town was all alive with business and bustle, though the sun now gilded only the upper half of the church spire, having left the housetops and loftiest trees in shadow. The scene was cheerful and animated, in spite of the somber shade between the high brick buildings. Here were pompous merchants, in white wigs and laced velvet; the bronzed faces of sea captains; the foreign garb and air of Spanish creoles; and the disdainful port of natives of Old England; all contrasted with the rough aspect of one or two back settlers, negotiating sales of timber from forests where axe had never sounded. Sometimes a lady passed, swelling roundly forth in an embroidered petticoat, balancing her steps in high-heeled shoes, and courtesying with lofty grace to the punctilious obeisances of the gentlemen. The life of the town seemed to have its very center not far from an old mansion that stood somewhat back from the pavement, surrounded by neglected grass, with a strange air of loneliness, rather deepened than dispelled by the throng so near it. Its site would have been suitably occupied by a magnificent Exchange or a brick block, lettered all over with various signs; or the large house itself might have been a noble tavern, with the "King's Arms" swinging before it, and guests in every chamber, instead of the present solitude. But owing to some dispute about the right of inheritance, the mansion had been long without a tenant, decaying from year to year, and throwing the stately gloom of its shadow over the busiest part of the town. Such was the scene, and such the time, when a figure unlike any that have been described was observed at a distance down the street.

"I espy a strange sail, yonder," remarked a Liverpool captain. "That woman in the long white garment!"

The sailor seemed much struck by the object, as were several others who, at the same moment, caught a glimpse of the figure that had attracted his notice. Almost immediately the various topics of conversation gave place to speculations, in an undertone, on this onwonted occurrence.

"Can there be a funeral so late this afternoon?" inquired some.

They looked for the signs of death at every door—the sexton, the hearse, the assemblage of black-clad relatives—all that makes up the woeful pomp of funerals. They raised their eyes, also, to the sun-gilt spire of the church, and wondered that no clang proceeded from its bell, which had always tolled till now when this figure appeared in the light of day. But none had heard that a corpse was to be borne to its home that afternoon, nor was there any token of a funeral, except the apparition of the "Old Maid in the Winding Sheet."

"What may this portend?" asked each man of his neighbor.

All smiled as they put the question, yet with a certain trouble in their eyes, as if pestilence or some other wide calamity were prognosticated by the untimely intrusion among the living of one whose presence had always been associated with death and woe. What a comet is to the earth was that sad woman to the town. Still she moved on, while the hum of surprise was hushed at her approach, and the proud and the humble stood aside, that her white garment might not wave against them. It was a long, loose robe, of spotless purity. Its wearer appeared very old, pale, emaciated, and feeble, yet glided onward without the unsteady pace of extreme age. At

one point of her course a little rosy boy burst forth from a
door, and ran, with open arms, toward the ghostly woman,
seeming to expect a kiss from her bloodless lips. She made a
slight pause, fixing her eye upon him with an expression of no
earthly sweetness, so that the child shivered and stood awe-
struck, rather than affrighted, while the Old Maid passed on.
Perhaps her garment might have been polluted even by an
infant's touch; perhaps her kiss would have been death to the
sweet boy within a year.

"She is but a shadow," whispered the superstitious. "The
child put forth his arms and could not grasp her robe!"

The wonder was increased when the Old Maid passed beneath the porch of the deserted mansion, ascended the moss-
covered steps, lifted the iron knocker, and gave three raps.
The people could only conjecture that some old remembrance,
troubling her bewildered brain, had impelled the poor woman
hither to visit the friends of her youth; all gone from their
home long since and forever, unless their guests still haunted it
—fit company for the "Old Maid in the Winding Sheet." An
elderly man approached the steps, and, reverently uncovering
his gray locks, essayed to explain the matter.

"None, madam," said he, "have dwelt in this house these
fifteen years agone—no, not since the death of old Colonel
Fenwicke, whose funeral you may remember to have followed.
His heirs, being ill agreed among themselves, have let the
mansion-house go to ruin."

The Old Maid looked slowly round with a slight gesture
of one hand, and a finger of the other upon her lip, appearing more shadow-like than ever in the obscurity of the porch.
But again she lifted the hammer, and gave, this time, a single
rap. Could it be that a footstep was now heard coming down
the staircase of the old mansion, which all conceived to have
been so long untenanted? Slowly, feebly, yet heavily, like the
pace of an aged and infirm person, the step approached, more
distinct on every downward stair, till it reached the portal.
The bar fell on the inside; the door was opened. One upward
glance toward the church spire, whence the sunshine had just
faded, was the last that the people saw of the "Old Maid in
the Winding Sheet."

"Who undid the door?" asked many.

This question, owing to the depth of shadow beneath the
porch, no one could satisfactorily answer. Two or three aged
men, while protesting against an inference which might be

drawn, affirmed that the person within was a Negro, and bore a singular resemblance to old Cæsar, formerly a slave in the house, but freed by death some thirty years before.

"Her summons has waked up a servant of the old family," said one, half seriously.

"Let us wait here," replied another. "More guests will knock at the door, anon. But the gate of the graveyard should be thrown open!"

Twilight had overspread the town before the crowd began to separate, or the comments on this incident were exhausted. One after another was wending his way homeward, when a coach—no common spectacle in those days—drove slowly into the street. It was an old-fashioned equipage, hanging close to the ground, with arms on the panels, a footman behind, and a grave, corpulent coachman seated high in front—the whole giving an idea of solemn state and dignity. There was something awful in the heavy rumbling of the wheels. The coach rolled down the street, till, coming to the gateway of the deserted mansion, it drew up, and the footman sprang to the ground.

"Whose grand coach is this?" askèd a very inquisitive body.

The footman made no reply, but ascended the steps of the old house, gave three raps with the iron hammer, and returned to open the coach door. An old man, possessed of the heraldic lore so common in that day, examined the shield of arms on the panel.

"Azure, a lion's head erased, between three flower-de-luces," said he; then whispered the name of the family to whom these bearings belonged. The last inheritor of his honors was recently dead, after a long residence amid the splendor of the British court, where his birth and wealth had given him no mean station. "He left no child," continued the herald, "and these arms, being in a lozenge, betoken that the coach appertains to his widow."

Further disclosures, perhaps, might have been made, had not the speaker suddenly been struck dumb by the stern eye of an ancient lady who thrust forth her head from the coach, preparing to descend. As she emerged, the people saw that her dress was magnificent, and her figure dignified, in spite of age and infirmity—a stately ruin but with a look, at once, of pride and wretchedness. Her strong and rigid features had an awe about them, unlike that of the White Old Maid, but as of something evil. She passed up the steps, leaning on a

gold-headed cane; the door swung open as she ascended—
and the light of a torch glittered on the embroidery of her
dress, and gleamed on the pillars of the porch. After a momentary pause—a glance backward—and then a desperate effort—
she went in. The decipherer of the coat-of-arms had ventured
up the lowest step, and shrinking back immediately, pale and
tremulous, affirmed that the torch was held by the very image
of old Cæsar.

"But such a hideous grin," added he, "was never seen on
the face of mortal man, black or white! It will haunt me till
my dying day."

Meantime, the coach had wheeled round, with a prodigious
clatter on the pavement, and rumbled up the street, disappearing in the twilight, while the ear still tracked its course.
Scarcely was it gone, when the people began to question
whether the coach and attendants, the ancient lady, the specter
of old Cæsar, and the Old Maid herself, were not all a strangely
combined delusion, with some dark purport in its mystery.
The whole town was astir, so that, instead of dispersing, the
crowd continually increased, and stood gazing up at the windows of the mansion, now silvered by the brightening moon.
The elders, glad to indulge the narrative propensity of age,
told of the long-faded splendor of the family, the entertainments they had given, and the guests, the greatest of the land,
and even titled and noble ones from abroad, who had passed
beneath that portal. These graphic reminiscences seemed to
call up the ghosts of those to whom they referred. So strong
was the impression on some of the more imaginative hearers,
that two or three were seized with trembling fits, at one and
the same moment, protesting that they had distinctly heard
three other raps of the iron knocker.

"Impossible!" exclaimed others. "See! The moon shines
beneath the porch, and shows every part of it, except in the
narrow shade of that pillar. There is no one there!"

"Did not the door open?" whispered one of these fanciful
persons.

"Didst thou see it, too?" said his companion, in a startled
tone.

But the general sentiment was opposed to the idea that a
third visitant had made application at the door of the deserted
house. A few, however, adhered to this new marvel, and even
declared that a red gleam like that of a torch had shone
through the great front window, as if the Negro were lighting

a guest up the staircase. This, too, was pronounced a mere fantasy. But at once the whole multitude started, and each man beheld his own terror painted in the faces of all the rest.

"What an awful thing is this!" cried they.

A shriek too fearfully distinct for doubt had been heard within the mansion, breaking forth suddenly, and succeeded by a deep stillness, as if a heart had burst in giving it utterance. The people knew not whether to fly from the very sight of the house, or to rush trembling in, and search out the strange mystery. Amid their confusion and affright, they were somewhat reassured by the appearance of their clergyman, a venerable patriarch, and equally a saint, who had taught them and their fathers the way to Heaven for more than the space of an ordinary lifetime. He was a reverend figure, with long, white hair upon his shoulders, a white beard upon his breast, and a back so bent over his staff that he seemed to be looking downward continually, as if to choose a proper grave for his weary frame. It was some time before the good old man, being deaf and of impaired intellect, could be made to comprehend such portions of the affair as were comprehensible at all. But, when possessed of the facts, his energies assumed unexpected vigor.

"Verily," said the old gentleman, "it will be fitting that I enter the mansion-house of the worthy Colonel Fenwicke, lest any harm should have befallen that true Christian woman whom ye call the 'Old Maid in the Winding Sheet.' "

Behold, then, the venerable clergyman ascending the steps of the mansion, with a torch-bearer behind him. It was the elderly man who had spoken to the Old Maid, and the same who had afterward explained the shield of arms and recognized the features of the Negro. Like their predecessors, they gave three raps with the iron hammer.

"Old Cæsar cometh not," observed the priest. "Well I wot he no longer doth service in this mansion."

"Assuredly, then, it was something worse, in old Cæsar's likeness!" said the other adventurer.

"Be it as God wills," answered the clergyman. "See! my strength, though it be much decayed, hath sufficed to open this heavy door. Let us enter and pass up the staircase."

Here occurred a singular exemplification of the dreamy state of a very old man's mind. As they ascended the wide flight of stairs, the aged clergyman appeared to move with caution, occasionally standing aside, and oftener bending his head, as it were in salutation, thus practicing all the gestures of one who makes his way through a throng. Reaching the head of the staircase, he looked around with sad and solemn benignity, laid aside his staff, bared his hoary locks, and was evidently on the point of commencing a prayer.

"Reverend sir," said his attendant, who conceived this a very suitable prelude to their further search, "would it not be well that the people join with us in prayer?"

"Welladay!" cried the old clergyman, staring strangely around him. "Art thou here with me, and none other? Verily, past times were present to me, and I deemed that I was to make a funeral prayer, as many a time heretofore, from the head of this staircase. Of a truth, I saw the shades of many that are gone. Yea, I have prayed at their burials, one after another, and the 'Old Maid in the Winding Sheet' hath seen them to their graves!"

Being now more thoroughly awake to their present purpose, he took his staff and struck forcibly on the floor, till there came an echo from each deserted chamber, but no menial to answer their summons. They therefore walked along the passage, and again paused, opposite to the great front window through which was seen the crowd, in the shadow and partial moonlight of the street beneath. On their right hand was the open door of a chamber, and a closed one on their left. The clergyman pointed his cane to the carved oak panel of the latter.

"Within that chamber," observed he, "a whole lifetime since, did I sit by the death-bed of a goodly young man, who, being now at the last gasp"—

Apparently there was some powerful excitement in the ideas which had now flashed across his mind. He snatched the torch from his companion's hand, and threw open the door with such sudden violence that the flame was extinguished, leaving them no other light than the moonbeams, which fell through two windows into the spacious chamber. It was sufficient to discover all that could be known. In a high-backed oaken arm-chair, upright, with her hands clasped across her breast, and her head thrown back, sat the "Old Maid in the Winding Sheet." The stately dame had fallen on her knees, with her forehead on the holy knees of the Old Maid, one hand upon the floor and the other pressed convulsively against her heart. It clutched a lock of hair, once sable, now discolored with a greenish mold. As the priest and layman advanced into the chamber, the Old Maid's features assumed such a semblance of shifting expression that they trusted to hear the whole mystery explained by a single word. But it was only the shadow of a tattered curtain waving betwixt the dead face and the moonlight.

"Both dead!" said the venerable man. "Then who shall divulge the secret? Methinks it glimmers to and fro in my mind, like the light and shadow across the Old Maid's face. And now 't is gone!"

The Fall of the House of Usher

by

EDGAR ALLAN POE

EDGAR ALLAN POE (1809–1849)

The Gothic personality of Edgar Allan Poe is inseparable from the black, nightmare world of his poetry and fiction. His insistence upon a first-person method of narration—whatever the particular characteristics of its *persona*—suggests how very much he desired to project his own being into his writing. The ghoul-haunted castles of Poe's stories, the necromantic mysteries of his creations, the harassed Byronic characters of his aesthetic world—all are the manifestations of his troubled soul, which resembled nothing so much as it did the tortured, turbulent psyche of the Gothic itself.

Yet these very facts have obscured the importance of Poe's literary genius. Critics who have been busy cataloguing his aberrations too often have neglected his artistic achievements, which made, after all, an amazing contribution to American literature. He was as responsible as any one man could be for the development of the modern short story. He opened the way for writers of detective fiction and broadened the possibilities of scientific fantasy. To him the French Symbolist poets willingly expressed their indebtedness, and it is doubtful if any psychological writer since the nineteenth century has been free of his influence.

Poe was a conscious literary craftsman. As an editor he demonstrated a remarkable talent for judgment; as a theorist he expounded the first important body of principles in American literature. What Poe sought most in art was effect. This demanded the creation of an atmosphere and mood that would stimulate an emotional response; it called for the development of a bond between the characters and reader that would induce a similitude in their reactions to the circumstances of the narrative. In every way, Poe's aesthetic theories were suited to the Gothic genre. Nowhere is the reader called upon to analyze the reality of the occurrences; nowhere is he expected to draw the fatal parallel between life and Gothic fiction.

Among Poe's important works are *Al Aaraaf, Tamerlane, and Minor Poems* (1829); *Tales of the Grotesque and Arabesque* (1840) in which "The Fall of the House of Usher" (1839) was reprinted; *The Raven and Other Poems* (1845); and *Tales* (1845).

Son cœur est un luth suspendu;
Sitôt qu'on le touche il rèsonne.

DE BÉRANGER.[1]

DURING the whole of a dull, dark, and soundless day in the autumn of the year, when the clouds hung oppressively low in the heavens, I had been passing alone, on horseback, through a singularly dreary tract of country, and at length found myself, as the shades of evening grew on, within view of the melancholy House of Usher. I know not how it was— but, with the first glimpse of the building, a sense of insufferable gloom pervaded my spirit. I say insufferable; for the feeling was unrelieved by any of that half-pleasurable, because poetic, sentiment, with which the mind usually receives even the sternest natural images of the desolate or terrible. I looked upon the scene before me—upon the mere house, and the simple landscape features of the domain—upon the bleak walls —upon the vacant eyelike windows—upon a few rank sedges— and upon a few white trunks of decayed trees—with an utter depression of soul which I can compare to no earthly sensation more properly than to the after-dream of the reveler upon opium—the bitter lapse into everyday life—the hideous dropping of the veil. There was an iciness, a sinking, a sickening of the heart—an unredeemed dreariness of thought which no goading of the imagination could torture into aught of the sublime. What was it—I paused to think—what was it that so unnerved me in the contemplation of the House of Usher? It was a mystery all insoluble; nor could I grapple with the shadowy fancies that crowded upon me as I pondered. I was forced to fall back upon the unsatisfactory conclusion, that while, beyond doubt, there *are* combinations of very simple natural objects which have the power of thus affecting us, still the analysis of this power lies among considerations beyond our depth. It was possible, I reflected, that a mere different arrangement of the particulars of the scene, of the details of the picture, would be sufficient to modify, or perhaps to annihilate its capacity for sorrowful impression; and, acting upon this idea, I reined my horse to the precipitous brink of a black and lurid tarn that lay in unruffled luster by the dwelling, and

[1] From "Le Refus" by Pierre Jean de Béranger: "His heart is a suspended lute; which resounds at once when it is touched."

gazed down—but with a shudder more thrilling than before—upon the remodeled and inverted images of the gray sedge, and the ghastly tree-stems, and the vacant and eyelike windows.

Nevertheless, in this mansion of gloom I now proposed to myself a sojourn of some weeks. Its proprietor, Roderick Usher, had been one of my boon companions in boyhood; but many years had elapsed since our last meeting. A letter, however, had lately reached me in a distant part of the country—a letter from him—which, in its wildly importunate nature, had admitted of no other than a personal reply. The MS. gave evidence of nervous agitation. The writer spoke of acute bodily illness—of a mental disorder which oppressed him—and of an earnest desire to see me, as his best, and indeed his only personal friend, with a view of attempting, by the cheerfulness of my society, some alleviation of his malady. It was the manner in which all this, and much more, was said—it was the apparent *heart* that went with his request—which allowed me no room for hesitation, and I accordingly obeyed forthwith what I still considered a very singular summons.

Although, as boys, we had been even intimate associates, yet I really knew little of my friend. His reserve had been always excessive and habitual. I was aware, however, that his very ancient family had been noted, time out of mind, for a peculiar sensibility of temperament, displaying itself through long ages in many works of exalted art, and manifested of late in repeated deeds of munificent yet unobtrusive charity, as well as in a passionate devotion to the intricacies, perhaps even more than to the orthodox and easily-recognizable beauties of musical science. I had learned, too, the very remarkable fact that the stem of the Usher race, all time-honored as it was, had put forth at no period any enduring branch; in other words, that the entire family lay in the direct line of descent, and had always, with very trifling and very temporary variation, so lain. It was this deficiency, I considered, while running over in thought the perfect keeping of the character of the premises with the accredited character of the people, and while speculating upon the possible influence which the one, in the long lapse of centuries, might have exercised upon the other—it was this deficiency perhaps of collateral issue, and the consequent undeviating transmission from sire to son of the patrimony with the name, which had at length so identified the two as to merge the original title of the estate in the quaint and equivocal appellation of the "House of Usher"—an appellation which seemed to include, in the minds of the peasantry who used it, both the family and the family mansion.

I have said that the sole effect of my somewhat childish experiment—that of looking down within the tarn—had been to deepen the first singular impression. There can be no doubt that the consciousness of the rapid increase of my superstition —for why should I not so term it?—served mainly to accelerate the increase itself. Such, I have long known, is the paradoxical law of all sentiments having terror as a basis; and it might have been for this reason only that, when I again uplifted my eyes to the house itself from its image in the pool, there grew in my mind a strange fancy—a fancy so ridiculous indeed that I but mention it to show the vivid force of the sensations which oppressed me. I had so worked upon my imagination as really to believe that about the whole mansion and domain there hung an atmosphere peculiar to themselves and their immediate vicinity—an atmosphere which had no affinity with the air of Heaven, but which had reeked up from the decayed trees, and the gray wall, and the silent tarn—a pestilent and mystic vapor, dull, sluggish, faintly discernible, and leaden-hued.

Shaking off from my spirit what *must* have been a dream, I scanned more narrowly the real aspect of the building. Its principal feature seemed to be that of an excessive antiquity. The discoloration of ages had been great. Minute fungi overspread the whole exterior, hanging in a fine tangled web-work from the eaves. Yet all this was apart from any extraordinary dilapidation. No portion of the masonry had fallen, and there appeared to be a wild inconsistency between its still perfect adaptation of parts and the crumbling condition of the individual stones. In this there was much that reminded me of the spacious totality of old woodwork which has rotted for long years in some neglected vault with no disturbance from the breath of the external air. Beyond this indication of extensive decay, however, the fabric gave little token of instability. Perhaps the eye of a scrutinizing observer might have discovered a barely perceptible fissure, which, extending from the roof of the building in front, made its way down the wall in a zigzag direction, until it became lost in the sullen waters of the tarn.

Noticing these things, I rode over a short causeway to the house. A servant in waiting took my horse, and I entered the Gothic archway of the hall. A valet, of stealthy step, thence conducted me in silence through many dark and intricate pas-

sages in my progress to the *studio* of his master. Much that I
encountered on the way contributed, I know not how, to
heighten the vague sentiments of which I have already spoken.
While the objects around me—while the carvings of the ceil-
ings, the somber tapestries of the walls, the ebon blackness of
the floors, and the phantasmagoric armorial trophies which
rattled as I strode, were but matters to which, or to such as
which, I had been accustomed from my infancy—while I
hesitated not to acknowledge how familiar was all this—I still
wondered to find how unfamiliar were the fancies which
ordinary images were stirring up. On one of the staircases I
met the physician of the family. His countenance, I thought,
wore a mingled expression of low cunning and perplexity. He
accosted me with trepidation and passed on. The valet now
threw open a door and ushered me into the presence of his
master.

The room in which I found myself was very large and lofty.
The windows were long, narrow, and pointed, and at so vast
a distance from the black oaken floor as to be altogether in-
accessible from within. Feeble gleams of encrimsoned light
made their way through the trellised panes, and served to
render sufficiently distinct the more prominent objects around;
the eye, however, struggled in vain to reach the remoter
angles of the chamber, or the recesses of the vaulted and
fretted ceiling. Dark draperies hung upon the walls. The general furniture was profuse, comfortless, antique, and tattered.
Many books and musical instruments lay scattered about, but
failed to give any vitality to the scene. I felt that I breathed
an atmosphere of sorrow. An air of stern, deep, and irredeem-
able gloom hung over and pervaded all.

Upon my entrance, Usher arose from a sofa on which he
had been lying at full length, and greeted me with a vivacious
warmth which had much in it, I at first thought, of an over-
done cordiality—of the constrained effort of the *ennuyé*[2] man
of the world. A glance, however, at his countenance convinced
me of his perfect sincerity. We sat down; and for some moments, while he spoke not, I gazed upon him with a feeling
half of pity, half of awe. Surely, man had never before so
terribly altered, in so brief a period, as had Roderick Usher!
It was with difficulty that I could bring myself to admit the
identity of the wan being before me with the companion of
my early boyhood. Yet the character of his face had been at all

[2] Bored.

times remarkable. A cadaverousness of complexion; an eye large, liquid, and luminous beyond comparison; lips somewhat thin and very pallid, but of a surpassingly beautiful curve; a nose of a delicate Hebrew model, but with a breadth of nostril unusual in similar formations; a finely molded chin, speaking, in its want of prominence, of a want of moral energy; hair of a more than web-like softness and tenuity; these features, with an inordinate expansion above the regions of the temple, made up altogether a countenance not easily to be forgotten. And now in the mere exaggeration of the prevailing character of these features, and of the expression they were wont to convey, lay so much of change that I doubted to whom I spoke. The now ghastly pallor of the skin, and the now miraculous luster of the eye, above all things startled and even awed me. The silken hair, too, had been suffered to grow all unheeded, and as, in its wild gossamer texture, it floated rather than fell about the face, I could not, even with effort, connect its Arabesque expression with any idea of simple humanity.

In the manner of my friend I was at once struck with an incoherence—an inconsistency; and I soon found this to arise from a series of feeble and futile struggles to overcome an habitual trepidancy—an excessive nervous agitation. For something of this nature I had indeed been prepared, no less by his letter than by reminiscences of certain boyish traits, and by conclusions deduced from his peculiar physical conformation and temperament. His action was alternately vivacious and sullen. His voice varied rapidly from a tremulous indecision (when the animal spirits seemed utterly in abeyance) to that species of energetic concision—that abrupt, weighty, unhurried, and hollow-sounding enunciation—that leaden, self-balanced and perfectly modulated guttural utterance which may be observed in the lost drunkard, or the irreclaimable eater of opium, during the periods of his most intense excitement.

It was thus that he spoke of the object of my visit, of his earnest desire to see me, and of the solace he expected me to afford him. He entered at some length into what he conceived to be the nature of his malady. It was, he said, a constitutional and a family evil, and one for which he despaired to find a remedy—a mere nervous affection, he immediately added, which would undoubtedly soon pass off. It displayed itself in a host of unnatural sensations. Some of these, as he detailed them, interested and bewildered me; although perhaps the terms and the general manner of the narration had their

weight. He suffered much from a morbid acuteness of the
senses; the most insipid food was alone endurable; he could
wear only garments of certain texture; the odors of all flowers
were oppressive; his eyes were tortured by even a faint light;
and there were but peculiar sounds, and these from stringed
instruments, which did not inspire him with horror.

To an anomalous species of terror I found him a bounden
slave. "I shall perish," said he, "I *must* perish in this deplorable folly. Thus, thus, and not otherwise, shall I be lost. I
dread the events of the future, not in themselves, but in their
results. I shudder at the thought of any, even the most trivial
incident, which may operate upon this intolerable agitation of
soul. I have indeed no abhorrence of danger, except in its
absolute effect—in terror. In this unnerved—in this pitiable
condition—I feel that the period will sooner or later arrive
when I must abandon life and reason together in some struggle
with the grim phantasm, FEAR."

I learned, moreover, at intervals, and through broken and
equivocal hints, another singular feature of his mental condition. He was enchained by certain superstitious impressions
in regard to the dwelling which he tenanted, and whence, for
many years, he had never ventured forth—in regard to an influence whose suppositious force was conveyed in terms too
shadowy here to be restated—an influence which some peculiarities in the mere form and substance of his family mansion,
had, by dint of long sufferance, he said, obtained over his
spirit—an effect which the *physique* of the gray walls and
turrets, and of the dim tarn into which they all looked down,
had at length brought about upon the *morale* of his existence.

He admitted, however, although with hesitation, that much
of the peculiar gloom which thus afflicted him could be traced
to a more natural and far more palpable origin—to the severe
and long-continued illness—indeed to the evidently approaching dissolution—of a tenderly beloved sister—his sole companion for long years—his last and only relative on earth.
"Her decease," he said, with a bitterness which I can never
forget, "would leave him (him the hopeless and the frail) the
last of the ancient race of the Ushers." While he spoke, the
lady Madeline (for so was she called) passed slowly through a
remote portion of the apartment, and, without having noticed
my presence, disappeared. I regarded her with an utter astonishment not unmingled with dread—and yet I found it impossible to account for such feelings. A sensation of stupor

oppressed me as my eyes followed her retreating steps. When a door at length closed upon her, my glance sought instinctively and eagerly the countenance of the brother—but he had buried his face in his hands, and I could only perceive that a far more than ordinary wanness had overspread the emaciated fingers through which trickled many passionate tears.

The disease of the lady Madeline had long baffled the skill of her physicians. A settled apathy, a gradual wasting away of the person, and frequent although transient affections of a partially cataleptical character, were the unusual diagnosis. Hitherto she had steadily borne up against the pressure of her malady, and had not betaken herself finally to bed; but, on the closing in of the evening of my arrival at the house, she succumbed (as her brother told me at night with inexpressible agitation) to the prostrating power of the destroyer; and I learned that the glimpse I had obtained of her person would thus probably be the last I should obtain—that the lady, at least while living, would be seen by me no more.

For several days ensuing her name was unmentioned by either Usher or myself; and during this period I was busied in earnest endeavors to alleviate the melancholy of my friend. We painted and read together, or I listened, as if in a dream, to the wild improvisations of his speaking guitar. And thus, as a closer and still closer intimacy admitted me more unreservedly into the recesses of his spirit, the more bitterly did I perceive the futility of all attempts at cheering a mind from which darkness, as if an inherent positive quality, poured forth upon all objects of the moral and physical universe in one unceasing radiation of gloom.

I shall ever bear about me a memory of the many solemn hours I thus spent alone with the master of the House of Usher. Yet I should fail in any attempt to convey an idea of the exact character of the studies or of the occupations in which he involved me or led me the way. An excited and highly distempered ideality threw a sulphurous luster over all. His long improvised dirges will ring forever in my ears. Among other things, I hold painfully in mind a certain singular perversion and amplification of the wild air of the last waltz of Von Weber.[8] From the paintings over which his elaborate fancy brooded, and which grew, touch by touch, into vaguenesses at which I shuddered the more thrillingly because I

[8] "The Last Waltz of Von Weber" is one of Karl Gottlieb Reissiger's *Danses Brilliantes* (1822).

shuddered knowing not why—from these paintings (vivid as their images now are before me) I would in vain endeavor to educe more than a small portion which should lie within the compass of merely written words. By the utter simplicity, by the nakedness of his designs, he arrested and overawed attention. If ever mortal painted an idea, that mortal was Roderick Usher. For me at least—in the circumstances then surrounding me—there arose out of the pure abstractions which the hypochondriac contrived to throw upon his canvas an intensity of intolerable awe, no shadow of which felt I ever yet in the contemplation of the certainly glowing yet too concrete reveries of Fuseli.[4]

One of the phantasmagoric conceptions of my friend partaking not so rigidly of the spirit of abstraction, may be shadowed forth, although feebly, in words. A small picture presented the interior of an immensely long and rectangular vault or tunnel, with low walls, smooth, white, and without interruption or device. Certain accessory points of the design served well to convey the idea that this excavation lay at an exceeding depth below the surface of the earth. No outlet was observed in any portion of its vast extent, and no torch, or other artificial sources of light was discernible, yet a flood of intense rays rolled throughout, and bathed the whole in a ghastly and inappropriate splendor.

I have just spoken of that morbid condition of the auditory nerve which rendered all music intolerable to the sufferer, with the exception of certain effects of stringed instruments. It was perhaps the narrow limits to which he thus confined himself upon the guitar which gave birth, in great measure, to the fantastic character of his performances. But the fervid *facility* of his *impromptus* could not be so accounted for. They must have been and were, in the notes, as well as in the words of his wild fantasies (for he not infrequently accompanied himself with rhymed-verbal improvisations), the result of that intense mental collectedness and concentration to which I have previously alluded as observable only in particular moments of the highest artificial excitement. The words of one of these rhapsodies I have easily remembered. I was perhaps the more forcibly impressed with it as he gave it, because, in the under or mystic current of its meaning, I fancied that I perceived, and for the first time, a full consciousness on the part of Usher,

[4] Johan Heinrich Fuseli (1742-1825), romantic artist, was born in Switzerland but made his fame in London.

of the tottering of his lofty reason upon her throne. The
verses, which were entitled "The Haunted Palace,"[5] ran very
nearly, if not accurately, thus:

I.

In the greenest of our valleys
  By good angels tenanted,
Once a fair and stately palace—
  Radiant palace—reared its head.
In the monarch Thought's dominion
  It stood there!
Never seraph spread a pinion
  Over fabric half so fair.

II.

Banners yellow, glorious, golden,
  On its roof did float and flow;
(This—all this—was in the olden
  Time long ago)
And every gentle air that dallied,
  In that sweet day,
Along the ramparts plumed and pallid,
  A winged odor went away.

III.

Wanderers in that happy valley
  Through two luminous windows saw
Spirits moving musically
  To a lute's well-tunéd law,
Round about a throne, where sitting
  (Porphyrogene!)[6]
In state his glory well befitting,
  The ruler of the realm was seen.

IV.

And all with pearl and ruby glowing
  Was the fair palace door,
Through which came flowing, flowing, flowing
  And sparkling evermore,

[5] Poe's poem was published earlier in the *Baltimore Museum* (April, 1839).
[6] "Born to the purple" or royal.

A troop of Echoes whose sweet duty
  Was but to sing,
In voices of surpassing beauty,
  The wit and wisdom of their king.

V.

But evil things, in robes of sorrow,
  Assailed the monarch's high estate;
(Ah, let us mourn, for never morrow
  Shall dawn upon his, desolate!)
And, round about his home, the glory
  That blushed and bloomed
Is but a dim-remembered story
  Of the old time entombed.

VI.

And travelers now within that valley,
  Through the red-litten windows, see
Vast forms that move fantastically
  To a discordant melody;
While, like a rapid ghastly river
  Through the pale door,
A hideous throng rush out forever,
  And laugh—but smile no more.

I well remember that suggestions arising from this ballad led us into a train of thought wherein there became manifest an opinion of Usher's, which I mention not so much on account of its novelty (for other men have thought thus), as on account of the pertinacity with which he maintained it. This opinion, in its general form, was that of the sentience of all vegetable things. But, in this disordered fancy, the idea had assumed a more daring character, and trespassed, under certain conditions, upon the kingdom of inorganization. I lack words to express the full extent, or the earnest *abandon* of his persuasion. The belief, however, was connected (as I have previously hinted) with the gray stones of the home of his forefathers. The conditions of the sentience had been here he imagined, fulfilled in the method of collocation of these stones —in the order of their arrangement, as well as in that of the many *fungi* which overspread them, and of the decayed trees which stood around—above all, in the long undisturbed endurance of this arrangement, and in its reduplication in the still waters of the tarn. Its evidence—the evidence of the sentience—was to be seen, he said (and I here started as he spoke), in the gradual yet certain condensation of an atmosphere of their own about the waters and the walls. The result was discoverable, he added, in that silent yet importunate and terrible influence which for centuries had molded the destinies of his family, and which made *him* what I now saw him— what he was. Such opinions need no comment, and I will make none.

Our books[7]—the books which for years had formed no small portion of the mental existence of the invalid—were, as might be supposed, in strict keeping with this character of phantasm. We pored together over such works as the *Ververt et Chartreuse* of Gresset; the *Belphegor* of Machiavelli; the *Heaven and Hell* of Swedenborg; the *Subterranean Voyage of Nicholas Klimm* by Holberg; the *Chiromancy* of Robert Flud, of Jean D'Indaginé, and of De la Chambre; the *Journey into the Blue Distance* of Tieck; and the *City of the Sun* of Campanella. One favorite volume was a small octavo edition of the *Directorium Inquisitorium,* by the Dominican Emyric de Gironne; and there were passages in Pomponius Mela, about the old African Satyrs and Œgpians, over which Usher would sit dreaming for hours. His chief delight, however, was found in the perusal of an exceedingly rare and curious book in quarto Gothic—the manual of a forgotten church—the *Vigiliae Mortuorum secundum Chorum Ecclesiae Maguntinae*.

I could not help thinking of the wild ritual of this work, and of its probable influence upon the hypochondriac, when, one evening, having informed me abruptly that the lady Madeline was no more, he stated his intention of preserving her corpse for a fortnight (previously to its final interment) in one of the numerous vaults within the main walls of the building. The worldly reason, however, assigned for this singular proceeding was one which I did not feel at liberty to dispute. The brother had been led to his resolution (so he told me) by consideration of the unusual character of the malady of the deceased, of certain obtrusive and eager inquiries on the part of her medical man,[8] and of the remote and exposed situation

---

[7] The list of books suggests Usher's absorption in the occult, mystical, and necromantic.

[8] Body-snatching to provide specimens for medical study was a common practice.

of the burial-ground of the family. I will not deny that when I called to mind the sinister countenance of the person whom I met upon the staircase on the day of my arrival at the house, I had no desire to oppose what I regarded as at best but a harmless and by no means an unnatural precaution.

At the request of Usher, I personally aided him in the arrangements for the temporary entombment. The body having been encoffined, we two alone bore it to its rest. The vault in which we placed it (and which had been so long unopened that our torches, half smothered in its oppressive atmosphere, gave us little opportunity for investigation) was small, damp, and entirely without means of admission for light, lying at great depth immediately beneath that portion of the building in which was my own sleeping apartment. It had been used apparently in remote feudal times for the worst purposes of a donjon-keep, and in later days as a place of deposit for powder or some other highly combustible substance, as a portion of its floor, and the whole interior of a long archway through which we reached it, were carefully sheathed with copper. The door, of massive iron, had been also similarly protected. Its immense weight caused an unusually sharp grating sound as it moved upon its hinges.

Having deposited our mournful burden upon trestles within this region of horror, we partially turned aside the yet unscrewed lid of the coffin and looked upon the face of the tenant. A striking similitude between the brother and sister now first arrested my attention, and Usher, divining perhaps my thoughts, murmured out some few words from which I learned that the deceased and himself had been twins, and that sympathies of a scarcely intelligible nature had always existed between them. Our glances, however, rested not long upon the dead—for we could not regard her unawed. The disease which had thus entombed the lady in the maturity of youth had left, as usual in all maladies of a strictly cataleptical character, the mockery of a faint blush upon the bosom and the face, and that suspiciously lingering smile upon the lip which is so terrible in death. We replaced and screwed down the lid, and having secured the door of iron, made our way with toil into the scarcely less gloomy apartments of the upper portion of the house.

And now, some days of bitter grief having elapsed, an observable change came over the features of the mental disorder of my friend. His ordinary manner had vanished. His ordinary occupations were neglected or forgotten. He roamed from chamber to chamber with hurried, unequal, and objectless step. The pallor of his countenance had assumed if possible a more ghastly hue—but the luminousness of his eye had utterly gone out. The once occasional huskiness of his tone was heard no more, and a tremulous quaver, as if of extreme terror, habitually characterized his utterance. There were times indeed when I thought his unceasingly agitated mind was laboring with some oppressive secret, to divulge which he struggled for the necessary courage. At times again I was obliged to resolve all into the mere inexplicable vagaries of madness, for I beheld him gazing upon vacancy for long hours in an attitude of the profoundest attention, as if listening to some imaginary sound. It was no wonder that his condition terrified—that it infected me. I felt creeping upon me, by slow yet certain degrees, the wild influences of his own fantastic yet impressive superstitions.

It was especially upon retiring to bed late in the night of the seventh or eighth day after the placing of the lady Madeline within the donjon that I experienced the full power of such feelings. Sleep came not near my couch—while the hours waned and waned away. I struggled to reason off the nervousness which had dominion over me. I endeavored to believe that much if not all of what I felt was due to the bewildering influence of the gloomy furniture of the room—of the dark and tattered draperies which, tortured into motion by the breath of a rising tempest, swayed fitfully to and fro upon the walls, and rustled uneasily about the decorations of the bed. But my efforts were fruitless. An irrepressible tremor gradually pervaded my frame, and at length there sat upon my very heart an incubus of utterly causeless alarm. Shaking this off with a gasp and a struggle I uplifted myself upon the pillows, and peering earnestly within the intense darkness of the chamber, hearkened—I know not why, except that an instinctive spirit prompted me—to certain low and indefinite sounds which came, through the pauses of the storm, at long intervals, I knew not whence. Overpowered by an intense sentiment of horror, unaccountable yet unendurable, I threw on my clothes with haste (for I felt that I should sleep no more during the night), and endeavored to arouse myself from the pitiable condition into which I had fallen, by pacing rapidly to and fro through the apartment.

I had taken but few turns in this manner, when a light step

on an adjoining staircase arrested my attention. I presently recognized it as that of Usher. In an instant afterward he rapped with a gentle touch at my door, and entered, bearing a lamp. His countenance was as usual cadaverously wan—but, moreover, there was a species of mad hilarity in his eyes—an evidently restrained *hysteria* in his whole demeanor. His air appalled me—but anything was preferable to the solitude which I had so long endured, and I even welcomed his presence as a relief.

"And you have not seen it?" he said, abruptly, after having stared about him for some moments in silence—"you have not then seen it?—but stay! you shall." Thus speaking, and having carefully shaded his lamp, he hurried to one of the casements, and threw it freely open to the storm.

The impetuous fury of the entering gust nearly lifted us from our feet. It was indeed a tempestuous yet sternly beautiful night, and one wildly singular in its terror and its beauty. A whirlwind had apparently collected its force in our vicinity, for there were frequent and violent alterations in the direction of the wind, and the exceeding density of the clouds (which hung so low as to press upon the turrets of the house) did not prevent our perceiving the life-like velocity with which they flew careering from all points against each other without passing away into the distance.

I say that even their exceeding density did not prevent our perceiving this—yet we had no glimpse of the moon or stars, nor was there any flashing forth of the lightning. But the under surfaces of the huge masses of agitated vapor, as well as all terrestrial objects immediately around us, were glowing in the unnatural light of a faintly luminous and distinctly visible gaseous exhalation which hung about and enshrouded the mansion.

"You must not—you shall not behold this!" said I, shudderingly, to Usher, as I led him with a gentle violence from the window to a seat. "These appearances which bewilder you are merely electrical phenomena not uncommon, or it may be that they have their ghastly origin in the rank miasma of the tarn. Let us close this casement; the air is chilling and dangerous to your frame. Here is one of your favorite romances. I will read, and you shall listen; and so we will pass away this terrible night together."

The antique volume which I had taken up was the "Mad

Trist" of Sir Launcelot Canning,[9] but I had called it a favorite of Usher's more in sad jest than in earnest; for in truth, there is little in its uncouth and unimaginative prolixity which could have had interest for the lofty and spiritual ideality of my friend. It was, however, the only book immediately at hand, and I indulged a vague hope that the excitement which now agitated the hypochondriac might find relief (for the history of mental disorder is full of similar anomalies) even in the extremeness of the folly which I should read. Could I have judged, indeed, by the wild overstrained air of vivacity with which he hearkened, or apparently hearkened, to the words of the tale, I might well have congratulated myself upon the success of my design.

I had arrived at that well-known portion of the story where Ethelred, the hero of the Trist, having sought in vain for peaceable admission into the dwelling of the hermit, proceeds to make good an entrance by force. Here, it will be remembered, the words of the narrative run thus:

"And Ethelred, who was by nature of a doughty heart, and who was now mighty withal, on account of the powerfulness of the wine which he had drunken, waited no longer to hold parley with the hermit, who in sooth was of an obstinate and maliceful turn, but feeling the rain upon his shoulders, and fearing the rising of the tempest, uplifted his mace outright, and with blows made quickly room in the plankings of the door for his gauntleted hand; and now pulling therewith sturdily, he so cracked and ripped, and tore all asunder, that the noise of the dry and hollow-sounding wood alarummed and reverberated throughout the forest."

At the termination of this sentence I started, and for a moment paused, for it appeared to me (although I at once concluded that my excited fancy had deceived me) that from some very remote portion of the mansion there came indistinctly to my ears what might have been, in its exact similarity of character, the echo (but a stifled and dull one certainly) of the very cracking and ripping sound which Sir Launcelot had so particularly described. It was beyond doubt the coincidence alone which had arrested my attention; for amid the rattling of the sashes of the casements, and the ordinary commingled noises of the still increasing storm, the

[9] This work has never been identified and is presumed to have been created by Poe.

sound in itself had nothing surely which should have interested or disturbed me. I continued the story:

"But the good champion Ethelred, now entering within the door, was soon enraged and amazed to perceive no signal of the maliceful hermit; but in the stead thereof, a dragon of a scaly and prodigious demeanor, and of a fiery tongue, which sate in guard before a palace of gold, with a floor of silver; and upon the wall there hung a shield of shining brass with this legend enwritten—

> Who entereth herein, a conqueror hath bin;
> Who slayeth the dragon, the shield he shall win.

And Ethelred uplifted his mace, and struck upon the head of the dragon, which fell before him, and gave up his pesty breath, with a shriek so horrid and harsh, and withal so piercing, that Ethelred had fain to close his ears with his hands against the dreadful noise of it, the like whereof was never before heard."

Here again I paused abruptly, and now with a feeling of wild amazement—for there could be no doubt whatever that in this instance I did actually hear (although from what direction it proceeded I found it impossible to say) a low and apparently distant, but harsh, protracted, and most unusual screaming or grating sound—the exact counterpart of what my fancy had already conjured up for the dragon's unnatural shriek as described by the romancer.

Oppressed, as I certainly was upon the occurrence of this second and most extraordinary coincidence, by a thousand conflicting sensations, in which wonder and extreme terror were predominate, I still retained sufficient presence of mind to avoid exciting by any observation the sensitive nervousness of my companion. I was by no means certain that he had noticed the sounds in question, although, assuredly, a strange alteration had during the last few minutes taken place in his demeanor. From a position fronting my own, he had gradually brought round his chair, so as to sit with his face to the door of the chamber; and thus I could but partially perceive his features, although I saw that his lips trembled as if he were murmuring inaudibly. His head had dropped upon his breast, yet I knew that he was not asleep, from the wide and rigid opening of the eye as I caught a glance of it in profile. The motion of his body too was at variance with this idea,—for he rocked from side to side with a gentle yet constant and uniform sway. Having rapidly taken notice of all this, I resumed the narrative of Sir Launcelot, which thus proceeded:

"And now, the champion having escaped from the terrible fury of the dragon, bethinking himself of the brazen shield, and of the breaking up of the enchantment which was upon it, removed the carcass from out of the way before him, and approached valorously over the silver pavement of the castle to where the shield was upon the wall; which in sooth tarried not for his full coming, but fell down at his feet upon the silver floor with a mighty great and terrible ringing sound."

No sooner had these syllables passed my lips, than—as if a shield of brass had indeed at the moment fallen heavily upon a floor of silver—I became aware of a distinct, hollow, metallic, and clangorous, yet apparently muffled, reverberation. Completely unnerved, I leaped to my feet, but the measured rocking movement of Usher was undisturbed. I rushed to the chair in which he sat. His eyes were bent fixedly before him, and throughout his whole countenance there reigned a stony rigidity. But, as I placed my hand upon his shoulder, there came a strong shudder over his whole person; a sickly smile quivered about his lips, and I saw that he spoke in a low, hurried, and gibbering murmur, as if unconscious of my presence. Bending closely over him, I at length drank in the hideous import of his words.

"Not hear it?—yes, I hear it, and *have* heard it. Long—long—long—many minutes, many hours, many days, have I heard it—yet I dared not—oh, pity me, miserable wretch that I am!—I dared not—I *dared* not speak! *We have put her living in the tomb!* Said I not that my senses were acute? I *now* tell you that I heard her first feeble movements in the hollow coffin. I heard them—many, many days ago—yet I dared not—*I dared not speak!* And now—to-night—Ethelred—ha! ha!—the breaking of the hermit's door, and the death-cry of the dragon, and the clangor of the shield!—say, rather, the rending of her coffin, and the grating of the iron hinges of her prison, and her struggles within the coppered archway of the vault. O whither shall I fly? Will she not be here anon? Is she not hurrying to upbraid me for my haste? Have I not heard her footstep on the stair? Do I not distinguish that heavy and horrible beating of her heart? Madman!" Here he sprang furiously to his feet, and shrieked out his syllables, as if in the effort he were giving up his soul—"*Madman! I tell you that she now stands without the door!*"

As if in the superhuman energy of his utterance there had been found the potency of a spell—the huge antique panels to which the speaker pointed, threw slowly back, upon the instant, their ponderous and ebony jaws. It was the work of the rushing gust—but then without those doors there *did* stand the lofty and enshrouded figure of the lady Madeline of Usher. There was blood upon her white robes, and the evidence of some bitter struggle upon every portion of her emaciated frame. For a moment she remained trembling and reeling to and fro upon the threshold—then, with a low moaning cry, fell heavily inward upon the person of her brother, and in her violent and now final death-agonies, bore him to the floor a corpse, and a victim to the terrors he had anticipated.

From that chamber and from that mansion I fled aghast. The storm was still abroad in all its wrath as I found myself crossing the old causeway. Suddenly there shot along the path a wild light, and I turned to see whence a gleam so unusual could have issued, for the vast house and its shadows were alone behind me. The radiance was that of the full, setting, and blood-red moon, which now shone vividly through that once barely-discernible fissure, of which I have before spoken as extending from the roof of the building in a zigzag direction to the base. While I gazed, this fissure rapidly widened; there came a fierce breath of the whirlwind; the entire orb of the satellite burst at once upon my sight; my brain reeled as I saw the mighty walls rushing asunder; there was a long tumultuous shouting sound like the voice of a thousand waters, and the deep and dark tarn at my feet closed sullenly and silently over the fragments of the *"House of Usher."*

Carmilla

by

SHERIDAN LE FANU

SHERIDAN LE FANU (1814–1873)

Although today he is remembered almost solely for his novel
Uncle Silas (1864) and the fact that he was Richard Brinsley
Sheridan's grand-nephew, Joseph Sheridan Le Fanu was a
master of the Victorian supernatural tale. His stories bristle
with a faith in the occult and mysterious, for Le Fanu never
was emotionally far from these. In his final years after the
death of his wife, he yielded completely to his impulses and
withdrew from Dublin social life into the private fantasies of
the recluse.

In "Carmilla," first published in *The Dark Blue* (1871), a
magazine, and then reprinted in his collection *In a Glass
Darkly* (1872), he is determined to demonstrate the victory of
the irrational over the rational mind. Non-believers, like the
General and Laura's father, are made to come to terms with
forces that are beyond their understanding, while medical men
must accept evidence that is outside the material of their
textbooks. To be sure, Le Fanu has to offer his own kind of
verisimilitude and does with his narrator's insistence that her
readers will think her story implausible because of the differences between her environment and theirs. Nevertheless, the
credibility ultimately depends on one's willingness to enter
into the Gothic spirit of the vampire story.

The vampire story itself is actually an extension of the
Gothic type. They share in mysterious occurrences, haunted
castles, and erotic experiences. The last is particularly important, for the link between a Gothic romance like Coleridge's
fragment of "Christabel" and Le Fanu's "Carmilla" is most
specific in terms of the Lesbian drives that mark the supernatural struggle in one woman's attempt to win over another.
Whether in relating stories of incest or homosexuality, the
Gothicists were liberating the most forbidden social impulses
and, through conventional happy endings, reassuring their
readers at the same time that all was right with the world.

Among Le Fanu's other works of note are *The House by
the Church-Yard* (1863); *Wylder's Hand* (1864), and the
Wyvern Mystery (1869).

PROLOGUE

UPON a paper attached to the narrative which follows, Dr. Hesselius has written a rather elaborate note, which he accompanies with a reference to his essay on the strange subject which the MS. illuminates.

The mysterious subject he treats, in that essay, with his usual learning and acumen, and with remarkable directness and condensation. It will form but a one volume of the series of that extraordinary man's collected papers.

As I publish the case, in this volume, simply to interest the "laity," I shall forestall the intelligent lady, who relates it, in nothing; and, after due consideration, I have determined, therefore, to abstain from presenting any *précis* of the learned doctor's reasoning, or extract from his statement on a subject which he describes as "involving, not improbably, some of the profoundest arcana of our dual existence, and its intermediates."

I was anxious, on discovering this paper, to reopen the correspondence commenced by Dr. Hesselius, so many years before, with a person so clever and careful as his informant seems to have been. Much to my regret, however, I found that she had died in the interval.

She, probably, could have added little to the narrative which she communicates in the following pages, with, so far as I can pronounce, such a conscientious particularity.

I. AN EARLY FRIGHT

IN Styria,[1] we, though by no means magnificent people, inhabit a castle, or schloss. A small income, in that part of the world, goes a great way. Eight or nine hundred a year does wonders. Scantily enough ours would have answered among wealthy people at home. My father is English, and I bear an English name, although I never saw England. But, in this lonely and primitive place, where everything is so marvelously cheap, I really don't see how ever so much more money would at all materially add to our comforts, or even luxuries.

My father was in the Austrian service, and retired upon a

---

[1] A province in Southeast Austria.

pension and his patrimony, and purchased this feudal residence, and the small estate on which it stands, a bargain.

Nothing can be more picturesque or solitary. It stands on a slight eminence in a forest. The road, very old and narrow, passes in front of its drawbridge, never raised in my time, and its moat, stocked with perch, and sailed over by many swans, and floating on its surface white fleets of water-lilies.

Over all this the schloss shows its many-windowed front; its towers, and its Gothic chapel.

The forest opens in an irregular and very picturesque glade before its gate, and at the right a steep Gothic bridge carries the road over a stream that winds in deep shadow through the wood.

I have said that this is a very lonely place. Judge whether I say truth. Looking from the hall door toward the road, the forest in which our castle stands extends fifteen miles to the right, and twelve to the left. The nearest inhabited village is about seven of your English miles to the left. The nearest inhabited schloss of any historic associations, is that of old General Spielsdorf, nearly twenty miles away to the right.

I have said "the nearest *inhabited* village," because there is, only three miles westward, that is to say in the direction of General Spielsdorf's schloss, a ruined village, with its quaint little church, now roofless, in the aisle of which are the moldering tombs of the proud family of Karnstein, now extinct, who once owned the equally-desolate château which, in the thick of the forest, overlooks the silent ruins of the town.

Respecting the cause of the desertion of this striking and melancholy spot, there is a legend which I shall relate to you another time.

I must tell you now, how very small is the party who constitute the inhabitants of our castle. I don't include servants, or those dependants who occupy rooms in the buildings attached to the schloss. Listen, and wonder! My father, who is the kindest man on earth, but growing old; and I, at the date of my story, only nineteen. Eight years have passed since then. I and my father constituted the family at the schloss. My mother, a Styrian lady, died in my infancy, but I had a good-natured governess, who had been with me from, I might almost say, my infancy. I could not remember the time when her fat, benignant face was not a familiar picture in my memory. This was Madame Perrodon, a native of Berne, whose care and good nature in part supplied to me the loss of my mother, whom I do not even remember, so early I lost her. She made a third at our little dinner party. There was a fourth, Mademoiselle De Lafontaine, a lady such as you term, I believe, a "finishing governess." She spoke French and German, Madame Perrodon French and broken English, to which my father and I added English, which, partly to prevent its becoming a lost language among us, and partly from patriotic motives, we spoke every day. The consequence was a Babel, at which strangers used to laugh, and which I shall make no attempt to reproduce in this narrative. And there were two or three young lady friends besides, pretty nearly of my own age, who were occasional visitors, for longer or shorter terms; and these visits I sometimes returned.

These were our regular social resources; but of course there were chance visits from "neighbors" of only five or six leagues' distance. My life was, notwithstanding, rather a solitary one, I can assure you.

My gouvernantes had just so much control over me as you might conjecture such sage persons would have in the case of a rather spoiled girl, whose only parent allowed her pretty nearly her own way in everything.

The first occurrence in my existence, which produced a terrible impression upon my mind, which, in fact, never has been effaced, was one of the very earliest incidents of my life which I can recollect. Some people will think it so trifling that it should not be recorded here. You will see, however, by-and-by, why I mention it. The nursery, as it was called, though I had it all to myself, was a large room in the upper story of the castle, with a steep oak roof. I can't have been more than six years old, when one night I awoke, and looking round the room from my bed, failed to see the nursery-maid. Neither was my nurse there; and I thought myself alone. I was not frightened, for I was one of those happy children who are studiously kept in ignorance of ghost stories, of fairy tales, and of all such lore as makes us cover up our heads when the door creaks suddenly, or the flicker of an expiring candle makes the shadow of a bed-post dance upon the wall, nearer to our faces. I was vexed and insulted at finding myself, as I conceived, neglected, and I began to whimper, preparatory to a hearty bout of roaring; when to my surprise, I saw a solemn, but very pretty face looking at me from the side of the bed. It was that of a young lady who was kneeling, with her hands under the coverlet. I looked at her with a kind of pleased wonder, and ceased whimpering. She caressed me with her hands, and lay down beside me on the bed, and drew me toward her, smiling; I felt immediately delightfully soothed, and fell asleep again. I was wakened by a sensation as if two needles ran into my breast very deep at the same moment, and I cried loudly. The lady started back, with her eyes fixed on me, and then slipped down upon the floor, and, as I thought, hid herself under the bed.

I was now for the first time frightened, and I yelled with all my might and main. Nurse, nurserymaid, housekeeper, all came running in, and hearing my story, they made light of it, soothing me all they could meanwhile. But, child as I was, I could perceive that their faces were pale with an unwonted look of anxiety, and I saw them look under the bed, and about the room, and peep under tables and pluck open cupboards; and the housekeeper whispered to the nurse: "Lay your hand along that hollow in the bed; some one *did* lie there, so sure as you did not; the place is still warm."

I remember the nursery-maid petting me, and all three examining my chest, where I told them I felt the puncture, and pronouncing that there was no sign visible that any such thing had happened to me.

The housekeeper and the two other servants who were in charge of the nursery, remained sitting up all night; and from that time a servant always sat up in the nursery until I was about fourteen.

I was very nervous for a long time after this. A doctor was called in, he was pallid and elderly. How well I remember his long saturnine face, slightly pitted with smallpox, and his chestnut wig. For a good while, every second day, he came and gave me medicine, which of course I hated.

The morning after I saw this apparition I was in a state of terror, and could not bear to be left alone, daylight though it was, for a moment.

I remember my father coming up and standing at the bedside, and talking cheerfully, and asking the nurse a number of questions, and laughing very heartily at one of the answers; and patting me on the shoulder, and kissing me, and telling me not to be frightened, that it was nothing but a dream and could not hurt me.

But I was not comforted, for I knew the visit of the strange woman was *not* a dream; and I was *awfully* frightened.

I was a little consoled by the nursery-maid's assuring me

that it was she who had come and looked at me, and lain down beside me in the bed and that I must have been half-dreaming not to have known her face. But this, though supported by the nurse, did not quite satisfy me.

I remember, in the course of that day, a venerable old man, in a black cassock, coming into the room with the nurse and housekeeper, and talking a little to them, and very kindly to me; his face was very sweet and gentle, and he told me they were going to pray, and joined my hands together, and desired me to say, softly, while they were praying, "Lord, hear all good prayers for us, for Jesus' sake." I think these were the very words, for I often repeated them to myself, and my nurse used for years to make me say them in my prayers.

I remember so well the thoughtful sweet face of that white-haired old man, in his black cassock, as he stood in that rude, lofty, brown room, with the clumsy furniture of a fashion three hundred years old, about him, and the scanty light entering its shadowy atmosphere through the small lattice. He kneeled, and the three women with him, and he prayed aloud with an earnest quavering voice for, what appeared to me, a long time. I forget all my life preceding that event, and for some time after it is all obscure also; but the scenes I have just described stand out vivid as the isolated pictures of the phantasmagoria surrounded by darkness.

II. A GUEST

I am now going to tell you something so strange that it will require all your faith in my veracity to believe my story. It is not only true, nevertheless, but truth of which I have been an eye-witness.

It was a sweet summer evening, and my father asked me, as he sometimes did, to take a little ramble with him along that beautiful forest vista which I have mentioned as lying in front of the schloss.

"General Spielsdorf cannot come to us so soon as I had hoped," said my father, as we pursued our walk.

He was to have paid us a visit of some weeks, and we had expected his arrival next day. He was to have brought with him a young lady, his niece and ward, Mademoiselle Rhein-feldt, whom I had never seen, but whom I had heard described as a very charming girl, and in whose society I had promised myself many happy days. I was more disappointed than a young lady living in a town, or a bustling neighborhood can possibly imagine. This visit, and the new acquaintance it promised, had furnished my daydream for many weeks.

"And how soon does he come?" I asked.

"Not till autumn. Not for two months, I dare say," he answered. "And I am very glad now, dear, that you never knew Mademoiselle Rheinfeldt."

"And why?" I asked, both mortified and curious.

"Because the poor young lady is dead," he replied. "I quite forgot I had not told you, but you were not in the room when I received the General's letter this evening."

I was very much shocked. General Spielsdorf had mentioned in his first letter, six or seven weeks before, that she was not so well as he would wish her, but there was nothing to suggest the remotest suspicion of danger.

"Here is the General's letter," he said, handing it to me. "I am afraid he is in great affliction; the letter appears to me to have been written very nearly in distraction."

We sat down on a rude bench, under a group of magnificent lime trees. The sun was setting with all its melancholy splendor behind the sylvan horizon, and the stream that flows beside our home, and passes under the steep old bridge I have mentioned, wound through many a group of noble trees, almost at our feet, reflecting in its current the fading crimson of the sky. General Spielsdorf's letter was so extraordinary, so vehement, and in some places so self-contradictory, that I read it twice over—the second time aloud to my father—and was still unable to account for it, except by supposing that grief had unsettled his mind.

It said, "I have lost my darling daughter, for as such I loved her. During the last days of dear Bertha's illness I was not able to write to you. Before then I had no idea of her danger. I have lost her, and now learn *all*, too late. She died in the peace of innocence, and in the glorious hope of a blessed futurity. The fiend who betrayed our infatuated hospitality has done it all. I thought I was receiving into my house innocence, gaiety, a charming companion for my lost Bertha. Heavens! What a fool have I been! I thank God my child died without a suspicion of the cause of her sufferings. She is gone without so much as conjecturing the nature of her illness, and the accursed passion of the agent of all this misery. I devote my remaining days to tracking and extinguishing a monster. I am told I may hope to accomplish my righteous and merciful purpose. At present there is scarcely a gleam of light to guide me. I curse my conceited incredulity, my despicable affectation of superiority, my blindness, my obstinacy—all—too late. I cannot write or talk collectedly now. I am distracted. So soon as I shall have a little recovered, I mean to devote myself for a time to inquiry, which may possibly lead me as far as Vienna. Some time in the autumn, two months hence, or earlier if I live, I will see you—that is, if you permit me; I will then tell you all that I scarce dare put upon paper now. Farewell. Pray for me, dear friend."

In these terms ended this strange letter. Though I had never seen Bertha Rheinfeldt, my eyes filled with tears at the sudden intelligence; I was startled, as well as profoundly disappointed.

The sun had now set, and it was twilight by the time I had returned the General's letter to my father.

It was a soft clear evening, and we loitered, speculating upon the possible meanings of the violent and incoherent sentences which I had just been reading. We had nearly a mile to walk before reaching the road that passes the schloss in front, and by that time the moon was shining brilliantly. At the drawbridge we met Madame Perrodon and Mademoiselle De Lafontaine, who had come out, without their bonnets, to enjoy the exquisite moonlight.

We heard their voices gabbling in animated dialogue as we approached. We joined them at the drawbridge, and turned about to admire with them the beautiful scene.

The glade through which we had just walked lay before us. At our left the narrow road wound away under clumps of lordly trees, and was lost to sight amid the thickening forest. At the right the same road crosses the steep and picturesque bridge, near which stands a ruined tower, which once guarded that pass; and beyond the bridge an abrupt eminence rises, covered with trees, and showing in the shadow some gray ivy-clustered rocks.

Over the sward and low grounds, a thin film of mist was stealing, like smoke, marking the distances with a transparent veil; and here and there we could see the river faintly flashing in the moonlight.

No softer, sweeter scene could be imagined. The news I had just heard made it melancholy; but nothing could disturb its character of profound serenity, and the enchanted glory and vagueness of the prospect.

My father, who enjoyed the picturesque, and I, stood look-ing in silence over the expanse beneath us. The two good governesses, standing a little way behind us, discoursed upon the scene, and were eloquent upon the moon.

Madame Perrodon was fat, middle-aged, and romantic, and talked and sighed poetically. Mademoiselle De Lafontaine—in right of her father, who was a German, assumed to be psychological, metaphysical, and something of a mystic—now declared that when the moon shone with a light so intense it was well known that it indicated a special spiritual activity. The effect of the full moon in such a state of brilliancy was manifold. It acted on dreams, it acted on lunacy, it acted on nervous people; it had marvelous physical influences con-nected with life. Mademoiselle related that her cousin, who was mate of a merchant ship, having taken a nap on deck on such a night, lying on his back, with his face full in the light of the moon, had wakened, after a dream of an old woman clawing him by the cheek, with his features horribly drawn to one side; and his countenance had never quite recovered its equilibrium.

"The moon, this night," she said, "is full of odylic[2] and magnetic influence—and see, when you look behind you at the front of the schloss, how all its windows flash and twinkle with that silvery splendor, as if unseen hands had lighted up the rooms to receive fairy guests."

There are indolent states of the spirits in which, indisposed to talk ourselves, the talk of others is pleasant to our listless ears; and I gazed on, pleased with the tinkle of the ladies' conversation.

"I have got into one of my moping moods to-night," said my father, after a silence, and quoting Shakespeare, whom, by way of keeping up our English, he used to read aloud, he said:—

> " ' In truth I know not why I am so sad:
>   It wearies me; you say it wearies you;
>   But how I got it—came by it.'[3]

"I forget the rest. But I feel as if some great misfortune were hanging over us. I suppose the poor General's afflicted letter has had something to do with it."

[2] *Od* was a hypothetical force supposedly pervading all nature, particularly present in sensitive people. Baron von Reichenbach (1788-1869) proposed the theory to explain such phenomena as mesmerism and animal magnetism.
[3] *The Merchant of Venice.* Act I, Scene 1.

At this moment the unwonted sound of carriage wheels and many hoofs upon the road, arrested our attention.

They seemed to be approaching from the high ground overlooking the bridge, and very soon the equipage emerged from that point. Two horsemen first crossed the bridge, then came a carriage drawn by four horses, and two men rode behind.

It seemed to be a traveling carriage of a person of rank; and we were all immediately absorbed in watching that very unusual spectacle. It became, in a few moments, greatly more interesting, for just as the carriage had passed the summit of the steep bridge, one of the leaders, taking fright, communicated his panic to the rest, and, after a plunge or two, the whole team broke into a wild gallop together, and dashing between the horsemen who rode in front, came thundering along the road toward us with the speed of a hurricane.

The excitement of the scene was made more painful by the clear, long-drawn screams of a female voice from the carriage window.

We all advanced in curiosity and horror; my father in silence, the rest with various ejaculations of terror.

Our suspense did not last long. Just before you reach the castle drawbridge, on the route they were coming, there stands by the roadside a magnificent lime tree, on the other stands an ancient stone cross, at sight of which the horses, now going at a pace that was perfectly frightful, swerved so as to bring the wheel over the projecting roots of the tree.

I knew what was coming. I covered my eyes, unable to see it out, and turned my head away; at the same moment I heard a cry from my lady friends, who had gone on a little.

Curiosity opened my eyes, and I saw a scene of utter confusion. Two of the horses were on the ground, the carriage lay upon its side, with two wheels in the air; the men were busy removing the traces, and a lady, with a commanding air and figure had got out, and stood with clasped hands, raising the handkerchief that was in them every now and then to her eyes. Through the carriage door was now lifted a young lady, who appeared to be lifeless. My dear old father was already beside the elder lady, with his hat in his hand, evidently tendering his aid and the resources of his schloss. The lady did not appear to hear him, or to have eyes for anything but the slender girl who was being placed against the slope of the bank.

I approached; the young lady was apparently stunned, but she was certainly not dead. My father, who piqued himself on being something of a physician, had just had his fingers to her wrist and assured the lady, who declared herself her mother, that her pulse, though faint and irregular, was undoubtedly still distinguishable. The lady clasped her hands and looked upward, as if in a momentary transport of gratitude; but immediately she broke out again in that theatrical way which is, I believe, natural to some people.

She was what is called a fine-looking woman for her time of life, and must have been handsome; she was tall, but not thin, and dressed in black velvet, and looked rather pale, but with a proud and commanding countenance, though now agitated strangely.

"Was ever being so born to calamity?" I heard her say, with clasped hands, as I came up. "Here am I, on a journey of life and death, in prosecuting which to lose an hour is possibly to lose all. My child will not have recovered sufficiently to resume her route for who can say how long. I must leave her; I cannot, dare not, delay. How far on, sir, can you tell, is the nearest village? I must leave her there; and shall not see my darling, or even hear of her till my return, three months hence."

I plucked my father by the coat, and whispered earnestly in his ear, "Oh! papa, pray ask her to let her stay with us—it would be so delightful. Do, pray."

"If madame will entrust her child to the care of my daughter, and of her good gouvernante, Madame Perrodon, and permit her to remain as our guest, under my charge, until her return, it will confer a distinction and an obligation upon us, and we shall treat her with all the care and devotion which so sacred a trust deserves."

"I cannot do that, sir, it would be to task your kindness and chivalry too cruelly," said the lady, distractedly.

"It would, on the contrary, be to confer on us a very great kindness at the moment when we most need it. My daughter has just been disappointed by a cruel misfortune, in a visit from which she had long anticipated a great deal of happiness. If you confide this young lady to our care it will be her best consolation. The nearest village on your route is distant, and affords no such inn as you think of placing your daughter at; you cannot allow her to continue her journey for any considerable distance without danger. If, as you say, you cannot suspend your journey, you must part with her to-night, and nowhere could you do so with more honest assurances of care and tenderness than here."

There was something in this lady's air and appearance so distinguished, and even imposing, and in her manner so engaging, as to impress one, quite apart from the dignity of her equipage, with a conviction that she was a person of consequence.

By this time the carriage was replaced in its upright position, and the horses, quite tractable, in the traces again.

The lady threw on her daughter a glance which I fancied was not quite so affectionate as one might have anticipated from the beginning of the scene; then she beckoned slightly to my father, and withdrew two or three steps with him out of hearing; and talked to him with a fixed and stern countenance, not at all like that with which she had hitherto spoken.

I was filled with wonder that my father did not seem to perceive the change, and also unspeakably curious to learn what it could be that she was speaking, almost in his ear, with so much earnestness and rapidity.

Two or three minutes at most, I think, she remained thus employed, then she turned and a few steps brought her to where her daughter lay, supported by Madame Perrodon. She kneeled beside her for a moment and whispered, as madame supposed, a little benediction in her ear; then hastily kissing her, she stepped into her carriage, the door was closed, the footmen in stately liveries jumped up behind, the outriders spurred on, the postilions cracked their whips, the horses plunged and broke suddenly into a furious canter that threatened soon again to become a gallop, and the carriage whirled away, followed at the same rapid pace by the two horsemen in the rear.

III. WE COMPARE NOTES

WE followed the *cortége* with our eyes until it was swiftly lost to sight in the misty wood; and the very sound of the hoofs and wheels died away in the silent night air.

Nothing remained to assure us that the adventure had not been an illusion of a moment but the young lady, who just at that moment opened her eyes. I could not see, for her face was turned from me, but she raised her head, evidently looking about her, and I heard a very sweet voice ask complainingly, "Where is mamma?"

Our good Madame Perrodon answered tenderly, and added some comfortable assurances.

I then heard her ask:

"Where am I? What is this place?" and after that she said, "I don't see the carriage; and Matska, where is she?"

Madame answered all her questions in so far as she understood them; and gradually the young lady remembered how the misadventure came about, and was glad to hear that no one in, or in attendance on, the carriage was hurt; and on learning that her mamma had left her here, till her return in about three months, she wept.

I was going to add my consolations to those of Madame Perrodon when Mademoiselle De Lafontaine placed her hand upon my arm, saying:

"Don't approach, one at a time is as much as she can at present converse with; a very little excitement would possibly overpower her now."

As soon as she is comfortably in bed, I thought, I will run up to her room and see her.

My father in the meantime had sent a servant on horseback for the physician, who lived about two leagues away; and a bedroom was being prepared for the young lady's reception.

The stranger now rose, and leaning on madame's arm, walked slowly over the drawbridge and into the castle gate.

In the hall, servants waited to receive her, and she was conducted forthwith to her room.

The room we usually sat in as our drawing-room is long, having four windows, that looked over the moat and drawbridge, upon the forest scene I have just described.

It is furnished in old carved oak, with large carved cabinets, and the chairs are cushioned with crimson Utrecht velvet. The walls are covered with tapestry, and surrounded with great gold frames, the figures being as large as life, in ancient and very curious costume, and the subjects represented are hunting, hawking and generally festive. It is not too stately to be extremely comfortable; and here we had our tea, for with his usual patriotic leanings he insisted that the national beverage should make its appearance regularly with our coffee and chocolate.

We sat here this night, and with candles lighted, were talking over the adventure of the evening.

Madame Perrodon and Mademoiselle De Lafontaine were both of our party. The young stranger had hardly lain down in her bed when she sank into a deep sleep; and those ladies had left her in the care of a servant.

"How do you like our guest?" I asked, as soon as madame entered. "Tell me all about her?"

"I like her extremely," answered madame, "she is, I almost think the prettiest creature I ever saw; about your age, and so gentle and nice."

"She is absolutely beautiful," threw in mademoiselle, who had peeped for a moment into the stranger's room.

"And such a sweet voice!" added Madame Perrodon.

"Did you remark a woman in the carriage, after it was set up again, who did not get out," inquired mademoiselle, "but only looked from the window?"

No, we had not seen her.

Then she described a hideous black woman, with a sort of colored turban on her head, who was gazing all the time from the carriage window, nodding and grinning derisively toward the ladies, with gleaming eyes and large white eyeballs, and her teeth set as if in fury.

"Did you remark what an ill-looking pack of men the servants were?" asked madame.

"Yes," said my father, who had just come in, "ugly, hang-dog looking fellows, as ever I beheld in my life. I hope they mayn't rob the poor lady in the forest. They are clever rogues, however; they got everything to rights in a minute."

"I dare say they are worn out with too long traveling," said madame. "Besides looking wicked, their faces were so strangely lean, and dark, and sullen. I am very curious, I own; but I dare say the young lady will tell us all about it to-morrow, if she is sufficiently recovered."

"I don't think she will," said my father, with a mysterious smile, and a little nod of his head, as if he knew more about it than he cared to tell us.

This made me all the more inquisitive as to what had passed between him and the lady in the black velvet, in the brief but earnest interview that had immediately preceded her departure.

We were scarcely alone, when I entreated him to tell me. He did not need much pressing.

"There is no particular reason why I should not tell you. She expressed a reluctance to trouble us with the care of her daughter, saying she was in delicate health, and nervous, but not subject to any kind of seizure—she volunteered that—nor to any illusion; being, in fact, perfectly sane."

"How very odd to say all that!" I interpolated. "It was so unnecessary."

"At all events it was *said*," he laughed, "and as you wish to know all that passed, which was indeed very little, I tell you. She then said, 'I am making a long journey of *vital* importance' —she emphasized the word—'rapid and secret; I shall return for my child in three months; in the meantime, she will be silent as to who we are, whence we come, and whither we are traveling.' That is all she said. She spoke very pure French. When she said the word 'secret,' she paused for a few seconds, looking sternly, her eyes fixed on mine. I fancy she makes a great point of that. You saw how quickly she was gone. I hope I have not done a very foolish thing, in taking charge of the young lady."

For my part, I was delighted. I was longing to see and talk to her; and only waiting till the doctor should give me leave. You, who live in towns, can have no idea how great an event the introduction of a new friend is, in such a solitude as surrounded us.

The doctor did not arrive till nearly one o'clock; but I could no more have gone to my bed and slept, than I could have overtaken, on foot, the carriage in which the princess in black velvet had driven away.

When the physician came down to the drawing-room, it was to report very favorably upon his patient. She was now sitting up, her pulse quite regular, apparently perfectly well. She had sustained no injury, and the little shock to her nerves had passed away quite harmlessly. There could be no harm certainly in my seeing her, if we both wished it; and, with this permission, I sent, forthwith, to know whether she would allow me to visit her for a few minutes in her room.

The servant returned immediately to say that she desired nothing more.

You may be sure I was not long in availing myself of this permission.

Our visitor lay in one of the handsomest rooms in the schloss. It was, perhaps a little stately. There was a somber piece of tapestry opposite the foot of the bed, representing Cleopatra with the asps to her bosom; and other solemn classic scenes were displayed, a little faded, upon the other walls. But there was gold carving, and rich and varied color enough in the

other decorations of the room, to more than redeem the gloom
of the old tapestry.

There were candles at the bedside. She was sitting up; her
slender pretty figure enveloped in the soft silk dressing-gown,
embroidered with flowers, and lined with thick quilted silk,
which her mother had thrown over her feet as she lay upon
the ground.

What was it that, as I reached the bedside and had just
begun my little greeting, struck me dumb in a moment, and
made me recoil a step or two from before her? I will tell you.

I saw the very face which had visited me in my childhood
at night, which remained so fixed in my memory, and on
which I had for so many years so often ruminated with
horror, when no one suspected of what I was thinking.

It was pretty, even beautiful; and when I first beheld it,
wore the same melancholy expression.

But this almost instantly lighted into a strange fixed smile
of recognition.

There was a silence of fully a minute, and then at length
she spoke; *I* could not.

"How wonderful!" she exclaimed. "Twelve years ago, I saw
your face in a dream, and it has haunted me ever since."

"Wonderful indeed!" I repeated, overcoming with an effort
the horror that had for a time suspended my utterances.
"Twelve years ago, in vision or reality, *I* certainly saw you.
I could not forget your face. It has remained before my eyes
ever since."

Her smile had softened. Whatever I had fancied strange
in it, was gone, and it and her dimpling cheeks were now
delightfully pretty and intelligent.

I felt reassured, and continued more in the vein which hospitality indicated, to bid her welcome, and to tell her how
much pleasure her accidental arrival had given us all, and
especially what a happiness it was to me.

I took her hand as I spoke. I was a little shy, as lonely
people are, but the situation made me eloquent, and even
bold. She pressed my hand, she laid hers upon it, and her eyes
glowed, as, looking hastily into mine, she smiled again, and
blushed.

She answered my welcome very prettily. I sat down beside
her, still wondering; and she said:

"I must tell you my vision about you; it is so very strange
that you and I should have had, each of the other so vivid a

dream, that each should have seen, I you and you me, looking as we do now, when of course we both were mere children. I was a child, about six years old, and I awoke from a confused and troubled dream, and found myself in a room, unlike my nursery, wainscoted clumsily in some dark wood, and with cupboards and bedsteads, and chairs, and benches placed about it. The beds were, I thought, all empty, and the room itself without any one but myself in it; and I, after looking about me for some time, and admiring especially an iron candlestick, with two branches, which I should certainly know again, crept under one of the beds to reach the window; but as I got from under the bed, I heard some one crying; and looking up, while I was still upon my knees, I saw *you*—most assuredly you—as I see you now; a beautiful young lady, with golden hair and large blue eyes, and lips—your lips—you, as you are here. Your looks won me; I climbed on the bed and put my arms about you, and I think we both fell asleep. I was aroused by a scream; you were sitting up screaming. I was frightened, and slipped down upon the ground, and, it seemed to me, lost consciousness for a moment; and when I came to myself, I was again in my nursery at home. Your face I have never forgotten since. I could not be misled by mere resemblance. You *are* the lady whom I then saw."

It was now my turn to relate my corresponding vision, which I did, to the undisguised wonder of my new acquaintance.

"I don't know which should be most afraid of the other," she said, again smiling. "If you were less pretty I think I should be very much afraid of you, but being as you are, and you and I both so young, I feel only that I have made your acquaintance twelve years ago, and have already a right to your intimacy; at all events, it does seem as if we were destined, from our earliest childhood, to be friends. I wonder whether you feel as strangely drawn toward me as I do to you; I have never had a friend—shall I find one now?" She sighed, and her fine dark eyes gazed passionately on me.

Now the truth is, I felt rather unaccountably toward the beautiful stranger. I did feel, as she said, "drawn toward her," but there was also something of repulsion. In this ambiguous feeling, however, the sense of attraction immensely prevailed. She interested and won me, she was so beautiful and so indescribably engaging.

I perceived now something of languor and exhaustion stealing over her, and hastened to bid her good-night.

"The doctor thinks," I added, "that you ought to have a maid to sit up with you to-night; one of ours is waiting, and you will find her a very useful and quiet creature."

"How kind of you, but I could not sleep, I never could with an attendant in the room. I shan't require any assistance—and, shall I confess my weakness, I am haunted with a terror of robbers. Our house was robbed once, and two servants murdered, so I always lock my door. It has become a habit—and you look so kind I know you will forgive me. I see there is a key in the lock."

She held me close in her pretty arms for a moment and whispered in my ear, "Good-night, darling, it is very hard to part with you, but good-night; to-morrow, but not early, I shall see you again."

She sank back on the pillow with a sigh, and her fine eyes followed me with a fond and melancholy gaze, and she murmured again "Good-night, dear friend."

Young people like, and even love, on impulse. I was flattered by the evident, though as yet undeserved, fondness she showed me. I liked the confidence with which she at once received me. She was determined that we should be very dear friends.

Next day came and we met again. I was delighted with my companion; that is to say, in many respects.

Her looks lost nothing in daylight—she was certainly the most beautiful creature I had ever seen, and the unpleasant remembrance of the face presented in my early dream, had lost the effect of the first unexpected recognition.

She confessed that she had experienced a similar shock on seeing me, and precisely the same faint antipathy that had mingled with my admiration of her. We now laughed together over our momentary horrors.

IV. HER HABITS—A SAUNTER

I told you that I was charmed with her in most particulars.

There were some that did not please me so well.

She was above the middle height of women. I shall begin by describing her. She was slender, and wonderfully graceful. Except that her movements were languid—*very* languid—indeed, there was nothing in her appearance to indicate an invalid. Her complexion was rich and brilliant; her features were small and beautifully formed; her eyes large, dark, and lustrous; her hair was quite wonderful, I never saw hair so magnificently thick and long when it was down about her shoulders; I have often placed my hands under it, and laughed with wonder at its weight. It was exquisitely fine and soft, and in color a rich very dark brown, with something of gold. I loved to let it down, tumbling with its own weight, as, in her room, she lay back in her chair talking in her sweet low voice, I used to fold and braid it, and spread it out and play with it. Heavens! If I had but known all!

I said there were particulars which did not please me. I have told you that her confidence won me the first night I saw her; but I found that she exercised with respect to herself, her mother, her history, everything in fact connected with her life, plans, and people, an ever-wakeful reserve. I dare say I was unreasonable, perhaps I was wrong; I dare say I ought to have respected the solemn injunction laid upon my father by the stately lady in black velvet. But curiosity is a restless and unscrupulous passion, and no one girl can endure, with patience, that hers should be baffled by another. What harm could it do anyone to tell me what I so ardently desired to know? Had she no trust in my good sense or honor? Why would she not believe me when I assured her, so solemnly, that I would not divulge one syllable of what she told me to any mortal breathing.

There was a coldness, it seemed to me, beyond her years, in her smiling melancholy persistent refusal to afford me the least ray of light.

I cannot say we quarreled upon this point, for she would not quarrel upon any. It was, of course, very unfair of me to press her, very ill-bred, but I really could not help it; and I might just as well have let it alone.

What she did tell me amounted, in my unconscionable estimation—to nothing.

It was all summed up in three very vague disclosures:

First.—Her name was Carmilla.

Second.—Her family was very ancient and noble.

Third.—Her home lay in the direction of the west.

She would not tell me the name of her family, nor their armorial bearings, nor the name of their estate, nor even that of the country they lived in.

You are not to suppose that I worried her incessantly on these subjects. I watched opportunity, and rather insinuated than urged my inquiries. Once or twice, indeed, I did attack her more directly. But no matter what my tactics, utter failure was invariably the result. Reproaches and caresses were all lost upon her. But I must add this, that her evasion was conducted with so pretty a melancholy and deprecation, with so many, and even passionate declarations of her liking for me, and trust in my honor, and with so many promises that I should at last know all, that I could not find it in my heart long to be offended with her.

She used to place her pretty arms about my neck, draw me to her, and laying her cheek to mine, murmur with her lips near my ear, "Dearest, your little heart is wounded; think me not cruel because I obey the irresistible law of my strength and weakness; if your dear heart is wounded, my wild heart bleeds with yours. In the rapture of my enormous humiliation I live in your warm life, and you shall die—die, sweetly die—into mine. I cannot help it; as I draw near to you, you, in your turn, will draw near to others, and learn the rapture of that cruelty, which yet is love; so, for a while, seek to know no more of me and mine, but trust me with all your loving spirit."

And when she had spoken such a rhapsody, she would press me more closely in her trembling embrace, and her lips in soft kisses gently glow upon my cheek.

Her agitations and her language were unintelligible to me.

From these foolish embraces, which were not of very frequent occurrence, I must allow, I used to wish to extricate myself; but my energies seemed to fail me. Her murmured words sounded like a lullaby in my ear, and soothed my resistance into a trance, from which I only seemed to recover myself when she withdrew her arms.

In these mysterious moods I did not like her. I experienced a strange tumultuous excitement that was pleasurable, ever and anon, mingled with a vague sense of fear and disgust. I had no distinct thoughts about her while such scenes lasted, but I was conscious of a love growing into adoration, and also of abhorrence. This I know is paradox, but I can make no other attempt to explain the feeling.

I now write, after an interval of more than ten years, with a trembling hand, with a confused and horrible recollection of certain occurrences and situations, in the ordeal through which I was unconsciously passing; though with a vivid and very sharp remembrance of the main current of my story. But, I suspect, in all lives there are certain emotional scenes, those in which our passions have been most wildly and terribly roused, that are of all others the most vaguely and dimly remembered.

Sometimes after an hour of apathy, my strange and beautiful companion would take my hand and hold it with a fond pressure, renewed again and again; blushing softly, gazing in my face with languid and burning eyes, and breathing so fast that her dress rose and fell with the tumultuous respiration. It was like the ardor of a lover; it embarrassed me; it was hateful and yet overpowering; and with gloating eyes she drew me to her, and her hot lips traveled along my cheek in kisses; and she would whisper, almost in sobs, "You are mine, you *shall* be mine, and you and I are one forever." Then she has thrown herself back in her chair, with her small hands over her eyes, leaving me trembling.

"Are we related," I used to ask; "what can you mean by all this? I remind you perhaps of some one whom you love; but you must not, I hate it; I don't know you—I don't know myself when you look so and talk so."

She used to sigh at my vehemence, then turn away and drop my hand.

Respecting these very extraordinary manifestations I strove in vain to form any satisfactory theory—I could not refer them to affectation or trick. It was unmistakably the momentary breaking out of suppressed instinct and emotion. Was she, notwithstanding her mother's volunteered denial, subject to brief visitations of insanity; or was there here a disguise and a romance? I had read in old story books of such things. What if a boyish lover had found his way into the house, and sought to prosecute his suit in masquerade, with the assistance of a clever old adventuress. But there were many things against this hypothesis, highly interesting as it was to my vanity.

I could boast of no little attentions such as masculine gallantry delights to offer. Between these passionate moments there were long intervals of commonplace, of gaiety, of brooding melancholy, during which, except that I detected her eyes so full of melancholy fire, following me, at times I might have been as nothing to her. Except in their brief periods of mysterious excitement her ways were girlish; and there was always a languor about her, quite incompatible with a masculine system in a state of health.

In some respects her habits were odd. Perhaps not so singular in the opinion of a town lady like you, as they appeared to us rustic people. She used to come down very late, generally not till one o'clock, she would then take a cup of chocolate, but eat nothing; we then went out for a walk, which was a mere saunter, and she seemed, almost immediately, exhausted, and either returned to the schloss or sat on one of the benches that were placed, here and there, among the trees. This was a bodily languor in which her mind did not sympathize. She was always an animated talker, and very intelligent.

She sometimes alluded for a moment to her own home, or mentioned an adventure or situation, or an early recollection, which indicated a people of strange manners, and described customs of which we knew nothing. I gathered from these chance hints that her native country was much more remote than I had at first fancied.

As we sat thus one afternoon under the trees a funeral passed us by. It was that of a pretty young girl, whom I had often seen, the daughter of one of the rangers of the forest. The poor man was walking behind the coffin of his darling; she was his only child, and he looked quite heartbroken. Peasants walking two-and-two came behind, they were singing a funeral hymn.

I rose to mark my respect as they passed, and joined in the hymn they were very sweetly singing.

My companion shook me a little roughly, and I turned surprised.

She said brusquely, "Don't you perceive how discordant that is?"

"I think it very sweet, on the contrary," I answered, vexed at the interruption, and very uncomfortable, lest the people who composed the little procession should observe and resent what was passing.

I resumed, therefore, instantly, and was again interrupted. "You pierce my ears," said Carmilla, almost angrily, and stopping her ears with her tiny fingers. "Besides, how can you tell that your religion and mine are the same; your forms wound me, and I hate funerals. What a fuss! Why, *you* must die— *everyone* must die; and all are happier when they do. Come home."

"My father has gone on with the clergyman to the churchyard. I thought you knew she was to be buried to-day."

"*She*? I don't trouble my head about peasants. I don't know who she is," answered Carmilla, with a flash from her fine eyes.

"She is the poor girl who fancied she saw a ghost a fortnight ago, and has been dying ever since, till yesterday, when she expired."

"Tell me nothing about ghosts. I shan't sleep to-night if you do."

"I hope there is no plague or fever coming; all this looks very like it," I continued. "The swineherd's young wife died only a week ago, and she thought something seized her by the throat as she lay in her bed, and nearly strangled her. Papa says such horrible fancies do accompany some forms of fever. She was quite well the day before. She sank afterward, and died before a week."

"Well, *her* funeral is over, I hope, and *her* hymn sung; and our ears shan't be tortured with that discord and jargon. It has made me nervous. Sit down here, beside me; sit close; hold my hand; press it hard—hard—harder."

We had moved a little back, and had come to another seat.

She sat down. Her face underwent a change that alarmed and even terrified me for a moment. It darkened, and became horribly livid; her teeth and hands were clenched, and she frowned and compressed her lips, while she stared down upon the ground at her feet, and trembled all over with a continued shudder as irrepressible as ague. All her energies seemed strained to suppress a fit, with which she was then breathlessly tugging; and at length a low convulsive cry of suffering broke from her, and gradually the hysteria subsided. "There! That comes of strangling people with hymns!" she said at last. "Hold me, hold me still. It is passing away."

And so gradually it did; and perhaps to dissipate the somber impression which the spectacle had left upon me, she became unusually animated and chatty; and so we got home.

This was the first time I had seen her exhibit any definable symptoms of that delicacy of health which her mother had spoken of. It was the first time, also, I had seen her exhibit anything like temper.

Both passed away like a summer cloud; and never but once afterward did I witness on her part a momentary sign of anger. I will tell you how it happened.

She and I were looking out of one of the long drawing-room windows, when there entered the courtyard, over the drawbridge, a figure of a wanderer whom I knew very well. He used to visit the schloss generally twice a year.

It was the figure of a hunchback, with the sharp lean features that generally accompany deformity. He wore a pointed black beard, and he was smiling from ear to ear, showing his white fangs. He was dressed in buff, black, and scarlet, and crossed with more straps and belts than I could count, from which hung all manner of things. Behind, he carried a magic-lantern, and two boxes, which I well knew, in one of which was a salamander, and in the other a mandrake. These monsters used to make my father laugh. They were compounded of parts of monkeys, parrots, squirrels, fish, and hedgehogs, dried and stitched together with great neatness and startling effect. He had a fiddle, a box of conjuring apparatus, a pair of foils and masks attached to his belt, several other mysterious cases dangling about him, and a black staff with copper ferrules in his hand. His companion was a rough spare dog, that followed at his heels, but stopped short, suspiciously at the drawbridge, and in a little while began to howl dismally.

In the meantime, the mountebank, standing in the midst of the courtyard, raised his grotesque hat, and made us a very ceremonious bow, paying his compliments very volubly in execrable French, and German not much better. Then, disengaging his fiddle, he began to scrape a lively air, to which he sang with a merry discord, dancing with ludicrous airs and activity, that made me laugh, in spite of the dog's howling.

Then he advanced to the window with many smiles and salutations, and his hat in his left hand, his fiddle under his arm, and with a fluency that never took breath, he grabbed a long advertisement of all his accomplishments, and the resources of the various arts which he placed at our service, and the curiosities and entertainments which it was in his power, at our bidding to display.

"Will your ladyships be pleased to buy an amulet against the oupire, which is going like the wolf, I hear, through these woods," he said, dropping his hat on the pavement. "They are dying of it right and left, and here is a charm that never fails; only pinned to the pillow, and you may laugh in his face."

These charms consisted of oblong slips of vellum, with cabalistic ciphers and diagrams upon them.

Carmilla instantly purchased one, and so did I.

He was looking up, and we were smiling down upon him, amused; at least, I can answer for myself. His piercing black eye, as he looked up in our faces, seemed to detect something that fixed for a moment his curiosity.

In an instant he unrolled a leather case, full of all manner of odd little steel instruments.

"See here, my lady," he said, displaying it, and addressing me, "I profess, among other things less useful, the art of dentistry. Plague take the dog!" he interpolated. "Silence, beast! He howls so that your ladyships can scarcely hear a word. Your noble friend, the young lady at your right, has the sharpest tooth—long, thin, pointed, like an awl, like a needle; ha, ha! With my sharp and long sight, as I look up, I have seen it distinctly; now if it happens to hurt the young lady, and I think it must, here am I, here are my file, my punch, my nippers; I will make it round and blunt, if her ladyship pleases; no longer the tooth of a fish, but of a beautiful young lady as she is. Hey? Is the young lady displeased? Have I been too bold? Have I offended her?"

The young lady, indeed, looked very angry as she drew back from the window.

"How dares that mountebank insult us so? Where is your father? I shall demand redress from him. My father would have had the wretch tied up to the pump, and flogged with a cartwhip, and burnt to the bones with the castle brand!"

She retired from the window a step or two, and sat down, and had hardly lost sight of the offender, when her wrath subsided as suddenly as it had risen, and she gradually recovered her usual tone, and seemed to forget the little hunchback and his follies.

My father was out of spirits that evening. On coming in he told us that there had been another case very similar to the two fatal ones which had lately occurred. The sister of a young peasant on his estate, only a mile away, was very ill, had been, as she described it, attacked very nearly in the same way, and was now slowly but steadily sinking.

"All this," said my father, "is strictly referable to natural causes. These poor people infect one another with their superstitions, and so repeat in imagination the images of terror that have infested their neighbors."

"But that very circumstance frightens one horribly," said Carmilla.

"How so?" inquired my father.

"I am so afraid of fancying I see such things; I think it would be as bad as reality."

"We are in God's hands; nothing can happen without His permission, and all will end well for those who love Him. He is our faithful creator; He has made us all, and will take care of us."

"Creator! *Nature!*" said the young lady in answer to my gentle father. "And this disease that invades the country is natural. Nature. All things spring from nature—don't they? All things in the Heaven, in the earth, and under the earth, act and live as nature ordains? I think so."

"The doctor said he would come here to-day," said my father, after a silence. "I want to know what he thinks about it, and what he thinks we had better do."

"Doctors never did me any good," said Carmilla.

"Then you have been ill?" I asked.

"More ill than ever you were," she answered.

"Long ago?"

"Yes, a long time. I suffered from this very illness; but I forget all but my pain and weaknesses, and they were not so bad as are suffered in other diseases."

"You were very young then?"

"I dare say; let us talk no more of it. You would not wound a friend?" She looked languidly in my eyes, and passed her arm round my waist lovingly, and led me out of the room. My father was busy over some papers near the window.

"Why does your papa like to frighten us?" said the pretty girl, with a sigh and a little shudder.

"He doesn't, dear Carmilla, it is the very furthest thing from his mind."

"Are you afraid, dearest?"

"I should be very much if I fancied there was any real danger of my being attacked as those poor people were."

"You are afraid to die?"

"Yes, every one is."

"But to die as lovers may—to die together, so that they may live together. Girls are caterpillars while they live in the world, to be finally butterflies when the summer comes; but in the meantime there are grubs and larvæ, don't you see— each with their peculiar propensities, necessities, and structure. So says Monsieur Buffon,[4] in his big book, in the next room."

Later in the day the doctor came, and was closeted with papa for some time. He was a skilful man, of sixty and upwards, he wore powder, and shaved his pale face as smooth as a pumpkin. He and papa emerged from the room together, and I heard papa laugh, and say as they came out:

[4] George Louis Leclerc, comte de Buffon (1707-1788) was a French naturalist whose lifetime work was his *Histoire naturelle* in forty-four volumes (1749-1804).

"Well, I do wonder at a wise man like you. What do you say to hippogriffs and dragons?"

The doctor was smiling, and made answer, shaking his head—

"Nevertheless, life and death are mysterious states, and we know little of the resources of either."

And so they walked on, and I heard no more. I did not then know what the doctor had been broaching, but I think I guess it now.

V. A WONDERFUL LIKENESS

THIS evening there arrived from Gratz the grave, dark-faced son of the picture-cleaner, with a horse and cart laden with two large packing-cases, having many pictures in each. It was a journey of ten leagues, and whenever a messenger arrived at the schloss from our little capital of Gratz, we used to crowd about him in the hall, to hear the news.

This arrival created in our secluded quarters quite a sensation. The cases remained in the hall, and the messenger was taken charge of by the servants till he had eaten his supper. Then with assistants, and armed with hammer, ripping chisel, and turnscrew, he met us in the hall, where we had assembled to witness the unpacking of the cases.

Carmilla sat looking listlessly on, while one after the other the old pictures, nearly all portraits, which had undergone the process of renovation, were brought to light. My mother was of an old Hungarian family, and most of these pictures, which were about to be restored to their places, had come to us through her.

My father had a list in his hand, from which he read, as the artist rummaged out the corresponding numbers. I don't know that the pictures were very good, but they were undoubtedly very old, and some of them very curious also. They had, for the most part, the merit of being now seen by me, I may say, for the first time; for the smoke and dust of time had all but obliterated them.

"There is a picture that I have not seen yet," said my father. "In one corner, at the top of it, is the name, as well as I could read, 'Marcia Karnstein,' and the date '1698'; and I am curious to see how it has turned out."

I remembered it; it was a small picture, about a foot and a

half high, and nearly square, without a frame; but it was so
blackened by age that I could not make it out.

The artist now produced it, with evident pride. It was quite
beautiful; it was startling; it seemed to live. It was the effigy
of Carmilla!

"Carmilla, dear, here is an absolute miracle. Here you are,
living, smiling, ready to speak, in this picture. Isn't it beautiful, papa? And see, even the little mole on her throat."

My father laughed, and said "Certainly it is a wonderful
likeness," but he looked away, and to my surprise seemed but
little struck by it, went on talking to the picture-cleaner, who
was also something of an artist, and discoursed with intelligence about the portraits or other works, which his art had
just brought into light and color, while I was more and more
lost in wonder the more I looked at the picture.

"Will you let me hang this picture in my room, papa?" I
asked.

"Certainly, dear," said he, smiling, "I'm very glad you think
it so like. It must be prettier even than I thought it, if it is."

The young lady did not acknowledge this pretty speech, did
not seem to hear it. She was leaning back in her seat, her fine
eyes under their long lashes gazing on me in contemplation,
and she smiled in a kind of rapture.

"And now you can read quite plainly the name that is written in the corner. It is not Marcia; it looks as if it was done
in gold. The name is Mircalla, Countess Karnstein, and this
is a little coronet over it, and underneath A.D. 1698. I am
descended from the Karnsteins; that is, mamma was."

"Ah!" said the lady, languidly, "so am I, I think, a very
long descent, very ancient. Are there any Karnsteins living
now?"

"None who bear the name, I believe. The family were
ruined, I believe, in some civil wars, long ago, but the ruins
of the castle are only about three miles away."

"How interesting!" she said, languidly. "But see what beautiful moonlight!" She glanced through the hall door, which
stood a little open. "Suppose you take a little ramble round
the court, and look down at the road and river."

"It is so like the night you came to us," I said.

She sighed, smiling.

She rose, and each with her arm about the other's waist, we
walked out upon the pavement.

In silence, slowly we walked down to the drawbridge, where the beautiful landscape opened before us.

"And so you were thinking of the night I came here?" she almost whispered. "Are you glad I came?"

"Delighted, dear Carmilla," I answered.

"And you ask for the picture you think like me, to hang in your room," she murmured with a sigh, as she drew her arm closer about my waist, and let her pretty head sink upon my shoulder.

"How romantic you are, Carmilla," I said. "Whenever you tell me your story, it will be made up chiefly of some one great romance."

She kissed me silently.

"I am sure, Carmilla, you have been in love; that there is, at this moment, an affair of the heart going on."

"I have been in love with no one, and never shall," she whispered, "unless it should be with you."

How beautiful she looked in the moonlight!

Shy and strange was the look with which she quickly hid her face in my neck and hair, with tumultuous sighs, that seemed almost to sob, and pressed in mine a hand that trembled.

Her soft cheek was glowing against mine. "Darling, darling," she murmured, "I live in you; and you would die for me, I love you so."

I started from her.

She was gazing on me with eyes from which all fire, all meaning had flown, and a face colorless and apathetic.

"Is there a chill in the air, dear?" she said drowsily. "I almost shiver; have I been dreaming? Let us come in. Come, come; come in."

"You look ill, Carmilla; a little faint. You certainly must take some wine," I said.

"Yes, I will. I'm better now. I shall be quite well in a few minutes. Yes, do give me a little wine," answered Carmilla, as we approached the door. "Let us look again for a moment; it is the last time, perhaps, I shall see the moonlight with you."

"How do you feel now, dear Carmilla? Are you really better?" I asked.

I was beginning to take alarm, lest she should have been stricken with the strange epidemic that they said had invaded the country about us.

"Papa would be grieved beyond measure," I added, "if he thought you were ever so little ill, without immediately letting us know. We have a very skilful doctor near this, the physician who was with papa today."

"I'm sure he is. I know how kind you all are; but, dear child, I am quite well again. There is nothing ever wrong with me, but a little weakness. People say I am languid; I am incapable of exertion; I can scarcely walk as far as a child of three years old; and every now and then the little strength I have falters, and I become as you have just seen me. But after all I am very easily set up again; in a moment I am perfectly myself. See how I have recovered."

So, indeed, she had; and she and I talked a great deal, and very animated she was; and the remainder of that evening passed without any recurrence of what I called her infatuations. I mean her crazy talk and looks, which embarrassed, and even frightened me.

But there occurred that night an event which gave my thoughts quite a new turn, and seemed to startle even Carmilla's languid nature into momentary energy.

VI. A VERY STRANGE AGONY

WHEN we got into the drawing-room, and had sat down to our coffee and chocolate, although Carmilla did not take any, she seemed quite herself again and madame, and Mademoiselle De Lafontaine, joined us, and made a little card party, in the course of which papa came in for what he called his "dish of tea."

When the game was over he sat down beside Carmilla on the sofa, and asked her, a little anxiously, whether she had heard from her mother since her arrival.

She answered "No."

He then asked her whether she knew where a letter would reach her at present.

"I cannot tell," she answered, ambiguously, "but I have been thinking of leaving you; you have been already too hospitable and too kind to me. I have given you an infinity of trouble, and I should wish to take a carriage to-morrow, and post in pursuit of her; I know where I shall ultimately find her, although I dare not tell you."

"But you must not dream of any such thing," exclaimed my father, to my great relief. "We can't afford to lose you so, and I won't consent to your leaving us, except under the care

of your mother, who was so good as to consent to your remaining with us till she should herself return. I should be quite
happy if I knew that you heard from her; but this evening
the accounts of the progress of the mysterious disease that has
invaded our neighborhood, grow even more alarming; and my
beautiful guest, I do feel the responsibility, unaided by advice
from your mother, very much. But I shall do my best; and
one thing is certain, that you must not think of leaving us
without her distinct direction to that effect. We should suffer
too much in parting from you to consent to it easily."

"Thank you, sir, a thousand times for your hospitality," she
answered, smiling bashfully. "You have all been too kind to
me; I have seldom been so happy in all my life before, as in
your beautiful château, under your care, and in the society of
your dear daughter."

So he gallantly, in his old-fashioned way, kissed her hand,
smiling, and pleased at her little speech.

I accompanied Carmilla as usual to her room, and sat and
chatted with her while she was preparing for bed.

"Do you think," I said, at length, "that you will ever confide
fully in me?"

She turned round smiling, but made no answer, only continued to smile on me.

"You won't answer that?" I said. "You can't answer pleasantly; I ought not to have asked you."

"You were quite right to ask me that, or anything. You do
not know how dear you are to me, or you could not think any
confidence too great to look for. But I am under vows, no nun
half so awfully, and I dare not tell my story yet, even to you.
The time is very near when you shall know everything. You
will think me cruel, very selfish, but love is always selfish;
the more ardent the more selfish. How jealous I am you cannot
know. You must come with me, loving me, to death; or else
hate me, and still come with me, and *hating* me through death
and after. There is no such word as indifference in my apathetic nature."

"Now, Carmilla, you are going to talk your wild nonsense
again," I said hastily.

"Not I, silly little fool as I am, and full of whims and
fancies; for your sake I'll talk like a sage. Were you ever at
a ball?"

"No; how you do run on. What is it like? How charming
it must be."

"I almost forget, it is years ago."

I laughed.

"You are not so old. Your first ball can hardly be forgotten yet."

"I remember everything about it—with an effort. I see it all, as divers see what is going on above them, through a medium, dense, rippling, but transparent. There occurred that night what has confused the picture, and made its colors faint. I was all but assassinated in my bed, wounded *here*," she touched her breast, "and never was the same since."

"Were you near dying?"

"Yes, very—a cruel love—strange love, that would have taken my life. Love will have its sacrifices. No sacrifice without blood. Let us go to sleep now; I feel so lazy. How can I get up just now and lock my door?"

She was lying with her tiny hands buried in her rich wavy hair, under her cheek, her little head upon the pillow, and her glittering eyes followed me wherever I moved, with a kind of shy smile that I could not decipher.

I bid her good-night, and crept from the room with an uncomfortable sensation.

I often wondered whether our pretty guest ever said her prayers. *I* certainly had never seen her upon her knees. In the morning she never came down until long after our family prayers were over, and at night she never left the drawing-room to attend our brief evening prayers in the hall.

If it had not been that it had casually come out in one of our careless talks that she had been baptised, I should have doubted her being a Christian. Religion was a subject on which I had never heard her speak a word. If I had known the world better, this particular neglect or antipathy would not have so much surprised me.

The precautions of nervous people are infectious, and persons of a like temperament are pretty sure, after a time, to imitate them. I had adopted Carmilla's habit of locking her bedroom door, having taken into my head all her whimsical alarms about midnight invaders, and prowling assassins. I had also adopted her precaution of making a brief search through her room, to satisfy herself that no lurking assassin or robber was "ensconced."

These wise measures taken, I got into my bed and fell asleep. A light was burning in my room. This was an old habit, of very early date, and which nothing could have tempted me to dispense with.

Thus fortified I might take my rest in peace. But dreams come through stone walls, light up dark rooms, or darken light ones, and their persons make their exits and their entrances as they please, and laugh at locksmiths.

I had a dream that night that was the beginning of a very strange agony.

I cannot call it a nightmare, for I was quite conscious of being asleep. But I was equally conscious of being in my room, and lying in bed, precisely as I actually was. I saw, or fancied I saw, the room and its furniture just as I had seen it last, except that it was very dark, and I saw something moving round the foot of the bed, which at first I could not accurately distinguish. But I soon saw that it was a sooty-black animal that resembled a monstrous cat. It appeared to me about four or five feet long, for it measured fully the length of the hearth-rug as it passed over it; and it continued to-ing and fro-ing with the lithe sinister restlessness of a beast in a cage. I could not cry out, although as you may suppose, I was terrified. Its pace was growing faster, and the room rapidly darker and darker, and at length so dark that I could no longer see anything of it but its eyes. I felt it spring lightly on the bed. The two broad eyes approached my face, and suddenly I felt a stinging pain as if two large needles darted, an inch or two apart, deep into my breast. I waked with a scream. The room was lighted by the candle that burned there all through the night, and I saw a female figure standing at the foot of the bed, a little at the right side. It was in a dark loose dress, and its hair was down and covered its shoulders. A block of stone could not have been more still. There was not the slightest stir of respiration. As I stared at it, the figure appeared to have changed its place, and was now nearer the door; then, close to it, the door opened, and it passed out.

I was now relieved, and able to breathe and move. My first thought was that Carmilla had been playing me a trick, and that I had forgotten to secure my door. I hastened to it, and found it locked as usual on the inside. I was afraid to open it—I was horrified. I sprang into my bed and covered my head up in the bedclothes, and lay there more dead than alive till morning.

VII. DESCENDING

IT would be vain my attempting to tell you the horror with which, even now, I recall the occurrence of that night. It was no such transitory terror as a dream leaves behind it. It seemed to deepen by time, and communicated itself to the room and the very furniture that had encompassed the apparition.

I could not bear next day to be alone for a moment. I should have told papa, but for two opposite reasons. At one time I thought he would laugh at my story, and I could not bear its being treated as a jest; and at another, I thought he might fancy that I had been attacked by the mysterious complaint which had invaded our neighborhood. I had myself no misgivings of the kind, and as he had been rather an invalid for some time, I was afraid of alarming him.

I was comfortable enough with my good-natured companions, Madame Perrodon, and the vivacious Mademoiselle Lafontaine. They both perceived that I was out of spirits and nervous, and at length I told them what lay so heavy at my heart.

Mademoiselle laughed, but I fancied that Madame Perrodon looked anxious.

"By-the-by," said mademoiselle, laughing, "the long lime tree walk, behind Carmilla's bedroom window, is haunted!"

"Nonsense!" exclaimed madame, who probably thought the theme rather inopportune, "and who tells that story, my dear?"

"Martin says that he came up twice, when the old yard-gate was being repaired before sunrise, and twice saw the same female figure walking down the lime tree avenue."

"So he well might, as long as there are cows to milk in the river fields," said madame.

"I daresay; but Martin chooses to be frightened, and never did I see fool *more* frightened."

"You must not say a word about it to Carmilla, because she can see down that walk from her room window," I interposed, "and she is, if possible, a greater coward than I."

Carmilla came down rather later than usual that day.

"I was so frightened last night," she said, so soon as we were together, "and I am sure I should have seen something dreadful if it had not been for that charm I bought from the poor little hunchback whom I called such hard names. I had a dream of something black coming round my bed, and I awoke in a perfect horror, and I really thought, for some seconds, I saw a dark figure near the chimney piece, but I felt under my pillow for my charm, and the moment my fingers touched it, the figure disappeared, and I felt quite certain, only that I had it by me, that something frightful would have made its appearance, and, perhaps, throttled me, as it did those poor people we heard of."

"Well, listen to me," I began, and recounted my adventure, at the recital of which she appeared horrified.

"And had you the charm near you?" she asked earnestly.

"No, I had dropped it into a china vase in the drawing-room, but I shall certainly take it with me to-night, as you have so much faith in it."

At this distance of time I cannot tell you, or even understand, how I overcame my horror so effectually as to lie alone in my room that night. I remember distinctly that I pinned the charm to my pillow. I fell asleep almost immediately, and slept even more soundly than usual all night.

Next night I passed as well. My sleep was delightfully deep and dreamless. But I wakened with a sense of lassitude and melancholy, which, however, did not exceed a degree that was almost luxurious.

"Well, I told you so," said Carmilla, when I described my quiet sleep, "I had such delightful sleep myself last night; I pinned the charm to the breast of my nightdress. It was too far away the night before. I am quite sure it was all fancy, except the dreams. I used to think that evil spirits made dreams, but our doctor told me it is no such thing. Only a fever passing by, or some other malady, as they often do, he said, knocks at the door, and not being able to get in, passes on, with that alarm."

"And what do you think the charm is?" said I.

"It has been fumigated or immersed in some drug, and is an antidote against the malaria," she answered.

"Then it acts only on the body?"

"Certainly; you don't suppose that evil spirits are frightened by bits of ribbon, or the perfumes of a druggist's shop? No, these complaints, wandering in the air, begin by trying the nerves, and so infect the brain; but before they can seize upon you, the antidote repels them. That I am sure is what the

charm has done for us. It is nothing magical, it is simply
natural."

I should have been happier if I could quite have agreed
with Carmilla, but I did my best, and the impression was a
little losing its force.

For some nights I slept profoundly; but still every morning
I felt the same lassitude, and a languor weighed upon me all
day. I felt myself a changed girl. A strange melancholy was
stealing over me, a melancholy that I would not have interrupted. Dim thoughts of death began to open, and an idea
that I was slowly sinking took gentle, and, somehow, not
unwelcome possession of me. If it was sad, the tone of mind
which this induced was also sweet. Whatever it might be, my
soul acquiesced in it.

I would not admit that I was ill, I would not consent to tell
my papa, or to have the doctor sent for.

Carmilla became more devoted to me than ever, and her
strange paroxysms of languid adoration more frequent. She
used to gloat on me with increasing ardor the more my
strength and spirits waned. This always shocked me like a
momentary glare of insanity.

Without knowing it, I was now in a pretty advanced stage
of the strangest illness under which mortal ever suffered. There
was an unaccountable fascination in its earlier symptoms that
more than reconciled me to the incapacitating effect of that
stage of the malady. This fascination increased for a time,
until it reached a certain point, when gradually a sense of the
horrible mingled itself with it, deepening as you shall hear,
until it discolored and perverted the whole state of my life.

The first change I experienced was rather agreeable. It was
very near the turning point from which began the descent of
Avernus.[5]

Certain vague and strange sensations visited me in my sleep.
The prevailing one was of that pleasant, peculiar cold thrill
which we feel in bathing, when we move against the current
of a river. This was soon accompanied by dreams that seemed
interminable, and were so vague that I could never recollect
their scenery and persons, or any one connected portion of
their action. But they left an awful impression, and a sense
of exhaustion, as if I had passed through a long period of
great mental exertion and danger. After all these dreams there

[5] Sulphuric lake through which both Odysseus and Aeneas entered the lower
regions; thus it is synonymous with Hell.

remained on waking a remembrance of having been in a place very nearly dark, and of having spoken to people whom I could not see; and especially of one clear voice, of a female's, very deep, that spoke as if at a distance, slowly, and producing always the same sensation of indescribable solemnity and fear. Sometimes there came a sensation as if a hand was drawn softly along my cheek and neck. Sometimes it was as if warm lips kissed me, and longer and more lovingly as they reached my throat, but there the caress fixed itself. My heart beat faster, my breathing rose and fell rapidly and full drawn; a sobbing, that rose into a sense of strangulation, supervened, and turned into a dreadful convulsion, in which my senses left me, and I became unconscious.

It was now three weeks since the commencement of this unaccountable state. My sufferings had, during the last week, told upon my appearance. I had grown pale, my eyes were dilated and darkened underneath, and the languor which I had long felt began to display itself in my countenance.

My father asked me often whether I was ill; but, with an obstinacy which now seems to me unaccountable, I persisted in assuring him that I was quite well.

In a sense this was true. I had no pain, I could complain of no bodily derangement. My complaint seemed to be one of the imagination, or the nerves, and, horrible as my sufferings were, I kept them, with a morbid reserve, very nearly to myself.

It could not be that terrible complaint which the peasants call the oupire, for I had now been suffering for three weeks, and they were seldom ill for much more than three days, when death put an end to their miseries.

Carmilla complained of dreams and feverish sensations, but by no means of so alarming a kind as mine. I say that mine were extremely alarming. Had I been capable of comprehending my condition, I would have invoked aid and advice on my knees. The narcotic of an unsuspected influence was acting upon me, and my perceptions were benumbed.

I am going to tell you now of a dream that led immediately to an odd discovery.

One night, instead of the voice I was accustomed to hear in the dark, I heard one, sweet and tender, and at the same time terrible, which said, "Your mother warns you to beware of the assassin." At the same time a light unexpectedly sprang up, and I saw Carmilla, standing near the foot of my bed, in her white nightdress, bathed, from her chin to her feet, in one great stain of blood.

I wakened with a shriek, possessed with the one idea that Carmilla was being murdered. I remember springing from my bed, and my next recollection is that of standing on the lobby, crying for help.

Madame and mademoiselle came scurrying out of their rooms in alarm; a lamp burned always in the lobby, and seeing me, they soon learned the cause of my terror.

I insisted on our knocking at Carmilla's door. Our knocking was unanswered. It soon became a pounding and an uproar. We shrieked her name, but all was vain.

We all grew frightened, for the door was locked. We hurried back, in panic, to my room. There we rang the bell long and furiously. If my father's room had been at that side of the house, we would have called him up at once to our aid. But, alas! he was quite out of hearing, and to reach him involved an excursion for which we none of us had courage.

Servants, however, soon came running up the stairs; I had got on my dressing-gown and slippers meanwhile, and my companions were already similarly furnished. Recognizing the voices of the servants on the lobby, we sallied out together; and having renewed, as fruitlessly, our summons at Carmilla's door, I ordered the men to force the lock. They did so, and we stood, holding our lights aloft, in the doorway, and so stared into the room.

We called her by name; but there was still no reply. We looked round the room. Everything was undisturbed. It was exactly in the state in which I left it on bidding her good night. But Carmilla was gone.

VIII. SEARCH

At sight of the room, perfectly undisturbed except for our violent entrance, we began to cool a little, and soon recovered our senses sufficiently to dismiss the men. It had struck mademoiselle that possibly Carmilla had been wakened by the uproar at her door, and in her first panic had jumped from her bed, and hid herself in a press, or behind a curtain, from which she could not, of course, emerge until the majordomo and his myrmidons had withdrawn. We now recommenced our search, and began to call her by name again.

It was all to no purpose. Our perplexity and agitation increased. We examined the windows, but they were secured. I implored of Carmilla, if she had concealed herself, to play this cruel trick no longer—to come out, and to end our anxieties. It was all useless. I was by this time convinced that she was not in the room, nor in the dressing-room, the door of which was still locked on this side. She could not have passed it. I was utterly puzzled. Had Carmilla discovered one of those secret passages which the old housekeeper said were known to exist in the schloss, although the tradition of their exact situation had been lost. A little time would, no doubt, explain all—utterly perplexed as, for the present, we were.

It was past four o'clock, and I preferred passing the remaining hours of darkness in madame's room. Daylight brought no solution of the difficulty.

The whole household, with my father at its head, was in a state of agitation next morning. Every part of the château was searched. The grounds were explored. Not a trace of the missing lady could be discovered. The stream was about to be dragged; my father was in distraction; what a tale to have to tell the poor girl's mother on her return. I, too, was almost beside myself, though my grief was quite of a different kind.

The morning was passed in alarm and excitement. It was now one o'clock, and still no tidings. I ran up to Carmilla's room, and found her standing at her dressing-table. I was astounded. I could not believe my eyes. She beckoned me to her with her pretty finger, in silence. Her face expressed extreme fear.

I ran to her in an ecstasy of joy; I kissed and embraced her again and again. I ran to the bell and rang it vehemently, to bring others to the spot, who might at once relieve my father's anxiety.

"Dear Carmilla, what has become of you all this time? We have been in agonies of anxiety about you," I exclaimed. "Where have you been? How did you come back?"

"Last night has been a night of wonders," she said.

"For mercy's sake, explain all you can."

"It was past two last night," she said, "when I went to sleep as usual in my bed, with my doors locked, that of the dressing-room, and that opening upon the gallery. My sleep was uninterrupted, and, so far as I know, dreamless; but I awoke just now on the sofa in the dressing-room there, and I found the door between the rooms open, and the other door forced.

How could all this have happened without my being wakened?
It must have been accompanied with a great deal of noise,
and I am particularly easily wakened; and how could I have
been carried out of my bed without my sleep having been
interrupted, I whom the slightest stir startles?"

By this time, madame, mademoiselle, my father, and a number of the servants were in the room. Carmilla was, of course,
overwhelmed with inquiries, congratulations, and welcomes.
She had but one story to tell, and seemed the least able of all
the party to suggest any way of accounting for what had
happened.

My father took a turn up and down the room, thinking.
I saw Carmilla's eye follow him for a moment with a sly, dark
glance.

When my father had sent the servants away, mademoiselle
having gone in search of a little bottle of valerian and sal-
volatile,[6] and there being no one now in the room with
Carmilla except my father, madame, and myself, he came to
her thoughtfully, took her hand very kindly, led her to the
sofa, and sat down beside her.

"Will you forgive me, my dear, if I risk a conjecture, and
ask a question?"

"Who can have a better right?" she said. "Ask what you
please, and I will tell you everything. But my story is simply
one of bewilderment and darkness. I know absolutely nothing.
Put any question you please. But you know, of course, the
limitations mamma has placed me under."

"Perfectly, my dear child. I need not approach the topics
on which she desires our silence. Now, the marvel of last night
consists in your having been removed from your bed and your
room without being wakened, and this removal having occurred apparently while the windows were still secured, and
the two doors locked upon the inside. I will tell you my
theory, and first ask you a question."

Carmilla was leaning on her hand dejectedly; madame and
I were listening breathlessly.

"Now, my question is this. Have you ever been suspected
of walking in your sleep?"

"Never since I was very young indeed."

"But you did walk in your sleep when you were young?"

"Yes; I know I did. I have been told so often by my old
nurse."

[6] Valerian is an herb used as a sedative; sal-volatile is smelling salts.

My father smiled and nodded.

"Well, what has happened is this. You got up in your sleep, unlocked the door, not leaving the key, as usual, in the lock, but taking it out and locking it on the outside; you again took the key out, and carried it away with you to some one of the five-and-twenty rooms on this floor, or perhaps upstairs or downstairs. There are so many rooms and closets, so much heavy furniture, and such accumulations of lumber, that it would require a week to search this old house thoroughly. Do you see, now, what I mean?"

"I do, but not all," she answered.

"And how, papa, do you account for her finding herself on the sofa in the dressing-room, which we had searched so carefully?"

"She came there after you had searched it, still in her sleep, and at last awoke spontaneously, and was as much surprised to find herself where she was as any one else. I wish all mysteries were as easily and innocently explained as yours, Carmilla," he said, laughing. "And so we may congratulate ourselves on the certainty that the most natural explanation of the occurrence is one that involves no drugging, no tampering with locks, no burglars, or poisoners, or witches—nothing that need alarm Carmilla, or any one else, for our safety."

Carmilla was looking charmingly. Nothing could be more beautiful than her tints. Her beauty was, I think, enhanced by that graceful languor that was peculiar to her. I think my father was silently contrasting her looks with mine, for he said:—

"I wish my poor Laura was looking more like herself," and he sighed.

So our alarms were happily ended, and Carmilla restored to her friends.

IX. THE DOCTOR

As Carmilla would not hear of an attendant sleeping in her room, my father arranged that a servant should sleep outside her door, so that she could not attempt to make another such excursion without being arrested at her own door.

That night passed quietly; and next morning early, the doctor, whom my father had sent for without telling me a word about it, arrived to see me.

Madame accompanied me to the library; and there the grave little doctor, with white hair and spectacles, whom I mentioned before, was waiting to receive me.

I told him my story, and as I proceeded he grew graver and graver.

We were standing, he and I, in the recess of one of the windows, facing one another. When my statement was over, he leaned with his shoulders against the wall, and with his eyes fixed on me earnestly, with an interest in which was a dash of horror.

After a minute's reflection, he asked madame if he could see my father.

He was sent for accordingly, and as he entered, smiling, he said:

"I dare say, doctor, you are going to tell me that I am an old fool for having brought you here; I hope I am."

But his smile faded into shadow as the doctor, with a very grave face, beckoned him to him.

He and the doctor talked for some time in the same recess where I had just conferred with the physician. It seemed an earnest and argumentative conversation. The room is very large, and I and madame stood together, burning with curiosity, at the further end. Not a word could we hear, however, for they spoke in a very low tone, and the deep recess of the window quite concealed the doctor from view, and very nearly my father, whose foot, arm, and shoulder only could we see; and the voices were, I suppose, all the less audible for the sort of closet which the thick wall and window formed.

After a time my father's face looked into the room; it was pale, thoughtful, and, I fancied, agitated.

"Laura, dear, come here for a moment. Madame, we shan't trouble you, the doctor says, at present."

Accordingly I approached, for the first time a little alarmed; for, although I felt very weak, I did not feel ill; and strength, one always fancies, is a thing that may be picked up when we please.

My father held out his hand to me as I drew near, but he was looking at the doctor, and he said:

"It certainly *is* very odd; I don't understand it quite. Laura, come here, dear; now attend to Doctor Spielsberg, and recollect yourself."

"You mentioned a sensation like that of two needles piercing the skin, somewhere about your neck, on the night when you experienced your first horrible dream. Is there still any soreness?"

"None at all," I answered.

"Can you indicate with your finger about the point at which you think this occurred?"

"Very little below my throat—*here*," I answered.

I wore a morning dress, which covered the place I pointed to.

"Now you can satisfy yourself," said the doctor. "You won't mind your papa's lowering your dress a very little. It is necessary, to detect a symptom of the complaint under which you have been suffering."

I acquiesced. It was only an inch or two below the edge of my collar.

"God bless me!—so it is," exclaimed my father, growing pale.

"You see it now with your own eyes," said the doctor, with a gloomy triumph.

"What is it?" I exclaimed, beginning to be frightened.

"Nothing, my dear young lady, but a small blue spot, about the size of the tip of your little finger; and now," he continued, turning to papa, "the question is what is best to be done?"

"Is there any danger?" I urged, in great trepidation.

"I trust not, my dear," answered the doctor. "I don't see why you should not recover. I don't see why you should not begin *immediately* to get better. That is the point at which the sense of strangulation begins?"

"Yes," I answered.

"And—recollect as well as you can—the same point was a kind of center of that thrill which you described just now, like the current of a cold stream running against you?"

"It may have been; I think it was."

"Ay, you see?" he added, turning to my father. "Shall I say a word to madame?"

"Certainly," said my father.

He called madame to him, and said:

"I find my young friend here far from well. It won't be of any great consequence, I hope; but it will be necessary that some steps be taken, which I will explain by-and-by; but in the meantime, madame, you will be so good as not to let Miss Laura be alone for one moment. That is the only direction I need give for the present. It is indispensable."

"We may rely upon your kindness, madame, I know," added my father.

Madame satisfied him eagerly.

"And you, dear Laura, I know you will observe the doctor's direction."

"I shall have to ask your opinion upon another patient, whose symptoms slightly resemble those of my daughter, that have just been detailed to you—very much milder in degree, but I believe quite of the same sort. She is a young lady—our guest; but as you say you will be passing this way again this evening, you can't do better than take your supper here, and you can then see her. She does not come down till the afternoon."

"I thank you," said the doctor. "I shall be with you, then, at about seven this evening."

And then they repeated their directions to me and to madame, and with this parting charge my father left us, and walked out with the doctor; and I saw them pacing together up and down between the road and the moat, on the grassy platform in front of the castle, evidently absorbed in earnest conversation.

The doctor did not return. I saw him mount his horse there, take his leave, and ride away eastward through the forest. Nearly at the same time I saw the man arrive from Dranfeld with the letters, and dismount and hand the bag to my father.

In the meantime, madame and I were both busy, lost in conjecture as to the reasons of the singular and earnest direction which the doctor and my father had concurred in imposing. Madame, as she afterward told me, was afraid the doctor apprehended a sudden seizure, and that, without prompt assistance, I might either lose my life in a fit, or at least be seriously hurt.

This interpretation did not strike me; and I fancied, perhaps luckily for my nerves, that the arrangement was prescribed simply to secure a companion, who would prevent my taking too much exercise, or eating unripe fruit, or doing any of the fifty foolish things to which young people are supposed to be prone.

About half-an-hour after my father came in—he had a letter in his hand—and said:

"This letter had been delayed; it is from General Spielsdorf. He might have been here yesterday, he may not come till to-morrow, or he may be here today."

He put the open letter into my hand; but he did not look pleased, as he used when a guest, especially one so much loved as the General, was coming. On the contrary, he looked as if he wished him at the bottom of the Red Sea. There was plainly something on his mind which he did not choose to divulge.

"Papa, darling, will you tell me this?" said I, suddenly laying my hand on his arm, and looking, I am sure, imploringly in his face.

"Perhaps," he answered, smoothing my hair caressingly over my eyes.

"Does the doctor think me very ill?"

"No, dear; he thinks, if right steps are taken, you will be quite well again, at least on the high road to a complete recovery, in a day or two," he answered, a little drily. "I wish our good friend, the General, had chosen any other time; that is, I wish you had been perfectly well to receive him."

"But do tell me, Papa," I insisted, "*what* does he think is the matter with me?"

"Nothing; you must not plague me with questions," he answered, with more irritation than I ever remember him to have displayed before; and seeing that I looked wounded, I suppose, he kissed me, and added, "You shall know all about it in a day or two; that is, all that *I* know. In the meantime, you are not to trouble your head about it."

He turned and left the room, but came back before I had done wondering and puzzling over the oddity of all this; it was merely to say that he was going to Karnstein, and had ordered the carriage to be ready at twelve, and that I and madame should accompany him; he was going to see the priest who lived near those picturesque grounds upon business, and as Carmilla had never seen them, she could follow, when she came down, with mademoiselle, who would bring materials for what you call a pic-nic, which might be laid for us in the ruined castle.

At twelve o'clock, accordingly, I was ready, and not long after, my father, madame and I set out upon our projected drive. Passing the drawbridge we turn to the right, and follow the road over the steep Gothic bridge, westward, to reach the deserted village and ruined castle of Karnstein.

No sylvan drive can be fancied prettier. The ground breaks into gentle hills and hollows, all clothed with beautiful wood, totally destitute of the comparative formality which artificial planting and early culture and pruning impart.

The irregularities of the ground often lead the road out of its course, and cause it to wind beautifully round the sides of broken hollows and the steeper sides of the hills, among varieties of ground almost inexhaustible.

Turning one of these points, we suddenly encountered our old friend, the General, riding toward us, attended by a mounted servant. His portmanteaus were following in a hired wagon, such as we term a cart.

The General dismounted as we pulled up, and, after the usual greetings, was easily persuaded to accept the vacant seat in the carriage, and send his horse on with his servant to the schloss.

X. BEREAVED

IT was about ten months since we had last seen him; but that time had sufficed to make an alteration of years in his appearance. He had grown thinner; something of gloom and anxiety had taken the place of that cordial serenity which used to characterize his features. His dark blue eyes, always penetrating, now gleamed with a sterner light from under his shaggy gray eyebrows. It was not such a change as grief alone usually induces, and angrier passions seemed to have had their share in bringing it about.

We had not long resumed our drive, when the General began to talk, with his usual soldierly directness, of the bereavement, as he termed it, which he had sustained in the death of his beloved niece and ward; and he then broke out in a tone of intense bitterness and fury, inveighing against the "hellish arts" to which she had fallen a victim, and expressing, with more exasperation than piety, his wonder that Heaven should tolerate so monstrous an indulgence of the lusts and malignity of Hell.

My father, who saw at once that something very extraordinary had befallen, asked him, if not too painful to him, to retail the circumstances which he thought justified the strong terms in which he expressed himself.

"I should tell you all with pleasure," said the General, "but you would not believe me."

"Why should I not?" he asked.

"Because," he answered testily, "you believe in nothing but what consists with your own prejudices and illusions. I remember when I was like you, but I have learned better."

"Try me," said my father; "I am not such a dogmatist as you suppose. Besides which, I very well know that you generally require proof for what you believe, and am, therefore, very strongly predisposed to respect your conclusions."

"You are right in supposing that I have not been led lightly into a belief in the marvelous—for what I have experienced *is* marvelous—and I have been forced by extraordinary evidence to credit that which ran counter, diametrically, to all my theories. I have been made the dupe of a preternatural conspiracy."

Notwithstanding his professions of confidence in the General's penetration, I saw my father, at this point, glance at the General, with, as I thought, a marked suspicion of his sanity.

The General did not see it, luckily. He was looking gloomily and curiously into the glades and vistas of the woods that were opening before us.

"You are going to the Ruins of Karnstein?" he said. "Yes, it is a lucky coincidence; do you know I was going to ask you to bring me there to inspect them. I have a special object in exploring. There is a ruined chapel, ain't there, with a great many tombs of that extinct family?"

"So there are—highly interesting," said my father. "I hope you are thinking of claiming the title and estates?"

My father said this gaily, but the General did not recollect the laugh, or even the smile, which courtesy exacts for a friend's joke; on the contrary, he looked grave and even fierce, ruminating on a matter that stirred his anger and horror.

"Something very different," he said, gruffly. "I mean to unearth some of those fine people. I hope, by God's blessing, to accomplish a pious sacrilege here, which will relieve our earth of certain monsters, and enable honest people to sleep in their beds without being assailed by murderers. I have strange things to tell you, my dear friend, such as I myself would have scouted as incredible a few months since."

My father looked at him again, but this time not with a glance of suspicion—with an eye, rather, of keen intelligence and alarm.

"The house of Karnstein," he said, "has been long extinct: a hundred years at least. My dear wife was maternally descended from the Karnsteins. But the name and title have long ceased to exist. The castle is a ruin; the very village is deserted; it is fifty years since the smoke of a chimney was seen there; not a roof left."

"Quite true. I have heard a great deal about that since I last saw you; a great deal that will astonish you. But I had better relate everything in the order in which it occurred," said the General. "You saw my dear ward—my child, I may call her. No creature could have been more beautiful, and only three months ago none more blooming."

"Yes, poor thing! When I saw her last she certainly was quite lovely," said my father. "I was grieved and shocked more than I can tell you, my dear friend; I knew what a blow it was to you."

He took the General's hand, and they exchanged a kind pressure. Tears gathered in the old soldier's eyes. He did not seek to conceal them. He said:

"We have been very old friends; I knew you would feel for me, childless as I am. She had become an object of very dear interest to me, and repaid my care by an affection that cheered my home and made my life happy. That is all gone. The years that remain to me on earth may not be very long; but by God's mercy I hope to accomplish a service to mankind before I die, and to subserve the vengeance of Heaven upon the fiends who have murdered my poor child in the spring of her hopes and beauty!"

"You said, just now, that you intended relating everything as it occurred," said my father. "Pray do; I assure you that it is not mere curiosity that prompts me."

By this time we had reached the point at which the Drunstall road, by which the General had come, diverges from the road which we were traveling to Karnstein.

"How far is it to the ruins?" inquired the General, looking anxiously forward.

"About half a league," answered my father. "Pray let us hear the story you were so good as to promise."

XI. THE STORY

"With all my heart," said the General, with an effort; and after a short pause in which to arrange his subject, he commenced one of the strangest narratives I ever heard.

"My dear child was looking forward with great pleasure to the visit you had been so good as to arrange for her to your charming daughter." Here he made me a gallant but melancholy bow. "In the meantime we had an invitation to my old friend the Count Carlsfeld, whose schloss is about six leagues to the other side of Karnstein. It was to attend the series of fêtes which, you remember, were given by him in honor of his illustrious visitor, the Grand Duke Charles."

"Yes; and very splendid, I believe, they were," said my father.

"Princely! But then his hospitalities are quite regal. He has Aladdin's lamp. The night from which my sorrow dates was devoted to a magnificent masquerade. The grounds were thrown open, the trees hung with colored lamps. There was such a display of fireworks as Paris itself had never witnessed. And such music—music, you know, is my weakness—such ravishing music! The finest instrumental band, perhaps, in the world, and the finest singers who could be collected from all the great operas in Europe. As you wandered through these fantastically illuminated grounds, the moon-lighted château throwing a rosy light from its long rows of windows, you would suddenly hear these ravishing voices stealing from the silence of some grove, or rising from boats upon the lake. I felt myself, as I looked and listened, carried back into the romance and poetry of my early youth.

"When the fireworks were ended, and the ball beginning, we returned to the noble suite of rooms that were thrown open to the dancers. A masked ball, you know, is a beautiful sight; but so brilliant a spectacle of the kind I never saw before.

"It was a very aristocratic assembly. I was myself almost the only 'nobody' present.

"My dear child was looking quite beautiful. She wore no mask. Her excitement and delight added an unspeakable charm to her features, always lovely. I remarked a young lady, dressed magnificently, but wearing a mask, who appeared to me to be observing my ward with extraordinary interest. I had seen her, earlier in the evening, in the great hall, and again, for a few minutes, walking near us, on the terrace under the castle windows, similarly employed. A lady, also masked, richly and gravely dressed, and with a stately air, like a person of rank, accompanied her as a chaperon. Had the young lady not worn a mask, I could, of course, have been much more certain upon the question whether she was really watching my poor darling. I am now well assured that she was.

"We were now in one of the *salons*. My poor dear child had been dancing, and was resting a little in one of the chairs near the door; I was standing near. The two ladies I have mentioned had approached, and the younger took the chair next my ward; while her companion stood beside me, and for a little time addressed herself, in a low tone, to her charge.

"Availing herself of the privilege of her mask, she turned to me, and in the tone of an old friend, and calling me by my name, opened a conversation with me, which piqued my curiosity a good deal. She referred to many scenes where she had met me—at Court, and at distinguished houses. She alluded to little incidents which I had long ceased to think of, but which, I found, had only lain in abeyance in my memory, for they instantly started into life at her touch.

"I became more and more curious to ascertain who she was, every moment. She parried my attempts to discover very adroitly and pleasantly. The knowledge she showed of many passages in my life seemed to me all but unaccountable; and she appeared to take a not unnatural pleasure in foiling my curiosity, and in seeing me flounder in my eager perplexity, from one conjecture to another.

"In the meantime the young lady, whom her mother called by the odd name of Millarca, when she once or twice addressed her, had, with the same ease and grace, got into conversation with my ward.

"She introduced herself by saying that her mother was a very old acquaintance of mine. She spoke of the agreeable audacity which a mask rendered practicable; she talked like a friend; she admired her dress, and insinuated very prettily her admiration of her beauty. She amused her with laughing criticisms upon the people who crowded the ballroom, and laughed at my poor child's fun. She was very witty and lively when she pleased, and after a time they had grown very good friends, and the young stranger lowered her mask, displaying a remarkably beautiful face. I had never seen it before, neither had my dear child. But though it was new to us, the features were so engaging, as well as lovely, that it was impossible not to feel the attraction powerfully. My poor child did so. I never saw anyone more taken with another at first sight, unless, indeed, it was the stranger herself, who seemed quite to have lost her heart to her.

"In the meantime, availing myself of the license of a masquerade, I put not a few questions to the elder lady.

" 'You have puzzled me utterly,' I said, laughing. 'Is that not enough? Won't you, now, consent to stand on equal terms, and do me the kindness to remove your mask?'

" 'Can any request be more unreasonable?' she replied. 'Ask a lady to yield an advantage! Beside, how do you know you should recognize me? Years make changes.'

" 'As you see,' I said, with a bow, and, I suppose, a rather melancholy little laugh.

" 'As philosophers tell us,' she said; 'and how do you know that a sight of my face would help you?'

" 'I should take chance for that,' I answered. 'It is vain trying to make yourself out an old woman; your figure betrays you.'

" 'Years, nevertheless, have passed since I saw you, rather since you saw me, for that is what I am considering. Millarca, there, is my daughter; I cannot then be young, even in the opinion of people whom time has taught to be indulgent, and I may not like to be compared with what you remember me. You have no mask to remove. You can offer me nothing in exchange.'

" 'My petition is to your pity, to remove it.'

" 'And mine to yours, to let it stay where it is,' she replied.

" 'Well, then, at least you will tell me whether you are French or German; you speak both languages so perfectly.'

" 'I don't think I shall tell you that, General; you intend a surprise, and are meditating the particular point of attack.'

" 'At all events, you won't deny this,' I said, 'that being honored by your permission to converse, I ought to know how to address you. Shall I say Madame la Comtesse?'

"She laughed, and she would, no doubt, have met me with another evasion—if, indeed, I can treat any occurrence in an interview every circumstance of which was prearranged, as I now believe, with the profoundest cunning, as liable to be modified by accident.

" 'As to that,' she began; but she was interrupted, almost as she opened her lips, by a gentleman, dressed in black, who looked particularly elegant and distinguished, with this drawback, that his face was the most deadly pale I ever saw, except in death. He was in no masquerade—in the plain evening dress of a gentleman; and he said without a smile, but with a courtly and unusually low bow:—

" 'Will Madame la Comtesse permit me to say a very few words which may interest her?'

"The lady turned quickly to him, and touched her lip in token of silence; she then said to me, 'Keep my place for me, General; I shall return when I have said a few words.'

"And with this injunction, playfully given, she walked a little aside with the gentleman in black, and talked for some minutes, apparently very earnestly. They then walked away slowly together in the crowd, and I lost them for some minutes.

"I spent the interval in cudgeling my brains for conjecture as to the identity of the lady who seemed to remember me so kindly, and I was thinking of turning about and joining in the conversation between my pretty ward and the Countess's daughter, and trying whether, by the time she returned, I might not have a surprise in store for her, by having her name, title, château, and estates at my fingers' ends. But at this moment she returned, accompanied by the pale man in black, who said:

" 'I shall return and inform Madame la Comtesse when her carriage is at the door.'

"He withdrew with a bow."

XII. A PETITION

" 'Then we are to lose Madame la Comtesse, but I hope only for a few hours,' I said, with a low bow.

" 'It may be that only, or it may be a few weeks. It was very unlucky his speaking to me just now as he did. Do you now know me?"

"I assured her I did not.

" 'You shall know me,' she said, 'but not at present. We are older and better friends than, perhaps, you suspect. I cannot yet declare myself. I shall in three weeks pass your beautiful schloss about which I have been making inquiries. I shall then look in upon you for an hour or two, and renew a friendship which I never think of without a thousand pleasant recollections. This moment a piece of news has reached me like a thunderbolt. I must set out now, and travel by a devious route, nearly a hundred miles, with all the dispatch I can possibly make. My perplexities multiply. I am only deterred by the compulsory reserve I practice as to my name from making a very singular request of you. My poor child has not quite recovered her strength. Her horse fell with her, at a hunt which she had ridden out to witness, her nerves have not yet recovered the shock, and our physician says that she must on no account exert herself for some time to come. We came here, in consequence, by very easy stages—hardly six leagues a day. I must now travel day and night, on a mission of life and death—a mission the critical and momentous nature of which I shall be able to explain to you when we meet, as I hope we shall, in a few weeks, without the necessity of any concealment.'

"She went on to make her petition, and it was in the tone of a person from whom such a request amounted to conferring, rather than seeking a favor. This was only in manner, and, as it seemed, quite unconsciously. Than the terms in which it was expressed, nothing could be more deprecatory. It was simply that I would consent to take charge of her daughter during her absence.

"This was, all things considered, a strange, not to say, an audacious request. She in some sort disarmed me, by stating and admitting everything that could be urged against it, and throwing herself entirely upon my chivalry. At the same moment, by a fatality that seems to have predetermined all that happened, my poor child came to my side, and, in an undertone, besought me to invite her new friend, Millarca, to pay us a visit. She had just been sounding her, and thought, if her mamma would allow her, she would like it extremely.

"At another time I should have told her to wait a little, until, at least, we knew who they were. But I had not a moment to think in. The two ladies assailed me together, and I must confess the refined and beautiful face of the young lady, about which there was something extremely engaging, as well as the elegance and fire of high birth, determined me; and quite overpowered, I submitted, and undertook too easily, the care of the young lady, whom her mother called Millarca.

"The Countess beckoned to her daughter, who listened with grave attention while she told her, in general terms, how suddenly and peremptorily she had been summoned, and also of the arrangement she had made for her under my care, adding that I was one of her earliest and most valued friends.

"I made, of course, such speeches as the case seemed to call for, and found myself, on reflection, in a position which I did not half like.

"The gentleman in black returned, and very ceremoniously conducted the lady from the room.

"The demeanor of this gentleman was such as to impress me with the conviction that the Countess was a lady of very much more importance than her modest title alone might have led me to assume.

"Her last charge to me was that no attempt was to be made to learn more about her than I might have already guessed, until her return. Our distinguished host, whose guest she was, knew her reasons.

"'But here,' she said, 'neither I nor my daughter could safely remain for more than a day. I removed my mask imprudently for a moment, about an hour ago, and, too late, I fancied you saw me. So I resolved to seek an opportunity of talking a little to you. Had I found that you *had* seen me, I should have thrown myself on your high sense of honor to keep my secret for some weeks. As it is, I am satisfied that you did not see me; but if you now *suspect*, or, on reflection, *should* suspect, who I am, I commit myself, in like manner, entirely to your honor. My daughter will observe the same secrecy, and I well know that you will, from time to time, remind her, lest she should thoughtlessly disclose it.'

"She whispered a few words to her daughter, kissed her hurriedly twice, and went away, accompanied by the pale gentleman in black, and disappeared in the crowd.

"'In the next room,' said Millarca, 'there is a window that looks upon the hall door. I should like to see the last of mamma, and to kiss my hand to her.'

"We assented, of course, and accompanied her to the window. We looked out, and saw a handsome old-fashioned carriage, with a troop of couriers and footmen. We saw the slim figure of the pale gentleman in black, as he held a thick velvet cloak, and placed it about her shoulders and threw the hood over her head. She nodded to him, and just touched his hand with hers. He bowed low repeatedly as the door closed, and the carriage began to move.

"'She is gone,' said Millarca, with a sigh.

"'She is gone,' I repeated to myself, for the first time—in the hurried moments that had elapsed since my consent—reflecting upon the folly of my act.

"'She did not look up,' said the young lady, plaintively.

"'The Countess had taken off her mask, perhaps, and did not care to show her face,' I said; 'and she could not know that you were in the window.'

"She sighed and looked in my face. She was so beautiful that

I relented. I was sorry I had for a moment repented of my hospitality, and I determined to make her amends for the unavowed churlishness of my reception.

"The young lady, replacing her mask, joined my ward in persuading me to return to the grounds, where the concert was soon to be renewed. We did so, and walked up and down the terrace that lies under the castle windows. Millarca became very intimate with us, and amused us with lively descriptions and stories of most of her great people whom we saw upon the terrace. I liked her more and more every minute. Her gossip, without being ill-natured, was extremely diverting to me, who had been so long out of the great world. I thought what life she would give to our sometimes lonely evenings at home.

" 'This ball was not over until the morning sun had almost reached the horizon. It pleased the Grand Duke to dance till then, so loyal people could not go away, or think of bed.

"We had just got through a crowded saloon, when my ward asked me what had become of Millarca. I thought she had been by her side, and she fancied she was by mine. The fact was, we had lost her.

"All my efforts to find her were vain. I feared that she had mistaken, in the confusion of a momentary separation from us, other people for her new friends, and had, possibly, pursued and lost them in the extensive grounds which were thrown open to us.

"Now, in its full force, I recognized a new folly in my having undertaken the charge of a young lady without so much as knowing her name; and fettered as I was by promises, of the reasons for imposing which I knew nothing, I could not even point my inquiries by saying that the missing young lady was the daughter of the Countess who had taken her departure a few hours before.

"Morning broke. It was clear daylight before I gave up my search. It was not till near two o'clock next day that we heard anything of my missing charge.

"At about that time a servant knocked at my niece's door, to say that he had been earnestly requested by a young lady, who appeared to be in great distress, to make out where she could find the General Baron Spielsdorf and the young lady, his daughter, in whose charge she had been left by her mother.

"There could be no doubt, notwithstanding the slight inaccuracy, that our young friend had turned up; and so she had. Would to Heaven we had lost her!

"She told my poor child a story to account for her having failed to recover us for so long. Very late, she said, she had got into the housekeeper's bedroom in despair of finding us, and had then fallen into a deep sleep which, long as it was, had hardly sufficed to recruit her strength after the fatigues of the ball.

"That day Millarca came home with us. I was only too happy, after all, to have secured so charming a companion for my dear girl.

XIII. THE WOODMAN

"There soon, however, appeared some drawbacks. In the first place, Millarca complained of extreme languor—the weakness that remained after her late illness—and she never emerged from her room till the afternoon was pretty far advanced. In the next place, it was accidentally discovered, although she always locked her door on the inside, and never disturbed the key from its place, till she admitted the maid to assist at her toilet, that she was undoubtedly sometimes absent from her room in the very early morning, and at various times later in the day, before she wished it to be understood that she was stirring. She was repeatedly seen from the windows of the schloss, in the first faint gray of the morning, walking through the trees, in an easterly direction, and looking like a person in a trance. This convinced me that she walked in her sleep. But this hypothesis did not solve the puzzle. How did she pass out from her room, leaving the door locked on the inside. How did she escape from the house without unbarring door or window?

"In the midst of my perplexities, an anxiety of a far more urgent kind presented itself.

"My dear child began to lose her looks and health, and that in a manner so mysterious, and even horrible, that I became thoroughly frightened.

"She was at first visited by appalling dreams; then, as she fancied, by a specter sometimes resembling Millarca, sometimes in the shape of a beast, indistinctly seen, walking round the foot of her bed, from side to side. Lastly came sensations. One, not unpleasant, but very peculiar, she said, resembled the flow of an icy stream against her breast. At a later time, she felt something like a pair of large needles pierce her, a little below the throat, with a very sharp pain. A few nights after, followed a gradual and convulsive sense of strangulation; then came unconsciousness."

I could hear distinctly every word the kind old General was saying, because by this time we were driving upon the short grass that spreads on either side of the road as you approach the roofless village which had not shown the smoke of a chimney for more than half a century.

You may guess how strangely I felt as I heard my own symptoms so exactly described in those which had been experienced by the poor girl who, but for the catastrophe which followed, would have been at that moment a visitor at my father's château. You may suppose, also, how I felt as I heard him detail habits and mysterious peculiarities which were, in fact, those of our beautiful guest, Carmilla!

A vista opened in the forest; we were on a sudden under the chimneys and gables of the ruined village, and the towers and battlements of the dismantled castle, round which gigantic trees are grouped, overhung us from a slight eminence.

In a frightened dream I got down from the carriage, and in silence, for we had each abundant matter for thinking; we soon mounted the ascent, and were among the spacious chambers, winding stairs, and dark corridors of the castle.

"And this was once the palatial residence of the Karnsteins!" said the old General at length, as from a great window he looked out across the village, and saw the wide, undulating expanse of forest. "It was a bad family, and here its blood-stained annals were written," he continued. "It is hard that they should, after death, continue to plague the human race with their atrocious lusts. That is the chapel of the Karnsteins, down there."

He pointed down to the gray walls of the Gothic building, partly visible through the foliage, a little way down the steep. "And I hear the axe of a woodman," he added, "busy among the trees that surround it; he possibly may give us the information of which I am in search, and point out the grave of Mircalla, Countess of Karnstein. These rustics preserve the local traditions of great families, whose stories die out among the rich and titled so soon as the families themselves become extinct."

"We have a portrait, at home, of Mircalla, the Countess Karnstein; should you like to see it?" asked my father.

"Time enough, dear friend," replied the General. "I believe that I have seen the original; and one motive which has led me to you earlier than I at first intended, was to explore the chapel which we are now approaching."

"What! See the Countess Mircalla," exclaimed my father. "Why, she has been dead more than a century!"

"Not so dead as you fancy, I am told," answered the General.

"I confess, General, you puzzle me utterly," replied my father, looking at him, I fancied, for a moment with a return of the suspicion I detected before. But although there was anger and detestation, at times, in the old General's manner, there was nothing flighty.

"There remains to me," he said, as we passed under the heavy arch of the Gothic church—for its dimensions would have justified its being so styled—"but one object which can interest me during the few years that remain to me on earth, and that is to wreak on her the vengeance which, I thank God, may still be accomplished by a mortal arm."

"What vengeance can you mean?" asked my father, in increasing amazement.

"I mean, to decapitate the monster," he answered, with a fierce flush, and a stamp that echoed mournfully through the hollow ruin, and his clenched hand was at the same moment raised, as if it grasped the handle of an axe, while he shook it ferociously in the air.

"What!" exclaimed my father, more than ever bewildered.

"To strike her head off."

"Cut her head off?"

"Aye, with a hatchet, with a spade, or with anything that can cleave through her murderous throat. You shall hear," he answered, trembling with rage. And hurrying forward he said:

"That beam will answer for a seat; your dear child is fatigued; let her be seated, and I will, in a few sentences, close my dreadful story."

The squared block of wood, which lay on the grass-grown pavement of the chapel, formed a bench on which I was very glad to seat myself, and in the meantime the General called to the woodman, who had been removing some boughs which leaned upon the old walls; and, axe in hand, the hardy old fellow stood before us.

He could not tell us anything of these monuments; but there

was an old man, he said, a ranger of this forest, at present sojourning in the house of the priest, about two miles away, who could point out every monument of the old Karnstein family; and, for a trifle, he undertook to bring him back with him, if we would lend him one of our horses, in little more than half-an-hour.

"Have you been long employed about this forest?" asked my father of the old man.

"I have been a woodman here," he answered in his *patois*,[7] under the forester, all my days; so has my father before me, and so on, as many generations as I can count up. I could show you the very house in the village here, in which my ancestors lived."

"How came the village to be deserted?" asked the General.

"It was troubled by *revenants*,[8] sir; several were tracked to their graves, there detected by the usual tests, and extinguished in the usual way, by decapitation, by the stake, and by burning; but not until many of the villagers were killed.

"But after all these proceedings according to law," he continued—"so many graves opened, and so many vampires deprived of their horrible animation—the village was not relieved. But a Moravian nobleman, who happened to be traveling this way, heard how matters were, and being skilled —as many people are in his country—in such affairs, he offered to deliver the village from its tormentor. He did so thus: There being a bright moon that night, he ascended, shortly after sunset, the tower of the chapel here, from whence he could distinctly see the churchyard beneath him; you can see it from that window. From this point he watched until he saw the vampire come out of his grave, and place near it the linen clothes in which he had been folded, and glide away toward the village to plague its inhabitants.

"The stranger, having seen all this, came down from the steeple, took the linen wrappings of the vampire, and carried them up to the top of the tower, which he again mounted. When the vampire returned from his prowlings and missed his clothes, he cried furiously to the Moravian, whom he saw at the summit of the tower, and who, in reply, beckoned him to ascend and take them. Whereupon the vampire, accepting his invitation, began to climb the steeple, and so soon as he had reached the battlements, the Moravian, with a stroke of

[7] Provincial dialect.
[8] Ghosts.

his sword, clove his skull in twain, hurling him down to the churchyard, whither, descending by the winding stairs, the stranger followed and cut his head off, and next day delivered it and the body to the villagers, who duly impaled and burned them.

"This Moravian nobleman had authority from the then head of the family to remove the tomb of Mircalla, Countess Karnstein, which he did effectually, so that in a little while its site was quite forgotten."

"Can you point out where it stood?" asked the General, eagerly.

The forester shook his head and smiled.

"Not a soul living could tell you that now," he said; "besides, they say her body was removed; but no one is sure of that either."

Having thus spoken, as time pressed, he dropped his axe and departed, leaving us to hear the remainder of the General's strange story.

XIV. THE MEETING

"My beloved child," he resumed, "was now growing rapidly worse. The physician who attended her had failed to produce the slightest impression upon her disease, for such I then supposed it to be. He saw my alarm, and suggested a consultation. I called in an abler physician, from Gratz. Several days elapsed before he arrived. He was a good and pious, as well as a learned man. Having seen my poor ward together, they withdrew to my library to confer and discuss. I, from the adjoining room, where I waited their summons, heard these two gentlemen's voices raised in something sharper than a strictly philosophical discussion. I knocked at the door and entered. I found the old physician from Gratz maintaining his theory. His rival was combating it with undisguised ridicule, accompanied with bursts of laughter. This unseemly manifestation subsided and the altercation ended on my entrance.

" 'Sir,' said my first physician, 'my learned brother seems to think that you want a conjuror, and not a doctor.'

" 'Pardon me,' said the old physician from Gratz, looking displeased, 'I shall state my own view of the case in my own way another time. I grieve, Monsieur le General, that by my skill and science I can be of no use. Before I go I shall do myself the honor to suggest something to you.'

"He seemed thoughtful, and sat down at a table, and began to write. Profoundly disappointed, I made my bow, and as I turned to go, the other doctor pointed over his shoulder to his companion who was writing, and then, with a shrug, significantly touched his forehead.

"This consultation, then, left me precisely where I was. I walked out into the grounds, all but distracted. The doctor from Gratz, in ten or fifteen minutes, overtook me. He apologized for having followed me, but said that he could not conscientiously take his leave without a few words more. He told me that he could not be mistaken; no natural disease exhibited the same symptoms; and that death was already very near. There remained, however, a day, or possibly two, of life. If the fatal seizure were at once arrested, with great care and skill her strength might possibly return. But all hung now upon the confines of the irrevocable. One more assault might extinguish the last spark of vitality which is, every moment, ready to die.

"'And what is the nature of the seizure you speak of?' I entreated.

"'I have stated all fully in this note, which I place in your hands, upon the distinct condition that you send for the nearest clergyman, and open my letter in his presence, and on no account read it till he is with you; you would despise it else, and it is a matter of life and death. Should the priest fail you, then, indeed, you may read it.'

"He asked me, before taking his leave finally, whether I would wish to see a man curiously learned upon the very subject, which, after I had read his letter, would probably interest me above all others, and he urged me earnestly to invite him to visit him there; and so took his leave.

"The ecclesiastic was absent, and I read the letter by myself. At another time, or in another case, it might have excited my ridicule. But into what quackeries will not people rush for a last chance, where all accustomed means have failed, and the life of a beloved object is at stake?

"Nothing, you will say, could be more absurd than the learned man's letter. It was monstrous enough to have consigned him to a madhouse. He said that the patient was suffering from the visits of a vampire! The punctures which she described as having occurred near the throat were, he insisted, the insertion of those two long, thin, and sharp teeth which, it is well known, are peculiar to vampires; and there could be no doubt, he added, as to the well-defined presence of the small livid mark which all concurred in describing as that induced by the demon's lips, and every symptom described by the sufferer was in exact conformity with those recorded in every case of a similar visitation.

"Being myself wholly skeptical as to the existence of any such portent as the vampire, the supernatural theory of the good doctor furnished, in my opinion, but another instance of learning and intelligence oddly associated with some one hallucination. I was so miserable, however, that, rather than try nothing, I acted upon the instructions of the letter.

"I concealed myself in the dark dressing-room, that opened upon the poor patient's room, in which a candle was burning, and watched there till she was fast asleep. I stood at the door, peeping through the small crevice, my sword laid on the table beside me, as my directions prescribed, until, a little after one, I saw a large black object, very ill-defined, crawl, as it seemed to me, over the foot of the bed, and swiftly spread itself up to the poor girl's throat, where it swelled, in a moment, into a great, palpitating mass.

"For a few moments I had stood petrified. I now sprang forward, with my sword in my hand. The black creature suddenly contracted toward the foot of the bed, glided over it, and, standing on the floor about a yard below the foot of the bed, with a glare of skulking ferocity and horror fixed on me, I saw Millarca. Speculating I know not what, I struck at her instantly with my sword; but I saw her standing near the door, unscathed. Horrified, I pursued, and struck again. She was gone! And my sword flew to shivers against the door.

"I can't describe to you all that passed on that horrible night. The whole house was up and stirring. The specter Millarca was gone. But her victim was sinking fast, and before the morning dawned, she died."

The old General was agitated. We did not speak to him. My father walked to some little distance, and began reading the inscriptions on the tombstones; and thus occupied, he strolled into the door of a side chapel to prosecute his researches. The General leaned against the wall, dried his eyes, and sighed heavily. I was relieved on hearing the voices of Carmilla and madame, who were at that moment approaching. The voices died away.

In this solitude, having just listened to so strange a story, connected, as it was, with the great and titled dead, whose monuments were moldering among the dust and ivy round us, and every incident of which bore so awfully upon my own mysterious case—in this haunted spot, darkened by the towering foliage that rose on every side, dense and high above its noiseless walls—a horror began to steal over me, and my heart sank as I thought that my friends were, after all, not about to enter and disturb this triste and ominous scene.

The old General's eyes were fixed on the ground, as he leaned with his hand upon the basement of a shattered monument.

Under a narrow, arched doorway, surmounted by one of those demoniacal grotesques in which the cynical and ghastly fancy of old Gothic carving delights, I saw very gladly the beautiful face and figure of Carmilla enter the shadowy chapel.

I was just about to rise and speak, and nodded smiling, in answer to her peculiarly engaging smile; when with a cry, the old man by my side caught up the woodman's hatchet, and started forward. On seeing him a brutalized change came over her features. It was an instantaneous and horrible transformation, as she made a crouching step backward. Before I could utter a scream, he struck at her with all his force, but she dived under his blow, and unscathed, caught him in her tiny grasp by the wrist. He struggled for a moment to release his arm, but his hand opened, the axe fell to the ground, and the girl was gone.

He staggered against the wall. His gray hair stood upon his head, a moisture shone over his face, as if he were at the point of death.

The frightful scene had passed in a moment. The first thing I recollect after, is madame standing before me, and impatiently repeating again and again, the question, "Where is Mademoiselle Carmilla?"

I answered at length, "I don't know—I can't tell—she went there," and I pointed to the door through which madame had just entered; "only a minute or two since."

"But I have been standing there, in the passage, ever since Mademoiselle Carmilla entered; and she did not return."

She then began to call "Carmilla" through every door and passage and from the windows, but no answer came.

"She called herself Carmilla?" asked the General, still agitated.

"Carmilla, yes," I answered.

"Aye," he said, "that is Millarca. That is the same person who long ago was called Mircalla, Countess Karnstein. Depart from this accursed ground, my poor child, as quickly as you can. Drive to the clergyman's house, and stay there till we come. Begone! May you never behold Carmilla more; you will not find her here."

XV. ORDEAL AND EXECUTION

As he spoke one of the strangest-looking men I ever beheld, entered the chapel at the door through which Carmilla had made her entrance and her exit. He was tall, narrow-chested, stooping, with high shoulders, and dressed in black. His face was brown and dried in with deep furrows; he wore an oddly-shaped hat with a broad leaf. His hair, long and grizzled, hung on his shoulders. He wore a pair of gold spectacles, and walked slowly, with an odd shambling gait, with his face sometimes turned up to the sky, and sometimes bowed down toward the ground, seemed to wear a perpetual smile; his long thin arms were swinging, and his lank hands, in old black gloves ever so much too wide for them, waving and gesticulating in utter abstraction.

"The very man!" exclaimed the General, advancing with manifest delight. "My dear baron, how happy I am to see you, I had no hope of meeting you so soon." He signed to my father, who had by this time returned, and leading the fantastic old gentleman, whom he called the baron, to meet him. He introduced him formally, and they at once entered into earnest conversation. The stranger took a roll of paper from his pocket, and spread it on the worn surface of a tomb that stood by. He had a pencil case in his fingers, with which he traced imaginary lines from point to point on the paper, which from their often glancing from it, together, at certain points of the building, I concluded to be a plan of the chapel. He accompanied, what I may term his lecture, with occasional readings from a dirty little book, whose yellow leaves were closely written over.

They sauntered together down the side aisle, opposite to the spot where I was standing, conversing as they went; then they begun measuring distances by paces, and finally they all stood together, facing a piece of the side-wall, which they began to examine with great minuteness; pulling off the ivy that clung over it, and rapping the plaster with the ends of their sticks, scraping here, and knocking there. At length they ascertained the existence of a broad marble tablet, with letters carved in relief upon it.

With the assistance of the woodman, who soon returned, a monumental inscription, and carved escutcheon, were disclosed. They proved to be those of the long lost monument of Mircalla, Countess Karnstein.

The old General, though not I fear given to the praying mood, raised his hands and eyes to Heaven, in mute thanksgiving for some moments.

"Tomorrow," I heard him say, "the commissioner will be here, and the inquisition will be held according to law."

Then turning to the old man with the gold spectacles, whom I have described, he shook him warmly by both hands and said:

"Baron, how can I thank you? How can we all thank you? You will have delivered this region from a plague that has scourged its inhabitants for more than a century. The horrible enemy, thank God, is at last tracked."

My father led the stranger aside, and the General followed. I knew that he had led them out of hearing, that he might relate my case, and I saw them glance often quickly at me, as the discussion proceeded.

My father came to me, kissed me again and again, and leading me from the chapel, said:

"It is time to return, but before we go home, we must add to our party the good priest, who lives but a little way from this; and persuade him to accompany us to the schloss."

In this quest we were successful: and I was glad, being unspeakably fatigued when we reached home. But my satisfaction was changed to dismay, on discovering that there were no tidings of Carmilla. Of the scene that had occurred in the ruined chapel, no explanation was offered to me, and it was clear that it was a secret which my father for the present determined to keep from me.

The sinister absence of Carmilla made the remembrance of the scene more horrible to me. The arrangements for that night were singular. Two servants and madame were to sit up in my room that night; and the ecclesiastic with my father kept watch in the adjoining dressing-room.

The priest had performed certain solemn rites that night, the purport of which I did not understand any more than I comprehended the reason of this extraordinary precaution taken for my safety during sleep.

I saw all clearly a few days later.

The disappearance of Carmilla was followed by the discontinuance of my nightly sufferings.

You have heard, no doubt, of the appalling superstition that prevails in Upper and Lower Styria, in Moravia, Silesia, in Turkish Servia, in Poland, even in Russia; the superstition, so we must call it, of the vampire.

If human testimony, taken with every care and solemnity, judicially, before commissions innumerable, each consisting of many members, all chosen for integrity and intelligence, and constituting reports more voluminous perhaps than exist upon any one other class of cases, is worth anything, it is difficult to deny, or even to doubt the existence of such a phenomenon as the vampire.

For my part I have heard no theory by which to explain what I myself have witnessed and experienced, other than that supplied by the ancient and well-attested belief of the country.

The next day the formal proceedings took place in the Chapel of Karnstein. The grave of the Countess Mircalla was opened; and the General and my father recognized each his perfidious and beautiful guest, in the face now disclosed to view. The features, though a hundred and fifty years had passed since her funeral, were tinted with the warmth of life. Her eyes were open; no cadaverous smell exhaled from the coffin. The two medical men, one officially present, the other on the part of the promotor of the inquiry, attested the marvelous fact, that there was a faint but appreciable respiration, and a corresponding action of the heart. The limbs were perfectly flexible, the flesh elastic; and the leaden coffin floated with blood, in which to a depth of seven inches, the body lay immersed. Here then, were all the admitted signs and proofs of vampirism. The body, therefore, in accordance with the ancient practice, was raised, and a sharp stake driven through the heart of the vampire, who uttered a piercing shriek at the moment, in all respects such as might escape from a living person in the last agony. Then the head was struck off, and a torrent of blood flowed from the severed neck. The body and head were next placed on a pile of wood, and reduced to ashes, which were thrown upon the river and borne away, and that territory has never since been plagued by the visits of a vampire.

My father has a copy of the report of the Imperial Commission, with the signatures of all who were present at these proceedings, attached in verification of the statement. It is from this official paper that I have summarized my account of this last shocking scene.

XVI. CONCLUSION

I write all this you suppose with composure. But far from it; I cannot think of it without agitation. Nothing but your earnest desire so repeatedly expressed, could have induced me to sit down to a task that has unstrung my nerves for months to come, and reinduced a shadow of the unspeakable horror which years after my deliverance continued to make my days and nights dreadful, and solitude insupportably terrific.

Let me add a word or two about that quaint Baron Vordenburg, to whose curious lore we are indebted for the discovery of the Countess Mircalla's grave.

He had taken up his abode in Gratz, where, living upon a mere pittance, which was all that remained to him of the once princely estates of his family, in Upper Styria, he devoted himself to the minute and laborious investigation of the marvelously authenticated tradition of vampirism. He had at his fingers' ends all the great and little works upon the subject. *Magia Posthuma, Phlegon de Mirabilibus, Augustinus de curâ pro Mortuis, Philosophicæ et Christianæ Cogitationes de Vampiris,* by John Christofer Herenberg; and a thousand others, among which I remember only a few of those which he lent to my father. He had a voluminous digest of all the judicial cases, from which he had extracted a system of principles that appear to govern—some always, and others occasionally only—the condition of the vampire. I may mention, in passing, that the deadly pallor attributed to that sort of *revenants,* is a mere melodramatic fiction. They present, in the grave, and when they show themselves in human society, the appearance of healthy life. When disclosed to light in their coffins, they exhibit all the symptoms that are enumerated as those which proved the vampire-life of the long-dead Countess Karnstein.

How they escape from their graves and return to them for certain hours every day, without displacing the clay or leaving any trace of disturbance in the state of the coffin or the cerements, has always been admitted to be utterly inexplicable. The amphibious existence of the vampire is sustained by daily renewed slumber in the grave. Its horrible lust for living blood supplies the vigor of its waking existence. The vampire is prone to be fascinated with an engrossing vehemence, resembling the passion of love, by particular persons. In pursuit of these it will exercise inexhaustible patience and stratagem, for access to a particular object may be obstructed in a hundred ways. It will never desist until it has satiated its passion, and drained the very life of its coveted victim. But it will, in these cases, husband and protract its murderous enjoyment with the refinement of an epicure, and heighten it by the gradual approaches of an artful courtship. In these cases it seems to yearn for something like sympathy and consent. In ordinary ones it goes direct to its object, overpowers with violence, and strangles and exhausts often at a single feast.

The vampire is, apparently, subject, in certain situations, to special conditions. In the particular instance of which I have given you a relation, Mircalla seemed to be limited to a name which, if not her real one, should at least reproduce, without the omission or addition of a single letter, those, as we say, anagrammatically, which compose it. *Carmilla* did this; so did *Millarca*.

My father related to the Baron Vordenburg, who remained with us for two or three weeks after the expulsion of Carmilla, the story about the Moravian nobleman and the vampire at Karnstein churchyard, and then he asked the Baron how he had discovered the exact position of the long-concealed tomb of the Countess Millarca? The Baron's grotesque features puckered up into a mysterious smile; he looked down, still smiling on his worn spectacle-case and fumbled with it. Then looking up, he said:

"I have many journals, and other papers, written by that remarkable man; the most curious among them is one treating of the visit of which you speak, to Karnstein. The tradition, of course, discolors and distorts a little. He might have been termed a Moravian nobleman, for he had changed his abode to that territory, and was, beside, a noble. But he was, in truth, a native of Upper Styria. It is enough to say that in very early youth he had been a passionate and favored lover of the beautiful Mircalla, Countess Karnstein. Her early death plunged him into inconsolable grief. It is the nature of vampires to increase and multiply, but according to an ascertained and ghostly law.

"Assume, at starting, a territory perfectly free from the pest. How does it begin, and how does it multiply itself? I will tell you. A person, more or less wicked, puts an end to himself. A suicide, under certain circumstances, becomes a vampire. That specter visits living people in their slumbers; *they* die, and almost invariably, in the grave, develop into vampires. This happened in the case of the beautiful Mircalla, who was haunted by one of those demons. My ancestor, Vordenburg, whose title I still bear, soon discovered this, and in the course of the studies to which he devoted himself, learned a great deal more.

"Among other things, he concluded that suspicion of vampirism would probably fall, sooner or later, upon the dead Countess, who in life had been his idol. He conceived a horror, be she what she might, of her remains being profaned by the outrage of a posthumous execution. He has left a curious paper to prove that the vampire, on its expulsion from its amphibious existence, is projected into a far more horrible life; and he resolved to save his once beloved Mircalla from this.

"He adopted the stratagem of a journey here, a pretended removal of her remains, and a real obliteration of her monument. When age had stolen upon him, and from the vale of years he looked back on the scenes he was leaving, he considered, in a different spirit, what he had done, and a horror took possession of him. He made the tracings and notes which have guided me to the very spot, and drew up a confession of the deception that he had practiced. If he had intended any further action in this matter, death prevented him; and the hand of a remote descendant has, too late for many, directed the pursuit to the lair of the beast."

We talked a little more, and among other things he said was this:

"One sign of the vampire is the power of the hand. The slender hand of Mircalla closed like a vise of steel on the General's wrist when he raised the hatchet to strike. But its power is not confined to its grasp; it leaves a numbness in the limb it seizes, which is slowly, if ever, recovered from."

The following spring my father took me on a tour through Italy. We remained away for more than a year. It was long before the terror of recent events subsided; and to this hour the image of Carmilla returns to memory with ambiguous alternations—sometimes the playful, languid, beautiful girl; sometimes the writhing fiend I saw in the ruined church; and often from a reverie I have started, fancying I heard the light step of Carmilla at the drawing-room door.

BIBLIOGRAPHY

The list includes works referred to in the introduction and notes in this edition and others recommended for further study of the Gothic and of authors represented in this collection.

BAILEY, J. O., "What Happens in 'The Fall of the House of Usher'?" *American Literature*. 1964.

BAKER, ERNEST A., *History of the English Novel*. Vols. IV and V. 1934.

BERRYMAN, JOHN, Introduction to *The Monk*. 1952.

BIRKHEAD, EDITH, *The Tale of Terror*. 1921.

BROWNE, NELSON, *Sheridan Le Fanu*. 1951.

CHASE, RICHARD, *The American Novel and Its Tradition*. 1957.

CLARK, KENNETH, *The Gothic Revival*. 1950.

CROSS, WILBUR L., *The Development of the English Novel*. 1911.

DAVIDSON, E. H., *Poe, A Critical Study*. 1957.

FIEDLER, LESLIE A., *Love and Death in the American Novel*. 1960.

FOGLE, R. H., *Hawthorne's Fiction: The Light and the Dark*. 1952.

FOSTER, JAMES R., *History of the Pre-Romantic Novel in England*. 1949.

GARRISON, JOSEPH M. JR., "The Function of Terror in the Work of Edgar Allan Poe," *American Quarterly*. 1966.

KETTON-CREMER, R. W., *Horace Walpole*. 1940.

LEVIN, HARRY, *The Power of Blackness*. 1958.

LEWIS, WILMARTH S., *Horace Walpole*. 1961.

Introduction to *The Castle of Otranto*. 1964.

MAYO, ROBERT D., "The Gothic Short Story in the Magazines," *Modern Language Review*. 1942.

The English Novel in the Magazines, 1740–1815. 1963.

NEILL, S. D., *A Short History of the English Novel*. 1952.

NELSON, LOWRY JR., "Night Thoughts on the Gothic Novel," *Yale Review*. 1963.

NITCHIE, ELIZABETH, *Mary Shelley, Author of "Frankenstein."* 1953.

PECK, LOUIS F., *A Life of Matthew Gregory Lewis*. 1961.

PRAZ, MARIO, *The Romantic Agony*. 1933.

QUINN, A. H., *Edgar Allan Poe*. 1941.

RAILO, EINO, *The Haunted Castle*. 1927.

REEVES, JOHN K., "The Mother of *Fatherless Fanny*," *English Literary History*. 1942.

SPACKS, PATRICIA M., *The Insistence of Horror: Aspects of the Supernatural in Eighteenth Century Poetry*. 1962.

SPECTOR, ROBERT D., *English Literary Periodicals and the Climate of Opinion During the Seven Years' War*. 1966.

Introduction to *Frankenstein*. 1967.

STEVENSON, LIONEL, *The English Novel: A Panorama*. 1960.

STEWART, RANDALL, *Nathaniel Hawthorne*. 1948.

SUMMERS, MONTAGUE, *A Gothic Bibliography*. 1941.

   The Gothic Quest. 1938.

TOMPKINS, J. M. S., *The Popular Novel in England, 1770–1800*. 1932.

TRAINER, JAMES, Introduction to *The Old English Baron*. 1967.

VARMA, DEVENDRA P., *Gothic Flame*. 1957.

WAGENKNECHT, EDWARD, *Cavalcade of the American Novel*. 1952.

   Edgar Allan Poe: The Man Behind the Legend. 1963.

WAGGONER, H. H., *Hawthorne, a Critical Study*. 1955.

Hair-raising happenings that guarantee nightmares!

You'll be fascinated by unearthly events, intrigued by stories of weird and bizarre occurrences, startled by terrifying tales that border fact and fiction, truth and fantasy. Look for these titles or use the handy coupon below. Go beyond time and space into the strange mysteries of all times!

☐	SEVEN MASTERPIECES OF GOTHIC HORROR by Robert Donald Spector, ed.	2465 •	$1.50
☐	THIS BAFFLING WORLD by John Godwin	8826 •	95¢
☐	DEVILS AND DEMONS by Rod Serling, ed.	8790 •	95¢
☐	TIMELESS STORIES FOR TODAY AND TOMORROW by Ray Bradbury, ed.	8162 •	95¢
☐	STRANGE WORLD by Frank Edwards	8045 •	95¢
☐	STRANGER THAN SCIENCE by Frank Edwards	8043 •	95¢
☐	GREAT TALES OF HORROR by Edgar Allan Poe	7859 •	75¢
☐	THIS BAFFLING WORLD III by John Godwin	7758 •	95¢
☐	50 GREAT HORROR STORIES by John Canning, ed.	7601 •	$1.50
☐	50 GREAT GHOST STORIES by John Canning, ed.	7577 •	$1.25
☐	THIS BAFFLING WORLD II by John Godwin	6918 •	95¢

Buy them at your local bookstore or use this handy coupon for ordering:

START A COLLECTION

With Bantam's fiction anthologies, you can begin almost anywhere. Choose from science fiction, classic literature, modern short stories, mythology, and more—all by both new and established writers in America and around the world.

THE NAMES THAT SPELL GREAT LITERATURE

Choose from today's most renowned world authors—every one an important addition to your personal library.

Hermann Hesse

☐	MAGISTER LUDI	5555	$1.50
☐	BENEATH THE WHEEL	5859	$1.25
☐	NARCISSUS AND GOLDMUND	6891	$1.75
☐	THE JOURNEY TO THE EAST	7362	$1.50
☐	ROSSHALDE	7370	$1.50
☐	DEMIAN	7734	$1.50
☐	GERTRUDE	7767	$1.50
☐	STEPPENWOLF	7979	$1.50
☐	SIDDHARTHA	8819	$1.50

Alexander Solzhenitsyn

☐	THE LOVE-GIRL AND THE INNOCENT	6600	$ .95
☐	ONE DAY IN THE LIFE OF IVAN DENISOVICH	6899	$1.25
☐	STORIES AND PROSE POEMS	7409	$1.50
☐	CANCER WARD	8271	$1.75
☐	AUGUST 1914	7677	$2.25

Jerzy Kosinski

☐	BEING THERE	2265	$1.50
☐	THE DEVIL TREE	7865	$1.50
☐	THE PAINTED BIRD	8257	$1.75
☐	STEPS	8709	$1.25

Doris Lessing

☐	THE GOLDEN NOTEBOOK	7747	$1.95
☐	THE FOUR-GATED CITY	7937	$1.95
☐	THE SUMMER BEFORE THE DARK	8360	$1.75

André Schwarz-Bart

☐	THE LAST OF THE JUST	7708	$1.50
☐	A WOMAN NAMED SOLITUDE	7880	$1.75

Buy them at your local bookstore or use this handy coupon for ordering:

Bantam Book Catalog

It lists over a thousand money-saving best-sellers originally priced from $3.75 to $15.00 —bestsellers that are yours now for as little as 50¢ to $2.95!

The catalog gives you a great opportunity to build your own private library at huge savings!

So don't delay any longer—send us your name and address and 25¢ (to help defray postage and handling costs).